>_ Enter a command:

>_

>_ NO/ONE is a multimedia story.

>_ Scan QR codes.
   Listen to each podcast episode.
   Read articles.

https://edgenews.substack.com/p/pittsburgh-belongs-to-noone

edge News Movies Food World Battle of San Francisco

edge Opinions

Pittsburgh belongs to NO/ONE

Digital activist promises accountability.

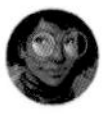

By Danielle Gaines
PITTSBURGH, CA

June 2 2022, 9:41am

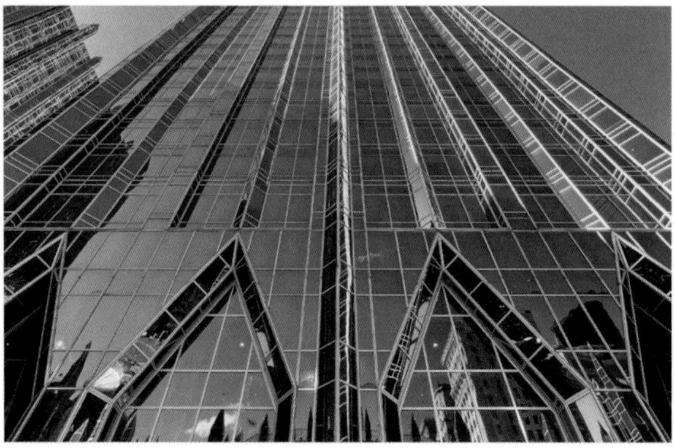

PPG Place | photo by Danielle Gaines

"The devil sometimes speaks the truth."

When people throw that old saying out, they usually mean it in a "don't take everything at face value" kind of way.

But when I say "the devil sometimes speaks the truth" today, I mean "sometimes the truth can only come from darkness... because sometimes the truth is dark."

The reality is, rich and powerful people in Pittsburgh play by a different set of rules. As we've seen time and time again, they can do whatever the hell they want, because they're protected from consequence. Immune to the "justice" system and above accountability.

So I admit, when an enigmatic digital activist—who refers to themselves as "NO/ONE"—offered up a narrative of impending accountability for this protected class... I wanted to believe it. I wanted to believe that this classist social construct we'd all seemingly just accepted could finally be disrupted.

A bit over a week ago, an email landed in my inbox. It contained a video—black text on a white background—promising that "no one is safe in the shadows."

Now, unfortunately... this isn't uncommon. Weirdos send through crazy shit—crazy, elaborate shit—more often than you'd think. And, from what I've gathered, this email went to every single Pittsburgh news outfit. Only to have them trash it like I probably should have.

But... I didn't. Because, despite its cringey presentation... I was curious to see how real they might be.

There are places most journalists don't go—either because they don't know how, or simply because they know better. Last century, these places were seedy back rooms in sketchy establishments. This century... they're on the dark web. A place this former hacktivist is comfortable navigating.

There, with true anonymous protection, exists a lot of truth. People can speak freely. In its own way, it's home to those with protected status... and least in the virtual world. And it was in this world, on a particular dark web forum known for being a hub for hardcore hackers... that I found them. A single post, promising to bring accountability to Pittsburgh, from the username NO/ONE, and featuring the same video.

I made contact. I revealed who I was and how I had gotten there. After verifying I was in fact a reporter, we messaged long enough for me to get a sense of their intentions. A confirmation of sorts that whoever NO/ONE was, meant business.

Were they really going to get the goods on the rich and powerful Yinzers?

Turns out... they've already started.

I was given what they called "a preview." Some of the "evidence" that'll be shared soon, relating to some pretty big Pittsburgh names.

And—assuming it's not faked somehow—it is damning. It's exactly what you think the rich fucks of Pittsburgh might be up to under cover of darkness. NO/ONE has the receipts.

I could tell you what I saw... but then I'd have to lawyer up.

Alternative... you could see for yourself.

NO/ONE gave me access to a website, where this alleged evidence will soon be shared, by way of a terminal command. They said I could share it with you all, if I wanted. So you could see for yourself. Come to your own conclusions.

But would that be crossing an ethical line?

Reality check, right? This material could be faked. It'd be an impressive set of forgeries if so, but it's not impossible.

But what are the alternatives? Trust that the media will get to the bottom of this? That they'll genuinely probe into the affairs of the rich and powerful? Trust that the police will investigate... and even if they do, trust that the courts will pursue justice?

I'm not that naïve. Which has brought me to a confronting realization: if the norms and the rules are holding back true accountability, then maybe it is time to find another path.

The dark truth is... we've needed someone to break the rules. For a long damn time.

NO/ONE seems willing to.

The website is:

http://00110000.info

The command to connect is:

terminal connect: accountability

I'd hoped to do some good for my favourite city with this platform, but if I'm being honest... the one thing digging into the real dirt in Pittsburgh has really done is confirm the truth: politicians, the cops, the mainstream media... they're not interested in holding the powerful to account. We're being screwed over and nobody will do anything about it. Unless we do first.

So, pay attention to the website. Wait for the drops. Come to your own conclusions.

My conclusion? I hope NO/ONE gets these guys. Whatever that means. Because we have nothing else left.

I'm not NO/ONE.

But I kinda wish I was.

TAGGED: NO/ONE, RICHARD ROE MURDERS, TRUE CRIME, PITTSBURGH

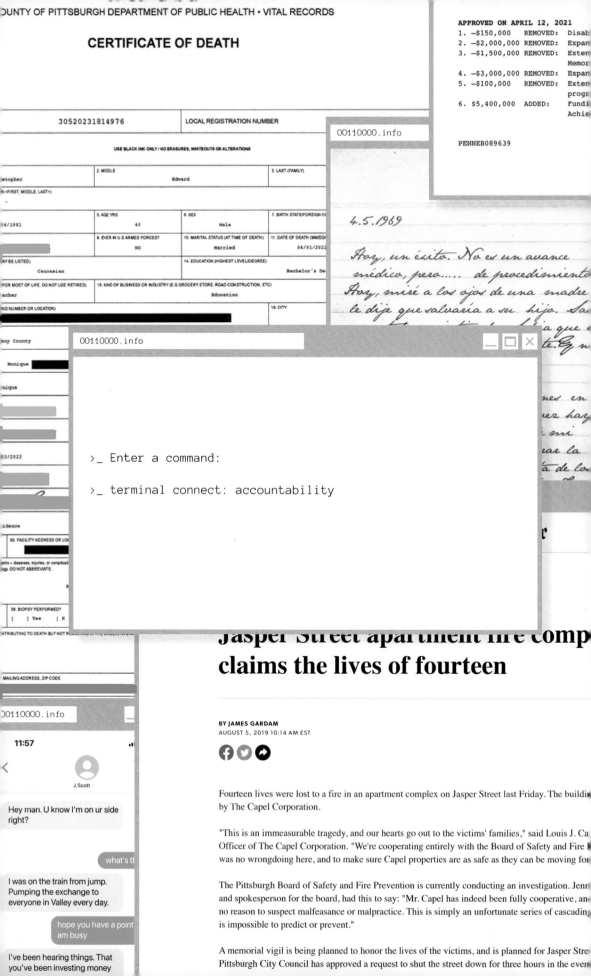

OUNTY OF PITTSBURGH DEPARTMENT OF PUBLIC HEALTH • VITAL RECORDS

CERTIFICATE OF DEATH

30520231814976	LOCAL REGISTRATION NUMBER

USE BLACK INK ONLY / NO ERASURES, WHITEOUTS OR ALTERATIONS

istopher	2. MIDDLE Edward		3. LAST (FAMILY)
A <FIRST, MIDDLE, LAST> –			
4/1981	5. AGE YRS 40	6. SEX Male	7. BIRTH STATE/FOREIGN CO
	9. EVER IN U.S ARMED FORCES? NO	10. MARITAL STATUS (AT TIME OF DEATH) Married	11. DATE OF DEATH (MM/DD/ 04/01/2022
AY BE LISTED) Caucasian		14. EDUCATION (HIGHEST LEVEL/DEGREE) Bachelor's De	
FOR MOST OF LIFE. DO NOT USE RETIRED) acher	16. KIND OF BUSINESS OR INDUSTRY (E.G GROCERY STORE, ROAD CONSTRUCTION, ETC) Education		
ND NUMBER OR LOCATION) [redacted]			19. CITY

ny County

Monique [redacted]

nique

03/2022

idence

50. FACILITY ADDRESS OR LO [redacted]

ents – diseases, injuries, or complicat
ogy. DO NOT ABBREVIATE:

56. BIOPSY PERFORMED?
[ ] Yes [X

NTRIBUTING TO DEATH BUT NOT R

MAILING ADDRESS, ZIP CODE

APPROVED ON APRIL 12, 2021

1. –$150,000 REMOVED: Disab
2. –$2,000,000 REMOVED: Expan
3. –$1,500,000 REMOVED: Exten Memor
4. –$3,000,000 REMOVED: Expan
5. –$100,000 REMOVED: Exten progr
6. $5,400,000 ADDED: Fundi Achie

PENNEB089639

00110000.info

4.5.1969

Hoy, un éxito. No es un avance médico, pero..... de procedimiento Hoy, miré a los ojos de una madre le dije que salvaría a su hijo. Sa

a que

te. Y n

nes en

ez hay

mi

ar la

a de lo

00110000.info

>_ Enter a command:

>_ terminal connect: accountability

Jasper Street apartment fire comp claims the lives of fourteen

BY JAMES GARDAM
AUGUST 5, 2019 10:14 AM EST

Fourteen lives were lost to a fire in an apartment complex on Jasper Street last Friday. The buildi by The Capel Corporation.

"This is an immeasurable tragedy, and our hearts go out to the victims' families," said Louis J. Ca Officer of The Capel Corporation. "We're cooperating entirely with the Board of Safety and Fire was no wrongdoing here, and to make sure Capel properties are as safe as they can be moving for

The Pittsburgh Board of Safety and Fire Prevention is currently conducting an investigation. Jenn and spokesperson for the board, had this to say: "Mr. Capel has indeed been fully cooperative, an no reason to suspect malfeasance or malpractice. This is simply an unfortunate series of cascadin is impossible to predict or prevent."

A memorial vigil is being planned to honor the lives of the victims, and is planned for Jasper Stre Pittsburgh City Council has approved a request to shut the street down for three hours in the even

00110000.info

11:57

J.Scott

Hey man. U know I'm on ur side right?

what's th

I was on the train from jump. Pumping the exchange to everyone in Valley every day.

hope you have a point am busy

I've been hearing things. That you've been investing money

s upgrade for Irvine Auditorium
ordable student housing project
ding for Dr. Theresa Howe
ship Program
versity bus route network
ding for campus safety
self-defense classes
ent Social Development and
ram 2023

PROPRIATIONS AMMENDMENT 04/12/22

1

04/05/1969

A success, today. Not a medical breakthrough, but... a
Today, I looked into a mother's eyes, and I told her I
child. I knew that I was lying. I knew the boy would d
And I felt nothing.

such situations, I have struggled. Not
rtance of my mission, but I struggled
l distance from the subjects. This tim
mply about experience. Perhaps I neede
ment sufficiently before I could hope

him— Cr
n bliste
is orga

but I ha
cess. It
crifice
child's
. Perhap
s part
e his pa
does no

conseq

00110000.info

VIEWPOINT

View Point Construction Group Inc.
Suite 5, 680 Grant St , Pittsburgh, PA 15219

info@viewpointconstruction.com
www.viewpointconstruction.com

August 5, 2019

Guess I didn't truly know who I was getting into bed with. More fool me, huh?

The fire safety board? Maybe the media, too? Jesus. Well, you know I won't talk. I've learned my lesson.

Me? I'll just have to live with the blood of fourteen innocent people on my hands. How the fuck am I supposed to take my kids to school tomorrow and act like I'm not responsible for the deaths of children who look just like them? Not to mention the other children going to sleep without parents tonight because YOU WANTED TO SAVE MONEY. I don't know how I'm going to live with myself.

I suppose I can just look to you for inspiration.

You make it look easy. Hope the money was worth it. You heartless fuck.

– Pat Wellman
Owner and General Manager
View Point Construction Group

and
xecu
ens
inve
e we
he sort that
day. The
vent.

00110000.info

J.Scott Cordon
Bankruptcy Lodgement
To: <All Staff>

Dear team,

Today, many of you received notifications that your employment is being terminated.

Unfortunately, more such notifications are to come. Earlier this morning, I authorized the lodgement of a bankruptcy filing for our or
company's darkest hour... or its end.

I can't get into the details regarding why this has occurred, for legal reasons.

Please know that all affected have my sympathies.

Regards,
– J. Scott Cordon
Chief Executive Officer

J. Scott Cordon
Chief Executive Officer

jcordon@coinholecrypto.com

>_ **No Suspect in Pharma CEO Murder**
SEPTEMBER 03 2022

written by Alejandro Rios
published on The Drop

"He said Colon was found dead, but wouldn't elaborate on motive or whether there was foul play."

>_ **Autopsy: Pharma CEO's death 'homicide,' investigation details begin to emerge**
SEPTEMBER 05 2022

written by Alejandro Rios
published on The Drop

"Colon suffered "multiple gunshot wounds" and his death was ruled a "homicide," according to a news release from the Allegheny County medical examiner's office."

>_ **Crypto boss found shot to death in alley**
OCTOBER 05 2022

written by Julia Paige & Alejandro Rios
published on The Drop

"Police haven't confirmed that the two killings are related, though they're investigating them as if they are."

>_ **Police sources: Ballistics match in Pharma, Crypto CEO murders**
OCTOBER 05 2022

written by Julia Paige
published on The Drop

"The ballistic report, dated the day after Lin was found shot to death, shows he and Colon were both likely shot by the same weapon."

>_ **101522 richard roe does not act for me.mp4**
OCTOBER 15 2022

published on http://00110000.info/

"*We must not degrade ourselves by resorting to violent murder.*"

>_ **Kemp - under cloud of suspicion - shot near home**
NOVEMBER 08 2022

written by Julia Paige
published on The Drop

"*Fire department officials said Kemp was taken by ambulance to Wexford Hospital where he was listed in good condition.*"

>_ **110922 no one is above the law.mp4**
NOVEMBER 09 2022

published on http://00110000.info/

"*This is now what our city needs. This will not heal us.*"

>_ **Richard Roe has a real name**
JANUARY 15 2023

written by Danielle Gaines
published on Edge News

"*Ask yourself why the police purposely withheld this information from the public? There is absolutely no reason to do that.*"

KNOWPEDIA
An Encyclopedia For Free

Aaron Kern

Article Talk | Read View source View history

Aaron James Kern (born April 15, 1994) is an American serial killer who murdered two men and injured three others in Pittsburgh, Pennsylvania between September and December 2022. His modus operandi consisted of shooting prominent locals that were threatened and doxed for their criminal conduct by the digital hacktivist NO/ONE. He used a .38 Special revolver, shooting them four times in the chest.

Kern was caught by a Pittsburgh Police SWAT team while hiding out in the Carrie Blast Furnaces during the winter of 2022. He is currently in police custody awaiting trial.

Aaron Kern

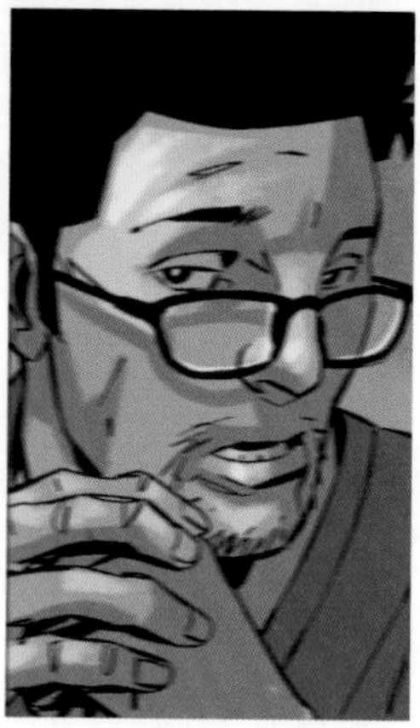

Born	April 15, 1994 (age 28) Pennsylvania, U.S.
Alias(es)	Richard Roe The Accountability Killer
Occupation	Carpenter
Years active	2022
Criminal status	Incarcerated
Conviction(s)	Pending trial
Criminal penalty	Pending
	Details
Victims	2 (Murdered) 3 (Attempted Murder)
Country	United States
State(s)	Pennsylvania
Apprehended	December 15, 2022

Early life [edit]

Born in Pennsylvania on April 15, 1994, to the son of a Pittsburgh police officer, not much is known of his childhood. By all accounts he was a precocious child who loved reading and excelled academically, until his mother passed away from cancer when he was twelve. The trauma of her death turned him into an introvert and disinterested student who barely graduated high school. He first came to the attention of law enforcement in 2008 when he was arrested for "minor in possession." However, a mix-up during his booking caused him to be entered into the system as Richard Roe. Aaron was ultimately released, and no charges were brought against him, some later claimed it was because he was the son of decorated police officer, Ben Kern.

Crimes [edit]

On the evening of September 2, 2022 Kern broke into the Squirrel Hill home of Julian Colon, 81. After locating him in the house, Kern shot Colon four times in the chest with a .38 Special revolver. The motive for the killing was unclear at the time as nothing was stolen from the home. Then, on October 4, 2022, Kern fatally shot Edwin Lin, 25, in the alley behind The Fairmont Hotel, leaving behind a graffiti note saying, "Held Accountable" and signed "Roe". Ballistics matched the shell casings left behind at both crime scenes, connecting the murders. Another, deeper, connection provided the motive as both men were threatened and then doxxed by the vigilante, NO/ONE.

A month later, on November 7, 2022, Kern attempted to murder the State Senator Noah Kemp inside his home. He was the third of four men doxed by NO/ONE, who intervened in the attack and saved Kemp's life. Kern fled the scene after shooting two Pittsburgh police officers called to the scene. They both survived.

Capture and alleged confession [edit]

The authorities had no suspects and no leads on Richard Roe's identity, until December 15, 2022, when they received a credible anonymous tip that led them to the Carrie Blast Furnaces. There, they located Aaron Kern squatting and, after a struggle, apprehended him. Items linking him to the crimes were found on the scene.

In an alleged taped confession recorded during a police interview after his capture, Kern cited the failure of the District Attorney's office and the entire justice department to hold the corrupt accountable as Kern's motive for the attacks.

Trial [edit]

Kern is in custody in Allegheny County Jail, awaiting trial.

Richard Roe [show]

Authority control [show]

>_ CHAPTER ONE
MARCH 2023

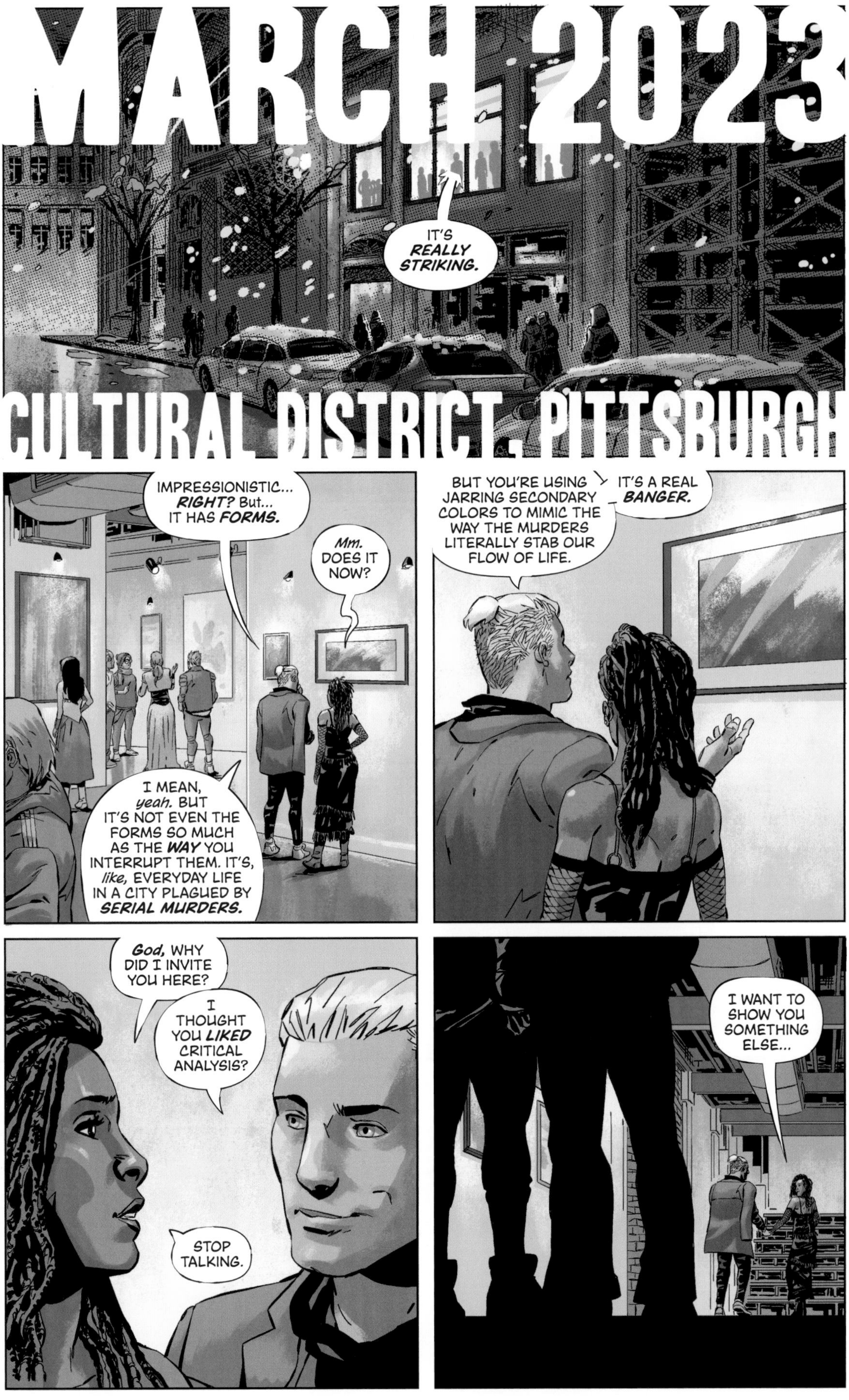
MARCH 2023
IT'S REALLY STRIKING.
CULTURAL DISTRICT, PITTSBURGH
IMPRESSIONISTIC... RIGHT? But... IT HAS FORMS.
Mm. DOES IT NOW?
I MEAN, yeah. BUT IT'S NOT EVEN THE FORMS SO MUCH AS THE WAY YOU INTERRUPT THEM. IT'S, like, EVERYDAY LIFE IN A CITY PLAGUED BY SERIAL MURDERS.
BUT YOU'RE USING JARRING SECONDARY COLORS TO MIMIC THE WAY THE MURDERS LITERALLY STAB OUR FLOW OF LIFE.
IT'S A REAL BANGER.
God, WHY DID I INVITE YOU HERE?
I THOUGHT YOU LIKED CRITICAL ANALYSIS?
STOP TALKING.
I WANT TO SHOW YOU SOMETHING ELSE...

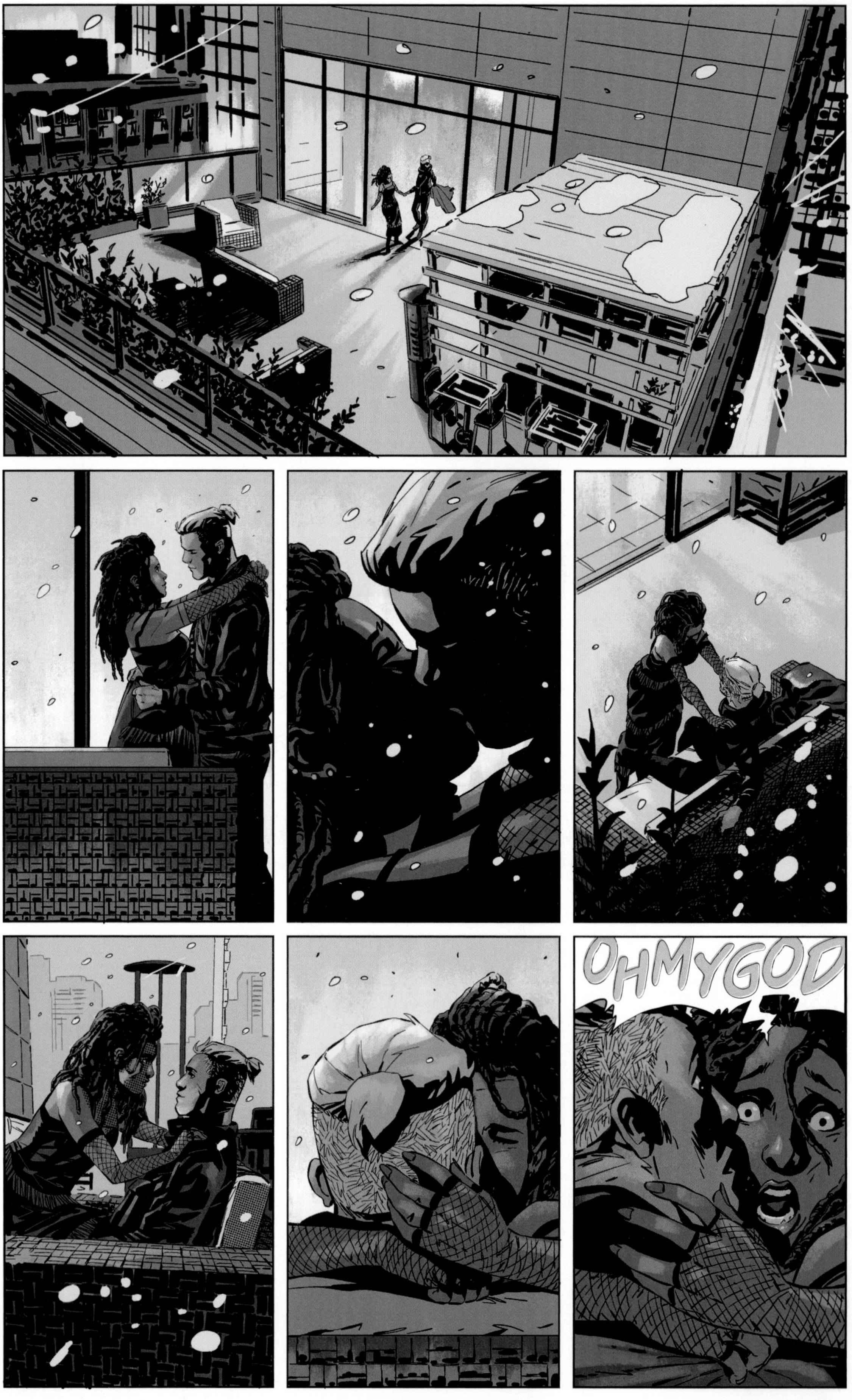
OHMYGOD

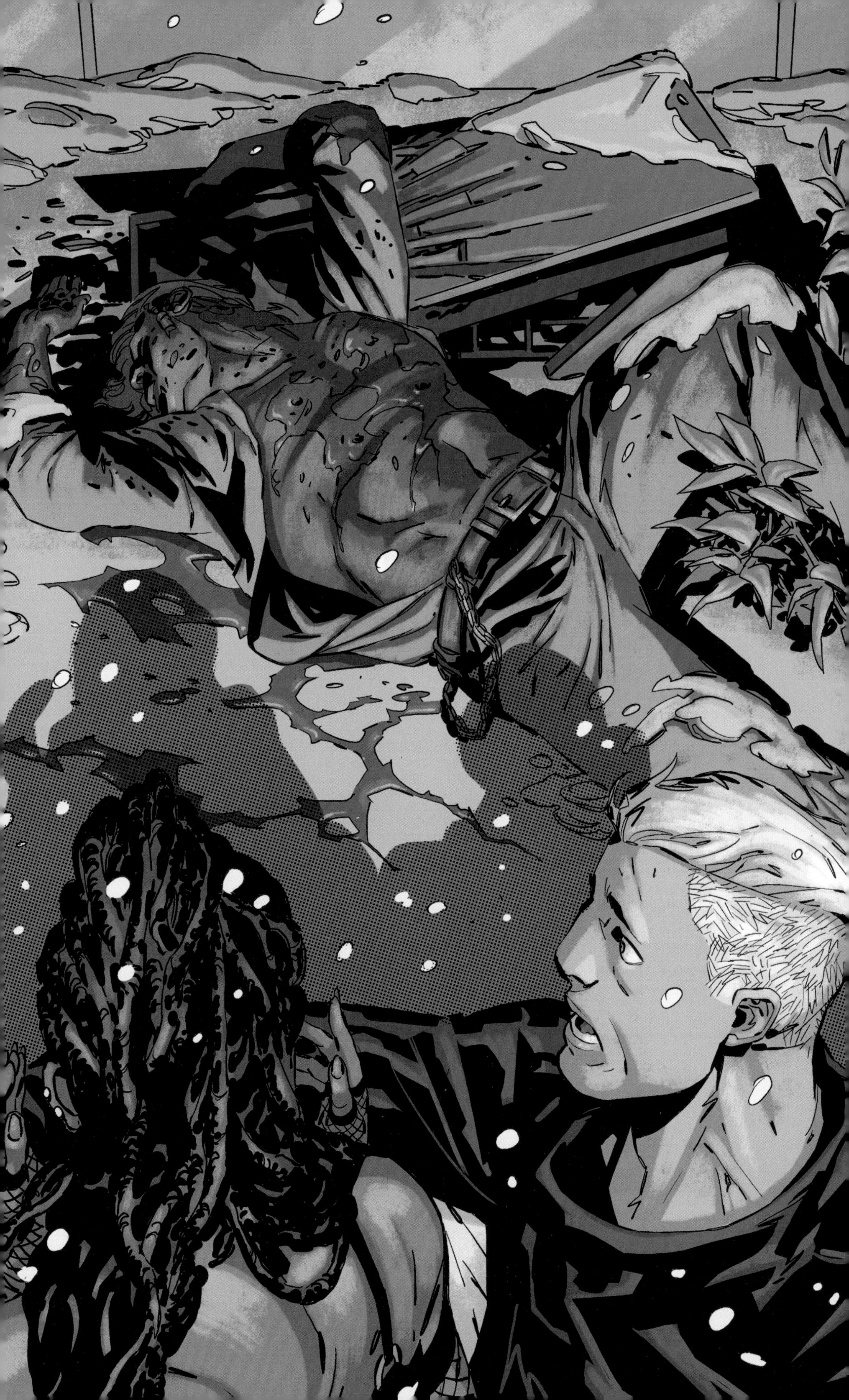

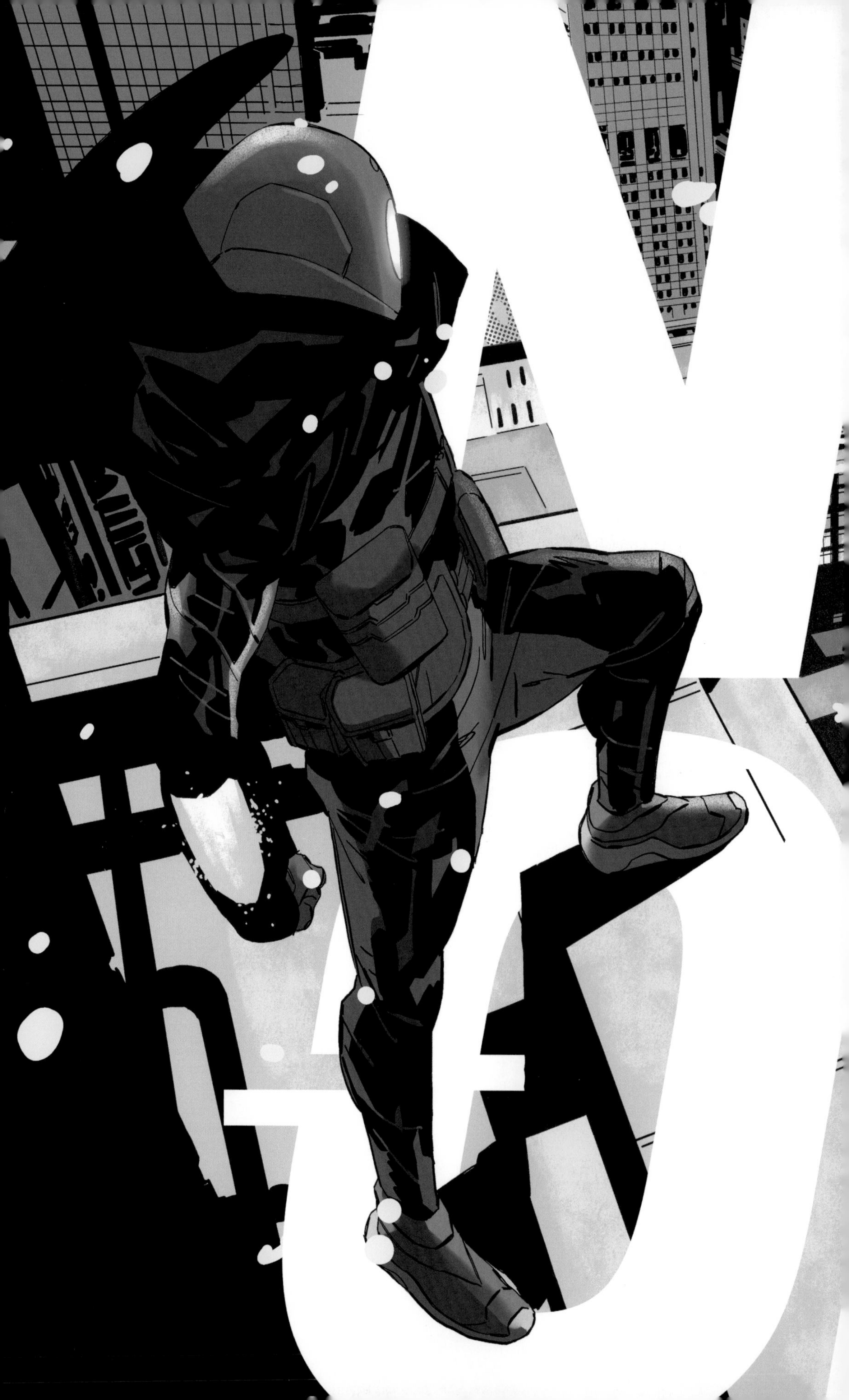

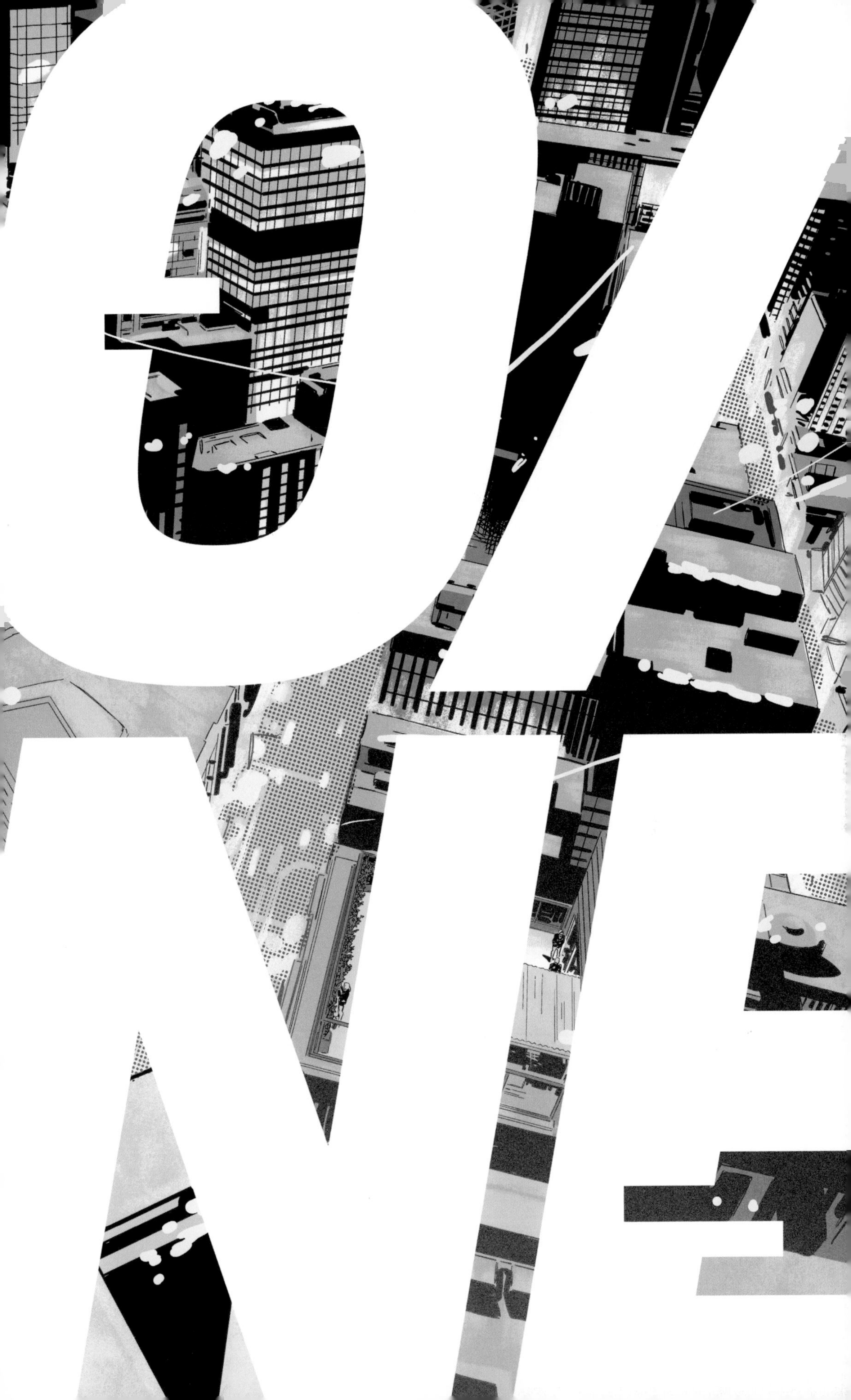

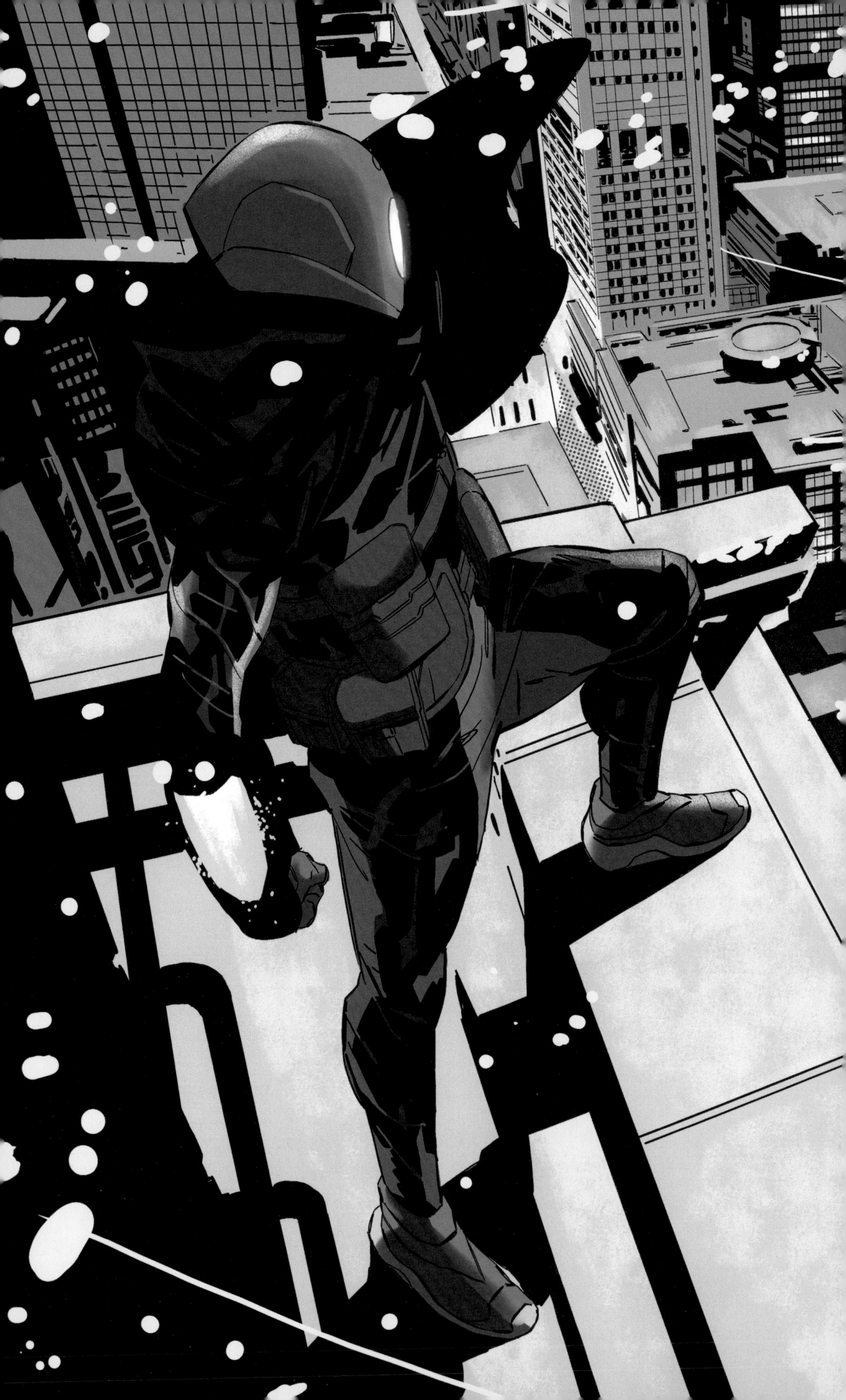

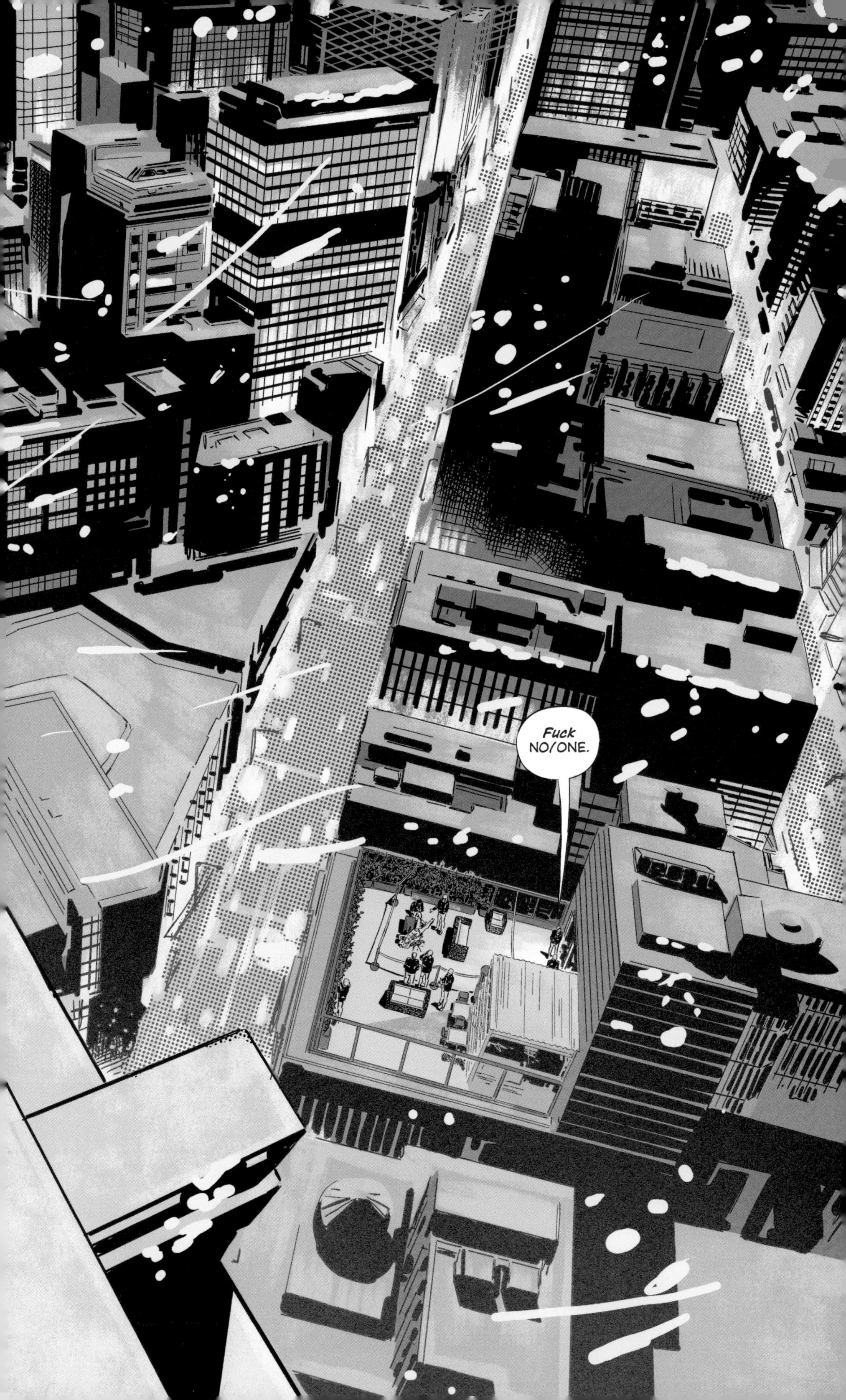
Fuck NO/ONE.

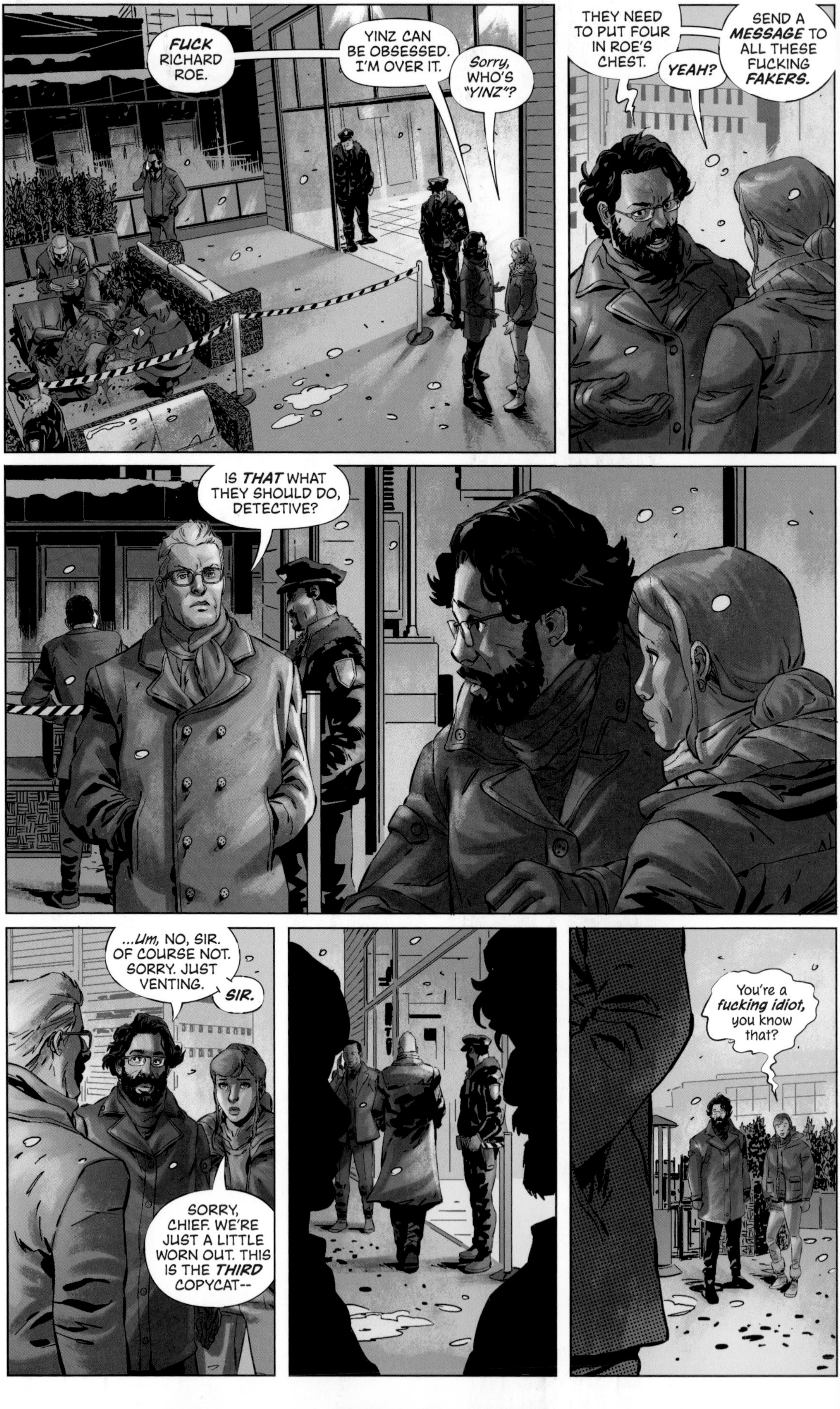

FUCK RICHARD ROE.
YINZ CAN BE OBSESSED. I'M OVER IT.
Sorry, WHO'S "YINZ"?
THEY NEED TO PUT FOUR IN ROE'S CHEST.
YEAH?
SEND A MESSAGE TO ALL THESE FUCKING FAKERS.
IS THAT WHAT THEY SHOULD DO, DETECTIVE?
...Um, NO, SIR. OF COURSE NOT. SORRY. JUST VENTING.
SIR.
SORRY, CHIEF. WE'RE JUST A LITTLE WORN OUT. THIS IS THE THIRD COPYCAT--
You're a fucking idiot, you know that?

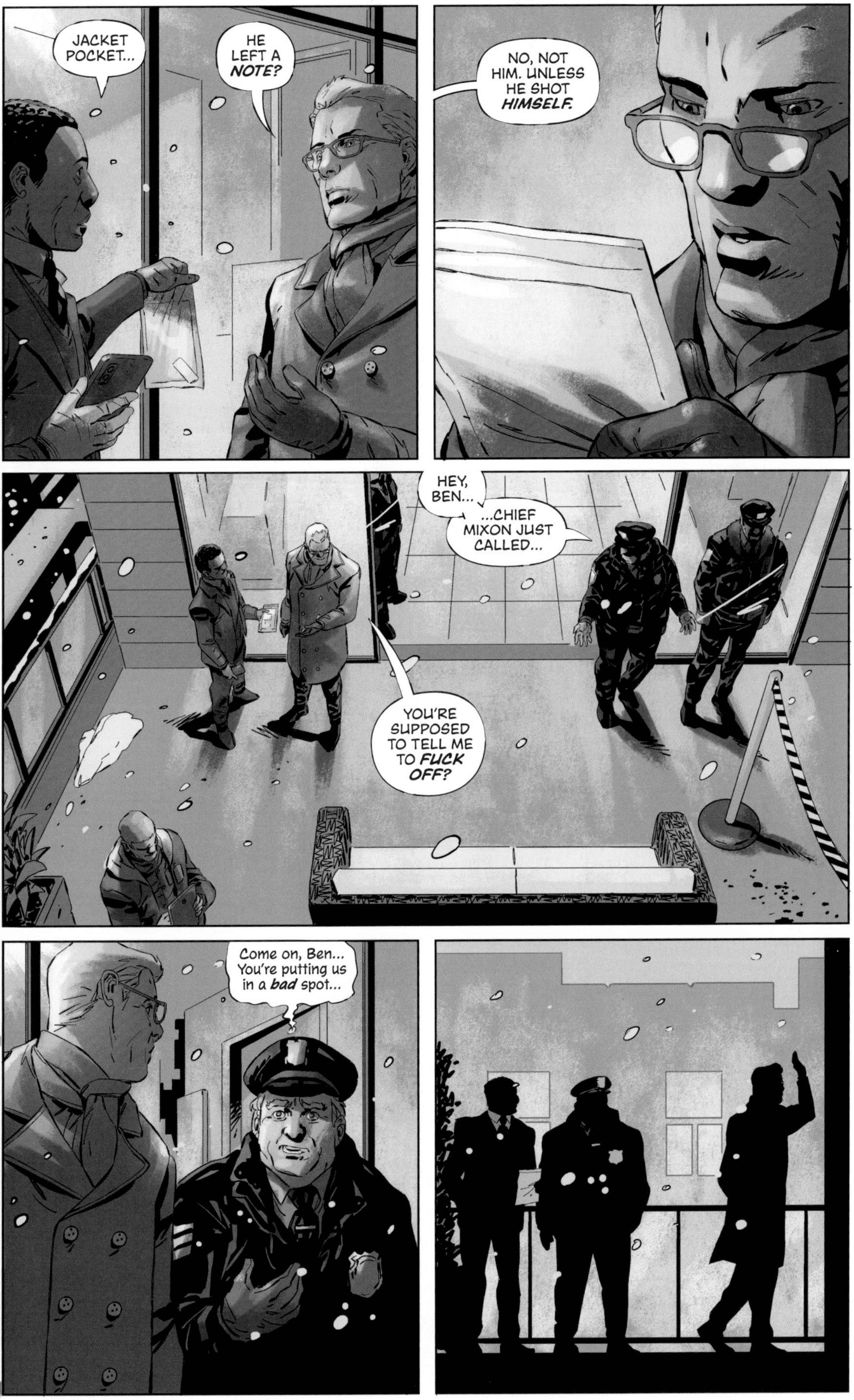
JACKET POCKET...
HE LEFT A NOTE?
NO, NOT HIM. UNLESS HE SHOT HIMSELF.
HEY, BEN...
...CHIEF MIXON JUST CALLED...
YOU'RE SUPPOSED TO TELL ME TO FUCK OFF?
Come on, Ben... You're putting us in a bad spot...

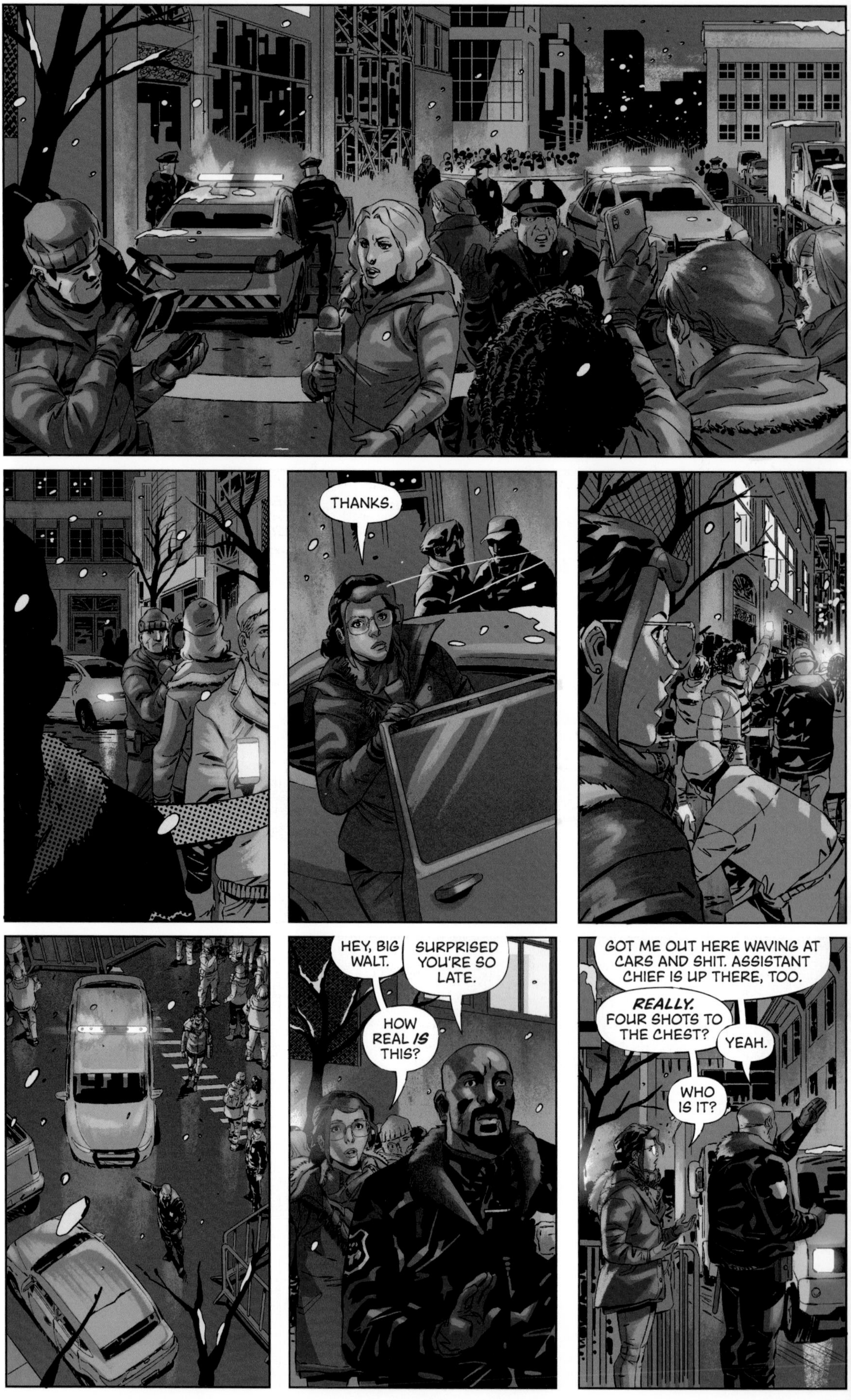
THANKS.
HEY, BIG WALT.
SURPRISED YOU'RE SO LATE.
HOW REAL *IS* THIS?
GOT ME OUT HERE WAVING AT CARS AND SHIT. ASSISTANT CHIEF IS UP THERE, TOO.
REALLY. FOUR SHOTS TO THE CHEST?
YEAH.
WHO IS IT?

I CAN'T TELL YOU THAT.

WALT, COME ON.

THEY HAVEN'T RELEASED THE NAME.

I JUST LEFT A PENS GAME TIED IN THE THIRD. *DANIELLE GAINES* IS HERE. I'M GOING TO FIND OUT ANYWAY. *WHO IS IT?*

LOUIS CAPEL.

Ah, shit.

Christ.

BEN KERN! BEN!

BEN, DID YOUR SON DO THIS?!

CHIEF KERN, WHAT DO YOU HAVE TO SAY TO ALL THE FAMILIES--?!

Paper Boss

Publisher wants to move forward. With YOU.

...

BZZT

Paper Boss

Publisher wants to move forward. With YOU.

...

Tell me you're in.

??????

Let's gooooooooooooooooo

Type a message

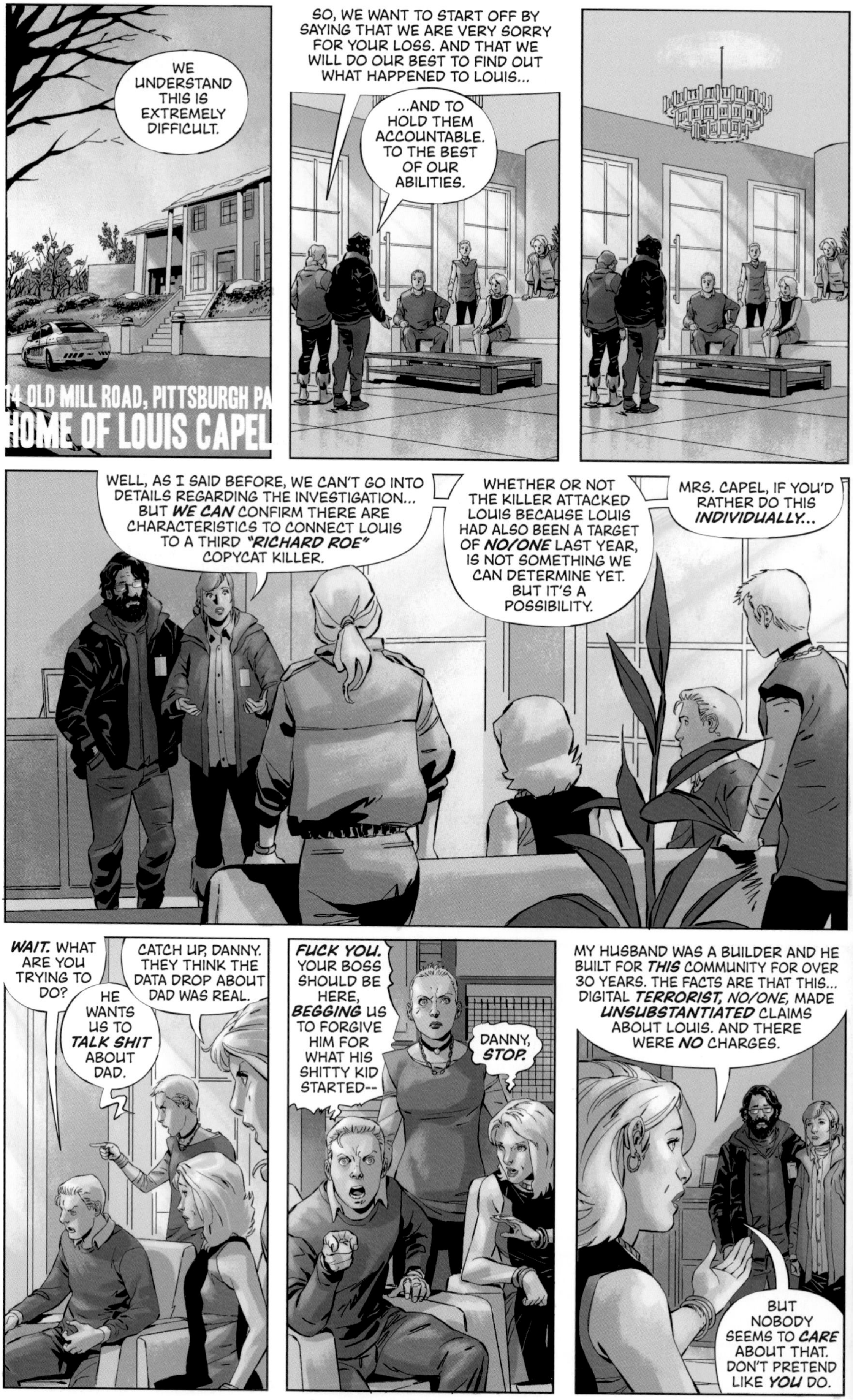

WE UNDERSTAND THIS IS EXTREMELY DIFFICULT.
14 OLD MILL ROAD, PITTSBURGH PA
HOME OF LOUIS CAPEL
SO, WE WANT TO START OFF BY SAYING THAT WE ARE VERY SORRY FOR YOUR LOSS. AND THAT WE WILL DO OUR BEST TO FIND OUT WHAT HAPPENED TO LOUIS...
...AND TO HOLD THEM ACCOUNTABLE. TO THE BEST OF OUR ABILITIES.
WELL, AS I SAID BEFORE, WE CAN'T GO INTO DETAILS REGARDING THE INVESTIGATION... BUT WE CAN CONFIRM THERE ARE CHARACTERISTICS TO CONNECT LOUIS TO A THIRD "RICHARD ROE" COPYCAT KILLER.
WHETHER OR NOT THE KILLER ATTACKED LOUIS BECAUSE LOUIS HAD ALSO BEEN A TARGET OF NO/ONE LAST YEAR, IS NOT SOMETHING WE CAN DETERMINE YET. BUT IT'S A POSSIBILITY.
MRS. CAPEL, IF YOU'D RATHER DO THIS INDIVIDUALLY...
WAIT. WHAT ARE YOU TRYING TO DO?
CATCH UP, DANNY. THEY THINK THE DATA DROP ABOUT DAD WAS REAL.
HE WANTS US TO TALK SHIT ABOUT DAD.
FUCK YOU. YOUR BOSS SHOULD BE HERE, BEGGING US TO FORGIVE HIM FOR WHAT HIS SHITTY KID STARTED--
DANNY, STOP.
MY HUSBAND WAS A BUILDER AND HE BUILT FOR THIS COMMUNITY FOR OVER 30 YEARS. THE FACTS ARE THAT THIS... DIGITAL TERRORIST, NO/ONE, MADE UNSUBSTANTIATED CLAIMS ABOUT LOUIS. AND THERE WERE NO CHARGES.
BUT NOBODY SEEMS TO CARE ABOUT THAT. DON'T PRETEND LIKE YOU DO.

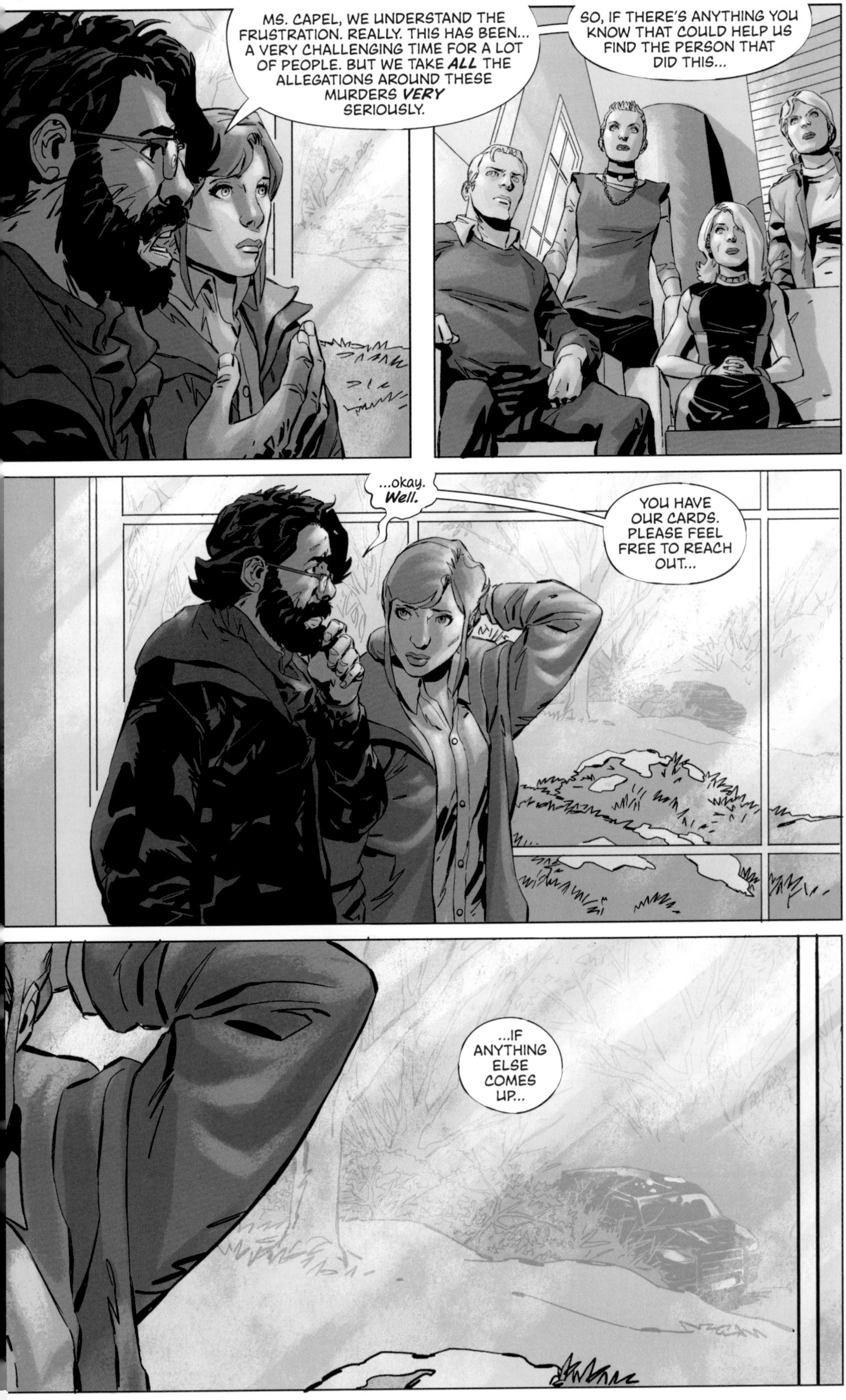
MS. CAPEL, WE UNDERSTAND THE FRUSTRATION. REALLY. THIS HAS BEEN... A VERY CHALLENGING TIME FOR A LOT OF PEOPLE. BUT WE TAKE ALL THE ALLEGATIONS AROUND THESE MURDERS VERY SERIOUSLY.
SO, IF THERE'S ANYTHING YOU KNOW THAT COULD HELP US FIND THE PERSON THAT DID THIS...
...okay. Well.
YOU HAVE OUR CARDS. PLEASE FEEL FREE TO REACH OUT...
...IF ANYTHING ELSE COMES UP...

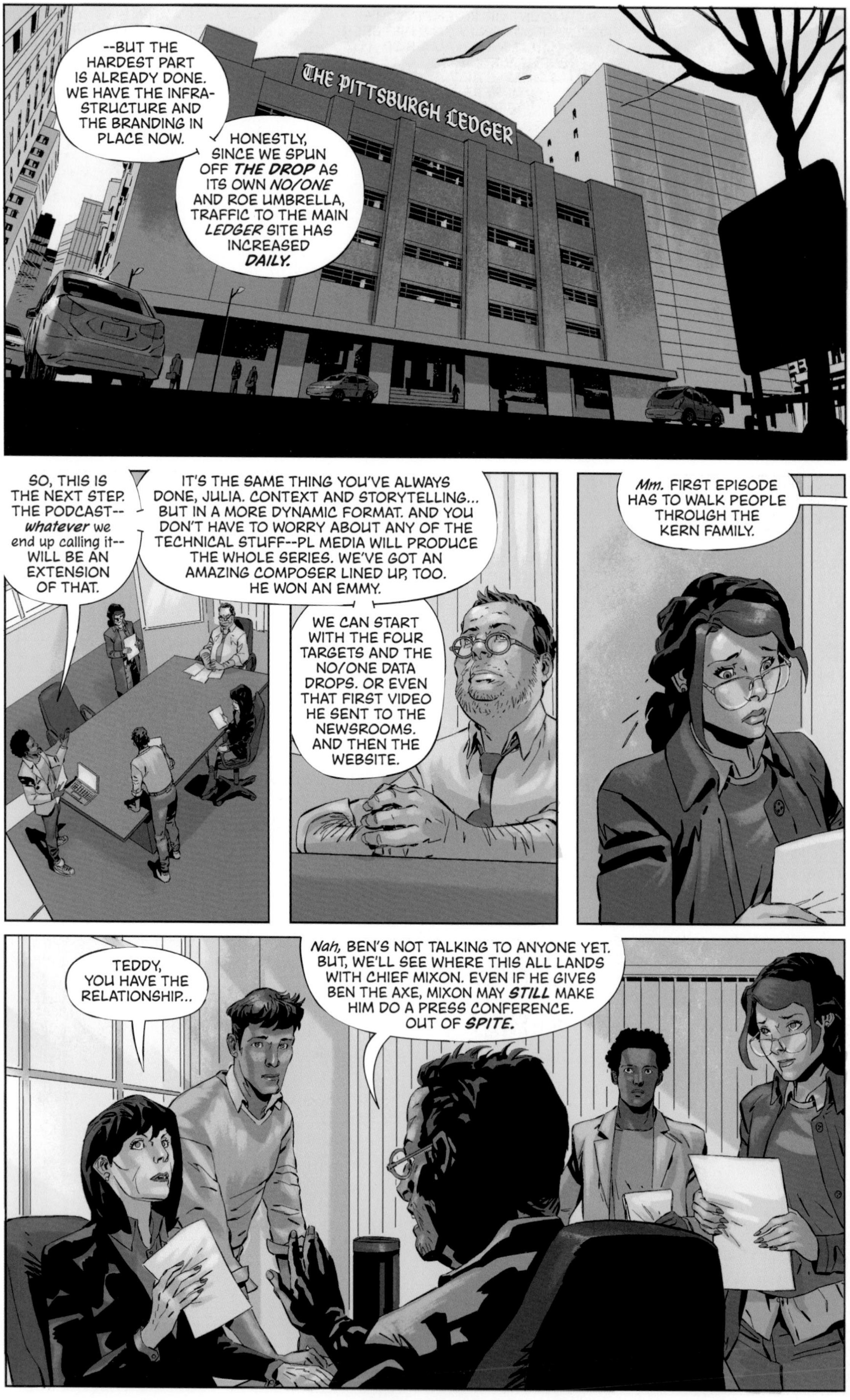

--BUT THE HARDEST PART IS ALREADY DONE. WE HAVE THE INFRA-STRUCTURE AND THE BRANDING IN PLACE NOW.
HONESTLY, SINCE WE SPUN OFF *THE DROP* AS ITS OWN *NO/ONE* AND ROE UMBRELLA, TRAFFIC TO THE MAIN *LEDGER* SITE HAS INCREASED *DAILY.*
THE PITTSBURGH LEDGER
SO, THIS IS THE NEXT STEP. THE PODCAST-- *whatever* we end up calling it-- WILL BE AN EXTENSION OF THAT.
IT'S THE SAME THING YOU'VE ALWAYS DONE, JULIA. CONTEXT AND STORYTELLING... BUT IN A MORE DYNAMIC FORMAT. AND YOU DON'T HAVE TO WORRY ABOUT ANY OF THE TECHNICAL STUFF--PL MEDIA WILL PRODUCE THE WHOLE SERIES. WE'VE GOT AN AMAZING COMPOSER LINED UP, TOO. HE WON AN EMMY.
WE CAN START WITH THE FOUR TARGETS AND THE NO/ONE DATA DROPS. OR EVEN THAT FIRST VIDEO HE SENT TO THE NEWSROOMS. AND THEN THE WEBSITE.
Mm. FIRST EPISODE HAS TO WALK PEOPLE THROUGH THE KERN FAMILY.
TEDDY, YOU HAVE THE RELATIONSHIP...
Nah, BEN'S NOT TALKING TO ANYONE YET. BUT, WE'LL SEE WHERE THIS ALL LANDS WITH CHIEF MIXON. EVEN IF HE GIVES BEN THE AXE, MIXON MAY *STILL* MAKE HIM DO A PRESS CONFERENCE. OUT OF *SPITE.*

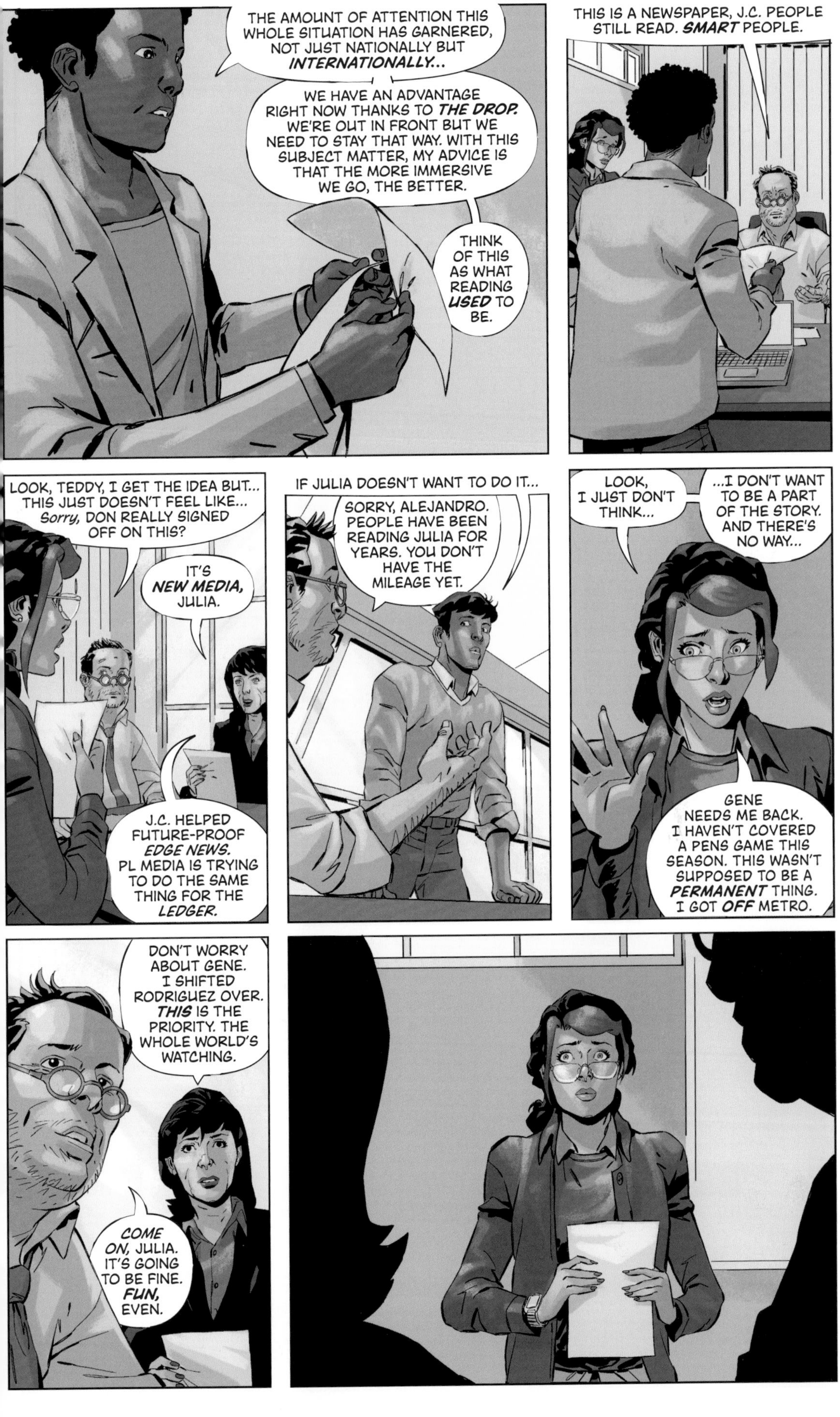
THE AMOUNT OF ATTENTION THIS WHOLE SITUATION HAS GARNERED, NOT JUST NATIONALLY BUT INTERNATIONALLY...
WE HAVE AN ADVANTAGE RIGHT NOW THANKS TO THE DROP. WE'RE OUT IN FRONT BUT WE NEED TO STAY THAT WAY. WITH THIS SUBJECT MATTER, MY ADVICE IS THAT THE MORE IMMERSIVE WE GO, THE BETTER.
THINK OF THIS AS WHAT READING USED TO BE.
THIS IS A NEWSPAPER, J.C. PEOPLE STILL READ. SMART PEOPLE.
LOOK, TEDDY, I GET THE IDEA BUT... THIS JUST DOESN'T FEEL LIKE... Sorry, DON REALLY SIGNED OFF ON THIS?
IT'S NEW MEDIA, JULIA.
J.C. HELPED FUTURE-PROOF EDGE NEWS. PL MEDIA IS TRYING TO DO THE SAME THING FOR THE LEDGER.
IF JULIA DOESN'T WANT TO DO IT...
SORRY, ALEJANDRO. PEOPLE HAVE BEEN READING JULIA FOR YEARS. YOU DON'T HAVE THE MILEAGE YET.
LOOK, I JUST DON'T THINK...
...I DON'T WANT TO BE A PART OF THE STORY. AND THERE'S NO WAY...
GENE NEEDS ME BACK. I HAVEN'T COVERED A PENS GAME THIS SEASON. THIS WASN'T SUPPOSED TO BE A PERMANENT THING. I GOT OFF METRO.
DON'T WORRY ABOUT GENE. I SHIFTED RODRIGUEZ OVER. THIS IS THE PRIORITY. THE WHOLE WORLD'S WATCHING.
COME ON, JULIA. IT'S GOING TO BE FINE. FUN, EVEN.

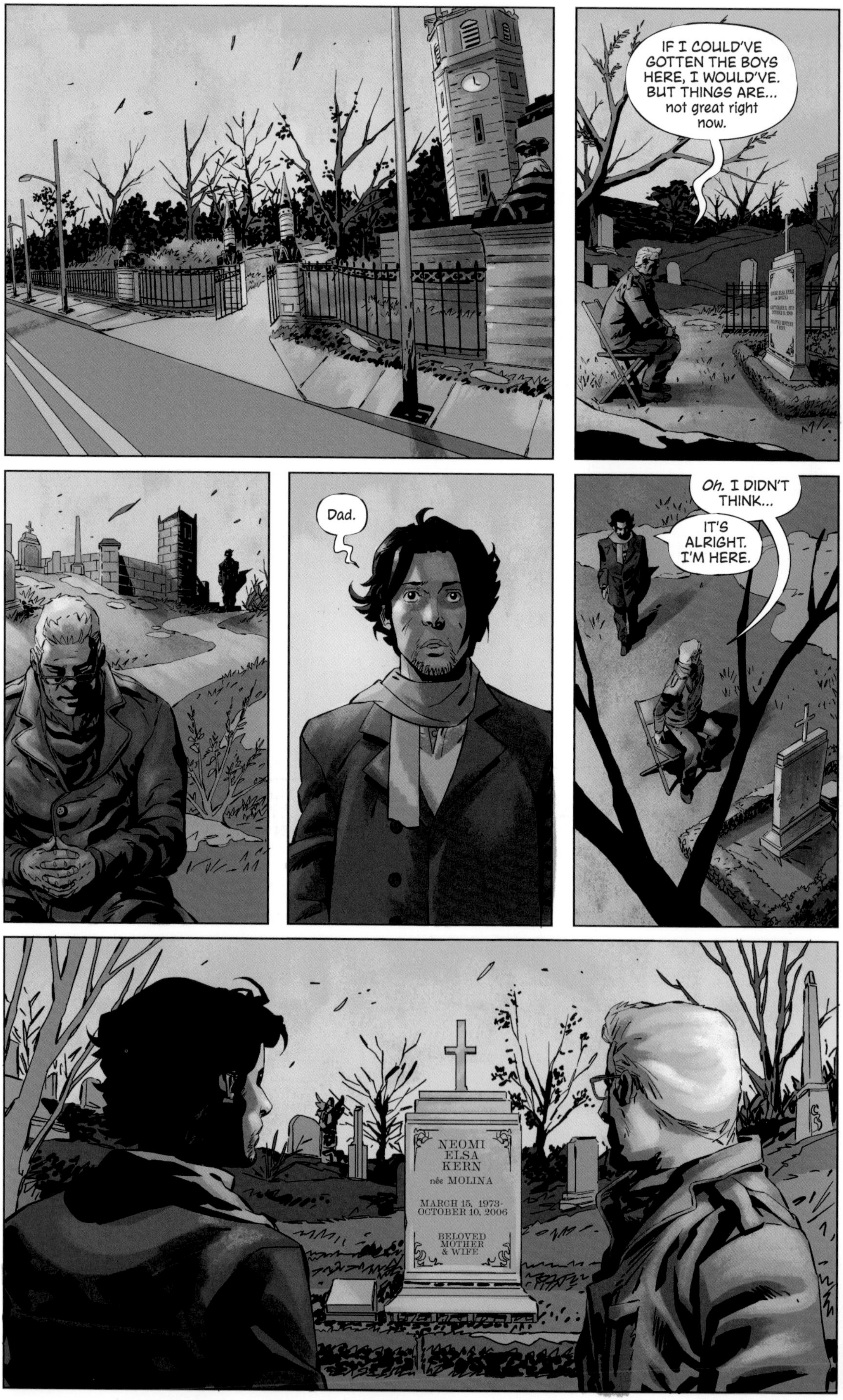
IF I COULD'VE GOTTEN THE BOYS HERE, I WOULD'VE. BUT THINGS ARE... not great right now.
Dad.
Oh. I DIDN'T THINK...
IT'S ALRIGHT. I'M HERE.
NEOMI ELSA KERN née MOLINA
MARCH 15, 1973- OCTOBER 10, 2006
BELOVED MOTHER & WIFE

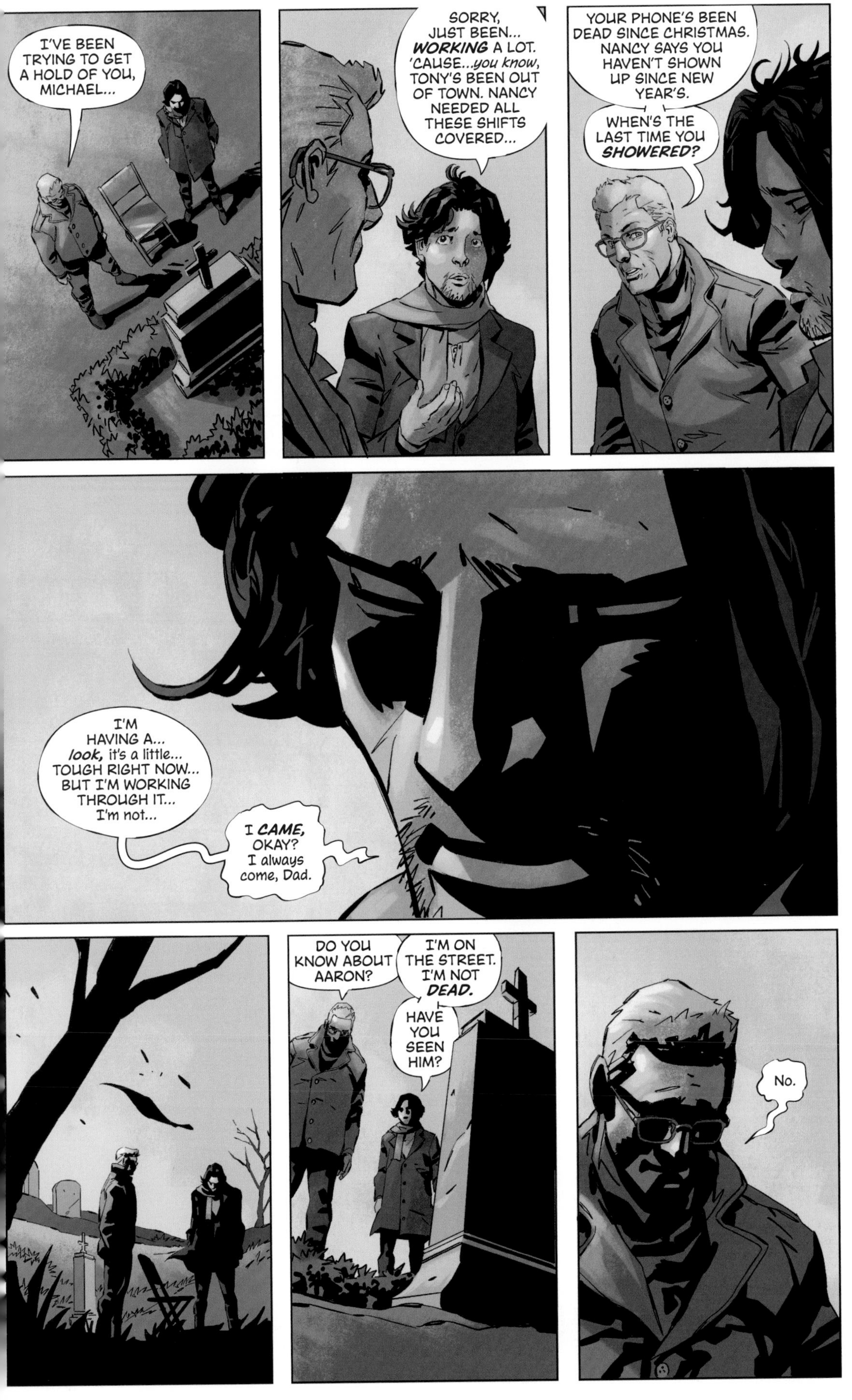

I'VE BEEN TRYING TO GET A HOLD OF YOU, MICHAEL...
SORRY, JUST BEEN... WORKING A LOT. 'CAUSE...you know, TONY'S BEEN OUT OF TOWN. NANCY NEEDED ALL THESE SHIFTS COVERED...
YOUR PHONE'S BEEN DEAD SINCE CHRISTMAS. NANCY SAYS YOU HAVEN'T SHOWN UP SINCE NEW YEAR'S.
WHEN'S THE LAST TIME YOU SHOWERED?
I'M HAVING A... look, it's a little... TOUGH RIGHT NOW... BUT I'M WORKING THROUGH IT... I'm not...
I CAME, OKAY? I always come, Dad.
DO YOU KNOW ABOUT AARON?
I'M ON THE STREET. I'M NOT DEAD.
HAVE YOU SEEN HIM?
No.

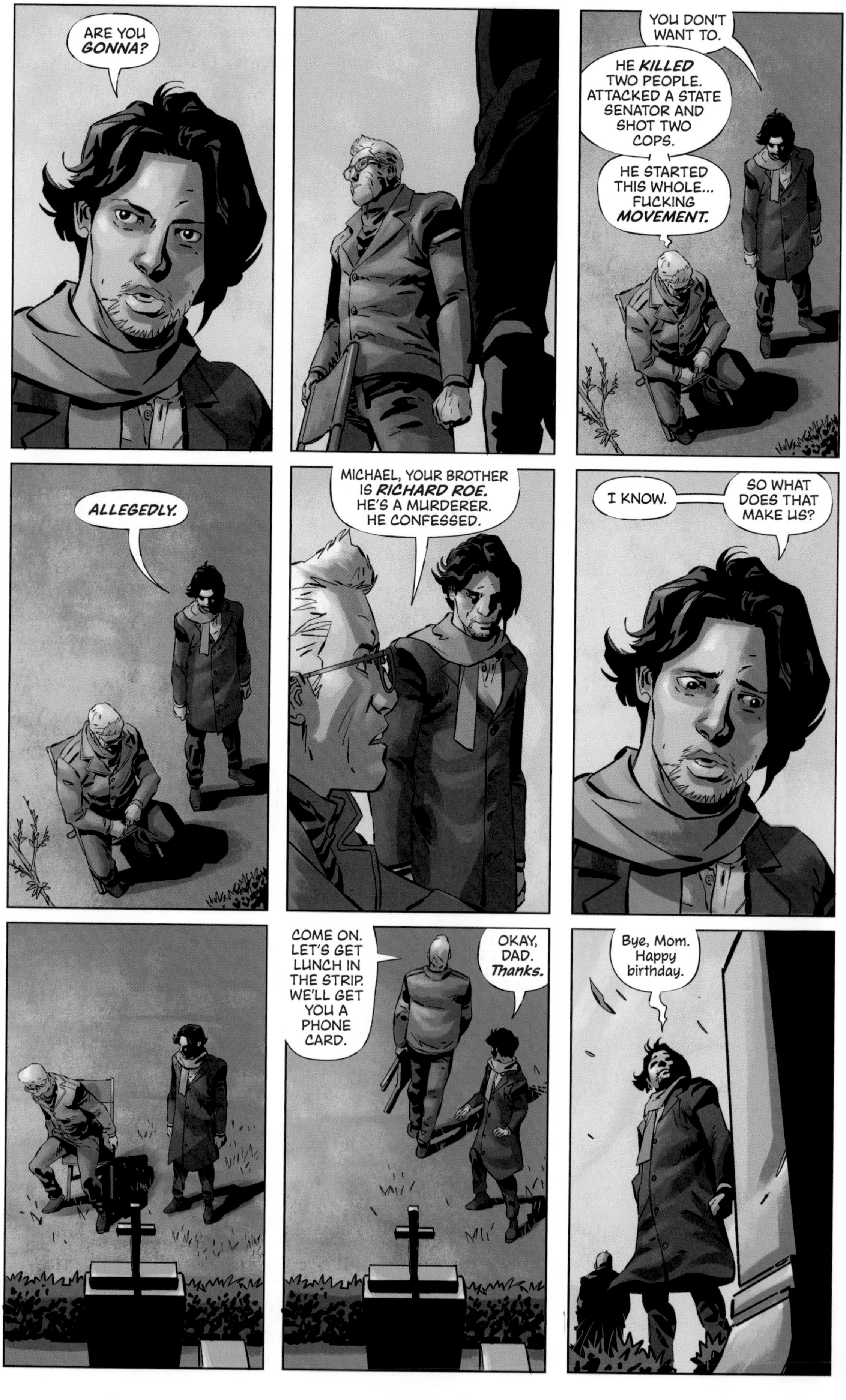
ARE YOU GONNA?
YOU DON'T WANT TO.
HE KILLED TWO PEOPLE. ATTACKED A STATE SENATOR AND SHOT TWO COPS.
HE STARTED THIS WHOLE... FUCKING MOVEMENT.
ALLEGEDLY.
MICHAEL, YOUR BROTHER IS RICHARD ROE. HE'S A MURDERER. HE CONFESSED.
I KNOW.
SO WHAT DOES THAT MAKE US?
COME ON. LET'S GET LUNCH IN THE STRIP. WE'LL GET YOU A PHONE CARD.
OKAY, DAD. Thanks.
Bye, Mom. Happy birthday.

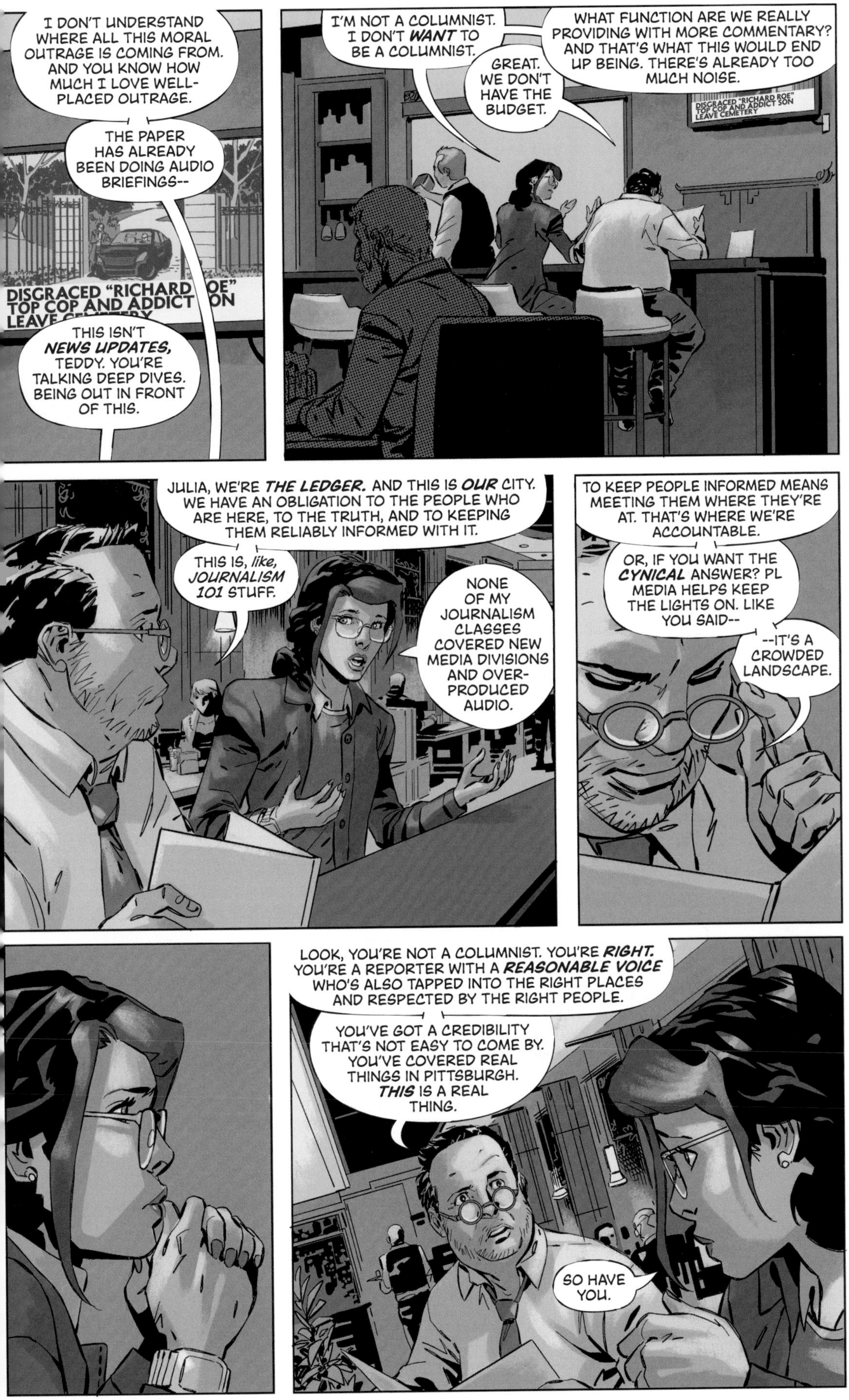
I DON'T UNDERSTAND WHERE ALL THIS MORAL OUTRAGE IS COMING FROM. AND YOU KNOW HOW MUCH I LOVE WELL-PLACED OUTRAGE.
THE PAPER HAS ALREADY BEEN DOING AUDIO BRIEFINGS--
DISGRACED "RICHARD ROE" TOP COP AND ADDICT SON LEAVE CEMETERY
THIS ISN'T NEWS UPDATES, TEDDY. YOU'RE TALKING DEEP DIVES. BEING OUT IN FRONT OF THIS.
I'M NOT A COLUMNIST. I DON'T WANT TO BE A COLUMNIST.
GREAT. WE DON'T HAVE THE BUDGET.
WHAT FUNCTION ARE WE REALLY PROVIDING WITH MORE COMMENTARY? AND THAT'S WHAT THIS WOULD END UP BEING. THERE'S ALREADY TOO MUCH NOISE.
DISGRACED "RICHARD ROE" TOP COP AND ADDICT SON LEAVE CEMETERY
JULIA, WE'RE THE LEDGER. AND THIS IS OUR CITY. WE HAVE AN OBLIGATION TO THE PEOPLE WHO ARE HERE, TO THE TRUTH, AND TO KEEPING THEM RELIABLY INFORMED WITH IT.
THIS IS, like, JOURNALISM 101 STUFF.
NONE OF MY JOURNALISM CLASSES COVERED NEW MEDIA DIVISIONS AND OVER-PRODUCED AUDIO.
TO KEEP PEOPLE INFORMED MEANS MEETING THEM WHERE THEY'RE AT. THAT'S WHERE WE'RE ACCOUNTABLE.
OR, IF YOU WANT THE CYNICAL ANSWER? PL MEDIA HELPS KEEP THE LIGHTS ON. LIKE YOU SAID--
--IT'S A CROWDED LANDSCAPE.
LOOK, YOU'RE NOT A COLUMNIST. YOU'RE RIGHT. YOU'RE A REPORTER WITH A REASONABLE VOICE WHO'S ALSO TAPPED INTO THE RIGHT PLACES AND RESPECTED BY THE RIGHT PEOPLE.
YOU'VE GOT A CREDIBILITY THAT'S NOT EASY TO COME BY. YOU'VE COVERED REAL THINGS IN PITTSBURGH. THIS IS A REAL THING.
SO HAVE YOU.

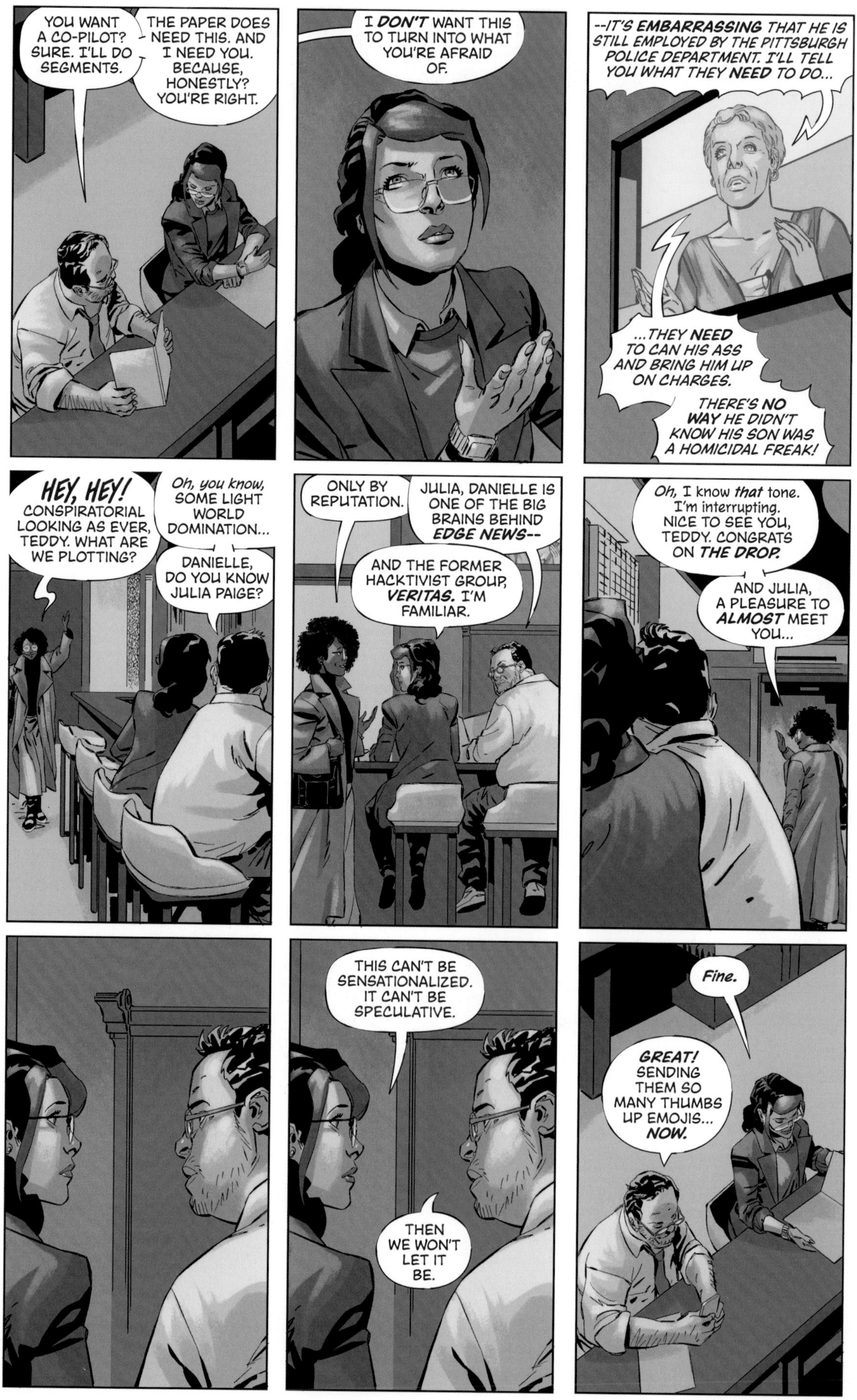
YOU WANT A CO-PILOT? SURE. I'LL DO SEGMENTS.
THE PAPER DOES NEED THIS. AND I NEED YOU. BECAUSE, HONESTLY? YOU'RE RIGHT.
I **DON'T** WANT THIS TO TURN INTO WHAT YOU'RE AFRAID OF.
--*IT'S* ***EMBARRASSING*** *THAT HE IS STILL EMPLOYED BY THE PITTSBURGH POLICE DEPARTMENT. I'LL TELL YOU WHAT THEY* ***NEED*** *TO DO...*
...THEY ***NEED*** *TO CAN HIS ASS AND BRING HIM UP ON CHARGES.*
THERE'S ***NO WAY*** *HE DIDN'T KNOW HIS SON WAS A HOMICIDAL FREAK!*
HEY, HEY! CONSPIRATORIAL LOOKING AS EVER, TEDDY. WHAT ARE WE PLOTTING?
Oh, you know, SOME LIGHT WORLD DOMINATION...
DANIELLE, DO YOU KNOW JULIA PAIGE?
ONLY BY REPUTATION.
JULIA, DANIELLE IS ONE OF THE BIG BRAINS BEHIND ***EDGE NEWS--***
AND THE FORMER HACKTIVIST GROUP, ***VERITAS.*** I'M FAMILIAR.
Oh, I know *that* tone. I'm interrupting. NICE TO SEE YOU, TEDDY. CONGRATS ON ***THE DROP.***
AND JULIA, A PLEASURE TO ***ALMOST*** MEET YOU...
THIS CAN'T BE SENSATIONALIZED. IT CAN'T BE SPECULATIVE.
THEN WE WON'T LET IT BE.
Fine.
GREAT! SENDING THEM SO MANY THUMBS UP EMOJIS... ***NOW.***

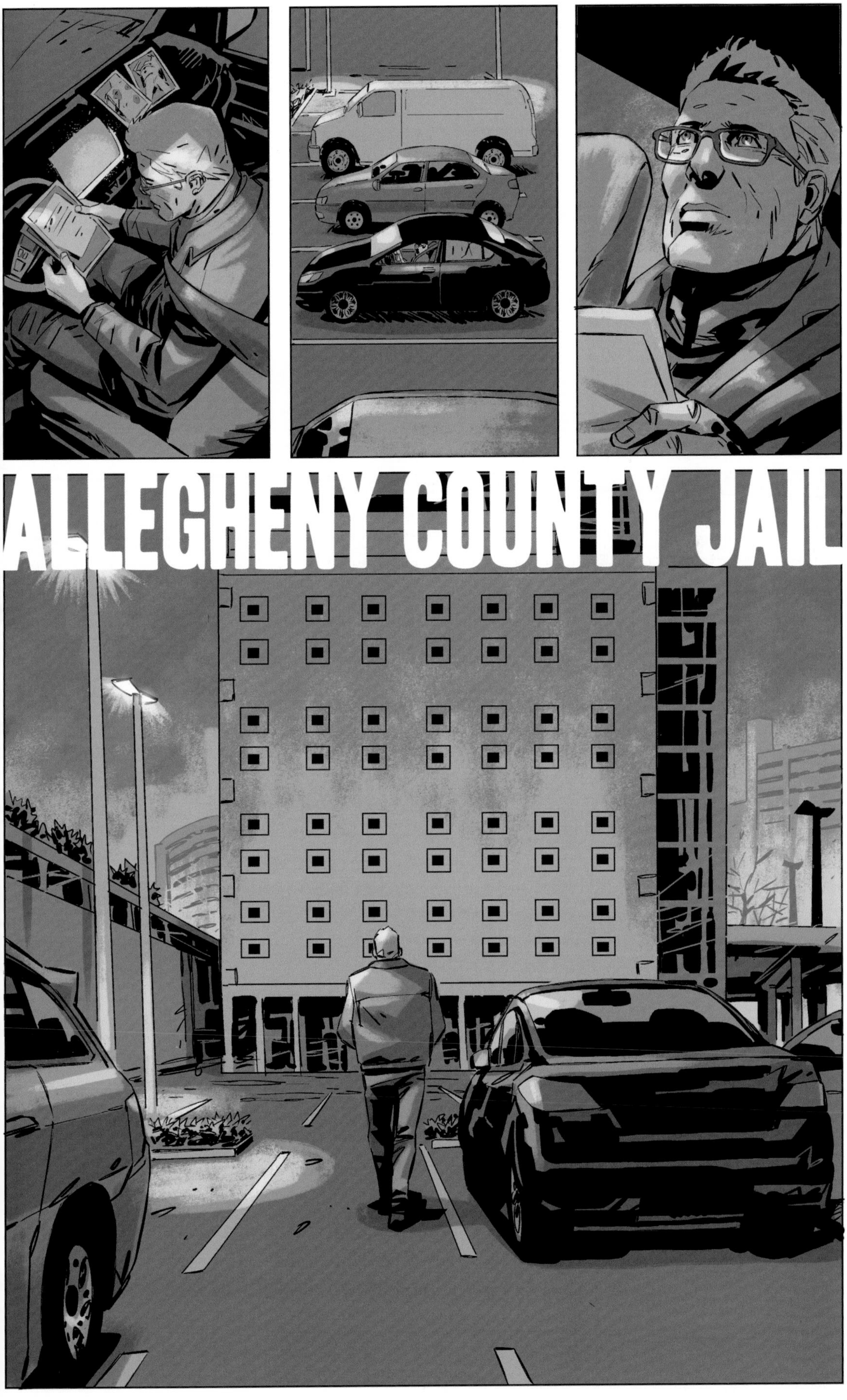
ALLEGHENY COUNTY JAIL

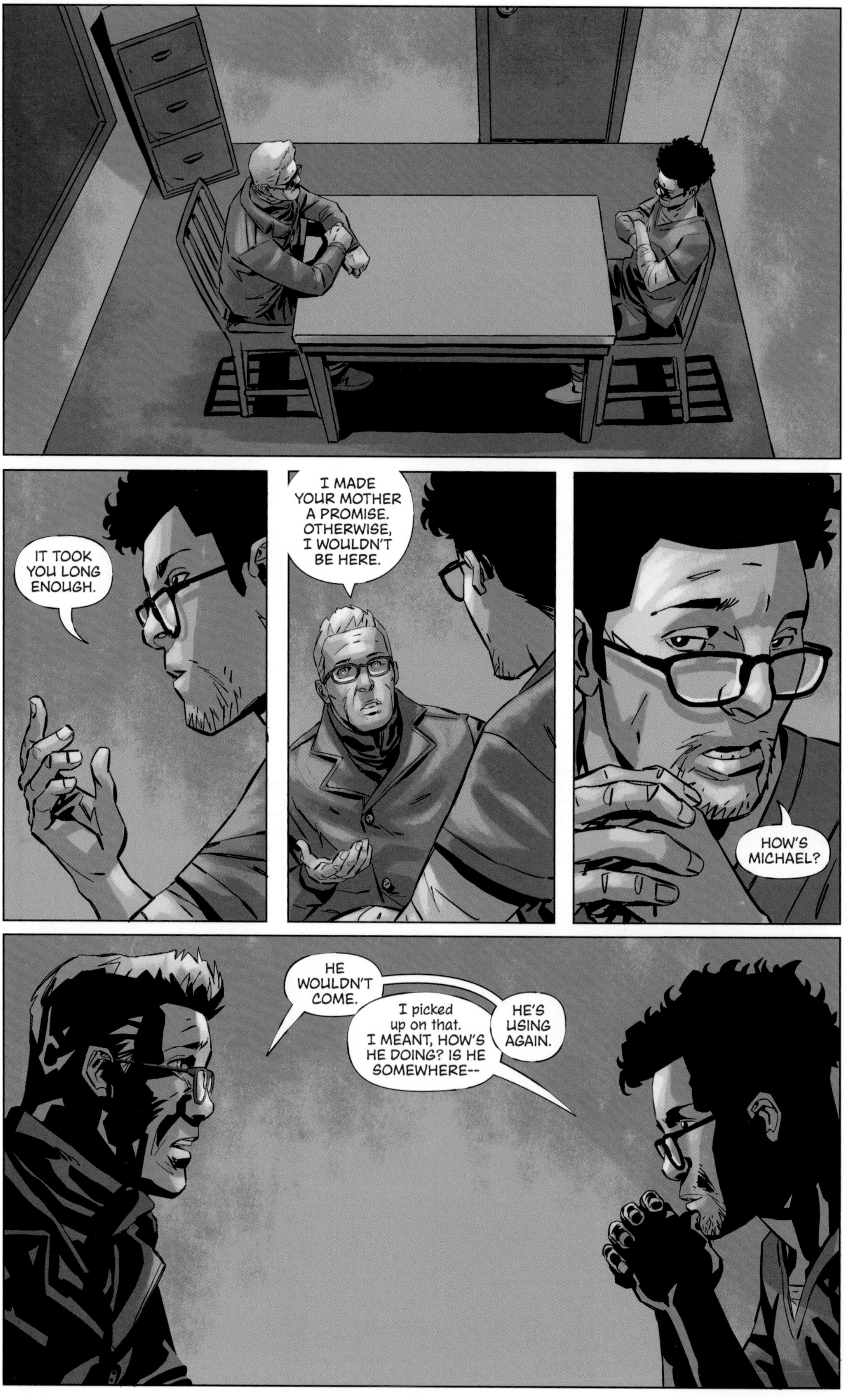
IT TOOK YOU LONG ENOUGH.
I MADE YOUR MOTHER A PROMISE. OTHERWISE, I WOULDN'T BE HERE.
HOW'S MICHAEL?
HE WOULDN'T COME.
I picked up on that. I MEANT, HOW'S HE DOING? IS HE SOMEWHERE--
HE'S USING AGAIN.

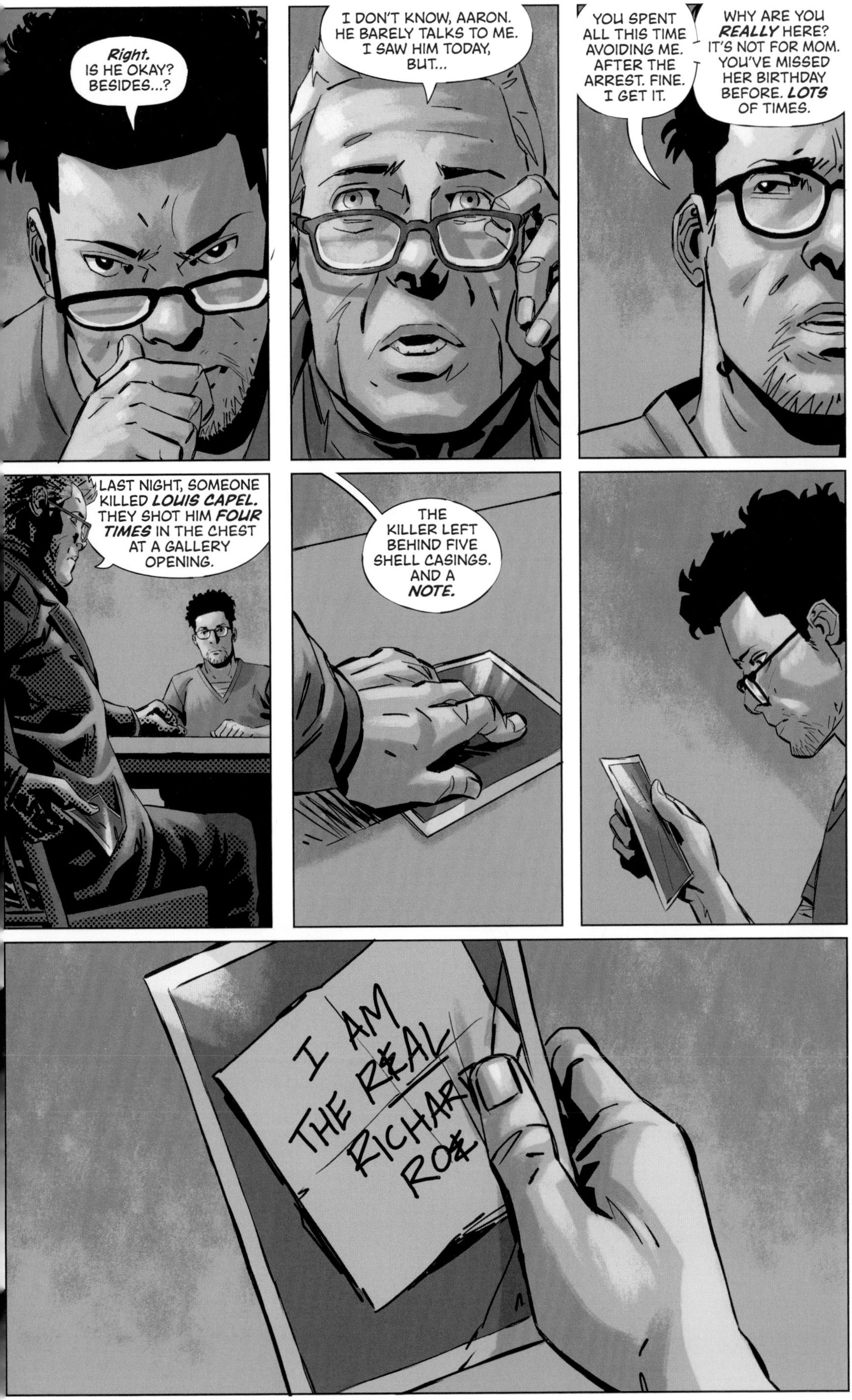
Right. IS HE OKAY? BESIDES...?
I DON'T KNOW, AARON. HE BARELY TALKS TO ME. I SAW HIM TODAY, BUT...
YOU SPENT ALL THIS TIME AVOIDING ME. AFTER THE ARREST. FINE. I GET IT.
WHY ARE YOU REALLY HERE? IT'S NOT FOR MOM. YOU'VE MISSED HER BIRTHDAY BEFORE. LOTS OF TIMES.
LAST NIGHT, SOMEONE KILLED LOUIS CAPEL. THEY SHOT HIM FOUR TIMES IN THE CHEST AT A GALLERY OPENING.
THE KILLER LEFT BEHIND FIVE SHELL CASINGS. AND A NOTE.
I AM THE REAL RICHARD ROE

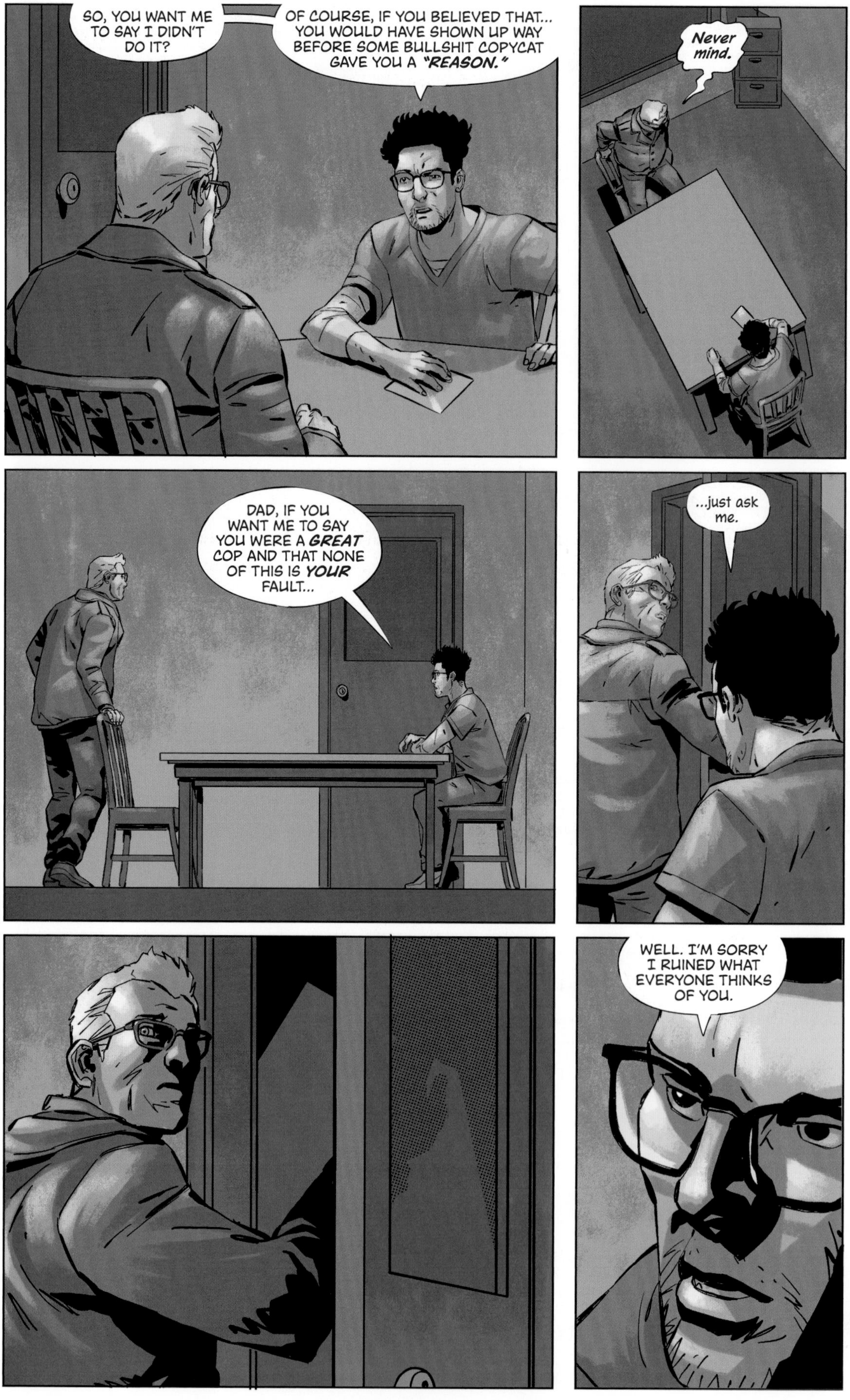
SO, YOU WANT ME TO SAY I DIDN'T DO IT?
OF COURSE, IF YOU BELIEVED THAT... YOU WOULD HAVE SHOWN UP WAY BEFORE SOME BULLSHIT COPYCAT GAVE YOU A "REASON."
Never mind.
DAD, IF YOU WANT ME TO SAY YOU WERE A GREAT COP AND THAT NONE OF THIS IS YOUR FAULT...
...just ask me.
WELL. I'M SORRY I RUINED WHAT EVERYONE THINKS OF YOU.

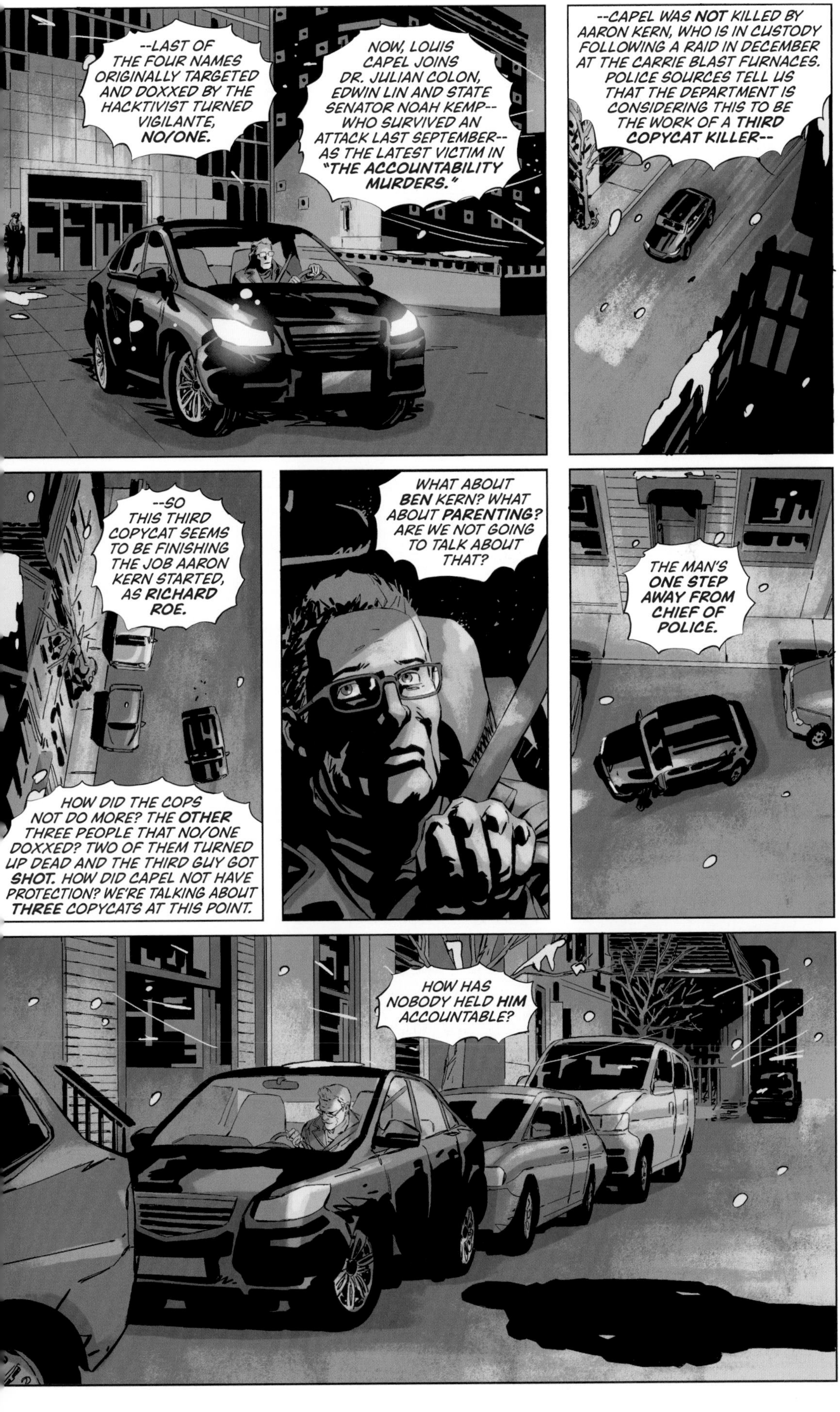
--LAST OF THE FOUR NAMES ORIGINALLY TARGETED AND DOXXED BY THE HACKTIVIST TURNED VIGILANTE, NO/ONE.
NOW, LOUIS CAPEL JOINS DR. JULIAN COLON, EDWIN LIN AND STATE SENATOR NOAH KEMP-- WHO SURVIVED AN ATTACK LAST SEPTEMBER-- AS THE LATEST VICTIM IN "THE ACCOUNTABILITY MURDERS."
--CAPEL WAS NOT KILLED BY AARON KERN, WHO IS IN CUSTODY FOLLOWING A RAID IN DECEMBER AT THE CARRIE BLAST FURNACES. POLICE SOURCES TELL US THAT THE DEPARTMENT IS CONSIDERING THIS TO BE THE WORK OF A THIRD COPYCAT KILLER--
--SO THIS THIRD COPYCAT SEEMS TO BE FINISHING THE JOB AARON KERN STARTED, AS RICHARD ROE.
HOW DID THE COPS NOT DO MORE? THE OTHER THREE PEOPLE THAT NO/ONE DOXXED? TWO OF THEM TURNED UP DEAD AND THE THIRD GUY GOT SHOT. HOW DID CAPEL NOT HAVE PROTECTION? WE'RE TALKING ABOUT THREE COPYCATS AT THIS POINT.
WHAT ABOUT BEN KERN? WHAT ABOUT PARENTING? ARE WE NOT GOING TO TALK ABOUT THAT?
THE MAN'S ONE STEP AWAY FROM CHIEF OF POLICE.
HOW HAS NOBODY HELD HIM ACCOUNTABLE?

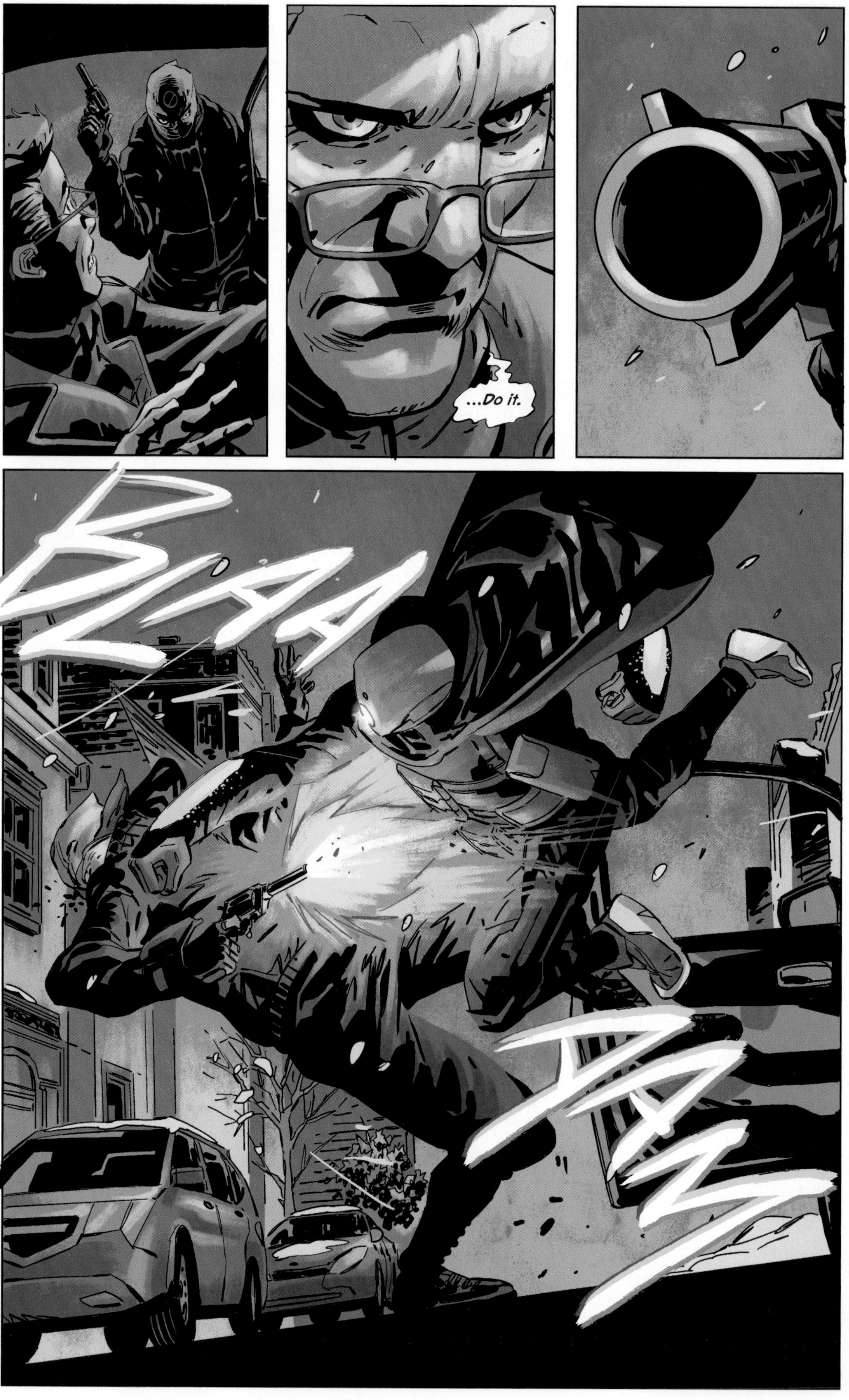
...Do it.

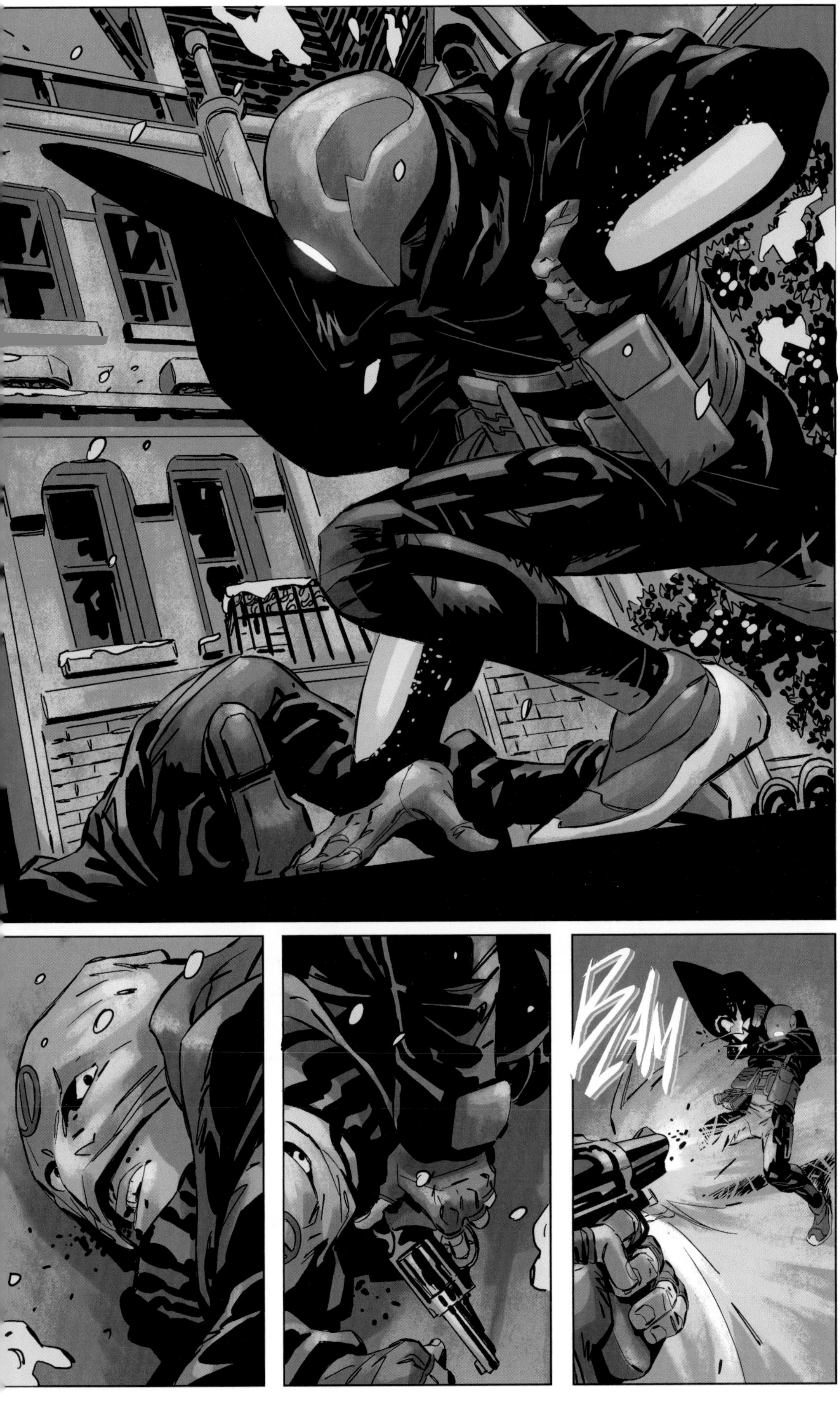
BLAM

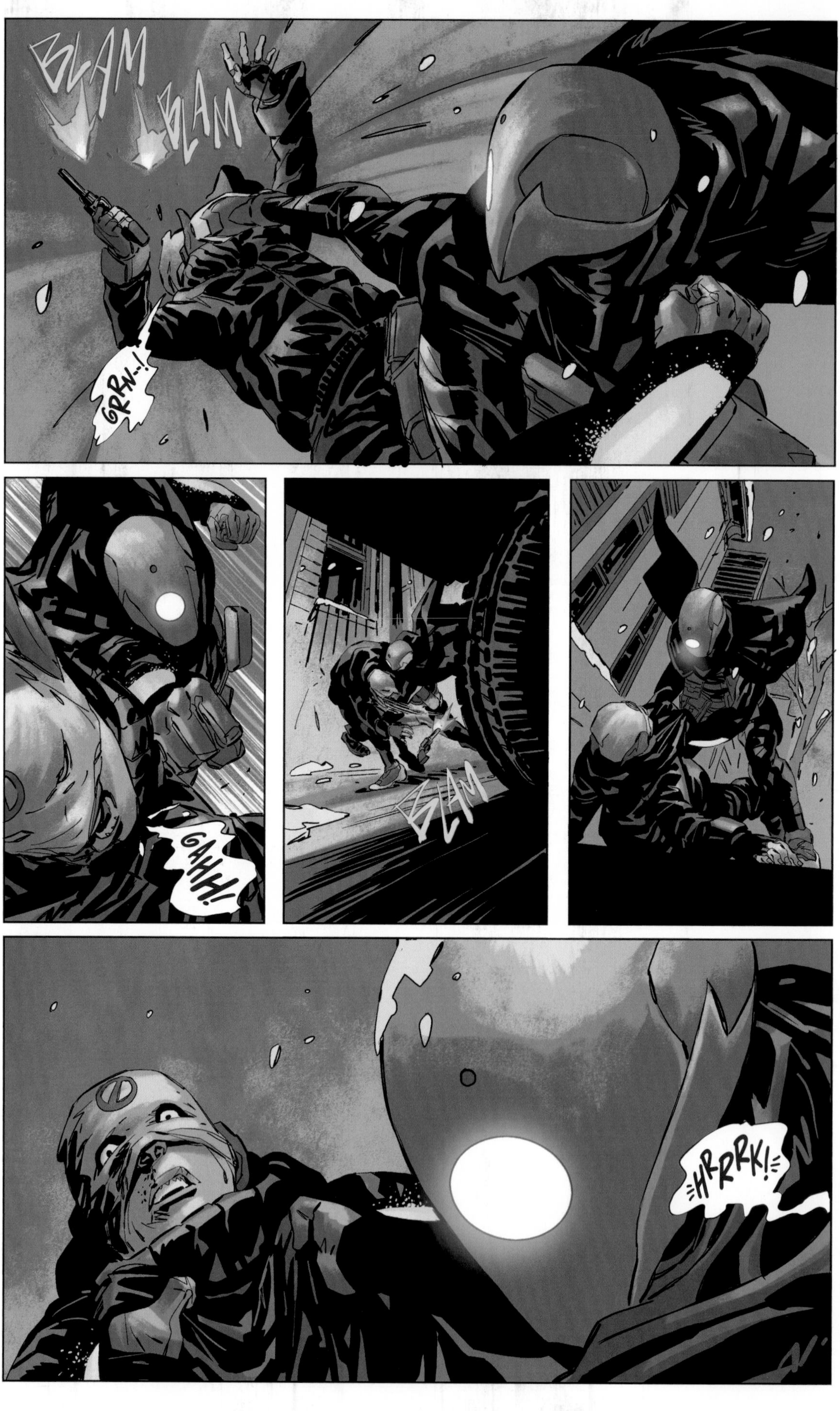
BLAM
BLAM
GRRN--!
GAHH!
BLAM
HRRRK!

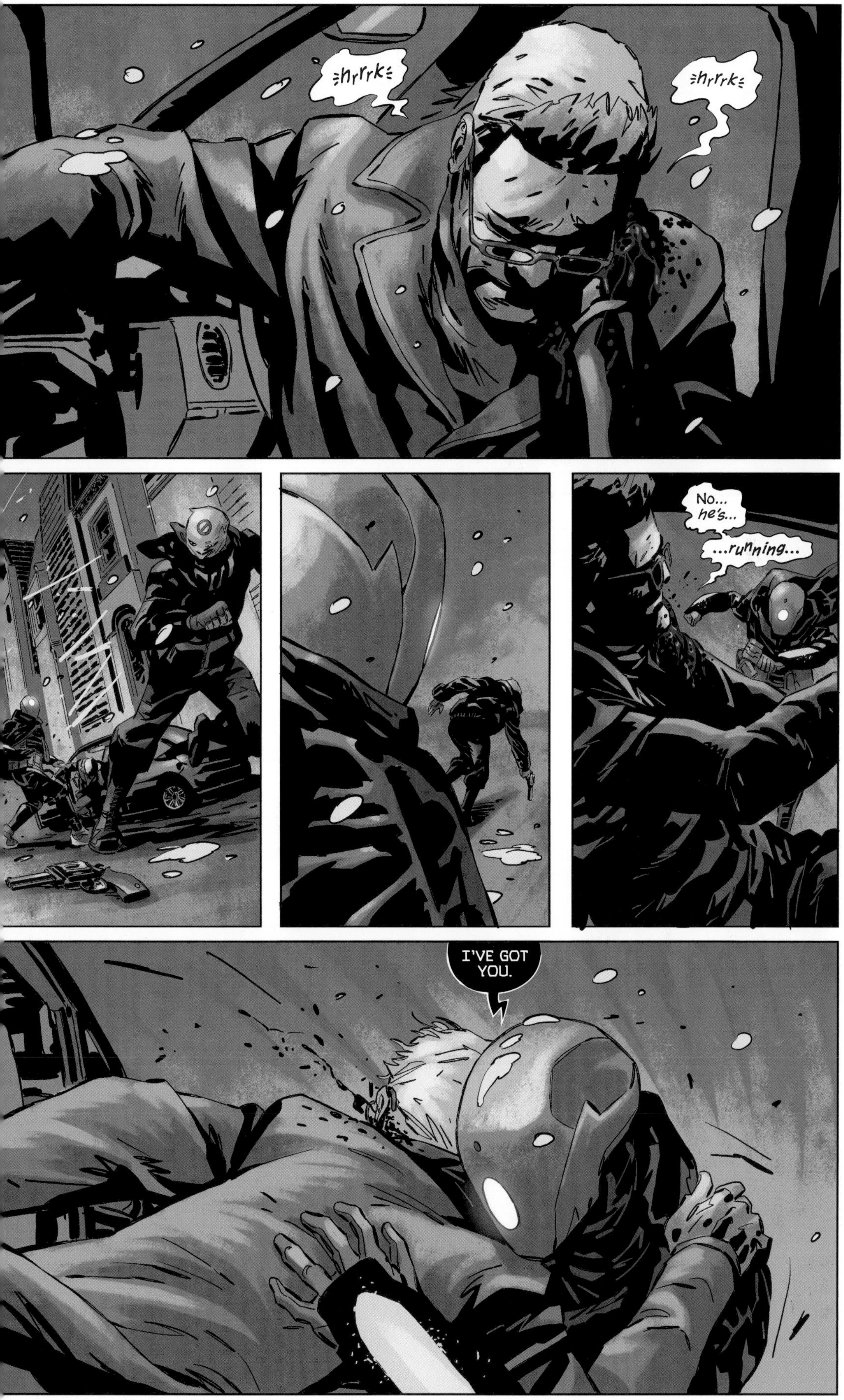
hrrrk
hrrrk
No... he's...
...running...
I'VE GOT YOU.

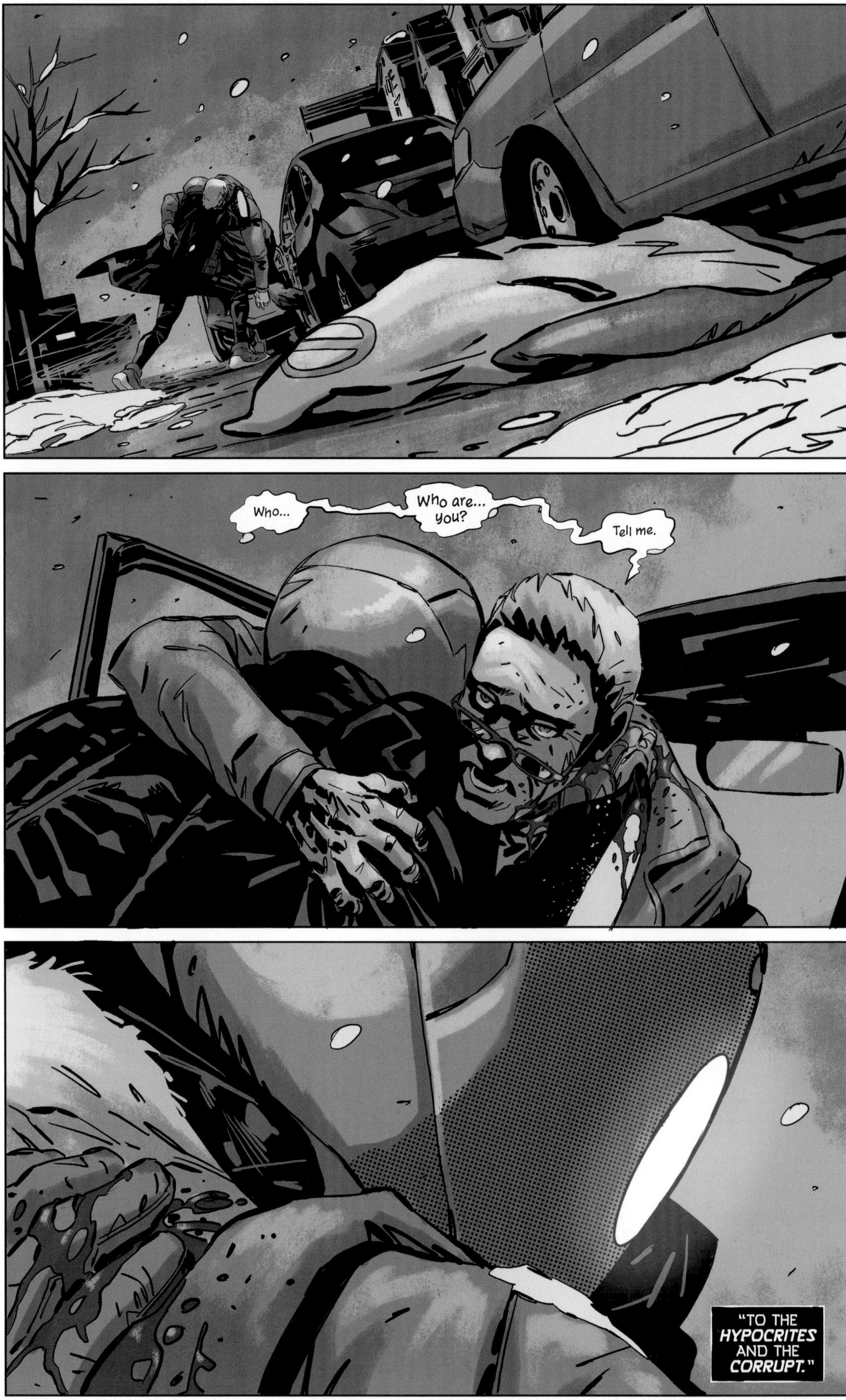
Who...
Who are... you?
Tell me.
"TO THE HYPOCRITES AND THE CORRUPT."

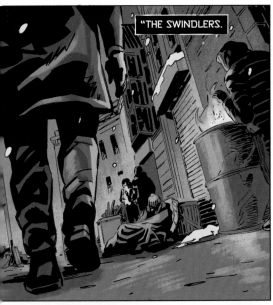

"THE SWINDLERS.

"THE PARASITES.

"ALL THOSE WHO TAKE FROM YOUR FELLOW MAN.

"BECAUSE-- LIKE ALL *MONSTERS*--

"--YOU BELIEVE YOURSELF SAFE IN THE SHADOWS.

"THIS MESSAGE IS FOR *YOU*."

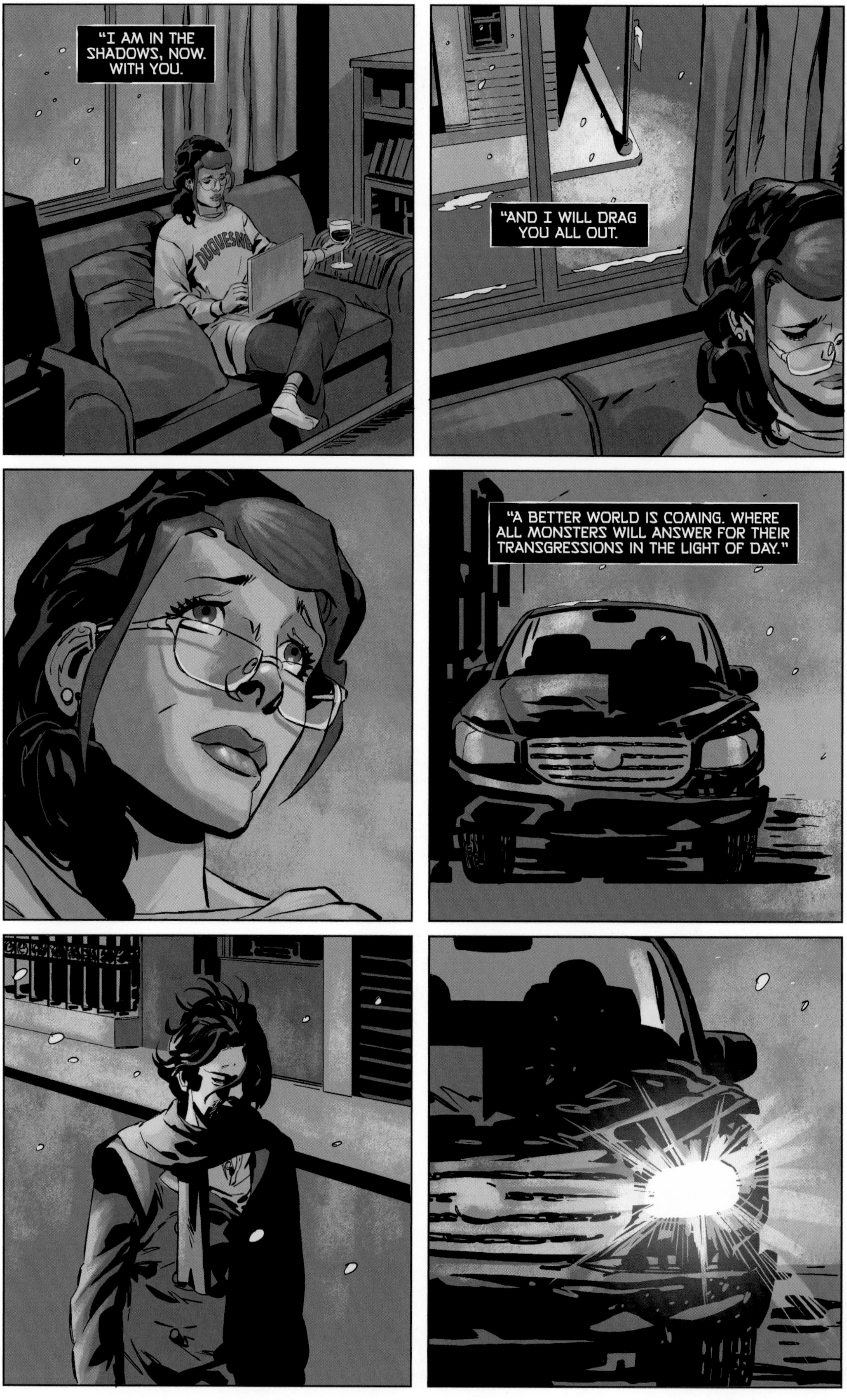
"I AM IN THE SHADOWS, NOW. WITH YOU.
DUQUESNE
"AND I WILL DRAG YOU ALL OUT.
"A BETTER WORLD IS COMING. WHERE ALL MONSTERS WILL ANSWER FOR THEIR TRANSGRESSIONS IN THE LIGHT OF DAY."

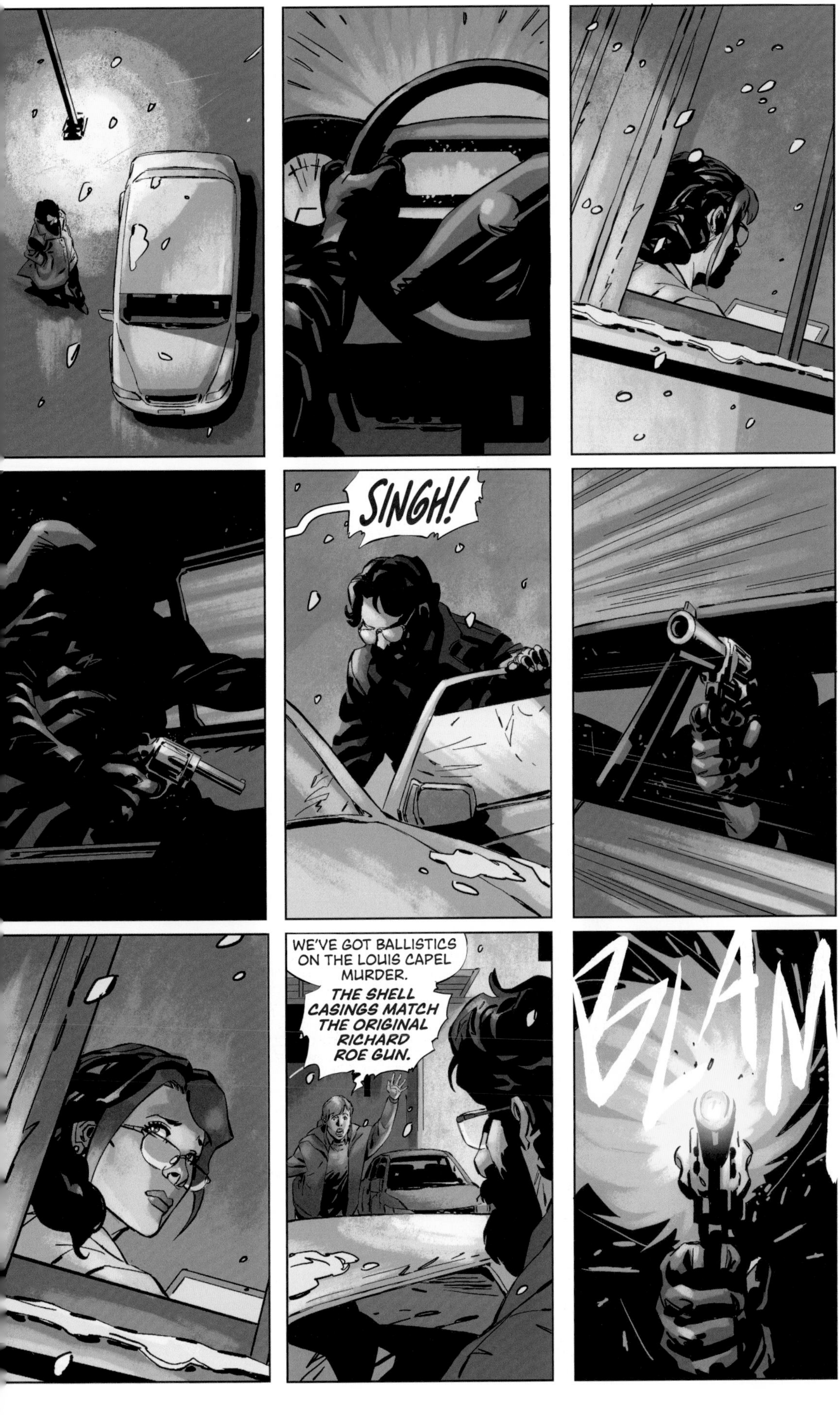
SINGH!
WE'VE GOT BALLISTICS ON THE LOUIS CAPEL MURDER.
THE SHELL CASINGS MATCH THE ORIGINAL RICHARD ROE GUN.
BLAM

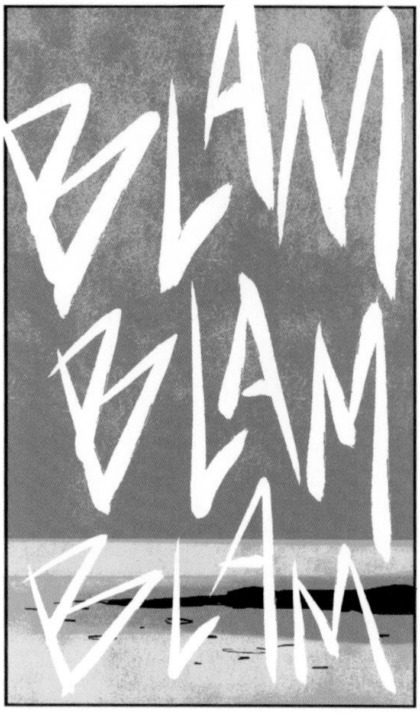
BLAM
BLAM
BLAM

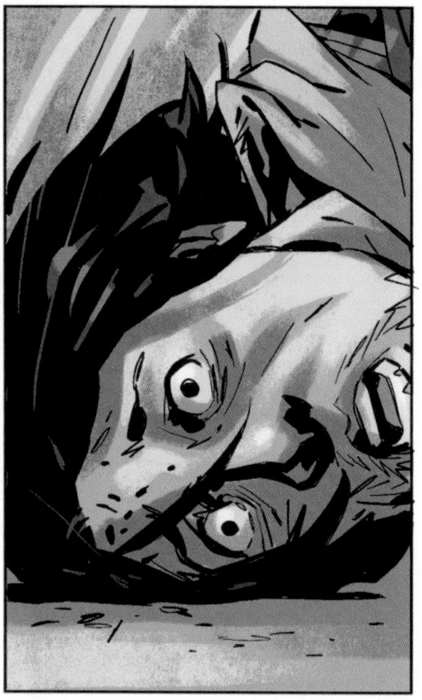

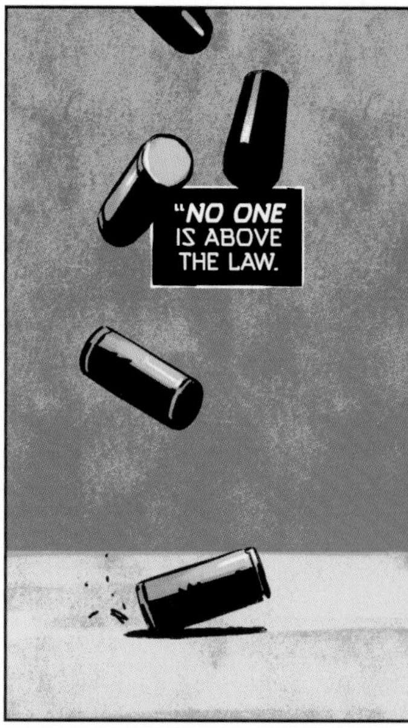
"NO ONE IS ABOVE THE LAW.

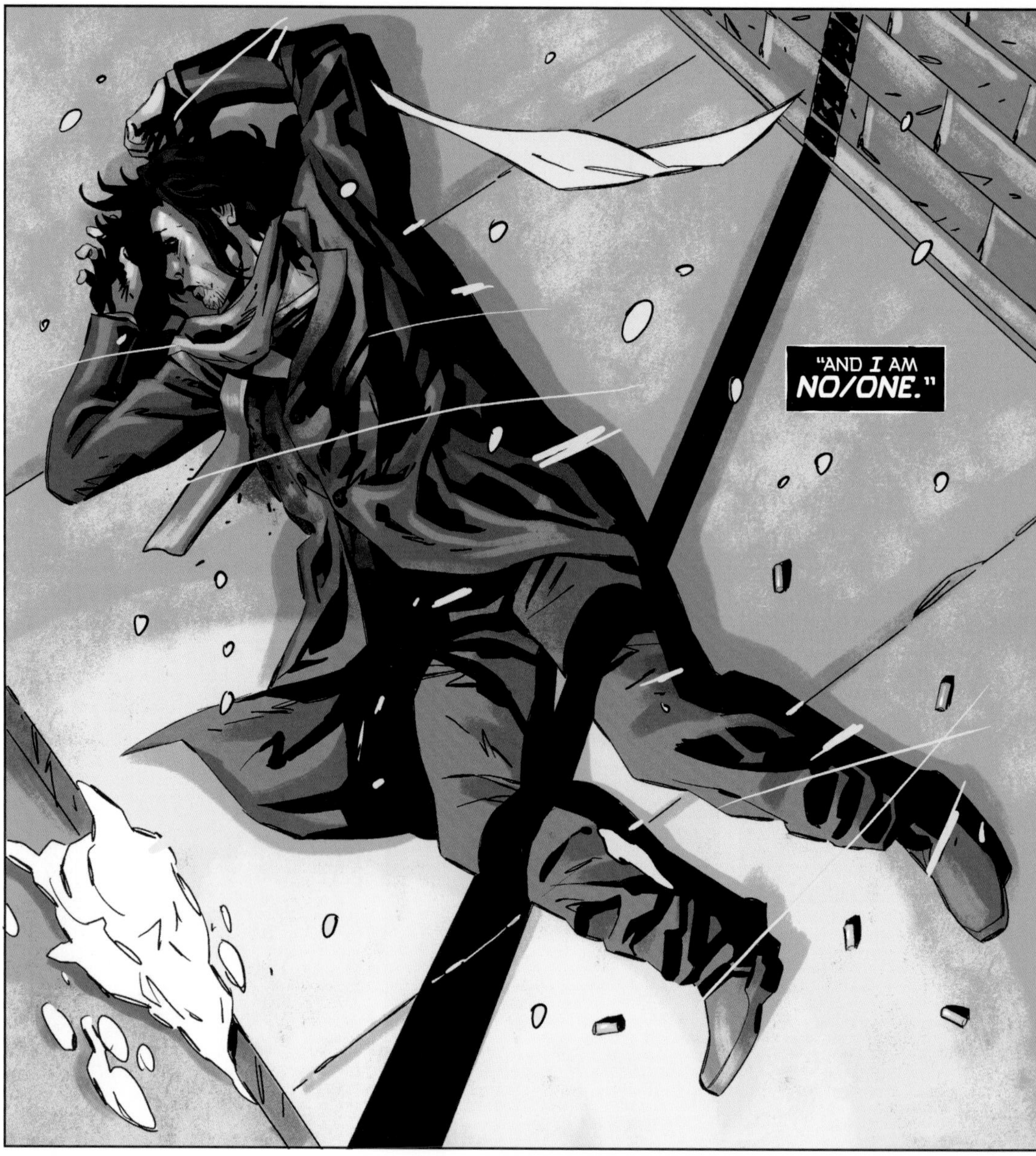
"AND I AM NO/ONE."

The Drop

PRESENTS

WHO IS NO/ONE
WITH/JULIA PAIGE

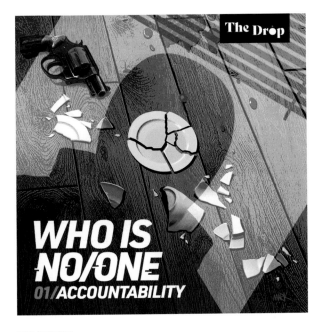

The Drop

WHO IS
NO/ONE
01/ACCOUNTABILITY

16 MARCH
01/Accountability
WHO IS NO/ONE

19:32   -15:32

>_ **Kern, police boss tied to "Accountability Murders," shot Wednesday**
MARCH 16 2023

written by Julia Paige & Alejandro Rios
published on The Drop

"Ben Kern, the department's assistant chief of operations, was shot once about 8 p.m. before someone intervened and the shooter fled."

>_ CHAPTER TWO
APRIL 2023

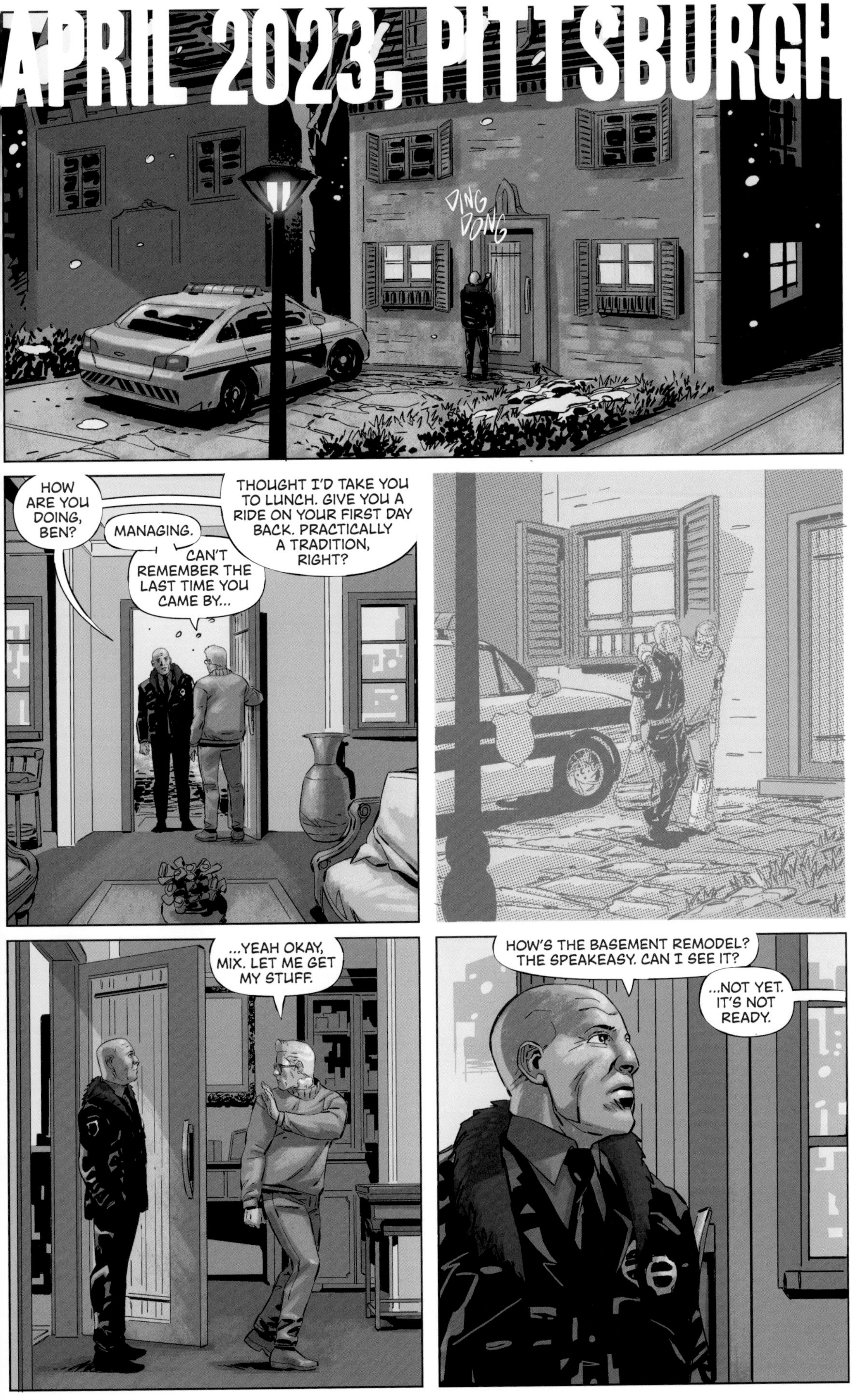

APRIL 2023, PITTSBURGH
DING DONG
HOW ARE YOU DOING, BEN?
MANAGING.
CAN'T REMEMBER THE LAST TIME YOU CAME BY...
THOUGHT I'D TAKE YOU TO LUNCH. GIVE YOU A RIDE ON YOUR FIRST DAY BACK. PRACTICALLY A TRADITION, RIGHT?
...YEAH OKAY, MIX. LET ME GET MY STUFF.
HOW'S THE BASEMENT REMODEL? THE SPEAKEASY. CAN I SEE IT?
...NOT YET. IT'S NOT READY.

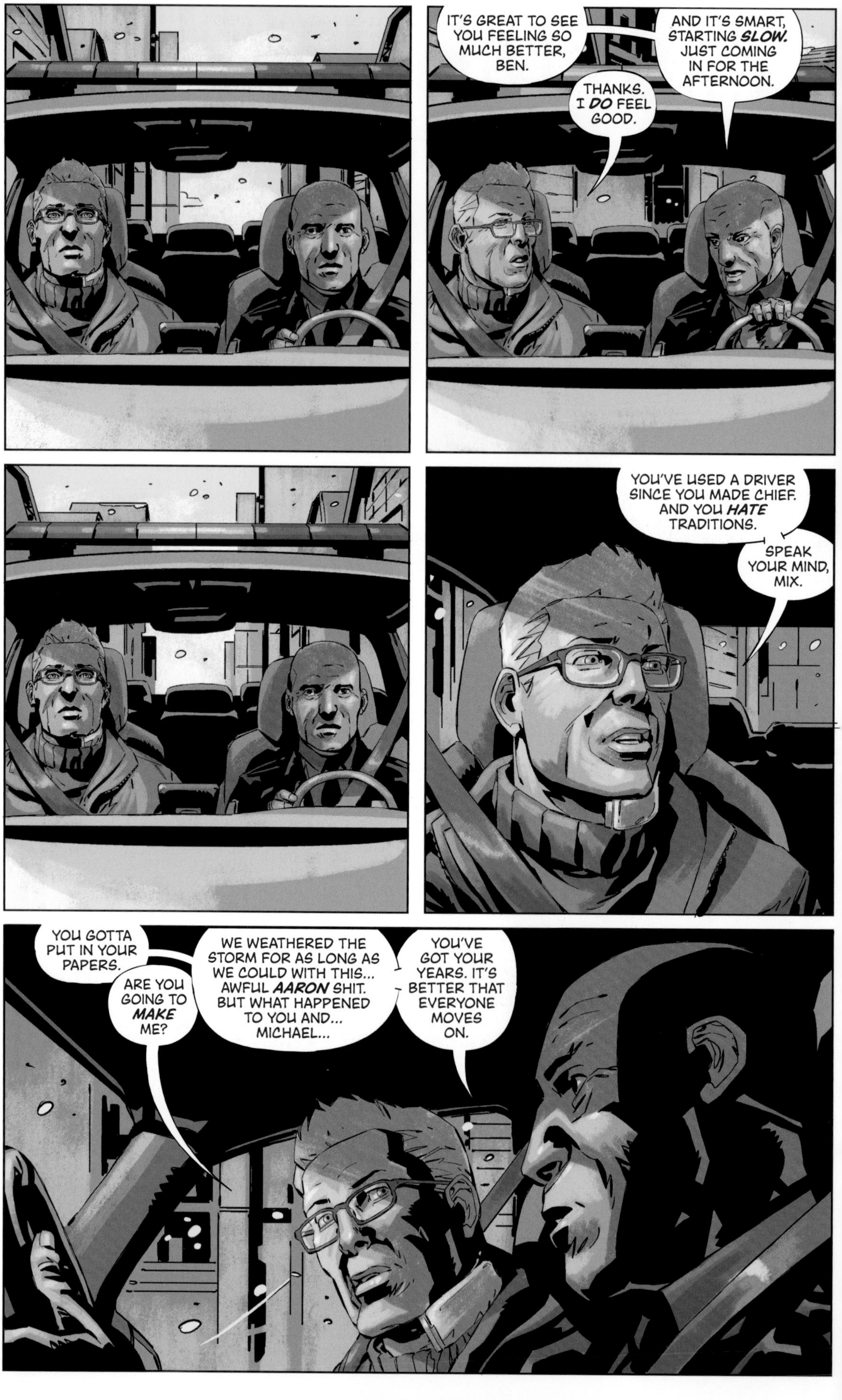
IT'S GREAT TO SEE YOU FEELING SO MUCH BETTER, BEN.
THANKS. I DO FEEL GOOD.
AND IT'S SMART, STARTING SLOW. JUST COMING IN FOR THE AFTERNOON.
YOU'VE USED A DRIVER SINCE YOU MADE CHIEF. AND YOU HATE TRADITIONS.
SPEAK YOUR MIND, MIX.
YOU GOTTA PUT IN YOUR PAPERS.
ARE YOU GOING TO MAKE ME?
WE WEATHERED THE STORM FOR AS LONG AS WE COULD WITH THIS... AWFUL AARON SHIT. BUT WHAT HAPPENED TO YOU AND... MICHAEL...
YOU'VE GOT YOUR YEARS. IT'S BETTER THAT EVERYONE MOVES ON.

NOT BETTER FOR *ME*. I NEED TO FIND WHO *MURDERED MY SON*.

YOU'RE *ASSISTANT CHIEF OPS*. THAT'S NOT EVEN YOUR *JOB*.

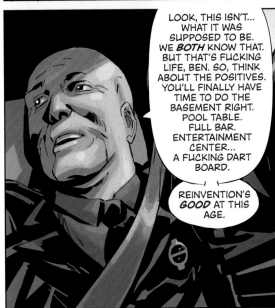

LOOK, THIS ISN'T... WHAT IT WAS SUPPOSED TO BE. WE *BOTH* KNOW THAT. BUT THAT'S FUCKING LIFE, BEN. SO, THINK ABOUT THE POSITIVES. YOU'LL FINALLY HAVE TIME TO DO THE BASEMENT RIGHT. POOL TABLE. FULL BAR. ENTERTAINMENT CENTER... A FUCKING DART BOARD.

REINVENTION'S *GOOD* AT THIS AGE.

REMEMBER WHAT NOEMI SAID, WE BETTER BE CHARGING COVER IF YOU'RE GONNA INVEST ALL THAT MONEY IN A CLUBHOUSE?

PLAYROOM. SHE CALLED IT A *PLAYROOM*.

BZZT BZZT

...*Fuck*.

DOWNTOWN
WHY ARE THEY NEVER ON THE FIRST FLOOR?
AND THE ELEVATOR'S OUT.
Fuck this.
huff
TRY BEING A SMOKER.
SO... huff IT'S THE SAME GUY?
OR SOMEONE WHO WANTS TO BE.
FOUR SHOTS TO THE CHEST. DROPPED SHELL CASINGS...
FIVE?
YEAH.
COULD BE OUR SAME COPYCAT.
OR IT COULD BE SOMEONE WHO LISTENED TO THE GODDAMN PODCAST. THEY MADE SUCH A BIG DEAL OUT OF THE FUCKING SHELL CASINGS.
THERE WAS A NOTE ON THIS ONE, TOO.
HEY, KATHY! SHOW SINGH AND HARPER THE NOTE.

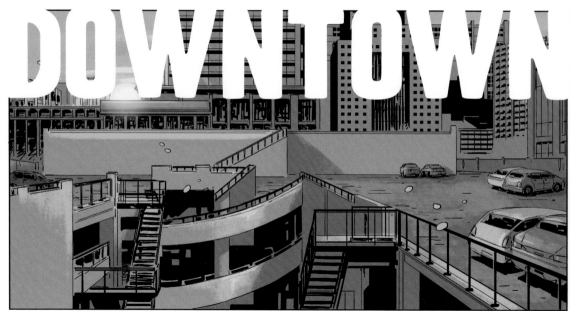

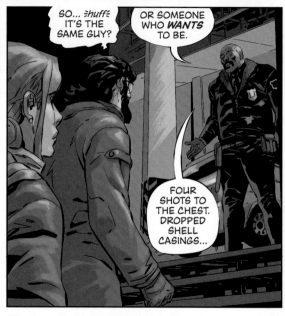

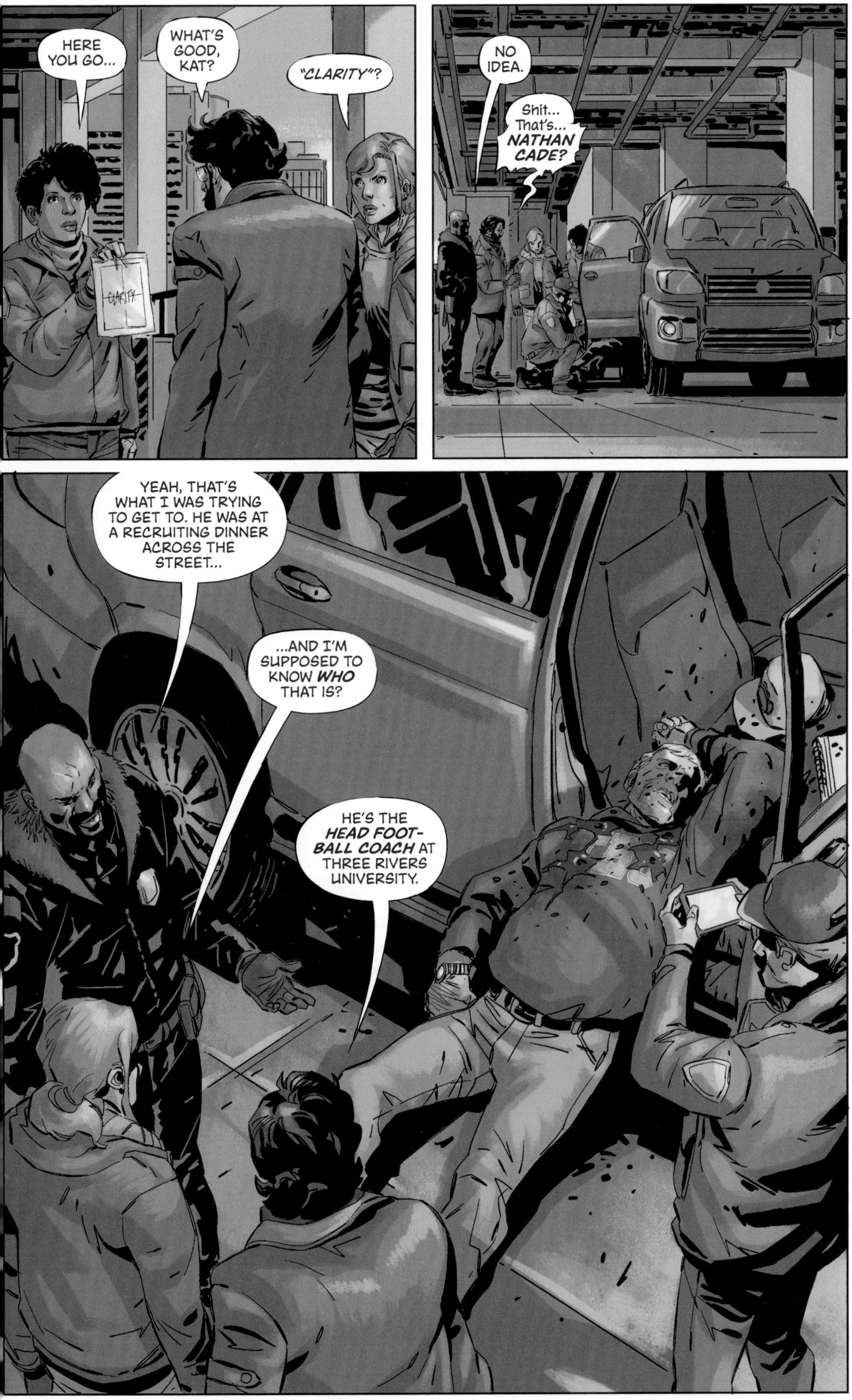
HERE YOU GO...
WHAT'S GOOD, KAT?
"CLARITY"?
CLARITY
NO IDEA.
Shit... That's... NATHAN CADE?
YEAH, THAT'S WHAT I WAS TRYING TO GET TO. HE WAS AT A RECRUITING DINNER ACROSS THE STREET...
...AND I'M SUPPOSED TO KNOW WHO THAT IS?
HE'S THE HEAD FOOTBALL COACH AT THREE RIVERS UNIVERSITY.

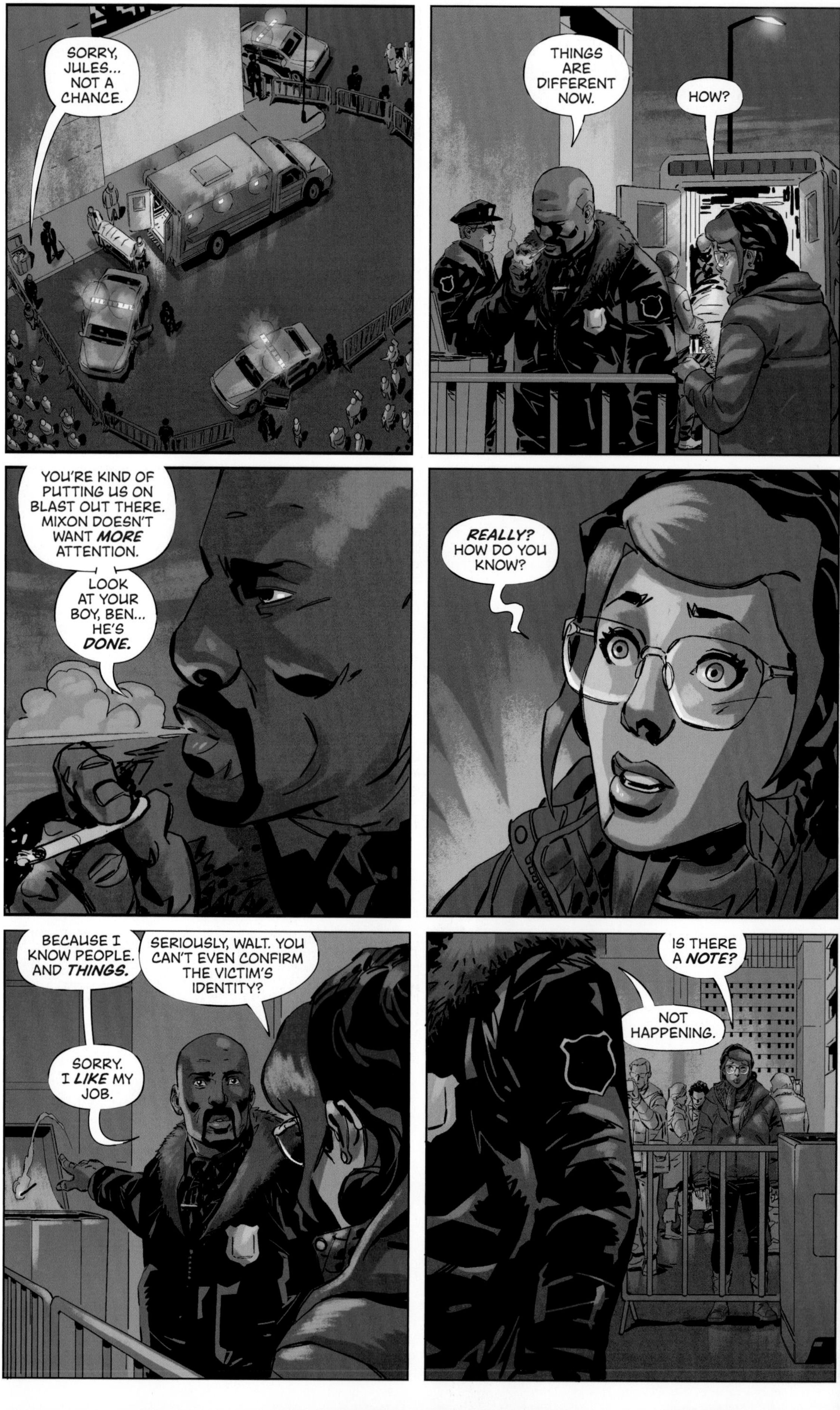
SORRY, JULES... NOT A CHANCE.
THINGS ARE DIFFERENT NOW.
HOW?
YOU'RE KIND OF PUTTING US ON BLAST OUT THERE. MIXON DOESN'T WANT MORE ATTENTION.
LOOK AT YOUR BOY, BEN... HE'S DONE.
REALLY? HOW DO YOU KNOW?
BECAUSE I KNOW PEOPLE. AND THINGS.
SERIOUSLY, WALT. YOU CAN'T EVEN CONFIRM THE VICTIM'S IDENTITY?
SORRY. I LIKE MY JOB.
IS THERE A NOTE?
NOT HAPPENING.

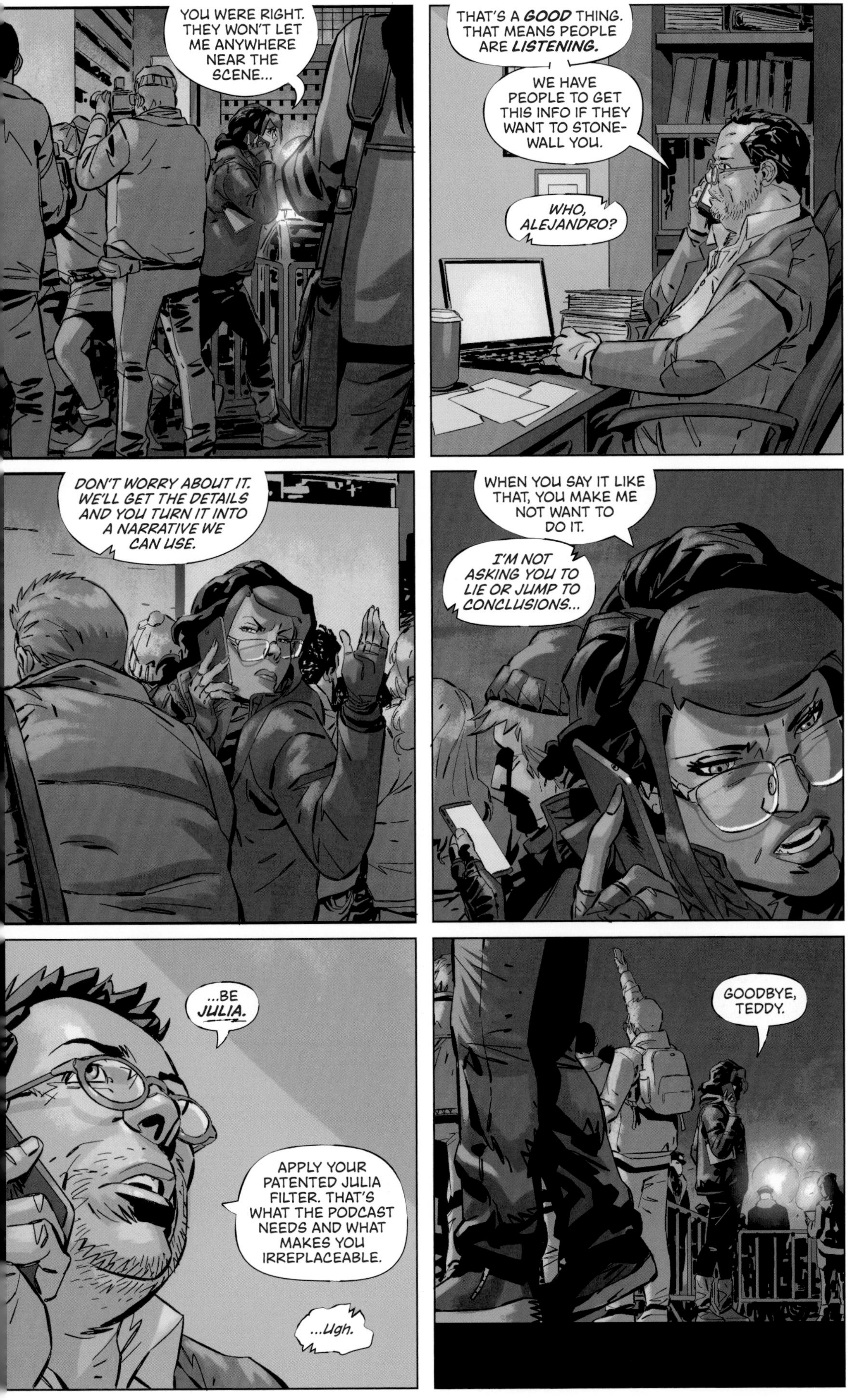
YOU WERE RIGHT. THEY WON'T LET ME ANYWHERE NEAR THE SCENE...
THAT'S A **GOOD** THING. THAT MEANS PEOPLE ARE **LISTENING.**
WE HAVE PEOPLE TO GET THIS INFO IF THEY WANT TO STONE-WALL YOU.
WHO, ALEJANDRO?
DON'T WORRY ABOUT IT. WE'LL GET THE DETAILS AND YOU TURN IT INTO A NARRATIVE WE CAN USE.
WHEN YOU SAY IT LIKE THAT, YOU MAKE ME NOT WANT TO DO IT.
I'M NOT ASKING YOU TO LIE OR JUMP TO CONCLUSIONS...
...BE JULIA.
APPLY YOUR PATENTED JULIA FILTER. THAT'S WHAT THE PODCAST NEEDS AND WHAT MAKES YOU IRREPLACEABLE.
...Ugh.
GOODBYE, TEDDY.

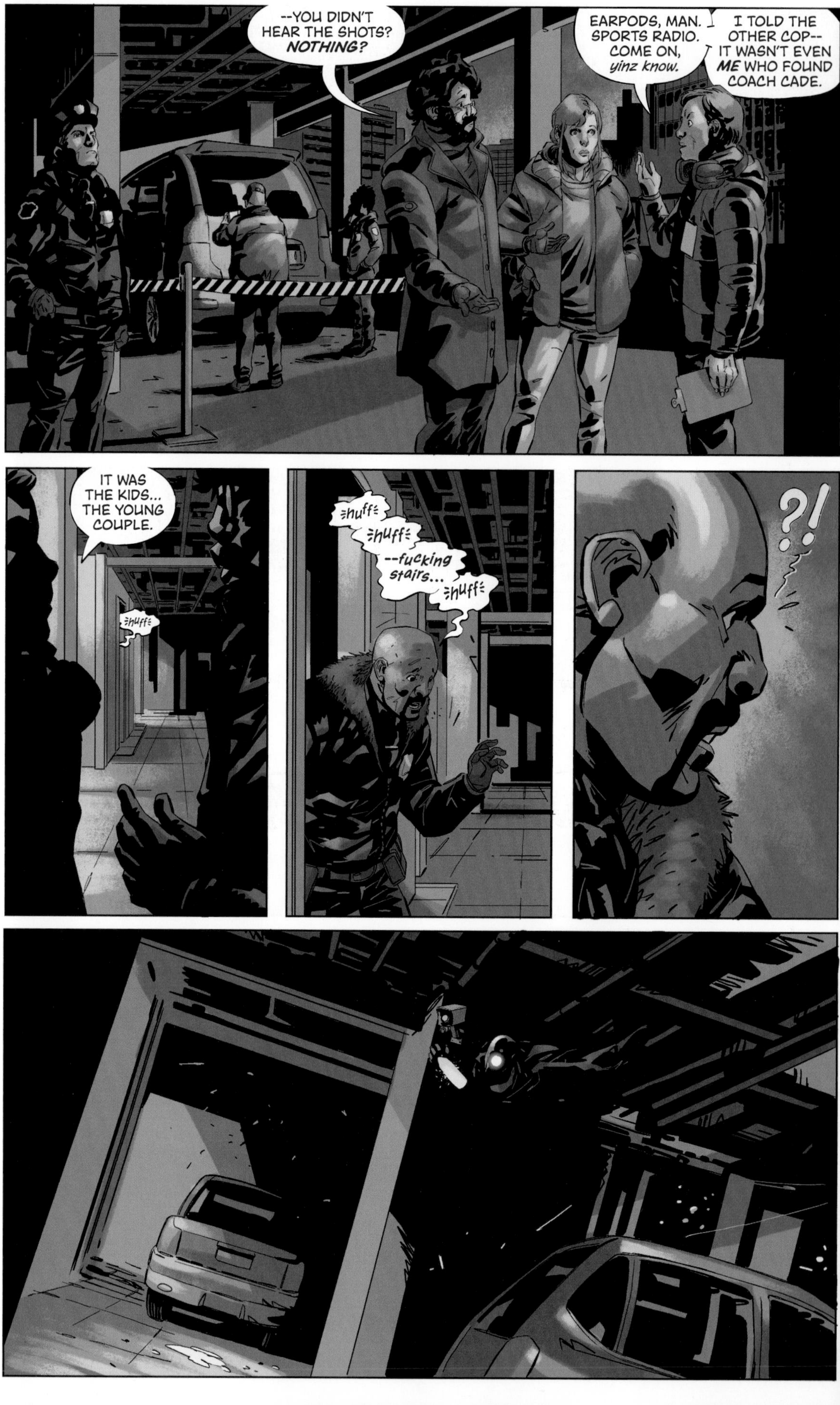
--YOU DIDN'T HEAR THE SHOTS? NOTHING?
EARPODS, MAN. SPORTS RADIO. COME ON, yinz know.
I TOLD THE OTHER COP-- IT WASN'T EVEN ME WHO FOUND COACH CADE.
IT WAS THE KIDS... THE YOUNG COUPLE.
huff
huff
huff
--fucking stairs...
huff
?!

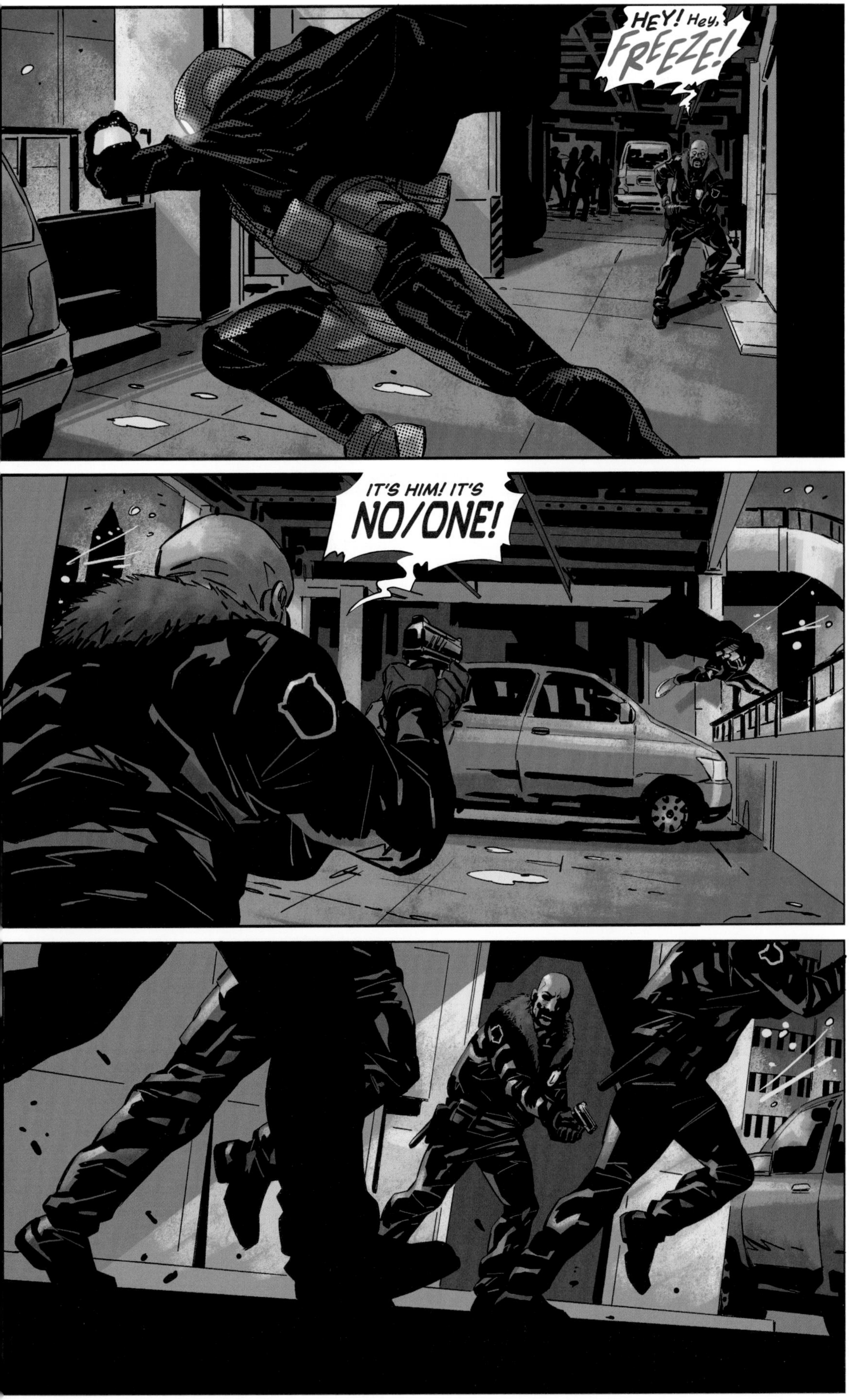
HEY! Hey, FREEZE!
IT'S HIM! IT'S NO/ONE!

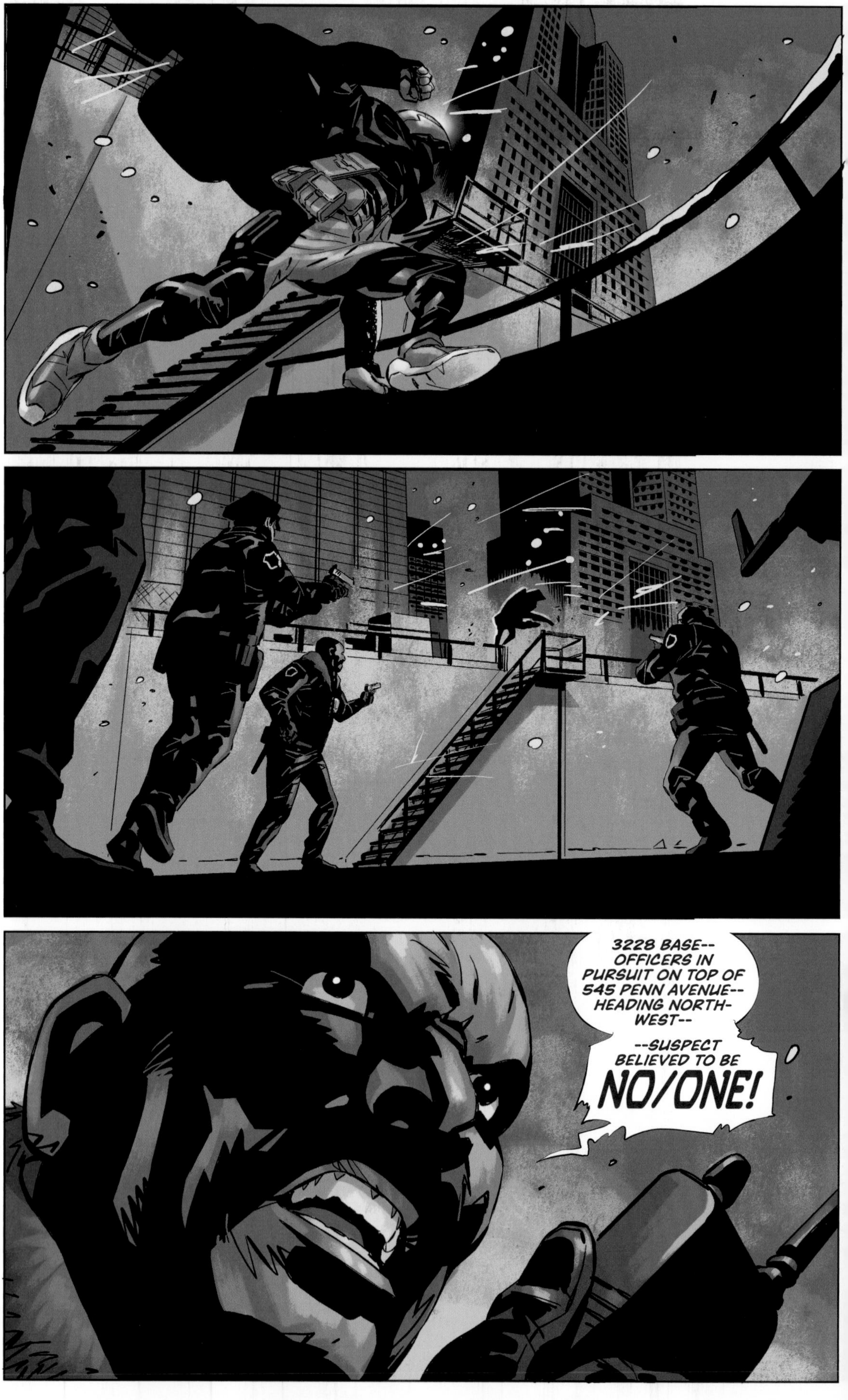
3228 BASE-- OFFICERS IN PURSUIT ON TOP OF 545 PENN AVENUE-- HEADING NORTH-WEST--
--SUSPECT BELIEVED TO BE NO/ONE!

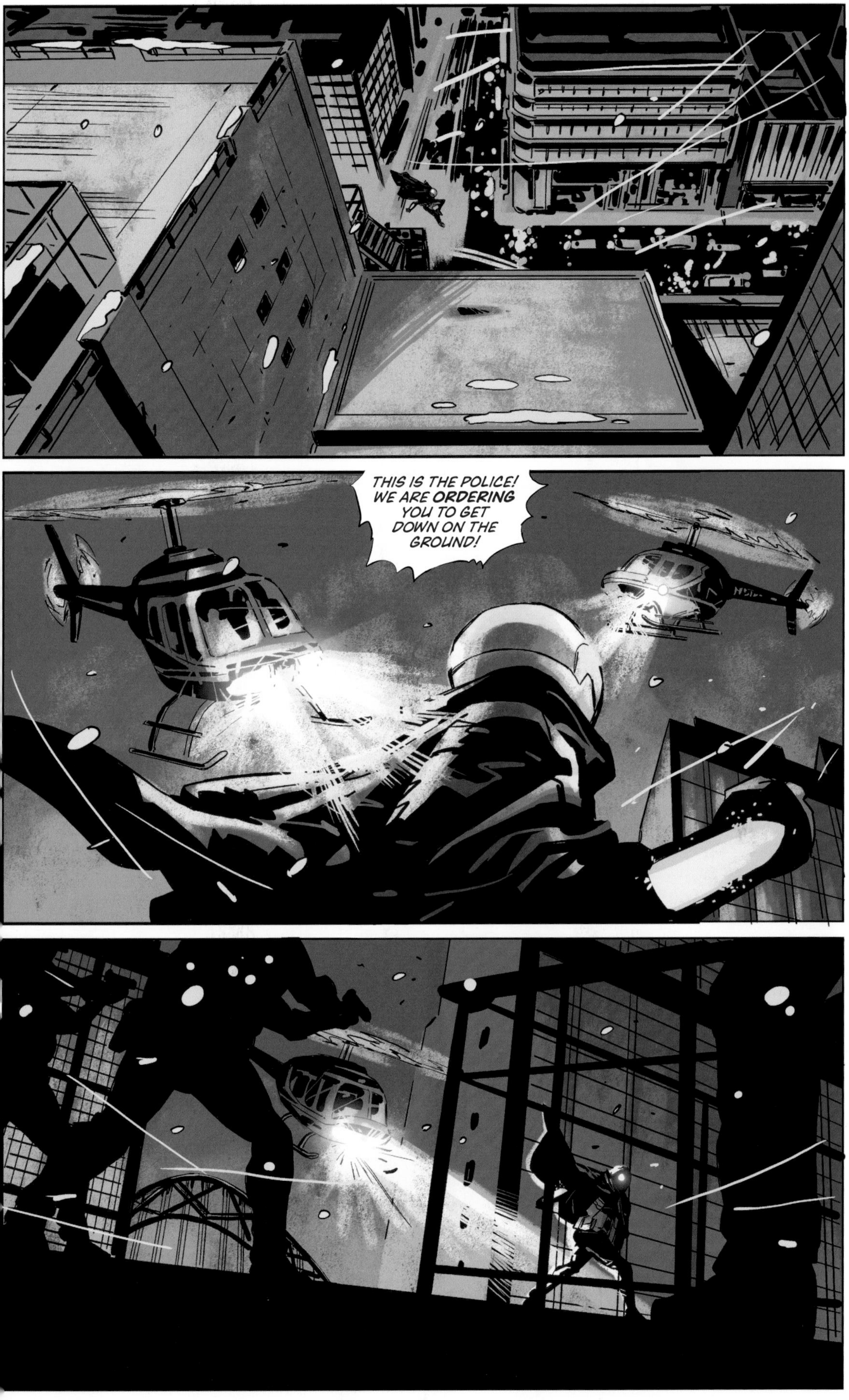
THIS IS THE POLICE! WE ARE ORDERING YOU TO GET DOWN ON THE GROUND!

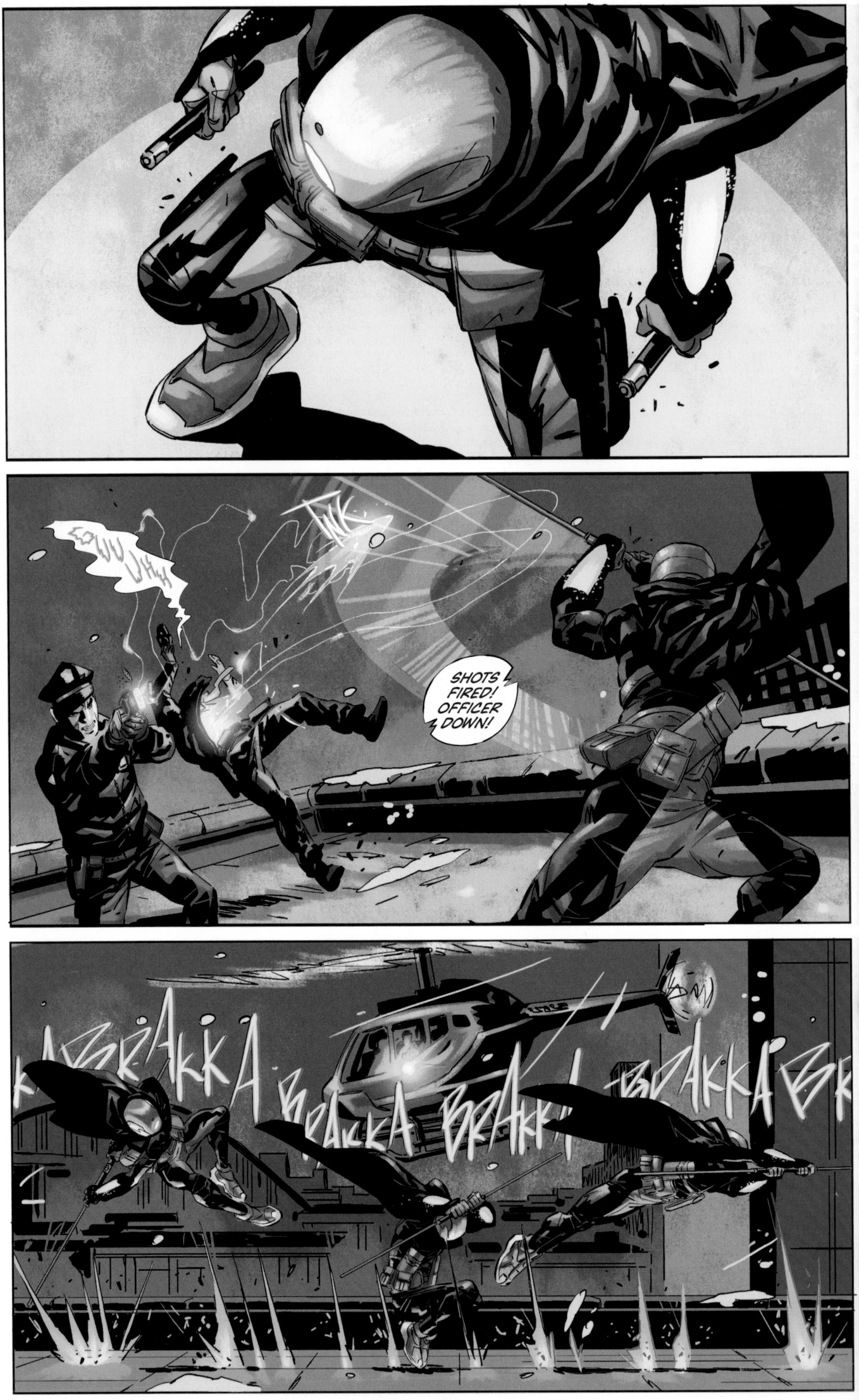
TINK
SHOTS FIRED! OFFICER DOWN!
BRAKKA BRAKKA BRAKKA BRAKKA BRAKKA

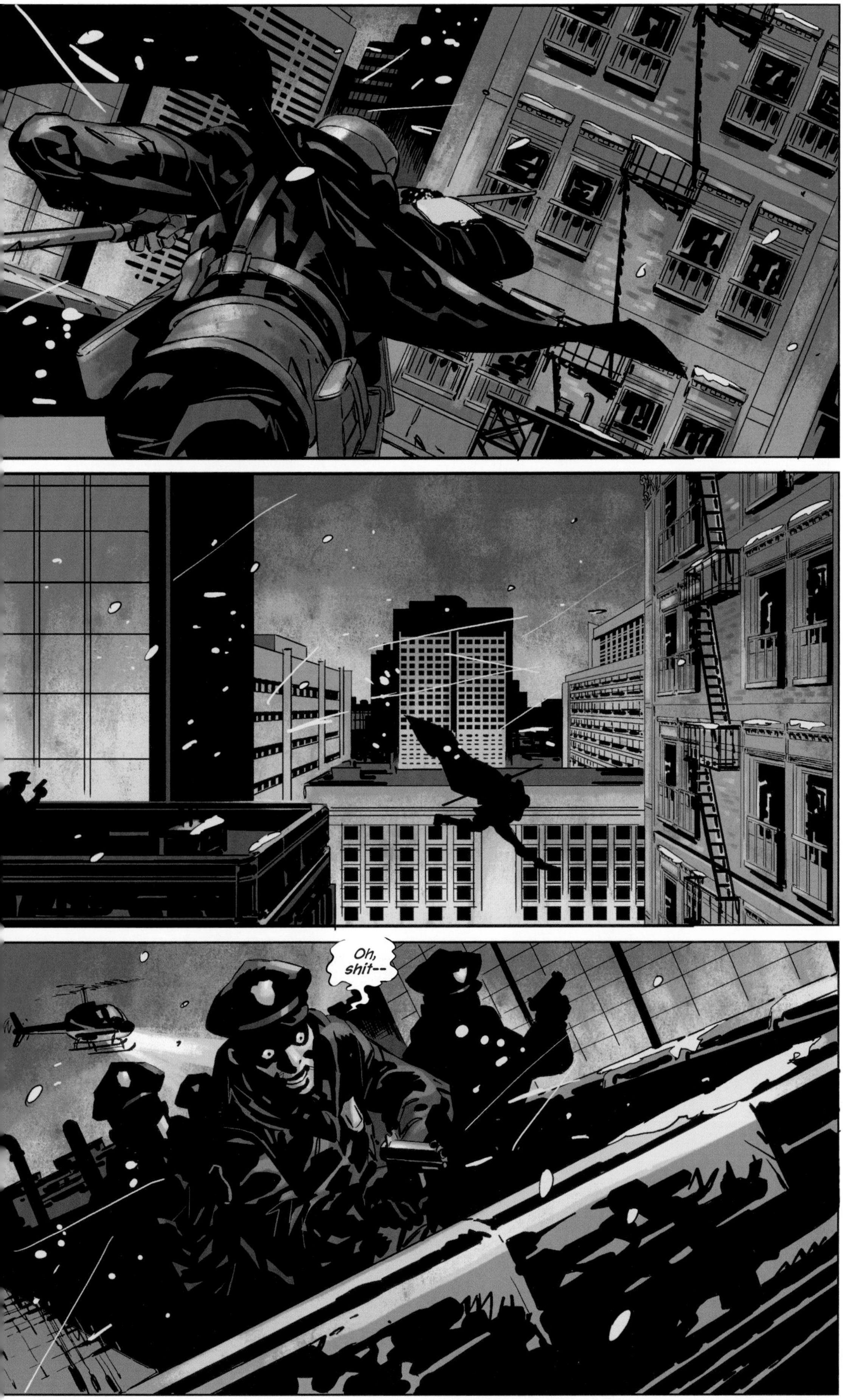
Oh, shit--

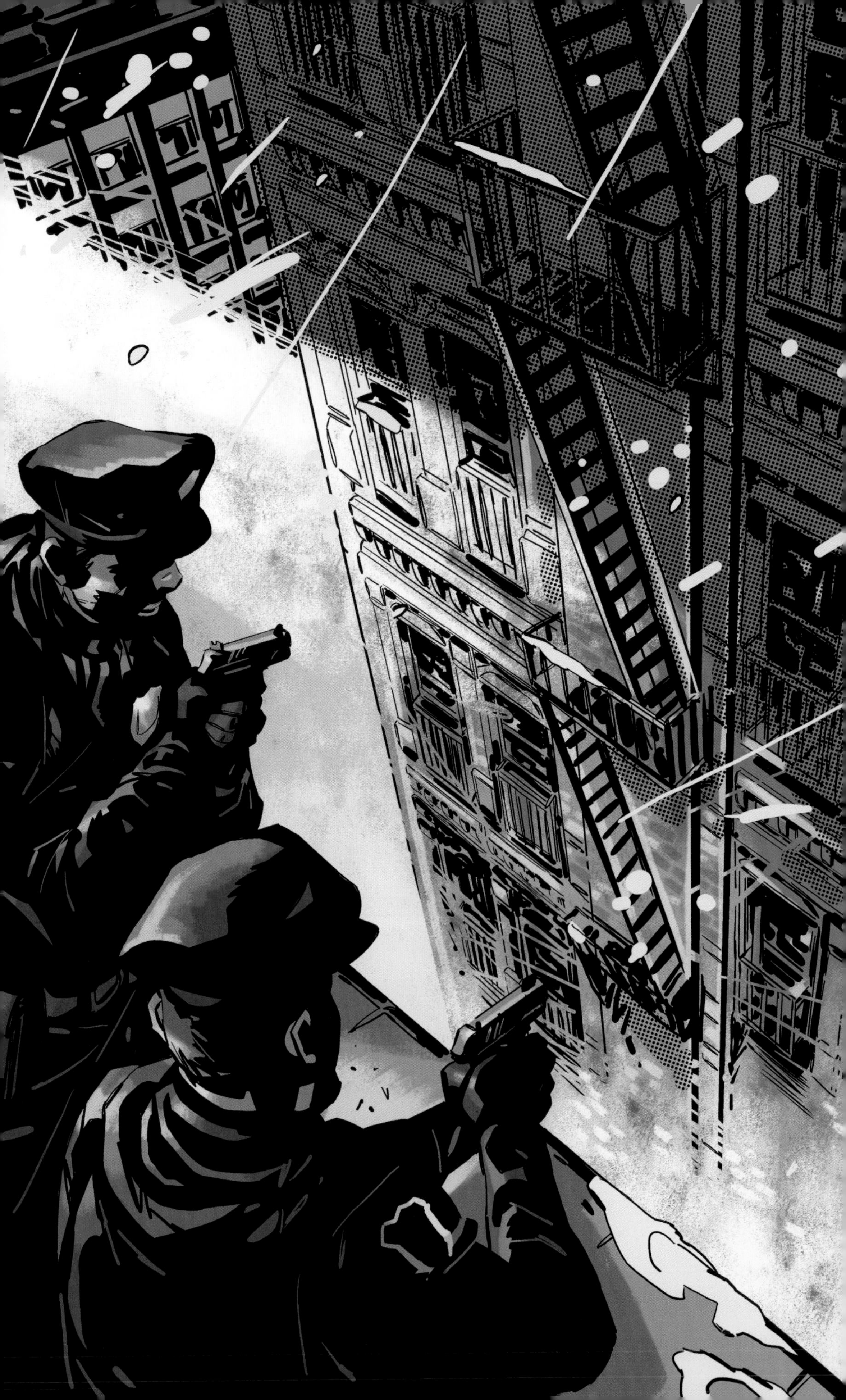

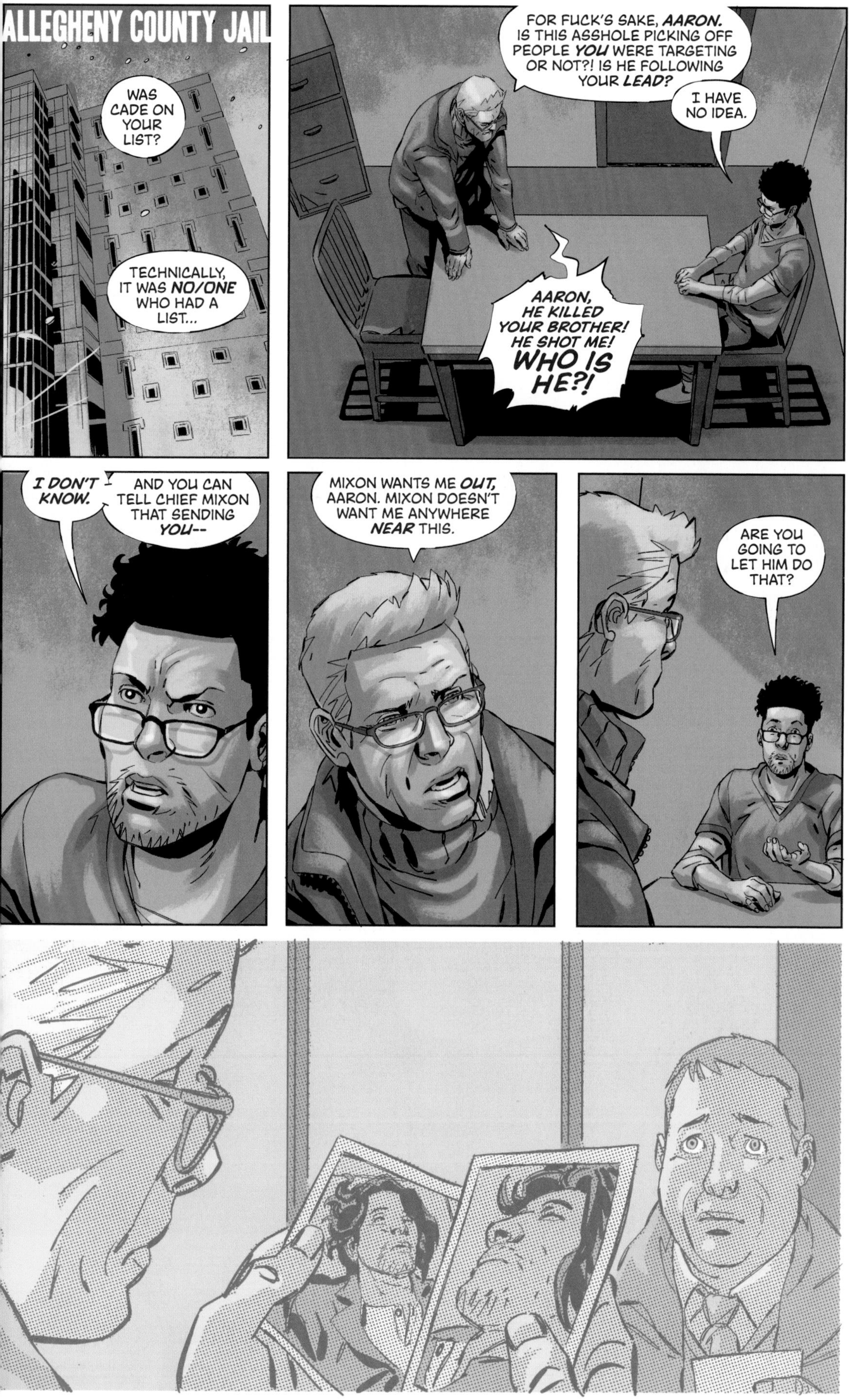
ALLEGHENY COUNTY JAIL
WAS CADE ON YOUR LIST?
TECHNICALLY, IT WAS NO/ONE WHO HAD A LIST...
FOR FUCK'S SAKE, AARON. IS THIS ASSHOLE PICKING OFF PEOPLE YOU WERE TARGETING OR NOT?! IS HE FOLLOWING YOUR LEAD?
I HAVE NO IDEA.
AARON, HE KILLED YOUR BROTHER! HE SHOT ME! WHO IS HE?!
I DON'T KNOW.
AND YOU CAN TELL CHIEF MIXON THAT SENDING YOU--
MIXON WANTS ME OUT, AARON. MIXON DOESN'T WANT ME ANYWHERE NEAR THIS.
ARE YOU GOING TO LET HIM DO THAT?

NOT UNTIL I CATCH THE MOTHERFUCKER THAT KILLED MICHAEL.

THEN SAY IT. SAY HOW MUCH *YOU* WANT MY HELP.

OF *COURSE* I WANT YOUR HELP! YOUR BROTHER'S *DEAD!* JESUS CHRIST, AREN'T *YOU* SUPPOSED TO BE THE ONE WHO WANTS *"ACCOUNTABILITY?!"*

Mm.

I HAD ABSOLUTELY NOTHING TO DO WITH CADE'S DEATH... BUT I SUSPECTED IT WAS COMING.

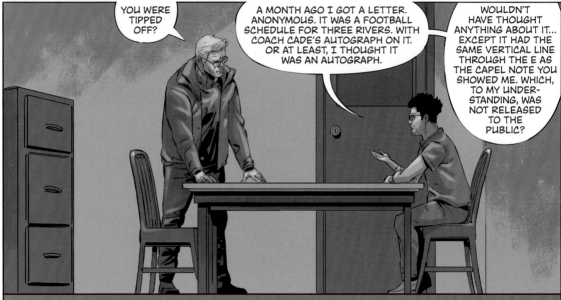

YOU WERE TIPPED OFF?

A MONTH AGO I GOT A LETTER. ANONYMOUS. IT WAS A FOOTBALL SCHEDULE FOR THREE RIVERS. WITH COACH CADE'S AUTOGRAPH ON IT. OR AT LEAST, I THOUGHT IT WAS AN AUTOGRAPH.

WOULDN'T HAVE THOUGHT ANYTHING ABOUT IT... EXCEPT IT HAD THE SAME VERTICAL LINE THROUGH THE E AS THE CAPEL NOTE YOU SHOWED ME. WHICH, TO MY UNDER-STANDING, WAS NOT RELEASED TO THE PUBLIC?

I AM THE REAL RICHARD RO&

A JOURNALIST FOR THE *LEDGER* CAME BY. ALEJANDRO SOME-THING. I PUT HIM ON MY VISITOR SHEET.

I TOLD HIM TO LOOK AT CADE. I DIDN'T SAY WHY. BUT MAYBE *HE* FOUND SOMETHING?

YOU JUST *GAVE* THIS TO A REPORTER...

YOU WERE IN THE HOSPITAL. I DIDN'T KNOW IF YOU'D COME BACK. For the record, I'm *glad* it was a graze.

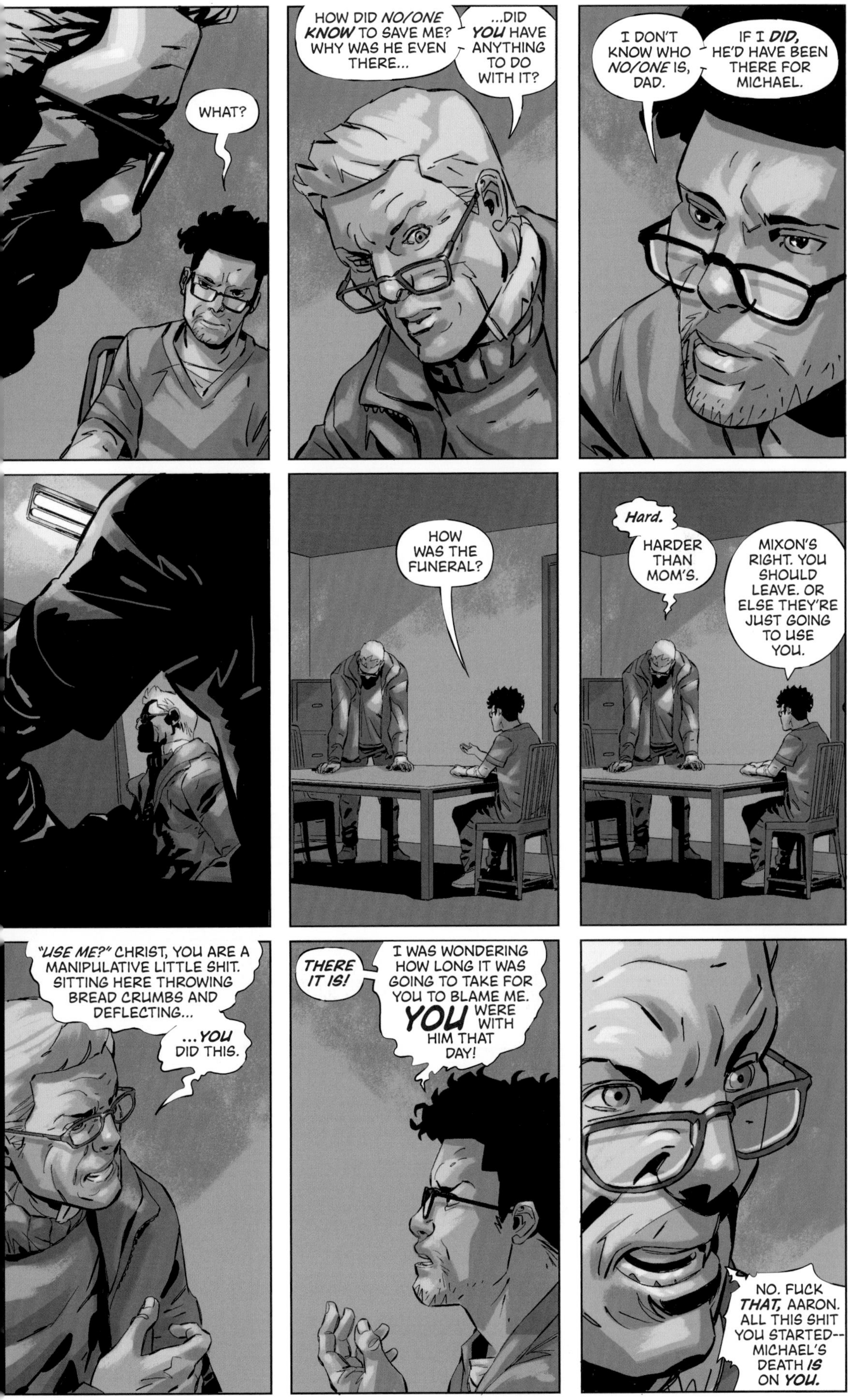
WHAT?
HOW DID NO/ONE KNOW TO SAVE ME? WHY WAS HE EVEN THERE...
...DID YOU HAVE ANYTHING TO DO WITH IT?
I DON'T KNOW WHO NO/ONE IS, DAD.
IF I DID, HE'D HAVE BEEN THERE FOR MICHAEL.
HOW WAS THE FUNERAL?
Hard.
HARDER THAN MOM'S.
MIXON'S RIGHT. YOU SHOULD LEAVE. OR ELSE THEY'RE JUST GOING TO USE YOU.
"USE ME?" CHRIST, YOU ARE A MANIPULATIVE LITTLE SHIT. SITTING HERE THROWING BREAD CRUMBS AND DEFLECTING...
...YOU DID THIS.
THERE IT IS!
I WAS WONDERING HOW LONG IT WAS GOING TO TAKE FOR YOU TO BLAME ME. YOU WERE WITH HIM THAT DAY!
NO. FUCK THAT, AARON. ALL THIS SHIT YOU STARTED-- MICHAEL'S DEATH IS ON YOU.

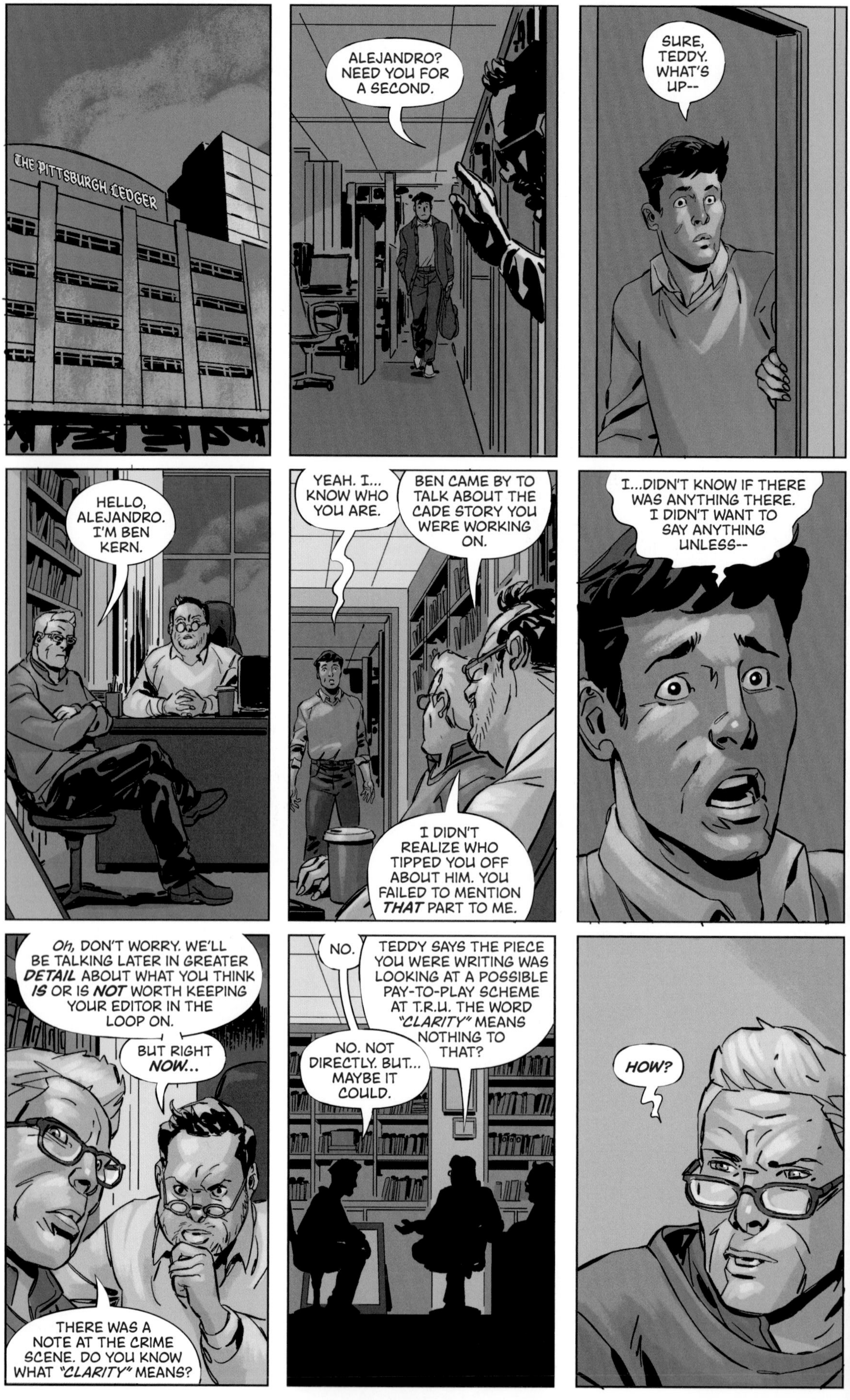
THE PITTSBURGH LEDGER
ALEJANDRO? NEED YOU FOR A SECOND.
SURE, TEDDY. WHAT'S UP--
HELLO, ALEJANDRO. I'M BEN KERN.
YEAH. I... KNOW WHO YOU ARE.
BEN CAME BY TO TALK ABOUT THE CADE STORY YOU WERE WORKING ON.
I DIDN'T REALIZE WHO TIPPED YOU OFF ABOUT HIM. YOU FAILED TO MENTION *THAT* PART TO ME.
I...DIDN'T KNOW IF THERE WAS ANYTHING THERE. I DIDN'T WANT TO SAY ANYTHING UNLESS--
Oh, DON'T WORRY. WE'LL BE TALKING LATER IN GREATER *DETAIL* ABOUT WHAT YOU THINK *IS* OR IS *NOT* WORTH KEEPING YOUR EDITOR IN THE LOOP ON.
BUT RIGHT *NOW...*
THERE WAS A NOTE AT THE CRIME SCENE. DO YOU KNOW WHAT *"CLARITY"* MEANS?
NO.
TEDDY SAYS THE PIECE YOU WERE WRITING WAS LOOKING AT A POSSIBLE PAY-TO-PLAY SCHEME AT T.R.U. THE WORD *"CLARITY"* MEANS NOTHING TO THAT?
NO. NOT DIRECTLY. BUT... MAYBE IT COULD.
HOW?

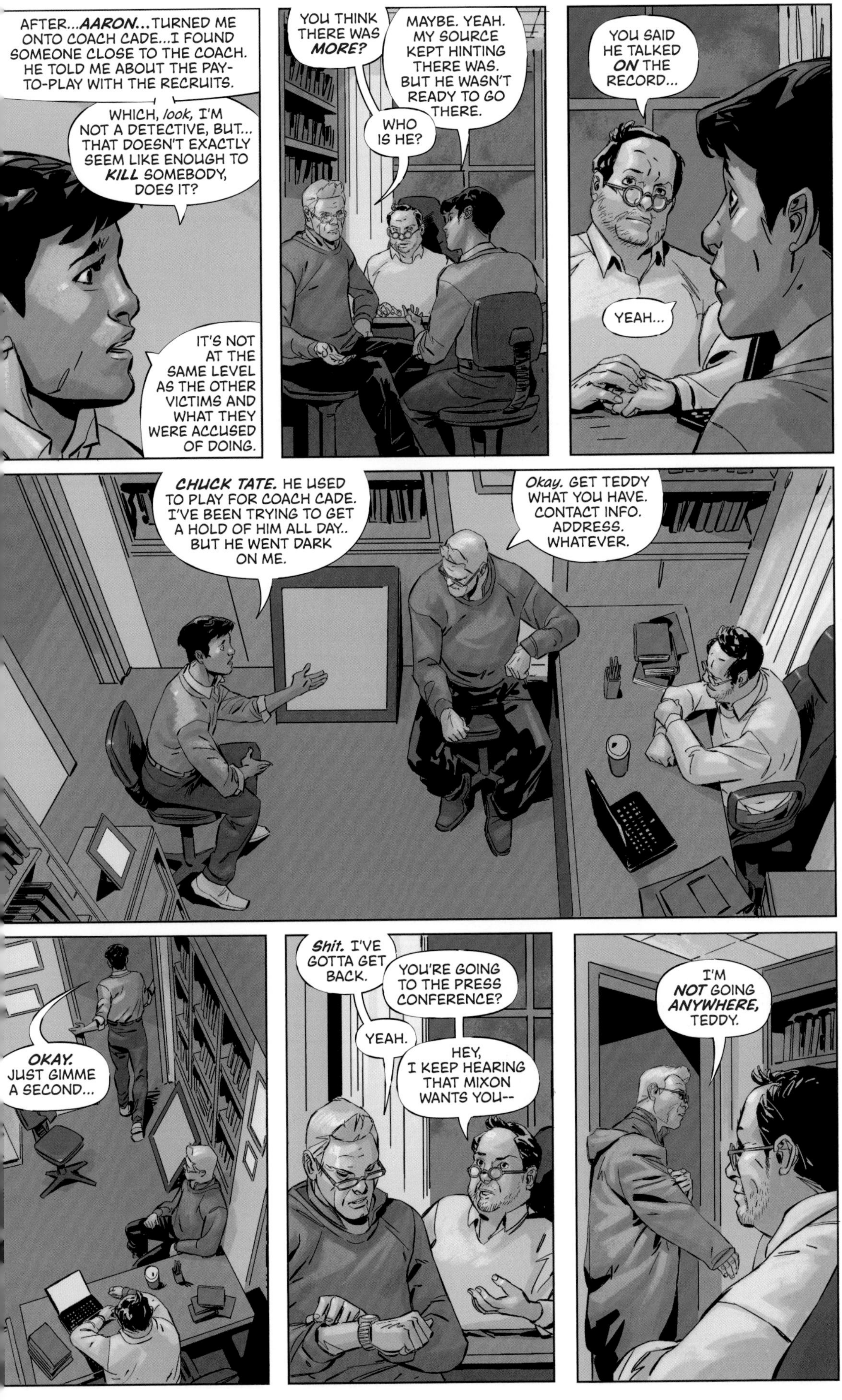
AFTER...AARON...TURNED ME ONTO COACH CADE...I FOUND SOMEONE CLOSE TO THE COACH. HE TOLD ME ABOUT THE PAY-TO-PLAY WITH THE RECRUITS.
WHICH, look, I'M NOT A DETECTIVE, BUT... THAT DOESN'T EXACTLY SEEM LIKE ENOUGH TO KILL SOMEBODY, DOES IT?
IT'S NOT AT THE SAME LEVEL AS THE OTHER VICTIMS AND WHAT THEY WERE ACCUSED OF DOING.
YOU THINK THERE WAS MORE?
MAYBE. YEAH. MY SOURCE KEPT HINTING THERE WAS. BUT HE WASN'T READY TO GO THERE.
WHO IS HE?
YOU SAID HE TALKED ON THE RECORD...
YEAH...
CHUCK TATE. HE USED TO PLAY FOR COACH CADE. I'VE BEEN TRYING TO GET A HOLD OF HIM ALL DAY.. BUT HE WENT DARK ON ME.
Okay. GET TEDDY WHAT YOU HAVE. CONTACT INFO. ADDRESS. WHATEVER.
OKAY. JUST GIMME A SECOND...
Shit. I'VE GOTTA GET BACK.
YOU'RE GOING TO THE PRESS CONFERENCE?
YEAH.
HEY, I KEEP HEARING THAT MIXON WANTS YOU--
I'M NOT GOING ANYWHERE, TEDDY.

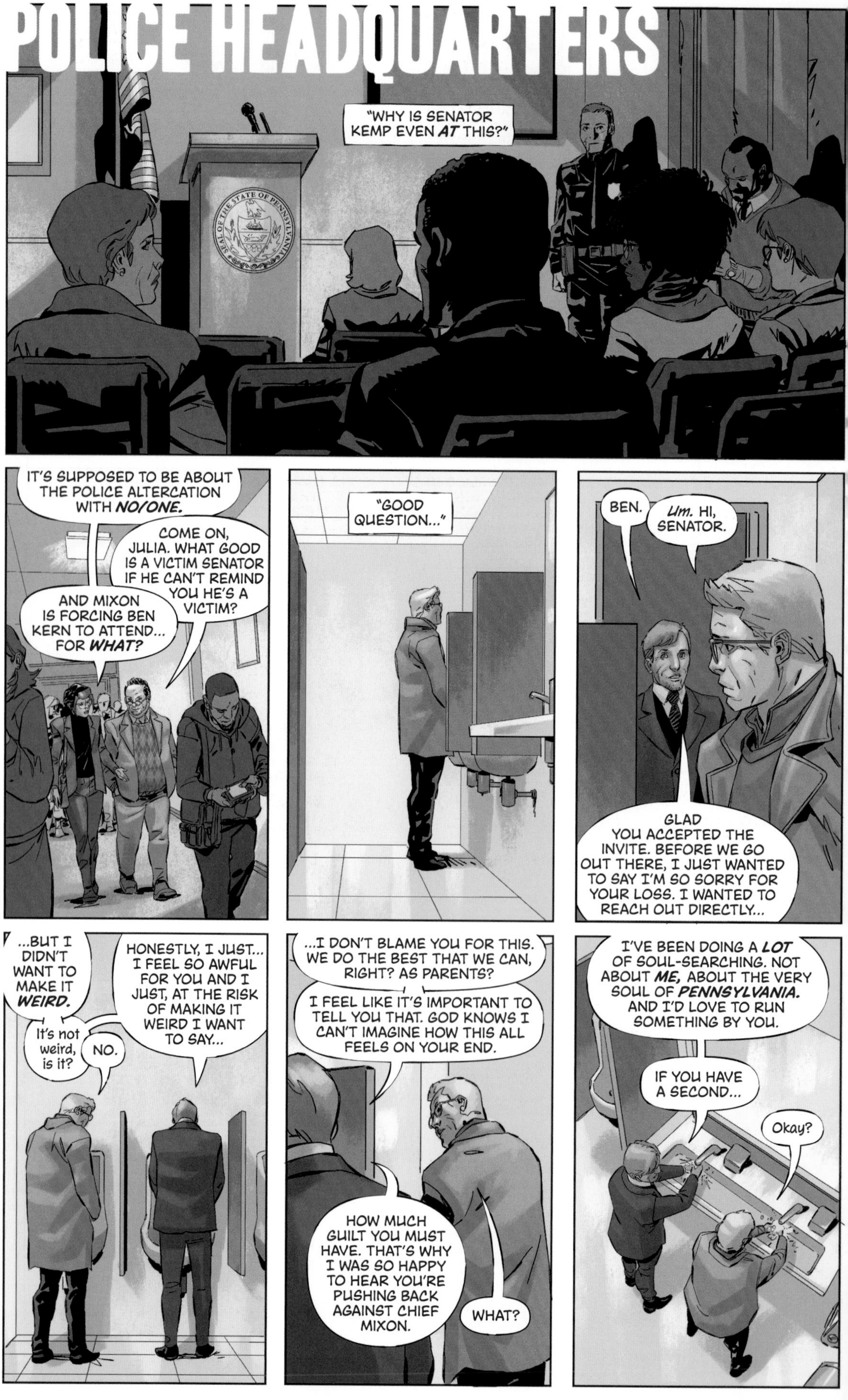
POLICE HEADQUARTERS
"WHY IS SENATOR KEMP EVEN *AT* THIS?"
IT'S SUPPOSED TO BE ABOUT THE POLICE ALTERCATION WITH *NO/ONE.*
COME ON, JULIA. WHAT GOOD IS A VICTIM SENATOR IF HE CAN'T REMIND YOU HE'S A VICTIM?
AND MIXON IS FORCING BEN KERN TO ATTEND... FOR *WHAT?*
"GOOD QUESTION..."
BEN.
Um. HI, SENATOR.
GLAD YOU ACCEPTED THE INVITE. BEFORE WE GO OUT THERE, I JUST WANTED TO SAY I'M SO SORRY FOR YOUR LOSS. I WANTED TO REACH OUT DIRECTLY...
...BUT I DIDN'T WANT TO MAKE IT *WEIRD.*
It's not weird, is it?
NO.
HONESTLY, I JUST... I FEEL SO AWFUL FOR YOU AND I JUST, AT THE RISK OF MAKING IT WEIRD I WANT TO SAY...
...I DON'T BLAME YOU FOR THIS. WE DO THE BEST THAT WE CAN, RIGHT? AS PARENTS?
I FEEL LIKE IT'S IMPORTANT TO TELL YOU THAT. GOD KNOWS I CAN'T IMAGINE HOW THIS ALL FEELS ON YOUR END.
HOW MUCH GUILT YOU MUST HAVE. THAT'S WHY I WAS SO HAPPY TO HEAR YOU'RE PUSHING BACK AGAINST CHIEF MIXON.
WHAT?
I'VE BEEN DOING A *LOT* OF SOUL-SEARCHING. NOT ABOUT *ME,* ABOUT THE VERY SOUL OF *PENNSYLVANIA.* AND I'D LOVE TO RUN SOMETHING BY YOU.
IF YOU HAVE A SECOND...
Okay?

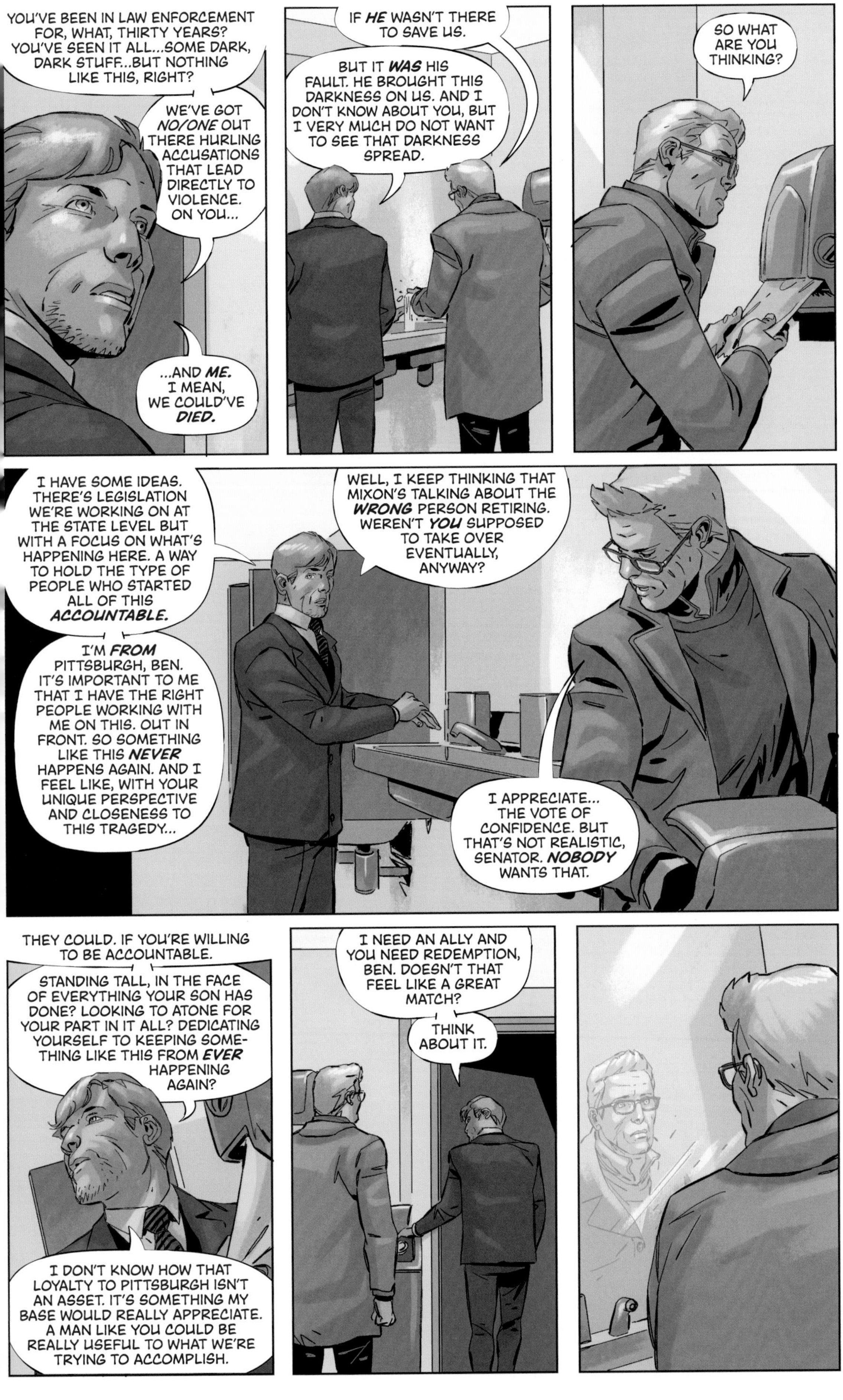
YOU'VE BEEN IN LAW ENFORCEMENT FOR, WHAT, THIRTY YEARS? YOU'VE SEEN IT ALL...SOME DARK, DARK STUFF...BUT NOTHING LIKE THIS, RIGHT?
WE'VE GOT NO/ONE OUT THERE HURLING ACCUSATIONS THAT LEAD DIRECTLY TO VIOLENCE. ON YOU...
...AND ME. I MEAN, WE COULD'VE DIED.
IF HE WASN'T THERE TO SAVE US.
BUT IT WAS HIS FAULT. HE BROUGHT THIS DARKNESS ON US. AND I DON'T KNOW ABOUT YOU, BUT I VERY MUCH DO NOT WANT TO SEE THAT DARKNESS SPREAD.
SO WHAT ARE YOU THINKING?
I HAVE SOME IDEAS. THERE'S LEGISLATION WE'RE WORKING ON AT THE STATE LEVEL BUT WITH A FOCUS ON WHAT'S HAPPENING HERE. A WAY TO HOLD THE TYPE OF PEOPLE WHO STARTED ALL OF THIS ACCOUNTABLE.
I'M FROM PITTSBURGH, BEN. IT'S IMPORTANT TO ME THAT I HAVE THE RIGHT PEOPLE WORKING WITH ME ON THIS. OUT IN FRONT. SO SOMETHING LIKE THIS NEVER HAPPENS AGAIN. AND I FEEL LIKE, WITH YOUR UNIQUE PERSPECTIVE AND CLOSENESS TO THIS TRAGEDY...
WELL, I KEEP THINKING THAT MIXON'S TALKING ABOUT THE WRONG PERSON RETIRING. WEREN'T YOU SUPPOSED TO TAKE OVER EVENTUALLY, ANYWAY?
I APPRECIATE... THE VOTE OF CONFIDENCE. BUT THAT'S NOT REALISTIC, SENATOR. NOBODY WANTS THAT.
THEY COULD. IF YOU'RE WILLING TO BE ACCOUNTABLE.
STANDING TALL, IN THE FACE OF EVERYTHING YOUR SON HAS DONE? LOOKING TO ATONE FOR YOUR PART IN IT ALL? DEDICATING YOURSELF TO KEEPING SOME-THING LIKE THIS FROM EVER HAPPENING AGAIN?
I DON'T KNOW HOW THAT LOYALTY TO PITTSBURGH ISN'T AN ASSET. IT'S SOMETHING MY BASE WOULD REALLY APPRECIATE. A MAN LIKE YOU COULD BE REALLY USEFUL TO WHAT WE'RE TRYING TO ACCOMPLISH.
I NEED AN ALLY AND YOU NEED REDEMPTION, BEN. DOESN'T THAT FEEL LIKE A GREAT MATCH?
THINK ABOUT IT.

--AT THAT TIME OFFICERS ENGAGED THE SUSPECT WHO FLED ON FOOT ACROSS THE TOP OF THE PARKING STRUCTURE, BEFORE ATTACKING OFFICER DILLON WITH A TASER-LIKE DEVICE.

FORTUNATELY, STATE POLICE WERE ABLE TO PROVIDE AIR SUPPORT AS OFFICERS CAME TO OFFICER DILLON'S AIDE. OFFICER DILLON WAS TREATED FOR HIS INJURIES EARLIER TONIGHT AND IS NOW HOME RESTING WITH HIS FAMILY.

AT THIS TIME OUR INVESTIGATORS ARE STILL TRYING TO DETERMINE *WHY NO/ONE* WAS IN THE PARKING STRUCTURE.

A GO-PRO CAMERA THAT A WITNESS SAYS WAS *IN NO/ONE'S* POSSESSION WAS RECOVERED FROM THE SCENE AFTER THE PURSUIT.

WE AREN'T SAYING THAT HE PLANTED THE CAMERA, OR THAT HE HAD ANYTHING TO DO WITH COACH CADE'S MURDER. THE INVESTIGATION IS ONGOING...

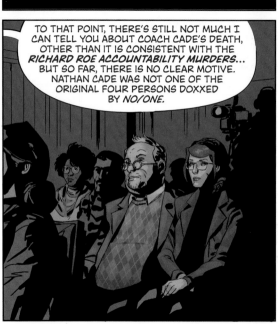

TO THAT POINT, THERE'S STILL NOT MUCH I CAN TELL YOU ABOUT COACH CADE'S DEATH, OTHER THAN IT IS CONSISTENT WITH THE *RICHARD ROE ACCOUNTABILITY MURDERS...* BUT SO FAR, THERE IS NO CLEAR MOTIVE. NATHAN CADE WAS NOT ONE OF THE ORIGINAL FOUR PERSONS DOXXED BY *NO/ONE*.

TO THAT POINT, ESTEEMED STATE SENATOR AND RICHARD ROE SURVIVOR *NOAH KEMP...* WOULD LIKE TO SAY A FEW WORDS.

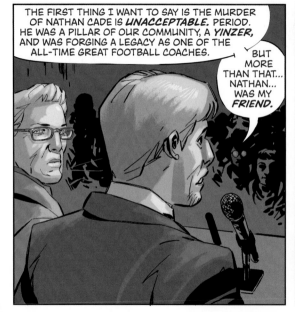

THE FIRST THING I WANT TO SAY IS THE MURDER OF NATHAN CADE IS *UNACCEPTABLE.* PERIOD. HE WAS A PILLAR OF OUR COMMUNITY, A *YINZER*, AND WAS FORGING A LEGACY AS ONE OF THE ALL-TIME GREAT FOOTBALL COACHES.

BUT MORE THAN THAT... NATHAN... WAS MY *FRIEND.*

AND HE DID NOT DESERVE TO HAVE HIS LIFE STOLEN BY ANOTHER OF THESE DOMESTIC TERRORISTS--

--BECAUSE THAT'S WHAT THIS COPYCAT IS-- *A DERANGED COWARD* WHO HAS CO-OPTED THE NONSENSE ACCOUNTABILITY MOVEMENT.

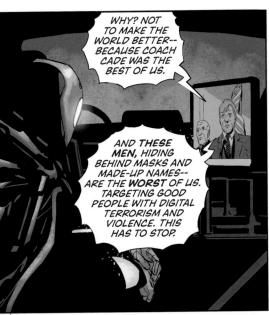

WHY? NOT TO MAKE THE WORLD BETTER-- BECAUSE COACH CADE WAS THE BEST OF US.

AND THESE MEN, HIDING BEHIND MASKS AND MADE-UP NAMES-- ARE THE WORST OF US. TARGETING GOOD PEOPLE WITH DIGITAL TERRORISM AND VIOLENCE. THIS HAS TO STOP.

WE MUST DO EVERY-THING IN OUR POWER TO MEET THIS SOCIETAL THREAT HEAD-ON... AND WITH FORCE.

"BECAUSE IF IT CAN HAPPEN TO COACH CADE, OR ME... OR THE BRAVE MEN AND WOMEN IN THE POLICE DEPARTMENT...

"...IT CAN HAPPEN TO YOU.

"I PLEDGE TO USE THE FULL WEIGHT OF OUR LEGISLATIVE SYSTEM TO ENSURE THAT EVERY PERSON IN OUR GREAT STATE HAS THE TOOLS TO PROTECT THEMSELVES."

THIS IS A NATION FOUNDED ON LIFE, LIBERTY, AND THE PURSUIT OF HAPPINESS. IF THE LAW DOES NOT ALLOW US TO DEFEND ANY OF THOSE, THEN IT'S THE LAW THAT HAS TO CHANGE, NOT US!

BUT I CAN'T DO THIS ALONE... WHICH IS WHY I AM ASSEMBLING A COALITION OF RIGHT-MINDED PEOPLE TO STEP UP AND MEET THE TIMES.

PEOPLE LIKE ASSISTANT CHIEF KERN, ANOTHER SURVIVOR WHO KNOWS BETTER THAN ANYONE WHAT IS AT STAKE...

...ISN'T THAT RIGHT, BEN?

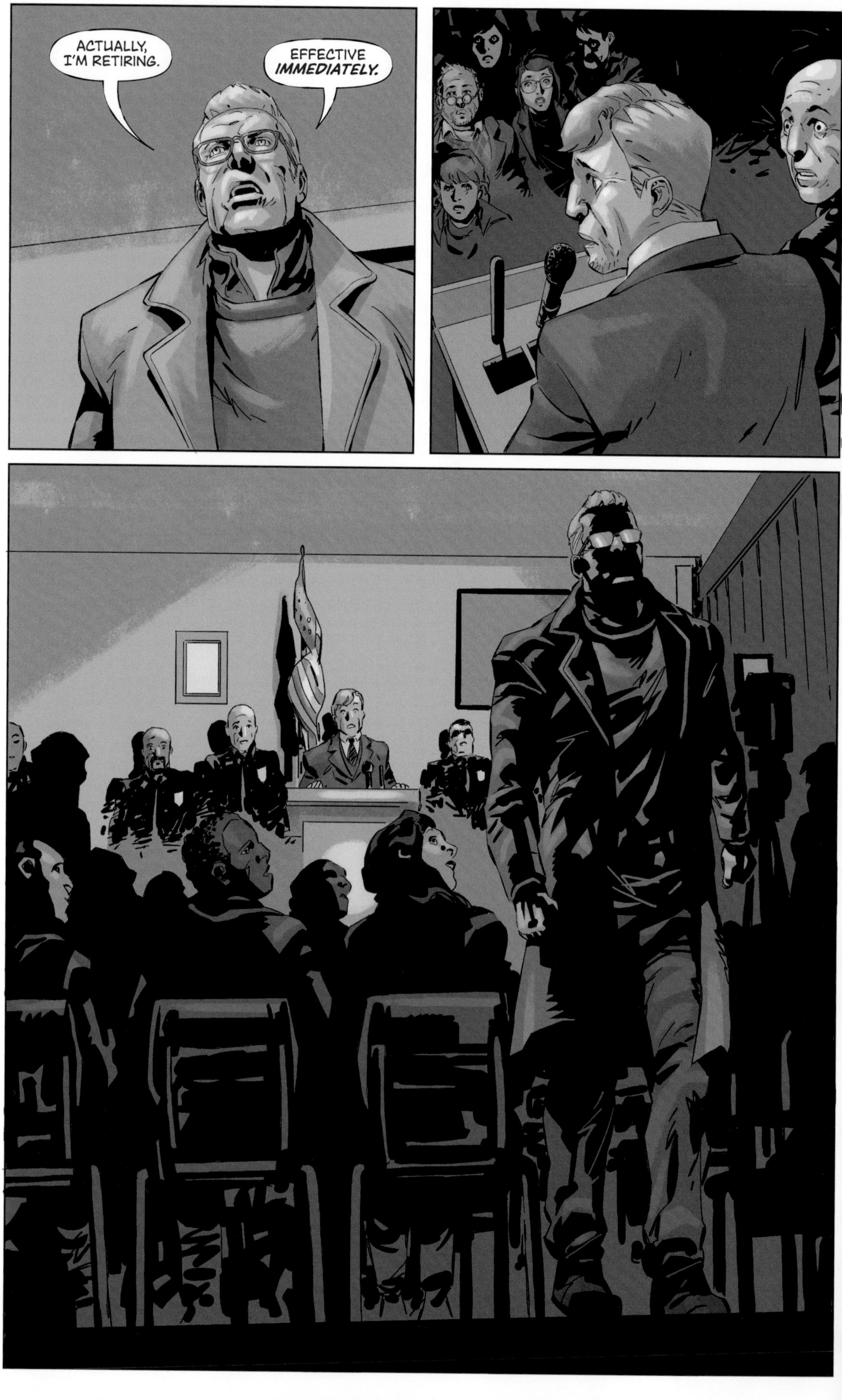
ACTUALLY, I'M RETIRING.
EFFECTIVE *IMMEDIATELY.*

>_ **NO/ONE spotted fleeing murder scene; police open fire after masked man "assaults" officers**
APRIL 20 2023

written by Julia Paige
published on The Drop

"Cade was found shot in a downtown parking garage Wednesday afternoon, just before dark."

The Dr⦁p

PRESENTS

WHO IS NO/ONE

WITH/JULIA PAIGE

The Dr⦁p

WHO IS NO/ONE
02/A FAMILY AFFAIR

21 APRIL

02/A Family Affair

WHO IS NO/ONE

4:30   -17:59

Listen on
Apple Podcasts

Listen on
Google Podcasts

LISTEN ON Spotify

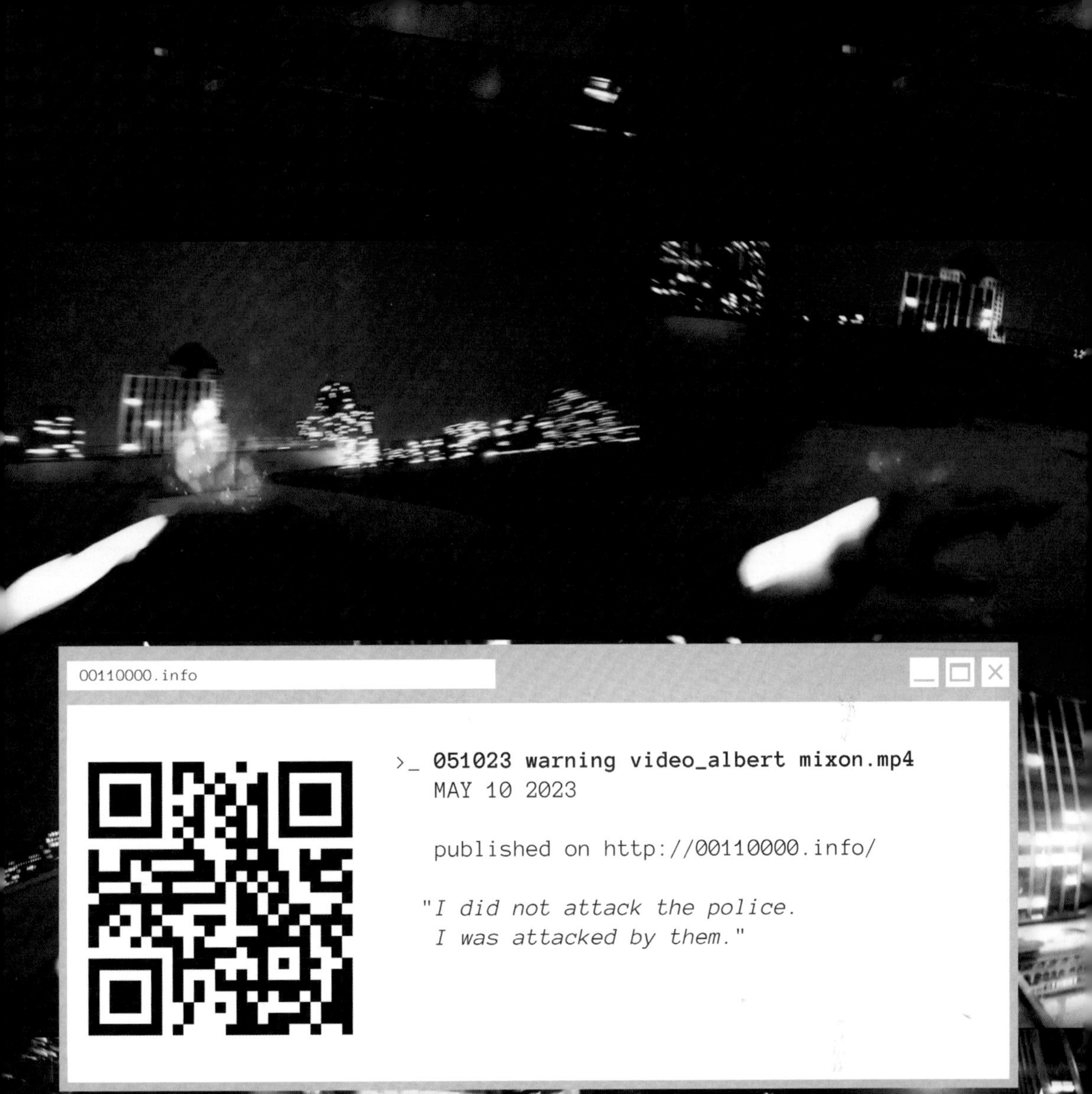

00110000.info

>_ **051023 warning video_albert mixon.mp4**
MAY 10 2023

published on http://00110000.info/

*"I did not attack the police.
I was attacked by them."*

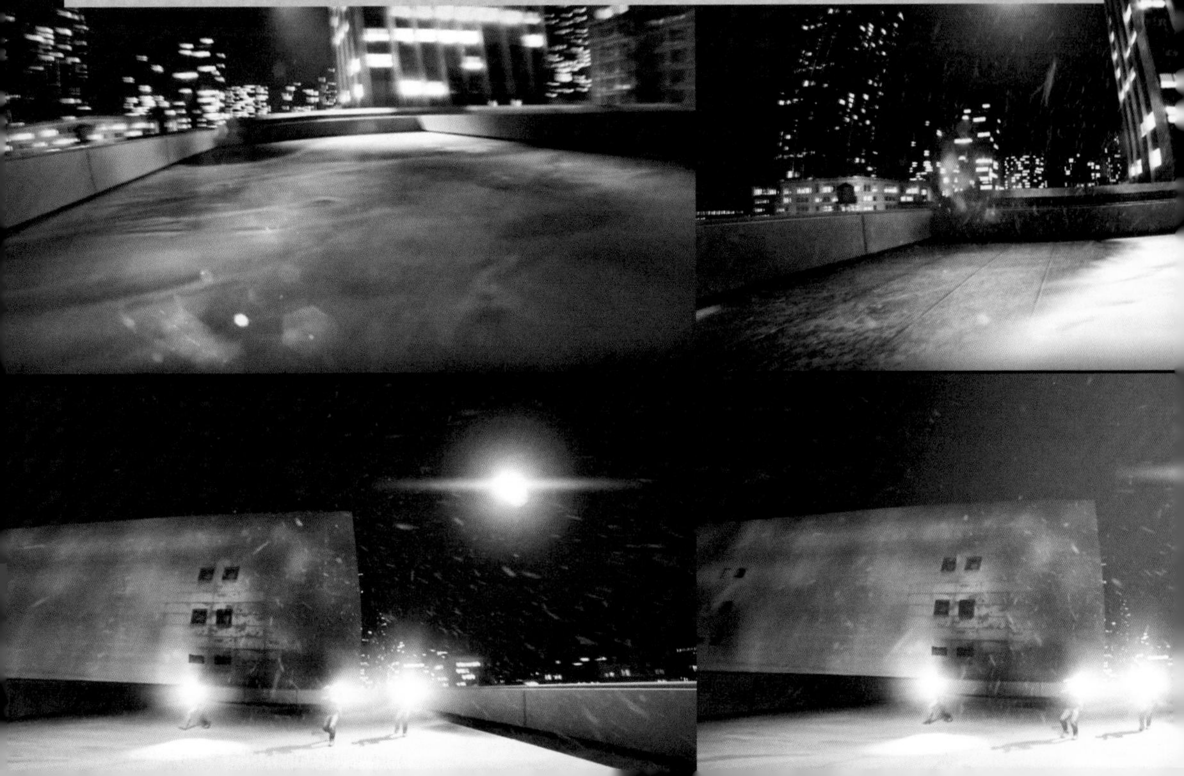

>_ **Under pressure from NO/ONE, Mixon revises key**
   details in police shooting narrative
   MAY 16 2023

   written by Julia Paige
   published on The Drop

   "Mixon didn't say why his account changed,
   and declined to answer most questions about
   the shooting."

>_ CHAPTER THREE
MAY 2023

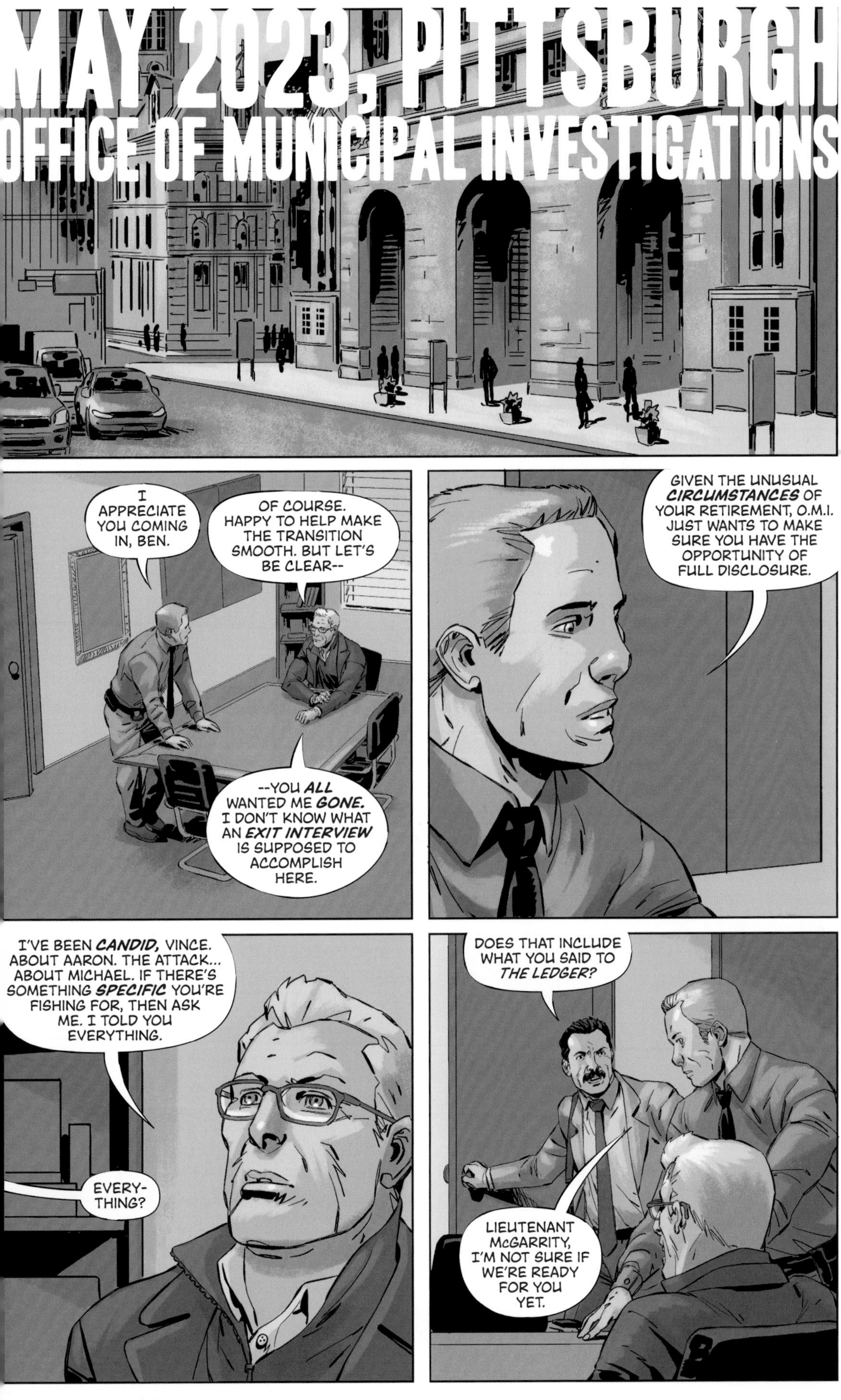
MAY 2023, PITTSBURGH
OFFICE OF MUNICIPAL INVESTIGATIONS
I APPRECIATE YOU COMING IN, BEN.
OF COURSE. HAPPY TO HELP MAKE THE TRANSITION SMOOTH. BUT LET'S BE CLEAR--
--YOU ALL WANTED ME GONE. I DON'T KNOW WHAT AN EXIT INTERVIEW IS SUPPOSED TO ACCOMPLISH HERE.
GIVEN THE UNUSUAL CIRCUMSTANCES OF YOUR RETIREMENT, O.M.I. JUST WANTS TO MAKE SURE YOU HAVE THE OPPORTUNITY OF FULL DISCLOSURE.
I'VE BEEN CANDID, VINCE. ABOUT AARON. THE ATTACK... ABOUT MICHAEL. IF THERE'S SOMETHING SPECIFIC YOU'RE FISHING FOR, THEN ASK ME. I TOLD YOU EVERYTHING.
EVERY-THING?
DOES THAT INCLUDE WHAT YOU SAID TO THE LEDGER?
LIEUTENANT McGARRITY, I'M NOT SURE IF WE'RE READY FOR YOU YET.

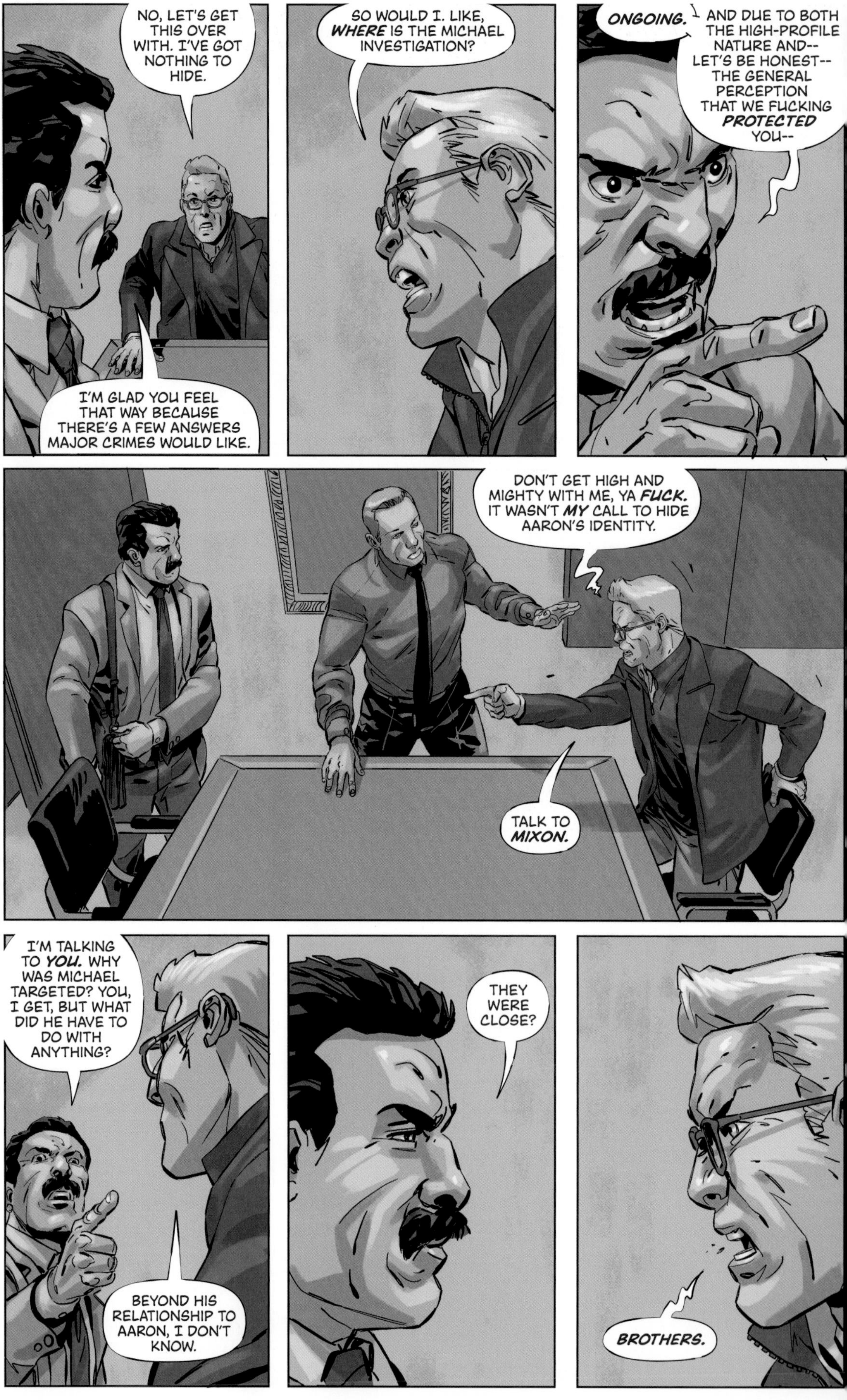
NO, LET'S GET THIS OVER WITH. I'VE GOT NOTHING TO HIDE.
I'M GLAD YOU FEEL THAT WAY BECAUSE THERE'S A FEW ANSWERS MAJOR CRIMES WOULD LIKE.
SO WOULD I. LIKE, *WHERE* IS THE MICHAEL INVESTIGATION?
ONGOING.
AND DUE TO BOTH THE HIGH-PROFILE NATURE AND-- LET'S BE HONEST-- THE GENERAL PERCEPTION THAT WE FUCKING *PROTECTED* YOU--
DON'T GET HIGH AND MIGHTY WITH ME, YA *FUCK.* IT WASN'T *MY* CALL TO HIDE AARON'S IDENTITY.
TALK TO *MIXON.*
I'M TALKING TO *YOU.* WHY WAS MICHAEL TARGETED? YOU, I GET, BUT WHAT DID HE HAVE TO DO WITH ANYTHING?
BEYOND HIS RELATIONSHIP TO AARON, I DON'T KNOW.
THEY WERE CLOSE?
BROTHERS.

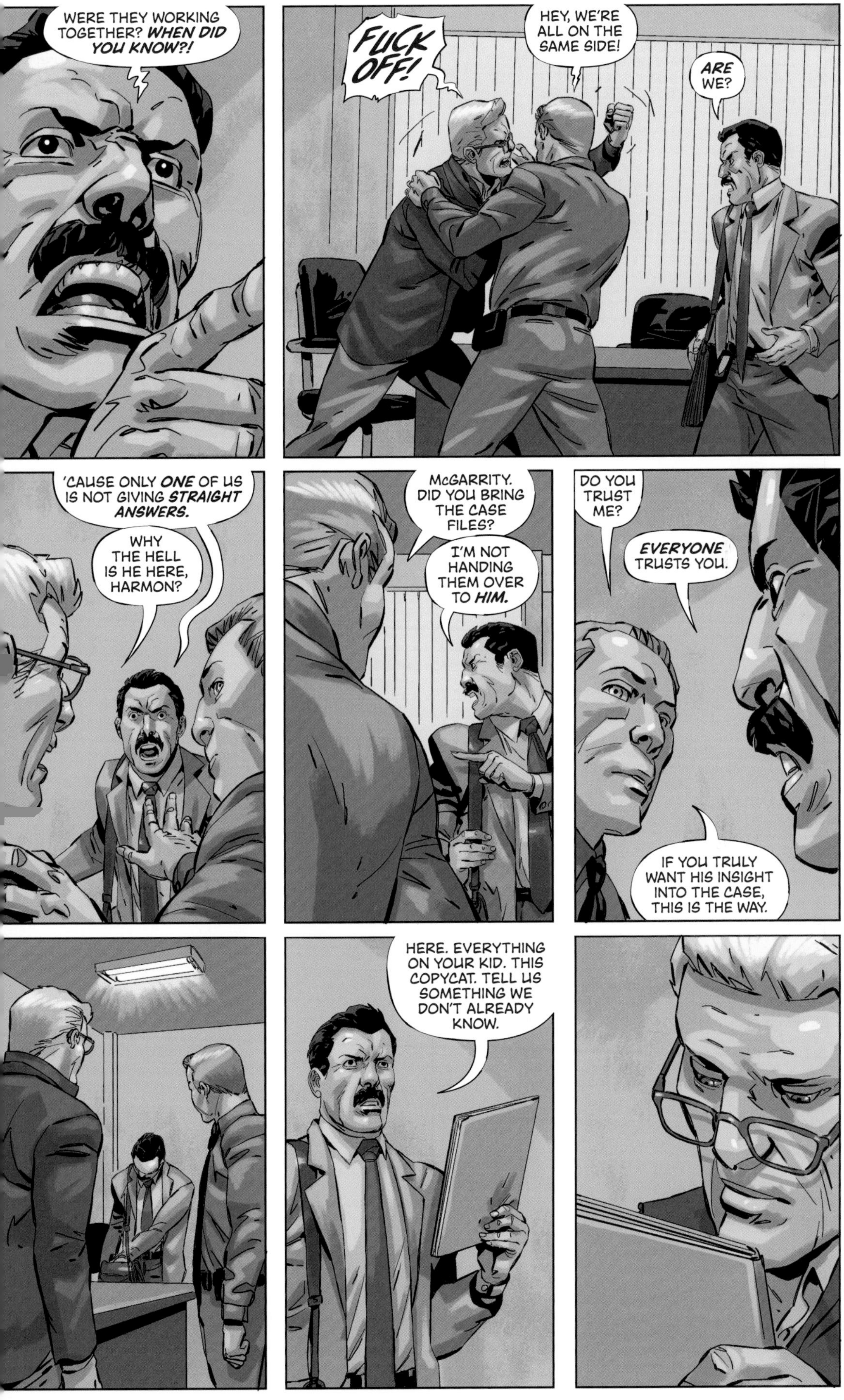

WERE THEY WORKING TOGETHER? WHEN DID YOU KNOW?!
FUCK OFF!
HEY, WE'RE ALL ON THE SAME SIDE!
ARE WE?
'CAUSE ONLY ONE OF US IS NOT GIVING STRAIGHT ANSWERS.
WHY THE HELL IS HE HERE, HARMON?
McGARRITY. DID YOU BRING THE CASE FILES?
I'M NOT HANDING THEM OVER TO HIM.
DO YOU TRUST ME?
EVERYONE TRUSTS YOU.
IF YOU TRULY WANT HIS INSIGHT INTO THE CASE, THIS IS THE WAY.
HERE. EVERYTHING ON YOUR KID. THIS COPYCAT. TELL US SOMETHING WE DON'T ALREADY KNOW.

BEN KERN IS NOT A VICTIM. HE'S **ANOTHER EXAMPLE** OF HOW WE PUT FAMILY LAST. HOW DID HE NOT KNOW HIS SON WAS A PSYCHOTIC KILLER?! MAYBE IF THEY WOULD'VE THROWN THE BOOK AT AARON WHEN HE WAS STILL A TEEN SCREW-UP, IT NEVER WOULD'VE GOTTEN THIS FAR.

THE PITTSBURGH LEDGER

HEY, TEDDY...

HEY.

YOU CAN'T HELP BUT WONDER ABOUT THE TIMING OF BEN'S RETIREMENT.

WAS THERE A CONFLICT OF INTEREST THAT MOTIVATED IT? WAS IT POLITICAL? WHY STEP DOWN NOW?

WHEN WE COME BACK, MORE BREAKING NEWS ON THE CHRIS O'NEIL SHOOTING...

WHY DO YOU STILL WATCH THAT SHIT?

KNOW THY ENEMY, JULES.

YOU KNOW, YOUR MOM, *uh*, EXCLUDED...

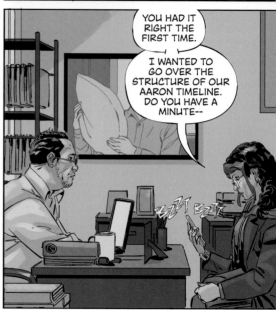

YOU HAD IT RIGHT THE FIRST TIME.

I WANTED TO GO OVER THE STRUCTURE OF OUR AARON TIMELINE. DO YOU HAVE A MINUTE--

BZZT BZZT

Hm.

WHAT?

BZZT BZZT

MOM

HI, MOM.

JULIA, DEAR--

I'M ON DEADLINE. CAN YOU JUST GET TO THE POINT?

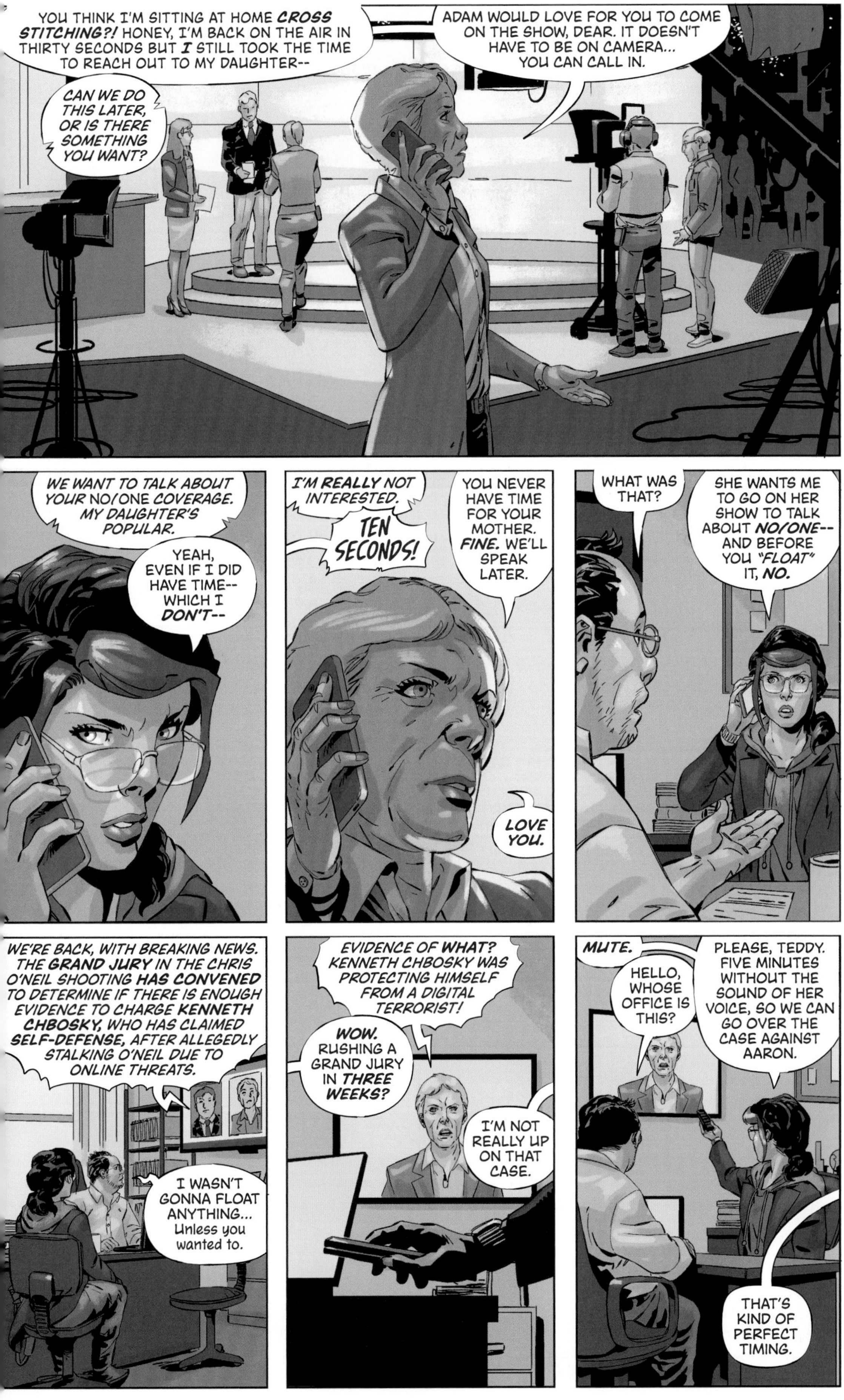
YOU THINK I'M SITTING AT HOME CROSS STITCHING?! HONEY, I'M BACK ON THE AIR IN THIRTY SECONDS BUT I STILL TOOK THE TIME TO REACH OUT TO MY DAUGHTER--
CAN WE DO THIS LATER, OR IS THERE SOMETHING YOU WANT?
ADAM WOULD LOVE FOR YOU TO COME ON THE SHOW, DEAR. IT DOESN'T HAVE TO BE ON CAMERA... YOU CAN CALL IN.
WE WANT TO TALK ABOUT YOUR NO/ONE COVERAGE. MY DAUGHTER'S POPULAR.
YEAH, EVEN IF I DID HAVE TIME-- WHICH I DON'T--
I'M REALLY NOT INTERESTED.
TEN SECONDS!
YOU NEVER HAVE TIME FOR YOUR MOTHER. FINE. WE'LL SPEAK LATER.
LOVE YOU.
WHAT WAS THAT?
SHE WANTS ME TO GO ON HER SHOW TO TALK ABOUT NO/ONE-- AND BEFORE YOU "FLOAT" IT, NO.
WE'RE BACK, WITH BREAKING NEWS. THE GRAND JURY IN THE CHRIS O'NEIL SHOOTING HAS CONVENED TO DETERMINE IF THERE IS ENOUGH EVIDENCE TO CHARGE KENNETH CHBOSKY, WHO HAS CLAIMED SELF-DEFENSE, AFTER ALLEGEDLY STALKING O'NEIL DUE TO ONLINE THREATS.
I WASN'T GONNA FLOAT ANYTHING... Unless you wanted to.
EVIDENCE OF WHAT? KENNETH CHBOSKY WAS PROTECTING HIMSELF FROM A DIGITAL TERRORIST!
WOW. RUSHING A GRAND JURY IN THREE WEEKS?
I'M NOT REALLY UP ON THAT CASE.
MUTE.
HELLO, WHOSE OFFICE IS THIS?
PLEASE, TEDDY. FIVE MINUTES WITHOUT THE SOUND OF HER VOICE, SO WE CAN GO OVER THE CASE AGAINST AARON.
THAT'S KIND OF PERFECT TIMING.

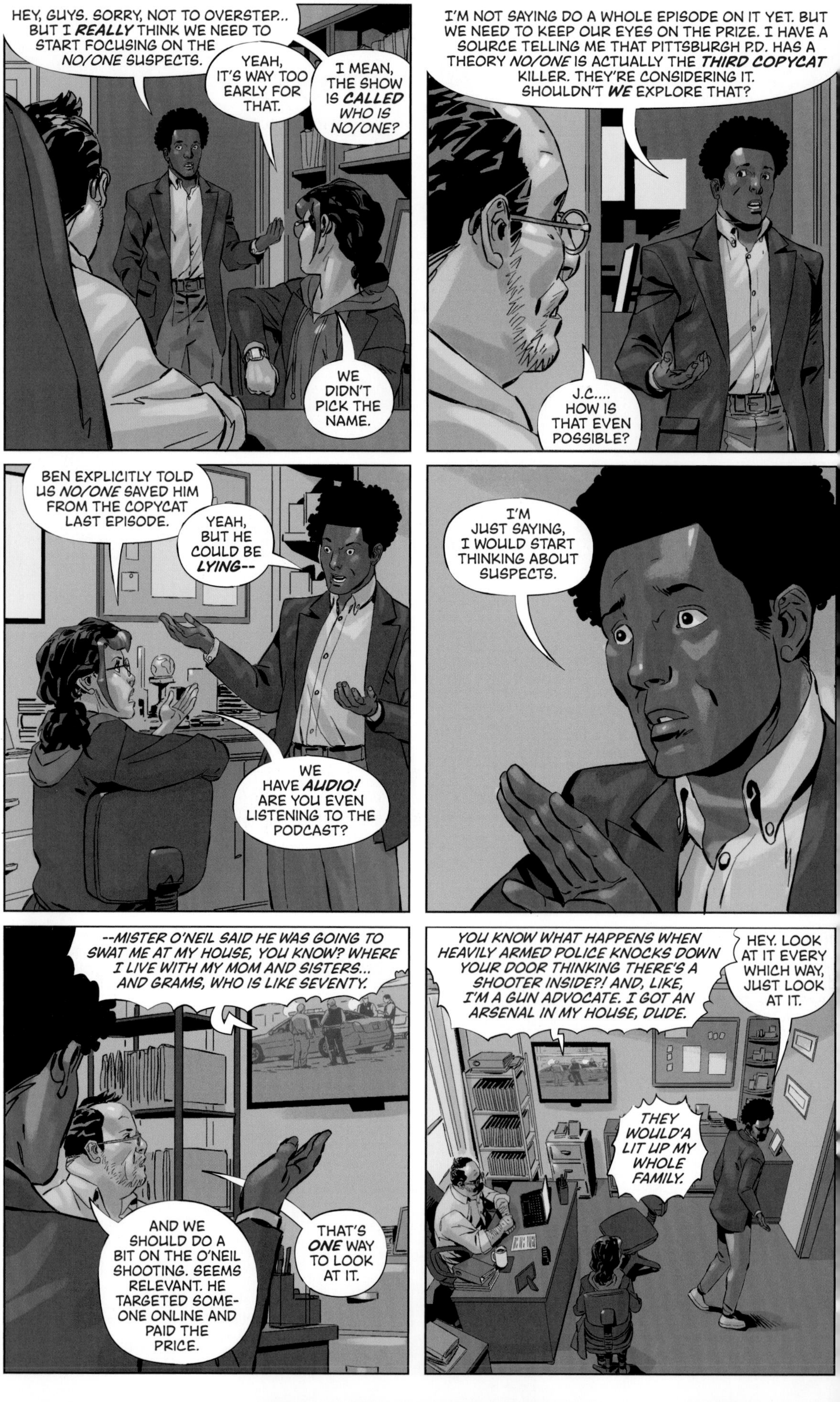
HEY, GUYS. SORRY, NOT TO OVERSTEP... BUT I REALLY THINK WE NEED TO START FOCUSING ON THE NO/ONE SUSPECTS.
YEAH, IT'S WAY TOO EARLY FOR THAT.
I MEAN, THE SHOW IS CALLED WHO IS NO/ONE?
WE DIDN'T PICK THE NAME.
I'M NOT SAYING DO A WHOLE EPISODE ON IT YET. BUT WE NEED TO KEEP OUR EYES ON THE PRIZE. I HAVE A SOURCE TELLING ME THAT PITTSBURGH P.D. HAS A THEORY NO/ONE IS ACTUALLY THE THIRD COPYCAT KILLER. THEY'RE CONSIDERING IT. SHOULDN'T WE EXPLORE THAT?
J.C.... HOW IS THAT EVEN POSSIBLE?
BEN EXPLICITLY TOLD US NO/ONE SAVED HIM FROM THE COPYCAT LAST EPISODE.
YEAH, BUT HE COULD BE LYING--
WE HAVE AUDIO! ARE YOU EVEN LISTENING TO THE PODCAST?
I'M JUST SAYING, I WOULD START THINKING ABOUT SUSPECTS.
--MISTER O'NEIL SAID HE WAS GOING TO SWAT ME AT MY HOUSE, YOU KNOW? WHERE I LIVE WITH MY MOM AND SISTERS... AND GRAMS, WHO IS LIKE SEVENTY.
AND WE SHOULD DO A BIT ON THE O'NEIL SHOOTING. SEEMS RELEVANT. HE TARGETED SOME-ONE ONLINE AND PAID THE PRICE.
THAT'S ONE WAY TO LOOK AT IT.
YOU KNOW WHAT HAPPENS WHEN HEAVILY ARMED POLICE KNOCKS DOWN YOUR DOOR THINKING THERE'S A SHOOTER INSIDE?! AND, LIKE, I'M A GUN ADVOCATE. I GOT AN ARSENAL IN MY HOUSE, DUDE.
HEY. LOOK AT IT EVERY WHICH WAY, JUST LOOK AT IT.
THEY WOULD'A LIT UP MY WHOLE FAMILY.

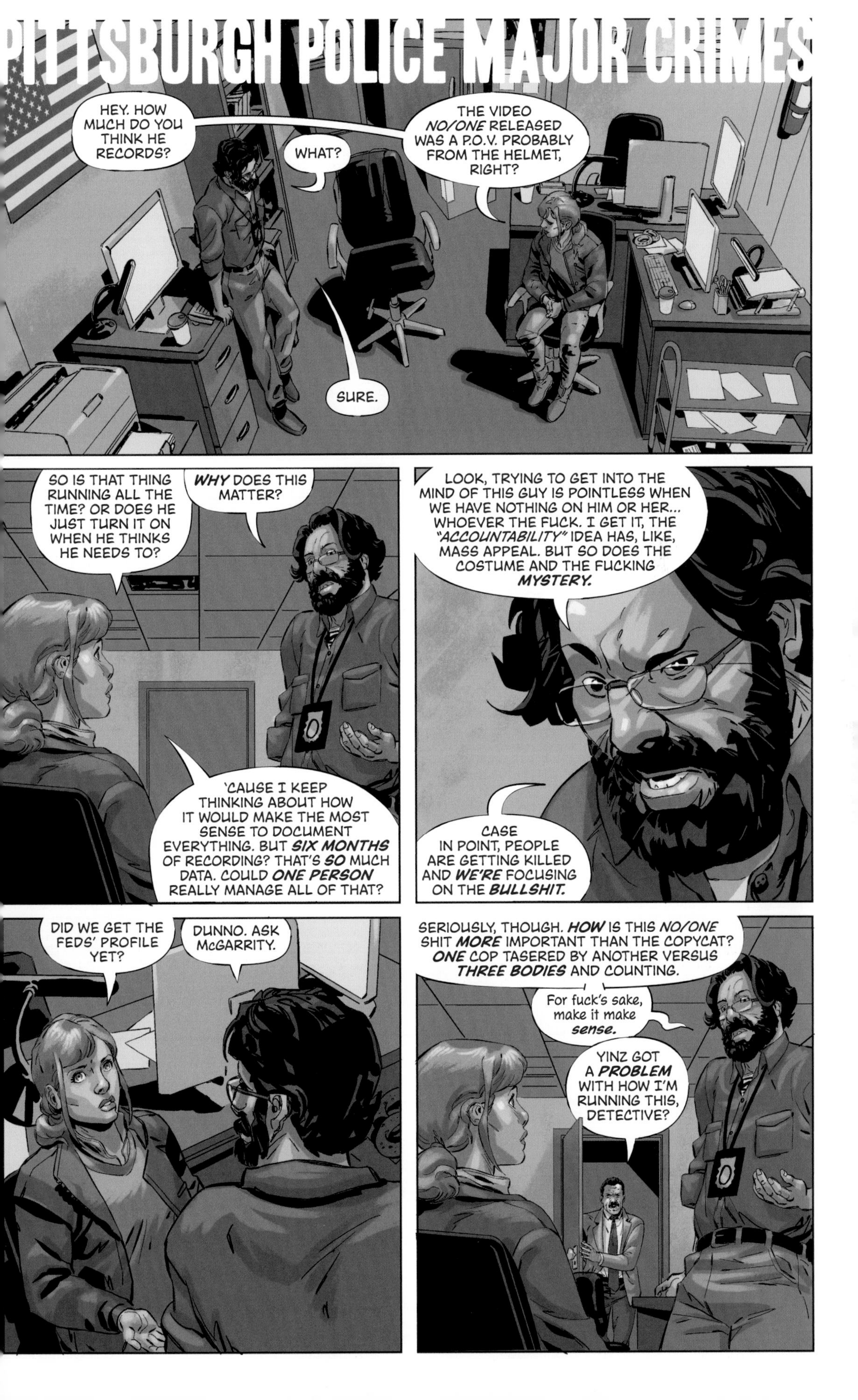
PITTSBURGH POLICE MAJOR CRIMES
HEY. HOW MUCH DO YOU THINK HE RECORDS?
WHAT?
THE VIDEO NO/ONE RELEASED WAS A P.O.V. PROBABLY FROM THE HELMET, RIGHT?
SURE.
SO IS THAT THING RUNNING ALL THE TIME? OR DOES HE JUST TURN IT ON WHEN HE THINKS HE NEEDS TO?
WHY DOES THIS MATTER?
'CAUSE I KEEP THINKING ABOUT HOW IT WOULD MAKE THE MOST SENSE TO DOCUMENT EVERYTHING. BUT SIX MONTHS OF RECORDING? THAT'S SO MUCH DATA. COULD ONE PERSON REALLY MANAGE ALL OF THAT?
LOOK, TRYING TO GET INTO THE MIND OF THIS GUY IS POINTLESS WHEN WE HAVE NOTHING ON HIM OR HER... WHOEVER THE FUCK. I GET IT, THE "ACCOUNTABILITY" IDEA HAS, LIKE, MASS APPEAL. BUT SO DOES THE COSTUME AND THE FUCKING MYSTERY.
CASE IN POINT, PEOPLE ARE GETTING KILLED AND WE'RE FOCUSING ON THE BULLSHIT.
DID WE GET THE FEDS' PROFILE YET?
DUNNO. ASK McGARRITY.
SERIOUSLY, THOUGH. HOW IS THIS NO/ONE SHIT MORE IMPORTANT THAN THE COPYCAT? ONE COP TASERED BY ANOTHER VERSUS THREE BODIES AND COUNTING.
For fuck's sake, make it make sense.
YINZ GOT A PROBLEM WITH HOW I'M RUNNING THIS, DETECTIVE?

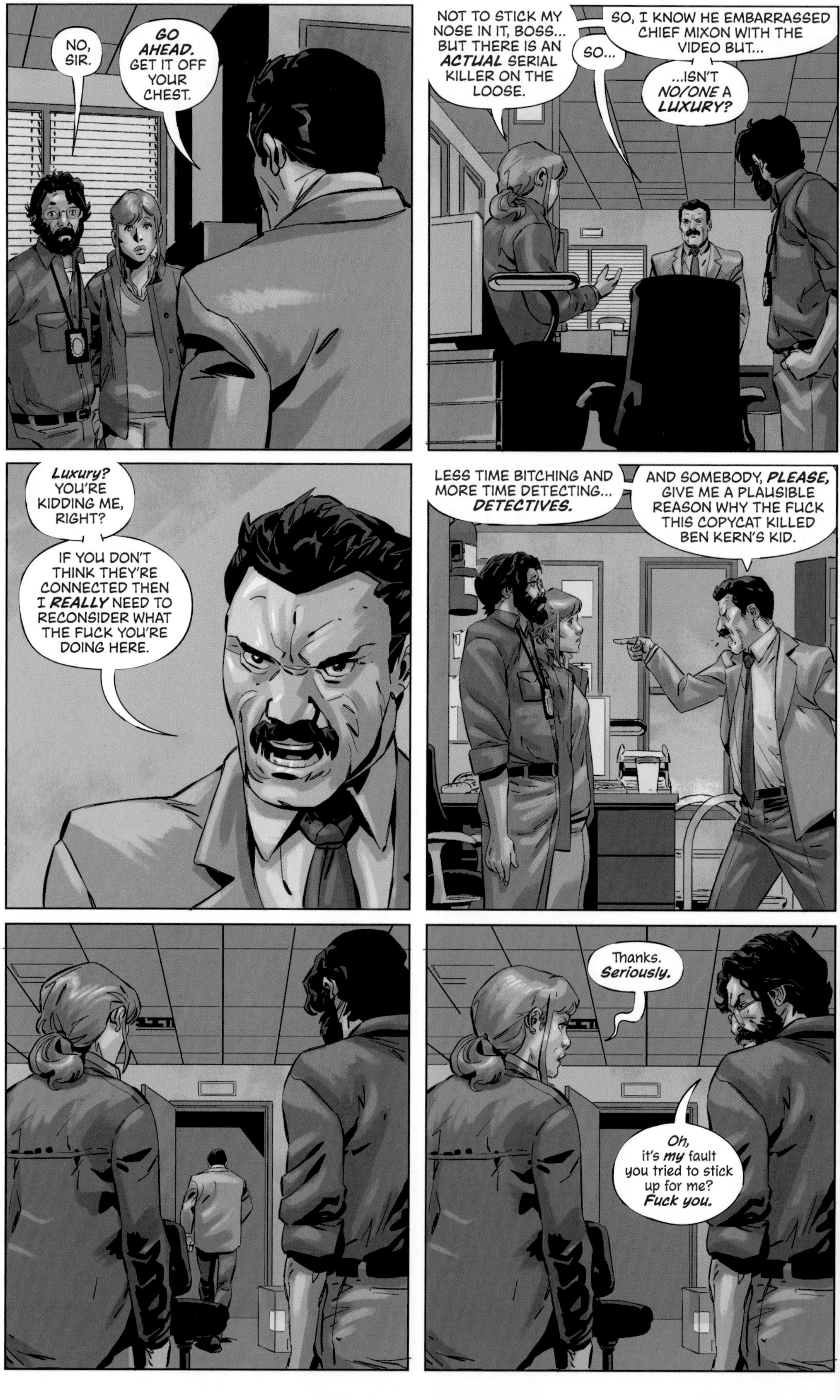
NO, SIR.
GO AHEAD. GET IT OFF YOUR CHEST.
NOT TO STICK MY NOSE IN IT, BOSS... BUT THERE IS AN ACTUAL SERIAL KILLER ON THE LOOSE.
SO...
SO, I KNOW HE EMBARRASSED CHIEF MIXON WITH THE VIDEO BUT...
...ISN'T NO/ONE A LUXURY?
Luxury? YOU'RE KIDDING ME, RIGHT?
IF YOU DON'T THINK THEY'RE CONNECTED THEN I REALLY NEED TO RECONSIDER WHAT THE FUCK YOU'RE DOING HERE.
LESS TIME BITCHING AND MORE TIME DETECTING... DETECTIVES.
AND SOMEBODY, PLEASE, GIVE ME A PLAUSIBLE REASON WHY THE FUCK THIS COPYCAT KILLED BEN KERN'S KID.
Thanks. Seriously.
Oh, it's my fault you tried to stick up for me? Fuck you.

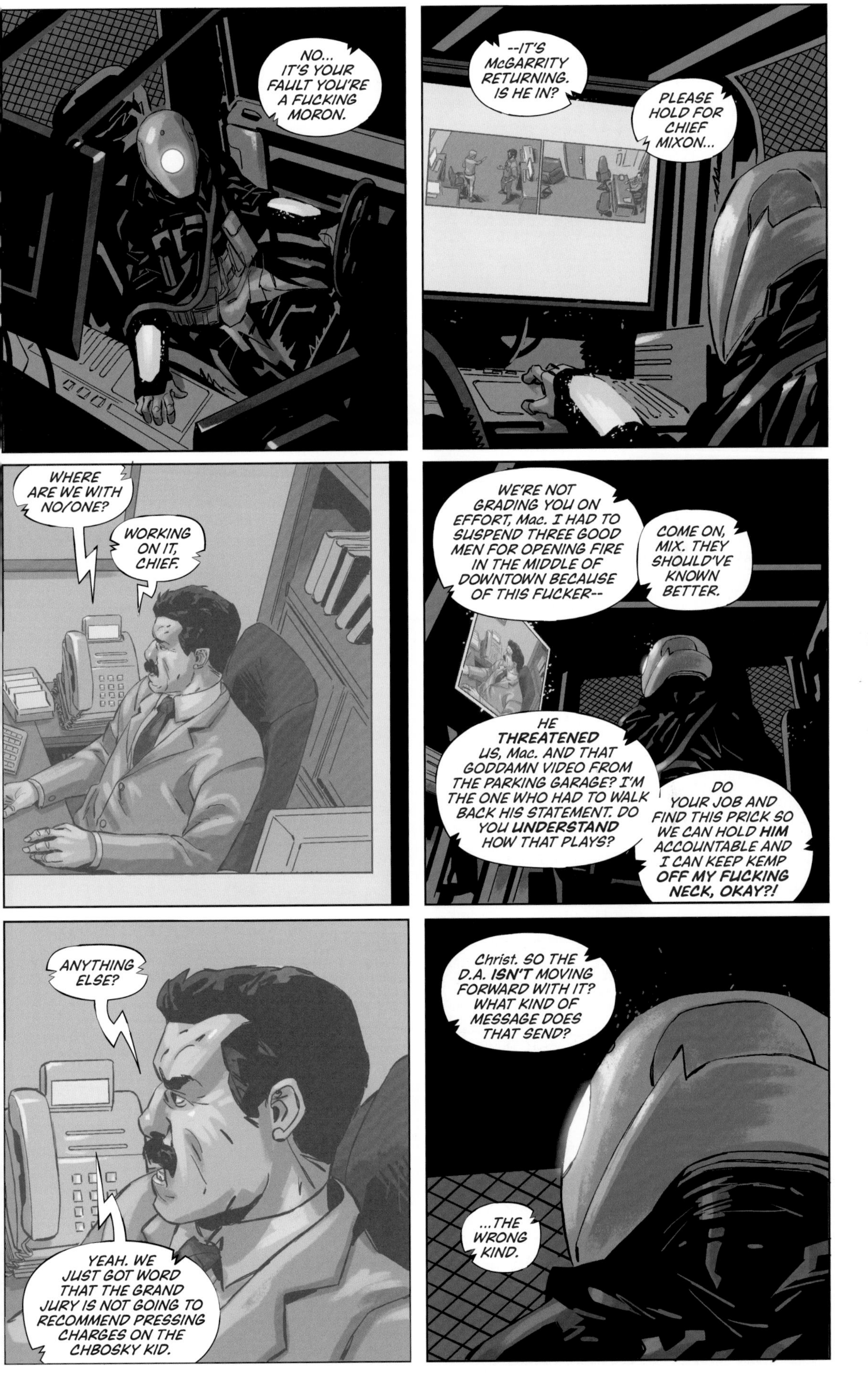
NO... IT'S YOUR FAULT YOU'RE A FUCKING MORON.
--IT'S McGARRITY RETURNING. IS HE IN?
PLEASE HOLD FOR CHIEF MIXON...
WHERE ARE WE WITH NO/ONE?
WORKING ON IT, CHIEF.
WE'RE NOT GRADING YOU ON EFFORT, Mac. I HAD TO SUSPEND THREE GOOD MEN FOR OPENING FIRE IN THE MIDDLE OF DOWNTOWN BECAUSE OF THIS FUCKER--
COME ON, MIX. THEY SHOULD'VE KNOWN BETTER.
HE **THREATENED** US, Mac. AND THAT GODDAMN VIDEO FROM THE PARKING GARAGE? I'M THE ONE WHO HAD TO WALK BACK HIS STATEMENT. DO YOU **UNDERSTAND** HOW THAT PLAYS?
DO YOUR JOB AND FIND THIS PRICK SO WE CAN HOLD **HIM** ACCOUNTABLE AND I CAN KEEP KEMP **OFF MY FUCKING NECK, OKAY?!**
ANYTHING ELSE?
YEAH. WE JUST GOT WORD THAT THE GRAND JURY IS NOT GOING TO RECOMMEND PRESSING CHARGES ON THE CHBOSKY KID.
Christ. SO THE D.A. **ISN'T** MOVING FORWARD WITH IT? WHAT KIND OF MESSAGE DOES THAT SEND?
...THE WRONG KIND.

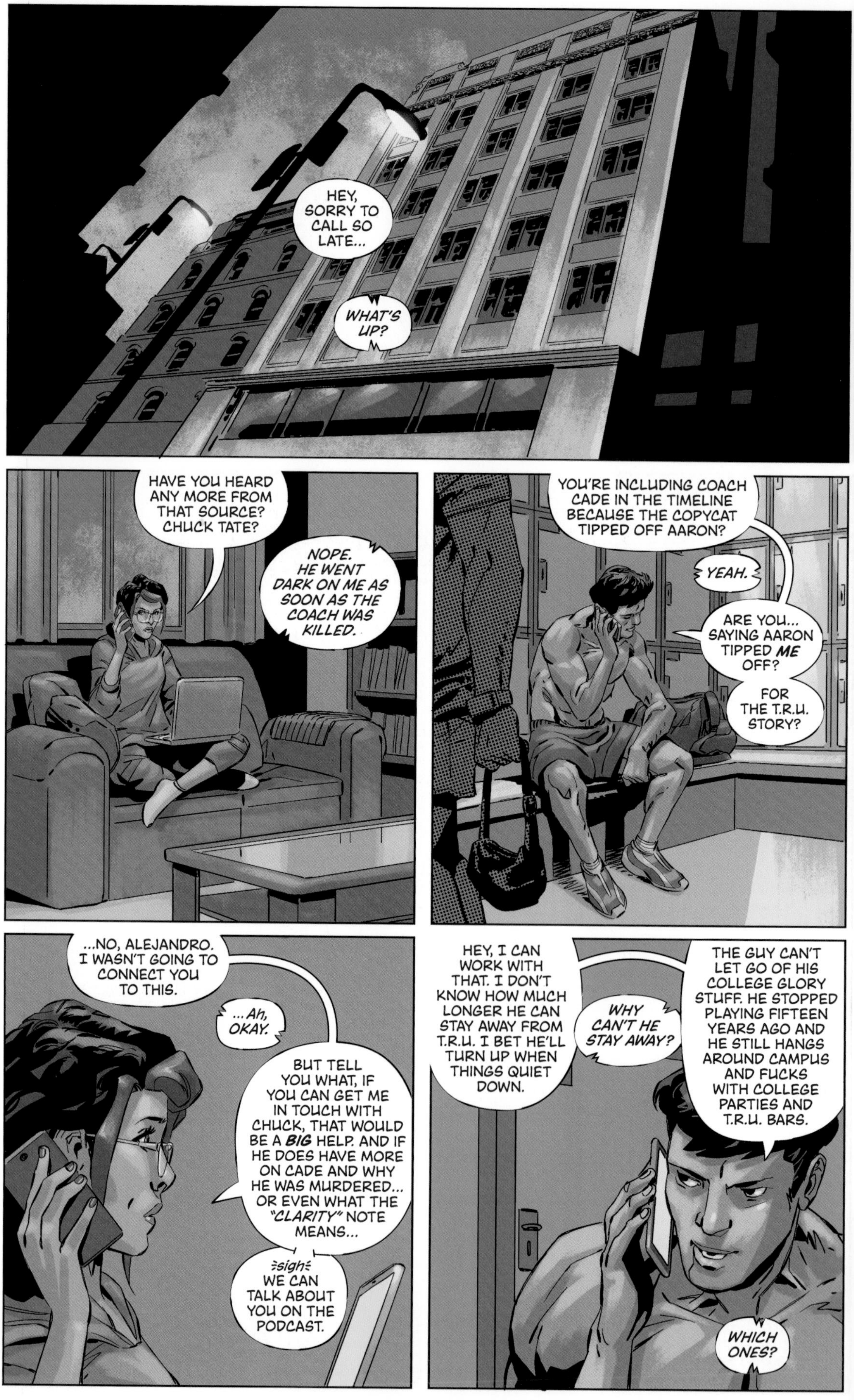
HEY, SORRY TO CALL SO LATE...
WHAT'S UP?
HAVE YOU HEARD ANY MORE FROM THAT SOURCE? CHUCK TATE?
NOPE. HE WENT DARK ON ME AS SOON AS THE COACH WAS KILLED.
YOU'RE INCLUDING COACH CADE IN THE TIMELINE BECAUSE THE COPYCAT TIPPED OFF AARON?
YEAH.
ARE YOU... SAYING AARON TIPPED ME OFF?
FOR THE T.R.U. STORY?
...NO, ALEJANDRO. I WASN'T GOING TO CONNECT YOU TO THIS.
...AH, OKAY.
BUT TELL YOU WHAT, IF YOU CAN GET ME IN TOUCH WITH CHUCK, THAT WOULD BE A BIG HELP. AND IF HE DOES HAVE MORE ON CADE AND WHY HE WAS MURDERED... OR EVEN WHAT THE "CLARITY" NOTE MEANS...
sigh WE CAN TALK ABOUT YOU ON THE PODCAST.
HEY, I CAN WORK WITH THAT. I DON'T KNOW HOW MUCH LONGER HE CAN STAY AWAY FROM T.R.U. I BET HE'LL TURN UP WHEN THINGS QUIET DOWN.
WHY CAN'T HE STAY AWAY?
THE GUY CAN'T LET GO OF HIS COLLEGE GLORY STUFF. HE STOPPED PLAYING FIFTEEN YEARS AGO AND HE STILL HANGS AROUND CAMPUS AND FUCKS WITH COLLEGE PARTIES AND T.R.U. BARS.
WHICH ONES?

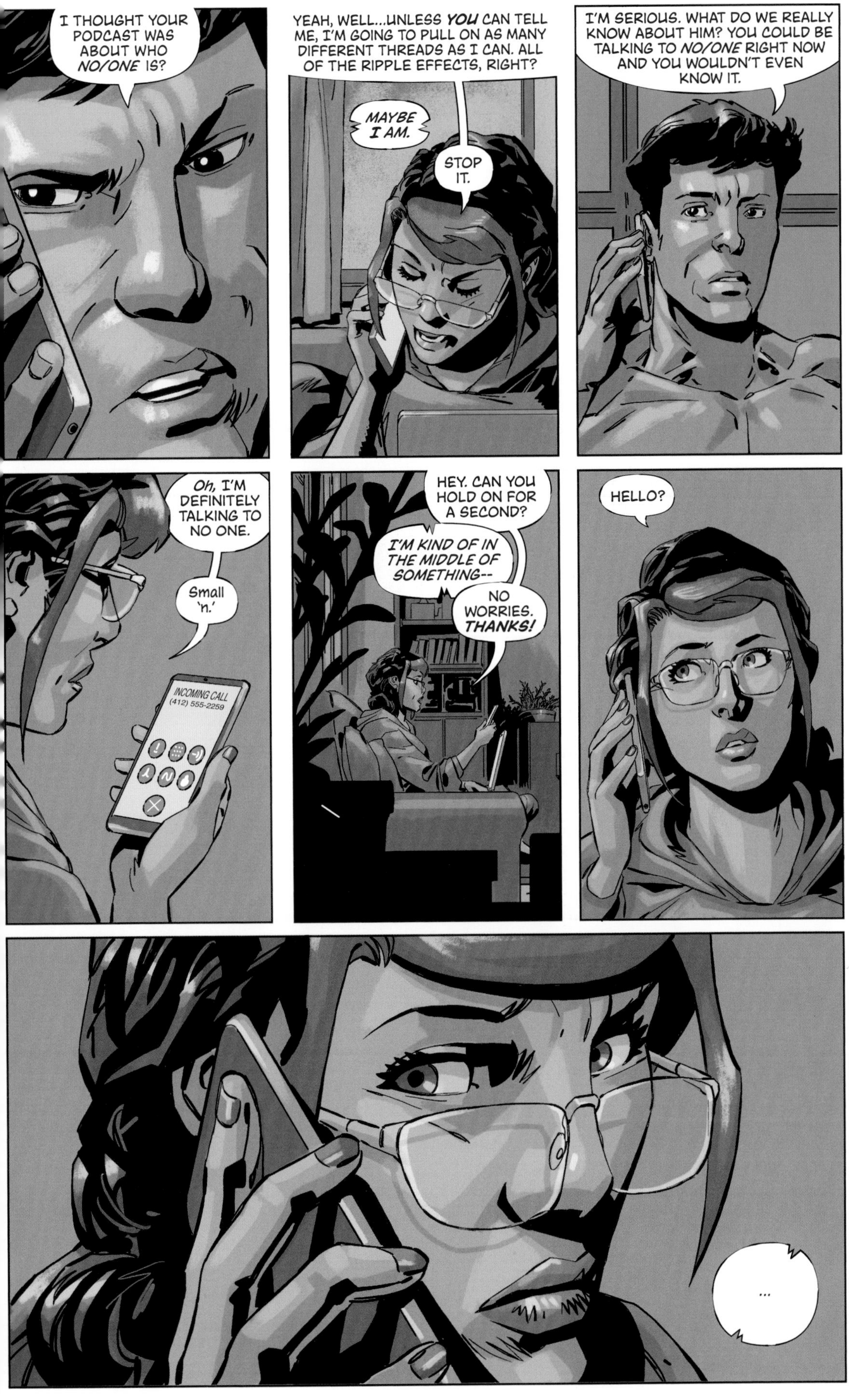
I THOUGHT YOUR PODCAST WAS ABOUT WHO *NO/ONE* IS?
YEAH, WELL...UNLESS ***YOU*** CAN TELL ME, I'M GOING TO PULL ON AS MANY DIFFERENT THREADS AS I CAN. ALL OF THE RIPPLE EFFECTS, RIGHT?
MAYBE I AM.
STOP IT.
I'M SERIOUS. WHAT DO WE REALLY KNOW ABOUT HIM? YOU COULD BE TALKING TO *NO/ONE* RIGHT NOW AND YOU WOULDN'T EVEN KNOW IT.
Oh, I'M DEFINITELY TALKING TO NO ONE.
Small 'n.'
INCOMING CALL
(412) 555-2259
HEY. CAN YOU HOLD ON FOR A SECOND?
I'M KIND OF IN THE MIDDLE OF SOMETHING--
NO WORRIES. ***THANKS!***
HELLO?
...

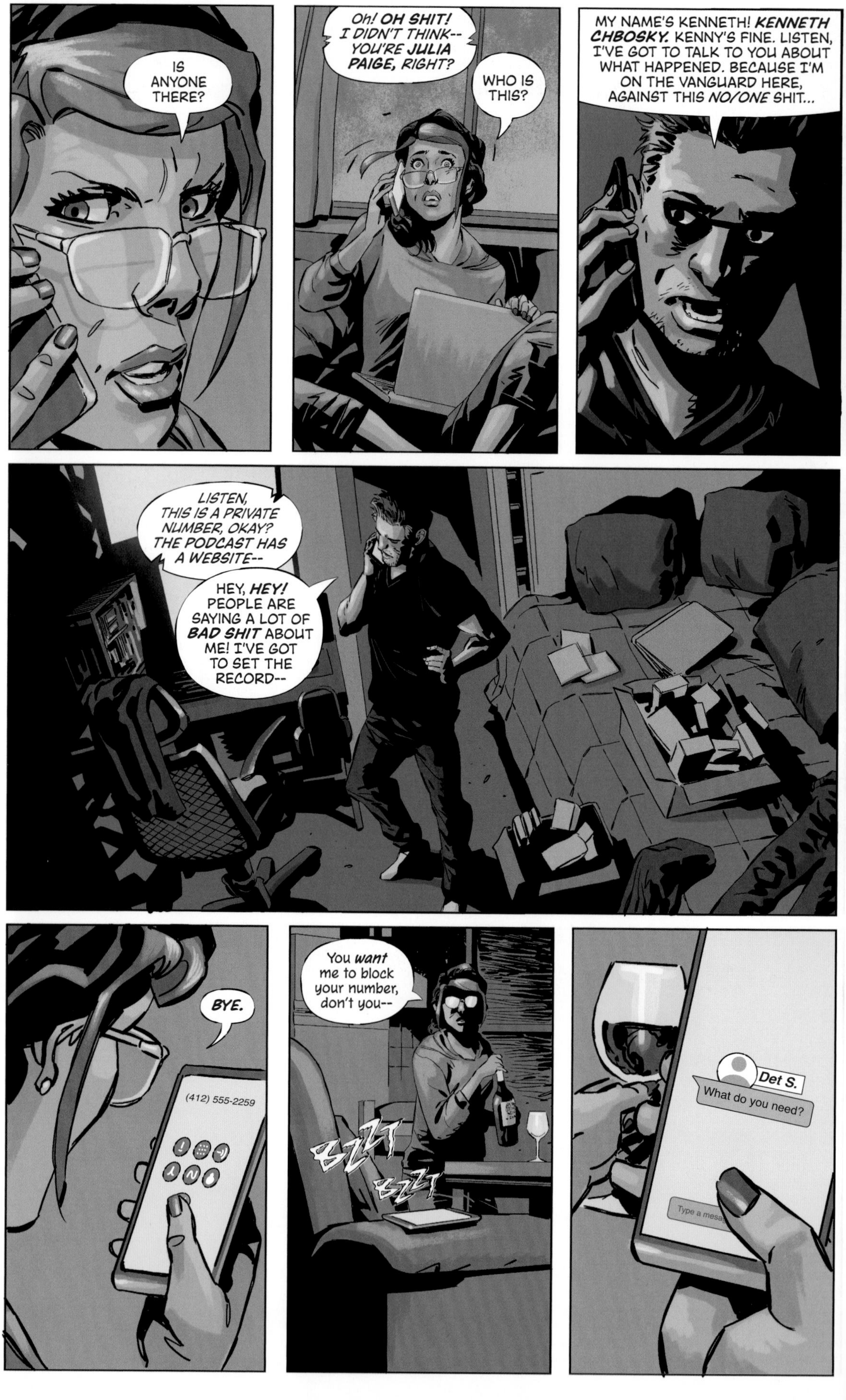
IS ANYONE THERE?
Oh! OH SHIT! I DIDN'T THINK-- YOU'RE JULIA PAIGE, RIGHT?
WHO IS THIS?
MY NAME'S KENNETH! KENNETH CHBOSKY. KENNY'S FINE. LISTEN, I'VE GOT TO TALK TO YOU ABOUT WHAT HAPPENED. BECAUSE I'M ON THE VANGUARD HERE, AGAINST THIS NO/ONE SHIT...
LISTEN, THIS IS A PRIVATE NUMBER, OKAY? THE PODCAST HAS A WEBSITE--
HEY, HEY! PEOPLE ARE SAYING A LOT OF BAD SHIT ABOUT ME! I'VE GOT TO SET THE RECORD--
BYE.
(412) 555-2259
You want me to block your number, don't you--
BZZZT
BZZZT
Det S.
What do you need?

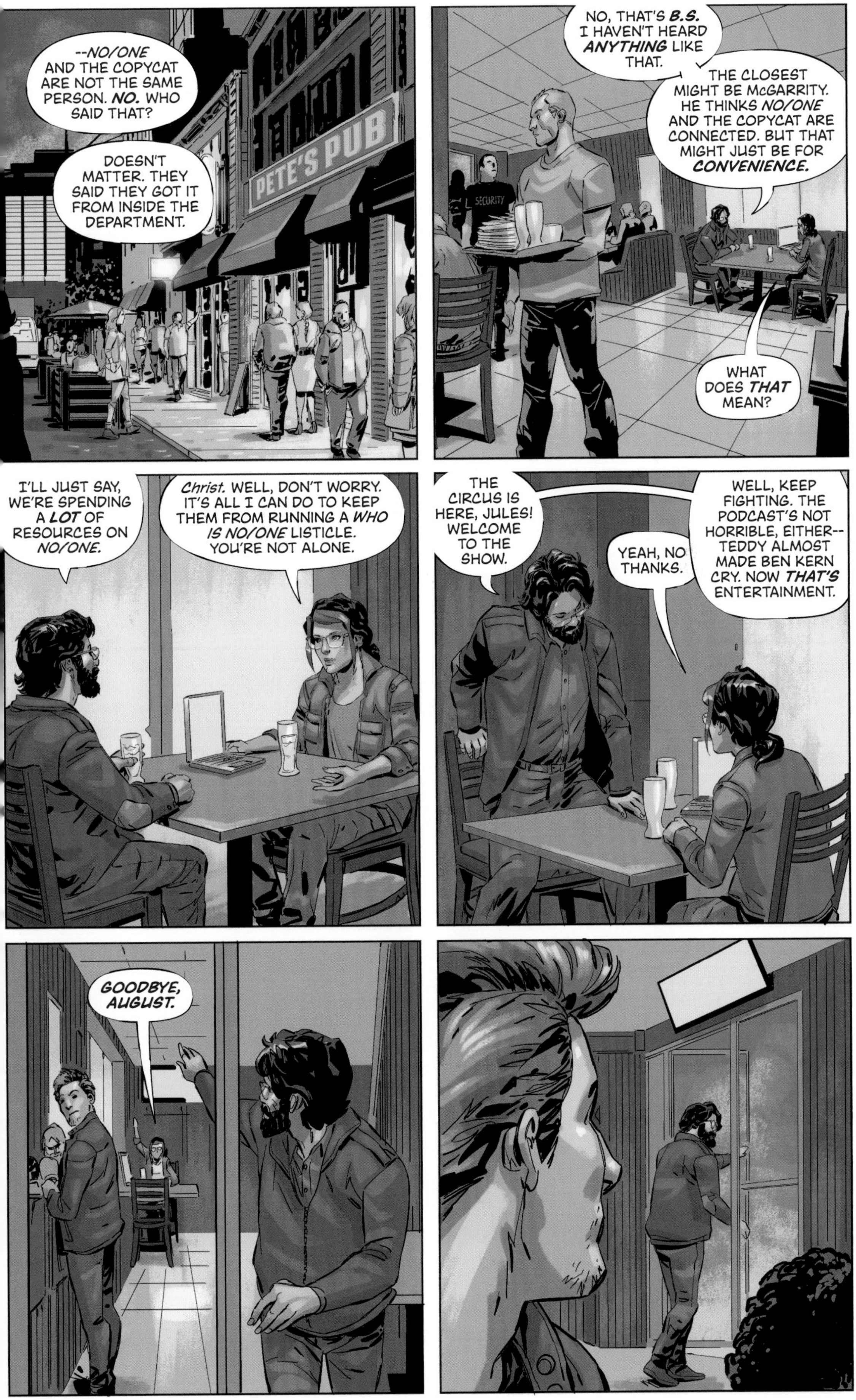
--NO/ONE AND THE COPYCAT ARE NOT THE SAME PERSON. NO. WHO SAID THAT?
DOESN'T MATTER. THEY SAID THEY GOT IT FROM INSIDE THE DEPARTMENT.
PETE'S PUB
NO, THAT'S B.S. I HAVEN'T HEARD ANYTHING LIKE THAT.
THE CLOSEST MIGHT BE McGARRITY. HE THINKS NO/ONE AND THE COPYCAT ARE CONNECTED. BUT THAT MIGHT JUST BE FOR CONVENIENCE.
SECURITY
WHAT DOES THAT MEAN?
I'LL JUST SAY, WE'RE SPENDING A LOT OF RESOURCES ON NO/ONE.
Christ. WELL, DON'T WORRY. IT'S ALL I CAN DO TO KEEP THEM FROM RUNNING A WHO IS NO/ONE LISTICLE. YOU'RE NOT ALONE.
THE CIRCUS IS HERE, JULES! WELCOME TO THE SHOW.
YEAH, NO THANKS.
WELL, KEEP FIGHTING. THE PODCAST'S NOT HORRIBLE, EITHER-- TEDDY ALMOST MADE BEN KERN CRY. NOW THAT'S ENTERTAINMENT.
GOODBYE, AUGUST.

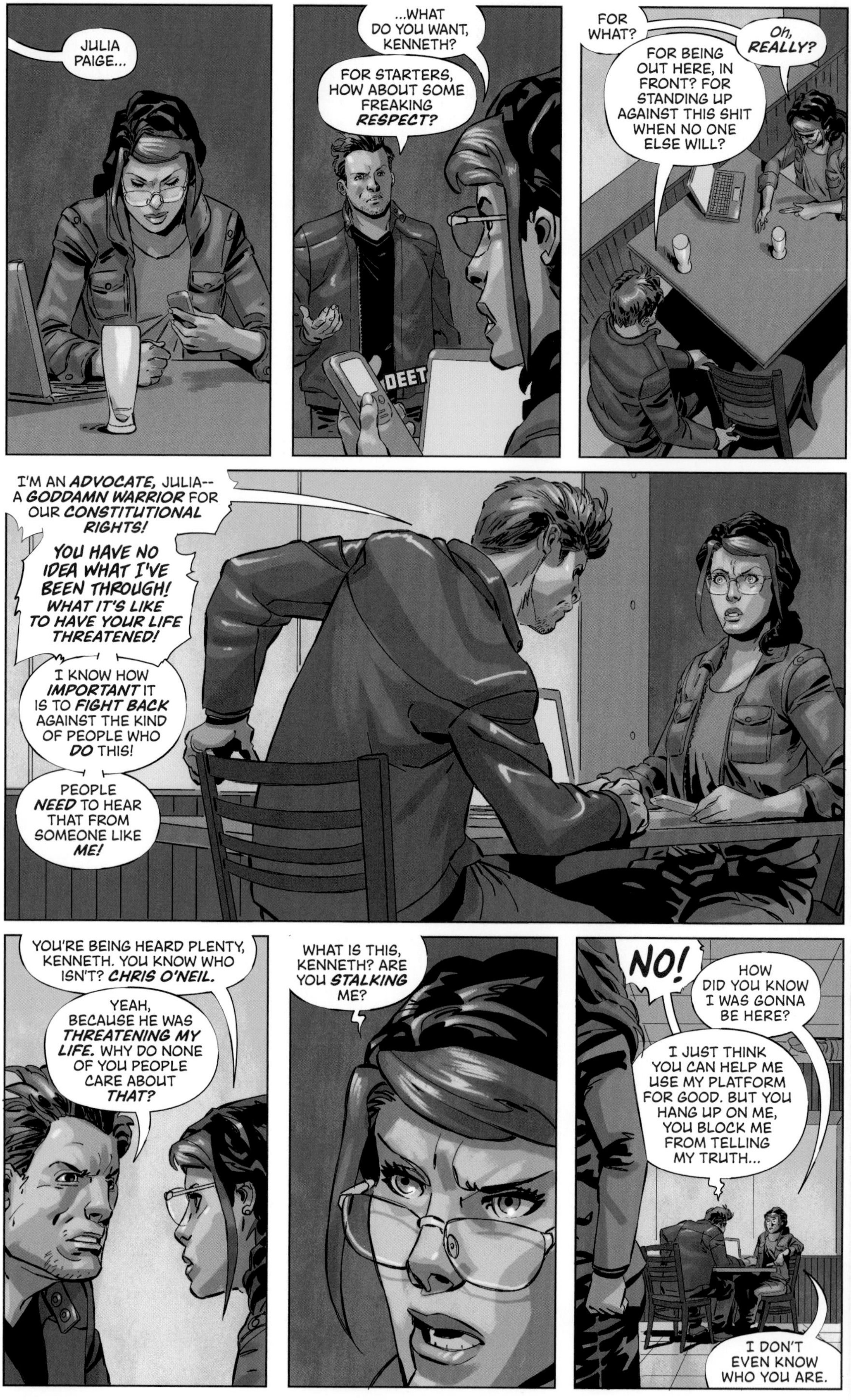
JULIA PAIGE...
...WHAT DO YOU WANT, KENNETH?
FOR STARTERS, HOW ABOUT SOME FREAKING RESPECT?
FOR WHAT?
Oh, REALLY?
FOR BEING OUT HERE, IN FRONT? FOR STANDING UP AGAINST THIS SHIT WHEN NO ONE ELSE WILL?
DEET
I'M AN ADVOCATE, JULIA-- A GODDAMN WARRIOR FOR OUR CONSTITUTIONAL RIGHTS!
YOU HAVE NO IDEA WHAT I'VE BEEN THROUGH! WHAT IT'S LIKE TO HAVE YOUR LIFE THREATENED!
I KNOW HOW IMPORTANT IT IS TO FIGHT BACK AGAINST THE KIND OF PEOPLE WHO DO THIS!
PEOPLE NEED TO HEAR THAT FROM SOMEONE LIKE ME!
YOU'RE BEING HEARD PLENTY, KENNETH. YOU KNOW WHO ISN'T? CHRIS O'NEIL.
YEAH, BECAUSE HE WAS THREATENING MY LIFE. WHY DO NONE OF YOU PEOPLE CARE ABOUT THAT?
WHAT IS THIS, KENNETH? ARE YOU STALKING ME?
NO!
HOW DID YOU KNOW I WAS GONNA BE HERE?
I JUST THINK YOU CAN HELP ME USE MY PLATFORM FOR GOOD. BUT YOU HANG UP ON ME, YOU BLOCK ME FROM TELLING MY TRUTH...
I DON'T EVEN KNOW WHO YOU ARE.

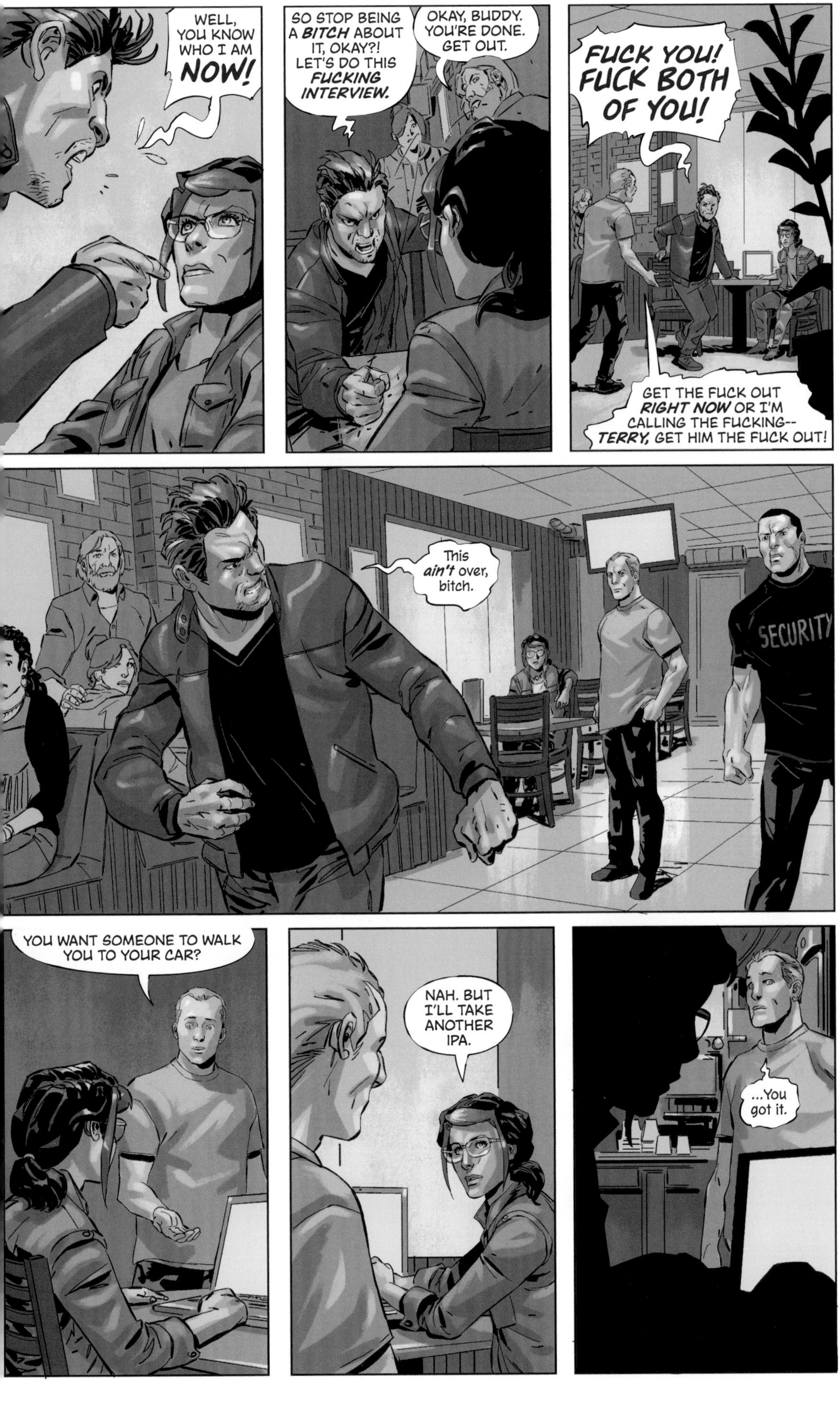
WELL, YOU KNOW WHO I AM NOW!
SO STOP BEING A BITCH ABOUT IT, OKAY?! LET'S DO THIS FUCKING INTERVIEW.
OKAY, BUDDY. YOU'RE DONE. GET OUT.
FUCK YOU! FUCK BOTH OF YOU!
GET THE FUCK OUT RIGHT NOW OR I'M CALLING THE FUCKING-- TERRY, GET HIM THE FUCK OUT!
This ain't over, bitch.
SECURITY
YOU WANT SOMEONE TO WALK YOU TO YOUR CAR?
NAH. BUT I'LL TAKE ANOTHER IPA.
...You got it.

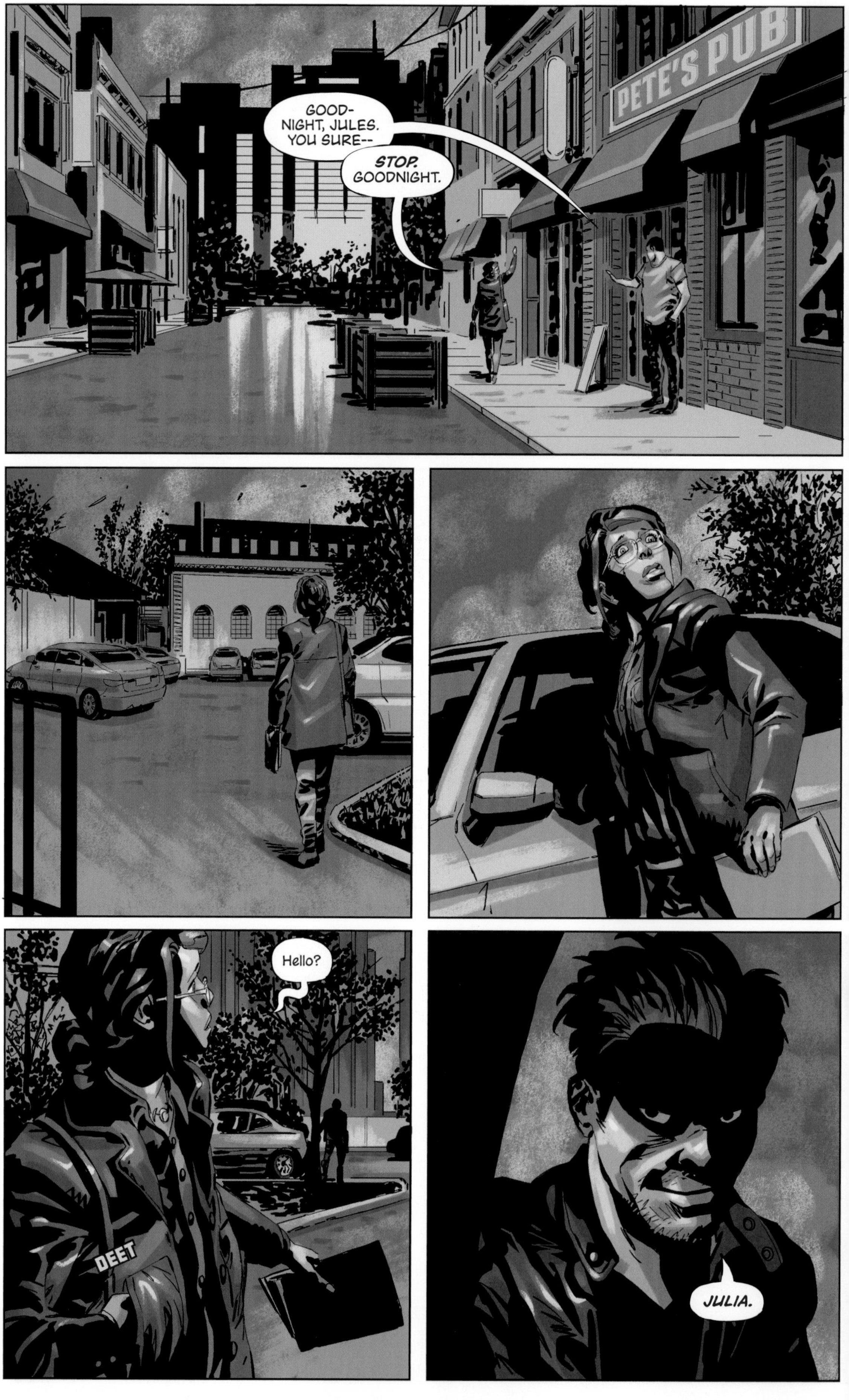
PETE'S PUB
GOOD-NIGHT, JULES. YOU SURE--
STOP. GOODNIGHT.
Hello?
DEET
JULIA.

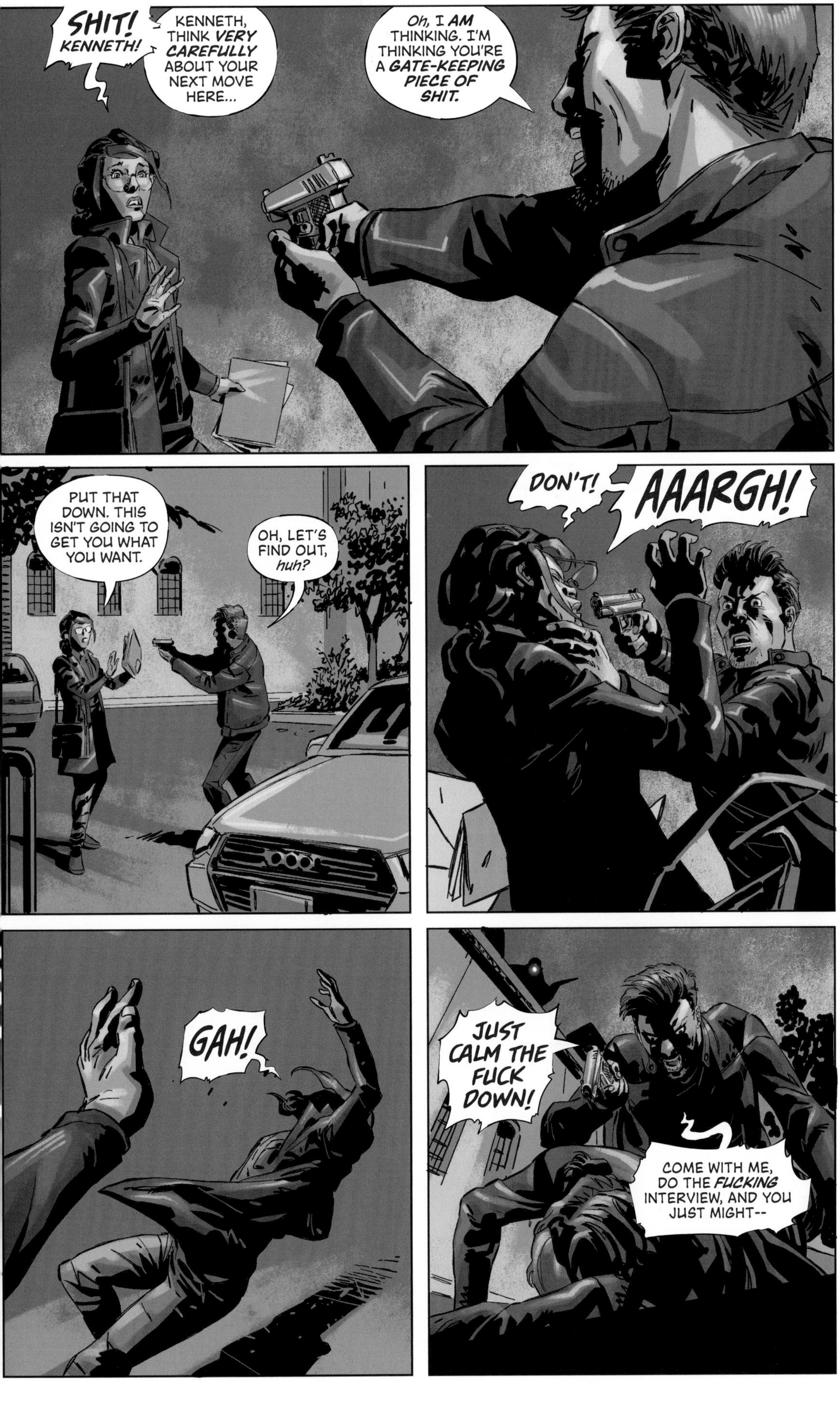
SHIT! KENNETH!
KENNETH, THINK VERY CAREFULLY ABOUT YOUR NEXT MOVE HERE...
Oh, I AM THINKING. I'M THINKING YOU'RE A GATE-KEEPING PIECE OF SHIT.
PUT THAT DOWN. THIS ISN'T GOING TO GET YOU WHAT YOU WANT.
OH, LET'S FIND OUT, huh?
DON'T!
AAARGH!
GAH!
JUST CALM THE FUCK DOWN!
COME WITH ME, DO THE FUCKING INTERVIEW, AND YOU JUST MIGHT--

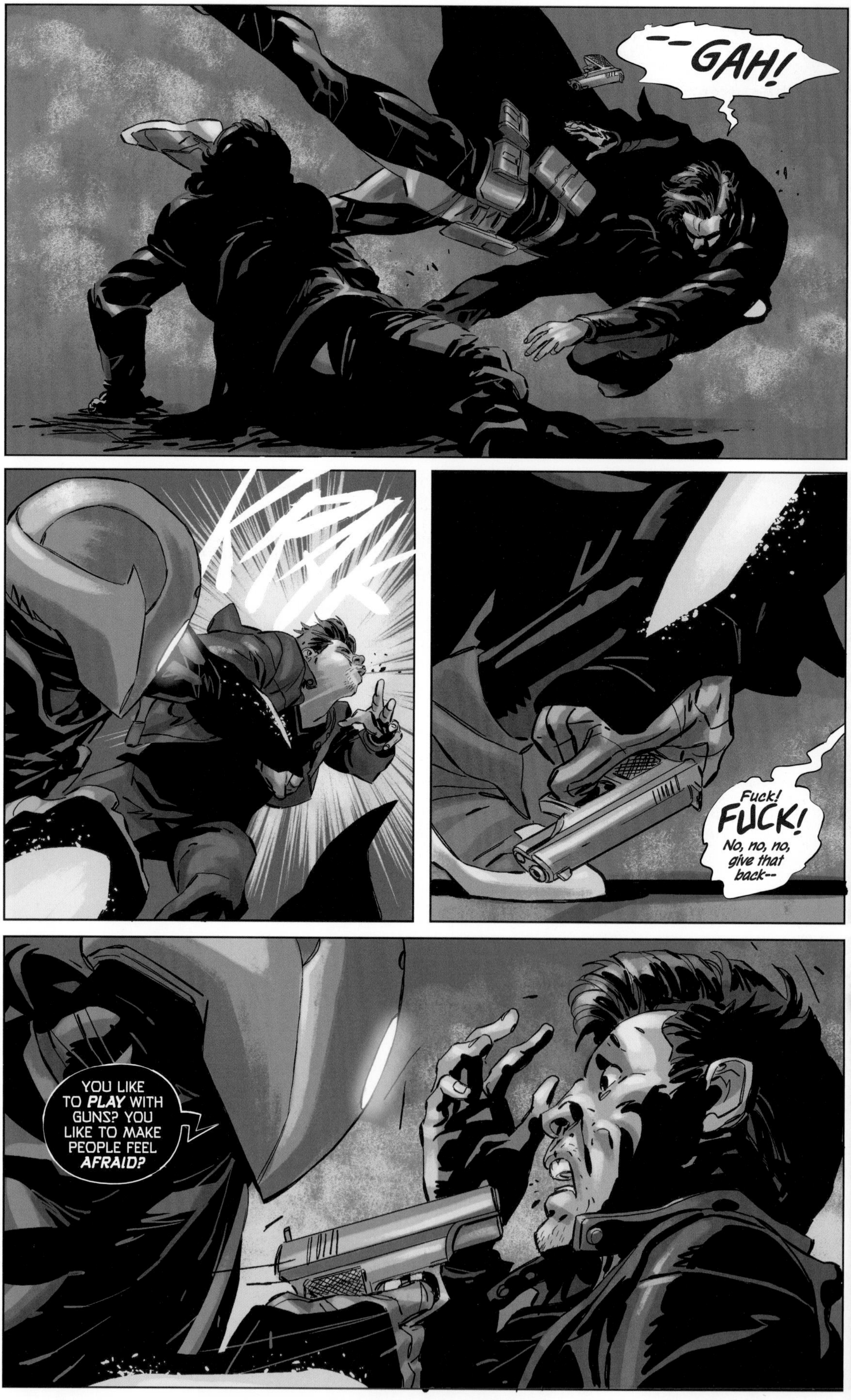
--GAH!
KRAK
Fuck! FUCK! No, no, no, give that back--
YOU LIKE TO PLAY WITH GUNS? YOU LIKE TO MAKE PEOPLE FEEL AFRAID?

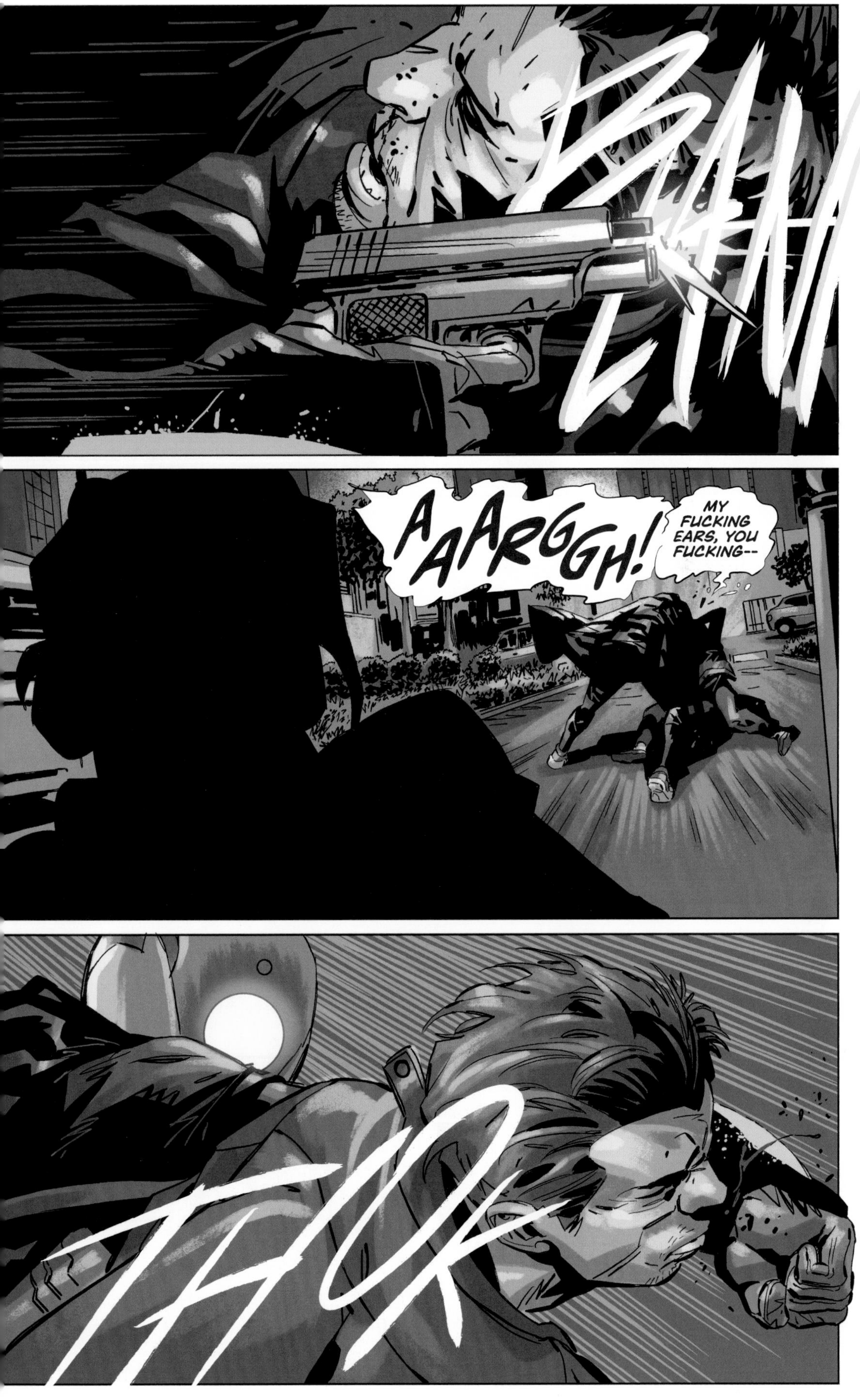
BLAM
AAARGGH!
MY FUCKING EARS, YOU FUCKING--
THOK

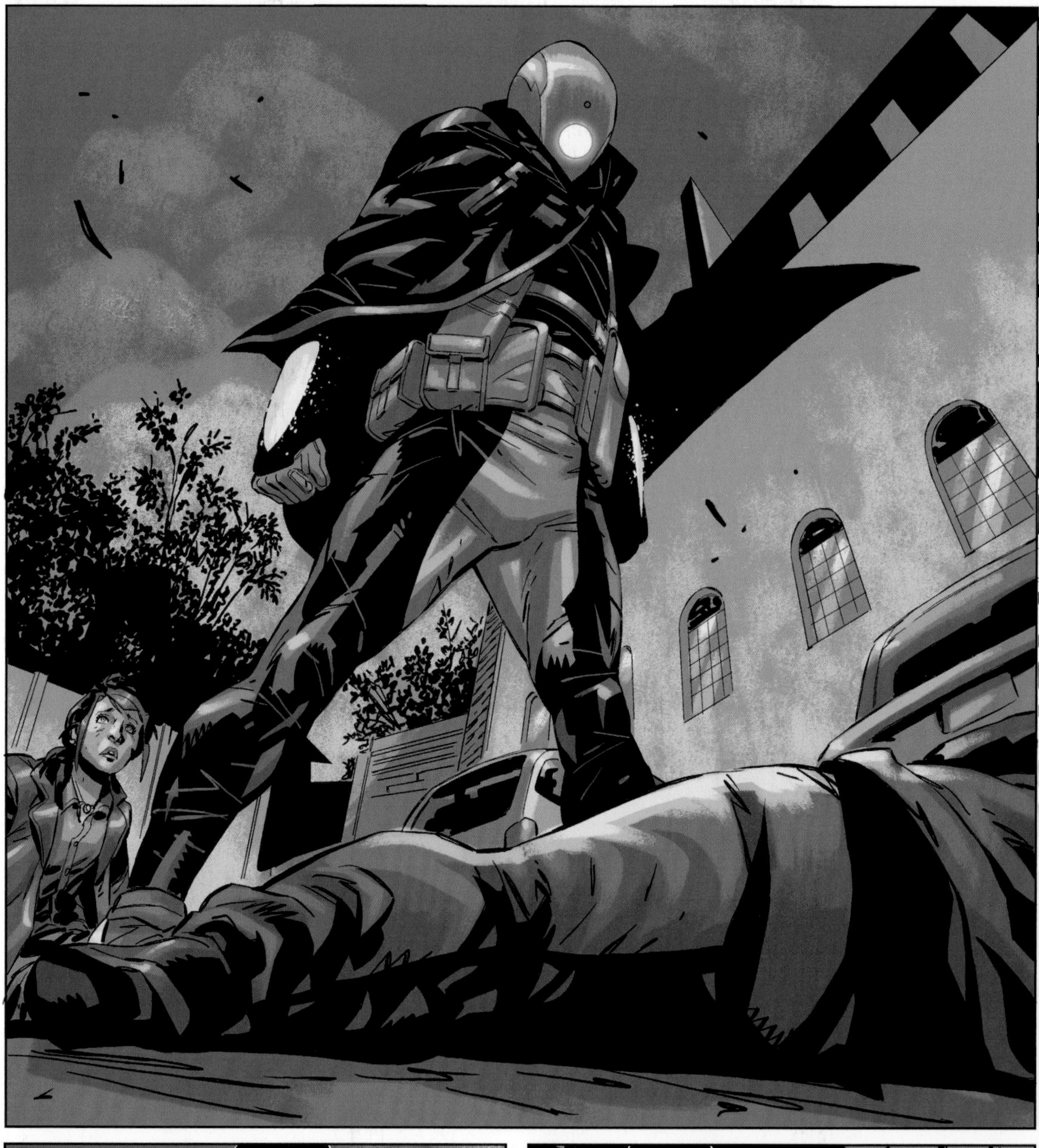

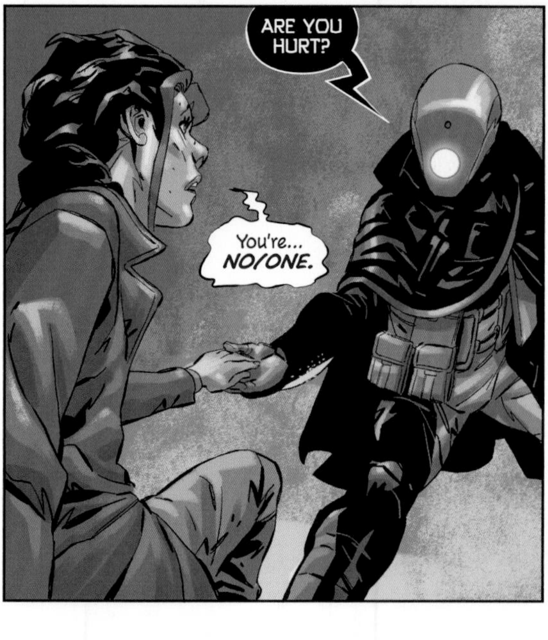

ARE YOU HURT?
You're... NO/ONE.

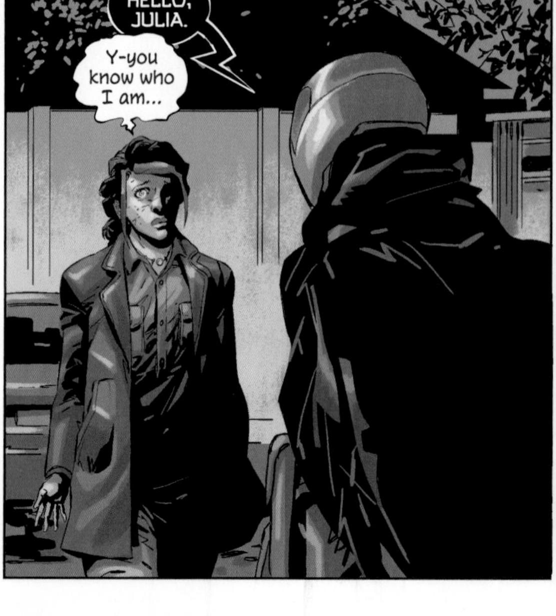

HELLO, JULIA.
Y-you know who I am...

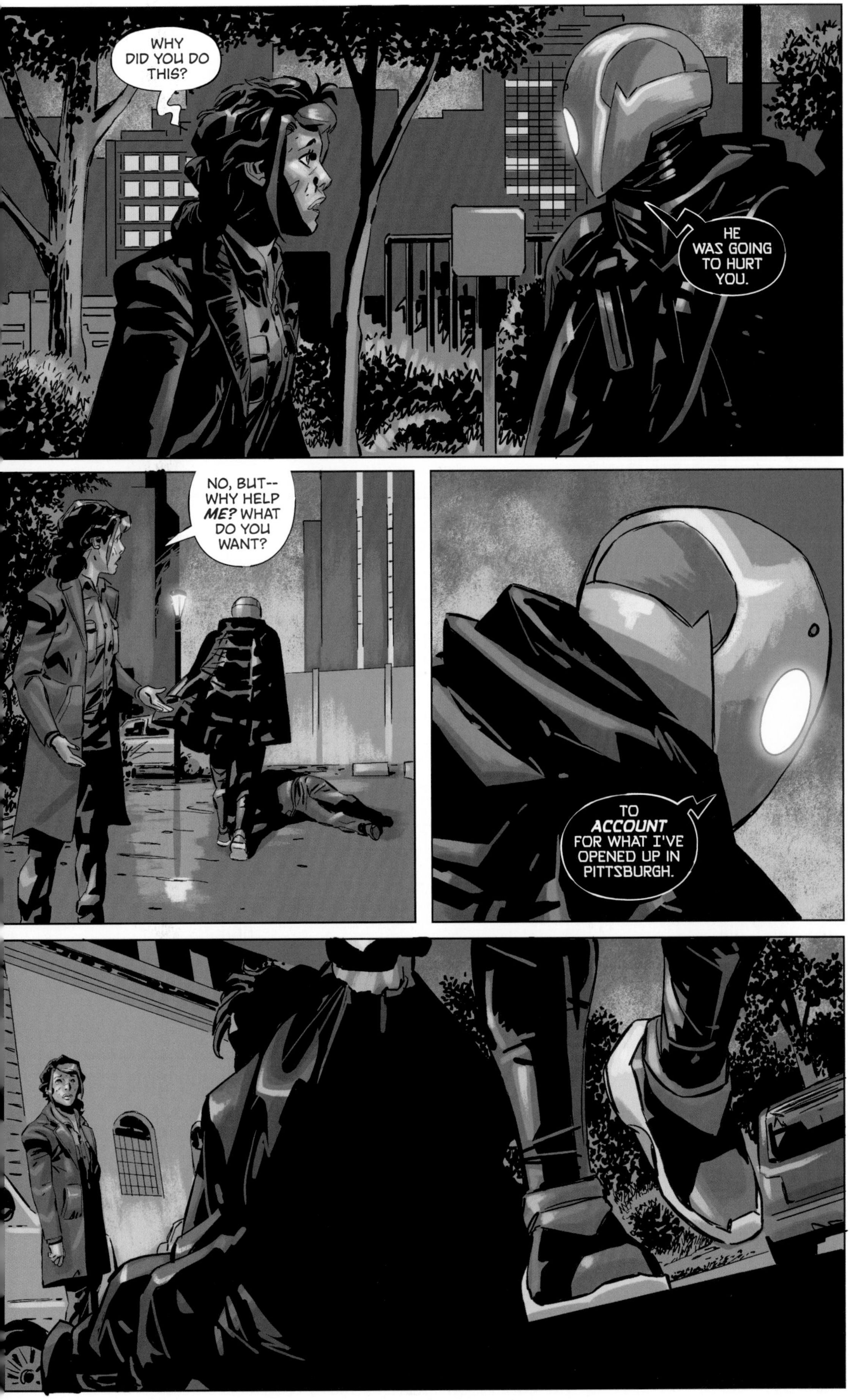
WHY DID YOU DO THIS?
HE WAS GOING TO HURT YOU.
NO, BUT-- WHY HELP *ME?* WHAT DO YOU WANT?
TO *ACCOUNT* FOR WHAT I'VE OPENED UP IN PITTSBURGH.

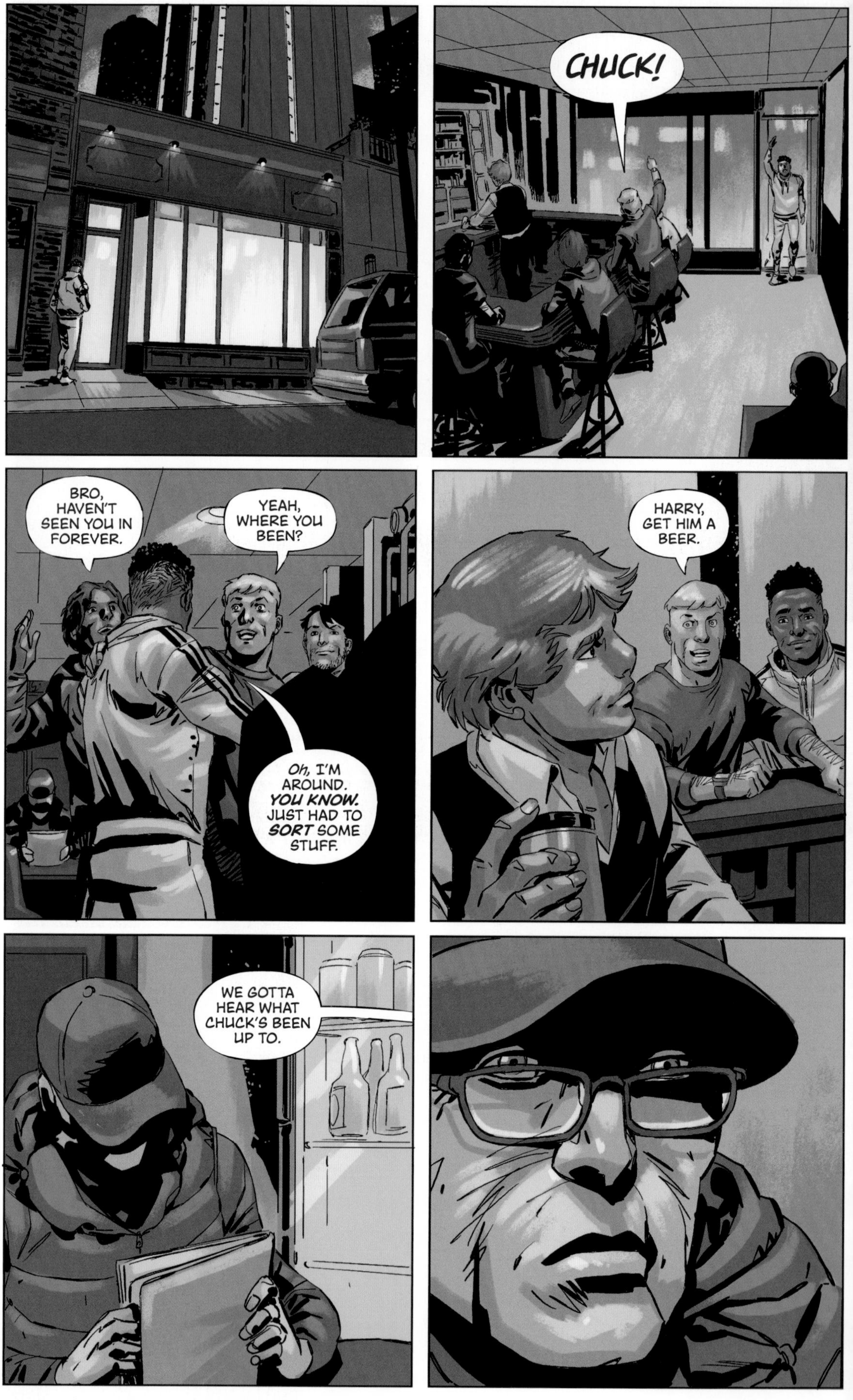
CHUCK!
BRO, HAVEN'T SEEN YOU IN FOREVER.
YEAH, WHERE YOU BEEN?
Oh, I'M AROUND. YOU KNOW. JUST HAD TO SORT SOME STUFF.
HARRY, GET HIM A BEER.
WE GOTTA HEAR WHAT CHUCK'S BEEN UP TO.

THE DROP

PRESENTS

WHO IS NO/ONE

WITH/ JULIA PAIGE

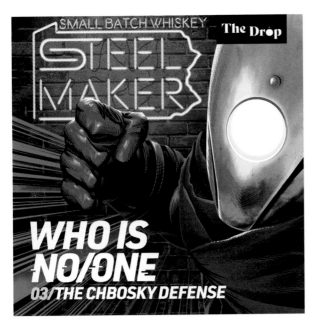

19 MAY

03/The Chbosky Defense

WHO IS NO/ONE

19:32   -15:32

KNOWPEDIA
An Encyclopedia For Free

Ben Kern

Article   Talk

Read   View source   View history

Benjamin Daryl Kern (born May 16, 1963) is a retired police officer, formerly serving as the Assistant Chief of Operations for the Pittsburgh Bureau of Police. A veteran of the department with over three decades as an officer, he is known for his undercover work infiltrating the Weiss Macht Brotherhood. His work helped prevent an act of domestic terrorism planned by a white supremacist gang targeting mosques throughout Pennsylvania in the mid 1990s. Recently, he is best known for being the father of suspected Accountability Killer, Aaron Kern.

Early life   [edit]

Kern is a native of East Allegheny, Pennsylvania. He attended East Allegheny High School and then Three Rivers University in Pittsburgh, where he received a B.A. in Criminal Justice. A third-generation officer, his father, Paul, was also a Pittsburgh policeman, retiring at the rank of Police Commander in 1993.

Career   [edit]

Kern was appointed to the Pittsburgh Bureau of Police in March 1988 after completing his degree and then graduating from the police academy. He served three years as a patrol officer in Zone 5 before joining the Narcotics Task Force. In 1995, Kern transferred to the Major Crimes Undercover Unit where he was assigned to infiltrate local white supremacist and militant hate groups. While working undercover cases, he was injured multiple times-- once from a knife wound sustained during a dispute with a Neo-Nazi gunrunner, and once in a car accident fleeing Pennsylvania State Police, during an unrelated warehouse raid in the Strip District. In 2003, he spent the final eight months of his undercover assignment with the Weiss Macht Brotherhood, and successfully stopped multiple coordinated attacks on area mosques while taking down the leadership of the white power group. In the process, his cover was blown and he was injured a third time-- shot twice by Macht Brotherhood enforcer Kaleb Roman, who was in turn slain by Pittsburgh Police Sergeant Albert Mixon in a violent shoot-out.

Ben Kern

Born	May 16, 1963 (age 59) Pittsburgh, U.S.
Department	Pittsburgh Bureau of Police
Years of Service	1988-2023
Rank	Officer (1988) Zone Commander (2009) Assistant Chief of Operations (2014-)
Awards	Medal of Valor (2003) Purple Heart (1998, 2001, 2003) Meritorious Service (2011)

After recovery and a promotion, Ben Kern transferred to Operations Division as a sergeant. He was elevated to lieutenant in October 2007 and to Zone Commander in July 2009, achieving the same rank that his father attained. By 2014 he was promoted to the rank of Assistant Chief of Operations, working under Chief of Police Mixon until his retirement in April 2023 under a cloud of suspicion stemming from his eldest son Aaron Kern's arrest for the Accountability Murders.

Controversy   [edit]

In December of 2022, suspected Accountability Killer Aaron Kern, was apprehended inside the Carrie Blast Furnaces. During the booking process, someone within the department booked him under the moniker Richard Roe, hiding his true identity and any connection to Ben Kern. Aaron remained in custody for a full month before Danielle Gaines of Edge News broke the story that Richard Roe was the son of the Pittsburgh Police Assistant Chief of Operations; although the department alleges an innocent clerical error was the cause, many in the media accused Ben Kern of forcing a cover up of his son's identity. To date, he denies any involvement, and will not discuss who was responsible.

Richard Roe attacks   [edit]

On March 15, 2023, Ben Kern was attacked in his car outside of his home by the suspected third copycat Accountability Killer, claiming to be the original Richard Roe. Ben was wounded in the neck by one shot from the assailant's .38 Special Revolver before the vigilante, NO/ONE, intervened to save his life. That same day, his youngest son, Michael Kern, was gunned down in the same manner. Michael died later that night from four gunshot wounds to the chest. Ben Kern made a full recovery and returned to active duty shortly before retiring.

Richard Roe	[show]

KNOWPEDIA
An Encyclopedia For Free

Kenneth Chbosky

Article Talk Read View source View history

Kenneth Michael Chbosky (born June 15, 2004) is an American man who gained national attention following his involvement in the death of Chris O'Neil, a fellow video game player who had threatened to SWAT him. Chbosky's legal defense, and subsequent acquittal, drew significant criticism from both commentators and legal experts.

Early life [edit]

Kenneth Chbosky was born and raised in Pittsburgh, Pennsylvania. The only child of Richard and Sandra Chbosky, his parents divorced when he was 12. He attended Terry Traditional Academy, where he struggled academically. After high school, Chbosky attempted to enlist in the United States Marine Corps but failed the Armed Services Vocational Aptitude Battery and was rejected. Unable to achieve his goal of military service, he turned to online gaming, where he became radicalized through extremist forums.

Death of Chris O'Neil [edit]

Kenneth Chbosky first entered the national spotlight after his involvement in the killing of Chris O'Neil, a fellow gamer who had threatened to SWAT him. Chbosky claimed preemptive self-defense, leading to the creation of the "Chbosky Defense," a controversial legal argument that contended Chbosky had acted to prevent imminent harm. His acquittal following the grand jury's refusal to indict him drew significant media attention and public debate around self-defense laws. The "Chbosky Defense" quickly became a flashpoint in conversations about preemptive violence and vigilante justice.

Julia Paige altercation [edit]

Chbosky's growing obsession with the media's portrayal of him culminated in an altercation with journalist Julia Paige at Pittsburgh bar Pete's Pub on May 15, 2023. Paige, notable for her writing about the Accountability Murders in Pittsburgh, was accosted by Chbosky, who believed she was part of a media conspiracy against him. During the encounter, Chbosky assaulted Paige, only to be subdued by the vigilante NO/ONE. This public confrontation brought additional attention to his increasingly unstable behavior and contributed to his arrest on charges of aggravated assault. Chbosky was released on bail while awaiting trial, but the incident further tarnished his public image and deepened public concern about online radicalization.

Controversy and legacy [edit]

Chbosky's story served as a flashpoint in debates over gun control, online radicalization, and self-defense laws. His initial acquittal in the Chris O'Neil shooting and the legal precedent set by the "Chbosky Defense" ignited fears about the normalization of preemptive violence, particularly in cases involving perceived rather than actual threats. The assault on Julia Paige only intensified these discussions, with Chbosky's radicalization often cited as a cautionary example of the dangers posed by unchecked extremist ideologies in online spaces.

In the aftermath of these events, the "Chbosky Defense" has been scrutinized as a troubling symptom of a society grappling with polarized views on personal safety, self-defense, and the limits of the law. While his legal journey is far from over, Kenneth Chbosky's actions have left a lasting impact on the national discourse surrounding preemptive violence and the influence of digital communities in shaping real-world aggression.

>_ **The problem with my daughter**
JUNE 20 2023

written by Alanna Paige
published on Edge News

*"Criminals are not complex, no matter how much
the media loves to romanticize them."*

>_ CHAPTER FOUR
JUNE 2023

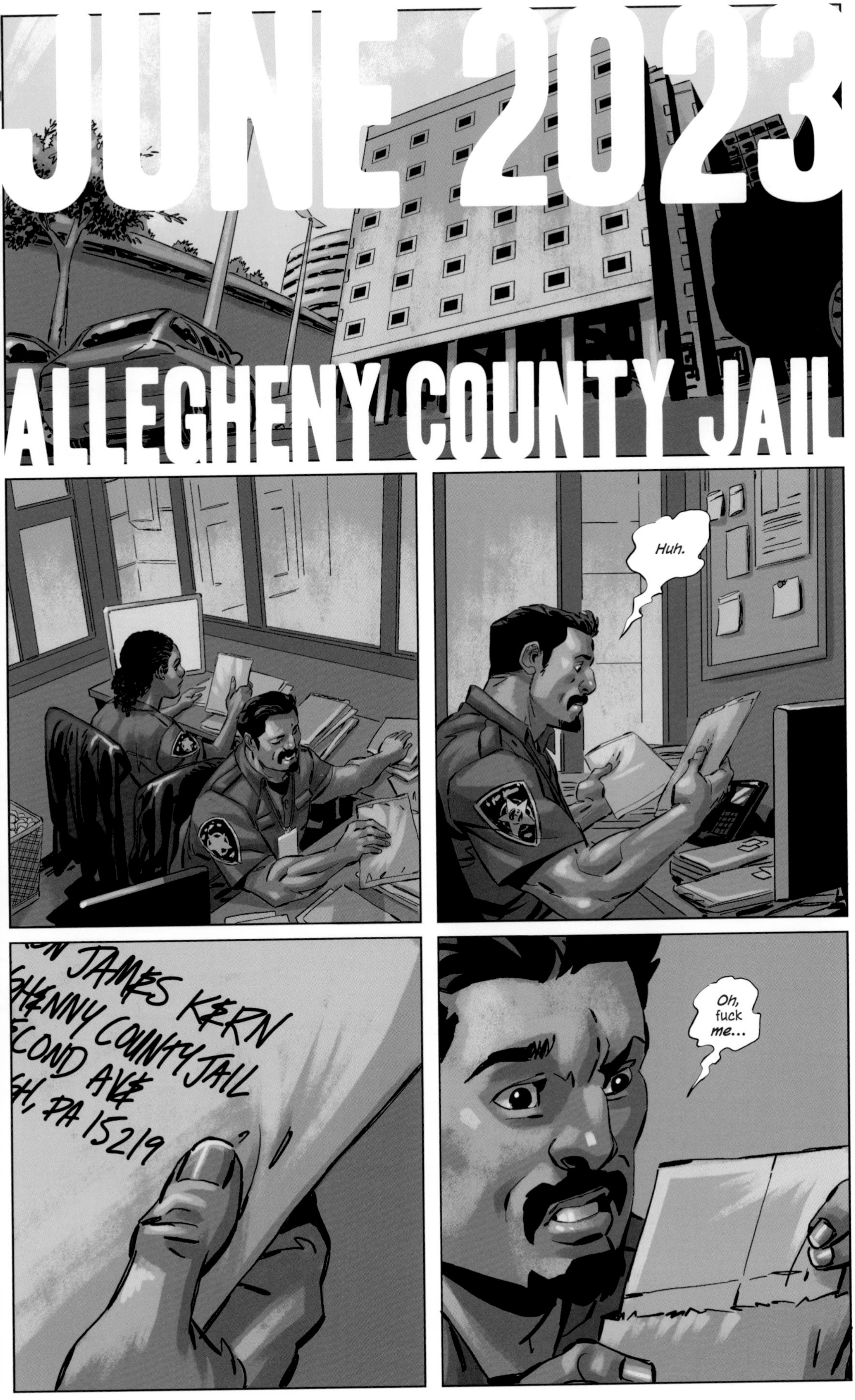
JUNE 2023
ALLEGHENY COUNTY JAIL
Huh.
JAMES KERN
HENNY COUNTY JAIL
ECOND AVE
H, PA 15219
Oh, fuck me...

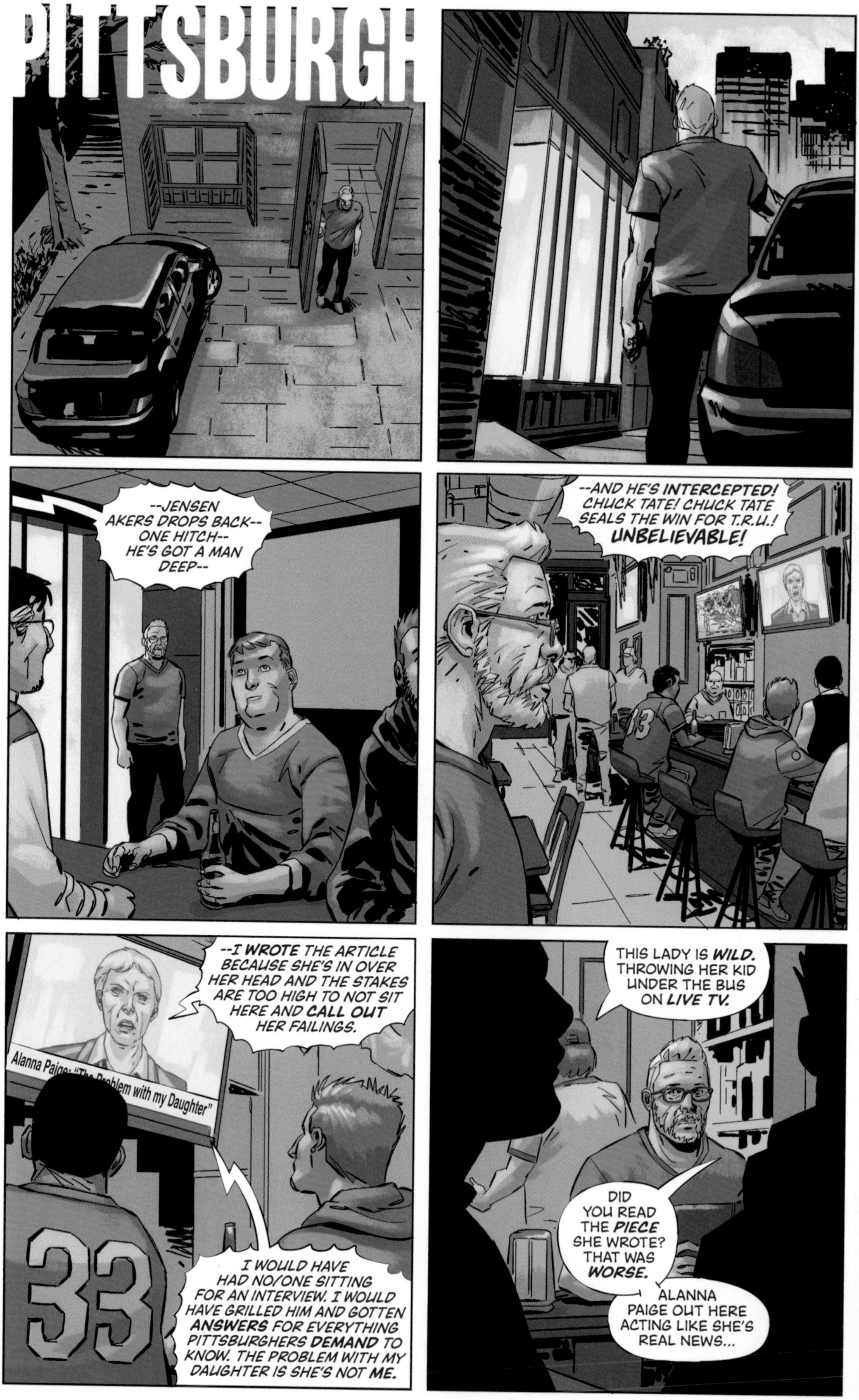
PITTSBURGH
--JENSEN AKERS DROPS BACK-- ONE HITCH-- HE'S GOT A MAN DEEP--
--AND HE'S INTERCEPTED! CHUCK TATE! CHUCK TATE SEALS THE WIN FOR T.R.U.! UNBELIEVABLE!
33
--I WROTE THE ARTICLE BECAUSE SHE'S IN OVER HER HEAD AND THE STAKES ARE TOO HIGH TO NOT SIT HERE AND CALL OUT HER FAILINGS.
Alanna Paige: "The Problem with my Daughter"
I WOULD HAVE HAD NO/ONE SITTING FOR AN INTERVIEW. I WOULD HAVE GRILLED HIM AND GOTTEN ANSWERS FOR EVERYTHING PITTSBURGHERS DEMAND TO KNOW. THE PROBLEM WITH MY DAUGHTER IS SHE'S NOT ME.
33
THIS LADY IS WILD. THROWING HER KID UNDER THE BUS ON LIVE TV.
DID YOU READ THE PIECE SHE WROTE? THAT WAS WORSE.
ALANNA PAIGE OUT HERE ACTING LIKE SHE'S REAL NEWS...

WHAT'S UP, BOYS?! WHERE'S THE FOOTBALL AT?

HEY, CHUCK!

WHAT'S BEEN GOING ON, MAN? HAVEN'T SEEN YOU THIS WEEK!

BUSY, *BUSY!* BUT I HAD SOME TIME TODAY TO SWING BY AND SEE THE CREW.

HOW YOU DOING, JIM?

WATCHING YOU CLOSE OUT THE BUCKEYES. CAN'T COMPLAIN.

Ah, THAT WAS A GOOD ONE.

YOU EVER GET SICK OF SEEING THESE?

No, sir. NOT GAMES LIKE *THAT.* FIESTA BOWL '02. TWO FORCED FUMBLES AND A PICK-SIX.

FELT INVINCIBLE. LIKE ME AND THE TEAM COULD DO *ANYTHING...*

--NOW, TURNING OUR ATTENTION BACK TO *COACH NATHAN CADE.*

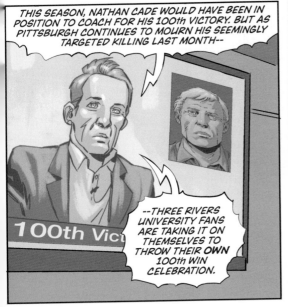

THIS SEASON, NATHAN CADE WOULD HAVE BEEN IN POSITION TO COACH FOR HIS 100th VICTORY. BUT AS PITTSBURGH CONTINUES TO MOURN HIS SEEMINGLY TARGETED KILLING LAST MONTH--

--THREE RIVERS UNIVERSITY FANS ARE TAKING IT ON THEMSELVES TO THROW THEIR *OWN* 100th WIN CELEBRATION.

100th Vic

THAT'S A *LOT* OF WINS.

COACH *WAS* T.R.U. FOOTBALL.

I BET YOU MISS HIM, *huh?*

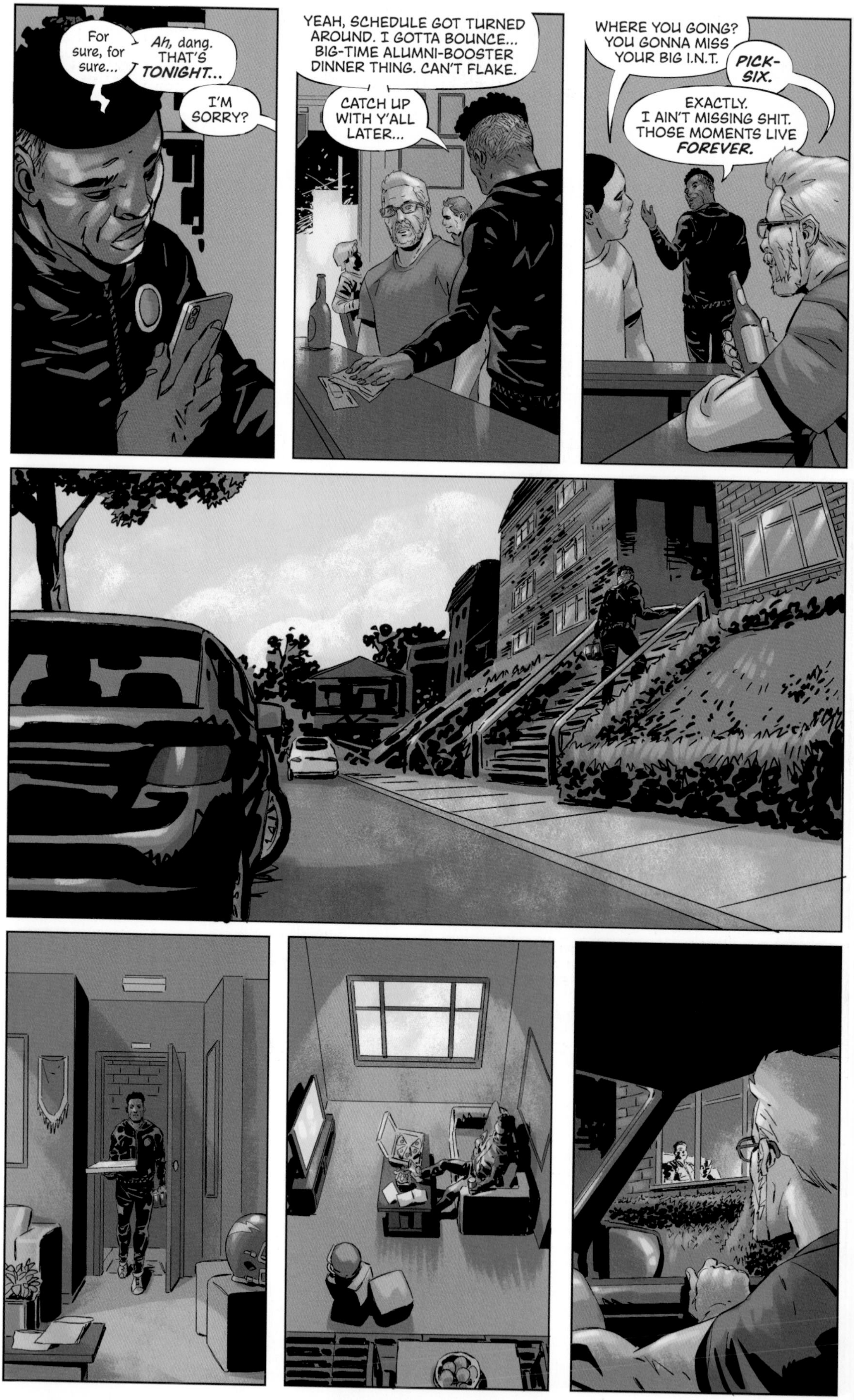

For sure, for sure...
Ah, dang. THAT'S ***TONIGHT...***
I'M SORRY?
YEAH, SCHEDULE GOT TURNED AROUND. I GOTTA BOUNCE... BIG-TIME ALUMNI-BOOSTER DINNER THING. CAN'T FLAKE.
CATCH UP WITH Y'ALL LATER...
WHERE YOU GOING? YOU GONNA MISS YOUR BIG I.N.T.
PICK-SIX.
EXACTLY. I AIN'T MISSING SHIT. THOSE MOMENTS LIVE ***FOREVER.***

ARE YOU GOING TO SAY SOMETHING? I KNOW YOU'RE *THINKING* ABOUT IT.

ABOUT *WHAT?*

THE ARTICLE.

THIS ISN'T THE PROPER FORUM FOR THAT.

AGREED. THE *LAST* THING YOU WANT TO DO IS TURN IT INTO A SOUNDBYTE--

JULIA!

DANIELLE.

HEY, JUST WANTED TO SAY... I *MEANT* TO TELL YOU ABOUT IT. FAIR WARNING AND ALL...

BUT YOU COULDN'T BE BOTHERED?

HONESTLY, I ACCIDENTALLY HIT PUBLISH, WHICH PUSHED IT LIVE BEFORE I MEANT TO.

IT DOESN'T MATTER *WHEN* YOU DID IT. YOU GAVE MY MOTHER A PLATFORM TO DRAG ME... WITHOUT GIVING ME A CHANCE TO DEFEND MYSELF.

THAT'S *FUCKED UP.* BUT I DON'T EXPECT ANY LESS FROM *EDGE NEWS.*

IS THAT RIGHT?

YEAH. *YOU'RE* PART OF THE PROBLEM.

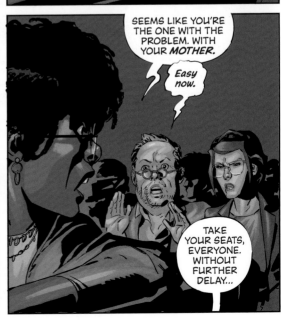

SEEMS LIKE YOU'RE THE ONE WITH THE PROBLEM. WITH YOUR *MOTHER.*

Easy now.

TAKE YOUR SEATS, EVERYONE. WITHOUT FURTHER DELAY...

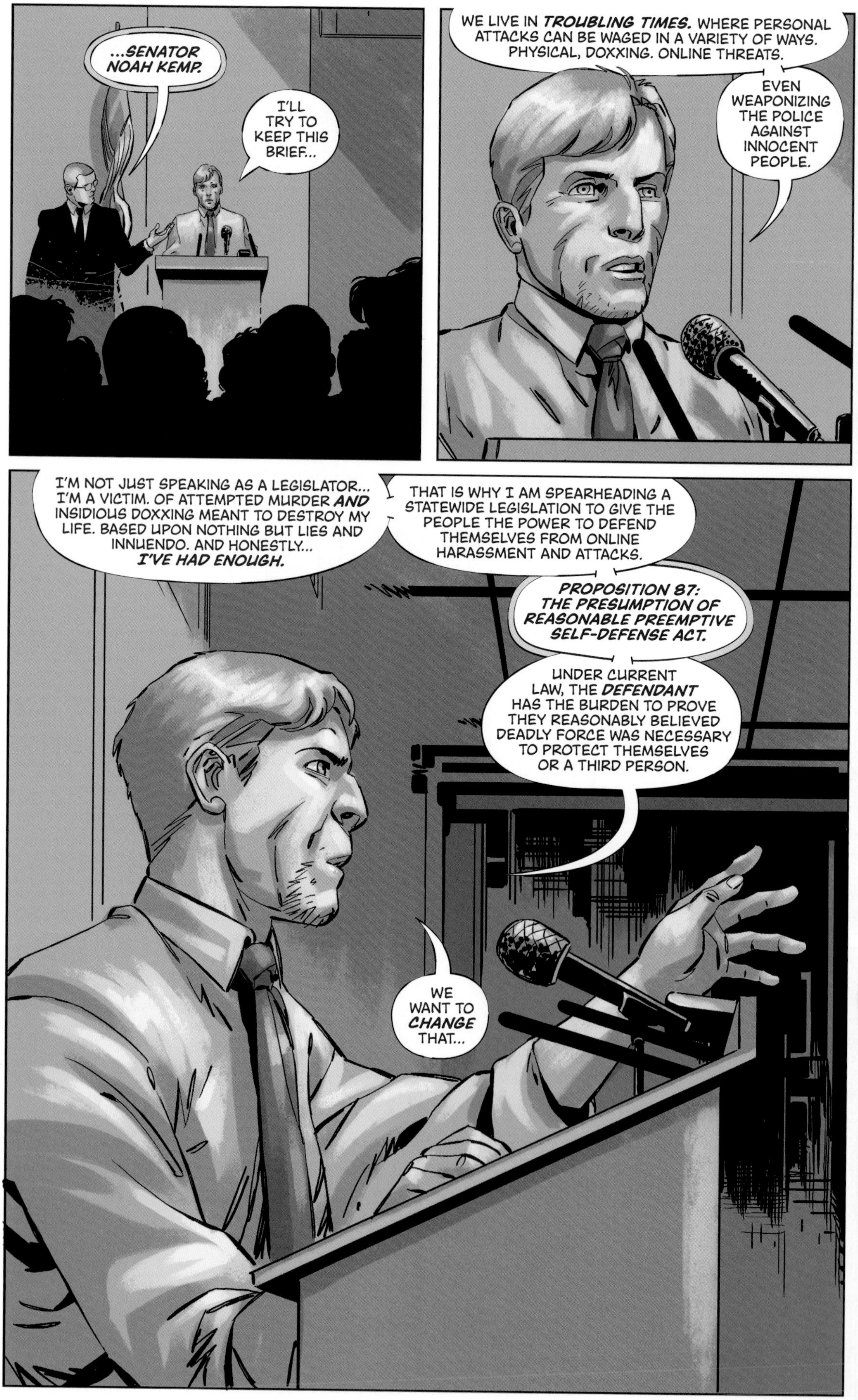
...SENATOR NOAH KEMP.
I'LL TRY TO KEEP THIS BRIEF...
WE LIVE IN TROUBLING TIMES. WHERE PERSONAL ATTACKS CAN BE WAGED IN A VARIETY OF WAYS. PHYSICAL, DOXXING. ONLINE THREATS.
EVEN WEAPONIZING THE POLICE AGAINST INNOCENT PEOPLE.
I'M NOT JUST SPEAKING AS A LEGISLATOR... I'M A VICTIM. OF ATTEMPTED MURDER AND INSIDIOUS DOXXING MEANT TO DESTROY MY LIFE. BASED UPON NOTHING BUT LIES AND INNUENDO. AND HONESTLY... I'VE HAD ENOUGH.
THAT IS WHY I AM SPEARHEADING A STATEWIDE LEGISLATION TO GIVE THE PEOPLE THE POWER TO DEFEND THEMSELVES FROM ONLINE HARASSMENT AND ATTACKS.
PROPOSITION 87: THE PRESUMPTION OF REASONABLE PREEMPTIVE SELF-DEFENSE ACT.
UNDER CURRENT LAW, THE DEFENDANT HAS THE BURDEN TO PROVE THEY REASONABLY BELIEVED DEADLY FORCE WAS NECESSARY TO PROTECT THEMSELVES OR A THIRD PERSON.
WE WANT TO CHANGE THAT...

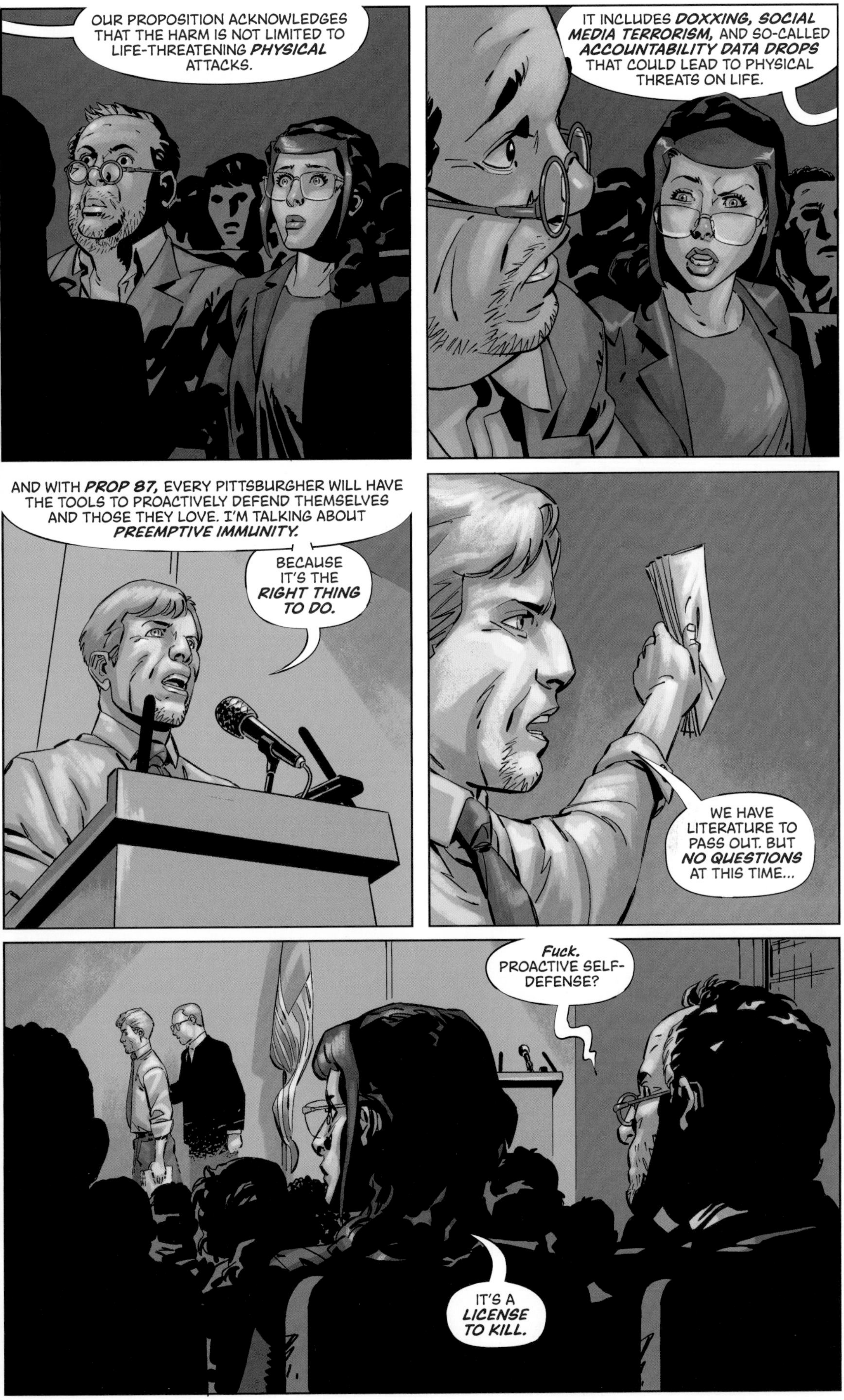

OUR PROPOSITION ACKNOWLEDGES THAT THE HARM IS NOT LIMITED TO LIFE-THREATENING *PHYSICAL* ATTACKS.
IT INCLUDES *DOXXING, SOCIAL MEDIA TERRORISM,* AND SO-CALLED *ACCOUNTABILITY DATA DROPS* THAT COULD LEAD TO PHYSICAL THREATS ON LIFE.
AND WITH *PROP 87,* EVERY PITTSBURGHER WILL HAVE THE TOOLS TO PROACTIVELY DEFEND THEMSELVES AND THOSE THEY LOVE. I'M TALKING ABOUT *PREEMPTIVE IMMUNITY.*
BECAUSE IT'S THE *RIGHT THING TO DO.*
WE HAVE LITERATURE TO PASS OUT. BUT *NO QUESTIONS* AT THIS TIME...
Fuck. PROACTIVE SELF-DEFENSE?
IT'S A *LICENSE TO KILL.*

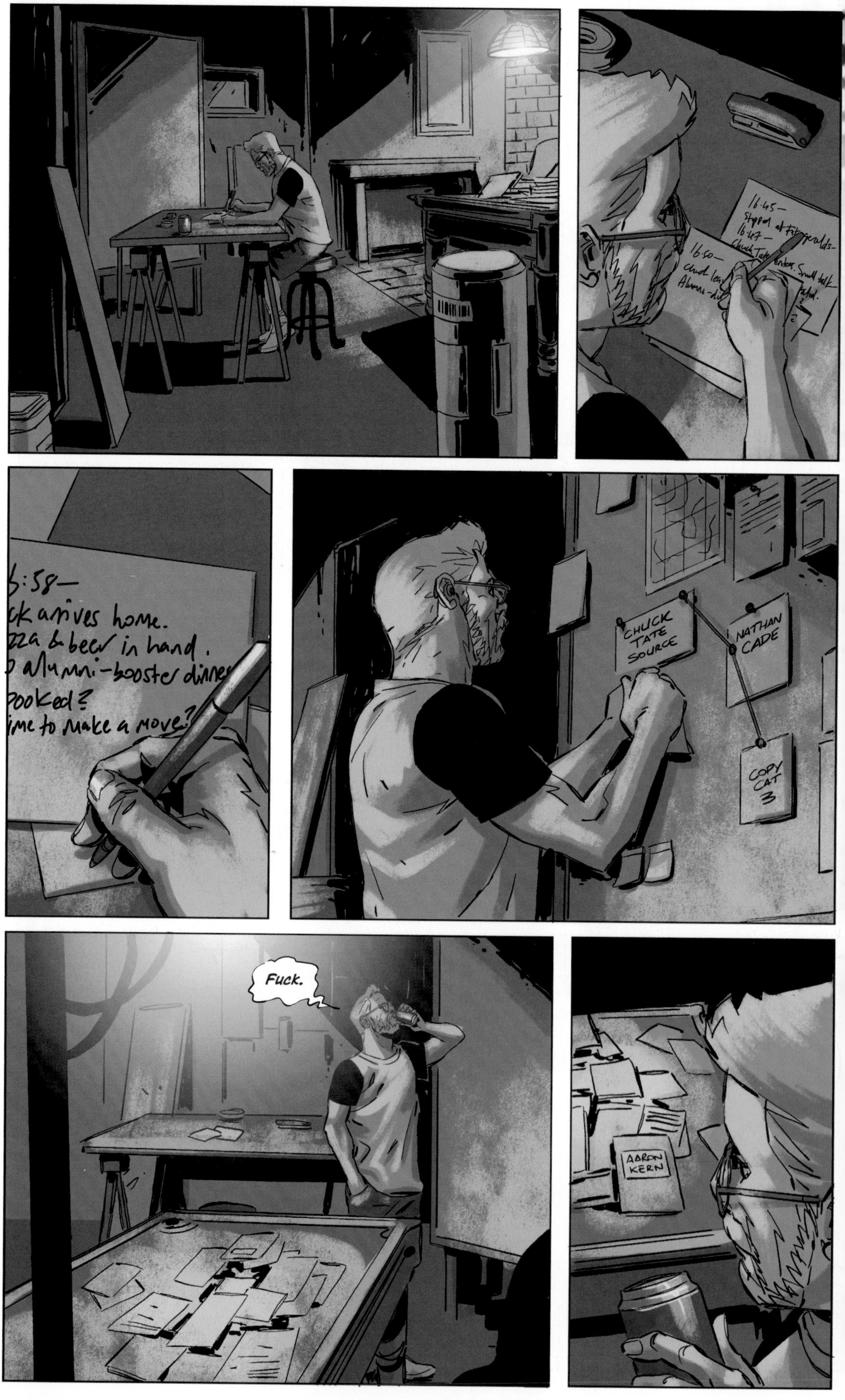
16:45—
Stopped at
16:47—
Chuck Tate
16:50—
Small talk
:58—
ck arrives home.
zza & beer in hand.
alumni-booster dinner
pooked?
ime to make a move?
CHUCK TATE SOURCE
NATHAN CADE
COPY CAT 3
Fuck.
AARON KERN

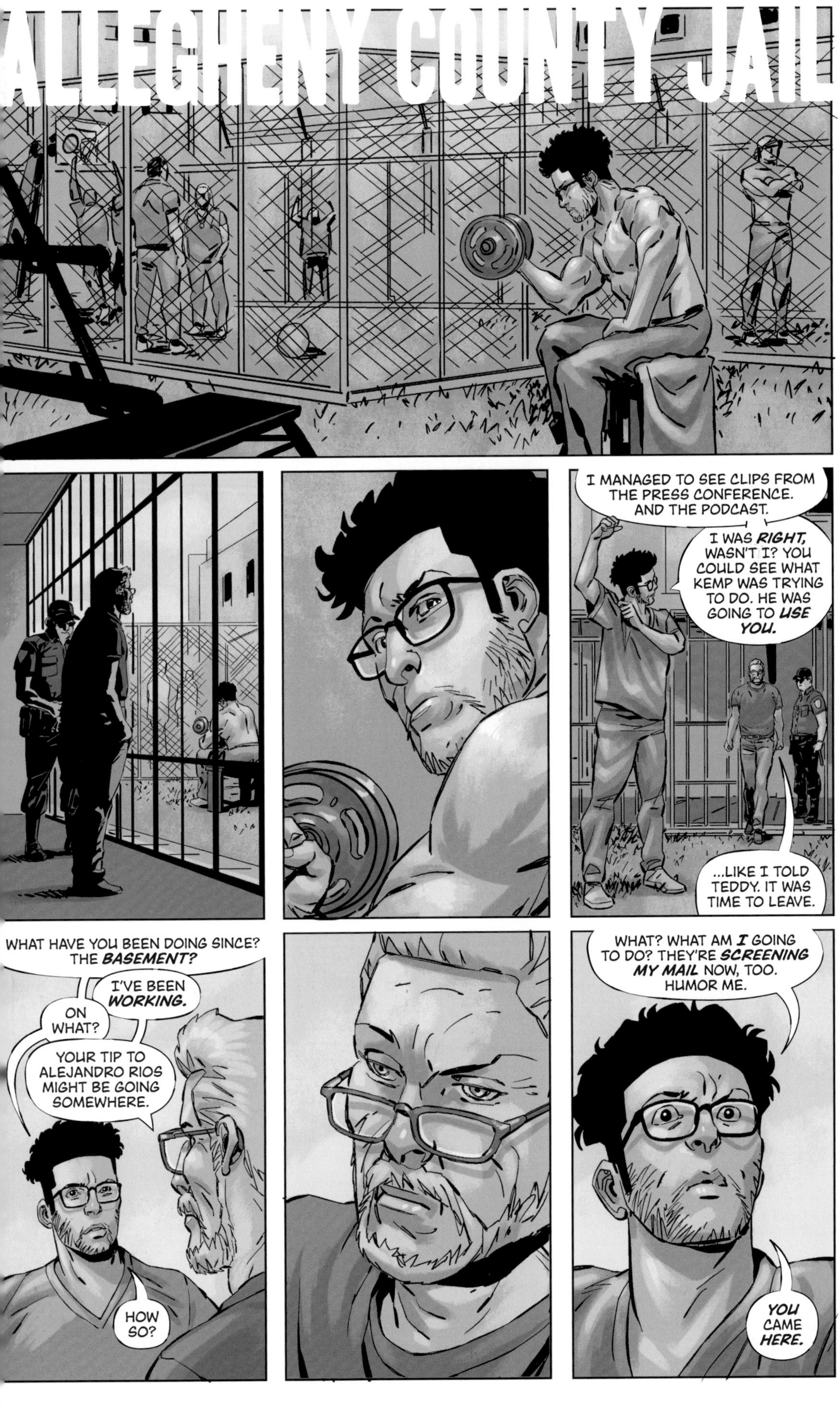

ALLEGHENY COUNTY JAIL
I MANAGED TO SEE CLIPS FROM THE PRESS CONFERENCE. AND THE PODCAST.
I WAS RIGHT, WASN'T I? YOU COULD SEE WHAT KEMP WAS TRYING TO DO. HE WAS GOING TO USE YOU.
...LIKE I TOLD TEDDY. IT WAS TIME TO LEAVE.
WHAT HAVE YOU BEEN DOING SINCE? THE BASEMENT?
I'VE BEEN WORKING.
ON WHAT?
YOUR TIP TO ALEJANDRO RIOS MIGHT BE GOING SOMEWHERE.
HOW SO?
WHAT? WHAT AM I GOING TO DO? THEY'RE SCREENING MY MAIL NOW, TOO. HUMOR ME.
YOU CAME HERE.

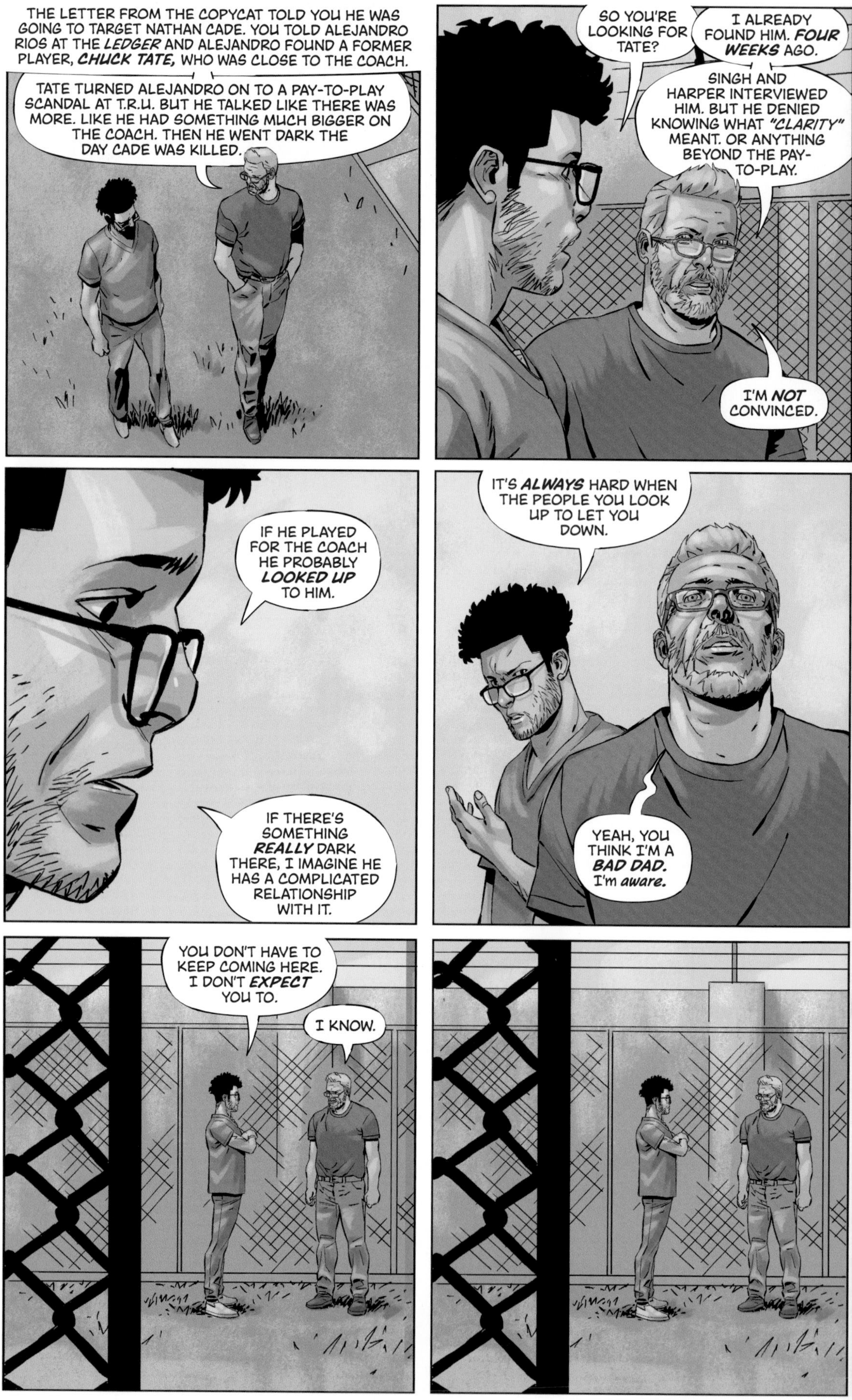
THE LETTER FROM THE COPYCAT TOLD YOU HE WAS GOING TO TARGET NATHAN CADE. YOU TOLD ALEJANDRO RIOS AT THE *LEDGER* AND ALEJANDRO FOUND A FORMER PLAYER, ***CHUCK TATE,*** WHO WAS CLOSE TO THE COACH.
TATE TURNED ALEJANDRO ON TO A PAY-TO-PLAY SCANDAL AT T.R.U. BUT HE TALKED LIKE THERE WAS MORE. LIKE HE HAD SOMETHING MUCH BIGGER ON THE COACH. THEN HE WENT DARK THE DAY CADE WAS KILLED.
SO YOU'RE LOOKING FOR TATE?
I ALREADY FOUND HIM. ***FOUR WEEKS*** AGO.
SINGH AND HARPER INTERVIEWED HIM. BUT HE DENIED KNOWING WHAT *"CLARITY"* MEANT. OR ANYTHING BEYOND THE PAY-TO-PLAY.
I'M ***NOT*** CONVINCED.
IF HE PLAYED FOR THE COACH HE PROBABLY ***LOOKED UP*** TO HIM.
IF THERE'S SOMETHING ***REALLY*** DARK THERE, I IMAGINE HE HAS A COMPLICATED RELATIONSHIP WITH IT.
IT'S ***ALWAYS*** HARD WHEN THE PEOPLE YOU LOOK UP TO LET YOU DOWN.
YEAH, YOU THINK I'M A ***BAD DAD.*** I'm ***aware.***
YOU DON'T HAVE TO KEEP COMING HERE. I DON'T ***EXPECT*** YOU TO.
I KNOW.

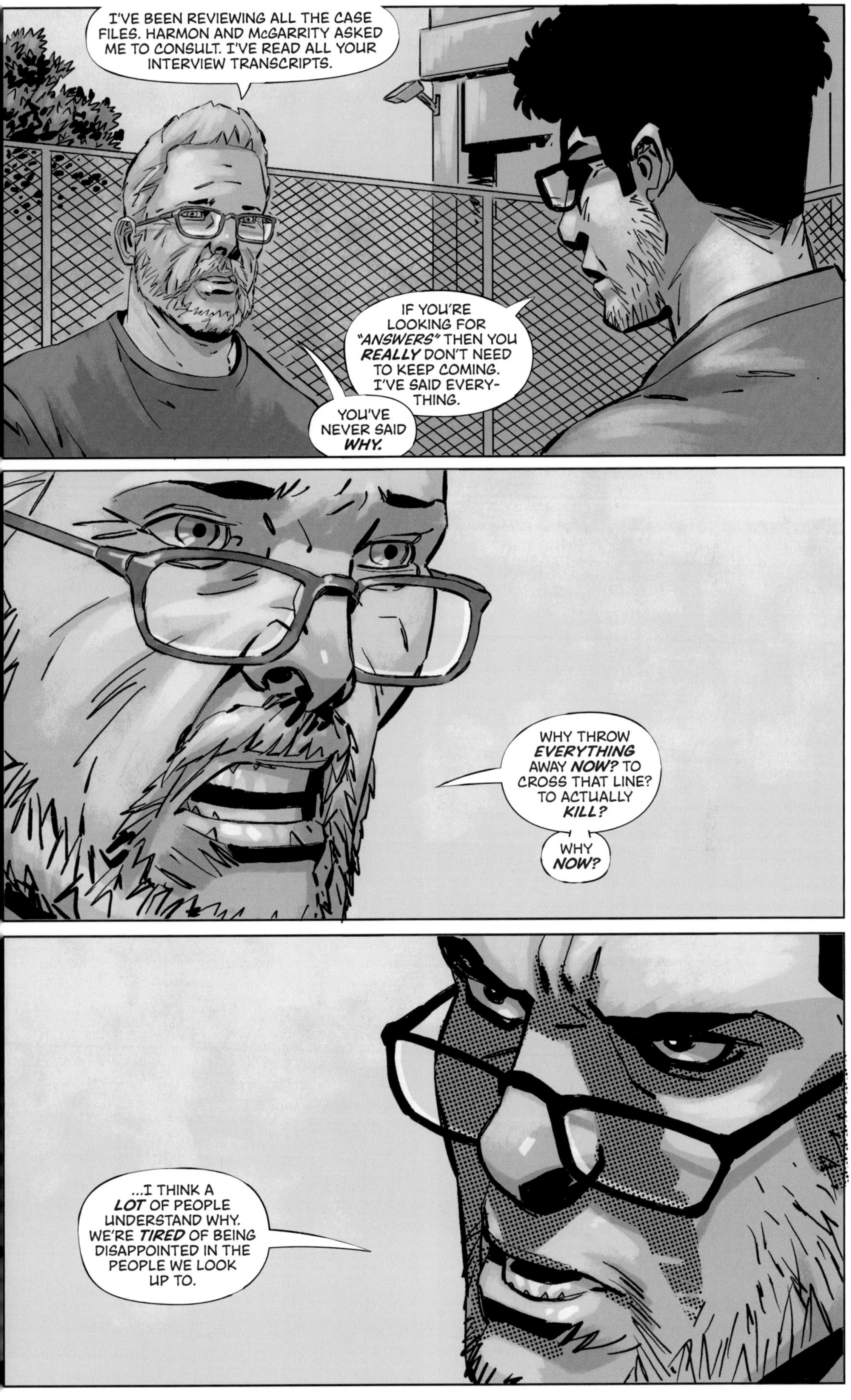
I'VE BEEN REVIEWING ALL THE CASE FILES. HARMON AND McGARRITY ASKED ME TO CONSULT. I'VE READ ALL YOUR INTERVIEW TRANSCRIPTS.
IF YOU'RE LOOKING FOR "ANSWERS" THEN YOU REALLY DON'T NEED TO KEEP COMING. I'VE SAID EVERY-THING.
YOU'VE NEVER SAID WHY.
WHY THROW EVERYTHING AWAY NOW? TO CROSS THAT LINE? TO ACTUALLY KILL?
WHY NOW?
...I THINK A LOT OF PEOPLE UNDERSTAND WHY. WE'RE TIRED OF BEING DISAPPOINTED IN THE PEOPLE WE LOOK UP TO.

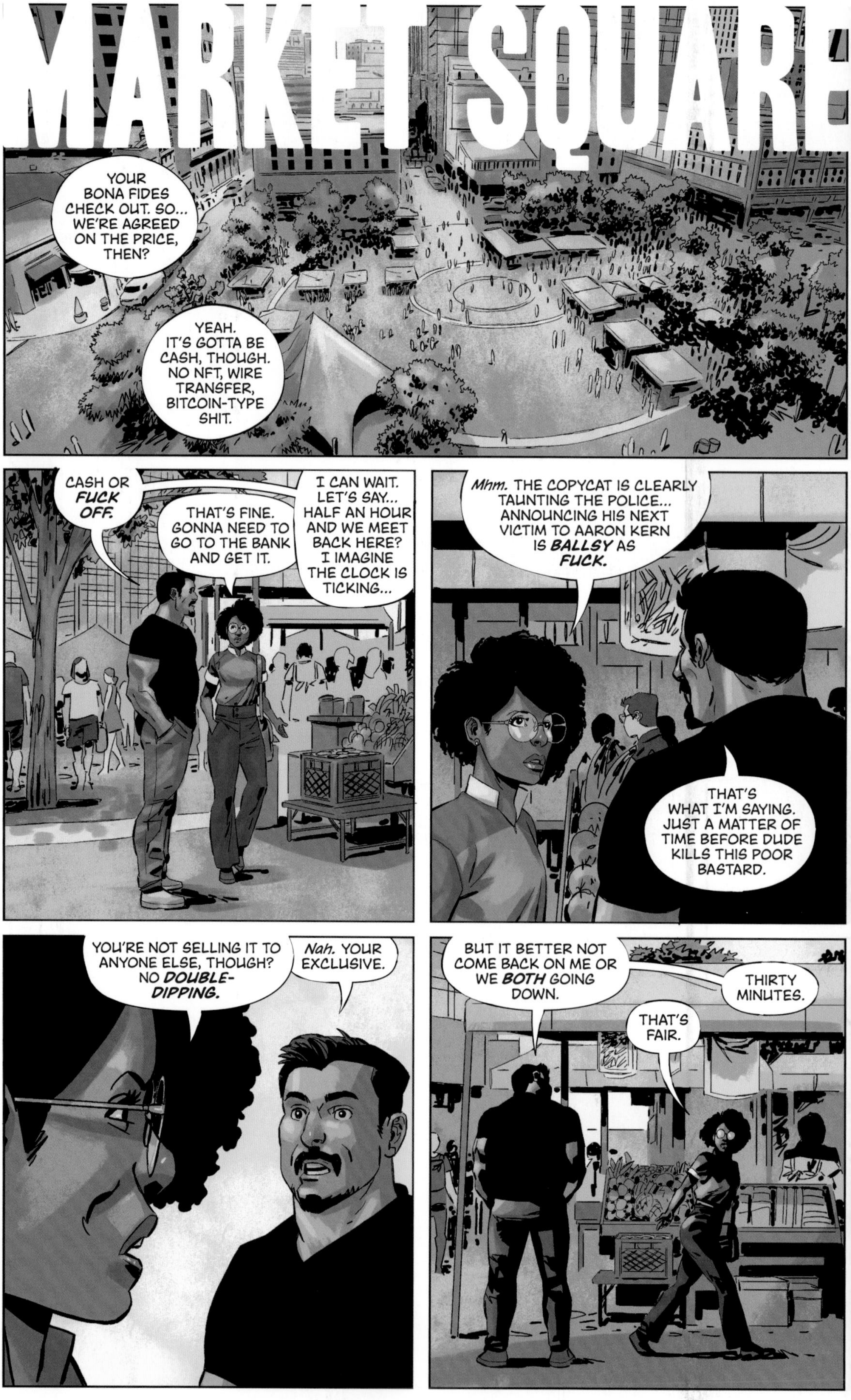
MARKET SQUARE
YOUR BONA FIDES CHECK OUT. SO... WE'RE AGREED ON THE PRICE, THEN?
YEAH. IT'S GOTTA BE CASH, THOUGH. NO NFT, WIRE TRANSFER, BITCOIN-TYPE SHIT.
CASH OR **FUCK OFF.**
THAT'S FINE. GONNA NEED TO GO TO THE BANK AND GET IT.
I CAN WAIT. LET'S SAY... HALF AN HOUR AND WE MEET BACK HERE? I IMAGINE THE CLOCK IS TICKING...
Mhm. THE COPYCAT IS CLEARLY TAUNTING THE POLICE... ANNOUNCING HIS NEXT VICTIM TO AARON KERN IS ***BALLSY*** AS ***FUCK.***
THAT'S WHAT I'M SAYING. JUST A MATTER OF TIME BEFORE DUDE KILLS THIS POOR BASTARD.
YOU'RE NOT SELLING IT TO ANYONE ELSE, THOUGH? NO ***DOUBLE-DIPPING.***
Nah. YOUR EXCLUSIVE.
BUT IT BETTER NOT COME BACK ON ME OR WE ***BOTH*** GOING DOWN.
THIRTY MINUTES.
THAT'S FAIR.

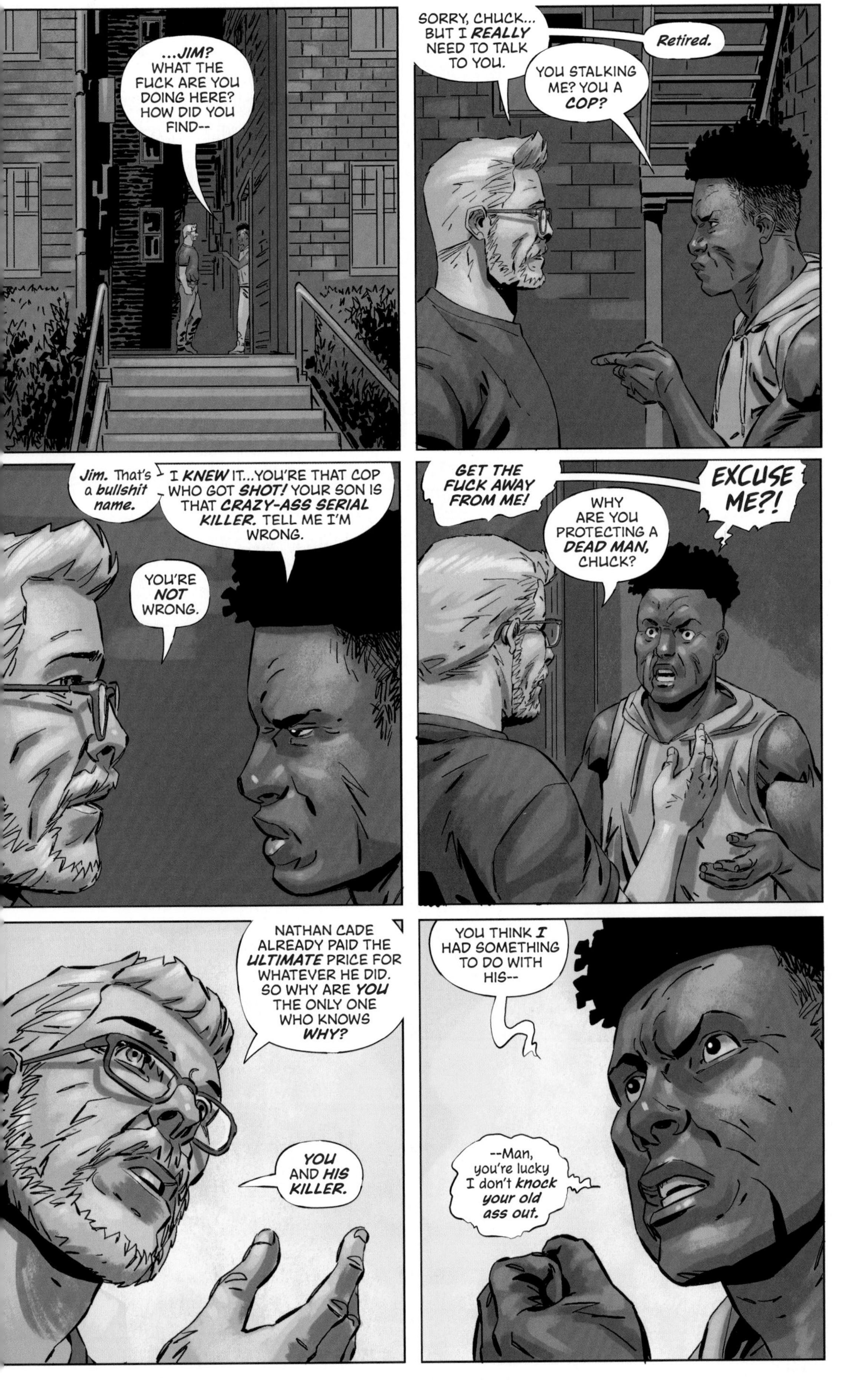
...JIM? WHAT THE FUCK ARE YOU DOING HERE? HOW DID YOU FIND--
SORRY, CHUCK... BUT I REALLY NEED TO TALK TO YOU.
Retired.
YOU STALKING ME? YOU A COP?
Jim. That's a bullshit name.
I KNEW IT...YOU'RE THAT COP WHO GOT SHOT! YOUR SON IS THAT CRAZY-ASS SERIAL KILLER. TELL ME I'M WRONG.
YOU'RE NOT WRONG.
GET THE FUCK AWAY FROM ME!
EXCUSE ME?!
WHY ARE YOU PROTECTING A DEAD MAN, CHUCK?
NATHAN CADE ALREADY PAID THE ULTIMATE PRICE FOR WHATEVER HE DID. SO WHY ARE YOU THE ONLY ONE WHO KNOWS WHY?
YOU AND HIS KILLER.
YOU THINK I HAD SOMETHING TO DO WITH HIS--
--Man, you're lucky I don't knock your old ass out.

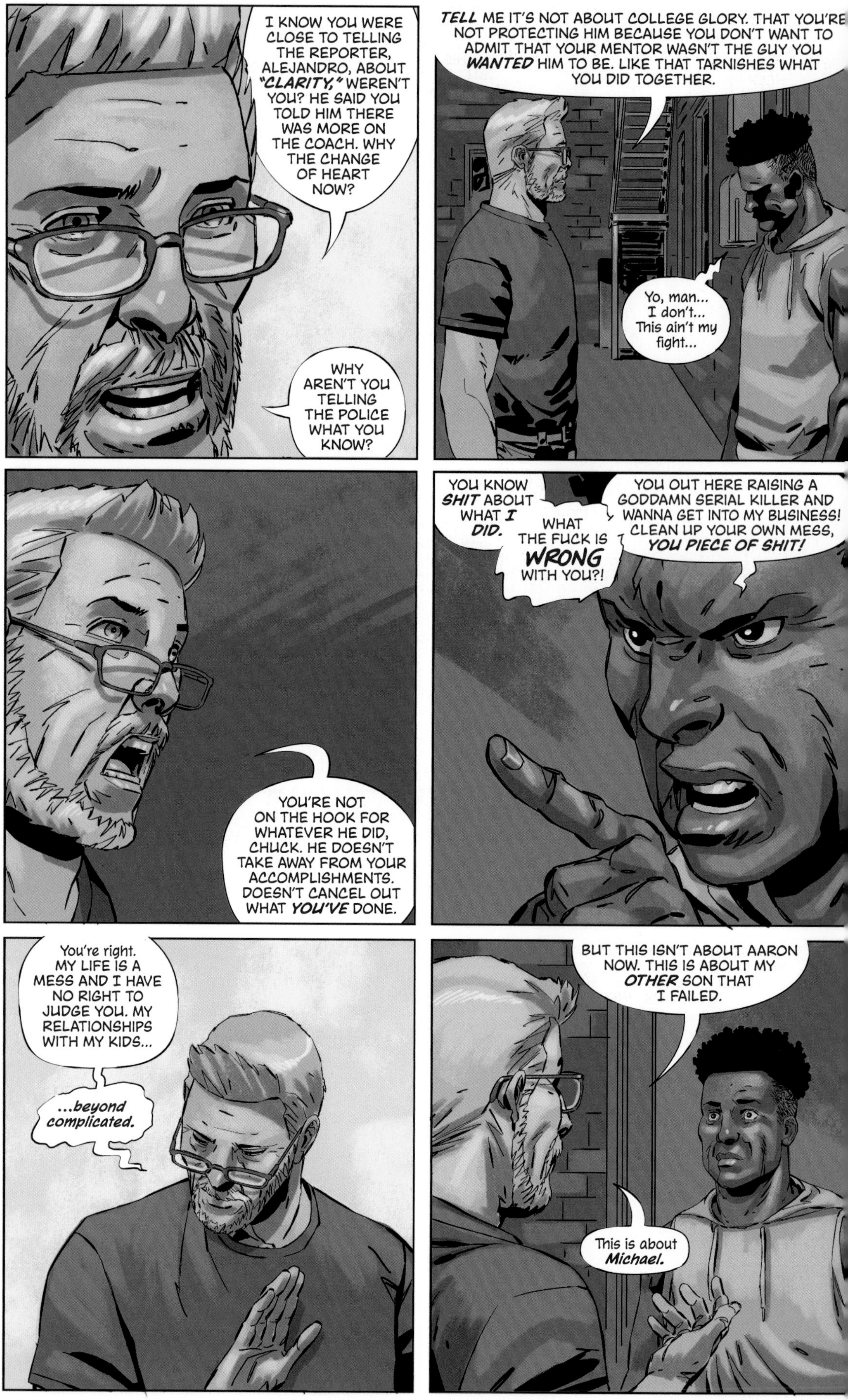

I KNOW YOU WERE CLOSE TO TELLING THE REPORTER, ALEJANDRO, ABOUT "CLARITY," WEREN'T YOU? HE SAID YOU TOLD HIM THERE WAS MORE ON THE COACH. WHY THE CHANGE OF HEART NOW?
WHY AREN'T YOU TELLING THE POLICE WHAT YOU KNOW?
TELL ME IT'S NOT ABOUT COLLEGE GLORY. THAT YOU'RE NOT PROTECTING HIM BECAUSE YOU DON'T WANT TO ADMIT THAT YOUR MENTOR WASN'T THE GUY YOU WANTED HIM TO BE. LIKE THAT TARNISHES WHAT YOU DID TOGETHER.
Yo, man... I don't... This ain't my fight...
YOU'RE NOT ON THE HOOK FOR WHATEVER HE DID, CHUCK. HE DOESN'T TAKE AWAY FROM YOUR ACCOMPLISHMENTS. DOESN'T CANCEL OUT WHAT YOU'VE DONE.
YOU KNOW SHIT ABOUT WHAT I DID.
WHAT THE FUCK IS WRONG WITH YOU?!
YOU OUT HERE RAISING A GODDAMN SERIAL KILLER AND WANNA GET INTO MY BUSINESS! CLEAN UP YOUR OWN MESS, YOU PIECE OF SHIT!
You're right. MY LIFE IS A MESS AND I HAVE NO RIGHT TO JUDGE YOU. MY RELATIONSHIPS WITH MY KIDS...
...beyond complicated.
BUT THIS ISN'T ABOUT AARON NOW. THIS IS ABOUT MY OTHER SON THAT I FAILED.
This is about Michael.

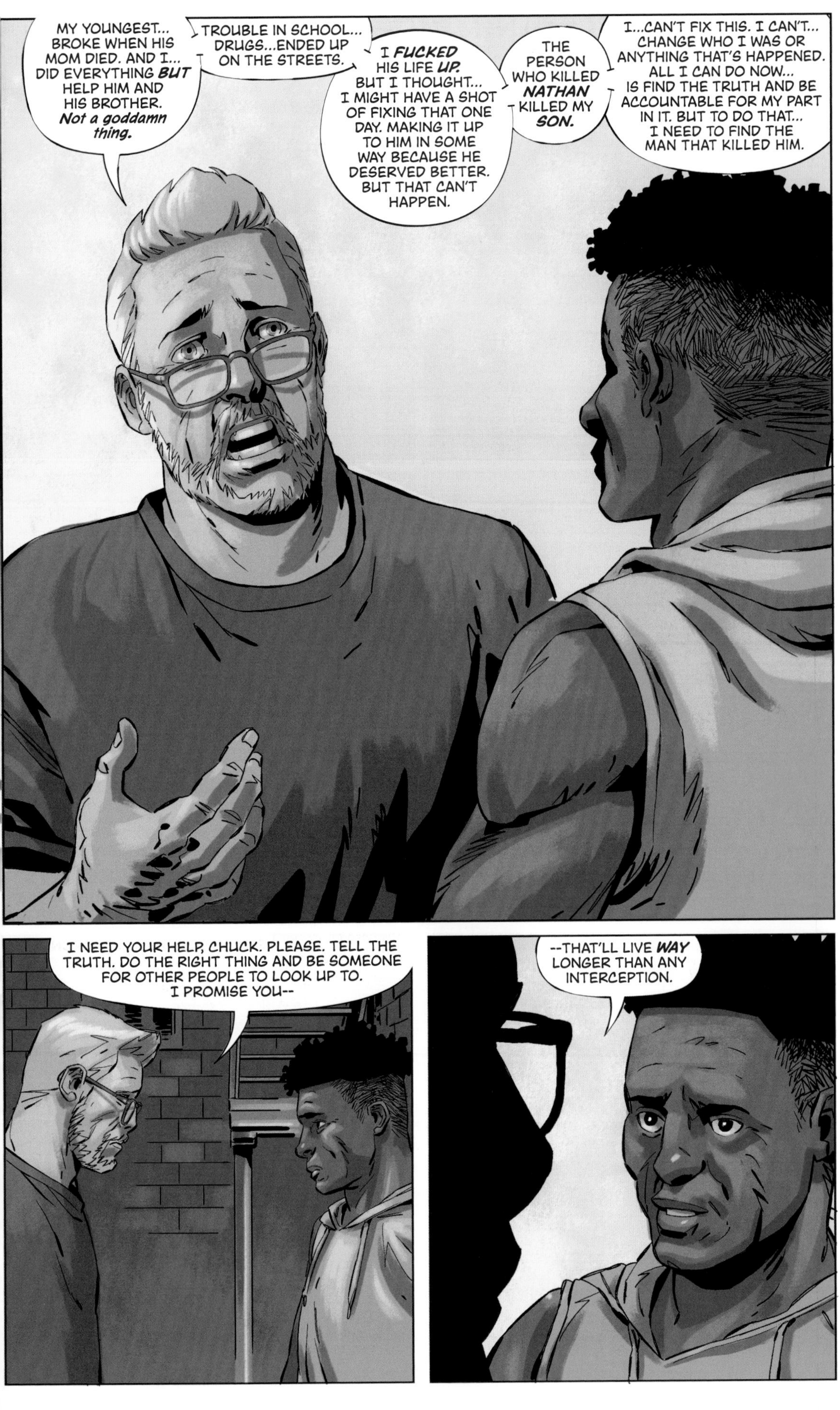
MY YOUNGEST... BROKE WHEN HIS MOM DIED. AND I... DID EVERYTHING ***BUT*** HELP HIM AND HIS BROTHER. ***Not a goddamn thing.***
TROUBLE IN SCHOOL... DRUGS...ENDED UP ON THE STREETS.
I ***FUCKED*** HIS LIFE ***UP.*** BUT I THOUGHT... I MIGHT HAVE A SHOT OF FIXING THAT ONE DAY. MAKING IT UP TO HIM IN SOME WAY BECAUSE HE DESERVED BETTER. BUT THAT CAN'T HAPPEN.
THE PERSON WHO KILLED ***NATHAN*** KILLED MY ***SON.***
I...CAN'T FIX THIS. I CAN'T... CHANGE WHO I WAS OR ANYTHING THAT'S HAPPENED. ALL I CAN DO NOW... IS FIND THE TRUTH AND BE ACCOUNTABLE FOR MY PART IN IT. BUT TO DO THAT... I NEED TO FIND THE MAN THAT KILLED HIM.
I NEED YOUR HELP, CHUCK. PLEASE. TELL THE TRUTH. DO THE RIGHT THING AND BE SOMEONE FOR OTHER PEOPLE TO LOOK UP TO. I PROMISE YOU--
--THAT'LL LIVE ***WAY*** LONGER THAN ANY INTERCEPTION.

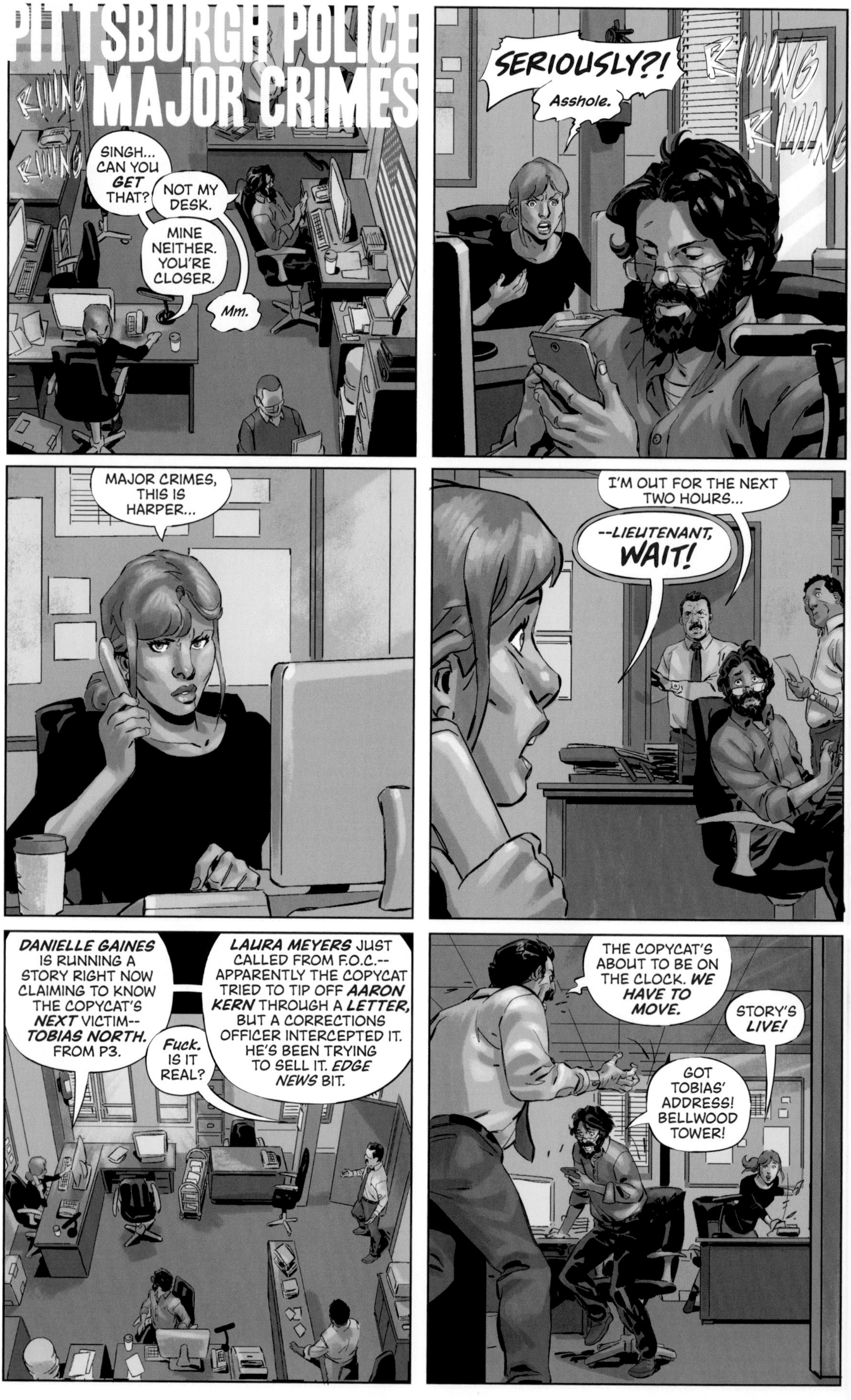
PITTSBURGH POLICE MAJOR CRIMES
RIIING
RIIING
SINGH... CAN YOU GET THAT?
NOT MY DESK.
MINE NEITHER. YOU'RE CLOSER.
Mm.
SERIOUSLY?!
Asshole.
RIIING
RIIING
MAJOR CRIMES, THIS IS HARPER...
I'M OUT FOR THE NEXT TWO HOURS...
--LIEUTENANT, WAIT!
DANIELLE GAINES IS RUNNING A STORY RIGHT NOW CLAIMING TO KNOW THE COPYCAT'S NEXT VICTIM-- TOBIAS NORTH. FROM P3.
Fuck. IS IT REAL?
LAURA MEYERS JUST CALLED FROM F.O.C.-- APPARENTLY THE COPYCAT TRIED TO TIP OFF AARON KERN THROUGH A LETTER, BUT A CORRECTIONS OFFICER INTERCEPTED IT. HE'S BEEN TRYING TO SELL IT. EDGE NEWS BIT.
THE COPYCAT'S ABOUT TO BE ON THE CLOCK. WE HAVE TO MOVE.
STORY'S LIVE!
GOT TOBIAS' ADDRESS! BELLWOOD TOWER!

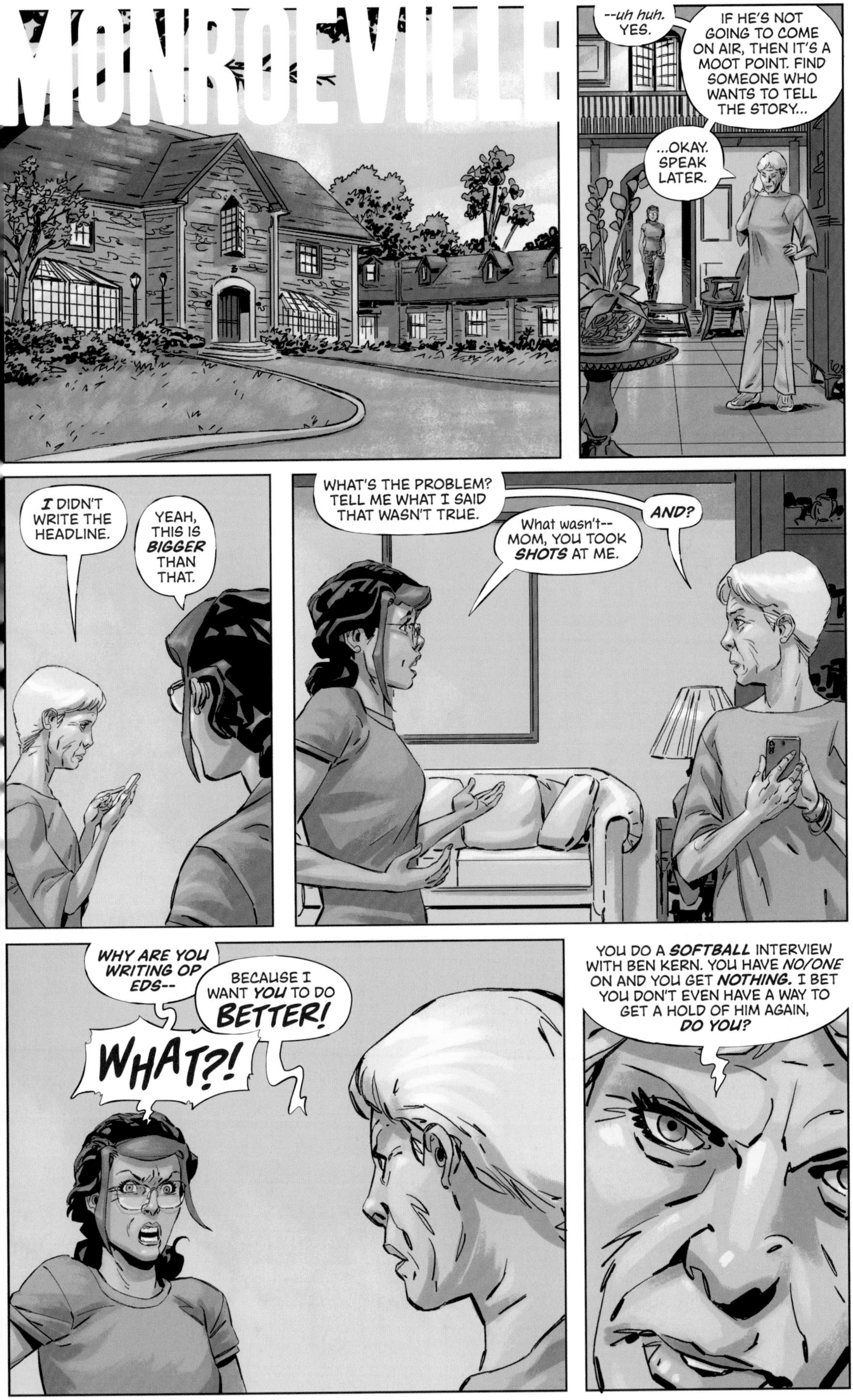
MONROEVILLE
--uh huh. YES.
IF HE'S NOT GOING TO COME ON AIR, THEN IT'S A MOOT POINT. FIND SOMEONE WHO WANTS TO TELL THE STORY...
...OKAY. SPEAK LATER.
I DIDN'T WRITE THE HEADLINE.
YEAH, THIS IS BIGGER THAN THAT.
WHAT'S THE PROBLEM? TELL ME WHAT I SAID THAT WASN'T TRUE.
What wasn't-- MOM, YOU TOOK SHOTS AT ME.
AND?
WHY ARE YOU WRITING OP EDS--
BECAUSE I WANT YOU TO DO BETTER!
WHAT?!
YOU DO A SOFTBALL INTERVIEW WITH BEN KERN. YOU HAVE NO/ONE ON AND YOU GET NOTHING. I BET YOU DON'T EVEN HAVE A WAY TO GET A HOLD OF HIM AGAIN, DO YOU?

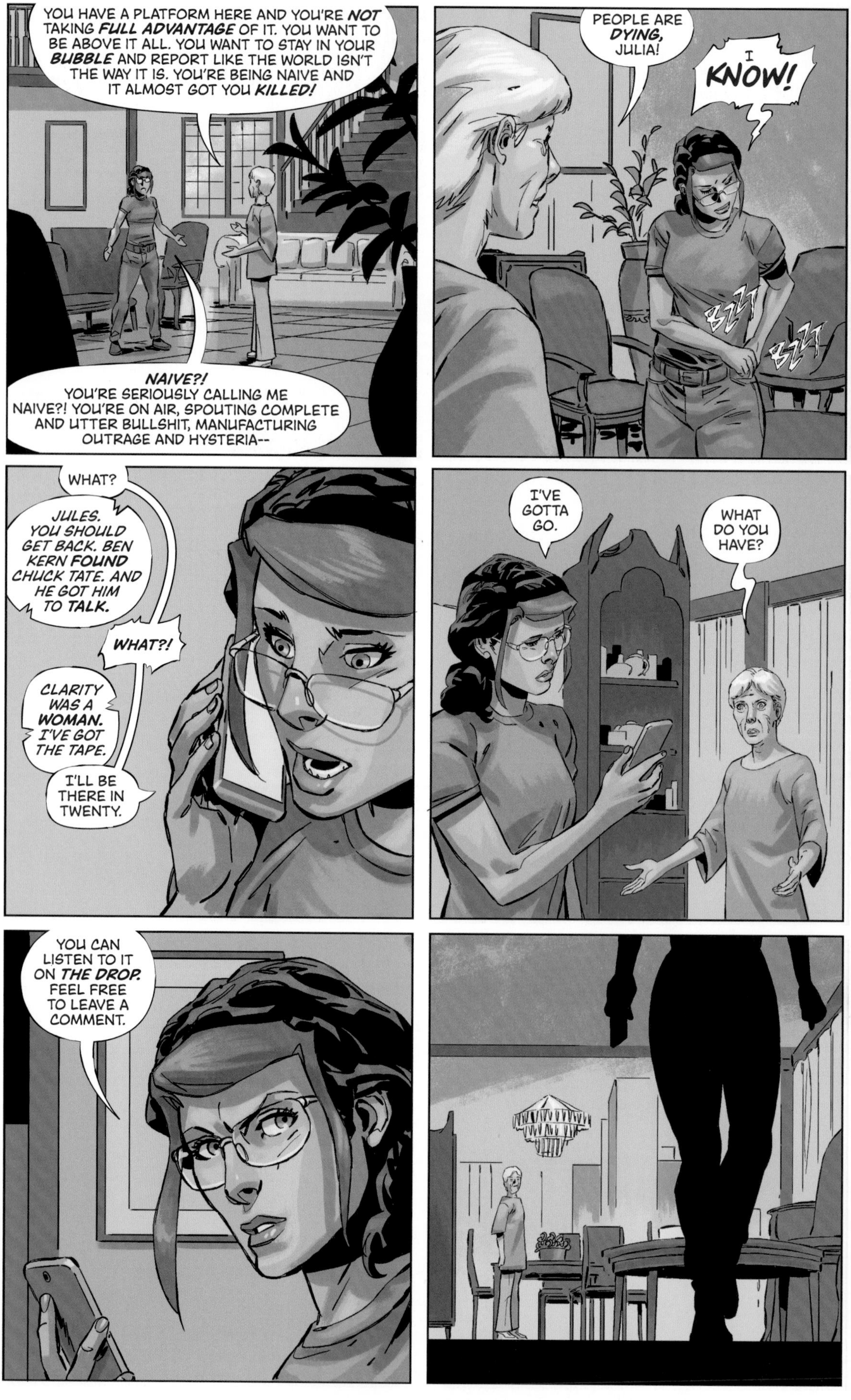
YOU HAVE A PLATFORM HERE AND YOU'RE NOT TAKING FULL ADVANTAGE OF IT. YOU WANT TO BE ABOVE IT ALL. YOU WANT TO STAY IN YOUR BUBBLE AND REPORT LIKE THE WORLD ISN'T THE WAY IT IS. YOU'RE BEING NAIVE AND IT ALMOST GOT YOU KILLED!
NAIVE?! YOU'RE SERIOUSLY CALLING ME NAIVE?! YOU'RE ON AIR, SPOUTING COMPLETE AND UTTER BULLSHIT, MANUFACTURING OUTRAGE AND HYSTERIA--
PEOPLE ARE DYING, JULIA!
I KNOW!
BZZT
BZZT
WHAT?
JULES. YOU SHOULD GET BACK. BEN KERN FOUND CHUCK TATE. AND HE GOT HIM TO TALK.
WHAT?!
CLARITY WAS A WOMAN. I'VE GOT THE TAPE.
I'LL BE THERE IN TWENTY.
I'VE GOTTA GO.
WHAT DO YOU HAVE?
YOU CAN LISTEN TO IT ON THE DROP. FEEL FREE TO LEAVE A COMMENT.

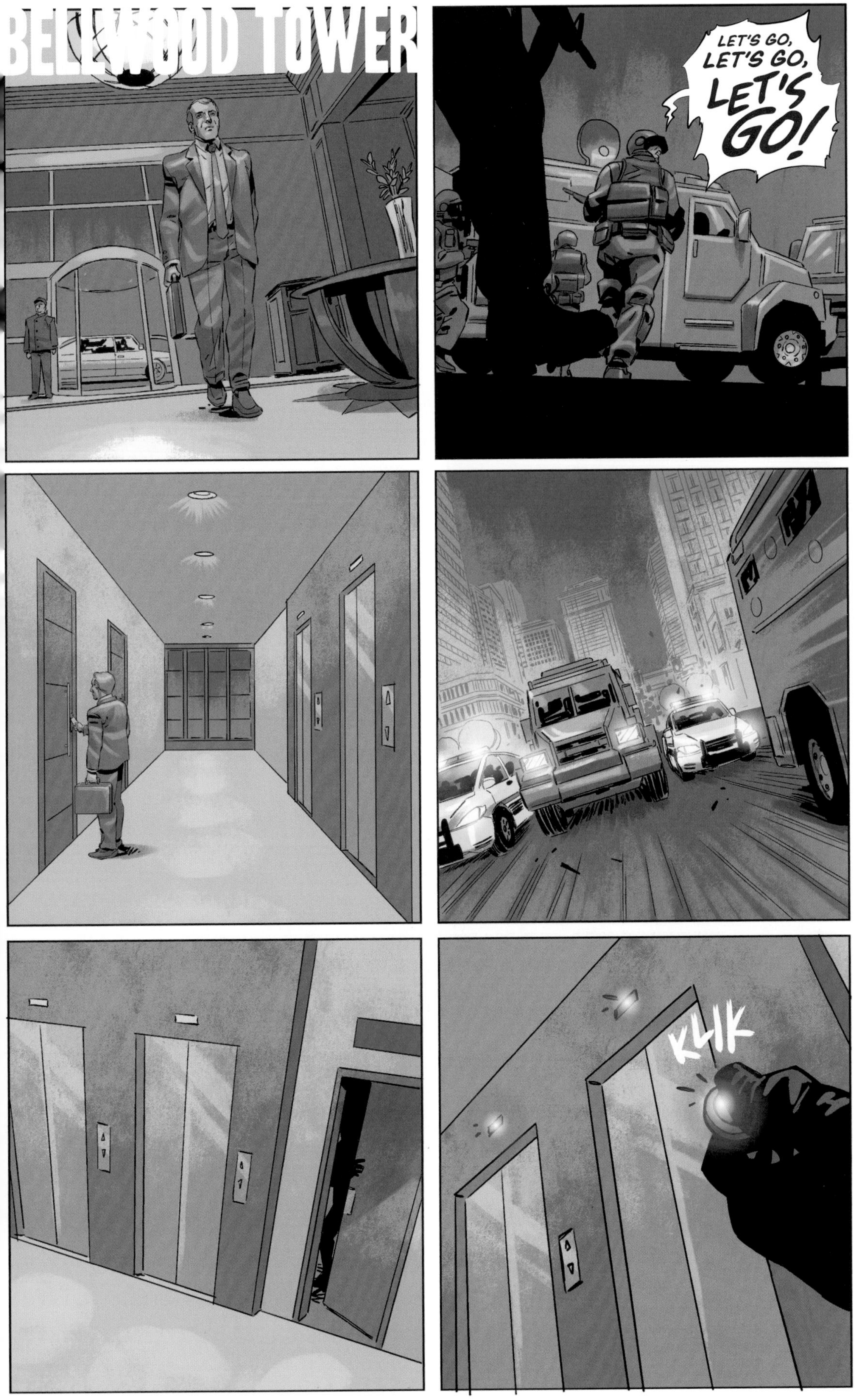
BELLWOOD TOWER
LET'S GO, LET'S GO, LET'S GO!
KLIK

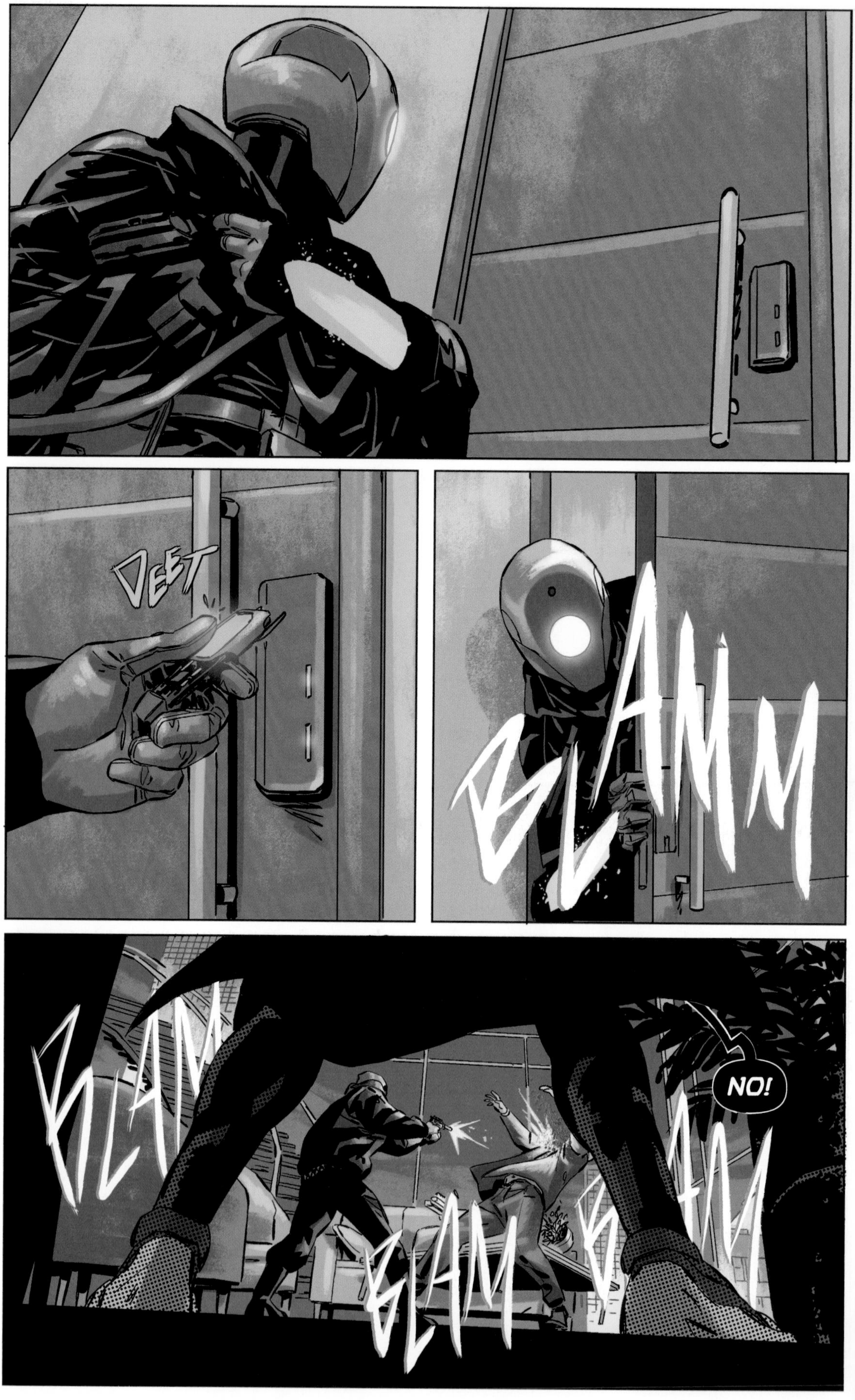
DEET
BLAMM
BLAM
NO!
BLAM
BLAM

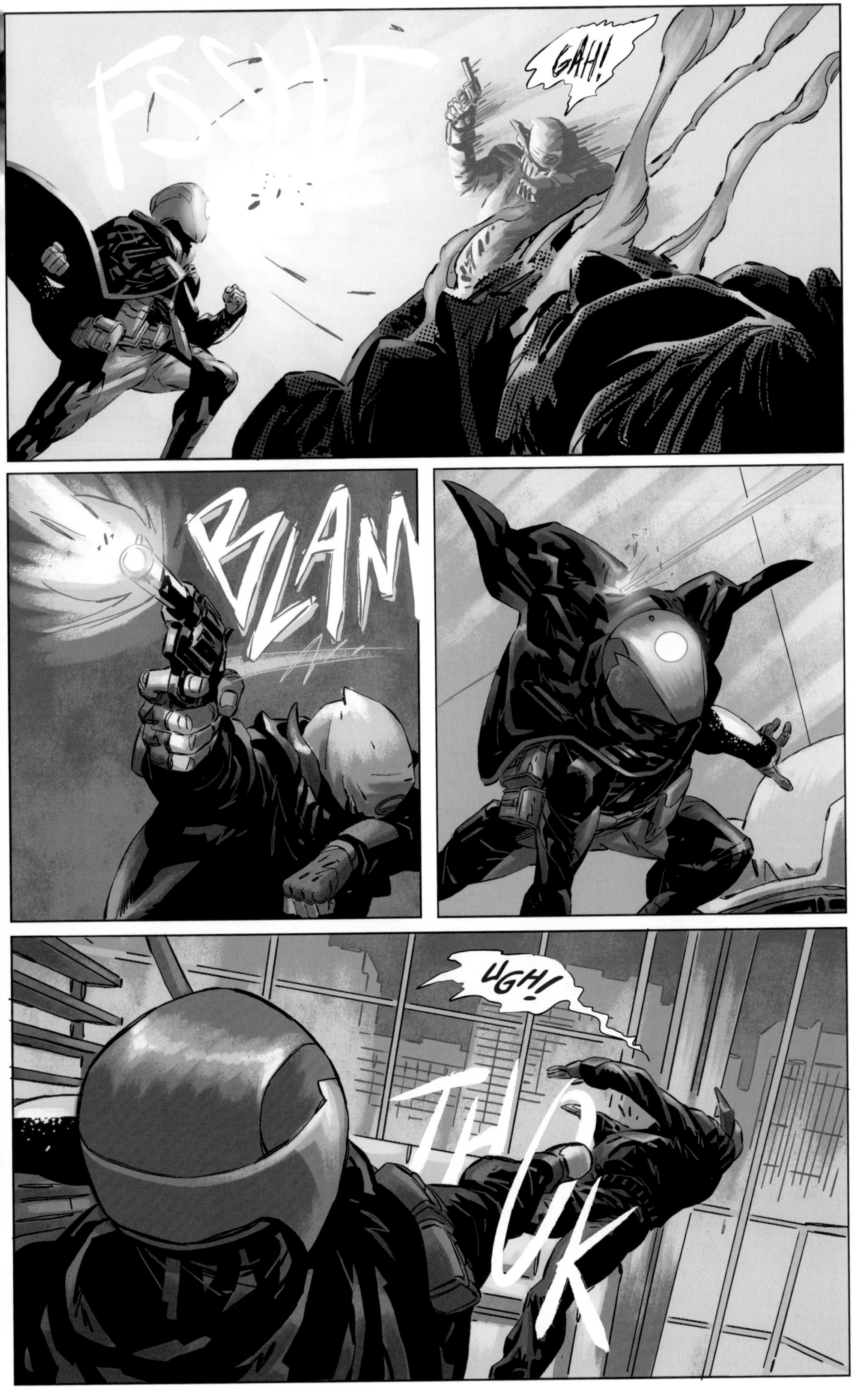
FSSHT
GAH!
BLAM
UGH!
THUK

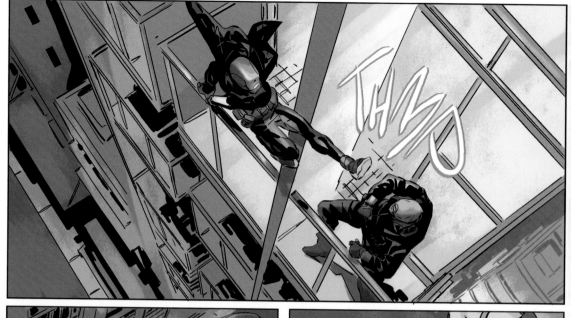

THWP

KKZZT

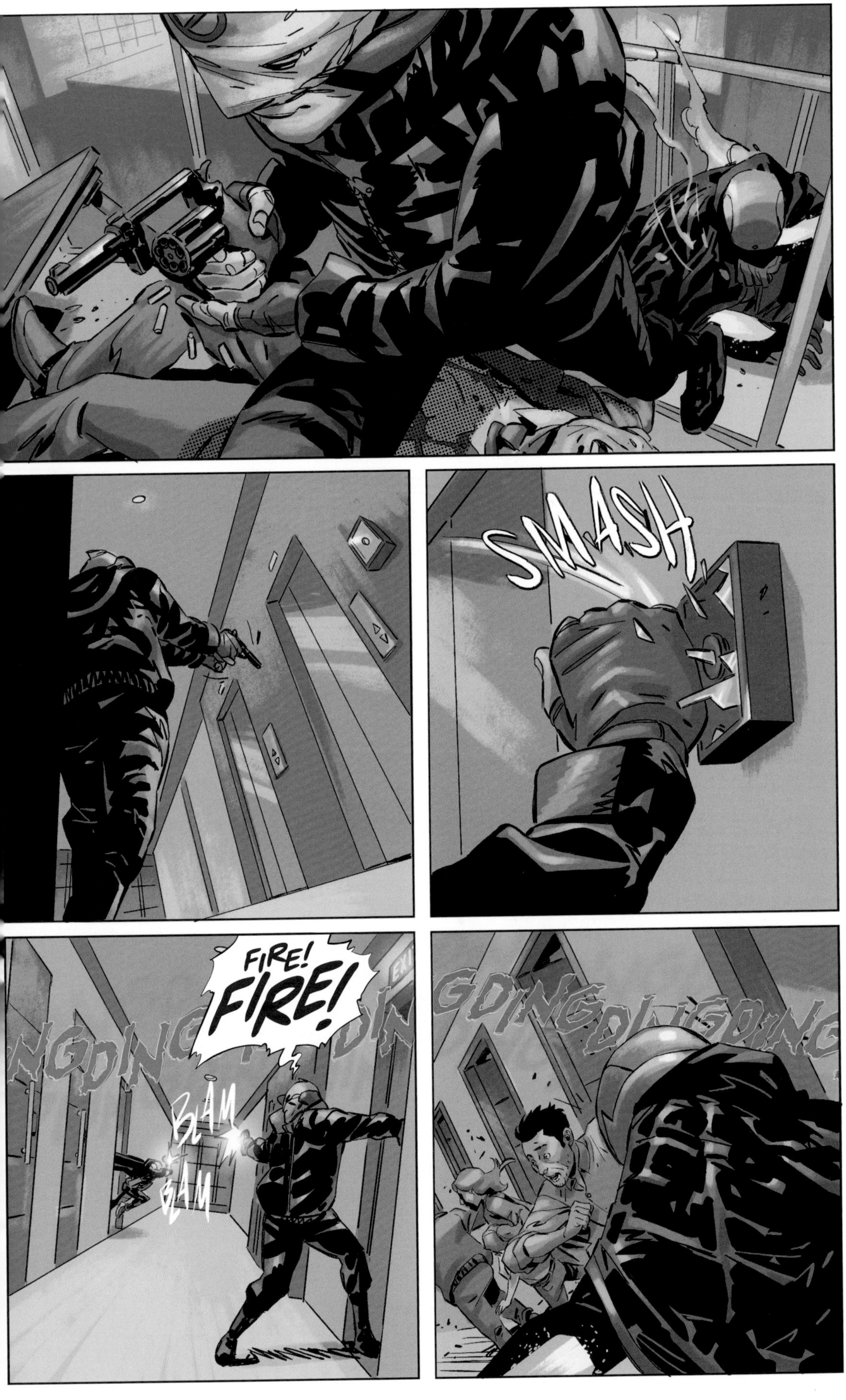
SMASH
FIRE! FIRE!
BLAM
BLAM

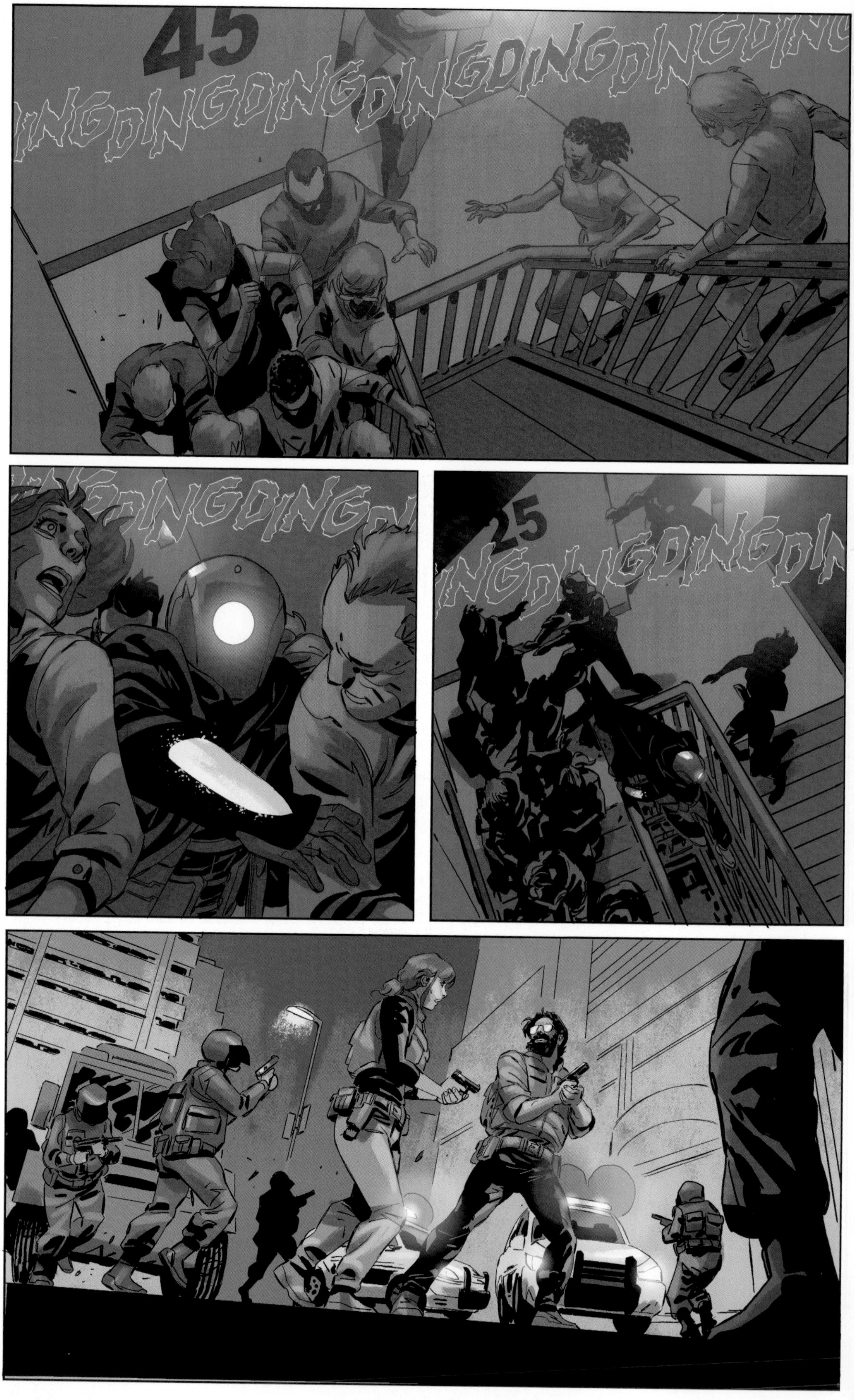
45
INGDINGDINGDINGDING
DINGDING
25
INGDINGDINGDIN

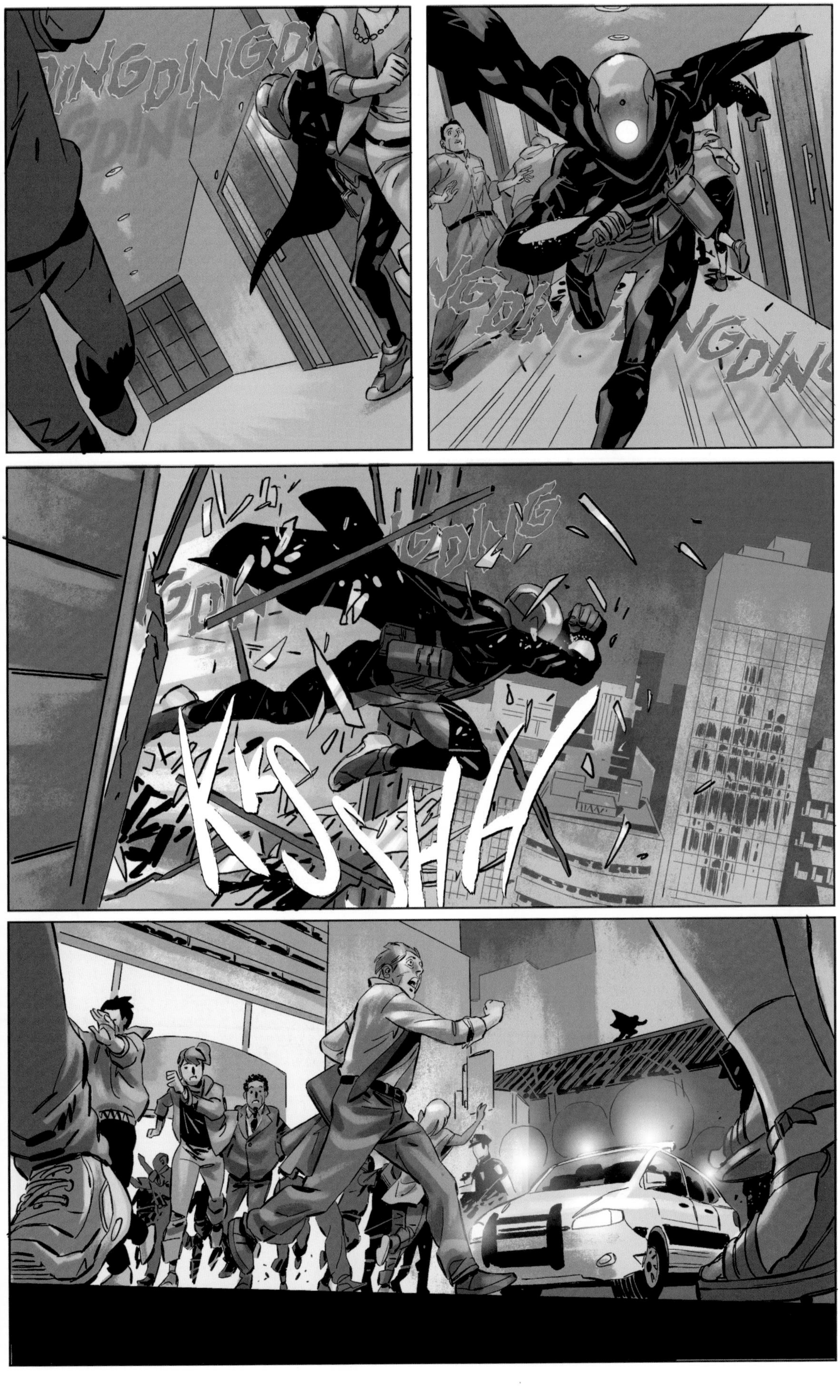
DINGDIN
GDING
KSSHH

NO CHUCK TONIGHT?

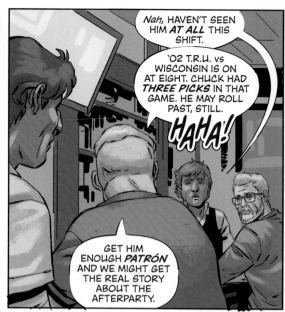

Nah, HAVEN'T SEEN HIM *AT ALL* THIS SHIFT.

'02 T.R.U. vs WISCONSIN IS ON AT EIGHT. CHUCK HAD *THREE PICKS* IN THAT GAME. HE MAY ROLL PAST, STILL.

HAHA!

GET HIM ENOUGH *PATRÓN* AND WE MIGHT GET THE REAL STORY ABOUT THE AFTERPARTY.

WHAT DO YOU MEAN?

DID HE EVER TELL YOU ABOUT SOMEONE NAMED *CLARITY?*

CHUCK TALKS WHEN HE DRINKS. ESPECIALLY WHEN HE GETS *EMO.* '02 WISCONSIN WAS HIS LAST GAME.

Nah, I DON'T THINK SO. WHAT IS THAT, LIKE AN EPIPHANY?

Yeah, if *only.*

ANOTHER ONE?

SURE.

I'VE GOT NOWHERE TO BE...

The Drøp

PRESENTS

WHO IS NO/ONE
WITH/ JULIA PAIGE

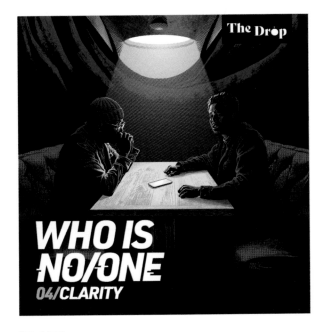

WHO IS NO/ONE
04/CLARITY

23 JUNE
04/Clarity
WHO IS NO/ONE

19:32   -15:32

>_ **EDGE NEWS EXCLUSIVE: Coach Cade's Shadowy**
Secrets & That 'WHO IS NO/ONE' Bombshell
Interview with Chuck Tate
JUNE 24 2023

written by Danielle Gaines
published on Edge News

"According to Tate, this was no random
accident—it was a tragedy swept under
the rug."

KNOWPEDIA
An Encyclopedia For Free

Chuck Tate

Article Talk Read View source View history

Chuck Tate (born August 16, 1980) is a former American Football player. He played cornerback at Three Rivers University before playing for the San Diego Chargers, New York Jets, and Pittsburgh Steelers.

Early life [edit]

Tate attended Saint Mary Preparatory High School in Malvern, PA where he played as a cornerback, safety, and wide receiver. He received All-State honors at cornerback as a Junior and Senior. He was also the starting shooting guard for the basketball team.

College career [edit]

Tate was named All-Big East Conference MVP in 2001 and 2002, and the Continental Tire Bowl MVP in 2002. He gained attention as a senior in a regionally televised game against the then-3rd ranked Virginia Tech Hokies by intercepting two passes for touchdowns and forcing a game-deciding fumble in the upset victory. That season he played in all 11 games, garnering 44 tackles, 6 interceptions, and 14 passes defended and earning the nickname "Lockdown" as he allowed zero touchdowns from opponents. In 2002 he concluded his college career with 29 starts, 106 tackles, 13 interceptions, and 30 passes defended.

Professional career [edit]

Despite a successful senior season, a subpar performance at the NFL combine sunk Tate's chances in the NFL draft. Unselected in the 7-round draft, his college coach Nathan Cade helped him land a spot on the San Diego Chargers. He was one of the last cuts of the preseason but made enough of an impression that he was signed mid-season by the New York Jets due to multiple injuries. After appearing in the last 4 games of 2003, Tate was waived in the following preseason.

In 2005 Tate landed on the Pittsburgh Steelers practice squad. He tore his Achilles tendon mid-season and was waived on December 16, 2005.

Following his playing career, Chuck Tate returned to Three Rivers University in 2009, in an advisory role under Coach Nathan Cade.

Nathan Cade murder allegations [edit]

Two months after the April 19, 2023 murder of Nathan Cade by the third Richard Roe copycat, Tate came forward with an accusation that Cade was responsible for the 2012 death of a sexworker known only as Clarity. He claimed to have found Cade with the dead woman and helped to dispose of the body in a city dump. Her identity is still unverified, pending an investigation by the Pittsburgh Police.

Chuck Tate

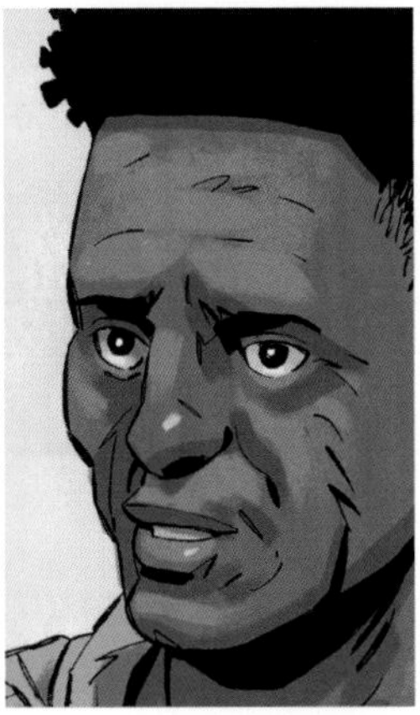

PERSONAL INFORMATION

Born	August 16, 1981 (age 47) Pittsburgh, U.S.
Height	6 ft (1.82 m)
Weight	190 lbs (86 kg)
Nicknames	Lockdown, Chuck

CAREER INFORMATION

High School	Saint Mary Prep Malvern, PA
College	Three Rivers University
NFL Draft	Undrafted

CAREER HISTORY

San Diego Chargers (2003)
New York Jets (2003-2004)*
Pittsburgh Steelers (2005)*
**offseason and/or practice squad member only*

CAREER HIGHLIGHTS & AWARDS

2x All-Big East (2001, 2002)
Big East Defensive Player of the Year (2002)
MVP Continental Tire Bowl (2002)

CAREER STATISTICS

Games Played	4
Tackles	3
Interceptions	1

Richard Roe [show]

Authority control [show]

>_ CHAPTER FIVE
JULY 2023

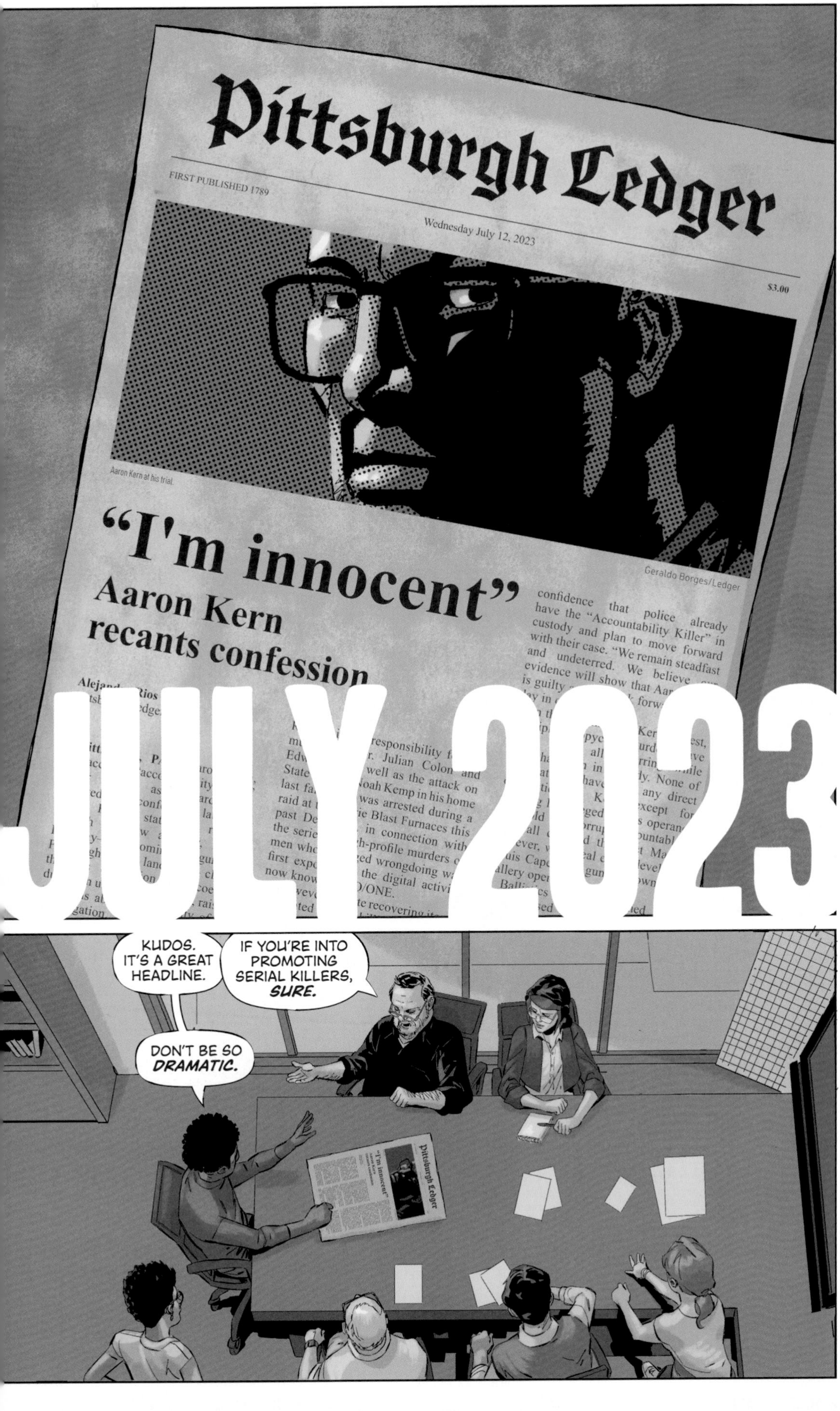

Pittsburgh Ledger
FIRST PUBLISHED 1789
Wednesday July 12, 2023
$3.00
Aaron Kern at his trial.
Geraldo Borges/Ledger
"I'm innocent"
Aaron Kern recants confession
confidence that police already have the "Accountability Killer" in custody and plan to move forward with their case. "We remain steadfast and undeterred. We believe
evidence will show that Aa
JULY 2023
KUDOS. IT'S A GREAT HEADLINE.
IF YOU'RE INTO PROMOTING SERIAL KILLERS, SURE.
DON'T BE SO DRAMATIC.
Pittsburgh Ledger
"I'm innocent"

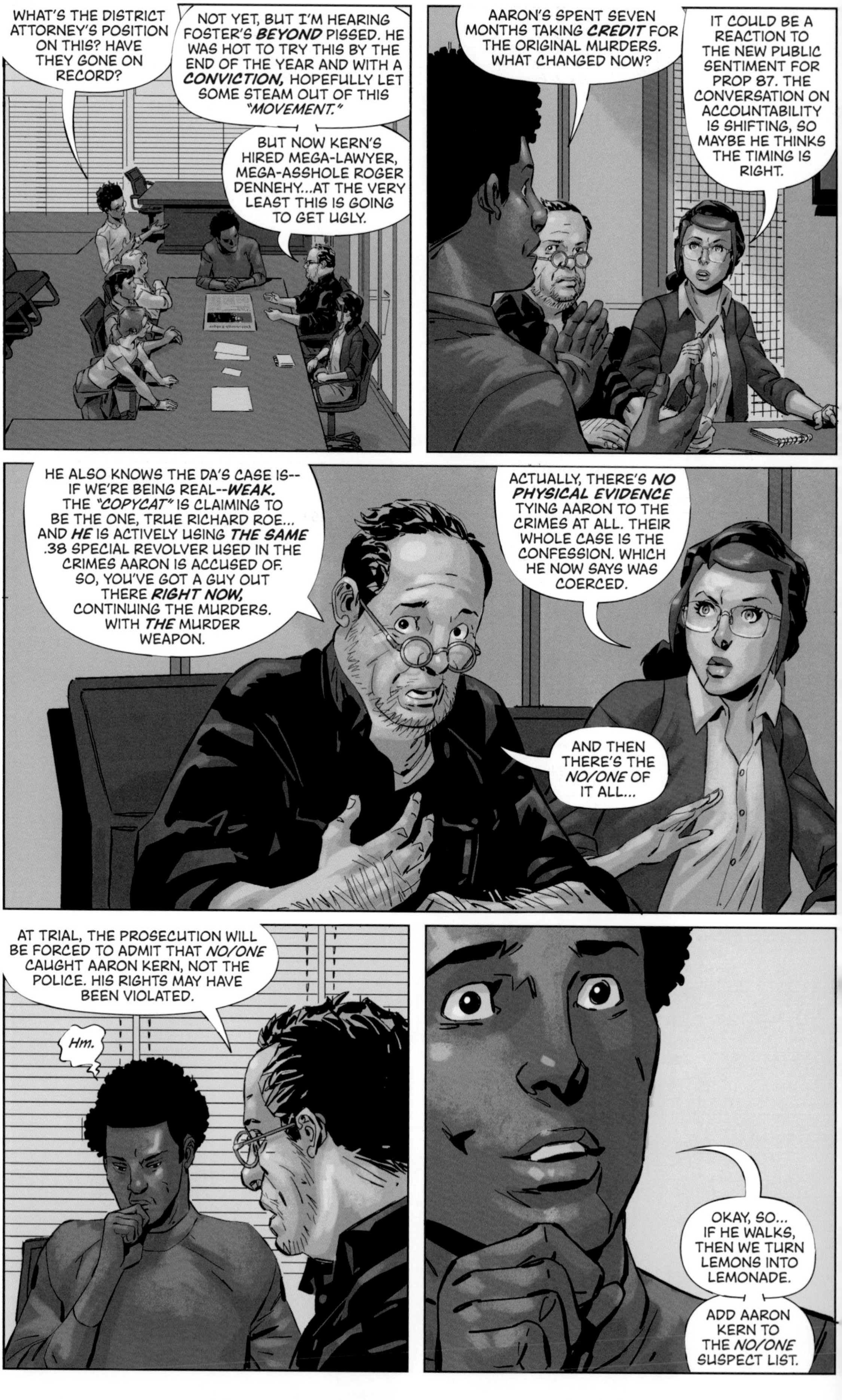
WHAT'S THE DISTRICT ATTORNEY'S POSITION ON THIS? HAVE THEY GONE ON RECORD?
NOT YET, BUT I'M HEARING FOSTER'S BEYOND PISSED. HE WAS HOT TO TRY THIS BY THE END OF THE YEAR AND WITH A CONVICTION, HOPEFULLY LET SOME STEAM OUT OF THIS "MOVEMENT."
BUT NOW KERN'S HIRED MEGA-LAWYER, MEGA-ASSHOLE ROGER DENNEHY...AT THE VERY LEAST THIS IS GOING TO GET UGLY.
AARON'S SPENT SEVEN MONTHS TAKING CREDIT FOR THE ORIGINAL MURDERS. WHAT CHANGED NOW?
IT COULD BE A REACTION TO THE NEW PUBLIC SENTIMENT FOR PROP 87. THE CONVERSATION ON ACCOUNTABILITY IS SHIFTING, SO MAYBE HE THINKS THE TIMING IS RIGHT.
HE ALSO KNOWS THE DA'S CASE IS-- IF WE'RE BEING REAL--WEAK. THE "COPYCAT" IS CLAIMING TO BE THE ONE, TRUE RICHARD ROE... AND HE IS ACTIVELY USING THE SAME .38 SPECIAL REVOLVER USED IN THE CRIMES AARON IS ACCUSED OF. SO, YOU'VE GOT A GUY OUT THERE RIGHT NOW, CONTINUING THE MURDERS. WITH THE MURDER WEAPON.
ACTUALLY, THERE'S NO PHYSICAL EVIDENCE TYING AARON TO THE CRIMES AT ALL. THEIR WHOLE CASE IS THE CONFESSION. WHICH HE NOW SAYS WAS COERCED.
AND THEN THERE'S THE NO/ONE OF IT ALL...
AT TRIAL, THE PROSECUTION WILL BE FORCED TO ADMIT THAT NO/ONE CAUGHT AARON KERN, NOT THE POLICE. HIS RIGHTS MAY HAVE BEEN VIOLATED.
Hm.
OKAY, SO... IF HE WALKS, THEN WE TURN LEMONS INTO LEMONADE.
ADD AARON KERN TO THE NO/ONE SUSPECT LIST.

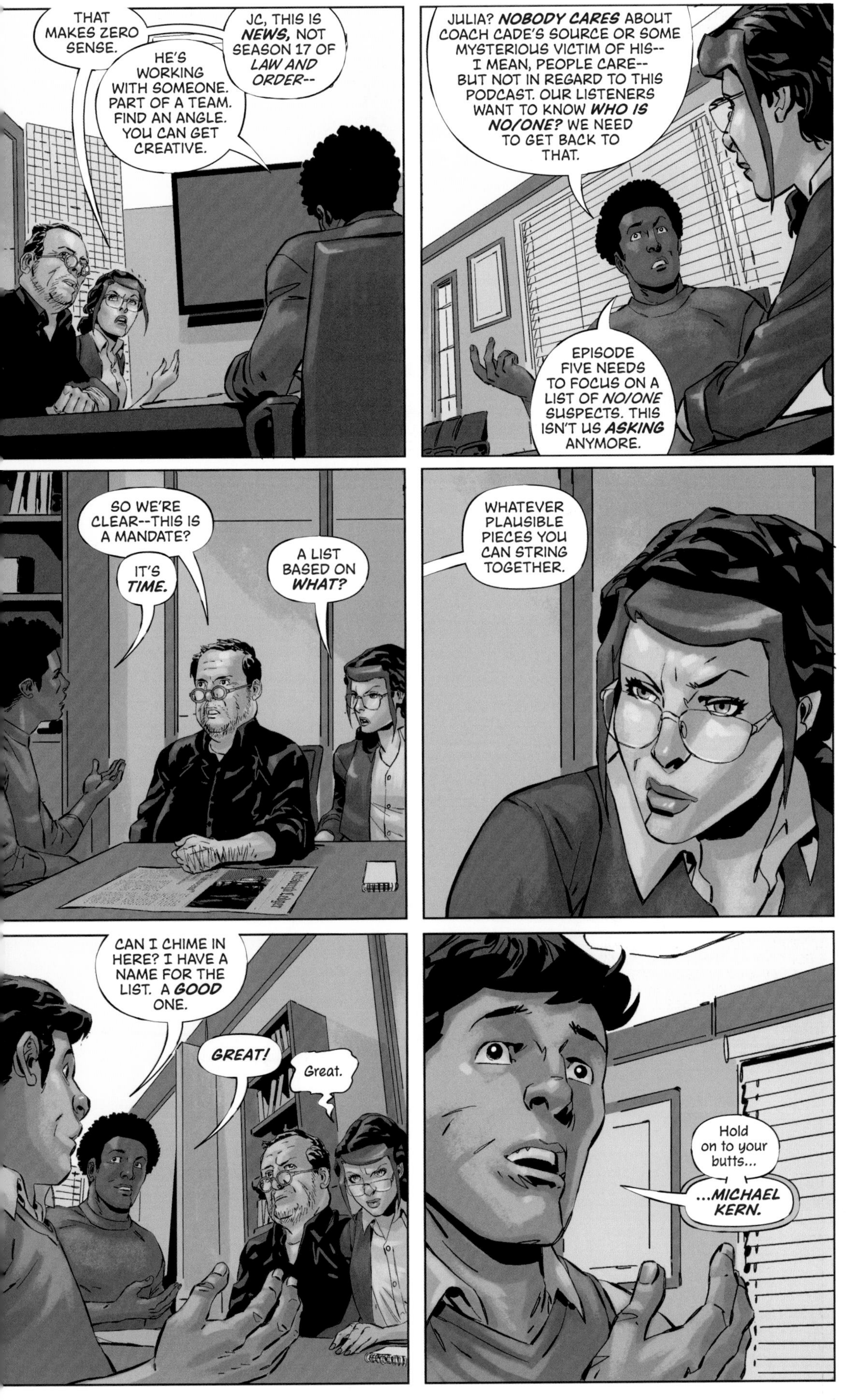
THAT MAKES ZERO SENSE.
HE'S WORKING WITH SOMEONE. PART OF A TEAM. FIND AN ANGLE. YOU CAN GET CREATIVE.
JC, THIS IS NEWS, NOT SEASON 17 OF LAW AND ORDER--
JULIA? NOBODY CARES ABOUT COACH CADE'S SOURCE OR SOME MYSTERIOUS VICTIM OF HIS-- I MEAN, PEOPLE CARE-- BUT NOT IN REGARD TO THIS PODCAST. OUR LISTENERS WANT TO KNOW WHO IS NO/ONE? WE NEED TO GET BACK TO THAT.
EPISODE FIVE NEEDS TO FOCUS ON A LIST OF NO/ONE SUSPECTS. THIS ISN'T US ASKING ANYMORE.
SO WE'RE CLEAR--THIS IS A MANDATE?
IT'S TIME.
A LIST BASED ON WHAT?
WHATEVER PLAUSIBLE PIECES YOU CAN STRING TOGETHER.
CAN I CHIME IN HERE? I HAVE A NAME FOR THE LIST. A GOOD ONE.
GREAT!
Great.
Hold on to your butts...
...MICHAEL KERN.

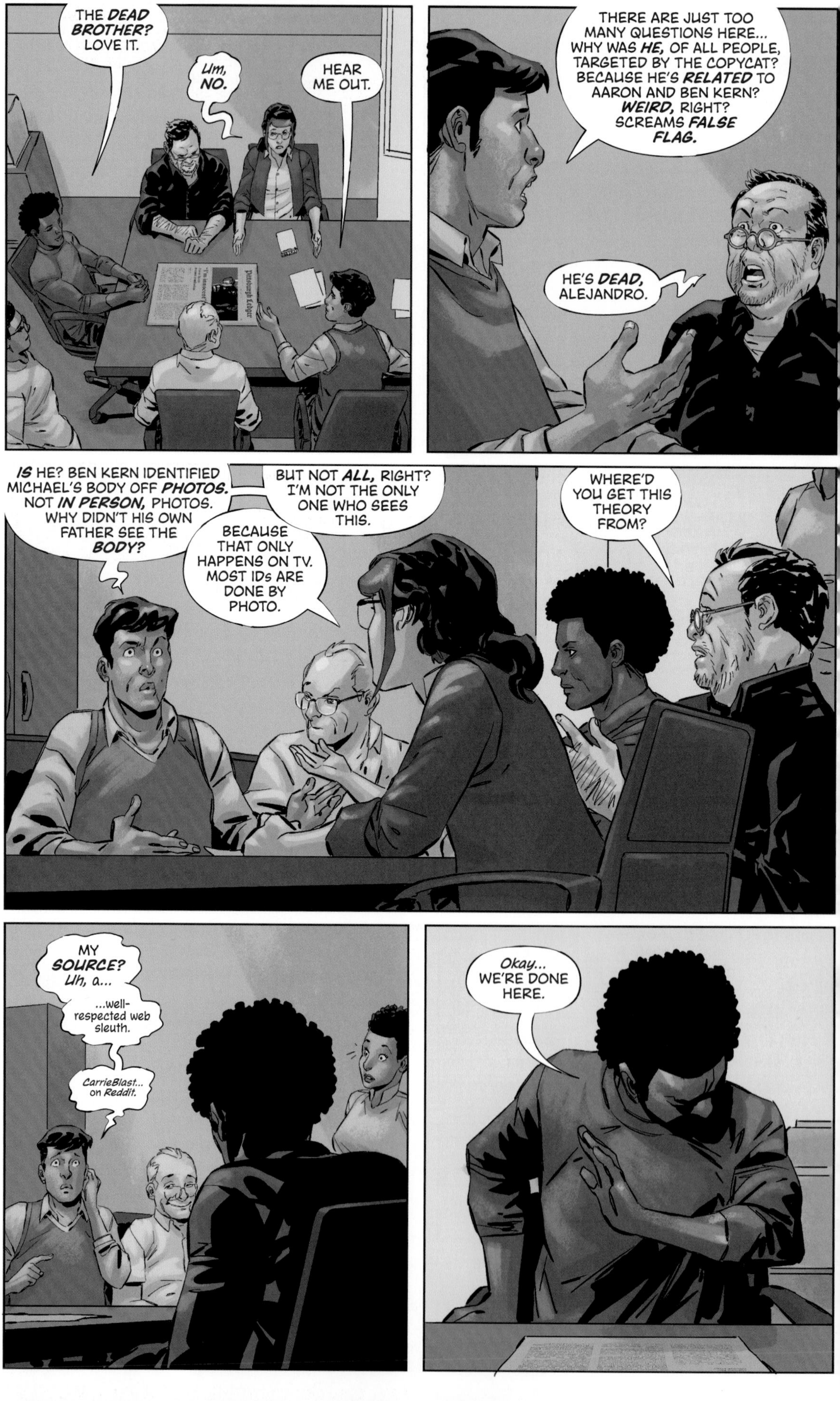
THE DEAD BROTHER? LOVE IT.
Um, NO.
HEAR ME OUT.
THERE ARE JUST TOO MANY QUESTIONS HERE... WHY WAS HE, OF ALL PEOPLE, TARGETED BY THE COPYCAT? BECAUSE HE'S RELATED TO AARON AND BEN KERN? WEIRD, RIGHT? SCREAMS FALSE FLAG.
HE'S DEAD, ALEJANDRO.
IS HE? BEN KERN IDENTIFIED MICHAEL'S BODY OFF PHOTOS. NOT IN PERSON, PHOTOS. WHY DIDN'T HIS OWN FATHER SEE THE BODY?
BECAUSE THAT ONLY HAPPENS ON TV. MOST IDs ARE DONE BY PHOTO.
BUT NOT ALL, RIGHT? I'M NOT THE ONLY ONE WHO SEES THIS.
WHERE'D YOU GET THIS THEORY FROM?
MY SOURCE? Uh, a...
...well-respected web sleuth.
CarrieBlast... on Reddit.
Okay... WE'RE DONE HERE.

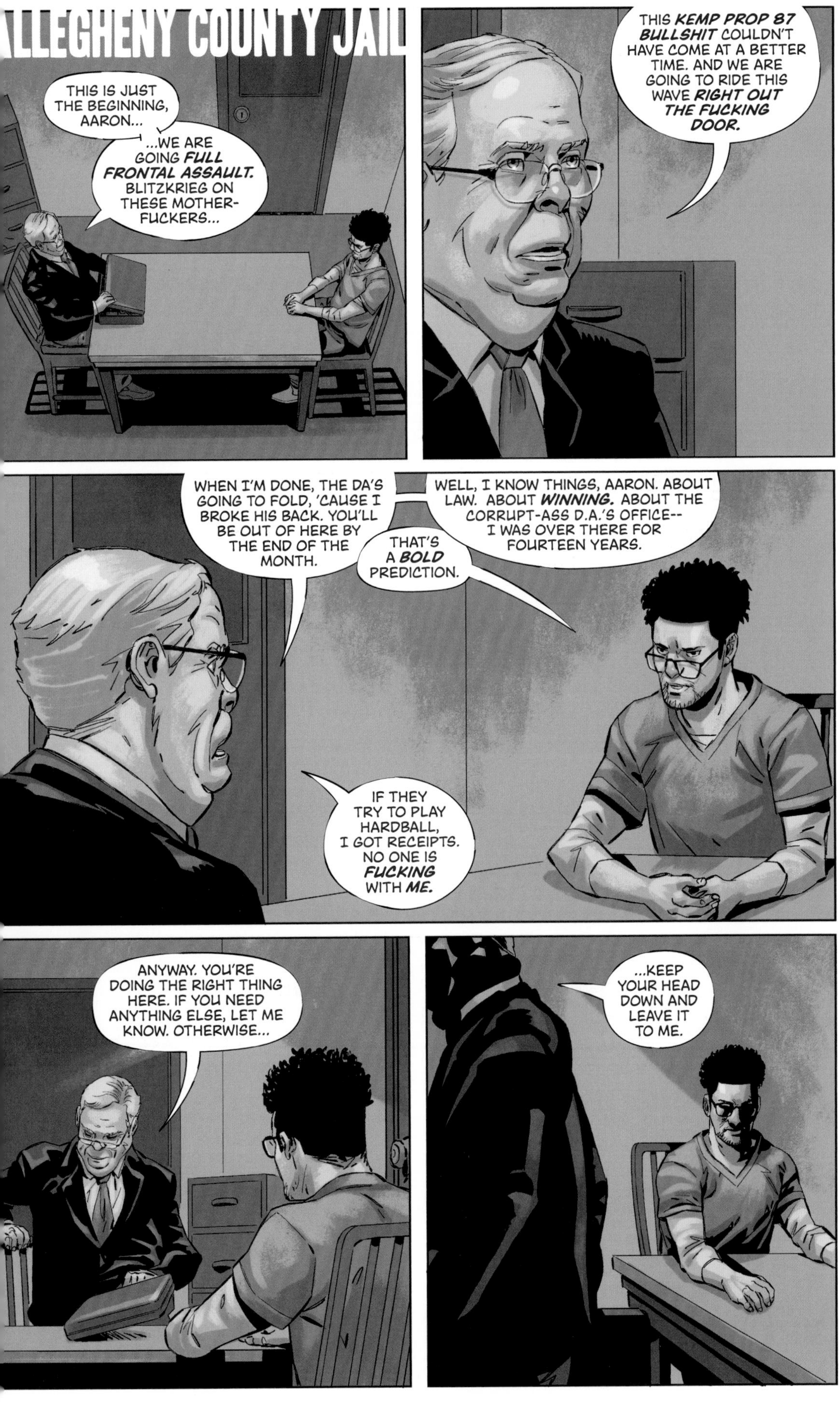
ALLEGHENY COUNTY JAIL
THIS IS JUST THE BEGINNING, AARON...
...WE ARE GOING FULL FRONTAL ASSAULT. BLITZKRIEG ON THESE MOTHER-FUCKERS...
THIS KEMP PROP 87 BULLSHIT COULDN'T HAVE COME AT A BETTER TIME. AND WE ARE GOING TO RIDE THIS WAVE RIGHT OUT THE FUCKING DOOR.
WHEN I'M DONE, THE DA'S GOING TO FOLD, 'CAUSE I BROKE HIS BACK. YOU'LL BE OUT OF HERE BY THE END OF THE MONTH.
WELL, I KNOW THINGS, AARON. ABOUT LAW. ABOUT WINNING. ABOUT THE CORRUPT-ASS D.A.'S OFFICE-- I WAS OVER THERE FOR FOURTEEN YEARS.
THAT'S A BOLD PREDICTION.
IF THEY TRY TO PLAY HARDBALL, I GOT RECEIPTS. NO ONE IS FUCKING WITH ME.
ANYWAY. YOU'RE DOING THE RIGHT THING HERE. IF YOU NEED ANYTHING ELSE, LET ME KNOW. OTHERWISE...
...KEEP YOUR HEAD DOWN AND LEAVE IT TO ME.

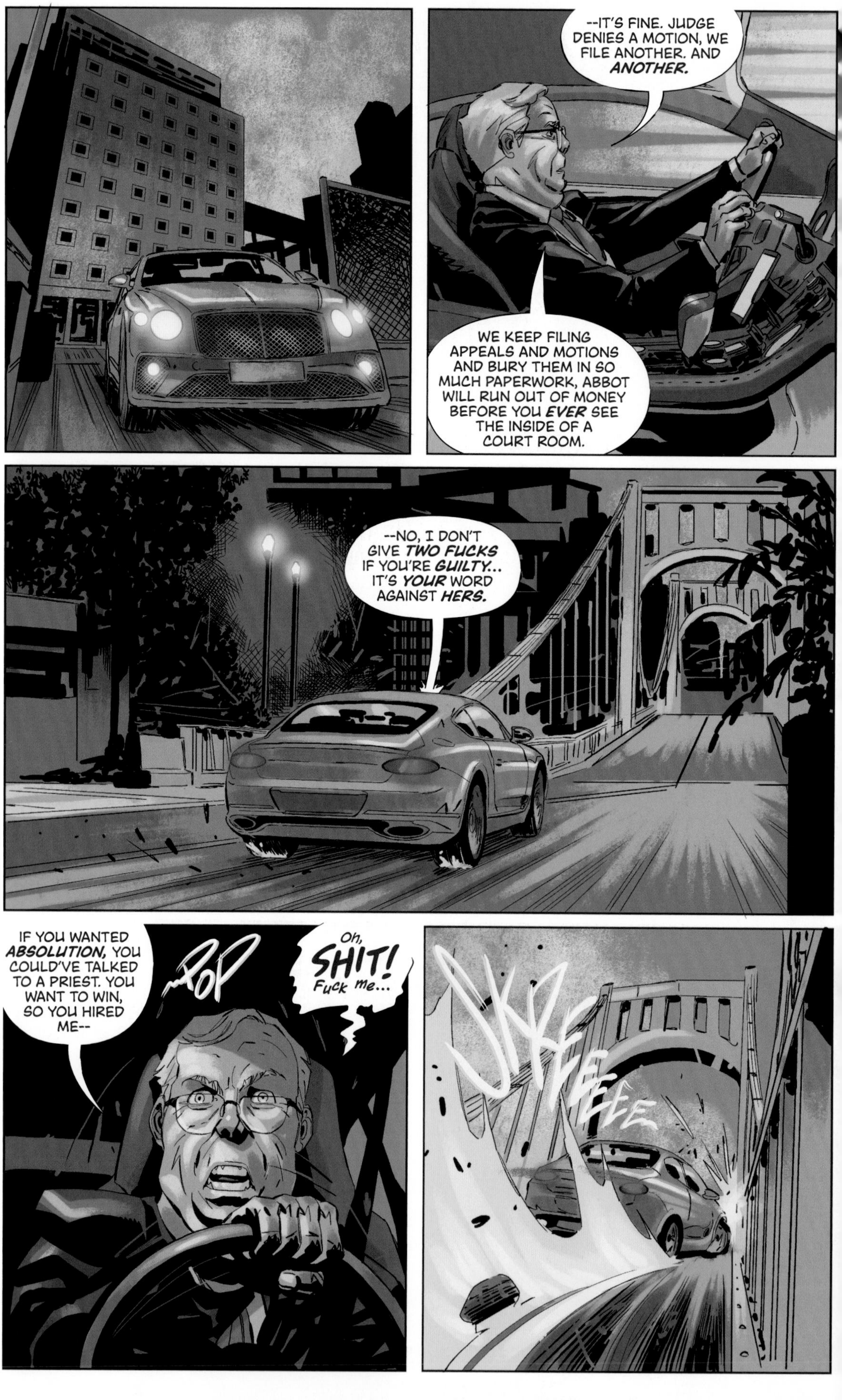
--IT'S FINE. JUDGE DENIES A MOTION, WE FILE ANOTHER. AND ANOTHER.
WE KEEP FILING APPEALS AND MOTIONS AND BURY THEM IN SO MUCH PAPERWORK, ABBOT WILL RUN OUT OF MONEY BEFORE YOU EVER SEE THE INSIDE OF A COURT ROOM.
--NO, I DON'T GIVE TWO FUCKS IF YOU'RE GUILTY... IT'S YOUR WORD AGAINST HERS.
IF YOU WANTED ABSOLUTION, YOU COULD'VE TALKED TO A PRIEST. YOU WANT TO WIN, SO YOU HIRED ME--
POP
Oh, SHIT! Fuck me...
SKREEEEEEE

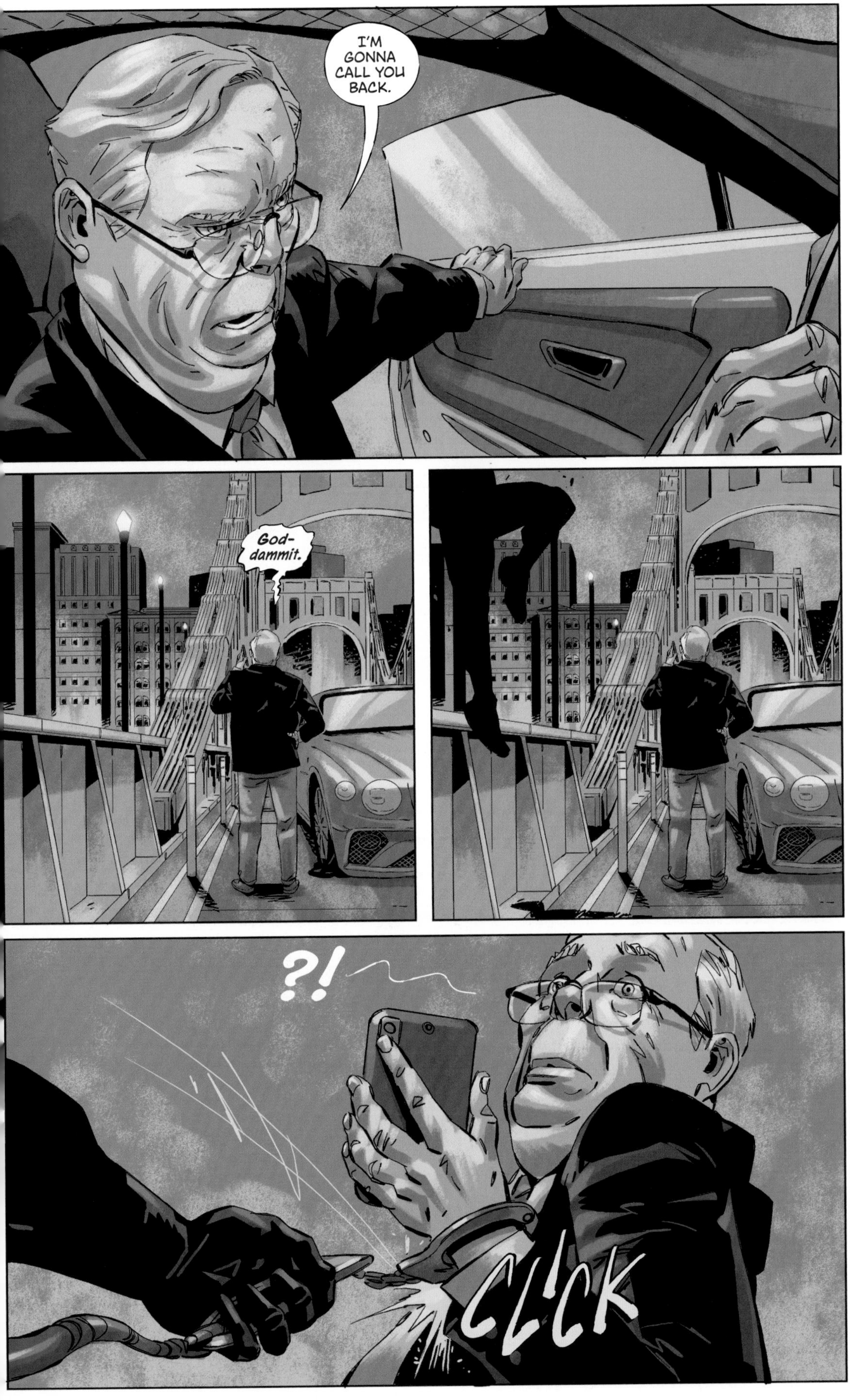
I'M GONNA CALL YOU BACK.
God-dammit.
?!
CLICK

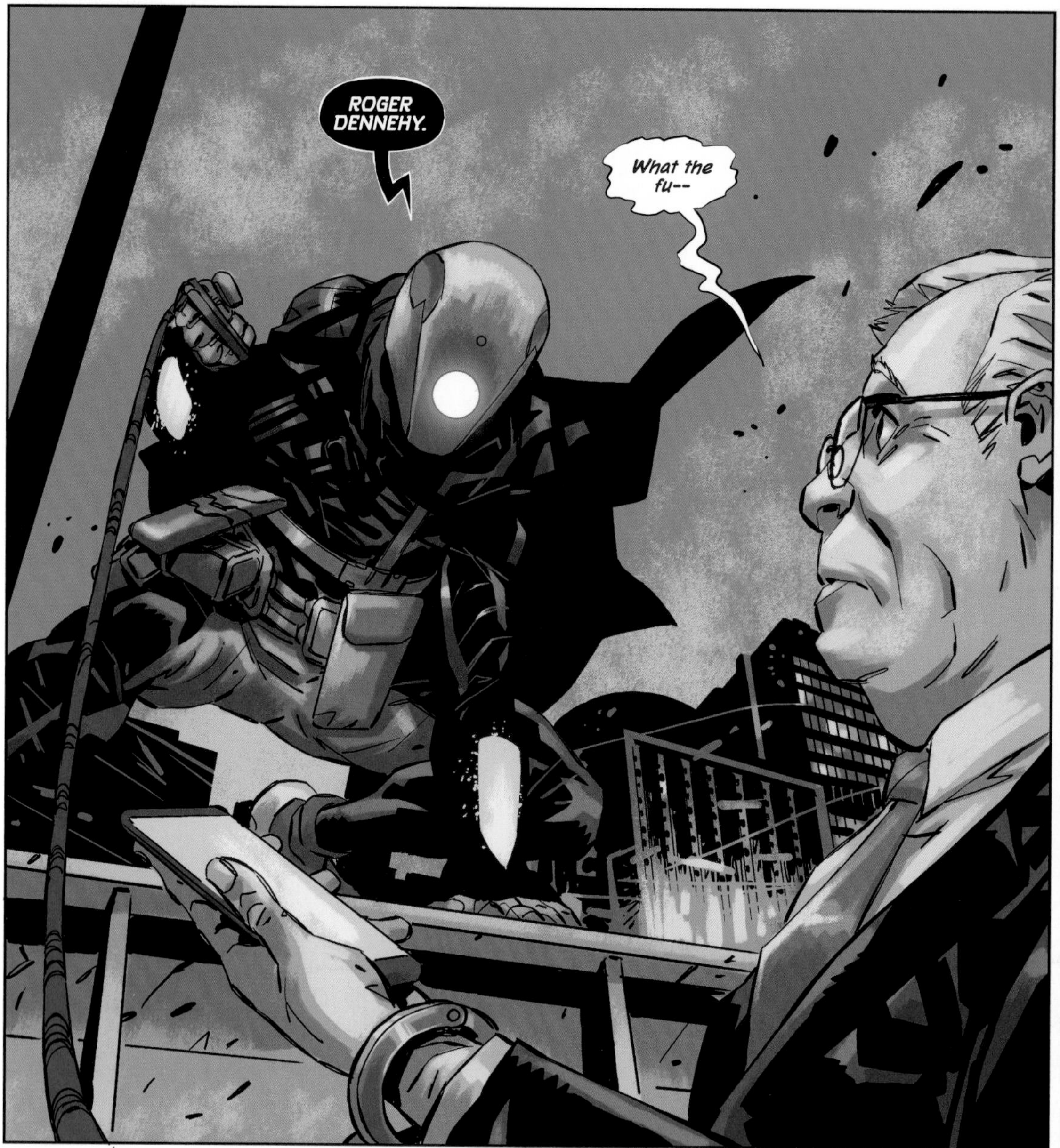
ROGER DENNEHY.
What the fu--
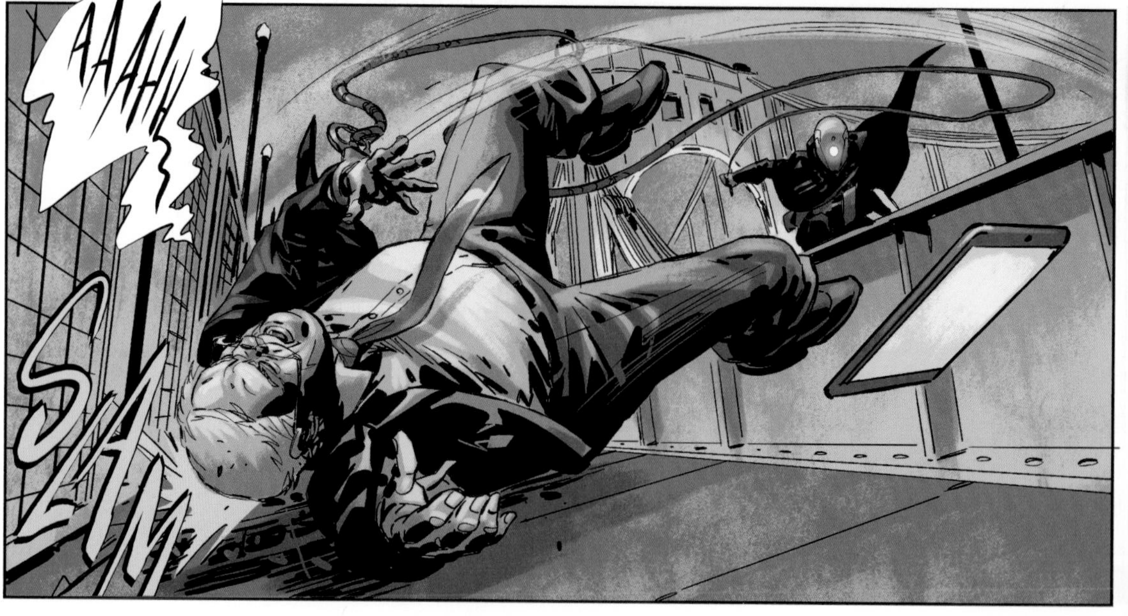
AAAHH
SLAM

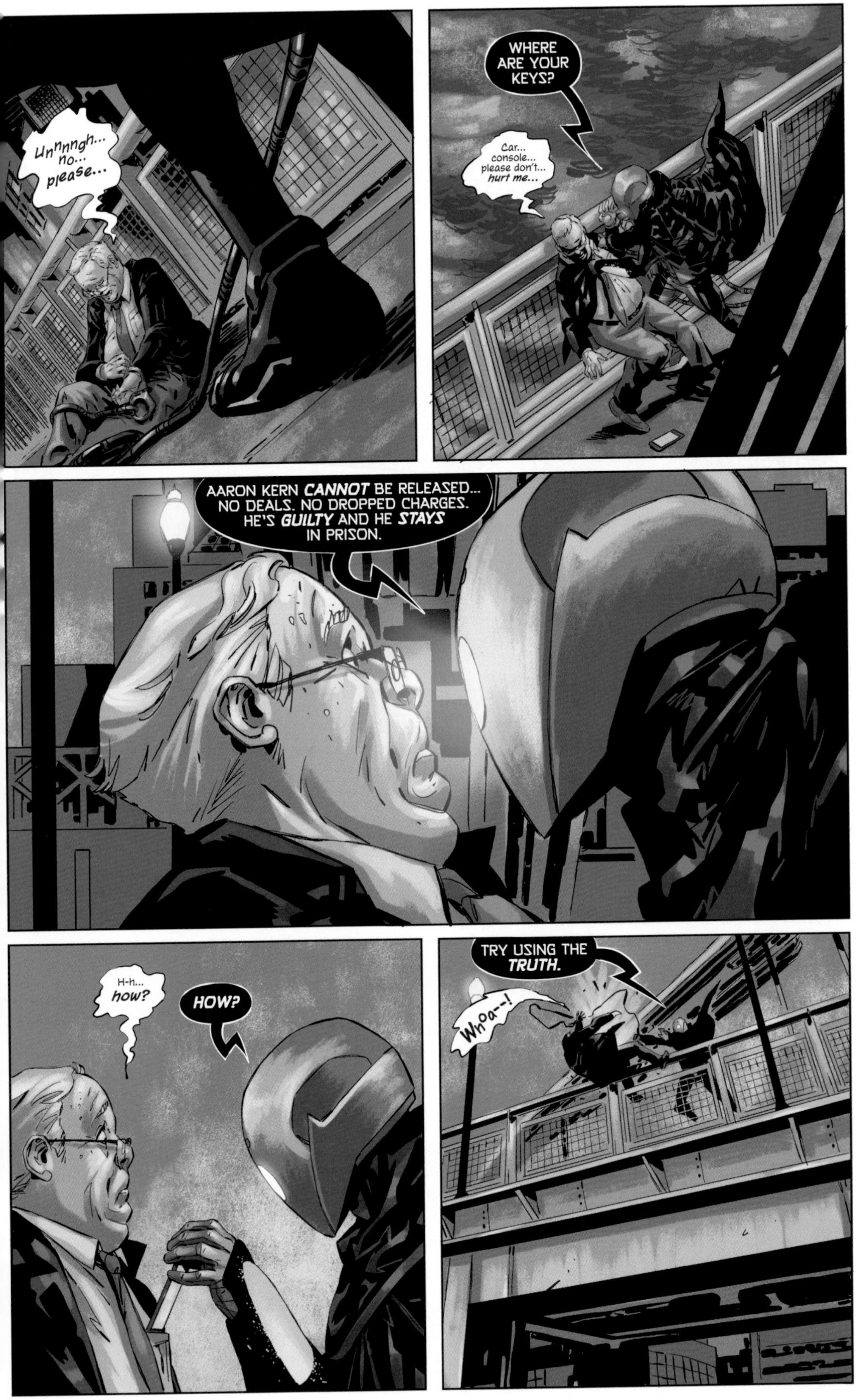
Unnnngh... no... please...
WHERE ARE YOUR KEYS?
Car... console... please don't... hurt me...
AARON KERN CANNOT BE RELEASED... NO DEALS. NO DROPPED CHARGES. HE'S GUILTY AND HE STAYS IN PRISON.
H-h... how?
HOW?
TRY USING THE TRUTH.
Whoa--!

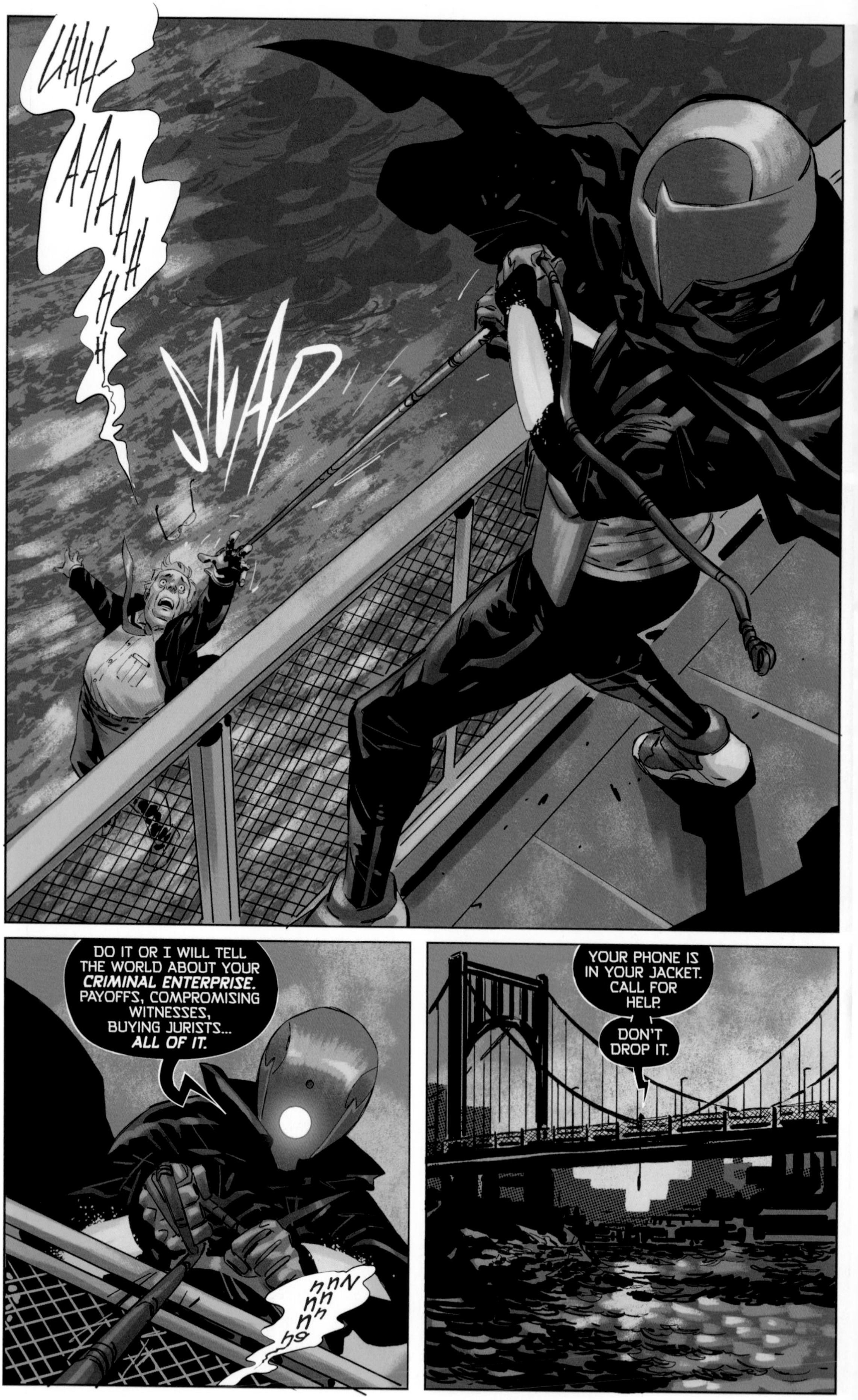
UHH-AAAAAHHHH
SNAP
DO IT OR I WILL TELL THE WORLD ABOUT YOUR ***CRIMINAL ENTERPRISE.*** PAYOFFS, COMPROMISING WITNESSES, BUYING JURISTS... ***ALL OF IT.***
Nnnnnnngh
YOUR PHONE IS IN YOUR JACKET. CALL FOR HELP.
DON'T DROP IT.

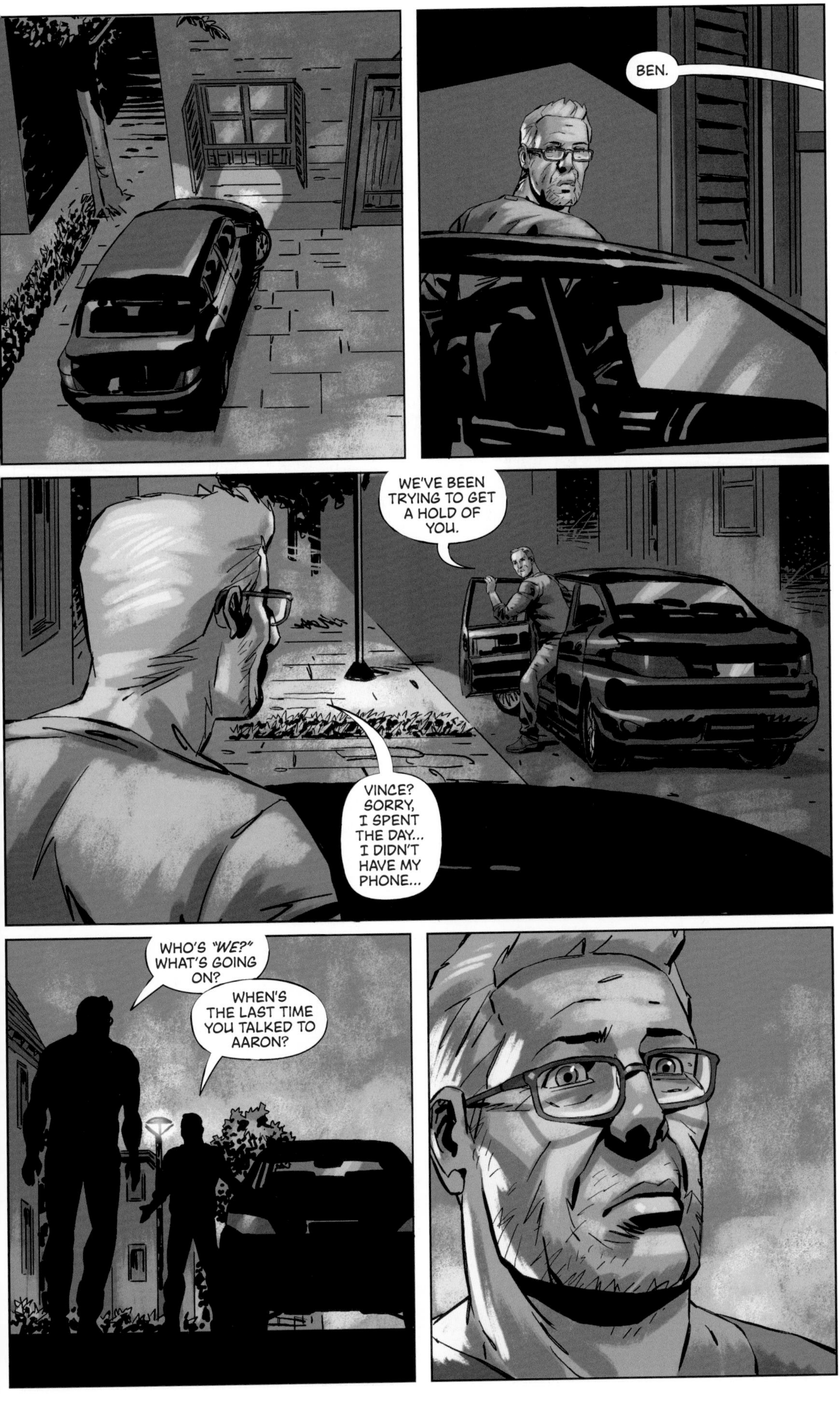
BEN.
WE'VE BEEN TRYING TO GET A HOLD OF YOU.
VINCE? SORRY, I SPENT THE DAY... I DIDN'T HAVE MY PHONE...
WHO'S "WE?" WHAT'S GOING ON?
WHEN'S THE LAST TIME YOU TALKED TO AARON?

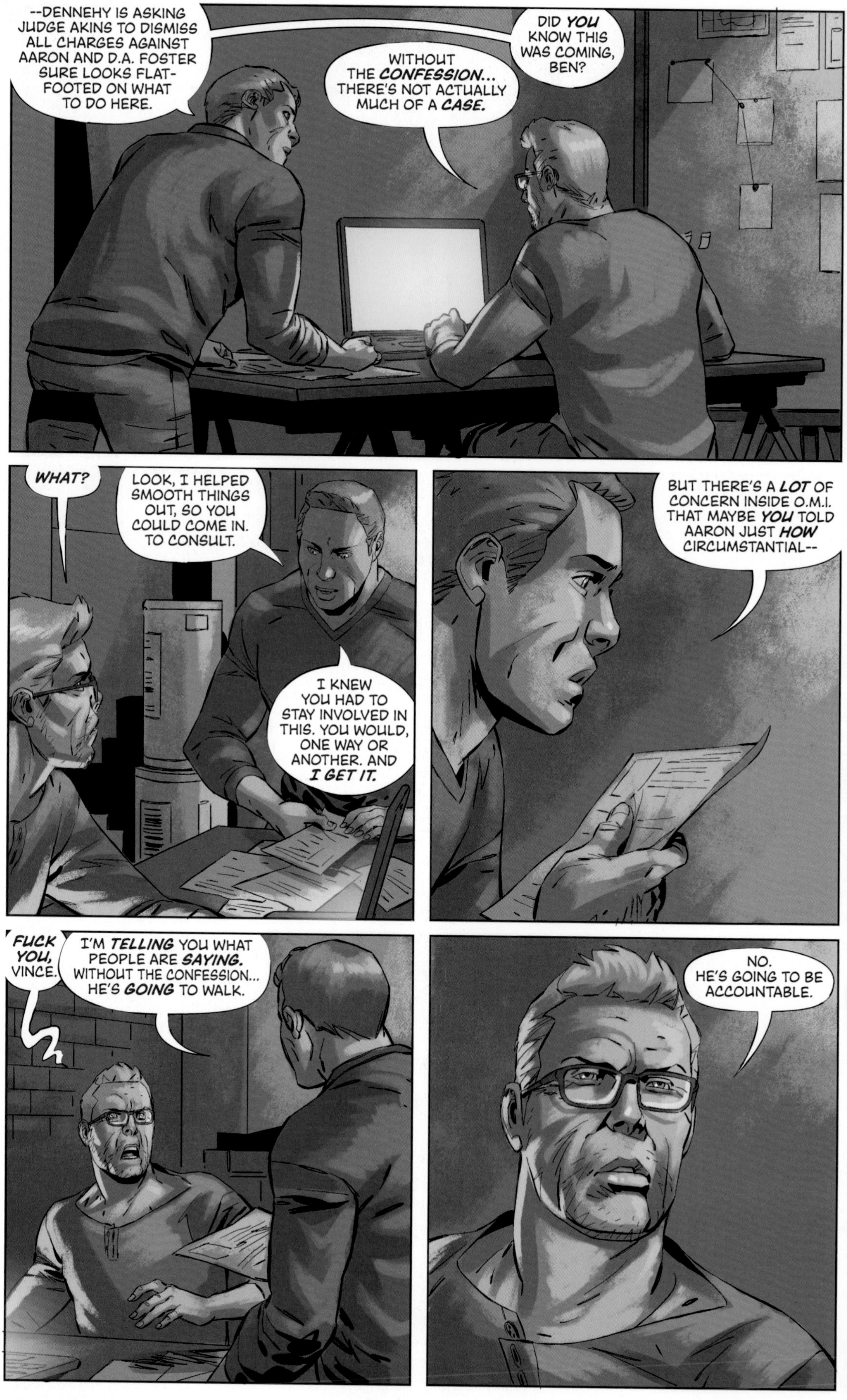
--DENNEHY IS ASKING JUDGE AKINS TO DISMISS ALL CHARGES AGAINST AARON AND D.A. FOSTER SURE LOOKS FLAT-FOOTED ON WHAT TO DO HERE.
WITHOUT THE CONFESSION... THERE'S NOT ACTUALLY MUCH OF A CASE.
DID YOU KNOW THIS WAS COMING, BEN?
WHAT?
LOOK, I HELPED SMOOTH THINGS OUT, SO YOU COULD COME IN. TO CONSULT.
I KNEW YOU HAD TO STAY INVOLVED IN THIS. YOU WOULD, ONE WAY OR ANOTHER. AND I GET IT.
BUT THERE'S A LOT OF CONCERN INSIDE O.M.I. THAT MAYBE YOU TOLD AARON JUST HOW CIRCUMSTANTIAL--
FUCK YOU, VINCE.
I'M TELLING YOU WHAT PEOPLE ARE SAYING. WITHOUT THE CONFESSION... HE'S GOING TO WALK.
NO. HE'S GOING TO BE ACCOUNTABLE.

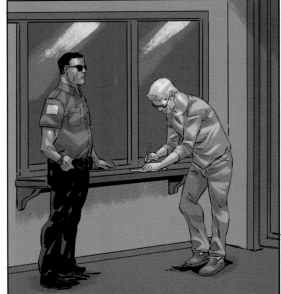

HAVE A SEAT. I'LL GO GET HIM...

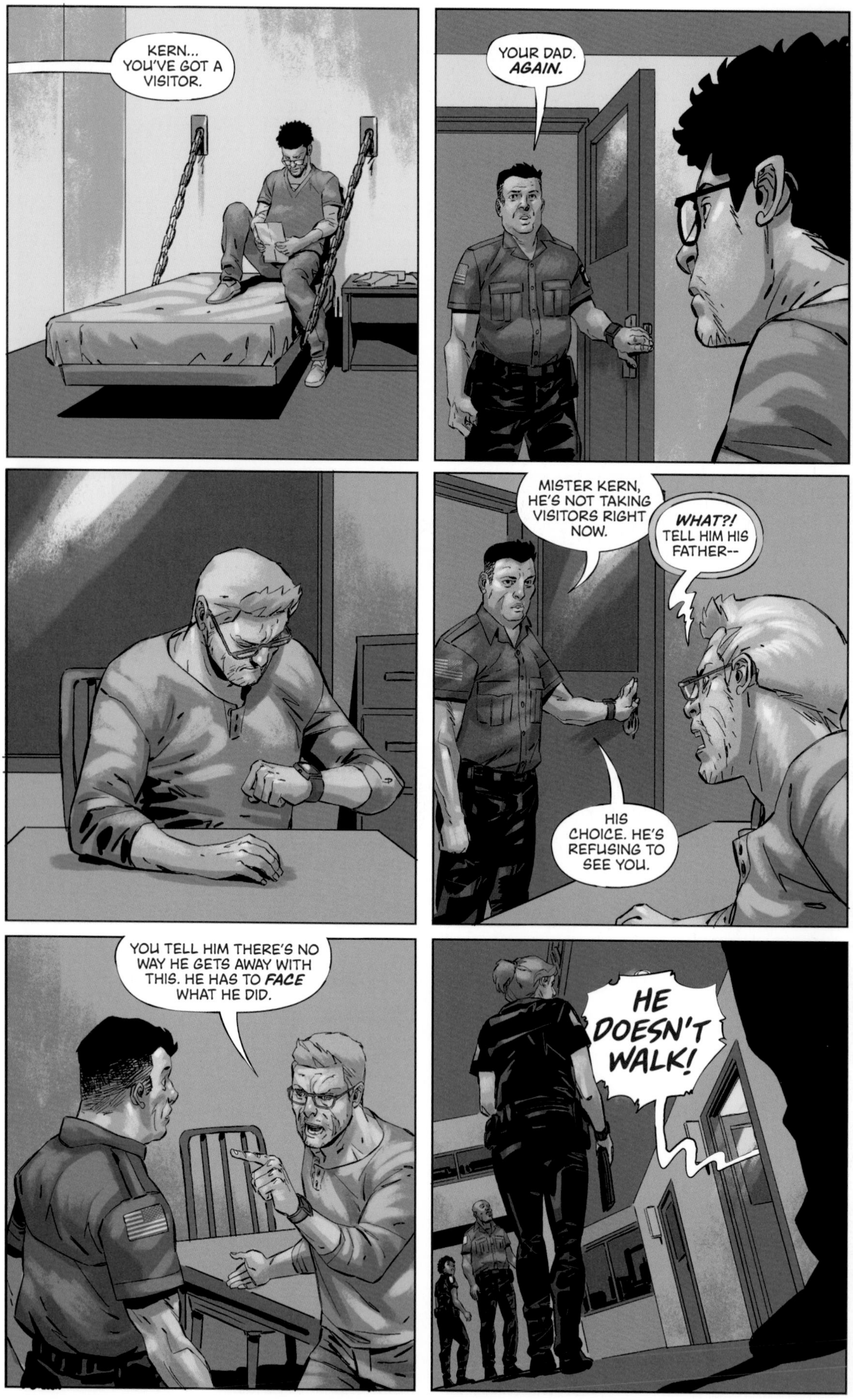
KERN... YOU'VE GOT A VISITOR.
YOUR DAD. AGAIN.
MISTER KERN, HE'S NOT TAKING VISITORS RIGHT NOW.
WHAT?! TELL HIM HIS FATHER--
HIS CHOICE. HE'S REFUSING TO SEE YOU.
YOU TELL HIM THERE'S NO WAY HE GETS AWAY WITH THIS. HE HAS TO FACE WHAT HE DID.
HE DOESN'T WALK!

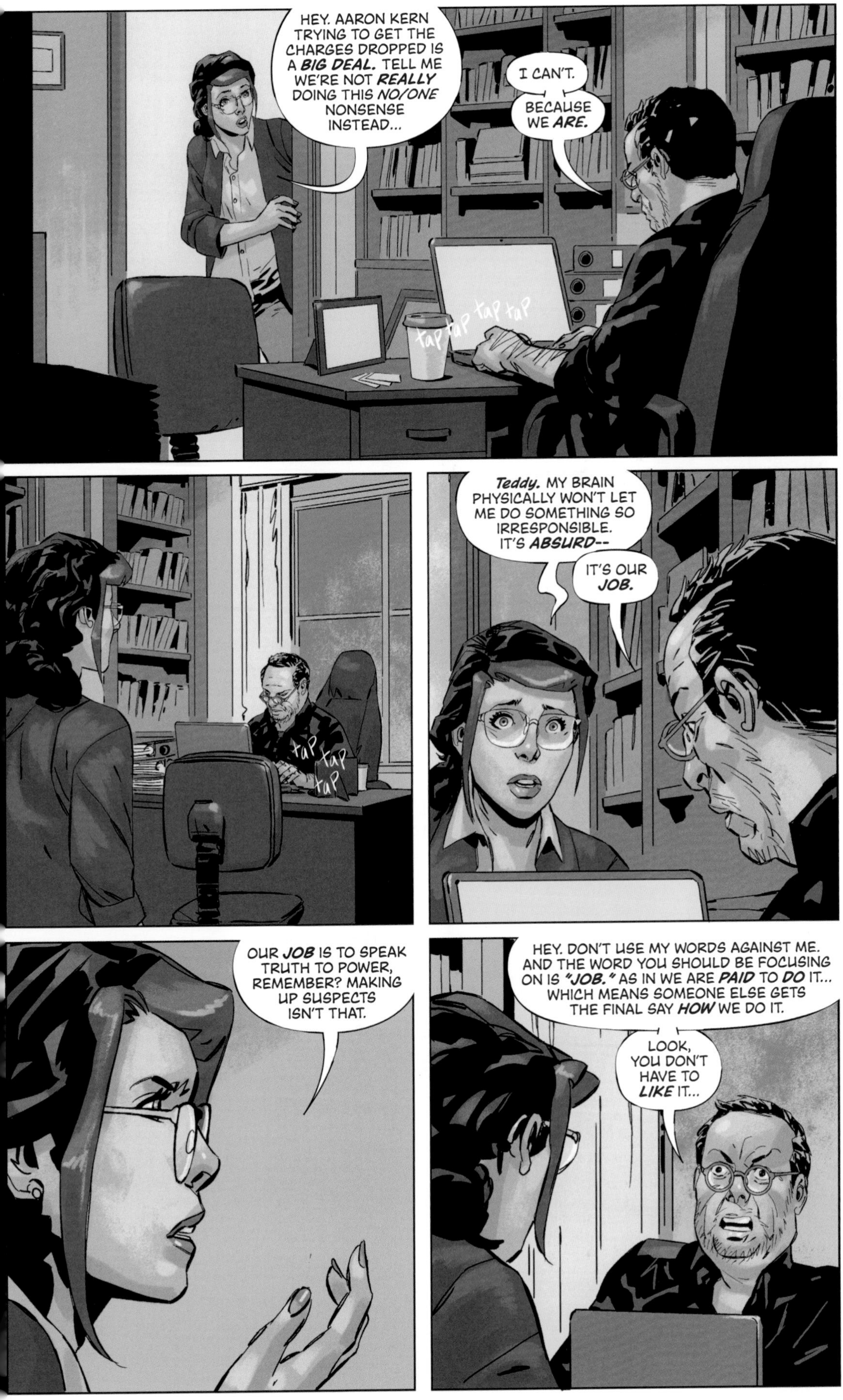
HEY. AARON KERN TRYING TO GET THE CHARGES DROPPED IS A BIG DEAL. TELL ME WE'RE NOT REALLY DOING THIS NO/ONE NONSENSE INSTEAD...
I CAN'T.
BECAUSE WE ARE.
tap tap tap tap
tap tap tap
Teddy. MY BRAIN PHYSICALLY WON'T LET ME DO SOMETHING SO IRRESPONSIBLE. IT'S ABSURD--
IT'S OUR JOB.
OUR JOB IS TO SPEAK TRUTH TO POWER, REMEMBER? MAKING UP SUSPECTS ISN'T THAT.
HEY. DON'T USE MY WORDS AGAINST ME. AND THE WORD YOU SHOULD BE FOCUSING ON IS "JOB." AS IN WE ARE PAID TO DO IT... WHICH MEANS SOMEONE ELSE GETS THE FINAL SAY HOW WE DO IT.
LOOK, YOU DON'T HAVE TO LIKE IT...

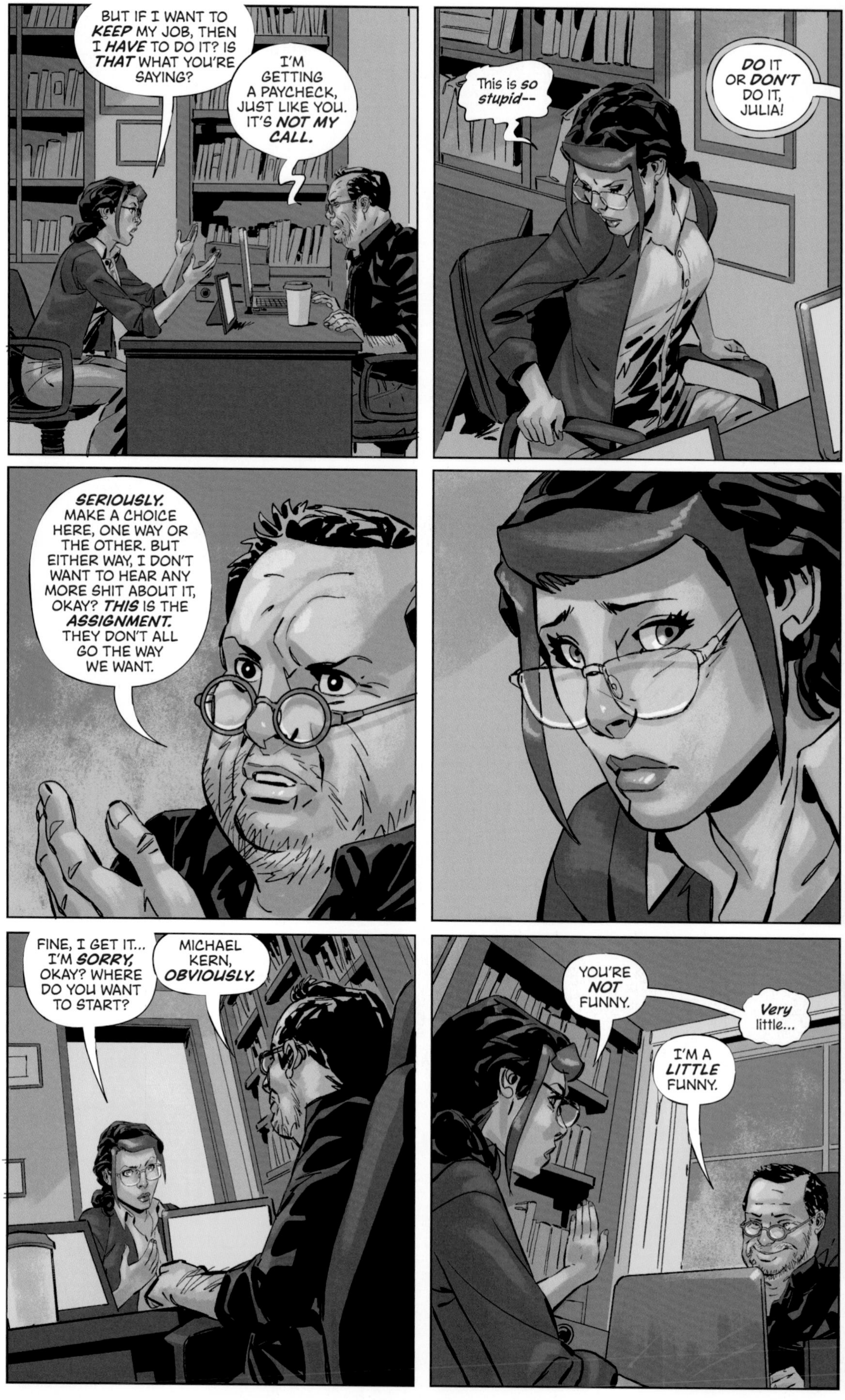
BUT IF I WANT TO KEEP MY JOB, THEN I HAVE TO DO IT? IS THAT WHAT YOU'RE SAYING?
I'M GETTING A PAYCHECK, JUST LIKE YOU. IT'S NOT MY CALL.
This is so stupid--
DO IT OR DON'T DO IT, JULIA!
SERIOUSLY. MAKE A CHOICE HERE, ONE WAY OR THE OTHER. BUT EITHER WAY, I DON'T WANT TO HEAR ANY MORE SHIT ABOUT IT, OKAY? THIS IS THE ASSIGNMENT. THEY DON'T ALL GO THE WAY WE WANT.
FINE, I GET IT... I'M SORRY, OKAY? WHERE DO YOU WANT TO START?
MICHAEL KERN, OBVIOUSLY.
YOU'RE NOT FUNNY.
I'M A LITTLE FUNNY.
Very little...

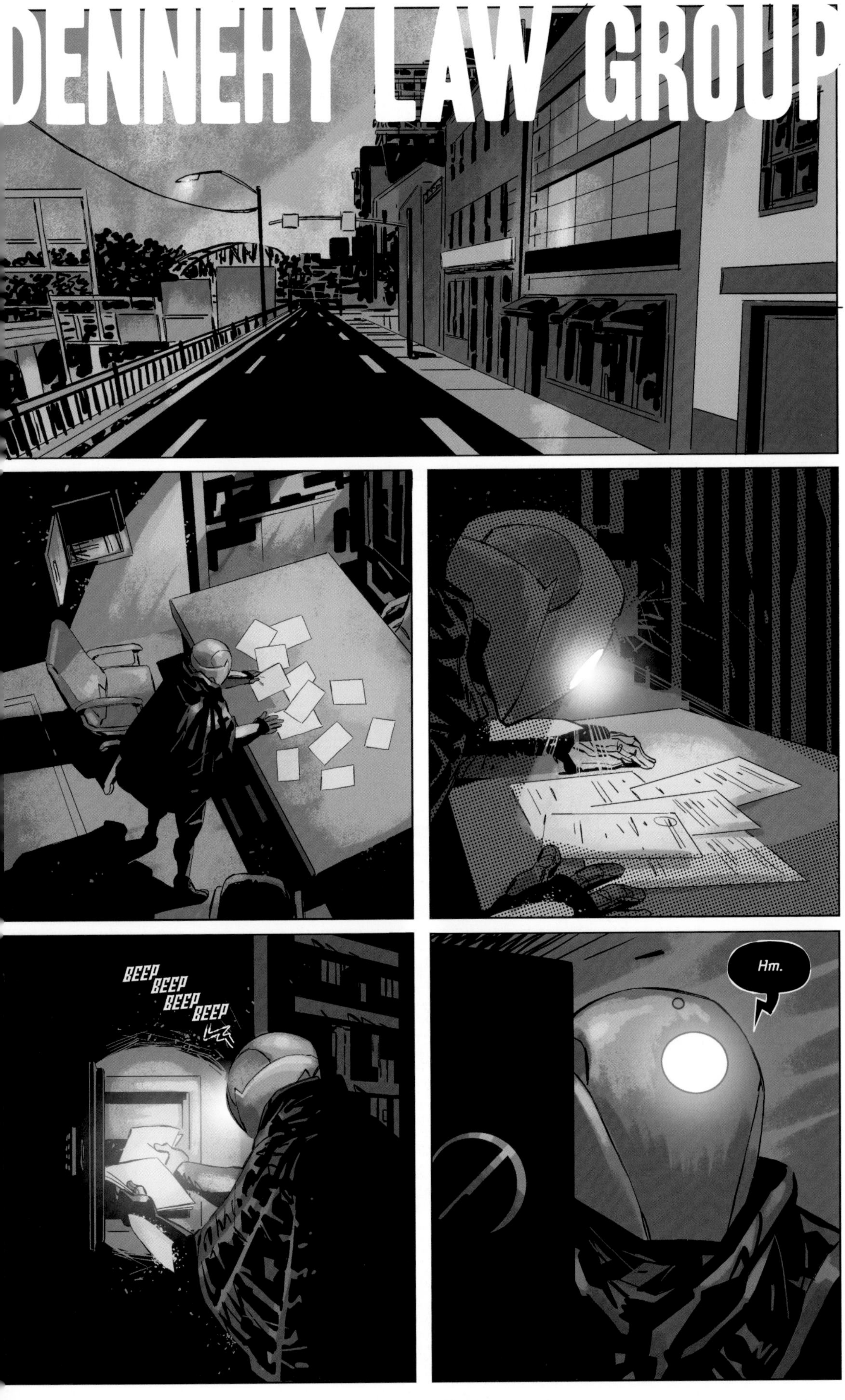
DENNEHY LAW GROUP
BEEP BEEP BEEP BEEP
Hm.

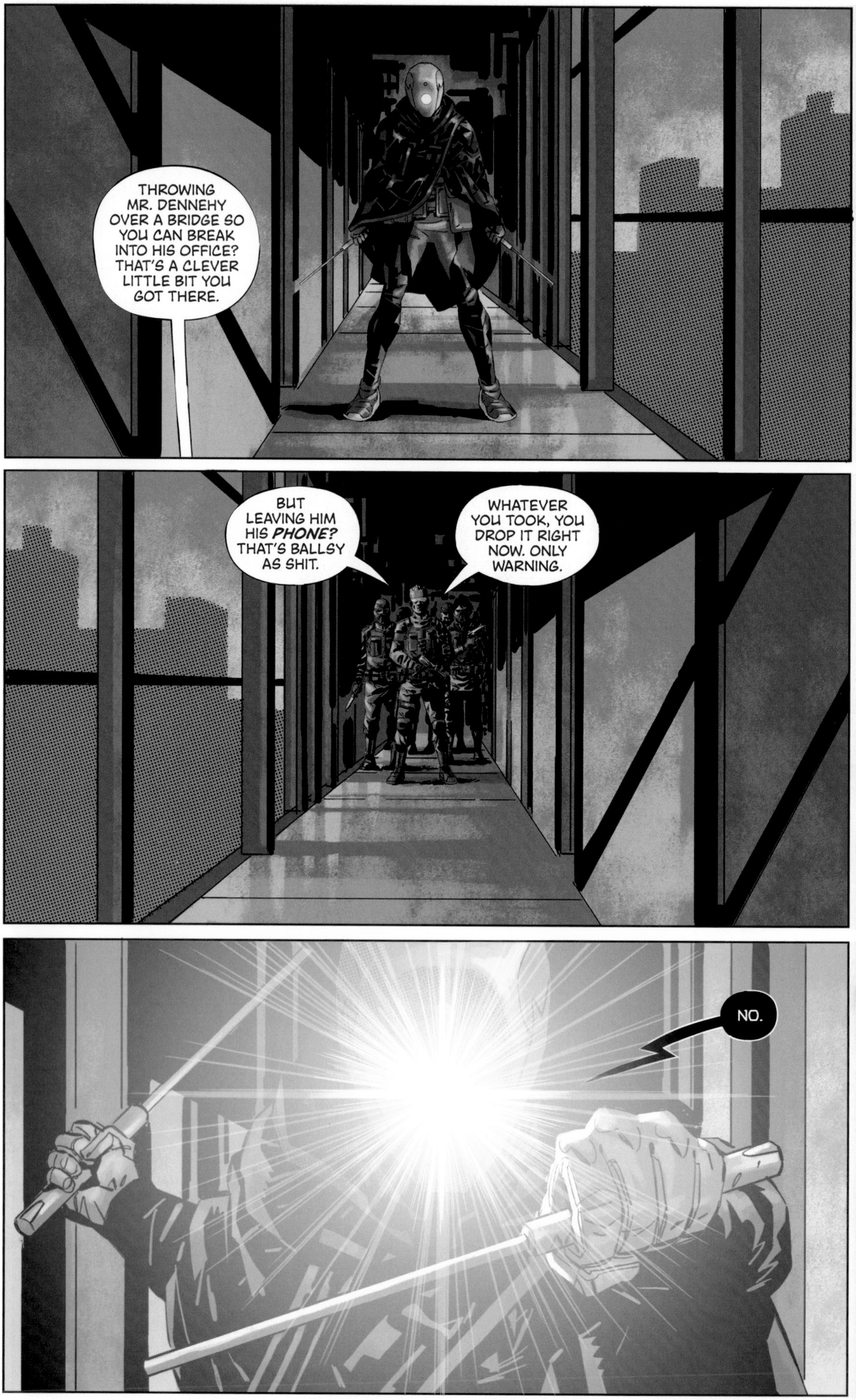
THROWING MR. DENNEHY OVER A BRIDGE SO YOU CAN BREAK INTO HIS OFFICE? THAT'S A CLEVER LITTLE BIT YOU GOT THERE.
BUT LEAVING HIM HIS *PHONE?* THAT'S BALLSY AS SHIT.
WHATEVER YOU TOOK, YOU DROP IT RIGHT NOW. ONLY WARNING.
NO.

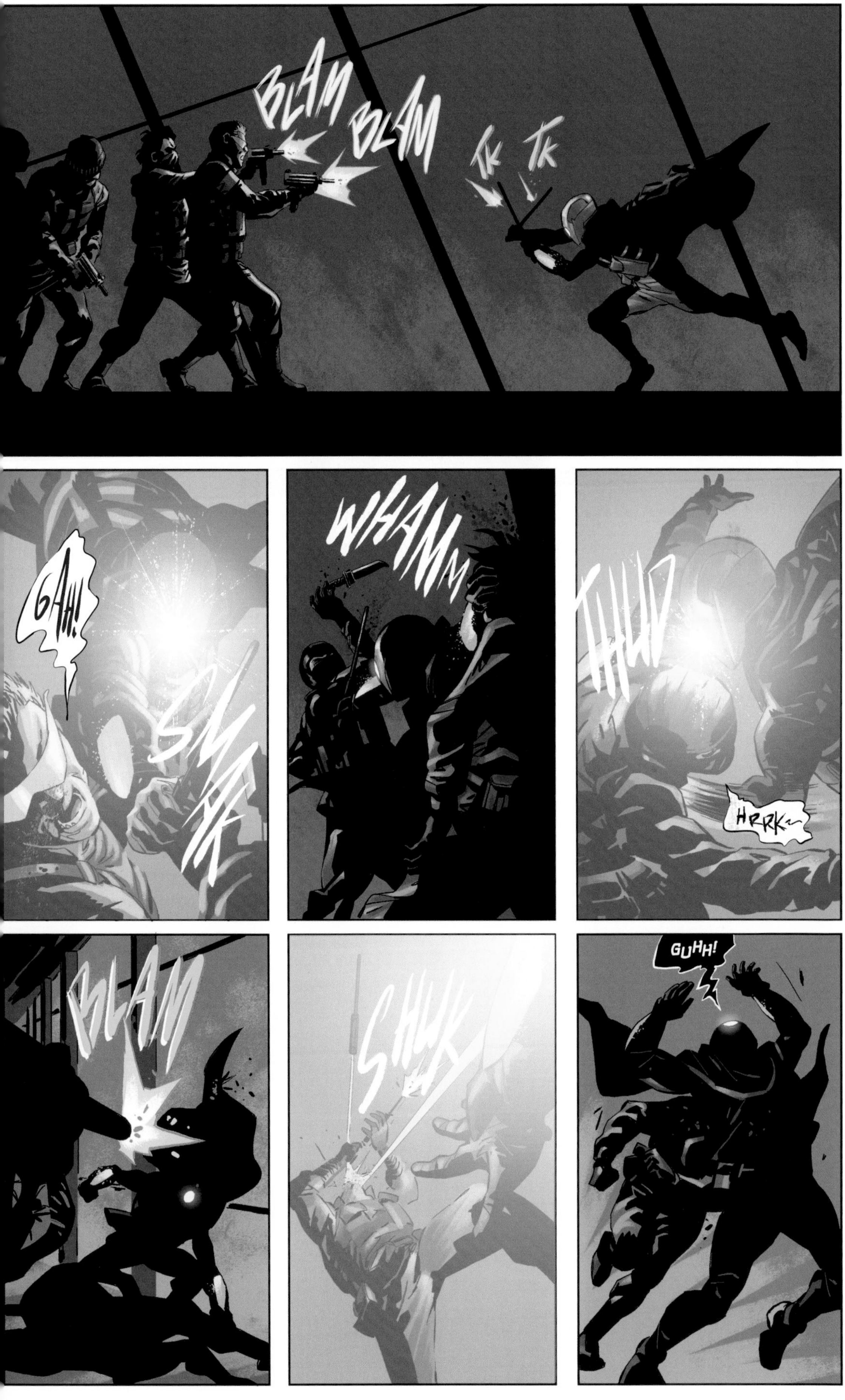
BLAM
BLAM
TK
TK
GAH!
SMAK
WHAMM
THUD
HRRK
BLAM
SHUK
GUHH!

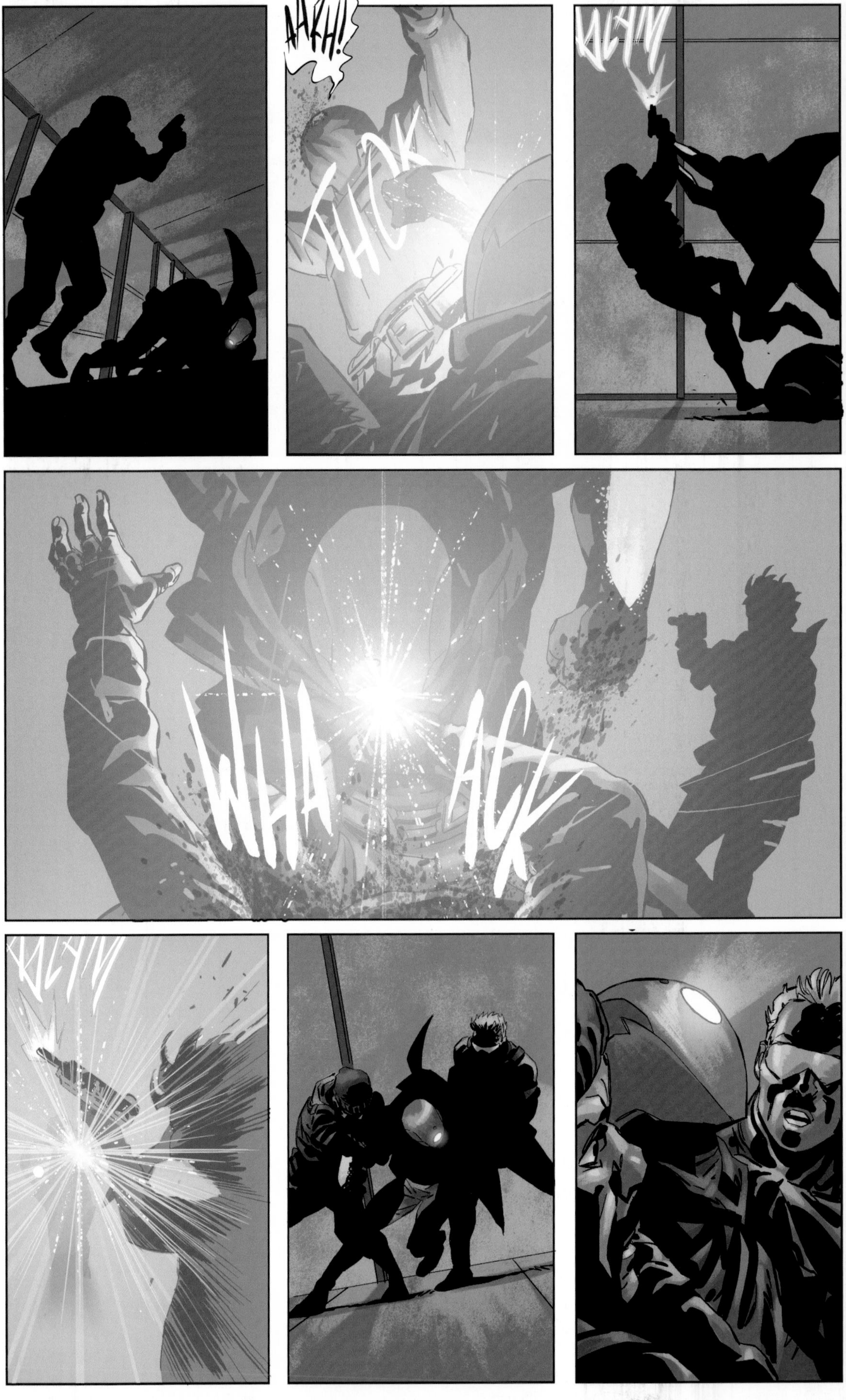
AARH!
THCK
WHA ACK

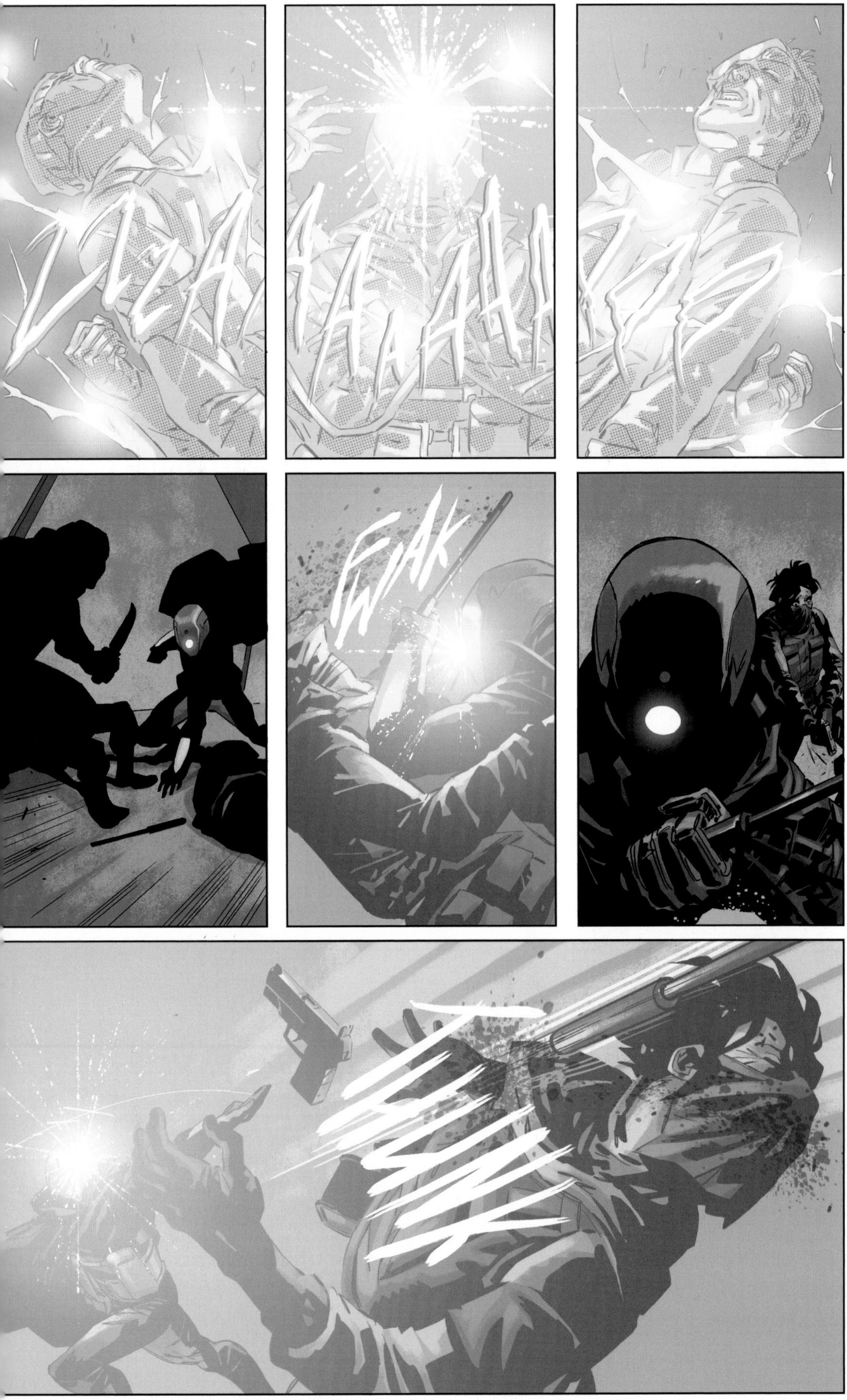
FWAK
THWUNK

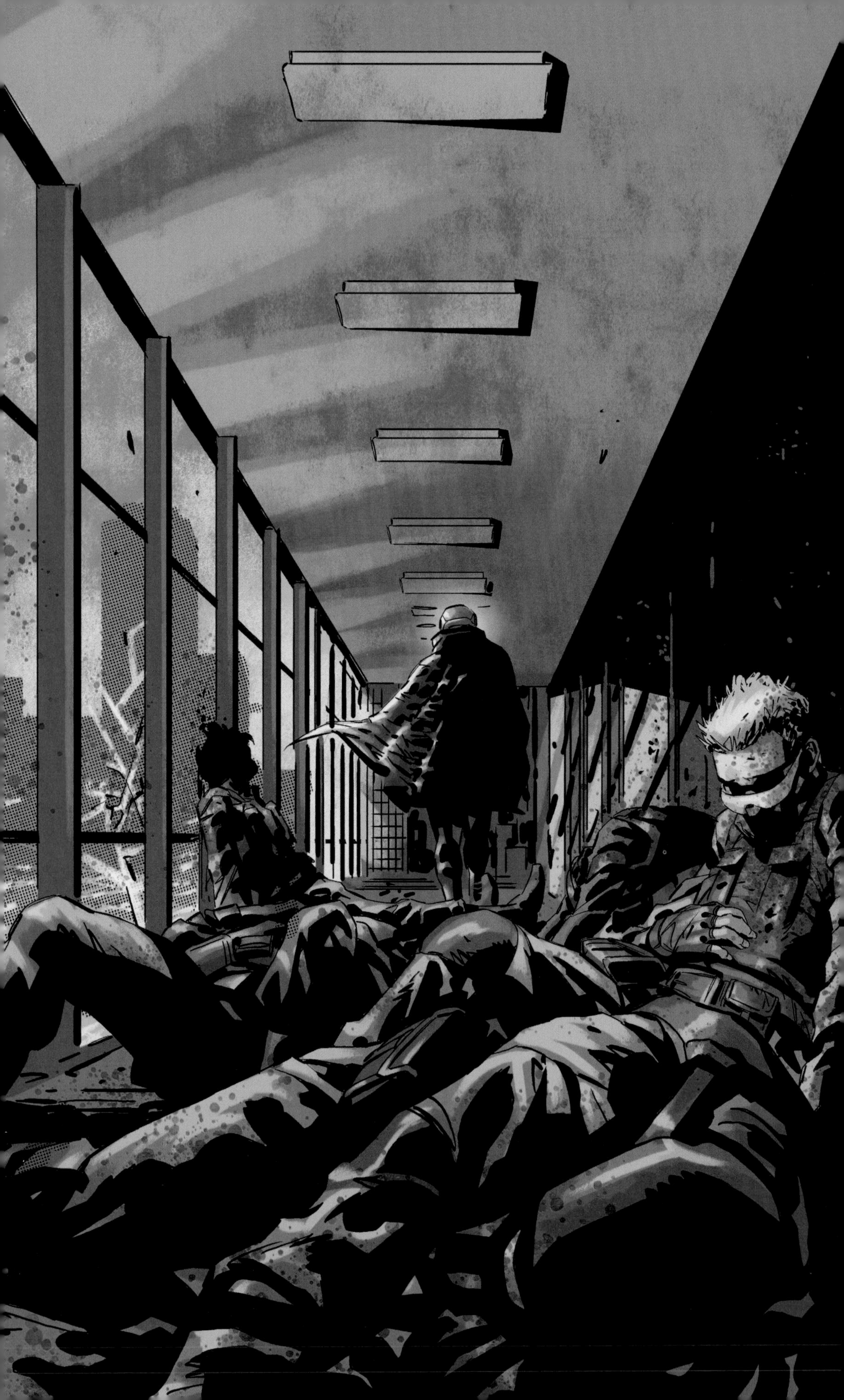

Aaron Kern charges dropped

Saturday July 15, 2023

Alejandro Rios
Pittsburgh Ledger

Pittsburgh, PA— Aaron Kern, otherwise known as Richard Roe and the alleged "Accountability Killer," is slated to be released from police custody today.

After recanting his confession earlier this week, defense attorney Roger Dennehy successfully petitioned Judge Akins to drop all charges against Kern, citing a lack of physical evidence and the questionable nature of his detention. With District Attorney Foster reportedly unprepared to proceed, Judge Akins granted the dismissal, leading to Kern's release. For now, it appears Kern will not face prosecution.

"In light of recent events, the active "convoy" events...

through physical intimidation," said District Attorney George Foster, during a press conference announcing the decision to not pursue charges against Kern. "Given the lack of physical evidence against Mister Kern and the questionable nature of his arrest, it is in the best interest and, more importantly, justice to...

Kern's developments ...g series ...ment, as well as ...ction between Kern ...ent killer.

Kern was originally apprehended during a raid at the Carrie Furnaces this ...

including real estate dev... Capel, Three Rivers coach Nathan Cade, P3... Tobias North, and, tragica... own brother. All of thes... have occurred while Kern... in custody.

But while the killer has le... notes claiming to be "the rea... Roe," this assailant also ma... alert Kern via a letter– that s... made its way past prison se... before the murder of Tobia... This connection raises... questions about the nature o... potential involvement and wh... might entail once he's relea... custody.

> *IT'S AN ABSOLUTE TRAGEDY THAT THE DA'S ENTIRE CASE RESTED UPON A NOW-RECANTED CONFESSION.*

> *ARE YOU TELLING ME THERE WAS NO PHYSICAL EVIDENCE LINKING HIM TO THE CRIMES?! NONE?!*

> *FAILURE TO PROSECUTE IS EITHER GROSS INCOMPETENCE OR WE HAVE THE MOST CORRUPT CRIMINAL JUSTICE SYSTEM IN PITTSBURGH HISTORY.*

> *AND I FOR ONE AM ABSOLUTELY DISGUSTED THAT A SICK SON OF A BITCH LIKE AARON KERN IS ALLOWED TO BREATHE FREE AIR.*

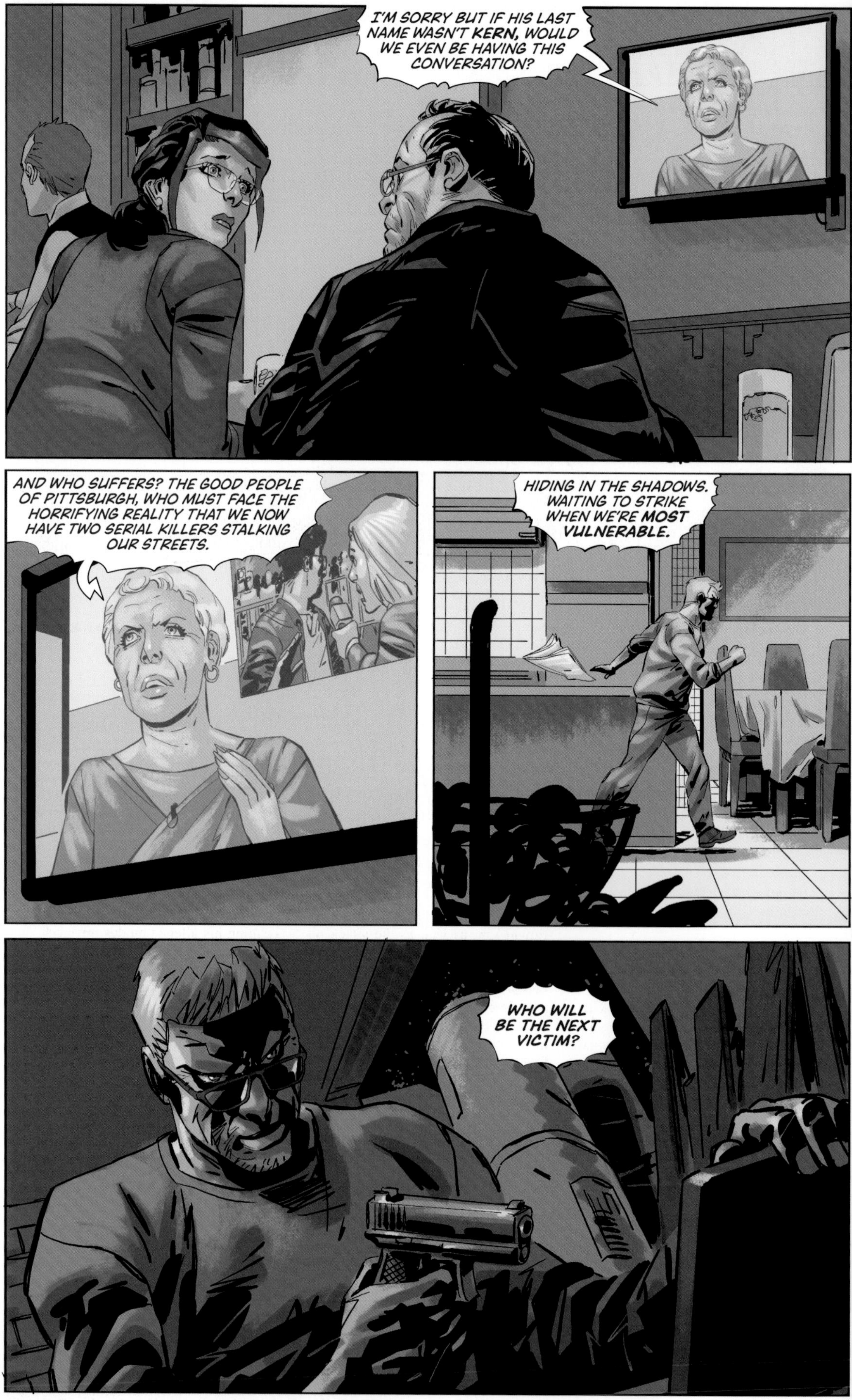
I'M SORRY BUT IF HIS LAST NAME WASN'T KERN, WOULD WE EVEN BE HAVING THIS CONVERSATION?
AND WHO SUFFERS? THE GOOD PEOPLE OF PITTSBURGH, WHO MUST FACE THE HORRIFYING REALITY THAT WE NOW HAVE TWO SERIAL KILLERS STALKING OUR STREETS.
HIDING IN THE SHADOWS. WAITING TO STRIKE WHEN WE'RE MOST VULNERABLE.
WHO WILL BE THE NEXT VICTIM?

Pittsburgh Ledger

FIRST PUBLISHED 1789   Wednesday July 12, 2023   **$3.00**

Aaron Kern at his trial.   Geraldo Borges/Ledger

"I'm innocent"
Aaron Kern recants confession

Alejandro Rios
Pittsburgh Ledger

Pittsburgh, PA— Aaron Kern, the accused "accountability killer" better known as Richard Roe, recanted his confession late last night. Kern's statement, relayed through his new attorney, Roger Dennehy– a prominent figure in Pittsburgh's legal landscape– claims that his confession was coerced during an unlawful detention, raising questions about the integrity of the investigation.

Kern, the son of former Pittsburgh Police Assistant Chief of Operations Ben Kern, had previously identified himself as the notorious Richard Roe, claiming responsibility for the murders of Dr. Julian Colon and Edwin Lin, as well as the attack on State Senator Noah Kemp in his home last fall. Kern was arrested during a raid at the Carrie Blast Furnaces this past December, in connection with the series of high-profile murders of men whose alleged wrongdoing was first exposed by the digital activist now known as NO/ONE.

However, despite recovering items associated with the killings, including a mask that fit the description of the one worn by Richard Roe, authorities did not recover the weapon used in the attacks.

District Attorney George Foster made a statement shortly after last night's dramatic turn, expressing confidence that police already have the "Accountability Killer" in custody and plan to move forward with their case. "We remain steadfast and undeterred. We believe our evidence will show that Aaron Kern is guilty and we look forward to our day in court."

In the months since Kern's arrest, multiple "copycat" murders have taken place, all occurring while Kern has been in custody. None of these attacks have bore any direct connection to Kern, except for echoing his alleged modus operandi to "hold the corrupt accountable." That all changed this past March, however, when real estate developer Louis Capel was gunned down at a gallery opening.

Ballistics tests matched the weapon used in Capel's murder to the .38 special revolver used in the murder of Dr. Colon and Edwin Lin last year. The same firearm has also been linked to the recent killings of Three Rivers University coach Nathan Cade and P3 executive Tobias North, as well as the tragic murder of Kern's own brother, Michael.

The killer has left notes claiming to be the original Richard Roe.

>_ **071223 aaron kern candid.mp3**
JULY 12 2023

published on http://00110000.info/

>_ **071323 warning video_roger dennehy.mp4**
JULY 13 2023

published on http://00110000.info/

*"You snatch justice from the wronged and rob
the community of healing."*

>_ **071523 roger dennehy**
JULY 15 2023

published on http://00110000.info/

>_ **071523 trust your instincts**
JULY 15 2023

published on http://00110000.info/

*"Trust your instincts. Aaron Kern is a
murderer."*

FIRST PUBLISHED 1789   Saturday July 15, 2023 $3.00

Aaron Kern charges dropped

Julia Paige
Pittsburgh Ledger

Pittsburgh, PA— Aaron Kern, otherwise known as Richard Roe and the alleged "Accountability Killer," is slated to be released from police custody today.

After recanting his confession earlier this week, defense attorney Roger Dennehy successfully petitioned Judge Akins to dismiss all charges against Kern, citing the lack of physical evidence and the questionable nature of his client's detention. With District Attorney Foster reportedly unprepared to proceed, Judge Akins granted the dismissal, leading to Kern's release. For now, it appears Kern will not face prosecution.

"In light of recent events, namely the active 'copycat' killer claiming to also be the original Richard Roe, we were informed by Mister Kern's attorney that their client is recanting his confession. They now maintain that said confession was coerced through physical intimidation," said District Attorney George Foster, during a press conference announcing the decision to not pursue charges against Kern. "Given the lack of physical evidence against Mister Kern and the questionable nature of his arrest, it is in the best interest of our office and, more importantly, the pursuit of justice to take a step back and reassess."

Further complicating Kern's release are recent developments surrounding the ongoing series of murders attributed to the accountability movement, as well as a potential connection between Kern and the current killer.

Kern was originally apprehended during a raid at the Carrie Blast Furnaces this past winter, with rumors swirling that NO/ONE assisted in his capture. But while investigators recovered several items associated with the original killings, they did not find the murder weapon. This weapon—known to be a .38 special revolver—has been linked to a string of recent murders, including real estate developer Louis Capel, Three Rivers University coach Nathan Cade, P3 executive Tobias North, and, tragically, Kern's own brother. All of these murders have occurred while Kern has been in custody.

But while the killer has left behind notes claiming to be "the real Richard Roe," this assailant also managed to alert Kern via a letter– that somehow made its way past prison screeners– before the murder of Tobias North. This connection raises troubling questions about the nature of Kern's potential involvement and what that might entail once he's released from custody.

Law enforcement is now scrambling to find new evidence that could definitively link Kern to any murders over the past year. The killer's notes, which seek to appropriate Kern's admitted identity, have further muddied the waters, complicating the investigation and blurring the lines between Kern's alleged actions and those of an apparent copycat.

Vigilante NO/ONE doxxes Kern attorney

Alejandro Rios
Pittsburgh Ledger

Pittsburgh, PA— In the wake of Aaron Kern recanting his confession, digital activist turned vigilante NO/ONE has released audio allegedly recorded during a private conversation between Kern and his father, former Pittsburgh Police Assistant Chief of Operations, Ben Kern. The recording, which surfaced just hours after Kern's hiring of high-profile defense attorney Roger Dennehy, appears to have been recorded during Kern's time in Allegheny County Jail.

The recording captures an emotional exchange between Aaron and Ben Kern. In it, Ben expresses concern for Aaron's brother, Michael, who has struggled with addiction. The conversation quickly shifts to the recent murder of real estate developer Louis Capel, with Aaron questioning his father's motivations for visiting him in prison.

As Ben reveals details about the murder—specifically the killer's chilling note declaring, "I AM THE REAL RICHARD ROE"—Aaron's skepticism about his father's intentions becomes evident. The tension escalates as Aaron suggests that his father only came to see him due to the actions of a "copycat" killer, reflecting a fractured family dynamic and seemingly bolstering Aaron's earlier confession that he was, in fact, the original Richard Roe.

In a subsequent statement posted to his website, NO/ONE then directly addressed Roger Dennehy, condemning him for defending what they describe as "corrupt interests." The digital activist's message warns Dennehy to recuse himself from the "Richard Roe" case, alleging that he has manipulated the justice system to protect wealthy and guilty clients.

Shortly after this warning, NO/ONE released files outlining alleged transgressions committed by Dennehy, including witness payoffs, bribery, and jury tampering. These allegations, if true, could have severe implications for Dennehy's career and the integrity of the legal process in Kern's case.

In a final chilling message, NO/ONE assured the people of Pittsburgh that they would not let Aaron Kern evade justice. "Aaron Kern is a murderer. Aaron Kern is guilty. He must face justice," the message stated, emphasizing their commitment to holding him accountable alongside the unnamed copycat killer.

As tensions surrounding the "accountability movement" continue to escalate, the interplay between Kern's release, NO/ONE's intervention, and the mounting pressure on Dennehy creates a volatile mix that could redefine the course of this high-profile case.

The Drop

PRESENTS

WHO IS NO/ONE
WITH/JULIA PAIGE

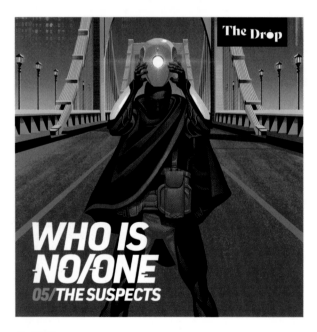

16 JULY

05/The Suspects

WHO IS NO/ONE

20:38   -4:15

Cops have no clue

Pittsburgh police struggle for leads in murder of Aaron Kern's attorney, Roger Dennehy

Alejandro Rios
Pittsburgh Ledger

Pittsburgh, PA— Following the release of Aaron Kern, alleged to be the original "Accountability Killer," Richard Roe, embattled defense attorney Roger Dennehy was found murdered in his upscale Shadyside home Saturday morning, echoing the patterns of earlier accountability killings. Like the other victims, Dennehy was shot four times in the chest, raising questions about the motives behind his death.

Dennehy's death comes on the heels of his successful representation of Kern, who had initially confessed to the Accountability murders but was released just over one week ago, after recanting his confession—a controversial decision that was met with public outrage and renewed scrutiny of Pittsburgh's criminal justice system. It also put Dennehy in the crosshairs of digital activist turned vigilante, NO/ONE, who released files outlining alleged transgressions committed by Dennehy, including witness payoffs, bribery, and jury tampering.

In the aftermath of Dennehy's murder, NO/ONE released a statement addressing the situation, asserting their non-involvement in Dennehy's death.

District Attorney George Foster condemned Dennehy's murder and addressed rumors circulating within Pittsburgh's legal community that some in his office might view Dennehy's death as convenient. "Roger Dennehy was a skilled attorney who served his clients, regardless of public opinion. The notion that anyone in law enforcement would be pleased by his death is not only false but deeply troubling," Foster said. "We are fully committed to assisting in the investigation to bring those responsible to justice."

Dennehy, who had built a lucrative career defending clients accused of everything from drug trafficking to murder, was no stranger to controversy. His success in the courtroom often made him a target of public disdain, with critics accusing him of enabling criminal behavior. However, colleagues remember him as a formidable legal mind who believed deeply in the right to a fair defense, regardless of the crime.

Dennehy's murder adds another layer of complexity to an already volatile situation. The timing of his death has led to widespread speculation about potential connections between the case and his assassination.

JULY 22 2023
PITTSBURGH LEDGER

>_ **072323 roger dennehy response.mp3**
JULY 23 2023

published on http://00110000.info/

*"This is not what our city needs.
This will not heal us."*

>_ CHAPTER SIX
AUGUST 2023

I HEAR YOU, BEN... I DO. BUT WE CAN'T DO IT.

PITTSBURGH POLICE HEADQUARTERS

LOOK, NOBODY WANTS TO NAIL YOUR KID MORE THAN ME-- *NO OFFENSE.* BUT THIS IS WAY TOO POLITICAL AT THIS POINT.

EVERYTHING'S POLITICAL.

ALL I'M ASKING YINZ TO DO IS PULL A COUPLE TRUSTED GUYS FROM THEIR USUAL DETAILS TO COVER FOR ME EVERY NOW AND THEN WHILE I GRAB A FEW HOURS' SLEEP. *THAT'S IT.* NO MORE THAN FOUR HOURS A DAY.

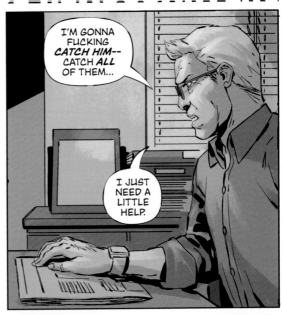

I'M GONNA FUCKING *CATCH HIM*-- CATCH *ALL* OF THEM...

I JUST NEED A LITTLE HELP.

THIS SHIT NEEDS TO *END.*

sburgh Gazett

Still no suspect in Dennehy murder

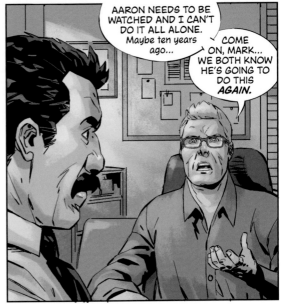

AARON NEEDS TO BE WATCHED AND I CAN'T DO IT ALL ALONE. Maybe ten years ago...

COME ON, MARK... WE BOTH KNOW HE'S GOING TO DO THIS *AGAIN.*

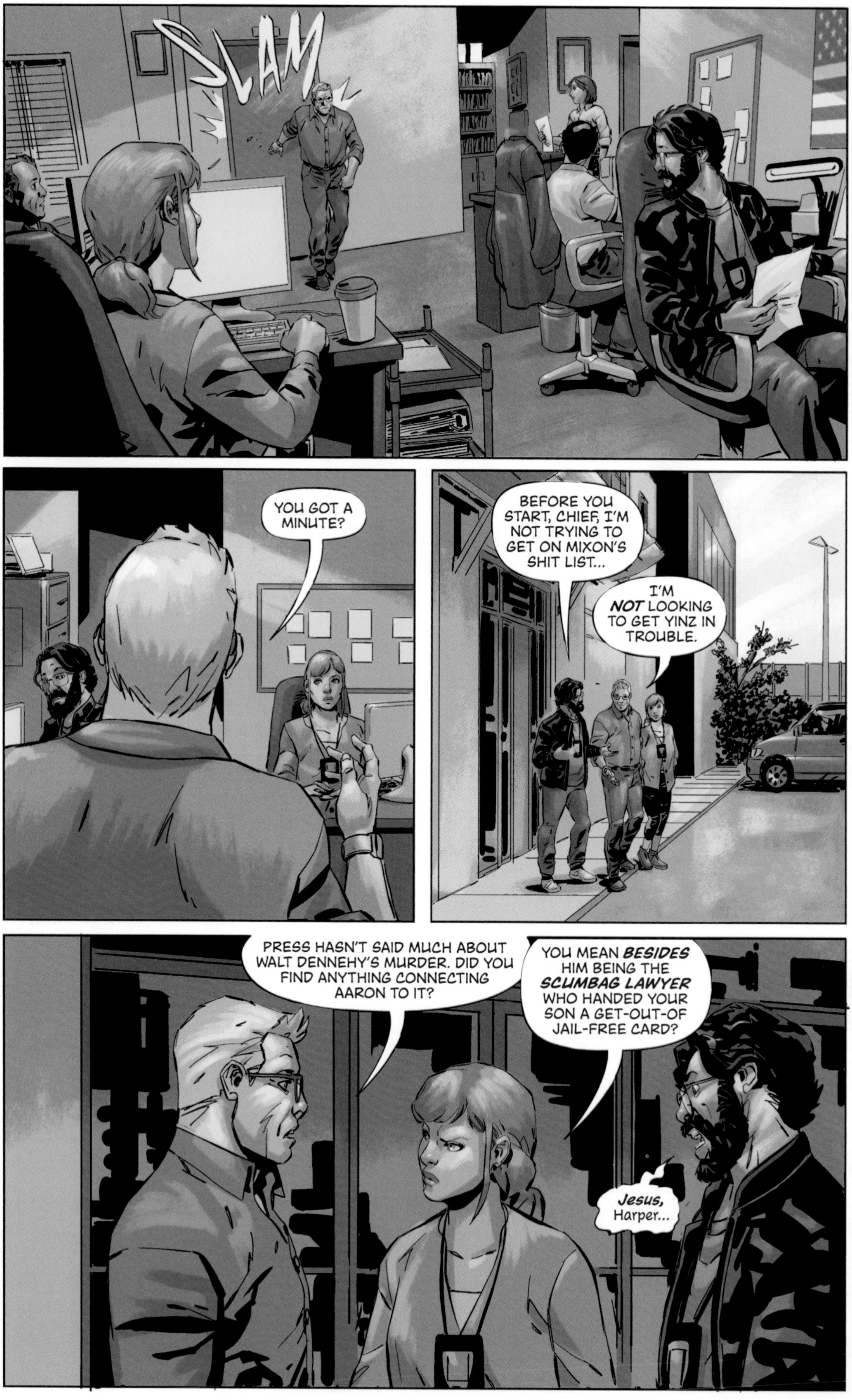
SLAM
YOU GOT A MINUTE?
BEFORE YOU START, CHIEF, I'M NOT TRYING TO GET ON MIXON'S SHIT LIST...
I'M NOT LOOKING TO GET YINZ IN TROUBLE.
PRESS HASN'T SAID MUCH ABOUT WALT DENNEHY'S MURDER. DID YOU FIND ANYTHING CONNECTING AARON TO IT?
YOU MEAN BESIDES HIM BEING THE SCUMBAG LAWYER WHO HANDED YOUR SON A GET-OUT-OF JAIL-FREE CARD?
Jesus, Harper...

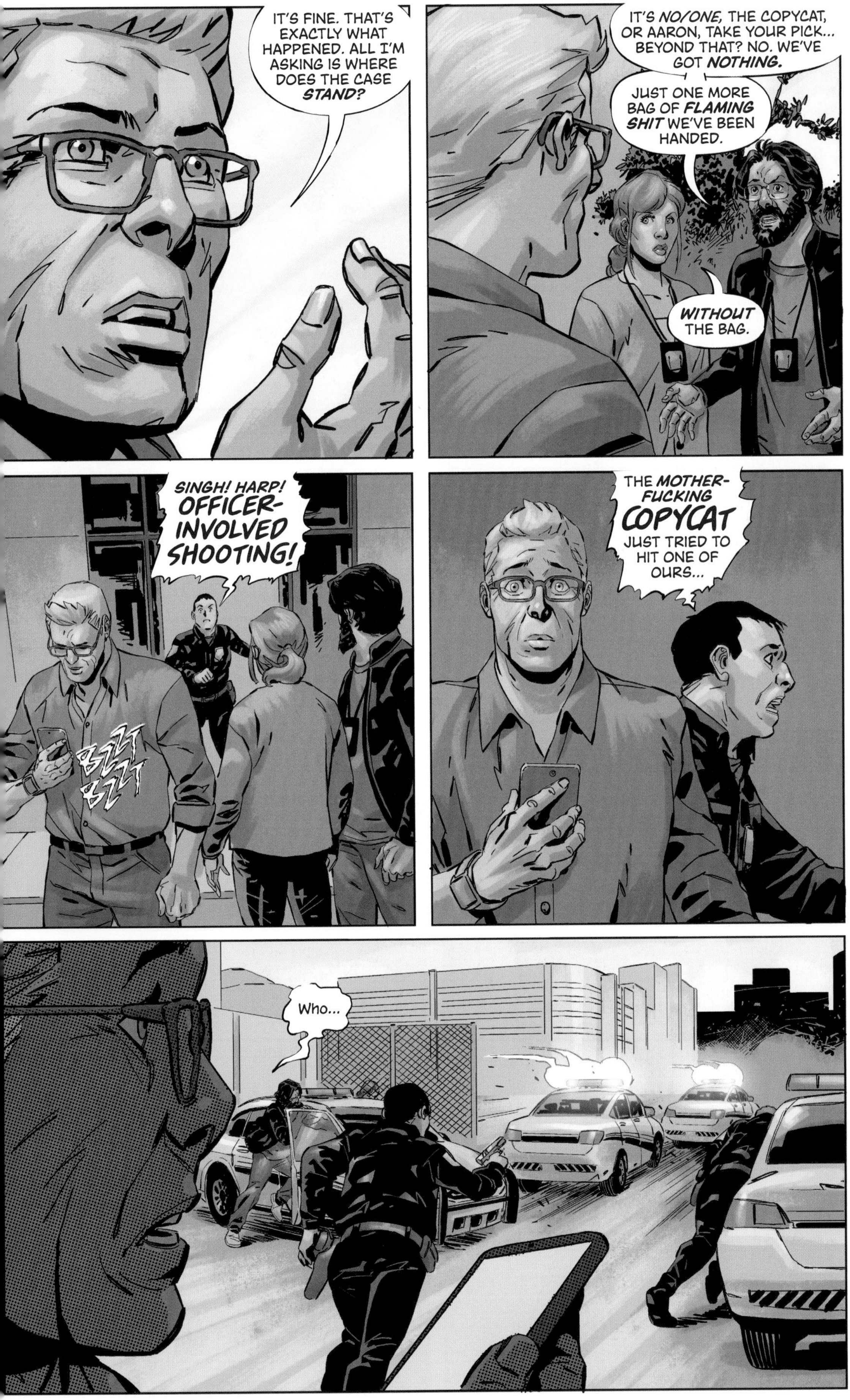
IT'S FINE. THAT'S EXACTLY WHAT HAPPENED. ALL I'M ASKING IS WHERE DOES THE CASE *STAND?*
IT'S *NO/ONE*, THE COPYCAT, OR AARON, TAKE YOUR PICK... BEYOND THAT? NO. WE'VE GOT *NOTHING.*
JUST ONE MORE BAG OF *FLAMING SHIT* WE'VE BEEN HANDED.
WITHOUT THE BAG.
SINGH! HARP! OFFICER-INVOLVED SHOOTING!
BZZT BZZT BZZT
THE *MOTHER-FUCKING* COPYCAT JUST TRIED TO HIT ONE OF OURS...
Who...

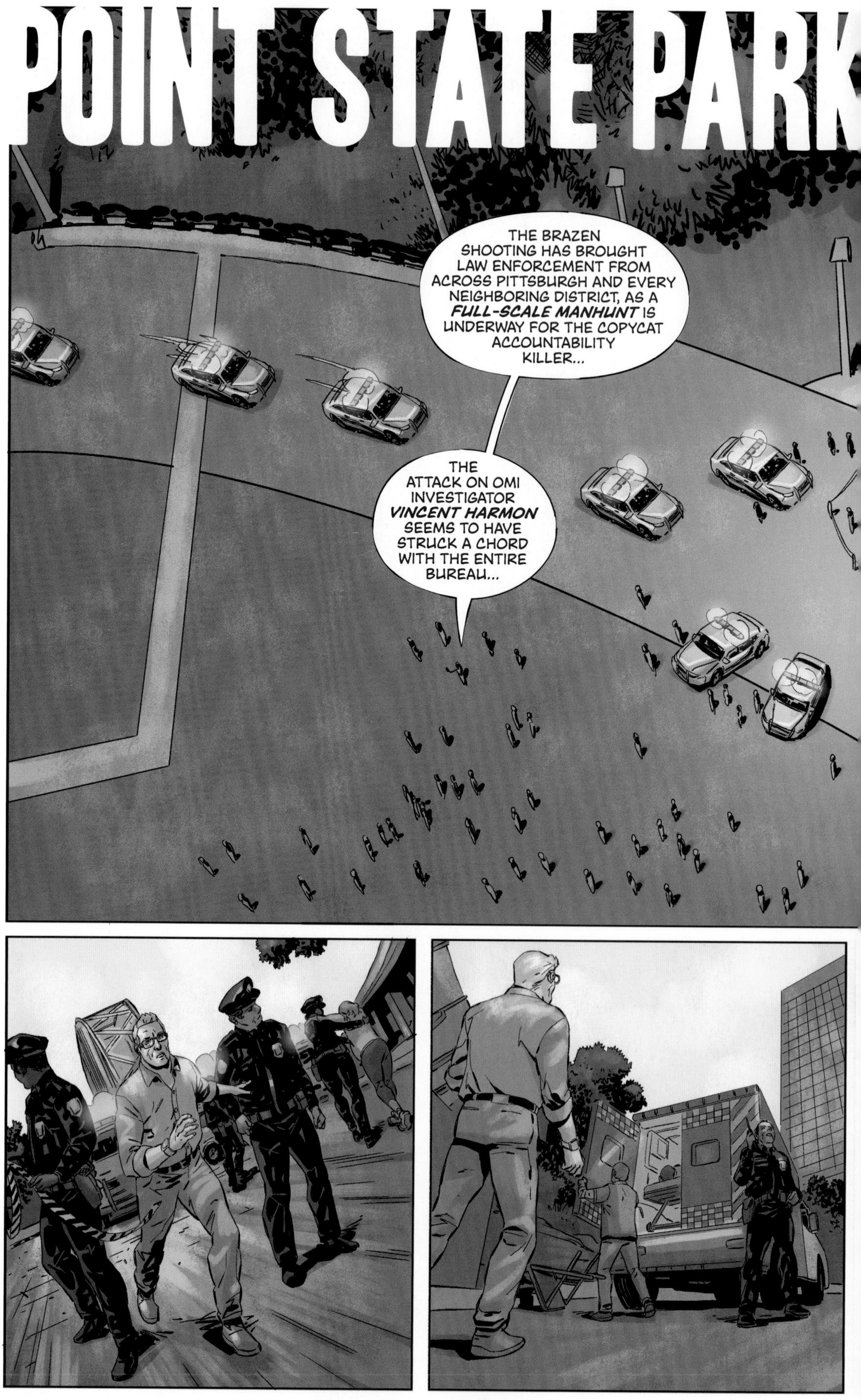
POINT STATE PARK
THE BRAZEN SHOOTING HAS BROUGHT LAW ENFORCEMENT FROM ACROSS PITTSBURGH AND EVERY NEIGHBORING DISTRICT, AS A FULL-SCALE MANHUNT IS UNDERWAY FOR THE COPYCAT ACCOUNTABILITY KILLER...
THE ATTACK ON OMI INVESTIGATOR VINCENT HARMON SEEMS TO HAVE STRUCK A CHORD WITH THE ENTIRE BUREAU...

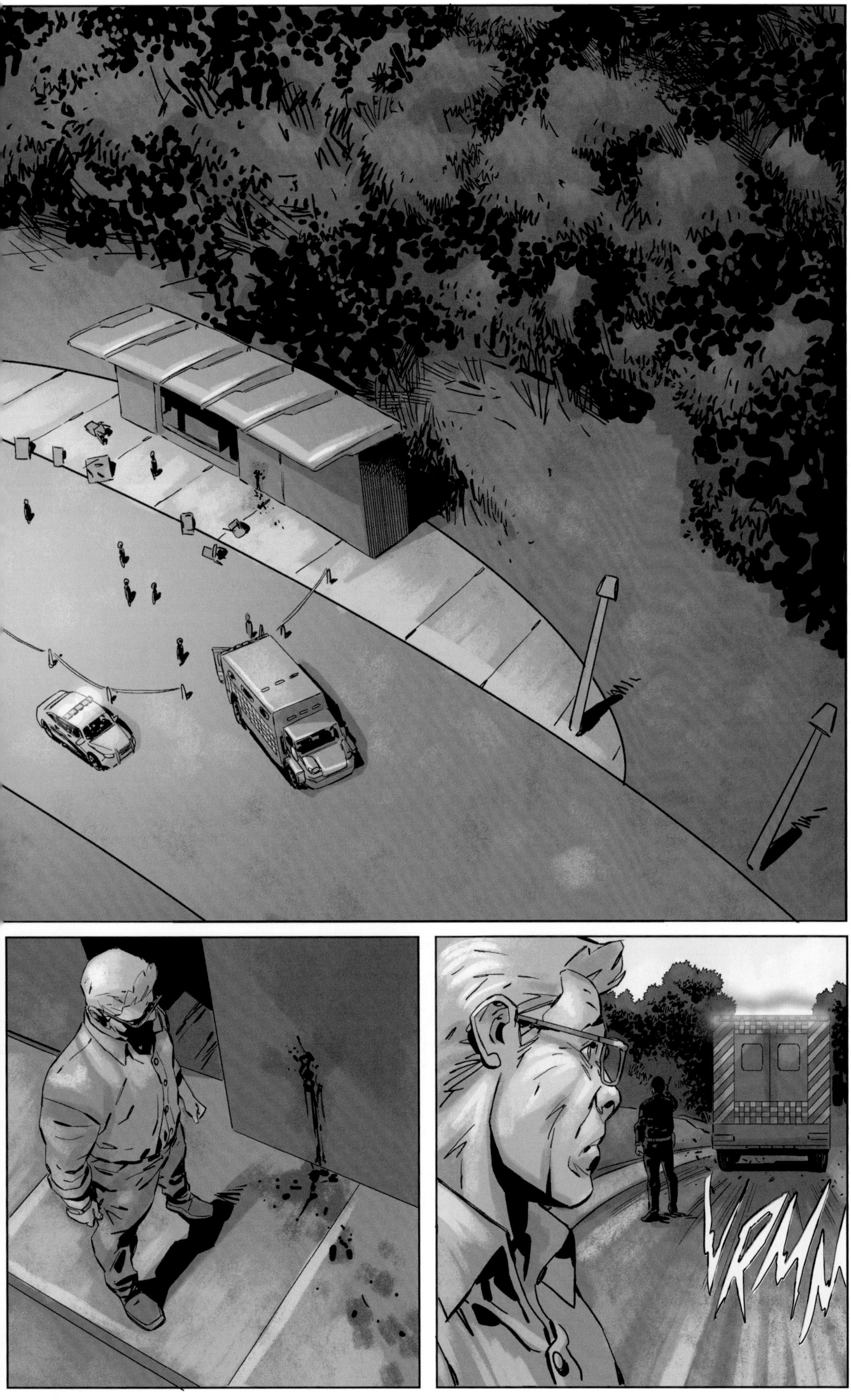
VRMM

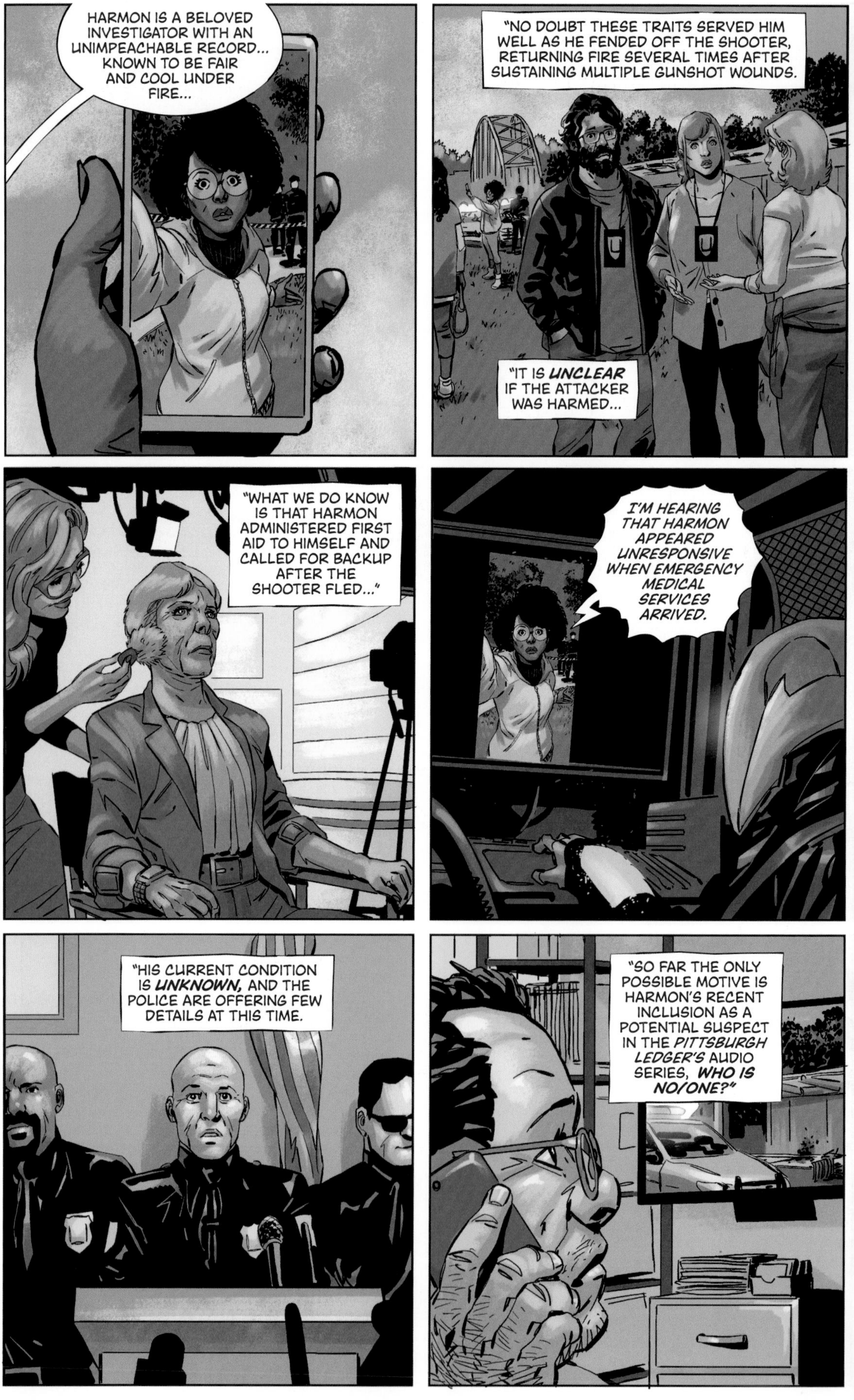
HARMON IS A BELOVED INVESTIGATOR WITH AN UNIMPEACHABLE RECORD... KNOWN TO BE FAIR AND COOL UNDER FIRE...
"NO DOUBT THESE TRAITS SERVED HIM WELL AS HE FENDED OFF THE SHOOTER, RETURNING FIRE SEVERAL TIMES AFTER SUSTAINING MULTIPLE GUNSHOT WOUNDS.
"IT IS UNCLEAR IF THE ATTACKER WAS HARMED...
"WHAT WE DO KNOW IS THAT HARMON ADMINISTERED FIRST AID TO HIMSELF AND CALLED FOR BACKUP AFTER THE SHOOTER FLED..."
I'M HEARING THAT HARMON APPEARED UNRESPONSIVE WHEN EMERGENCY MEDICAL SERVICES ARRIVED.
"HIS CURRENT CONDITION IS UNKNOWN, AND THE POLICE ARE OFFERING FEW DETAILS AT THIS TIME.
"SO FAR THE ONLY POSSIBLE MOTIVE IS HARMON'S RECENT INCLUSION AS A POTENTIAL SUSPECT IN THE PITTSBURGH LEDGER'S AUDIO SERIES, WHO IS NO/ONE?"

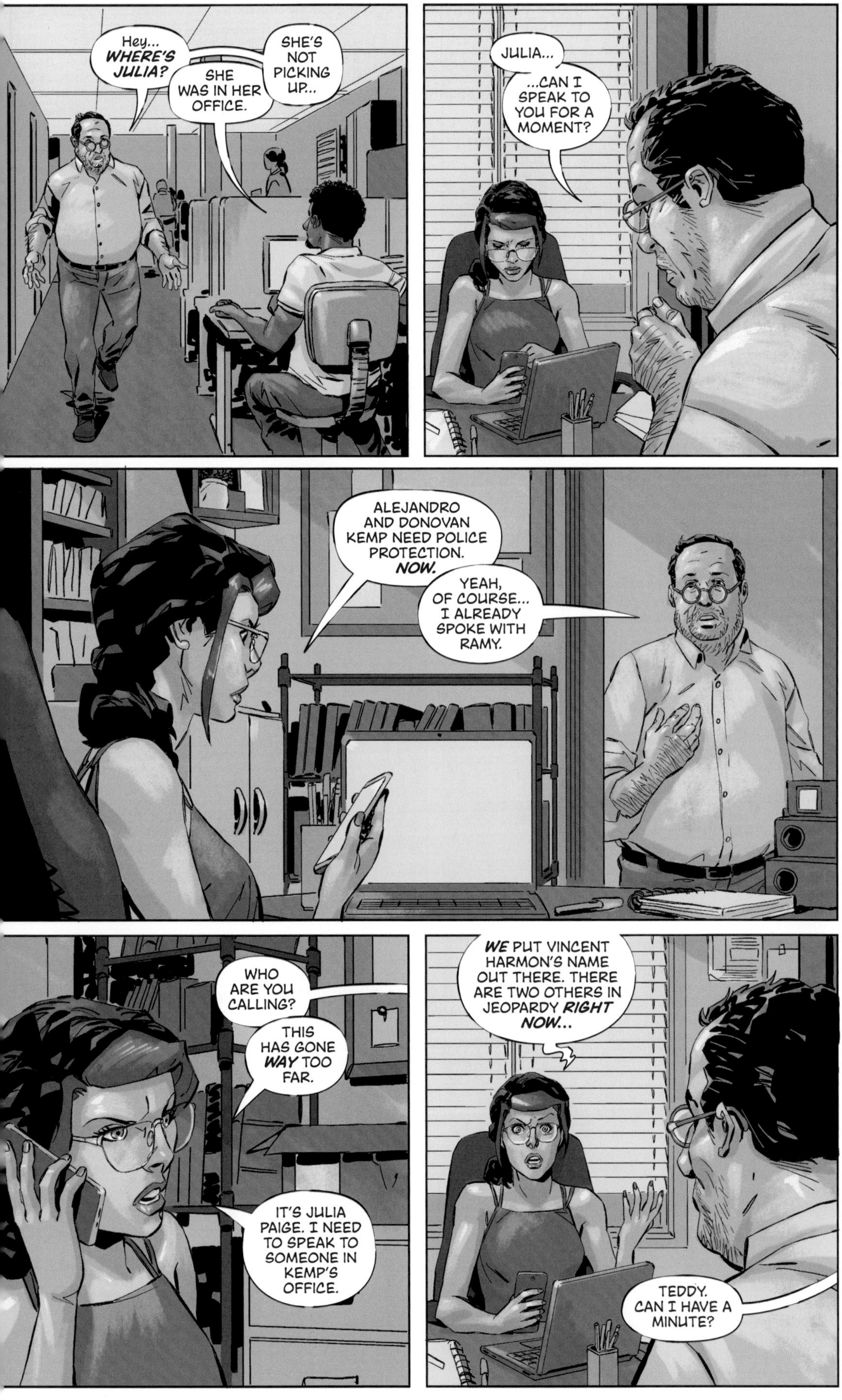

Hey... WHERE'S JULIA?
SHE'S NOT PICKING UP...
SHE WAS IN HER OFFICE.
JULIA...
...CAN I SPEAK TO YOU FOR A MOMENT?
ALEJANDRO AND DONOVAN KEMP NEED POLICE PROTECTION. NOW.
YEAH, OF COURSE... I ALREADY SPOKE WITH RAMY.
WHO ARE YOU CALLING?
THIS HAS GONE WAY TOO FAR.
IT'S JULIA PAIGE. I NEED TO SPEAK TO SOMEONE IN KEMP'S OFFICE.
WE PUT VINCENT HARMON'S NAME OUT THERE. THERE ARE TWO OTHERS IN JEOPARDY RIGHT NOW...
TEDDY. CAN I HAVE A MINUTE?

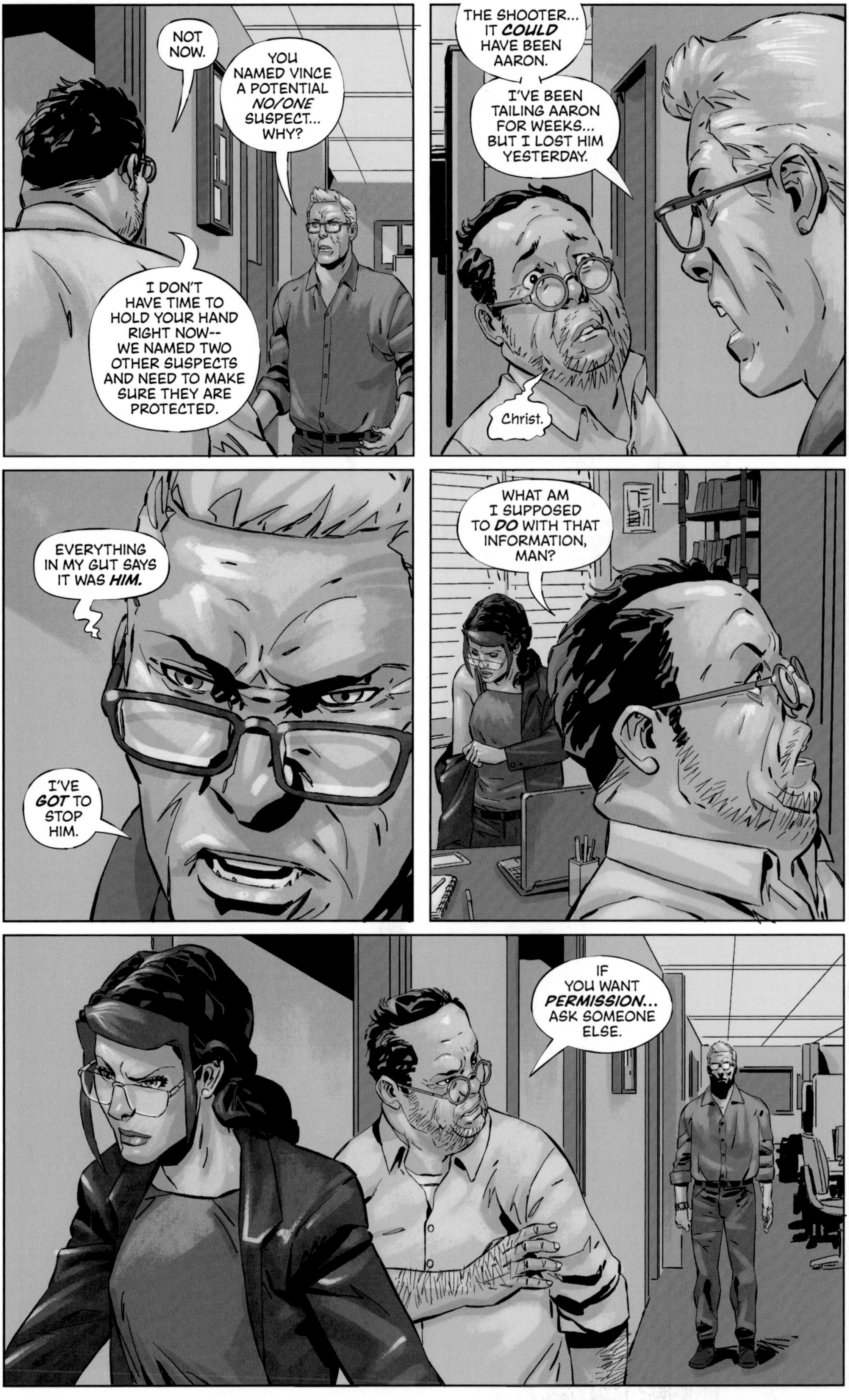
NOT NOW.
YOU NAMED VINCE A POTENTIAL *NO/ONE* SUSPECT... WHY?
I DON'T HAVE TIME TO HOLD YOUR HAND RIGHT NOW-- WE NAMED TWO OTHER SUSPECTS AND NEED TO MAKE SURE THEY ARE PROTECTED.
THE SHOOTER... IT ***COULD*** HAVE BEEN AARON.
I'VE BEEN TAILING AARON FOR WEEKS... BUT I LOST HIM YESTERDAY.
Christ.
EVERYTHING IN MY GUT SAYS IT WAS ***HIM.***
I'VE ***GOT*** TO STOP HIM.
WHAT AM I SUPPOSED TO ***DO*** WITH THAT INFORMATION, MAN?
IF YOU WANT ***PERMISSION...*** ASK SOMEONE ELSE.

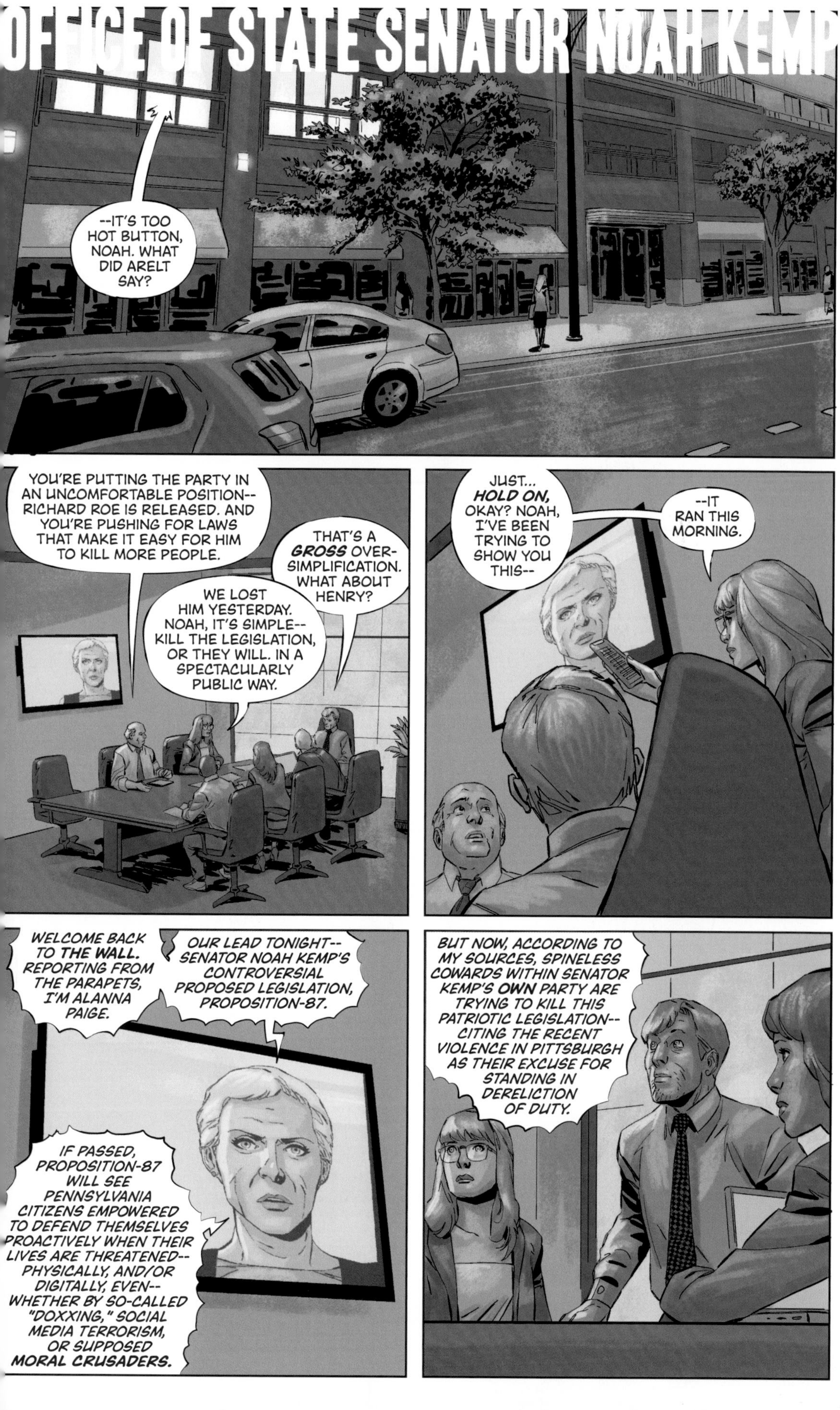
OFFICE OF STATE SENATOR NOAH KEMP
--IT'S TOO HOT BUTTON, NOAH. WHAT DID ARELT SAY?
YOU'RE PUTTING THE PARTY IN AN UNCOMFORTABLE POSITION-- RICHARD ROE IS RELEASED. AND YOU'RE PUSHING FOR LAWS THAT MAKE IT EASY FOR HIM TO KILL MORE PEOPLE.
THAT'S A GROSS OVER-SIMPLIFICATION. WHAT ABOUT HENRY?
WE LOST HIM YESTERDAY. NOAH, IT'S SIMPLE-- KILL THE LEGISLATION, OR THEY WILL. IN A SPECTACULARLY PUBLIC WAY.
JUST... HOLD ON, OKAY? NOAH, I'VE BEEN TRYING TO SHOW YOU THIS--
--IT RAN THIS MORNING.
WELCOME BACK TO THE WALL. REPORTING FROM THE PARAPETS, I'M ALANNA PAIGE.
OUR LEAD TONIGHT-- SENATOR NOAH KEMP'S CONTROVERSIAL PROPOSED LEGISLATION, PROPOSITION-87.
IF PASSED, PROPOSITION-87 WILL SEE PENNSYLVANIA CITIZENS EMPOWERED TO DEFEND THEMSELVES PROACTIVELY WHEN THEIR LIVES ARE THREATENED-- PHYSICALLY, AND/OR DIGITALLY, EVEN-- WHETHER BY SO-CALLED "DOXXING," SOCIAL MEDIA TERRORISM, OR SUPPOSED MORAL CRUSADERS.
BUT NOW, ACCORDING TO MY SOURCES, SPINELESS COWARDS WITHIN SENATOR KEMP'S OWN PARTY ARE TRYING TO KILL THIS PATRIOTIC LEGISLATION-- CITING THE RECENT VIOLENCE IN PITTSBURGH AS THEIR EXCUSE FOR STANDING IN DERELICTION OF DUTY.

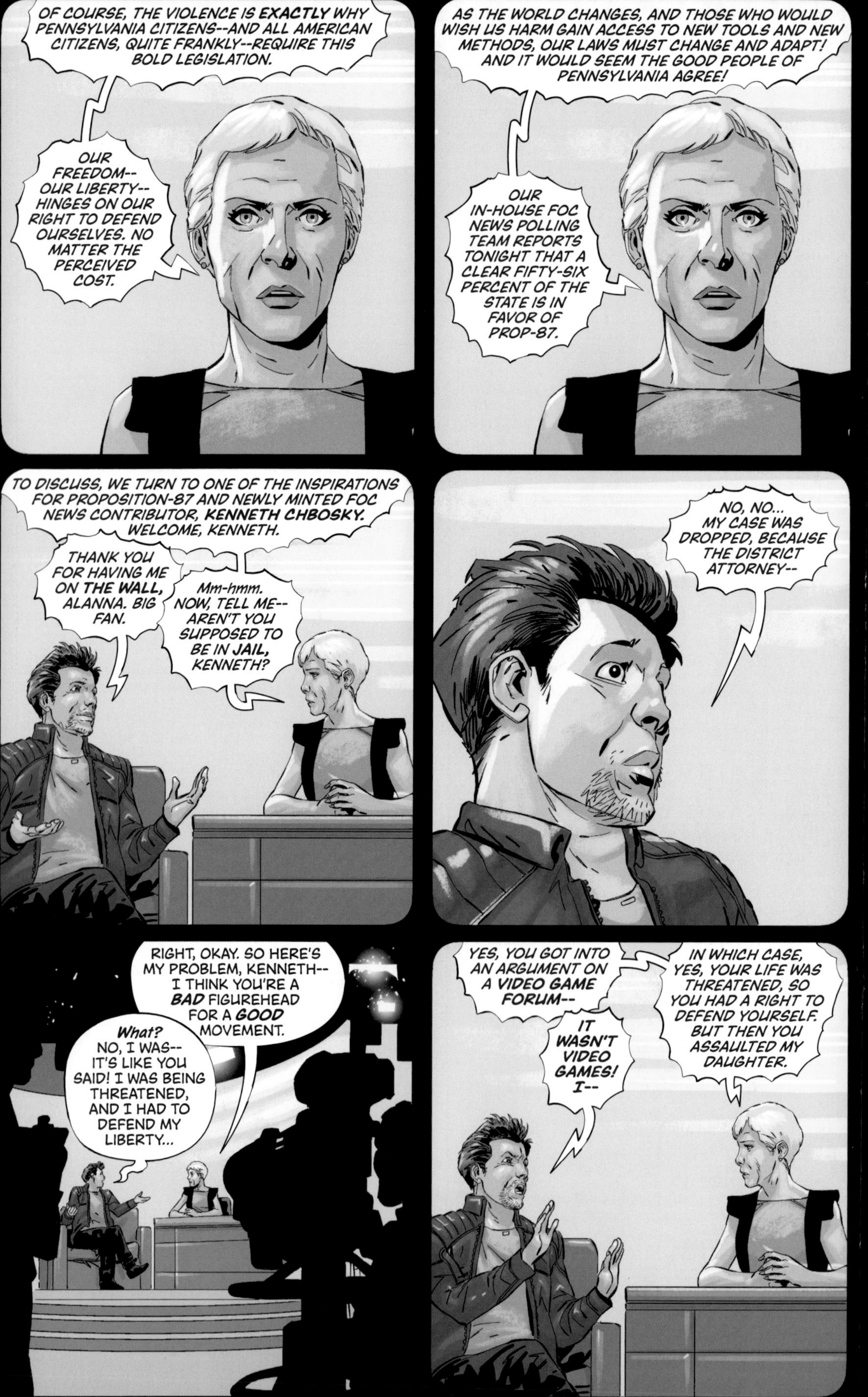
OF COURSE, THE VIOLENCE IS **EXACTLY** WHY PENNSYLVANIA CITIZENS--AND ALL AMERICAN CITIZENS, QUITE FRANKLY--REQUIRE THIS BOLD LEGISLATION.
OUR FREEDOM-- OUR LIBERTY-- HINGES ON OUR RIGHT TO DEFEND OURSELVES. NO MATTER THE PERCEIVED COST.
AS THE WORLD CHANGES, AND THOSE WHO WOULD WISH US HARM GAIN ACCESS TO NEW TOOLS AND NEW METHODS, OUR LAWS MUST CHANGE AND ADAPT! AND IT WOULD SEEM THE GOOD PEOPLE OF PENNSYLVANIA AGREE!
OUR IN-HOUSE FOC NEWS POLLING TEAM REPORTS TONIGHT THAT A CLEAR FIFTY-SIX PERCENT OF THE STATE IS IN FAVOR OF PROP-87.
TO DISCUSS, WE TURN TO ONE OF THE INSPIRATIONS FOR PROPOSITION-87 AND NEWLY MINTED FOC NEWS CONTRIBUTOR, **KENNETH CHBOSKY.** WELCOME, KENNETH.
THANK YOU FOR HAVING ME ON **THE WALL,** ALANNA. BIG FAN.
Mm-hmm. NOW, TELL ME-- AREN'T YOU SUPPOSED TO BE IN **JAIL,** KENNETH?
NO, NO... MY CASE WAS DROPPED, BECAUSE THE DISTRICT ATTORNEY--
RIGHT, OKAY. SO HERE'S MY PROBLEM, KENNETH-- I THINK YOU'RE A **BAD** FIGUREHEAD FOR A **GOOD** MOVEMENT.
What? NO, I WAS-- IT'S LIKE YOU SAID! I WAS BEING THREATENED, AND I HAD TO DEFEND MY LIBERTY...
YES, YOU GOT INTO AN ARGUMENT ON A **VIDEO GAME FORUM--**
IT WASN'T VIDEO GAMES! I--
IN WHICH CASE, YES, YOUR LIFE WAS THREATENED, SO YOU HAD A RIGHT TO DEFEND YOURSELF. BUT THEN YOU ASSAULTED MY DAUGHTER.

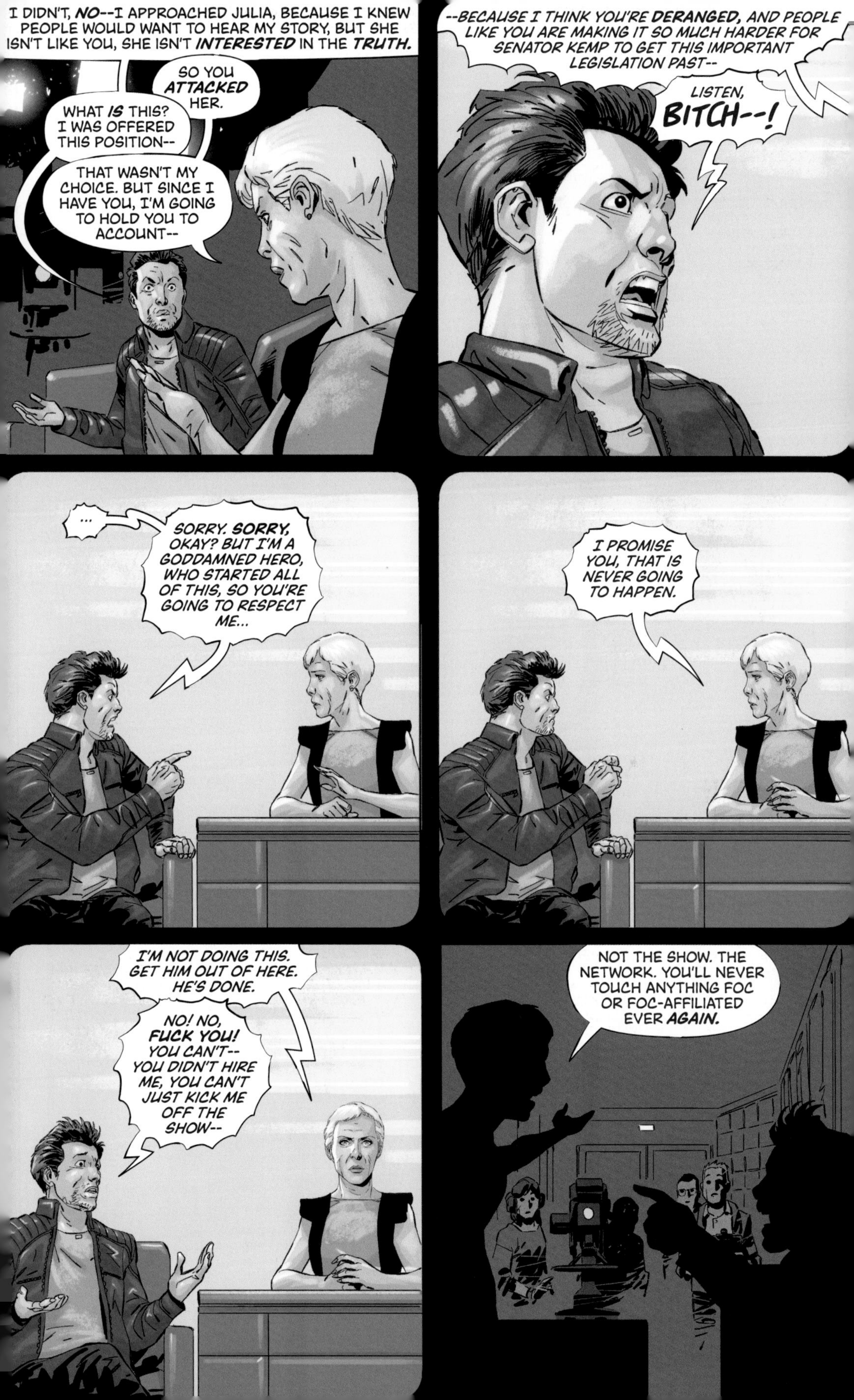
I DIDN'T, NO--I APPROACHED JULIA, BECAUSE I KNEW PEOPLE WOULD WANT TO HEAR MY STORY, BUT SHE ISN'T LIKE YOU, SHE ISN'T INTERESTED IN THE TRUTH.
SO YOU ATTACKED HER.
WHAT IS THIS? I WAS OFFERED THIS POSITION--
THAT WASN'T MY CHOICE. BUT SINCE I HAVE YOU, I'M GOING TO HOLD YOU TO ACCOUNT--
--BECAUSE I THINK YOU'RE DERANGED, AND PEOPLE LIKE YOU ARE MAKING IT SO MUCH HARDER FOR SENATOR KEMP TO GET THIS IMPORTANT LEGISLATION PAST--
LISTEN, BITCH--!
...
SORRY. SORRY, OKAY? BUT I'M A GODDAMNED HERO, WHO STARTED ALL OF THIS, SO YOU'RE GOING TO RESPECT ME...
I PROMISE YOU, THAT IS NEVER GOING TO HAPPEN.
I'M NOT DOING THIS. GET HIM OUT OF HERE. HE'S DONE.
NO! NO, FUCK YOU! YOU CAN'T-- YOU DIDN'T HIRE ME, YOU CAN'T JUST KICK ME OFF THE SHOW--
NOT THE SHOW. THE NETWORK. YOU'LL NEVER TOUCH ANYTHING FOC OR FOC-AFFILIATED EVER AGAIN.

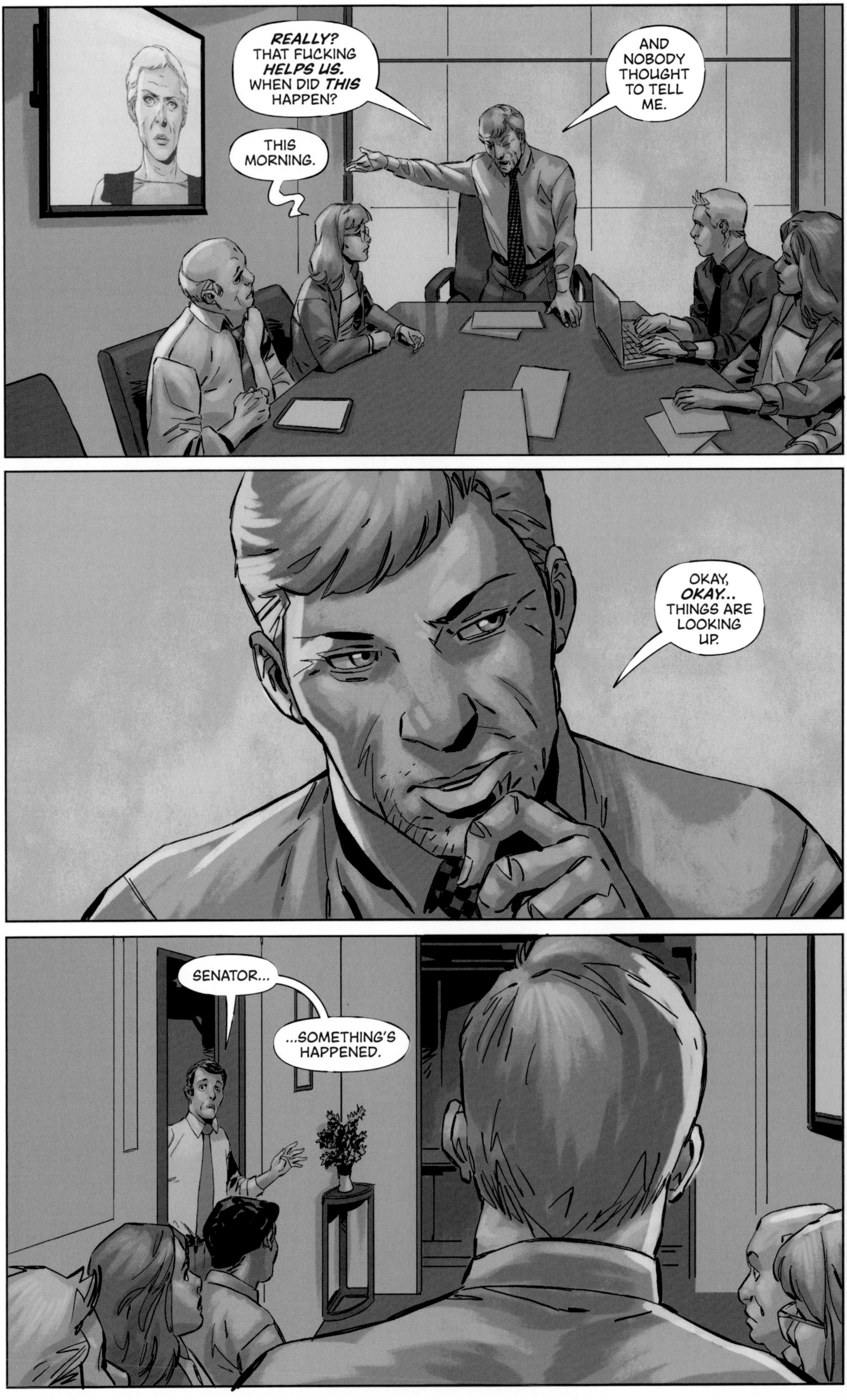
REALLY? THAT FUCKING HELPS US. WHEN DID THIS HAPPEN?
THIS MORNING.
AND NOBODY THOUGHT TO TELL ME.
OKAY, OKAY... THINGS ARE LOOKING UP.
SENATOR...
...SOMETHING'S HAPPENED.

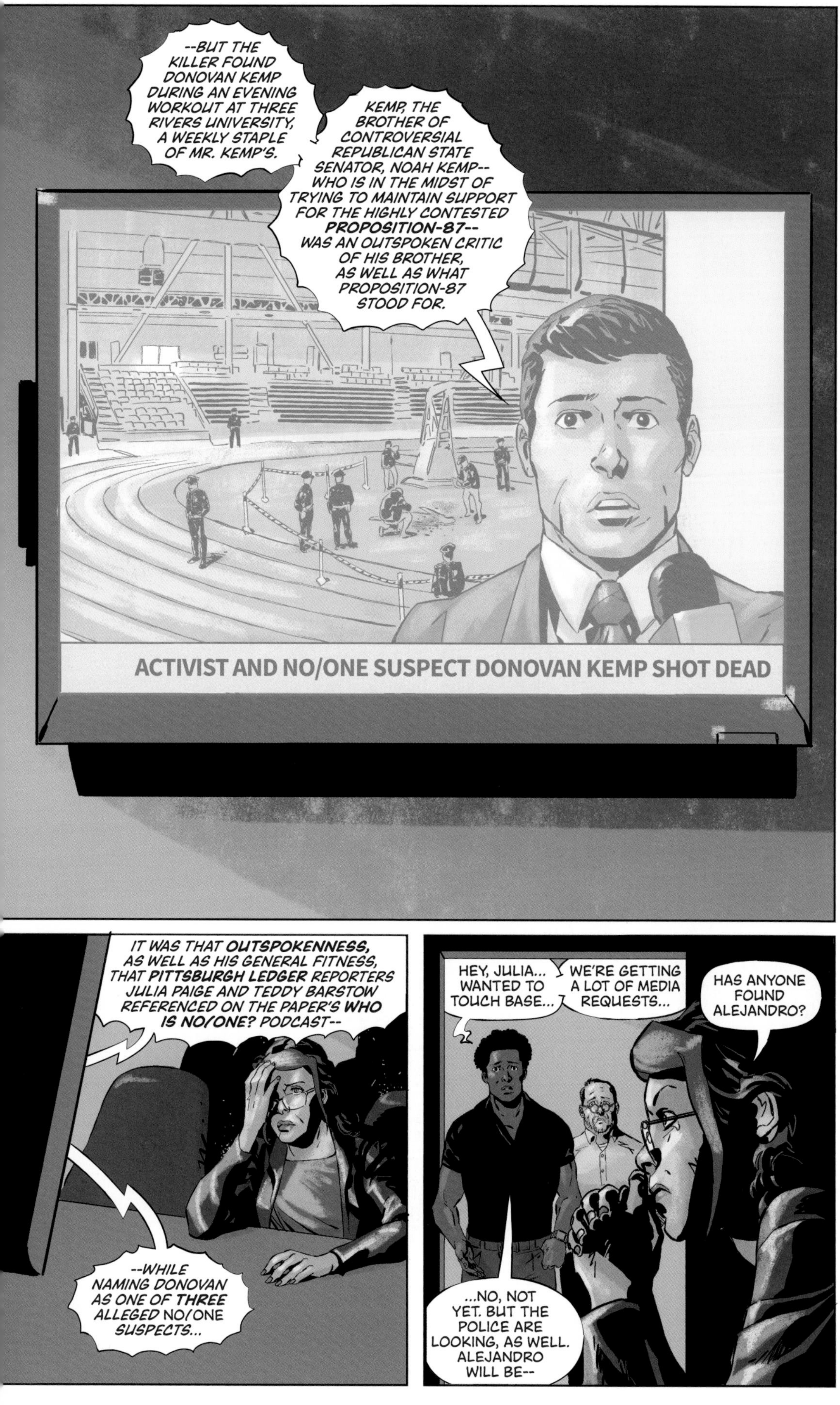
--BUT THE KILLER FOUND DONOVAN KEMP DURING AN EVENING WORKOUT AT THREE RIVERS UNIVERSITY, A WEEKLY STAPLE OF MR. KEMP'S.
KEMP, THE BROTHER OF CONTROVERSIAL REPUBLICAN STATE SENATOR, NOAH KEMP-- WHO IS IN THE MIDST OF TRYING TO MAINTAIN SUPPORT FOR THE HIGHLY CONTESTED **PROPOSITION-87--** WAS AN OUTSPOKEN CRITIC OF HIS BROTHER, AS WELL AS WHAT PROPOSITION-87 STOOD FOR.
ACTIVIST AND NO/ONE SUSPECT DONOVAN KEMP SHOT DEAD
IT WAS THAT **OUTSPOKENNESS,** AS WELL AS HIS GENERAL FITNESS, THAT **PITTSBURGH LEDGER** REPORTERS JULIA PAIGE AND TEDDY BARSTOW REFERENCED ON THE PAPER'S **WHO IS NO/ONE**? PODCAST--
--WHILE NAMING DONOVAN AS ONE OF **THREE** ALLEGED NO/ONE SUSPECTS...
HEY, JULIA... WANTED TO TOUCH BASE...
WE'RE GETTING A LOT OF MEDIA REQUESTS...
HAS ANYONE FOUND ALEJANDRO?
...NO, NOT YET. BUT THE POLICE ARE LOOKING, AS WELL. ALEJANDRO WILL BE--

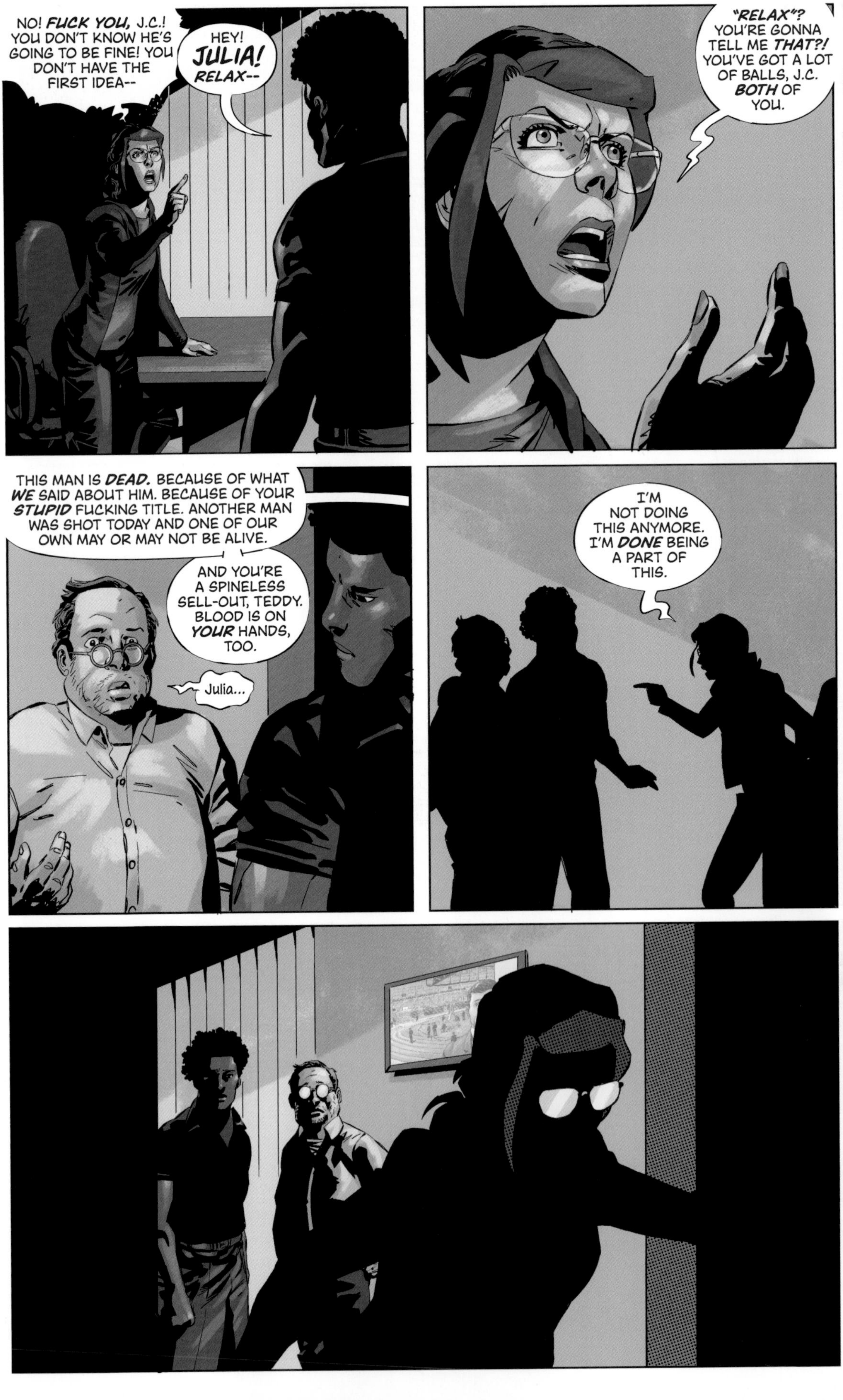
NO! FUCK YOU, J.C.! YOU DON'T KNOW HE'S GOING TO BE FINE! YOU DON'T HAVE THE FIRST IDEA--
HEY! JULIA! RELAX--
"RELAX"? YOU'RE GONNA TELL ME THAT?! YOU'VE GOT A LOT OF BALLS, J.C. BOTH OF YOU.
THIS MAN IS DEAD. BECAUSE OF WHAT WE SAID ABOUT HIM. BECAUSE OF YOUR STUPID FUCKING TITLE. ANOTHER MAN WAS SHOT TODAY AND ONE OF OUR OWN MAY OR MAY NOT BE ALIVE.
AND YOU'RE A SPINELESS SELL-OUT, TEDDY. BLOOD IS ON YOUR HANDS, TOO.
Julia...
I'M NOT DOING THIS ANYMORE. I'M DONE BEING A PART OF THIS.

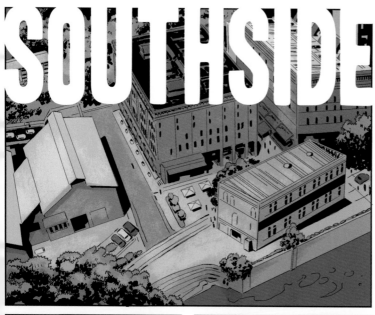

SOUTHSIDE

ALEJANDRO...

KLIK

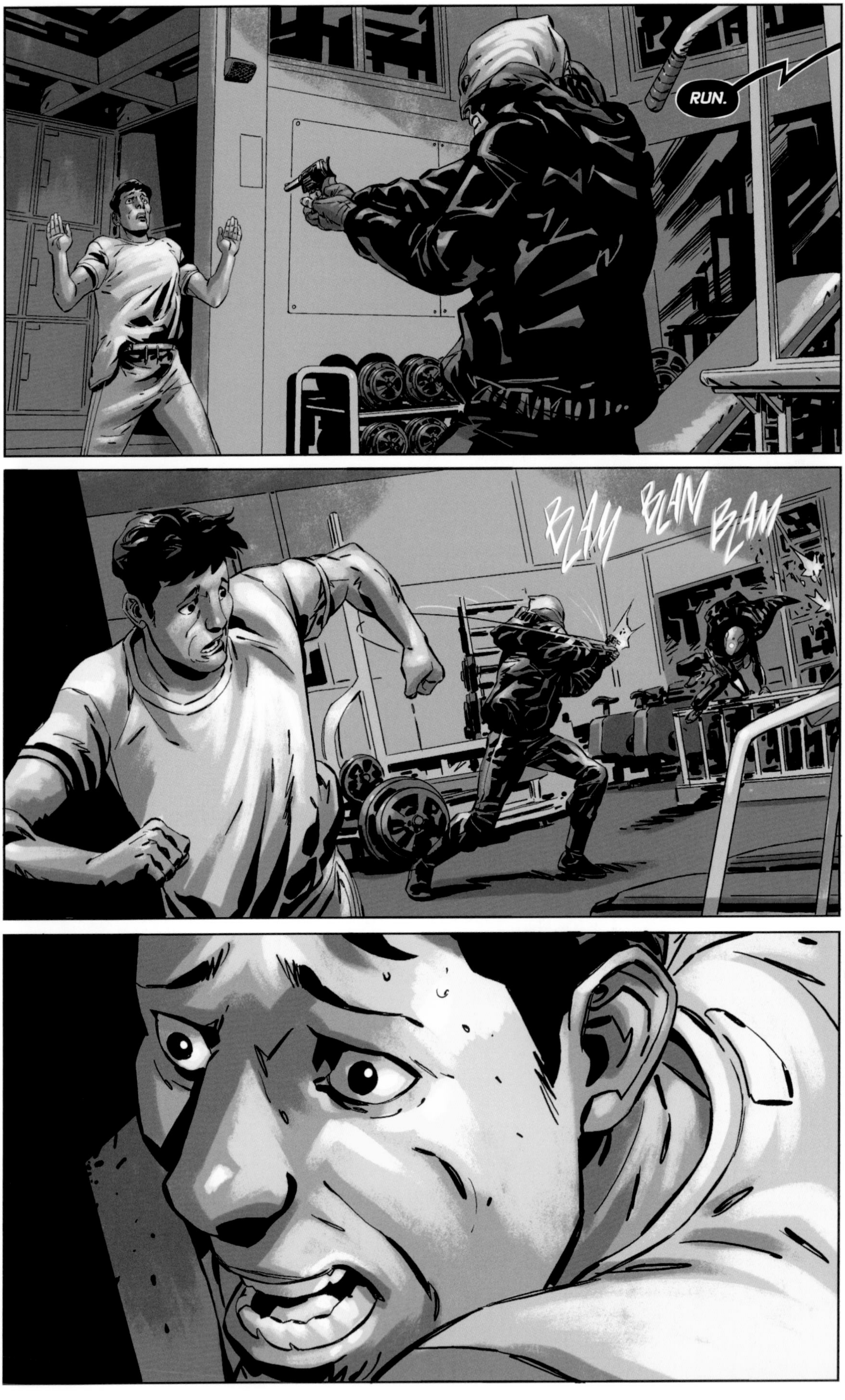
RUN.
BLAM BLAM BLAM

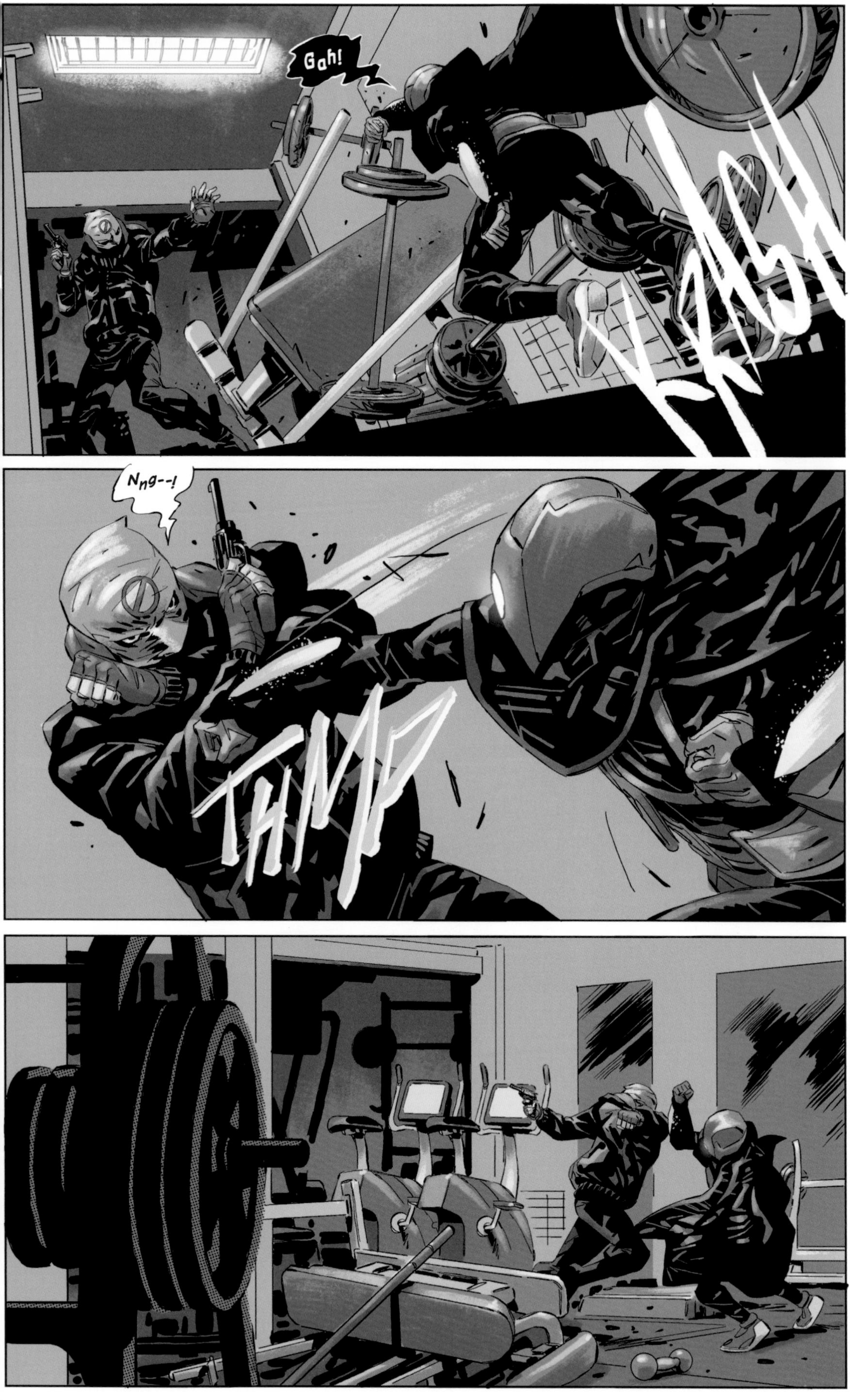
Gah!
KRASH
Nng--!
THMP

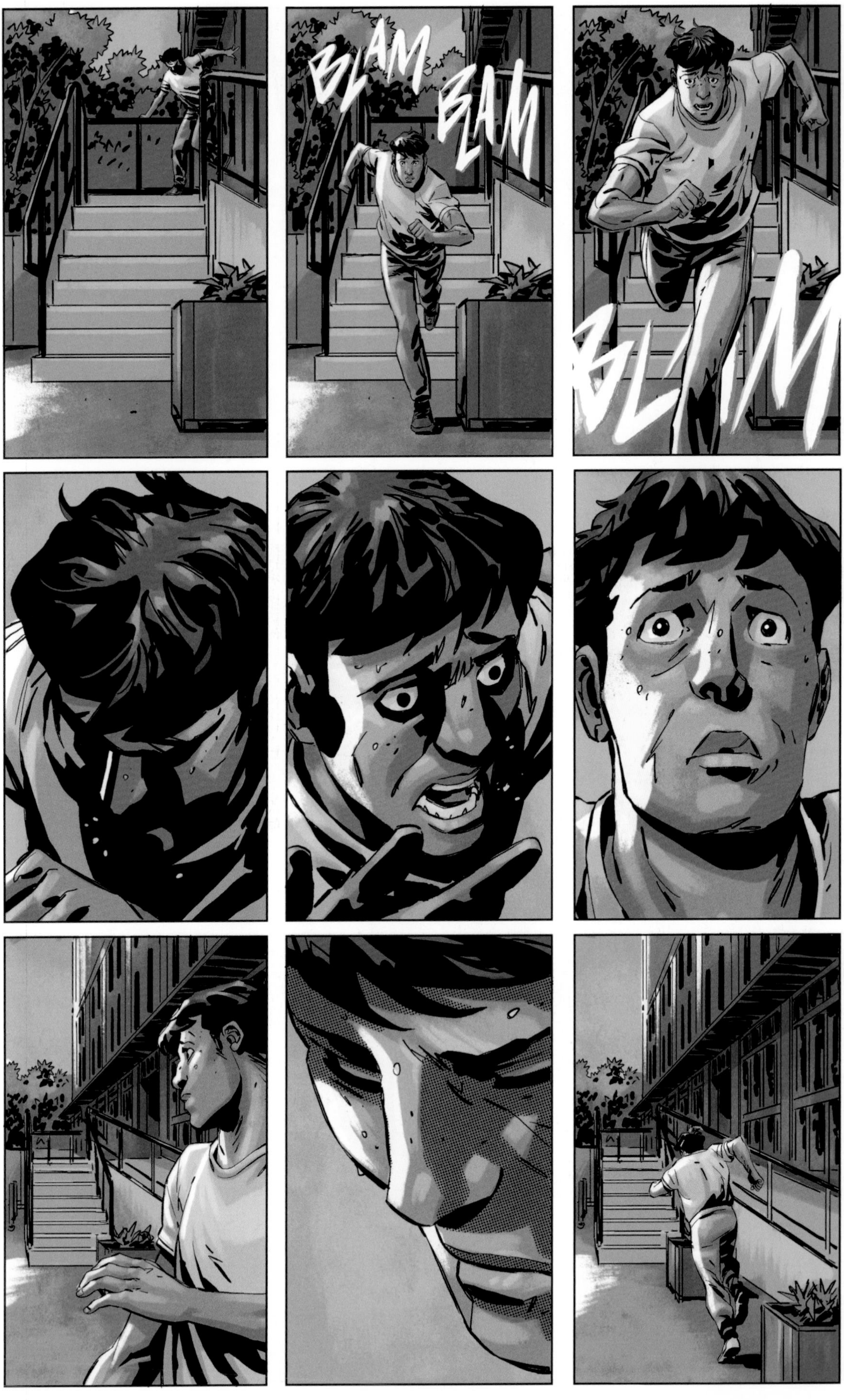
BLAM
BLAM
BLAM

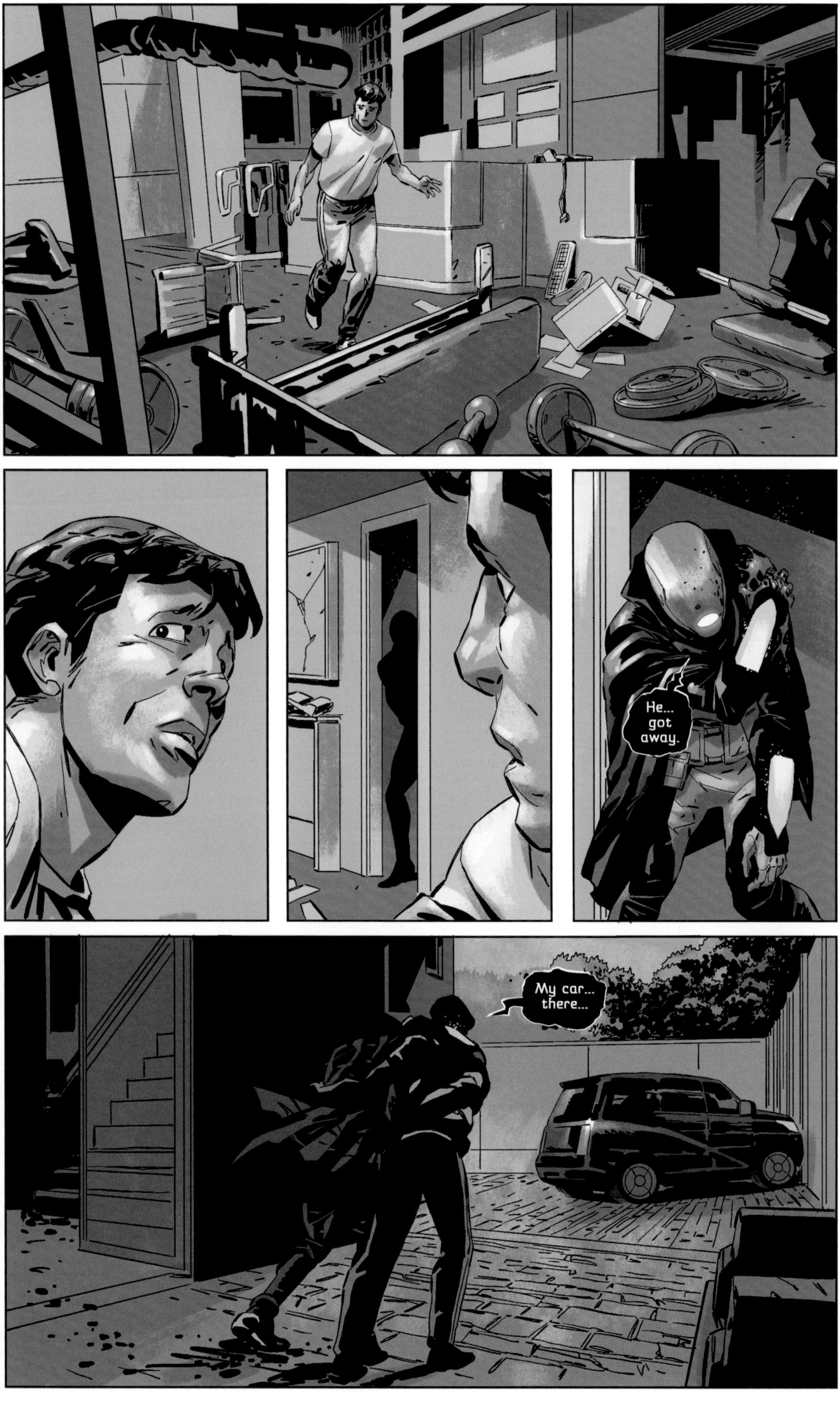
He... got away.
My car... there...

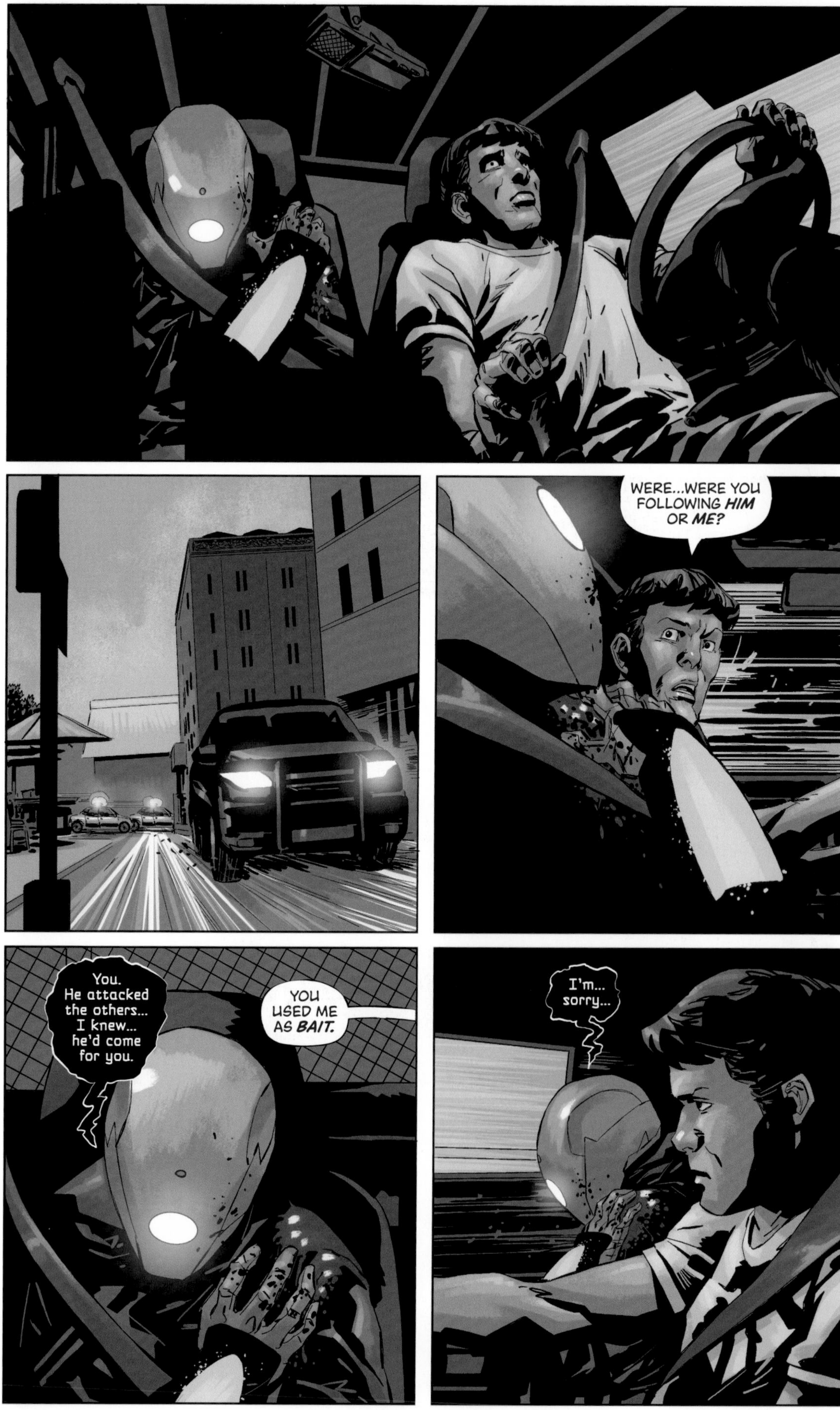
WERE...WERE YOU FOLLOWING HIM OR ME?
You. He attacked the others... I knew... he'd come for you.
YOU USED ME AS BAIT.
I'm... sorry...

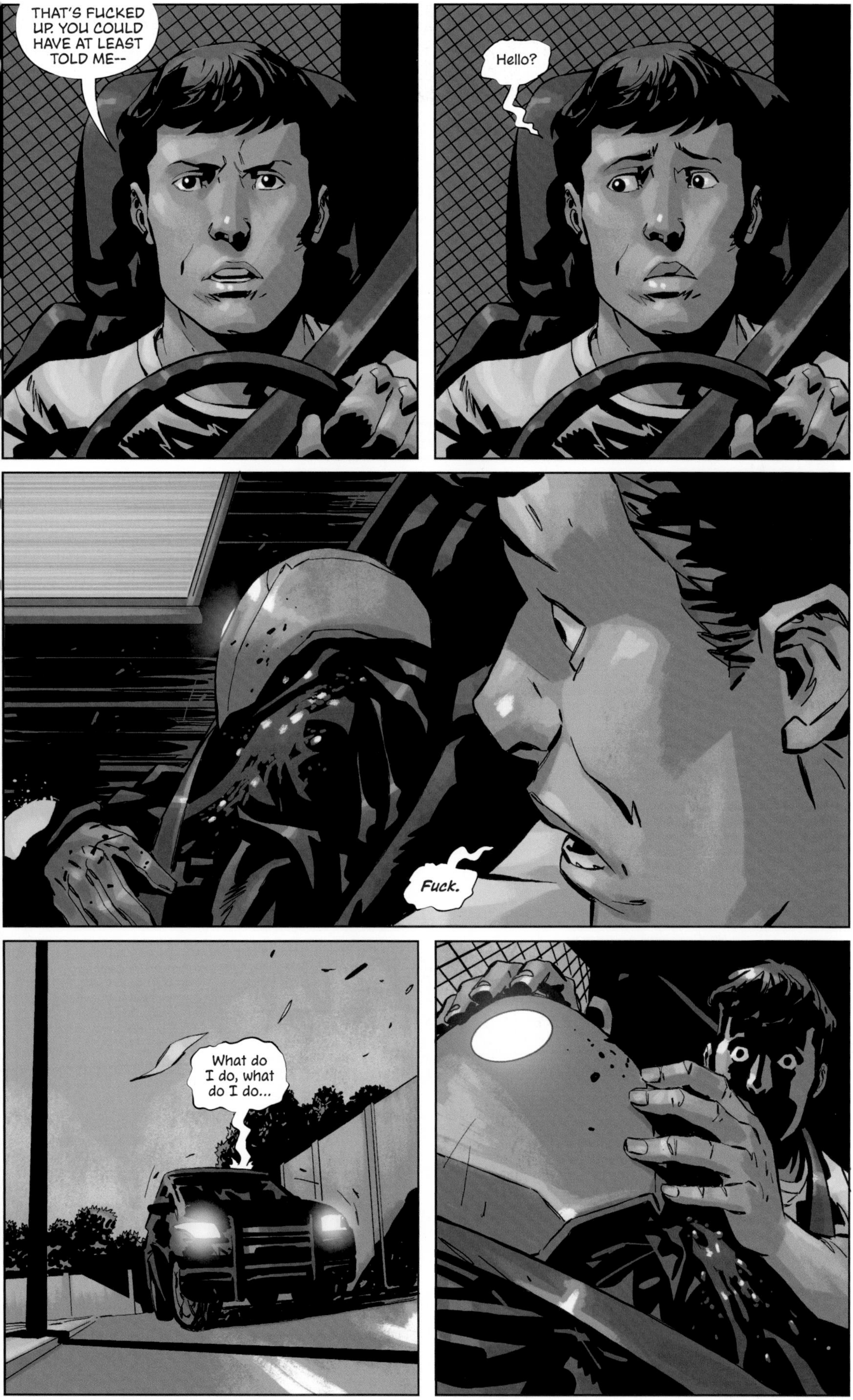
THAT'S FUCKED UP. YOU COULD HAVE AT LEAST TOLD ME--
Hello?
Fuck.
What do I do, what do I do...

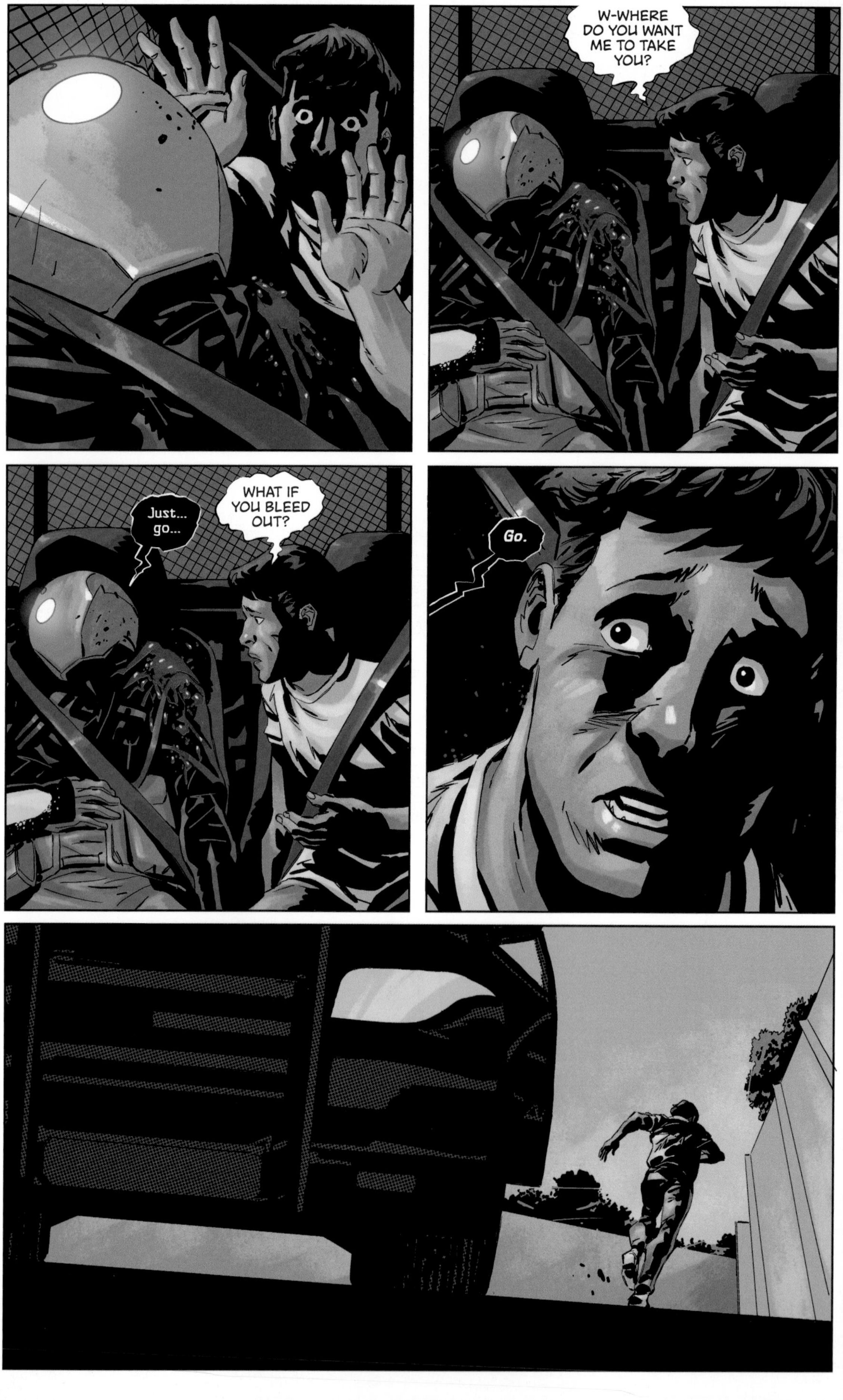
W-WHERE DO YOU WANT ME TO TAKE YOU?
Just... go...
WHAT IF YOU BLEED OUT?
Go.

Opinion

Pittsburgh Ledger

Attacks put podcast in the firing line

Julia Paige
Who Is NO/ONE podcast host

In the age of sensationalism, the line between reporting and exploitation often blurs, leading us—or those above us—to make choices that can prioritize ratings over integrity.

Recently, I found myself at a crossroads on this paper's WHO IS NO/ONE podcast, of which I am a co-host. In the rush and pressure to live up to the promise of the premise, we listed the names of three potential NO/ONE suspects, leading each of them into harm's way. While I initially voiced my objections, I ultimately surrendered to the pressure—compromising my own principles in the process. It's a decision I deeply regret.

Growing up as the daughter of a journalist, I have seen firsthand the impact that sensationalism can have on lives. I watched as someone close to me built a career from making decisions that often prioritized audience engagement over context. Watching this unfold taught me valuable lessons, but in this case, it didn't shield me from making the same mistakes myself.

My actions didn't just contribute to the public discourse; they inadvertently turned three innocent people into victims. And what's worse, it cost someone their life. I cannot help but think about the families left to grapple with the fallout. In particular, I owe an apology to the Kemp family, as well as Alejandro Rios and Officer Vince Harmon. They all deserved better.

This moment of reckoning has prompted me to rethink not only my approach to journalism but my place within it. Reporters have a responsibility to society and, just as important, to the subjects of our stories. Our duty is to shine a light on the truth, but not at the expense of those we cover. Sensationalism may draw viewers, but it also breeds mistrust and disillusionment.

I'm going to be taking some time away, but as I move forward, I commit to doing better. I hope, in time, I can rebuild the trust that was lost and strive for a standard that reflects the integrity we owe to our readers, our listeners and those we report on. The responsibility lies with us, the media, to remember that behind every headline, there is a human life—a life deserving of respect and dignity.

To the Kemp family, Alejandro Rios, and Officer Harmon, I apologize for my choices and ask for your understanding as I seek to do better. We all have a role to play in fostering a more compassionate and responsible landscape, and I am committed to being part of that change. Let's make sure that the stories we tell serve not just our ratings, but the truth.

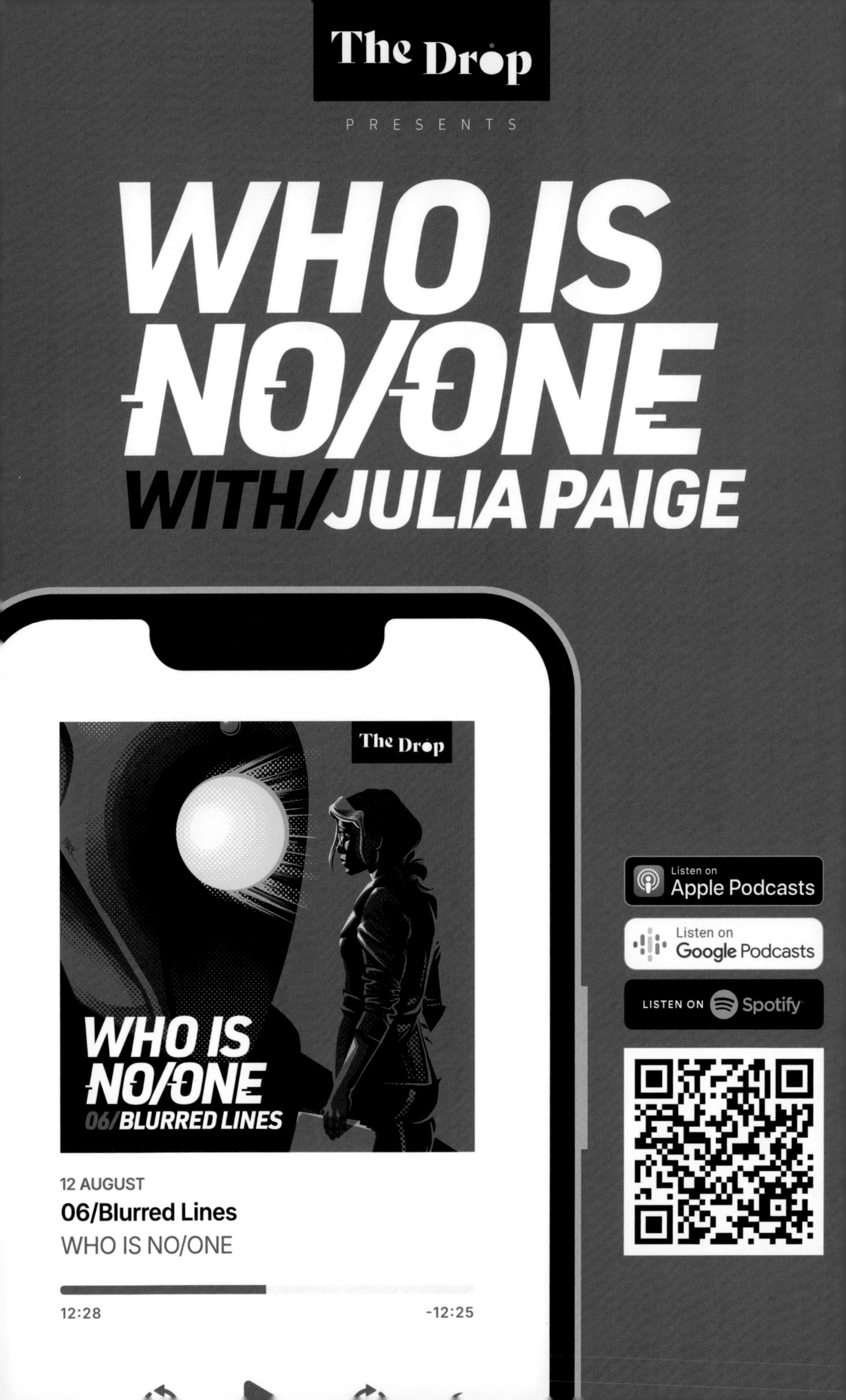

The Drop
PRESENTS
WHO IS NO/ONE
WITH/JULIA PAIGE
The Drop
WHO IS NO/ONE
06/BLURRED LINES
12 AUGUST
06/Blurred Lines
WHO IS NO/ONE
12:28
-12:25
Listen on Apple Podcasts
Listen on Google Podcasts
LISTEN ON Spotify

>_ **EDGE NEWS EXCLUSIVE: "Blurred Lines" – The Podcast Episode That Crossed Every Line**
AUGUST 13 2023

written by Danielle Gaines
published on Edge News

"It's not hard to imagine we're being played in a bigger game, and Teddy's too tangled in it to care."

KNOWPEDIA
An Encyclopedia For Free

Vincent Harmon

Article   Talk   Read   View source   View history

> **This article documents a current event.** Information may change rapidly as the event
> progresses, and initial news reports may be unreliable. The latest updates to this article may
> not reflect the most current information. Feel free to improve this article or discuss changes
> on the talk page, but please note that updates without valid and reliable references will be
> removed. (September 2023)

Vincent "Vince" Harmon (born September 17, 1975) is a highly respected investigator for the Pittsburgh Office of Municipal
Investigations. His career began in the military, where he served as an Army Ranger in Afghanistan. Upon his return to Pittsburgh,
Harmon joined the police force, eventually rising through the ranks due to his consistent bravery and dedication. He has been
commended for his integrity and his role in rooting out corruption within the police department through his work in internal
investigations.

Eagle Market Shooting   [edit]

Harmon gained widespread recognition in June 2017 when he heroically intervened during a mass shooting at a Big Eagle
supermarket in Ridgemont, Pennsylvania. While off duty, Harmon encountered an armed gunman who had already killed five
people and injured six others. Without hesitation, Harmon engaged the shooter and fatally shot him, preventing further casualties.
His actions saved the lives of many shoppers and earned him the Medal of Valor, cementing his status as a hero in the Pittsburgh
community.

Attempted assassination   [edit]

On August 5 2024, Vince Harmon became a target of the Richard Roe copycat killer. While off duty at Point State Park, he was
ambushed and shot four times with a .38 Special revolver, the weapon associated with the Accountability Murders.[citation needed]
Despite his injuries, Harmon returned fire, forcing the assailant to flee. He was later praised for his bravery by Pittsburgh Police
Chief Mixon, and he remains in stable condition.

Media speculation   [edit]

Harmon's reputation and military background led some commentators to believe he fit the profile of the masked vigilante known
as NO/ONE.[who?] His past heroism and commitment to holding law enforcement accountable align with the vigilante's mission.
With no concrete evidence, his connection to NO/ONE remains speculative, and Harmon continues to be a respected figure in
Pittsburgh's law enforcement community.

Richard Roe	[show]
Authority control	[show]

>_ CHAPTER SEVEN
SEPTEMBER 2023

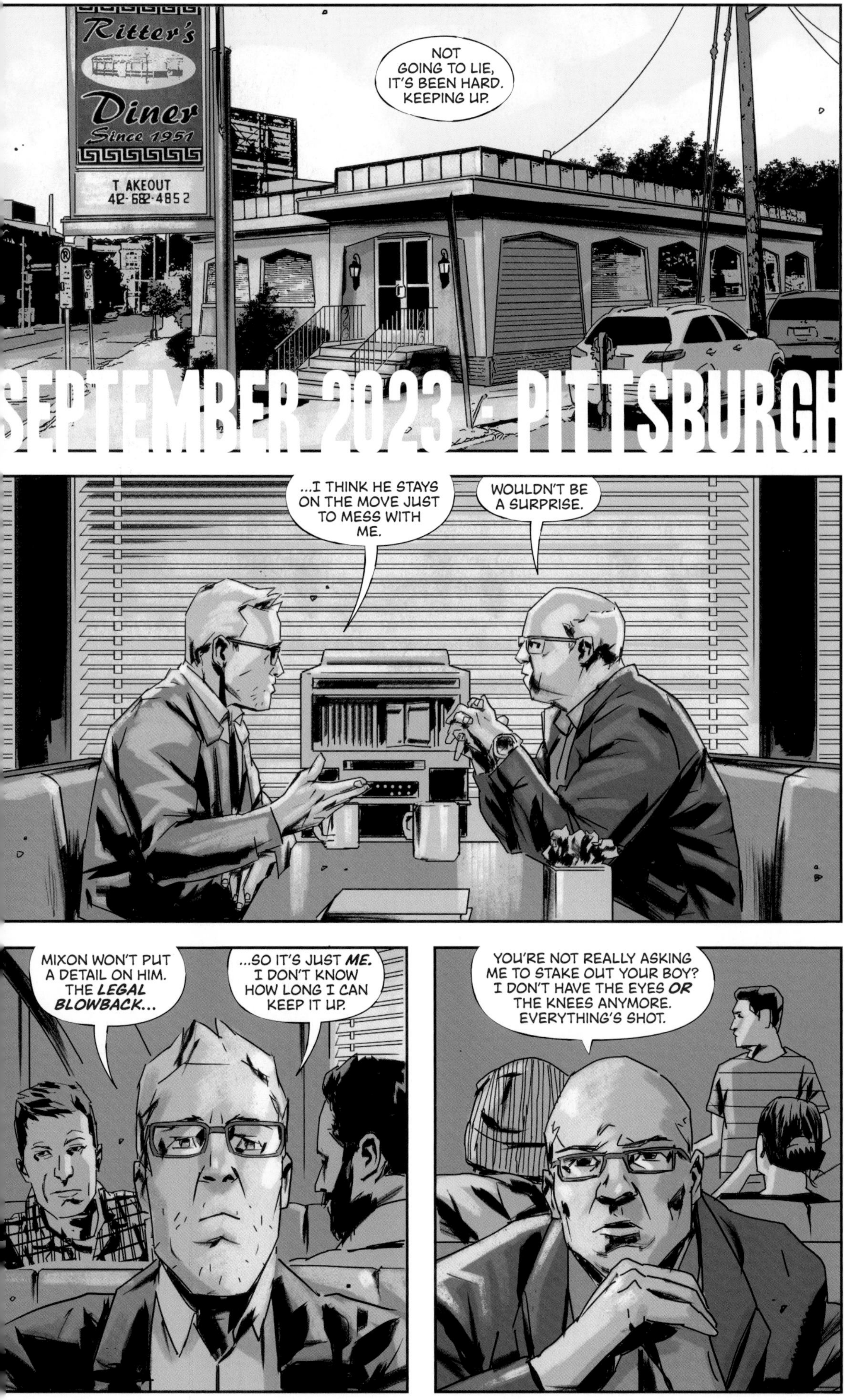
Ritter's Diner Since 1951
TAKEOUT
NOT GOING TO LIE, IT'S BEEN HARD. KEEPING UP.
SEPTEMBER 2023 · PITTSBURGH
...I THINK HE STAYS ON THE MOVE JUST TO MESS WITH ME.
WOULDN'T BE A SURPRISE.
MIXON WON'T PUT A DETAIL ON HIM. THE *LEGAL BLOWBACK...*
...SO IT'S JUST *ME.* I DON'T KNOW HOW LONG I CAN KEEP IT UP.
YOU'RE NOT REALLY ASKING ME TO STAKE OUT YOUR BOY? I DON'T HAVE THE EYES *OR* THE KNEES ANYMORE. EVERYTHING'S SHOT.

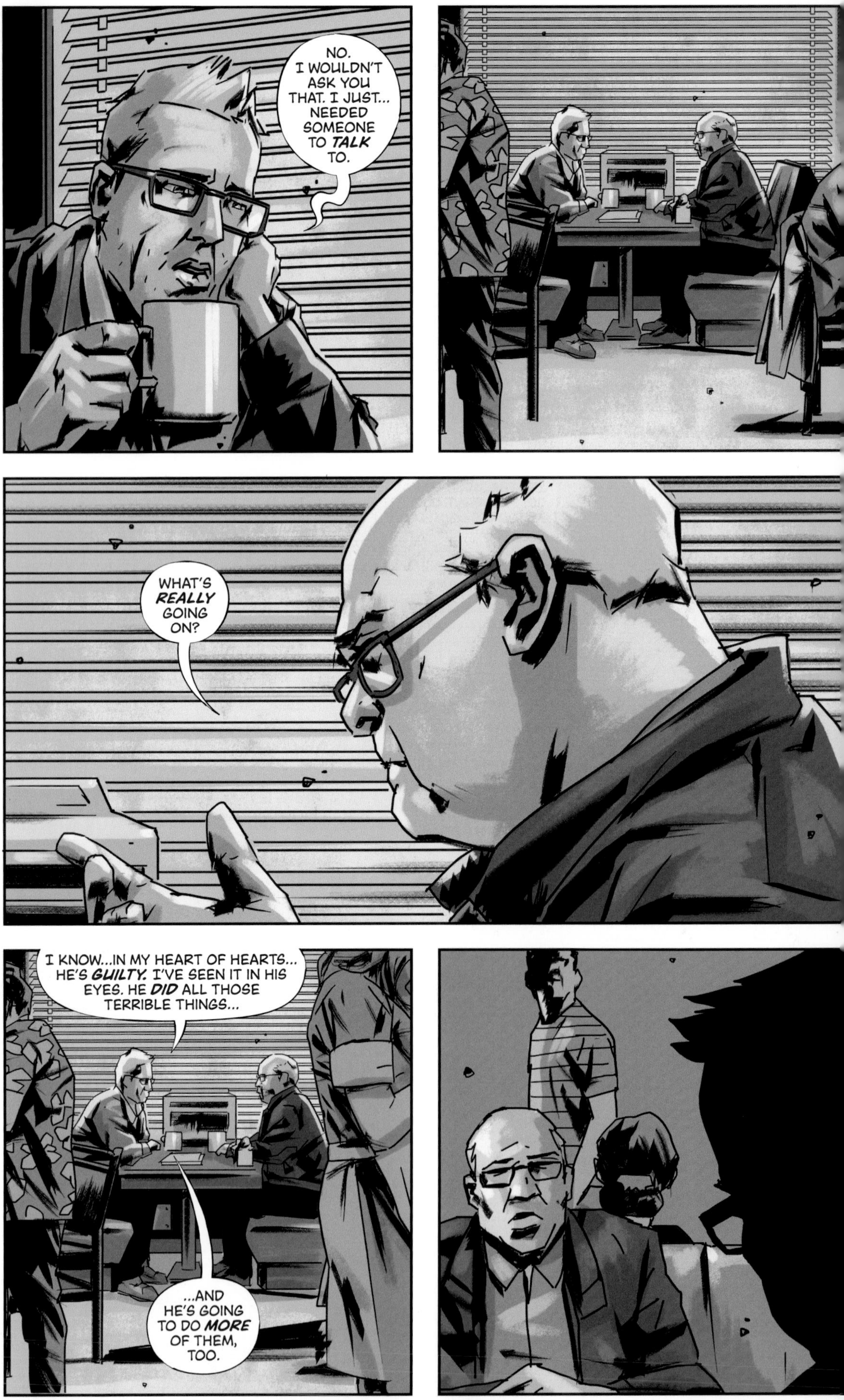
NO. I WOULDN'T ASK YOU THAT. I JUST... NEEDED SOMEONE TO TALK TO.
WHAT'S REALLY GOING ON?
I KNOW...IN MY HEART OF HEARTS... HE'S GUILTY. I'VE SEEN IT IN HIS EYES. HE DID ALL THOSE TERRIBLE THINGS...
...AND HE'S GOING TO DO MORE OF THEM, TOO.

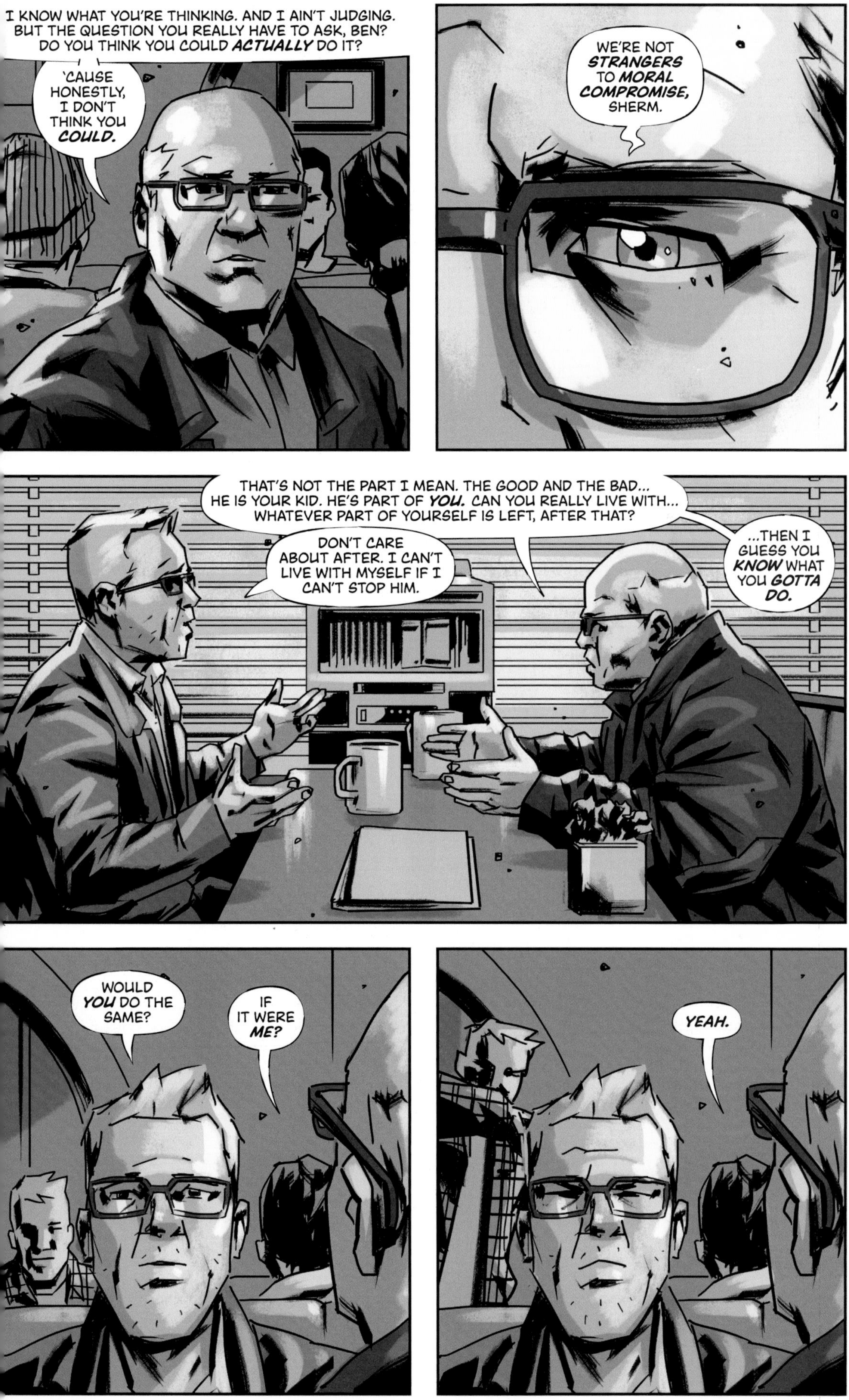
I KNOW WHAT YOU'RE THINKING. AND I AIN'T JUDGING. BUT THE QUESTION YOU REALLY HAVE TO ASK, BEN? DO YOU THINK YOU COULD ACTUALLY DO IT?
'CAUSE HONESTLY, I DON'T THINK YOU COULD.
WE'RE NOT STRANGERS TO MORAL COMPROMISE, SHERM.
DON'T CARE ABOUT AFTER. I CAN'T LIVE WITH MYSELF IF I CAN'T STOP HIM.
THAT'S NOT THE PART I MEAN. THE GOOD AND THE BAD... HE IS YOUR KID. HE'S PART OF YOU. CAN YOU REALLY LIVE WITH... WHATEVER PART OF YOURSELF IS LEFT, AFTER THAT?
...THEN I GUESS YOU KNOW WHAT YOU GOTTA DO.
WOULD YOU DO THE SAME?
IF IT WERE ME?
YEAH.

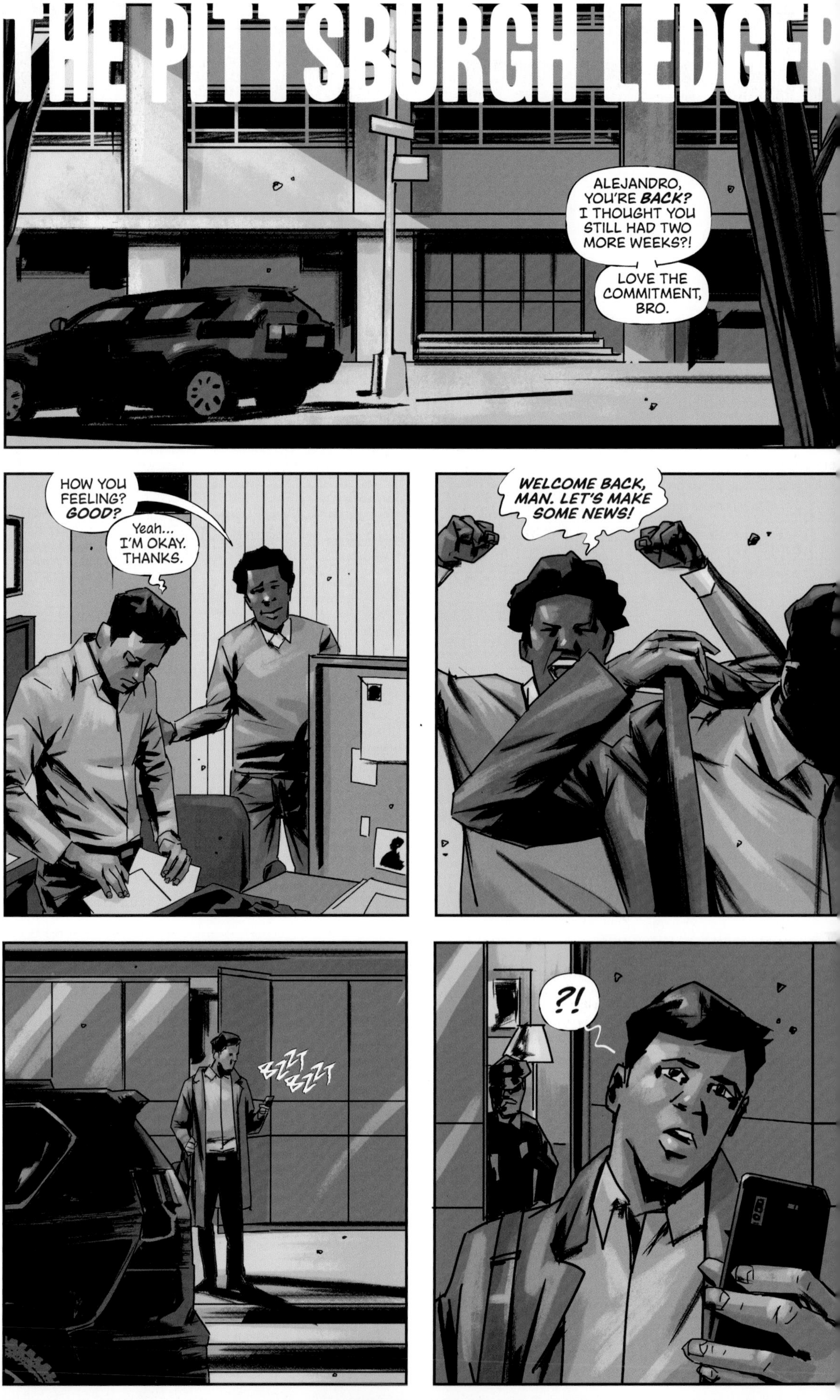
THE PITTSBURGH LEDGER
ALEJANDRO, YOU'RE BACK? I THOUGHT YOU STILL HAD TWO MORE WEEKS?!
LOVE THE COMMITMENT, BRO.
HOW YOU FEELING? GOOD?
Yeah... I'M OKAY. THANKS.
WELCOME BACK, MAN. LET'S MAKE SOME NEWS!
BZZZT BZZZT
?!

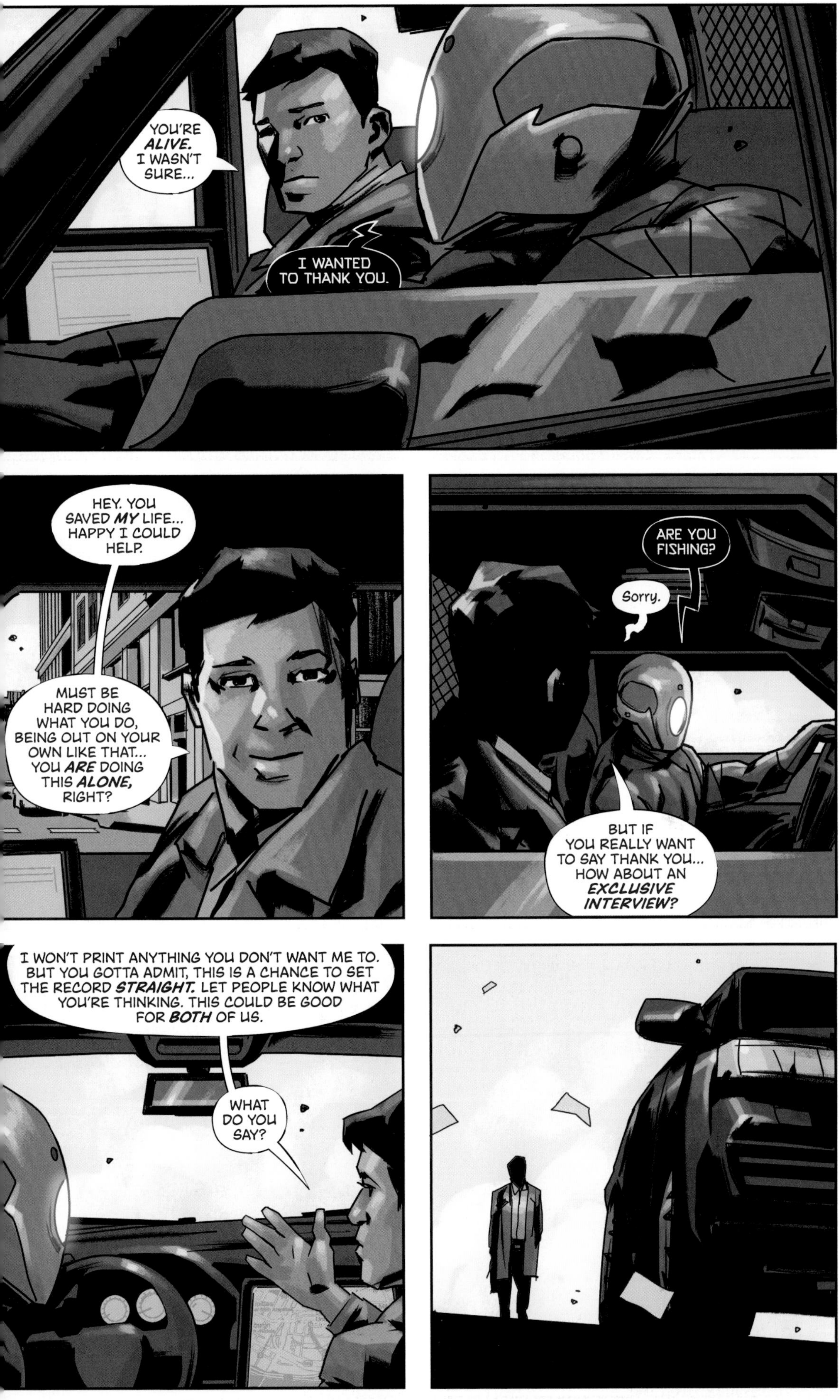
YOU'RE ALIVE. I WASN'T SURE...
I WANTED TO THANK YOU.
HEY. YOU SAVED MY LIFE... HAPPY I COULD HELP.
MUST BE HARD DOING WHAT YOU DO, BEING OUT ON YOUR OWN LIKE THAT... YOU ARE DOING THIS ALONE, RIGHT?
ARE YOU FISHING?
Sorry.
BUT IF YOU REALLY WANT TO SAY THANK YOU... HOW ABOUT AN EXCLUSIVE INTERVIEW?
I WON'T PRINT ANYTHING YOU DON'T WANT ME TO. BUT YOU GOTTA ADMIT, THIS IS A CHANCE TO SET THE RECORD STRAIGHT. LET PEOPLE KNOW WHAT YOU'RE THINKING. THIS COULD BE GOOD FOR BOTH OF US.
WHAT DO YOU SAY?

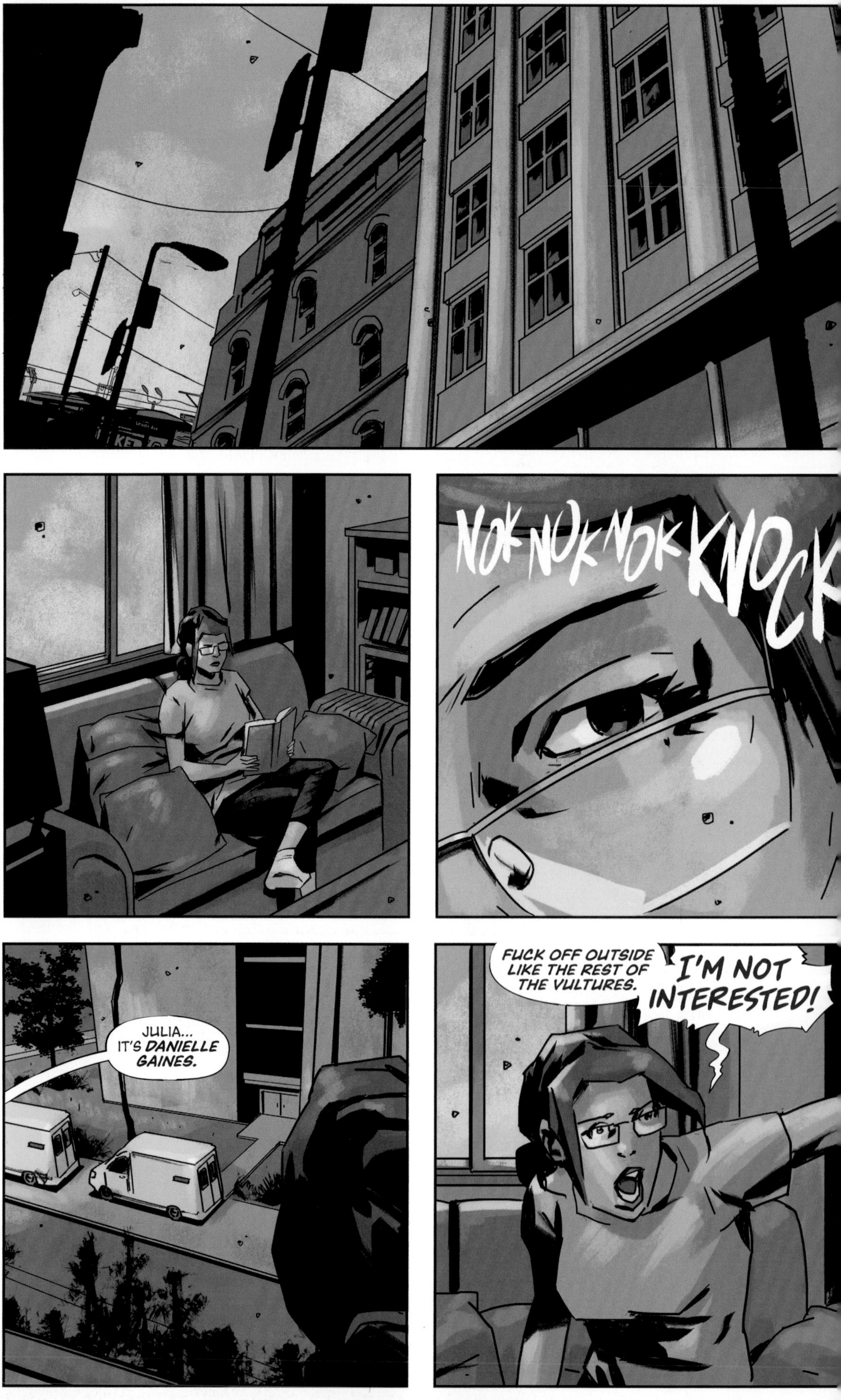
NOK NOK NOK KNOCK
JULIA... IT'S DANIELLE GAINES.
FUCK OFF OUTSIDE LIKE THE REST OF THE VULTURES.
I'M NOT INTERESTED!

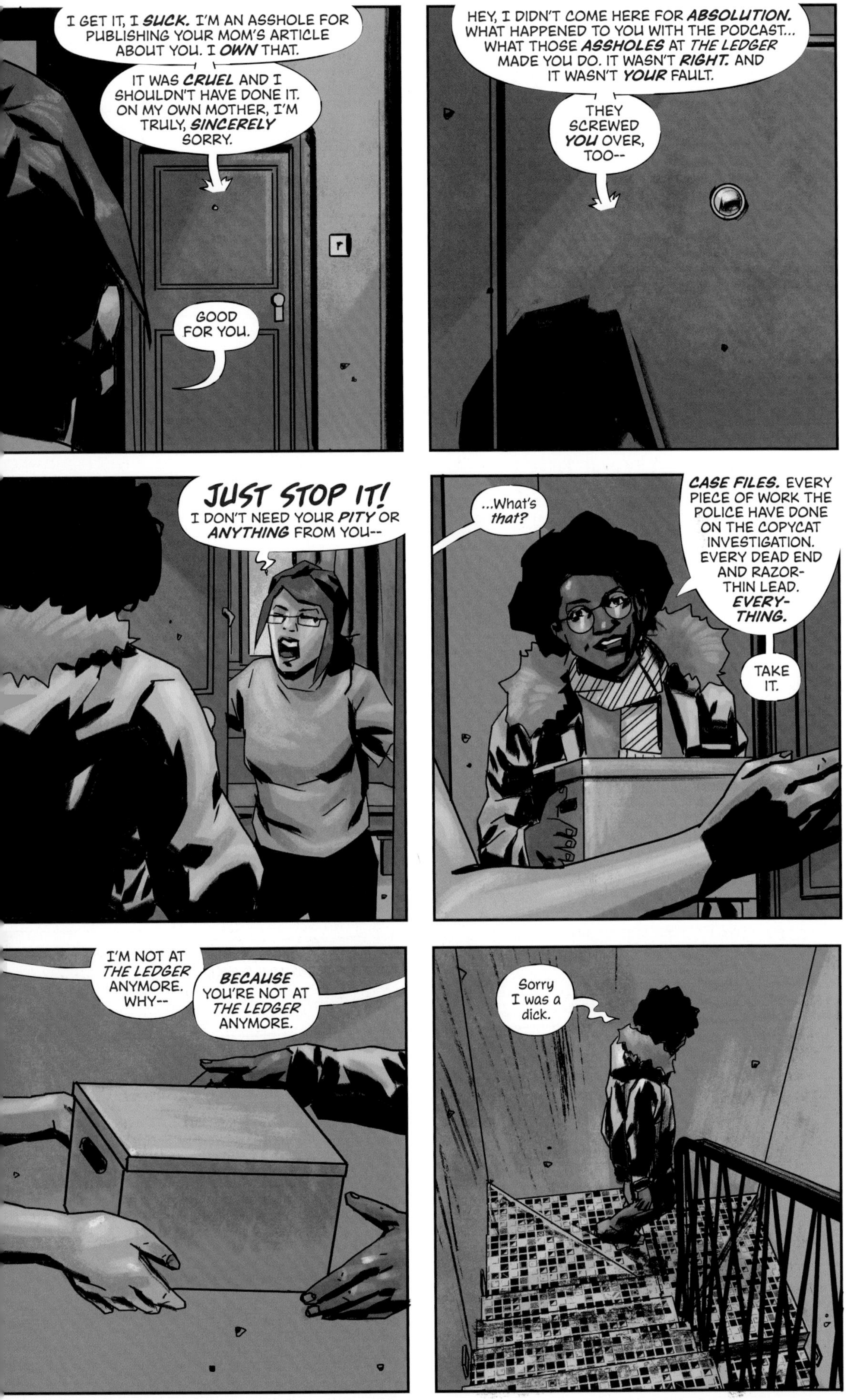

I GET IT, I SUCK. I'M AN ASSHOLE FOR PUBLISHING YOUR MOM'S ARTICLE ABOUT YOU. I OWN THAT.
IT WAS CRUEL AND I SHOULDN'T HAVE DONE IT. ON MY OWN MOTHER, I'M TRULY, SINCERELY SORRY.
GOOD FOR YOU.
HEY, I DIDN'T COME HERE FOR ABSOLUTION. WHAT HAPPENED TO YOU WITH THE PODCAST... WHAT THOSE ASSHOLES AT THE LEDGER MADE YOU DO. IT WASN'T RIGHT. AND IT WASN'T YOUR FAULT.
THEY SCREWED YOU OVER, TOO--
JUST STOP IT! I DON'T NEED YOUR PITY OR ANYTHING FROM YOU--
...What's that?
CASE FILES. EVERY PIECE OF WORK THE POLICE HAVE DONE ON THE COPYCAT INVESTIGATION. EVERY DEAD END AND RAZOR-THIN LEAD. EVERY-THING.
TAKE IT.
I'M NOT AT THE LEDGER ANYMORE. WHY--
BECAUSE YOU'RE NOT AT THE LEDGER ANYMORE.
Sorry I was a dick.

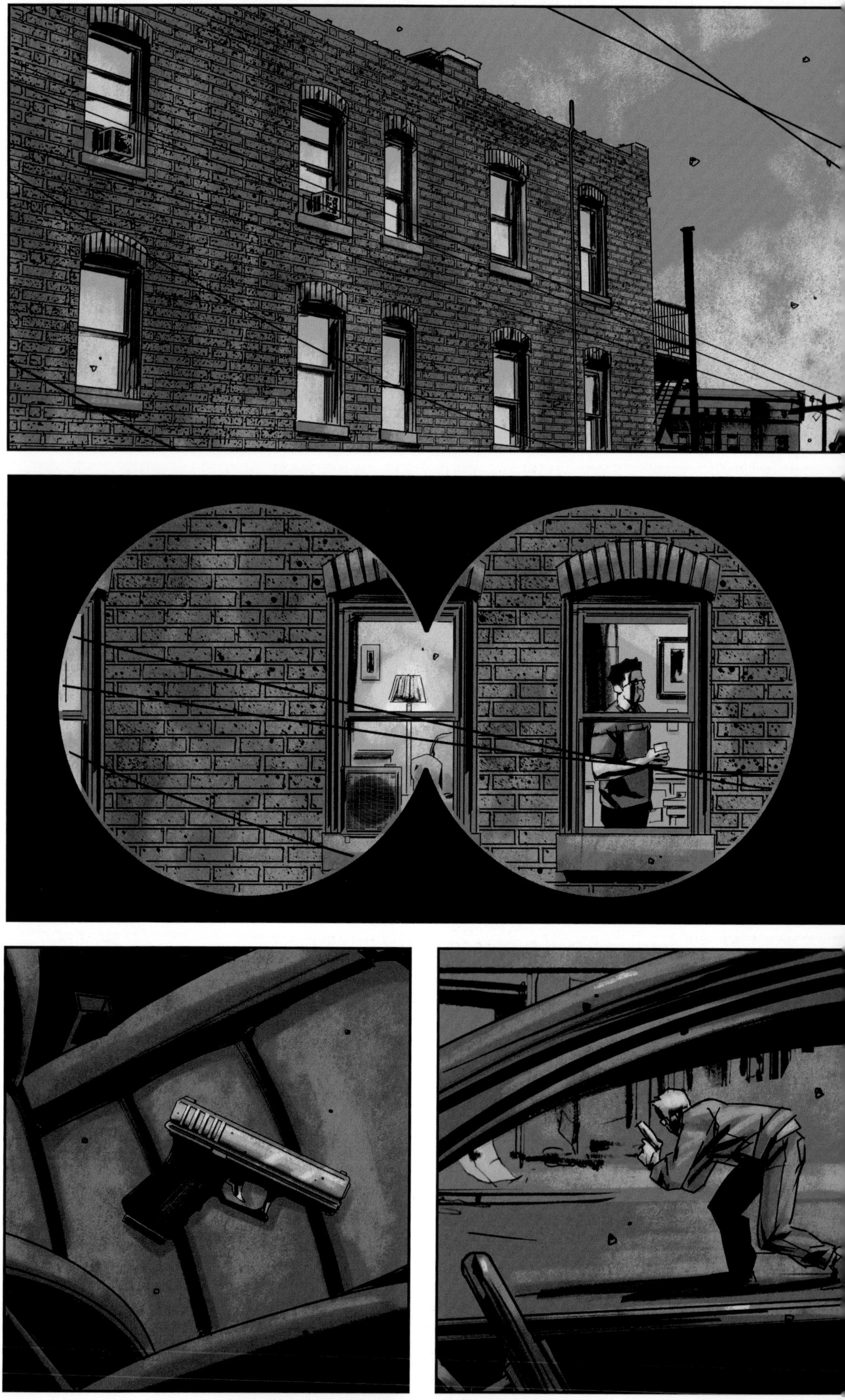

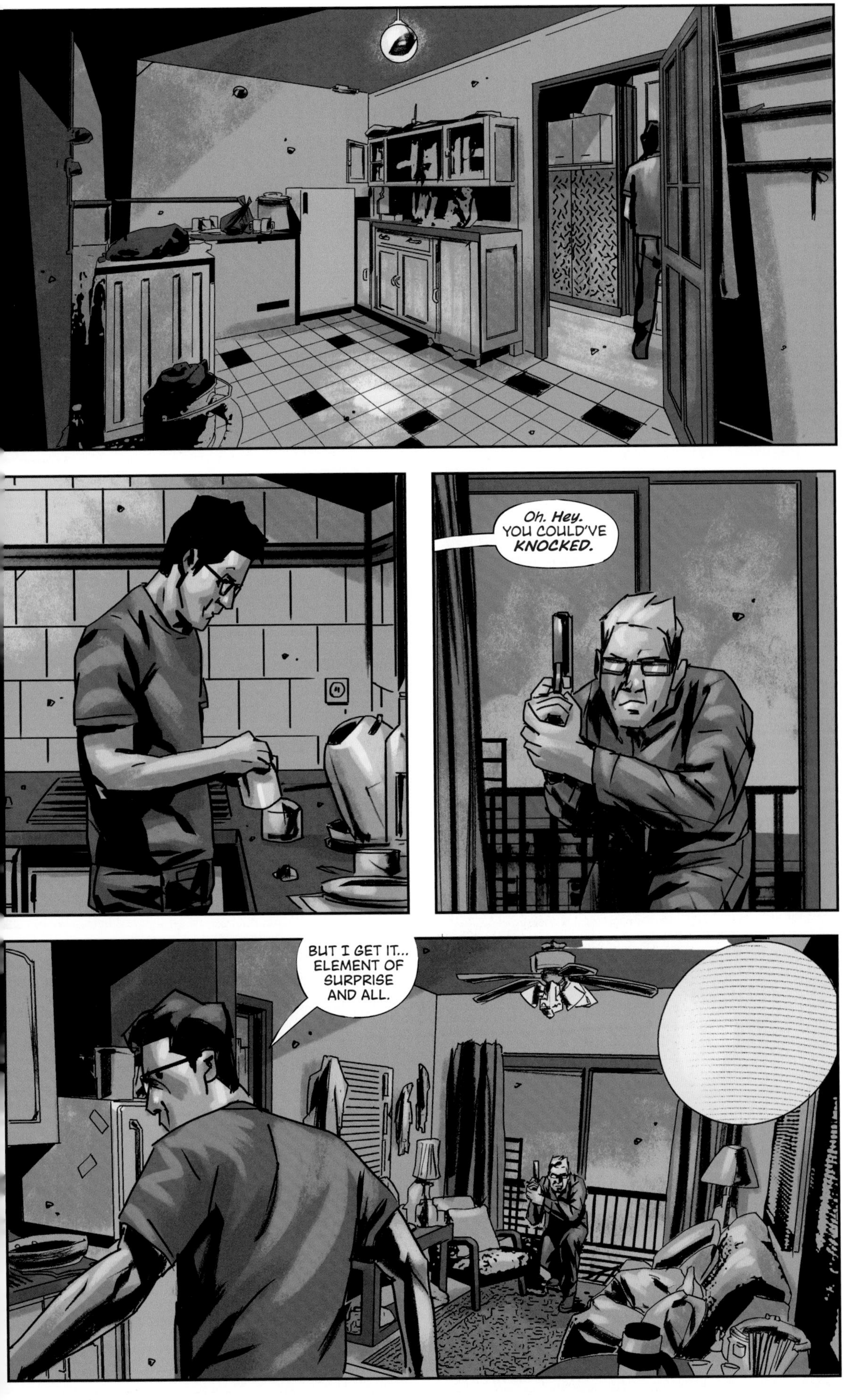
Oh. Hey. YOU COULD'VE KNOCKED.
BUT I GET IT... ELEMENT OF SURPRISE AND ALL.

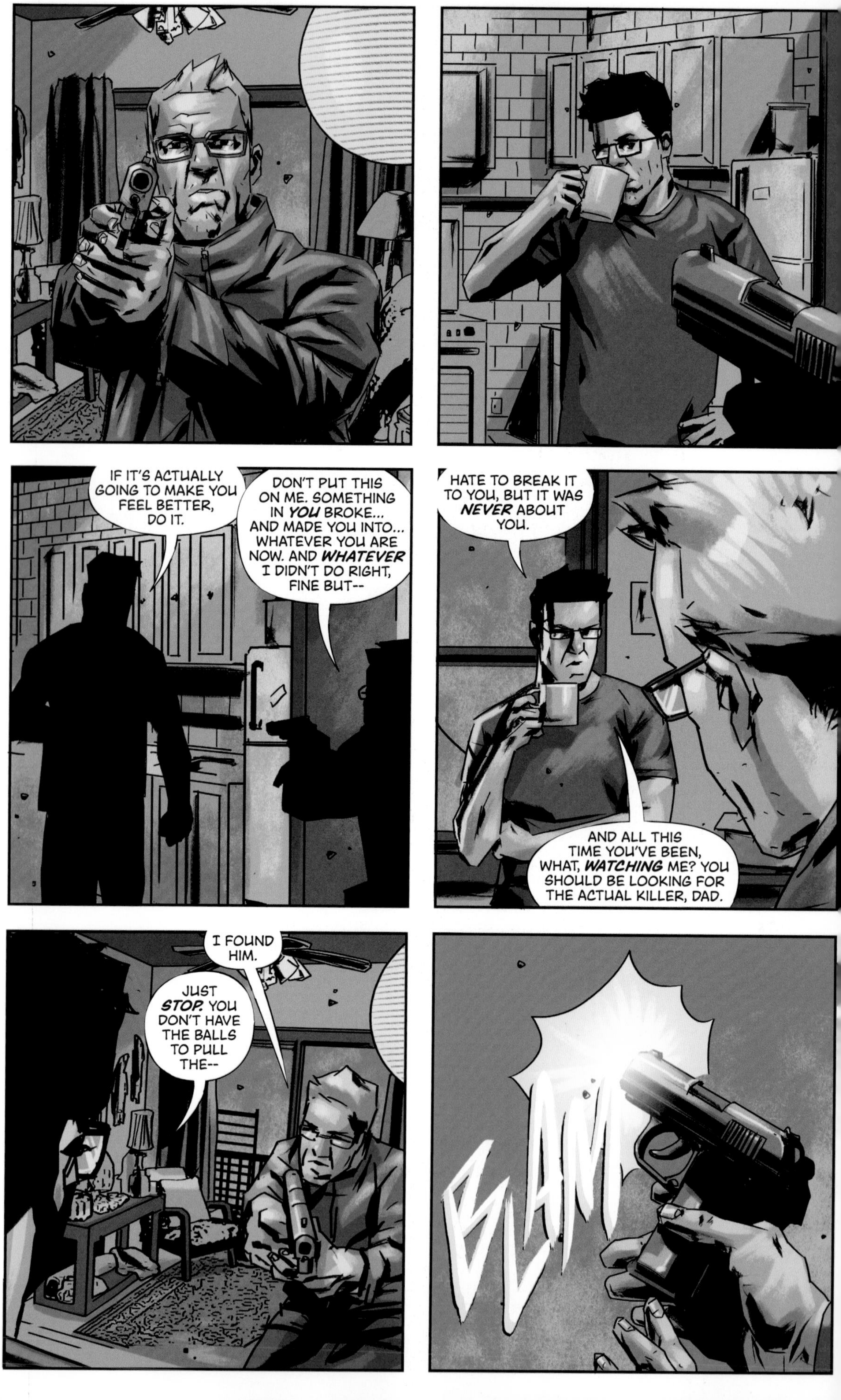
IF IT'S ACTUALLY GOING TO MAKE YOU FEEL BETTER, DO IT.
DON'T PUT THIS ON ME. SOMETHING IN *YOU* BROKE... AND MADE YOU INTO... WHATEVER YOU ARE NOW. AND *WHATEVER* I DIDN'T DO RIGHT, FINE BUT--
HATE TO BREAK IT TO YOU, BUT IT WAS *NEVER* ABOUT YOU.
AND ALL THIS TIME YOU'VE BEEN, WHAT, *WATCHING* ME? YOU SHOULD BE LOOKING FOR THE ACTUAL KILLER, DAD.
I FOUND HIM.
JUST *STOP.* YOU DON'T HAVE THE BALLS TO PULL THE--
BLAM

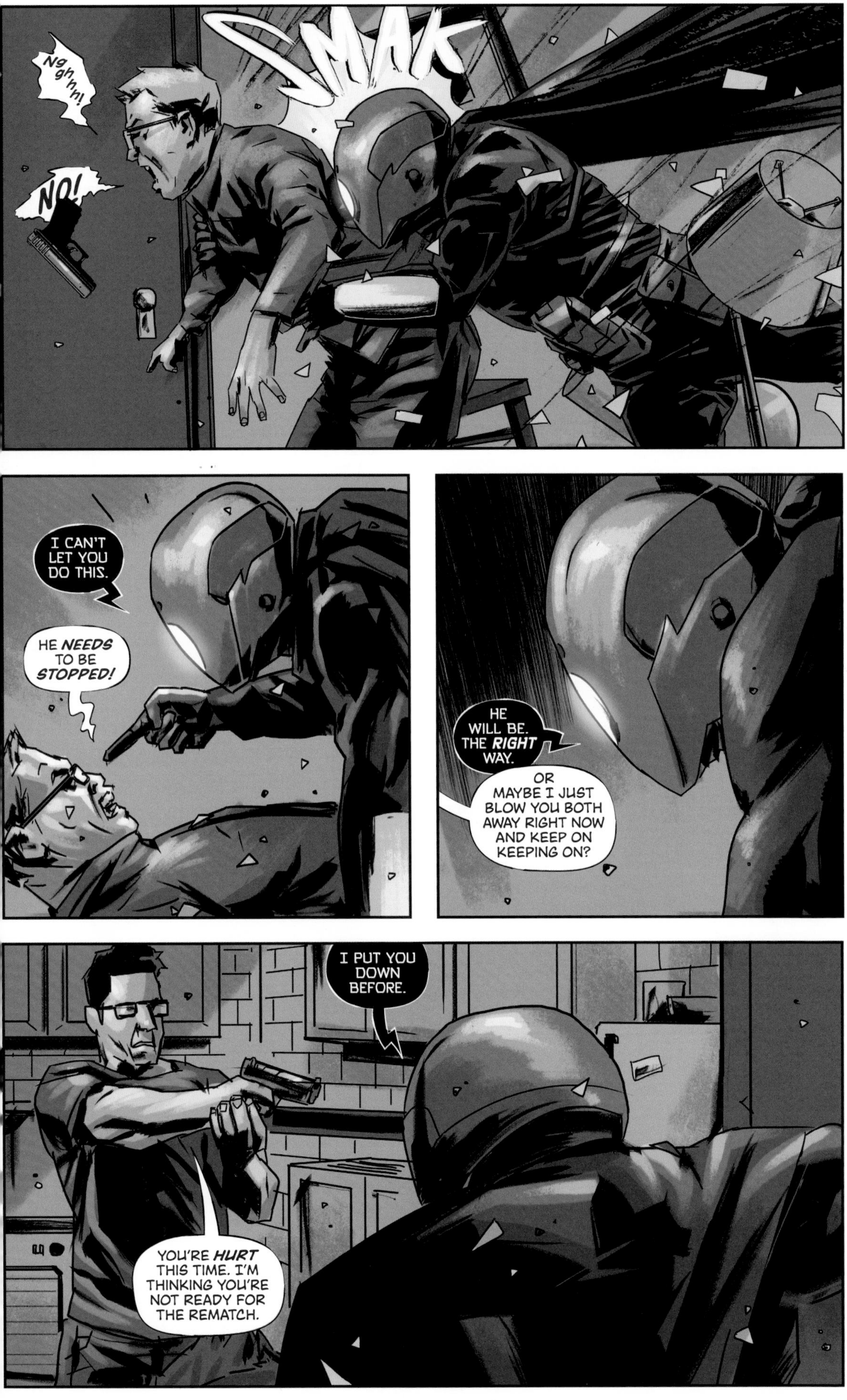
SMAK
Nghhh!
NO!
I CAN'T LET YOU DO THIS.
HE NEEDS TO BE STOPPED!
HE WILL BE. THE RIGHT WAY.
OR MAYBE I JUST BLOW YOU BOTH AWAY RIGHT NOW AND KEEP ON KEEPING ON?
I PUT YOU DOWN BEFORE.
YOU'RE HURT THIS TIME. I'M THINKING YOU'RE NOT READY FOR THE REMATCH.

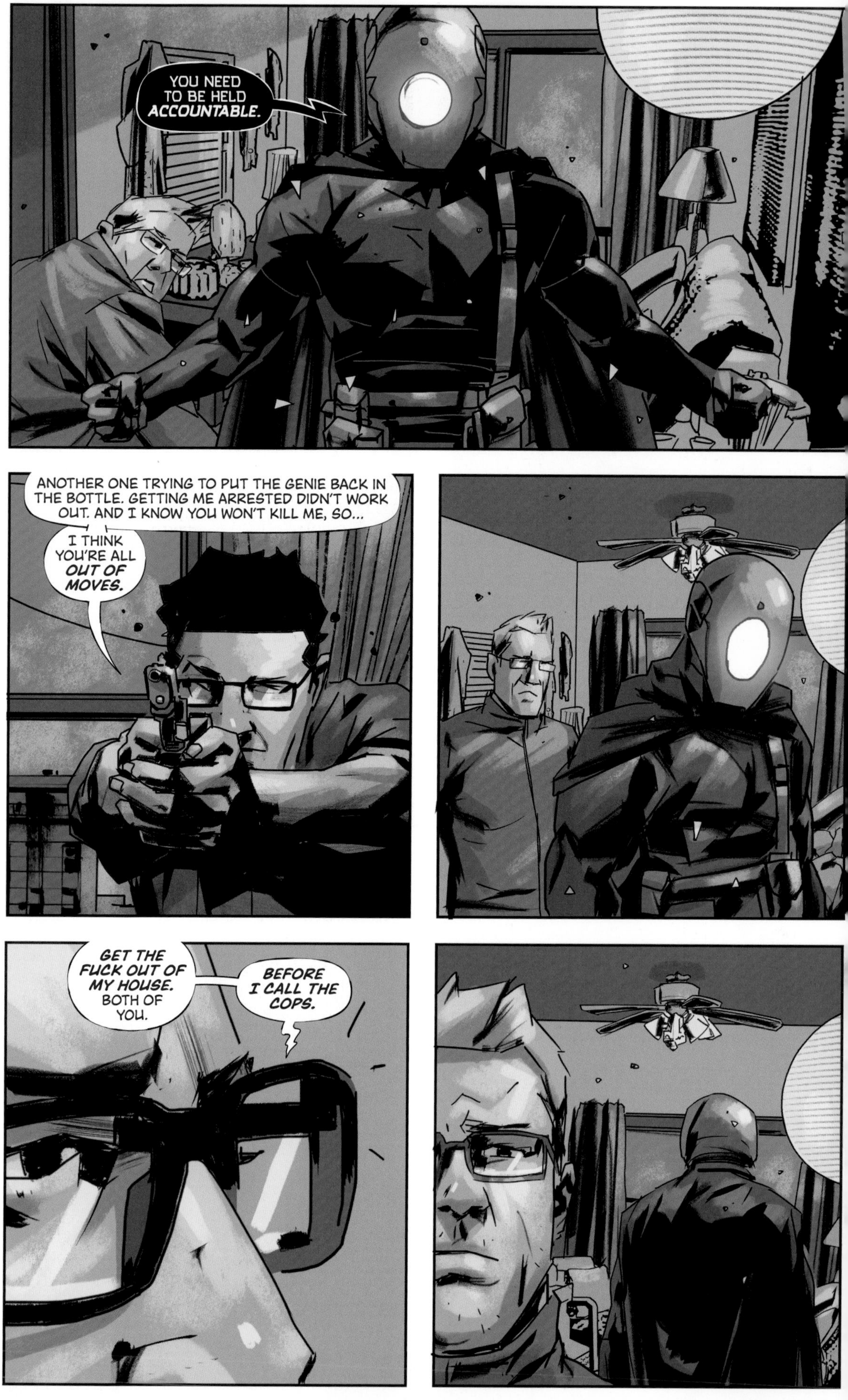
YOU NEED TO BE HELD ACCOUNTABLE.
ANOTHER ONE TRYING TO PUT THE GENIE BACK IN THE BOTTLE. GETTING ME ARRESTED DIDN'T WORK OUT. AND I KNOW YOU WON'T KILL ME, SO...
I THINK YOU'RE ALL OUT OF MOVES.
GET THE FUCK OUT OF MY HOUSE. BOTH OF YOU.
BEFORE I CALL THE COPS.

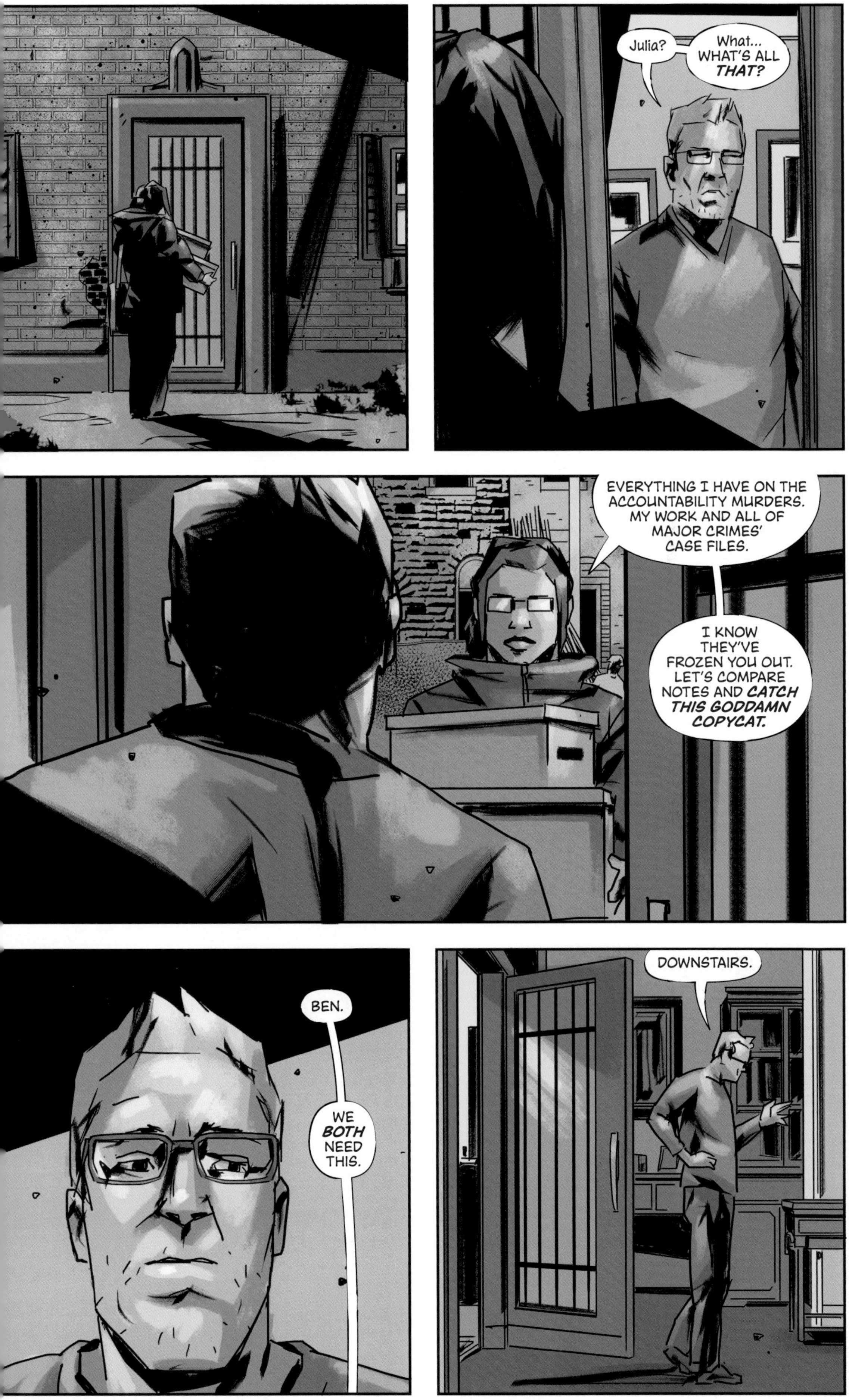
Julia?
What... WHAT'S ALL *THAT?*
EVERYTHING I HAVE ON THE ACCOUNTABILITY MURDERS. MY WORK AND ALL OF MAJOR CRIMES' CASE FILES.
I KNOW THEY'VE FROZEN YOU OUT. LET'S COMPARE NOTES AND ***CATCH THIS GODDAMN COPYCAT.***
BEN.
WE ***BOTH*** NEED THIS.
DOWNSTAIRS.

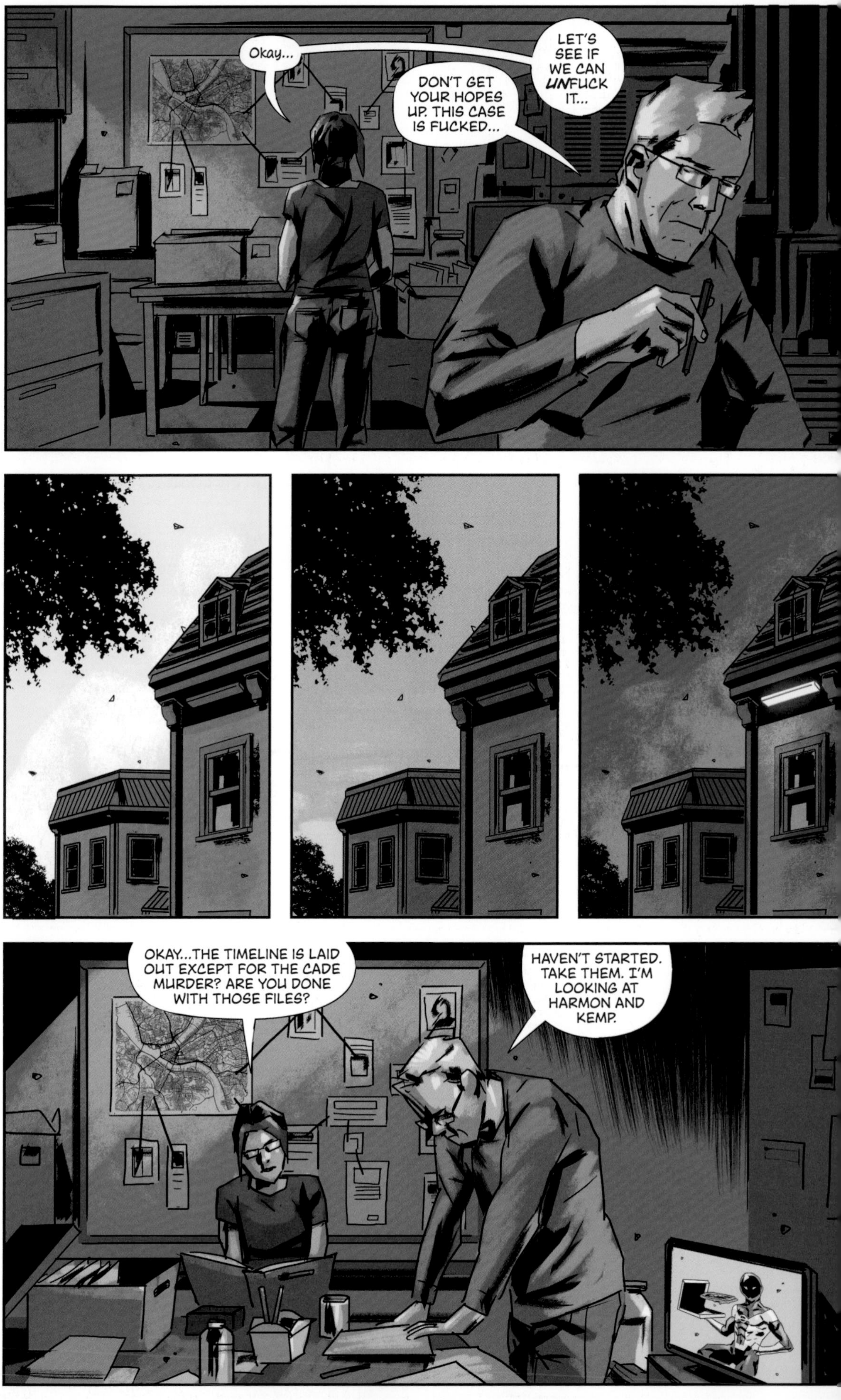
Okay...
DON'T GET YOUR HOPES UP. THIS CASE IS FUCKED...
LET'S SEE IF WE CAN UNFUCK IT...
OKAY...THE TIMELINE IS LAID OUT EXCEPT FOR THE CADE MURDER? ARE YOU DONE WITH THOSE FILES?
HAVEN'T STARTED. TAKE THEM. I'M LOOKING AT HARMON AND KEMP.

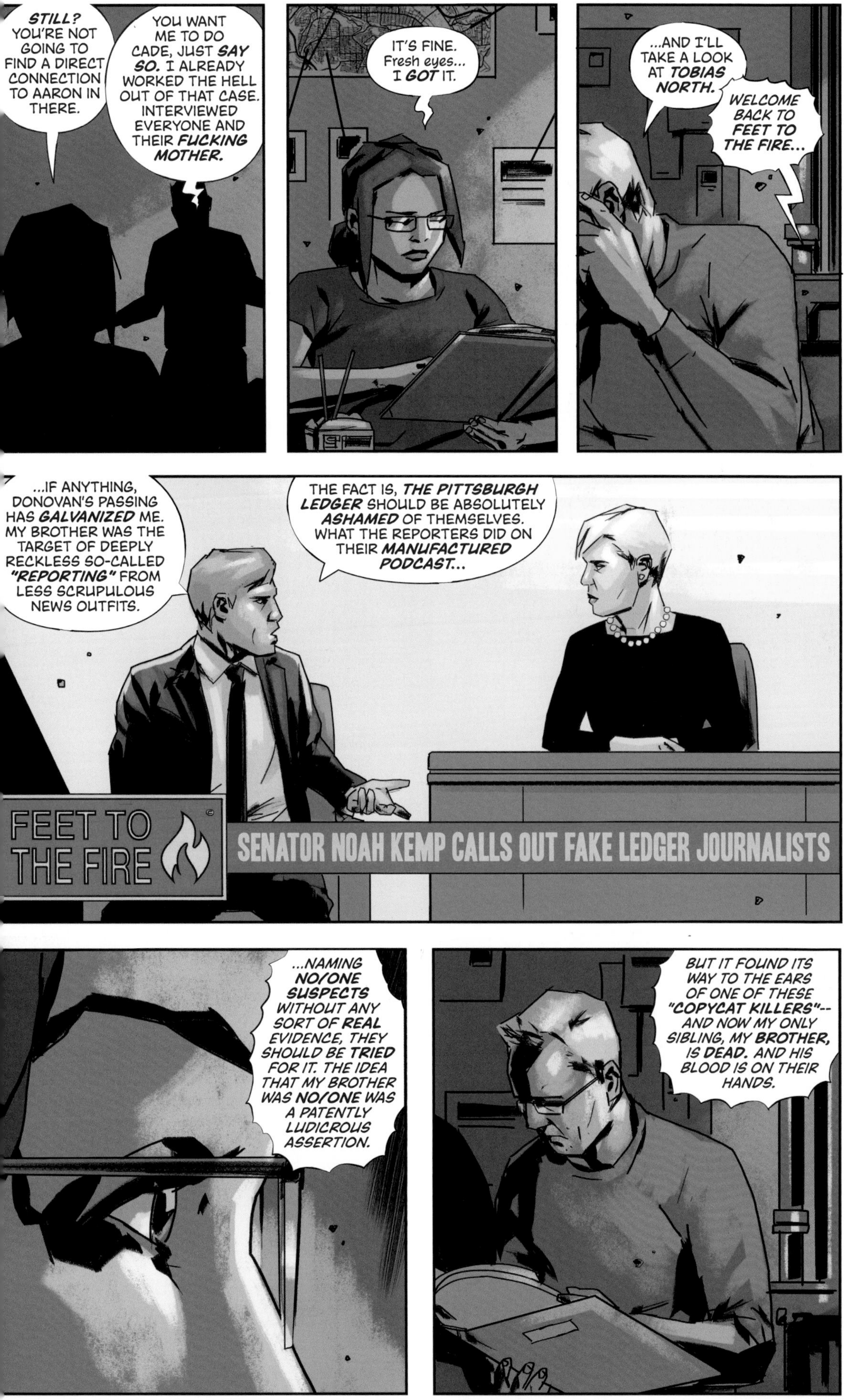
STILL? YOU'RE NOT GOING TO FIND A DIRECT CONNECTION TO AARON IN THERE.
YOU WANT ME TO DO CADE, JUST SAY SO. I ALREADY WORKED THE HELL OUT OF THAT CASE. INTERVIEWED EVERYONE AND THEIR FUCKING MOTHER.
IT'S FINE. Fresh eyes... I GOT IT.
...AND I'LL TAKE A LOOK AT TOBIAS NORTH.
WELCOME BACK TO FEET TO THE FIRE...
...IF ANYTHING, DONOVAN'S PASSING HAS GALVANIZED ME. MY BROTHER WAS THE TARGET OF DEEPLY RECKLESS SO-CALLED "REPORTING" FROM LESS SCRUPULOUS NEWS OUTFITS.
THE FACT IS, THE PITTSBURGH LEDGER SHOULD BE ABSOLUTELY ASHAMED OF THEMSELVES. WHAT THE REPORTERS DID ON THEIR MANUFACTURED PODCAST...
FEET TO THE FIRE
SENATOR NOAH KEMP CALLS OUT FAKE LEDGER JOURNALISTS
...NAMING NO/ONE SUSPECTS WITHOUT ANY SORT OF REAL EVIDENCE, THEY SHOULD BE TRIED FOR IT. THE IDEA THAT MY BROTHER WAS NO/ONE WAS A PATENTLY LUDICROUS ASSERTION.
BUT IT FOUND ITS WAY TO THE EARS OF ONE OF THESE "COPYCAT KILLERS"-- AND NOW MY ONLY SIBLING, MY BROTHER, IS DEAD. AND HIS BLOOD IS ON THEIR HANDS.

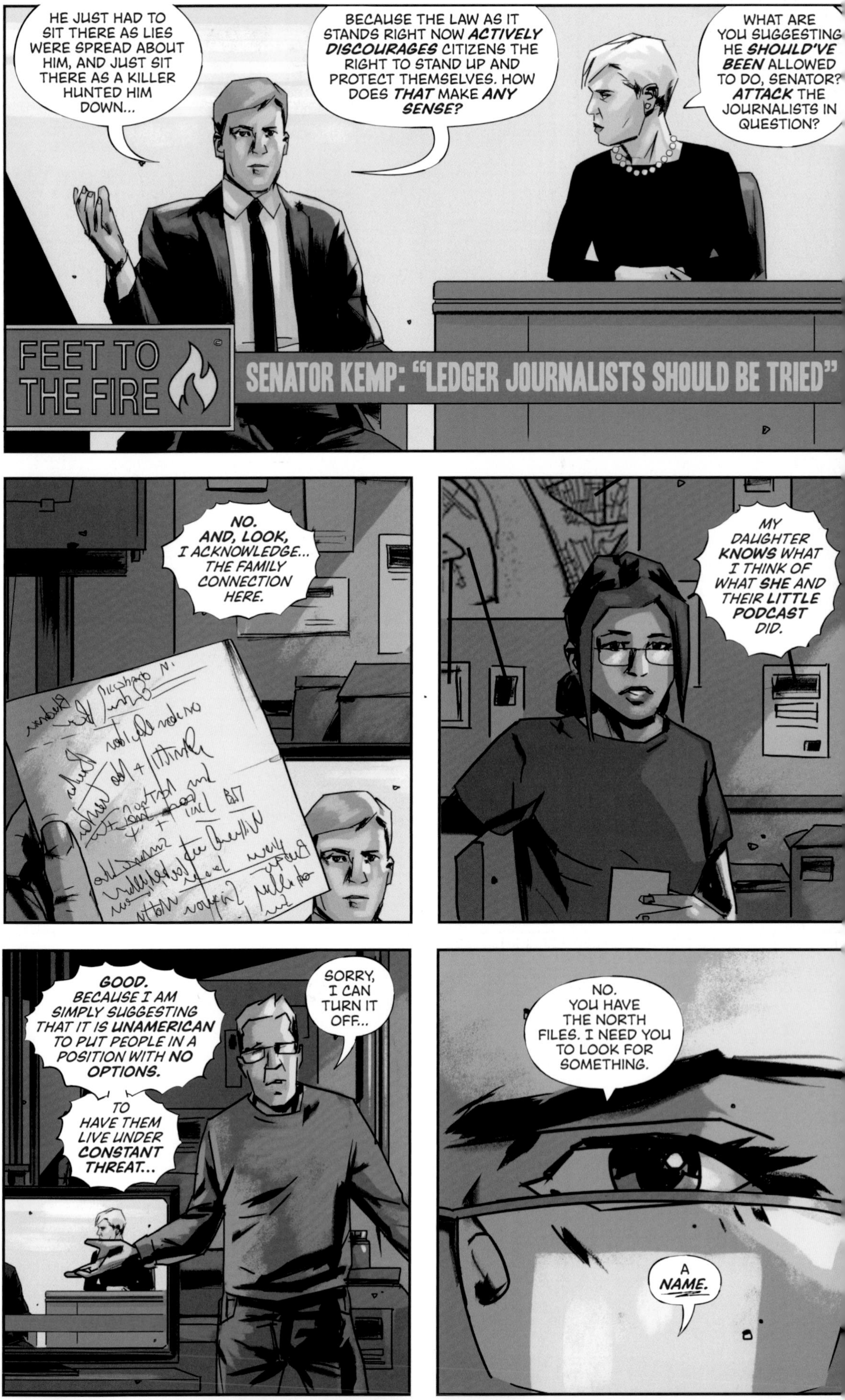
HE JUST HAD TO SIT THERE AS LIES WERE SPREAD ABOUT HIM, AND JUST SIT THERE AS A KILLER HUNTED HIM DOWN...
BECAUSE THE LAW AS IT STANDS RIGHT NOW ACTIVELY DISCOURAGES CITIZENS THE RIGHT TO STAND UP AND PROTECT THEMSELVES. HOW DOES THAT MAKE ANY SENSE?
WHAT ARE YOU SUGGESTING HE SHOULD'VE BEEN ALLOWED TO DO, SENATOR? ATTACK THE JOURNALISTS IN QUESTION?
FEET TO THE FIRE
SENATOR KEMP: "LEDGER JOURNALISTS SHOULD BE TRIED"
NO. AND, LOOK, I ACKNOWLEDGE... THE FAMILY CONNECTION HERE.
MY DAUGHTER KNOWS WHAT I THINK OF WHAT SHE AND THEIR LITTLE PODCAST DID.
GOOD. BECAUSE I AM SIMPLY SUGGESTING THAT IT IS UNAMERICAN TO PUT PEOPLE IN A POSITION WITH NO OPTIONS.
TO HAVE THEM LIVE UNDER CONSTANT THREAT...
SORRY, I CAN TURN IT OFF...
NO. YOU HAVE THE NORTH FILES. I NEED YOU TO LOOK FOR SOMETHING.
A NAME.

ON ONE SIDE, THE BAD GUYS, THEY CAN DO WHATEVER... AND THE GOOD SIDE ARE SUPPOSED TO PLAY WITH THEIR HANDS *TIED* BEHIND THEIR *BACKS?* PUNISHED, HAVING THE DECK TOTALLY STACKED *AGAINST* THEM...

...SIMPLY BECAUSE THEY *CHOOSE* TO BE *LAW-ABIDING* CITIZENS?

FEET TO THE FIRE

SENATOR KEMP: "...UN-AMERICAN TO PUT PEOPLE IN A POSITION WITH NO OPTIONS"

IS THAT THE SOCIETY *ANYONE* WANTS TO LIVE IN? IS THAT WHAT YOUR VIEWERS *WANT,* ALANNA?

NO. I CAN ASSURE YOU, SENATOR-- IT IS *NOT.* DO YOU THINK *YOU* CAN GET IT DONE?

MY COLLEAGUES CAN'T DENY THE NEED FOR CHANGE, NOT *NOW.* THEY CAN HEAR THE PEOPLE OF THIS GREAT STATE CHANTING OUTSIDE THEIR WINDOWS, *DEMANDING* THAT WE CODIFY THEIR NATURAL, *GOD-GIVEN* RIGHTS.

NOTHING WILL *STOP* ME. BECAUSE I'M DOING THIS FOR PENNSYLVANIA...

PROPOSITION-87 GAINS REN

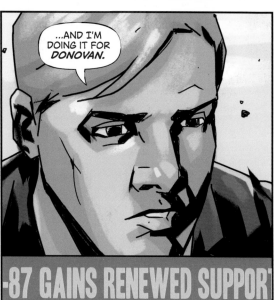

...AND I'M DOING IT FOR *DONOVAN.*

-87 GAINS RENEWED SUPPORT

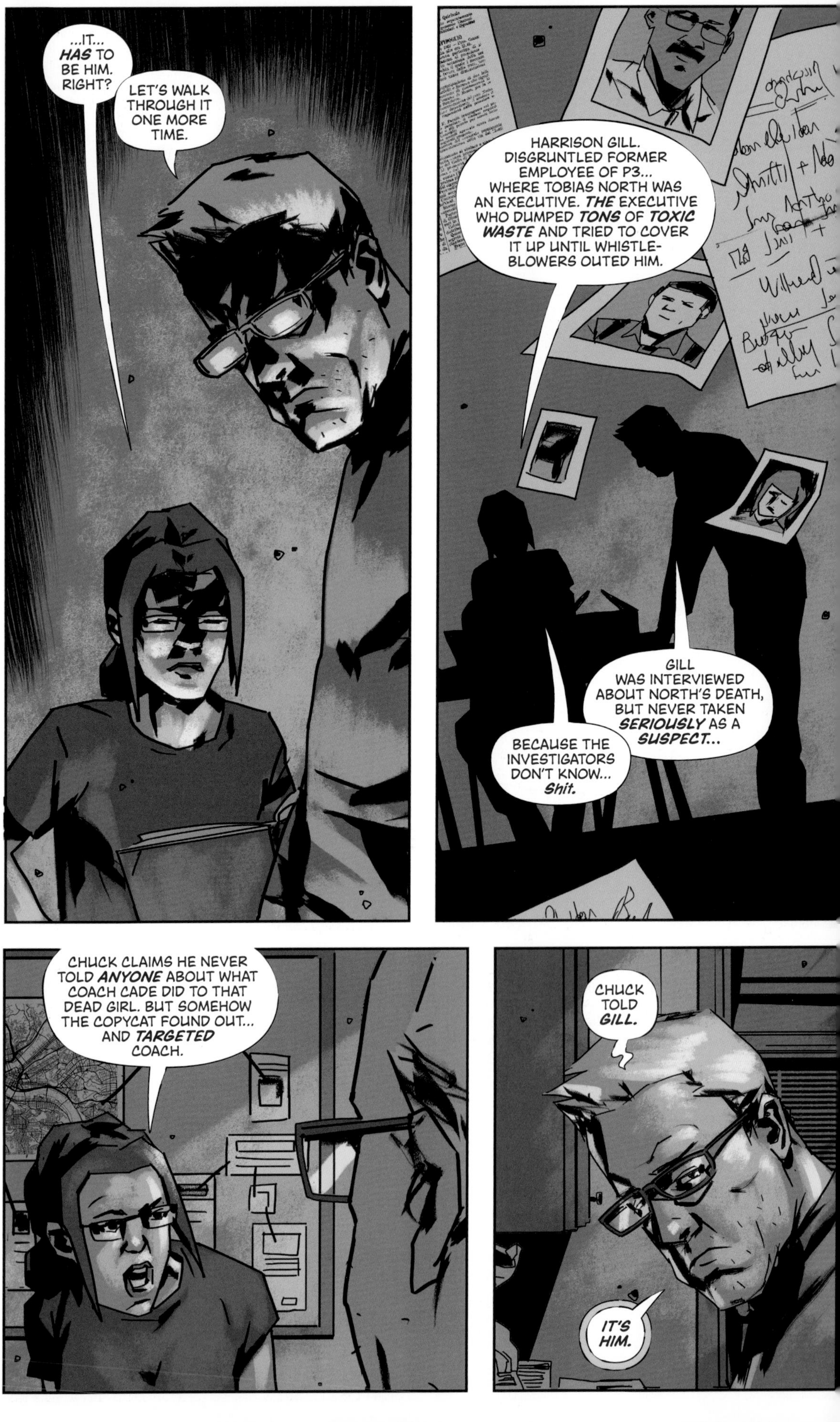
...IT... HAS TO BE HIM. RIGHT?
LET'S WALK THROUGH IT ONE MORE TIME.
HARRISON GILL. DISGRUNTLED FORMER EMPLOYEE OF P3... WHERE TOBIAS NORTH WAS AN EXECUTIVE. THE EXECUTIVE WHO DUMPED TONS OF TOXIC WASTE AND TRIED TO COVER IT UP UNTIL WHISTLE-BLOWERS OUTED HIM.
GILL WAS INTERVIEWED ABOUT NORTH'S DEATH, BUT NEVER TAKEN SERIOUSLY AS A SUSPECT...
BECAUSE THE INVESTIGATORS DON'T KNOW... Shit.
CHUCK CLAIMS HE NEVER TOLD ANYONE ABOUT WHAT COACH CADE DID TO THAT DEAD GIRL. BUT SOMEHOW THE COPYCAT FOUND OUT... AND TARGETED COACH.
CHUCK TOLD GILL.
IT'S HIM.

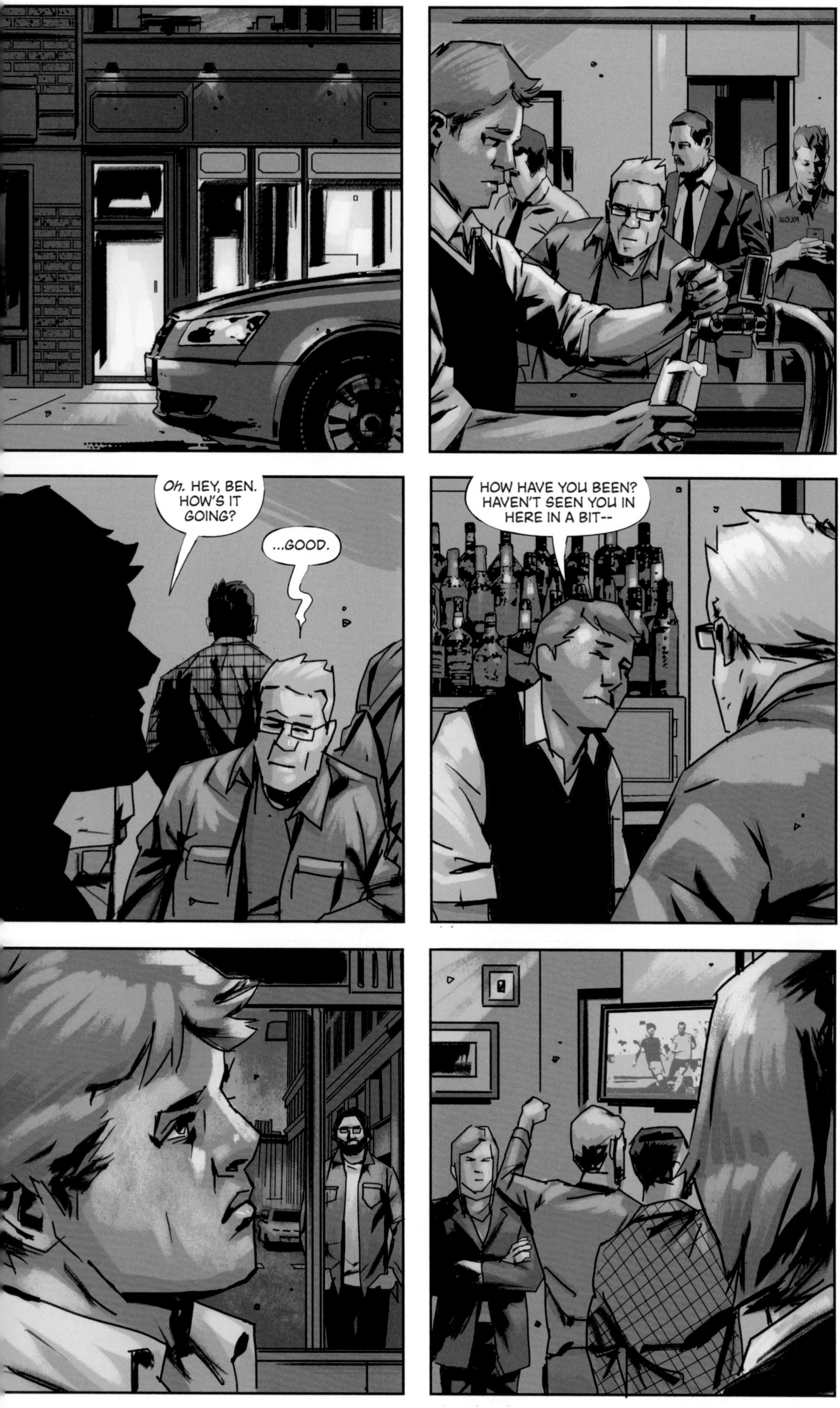
Oh. HEY, BEN. HOW'S IT GOING?
...GOOD.
HOW HAVE YOU BEEN? HAVEN'T SEEN YOU IN HERE IN A BIT--

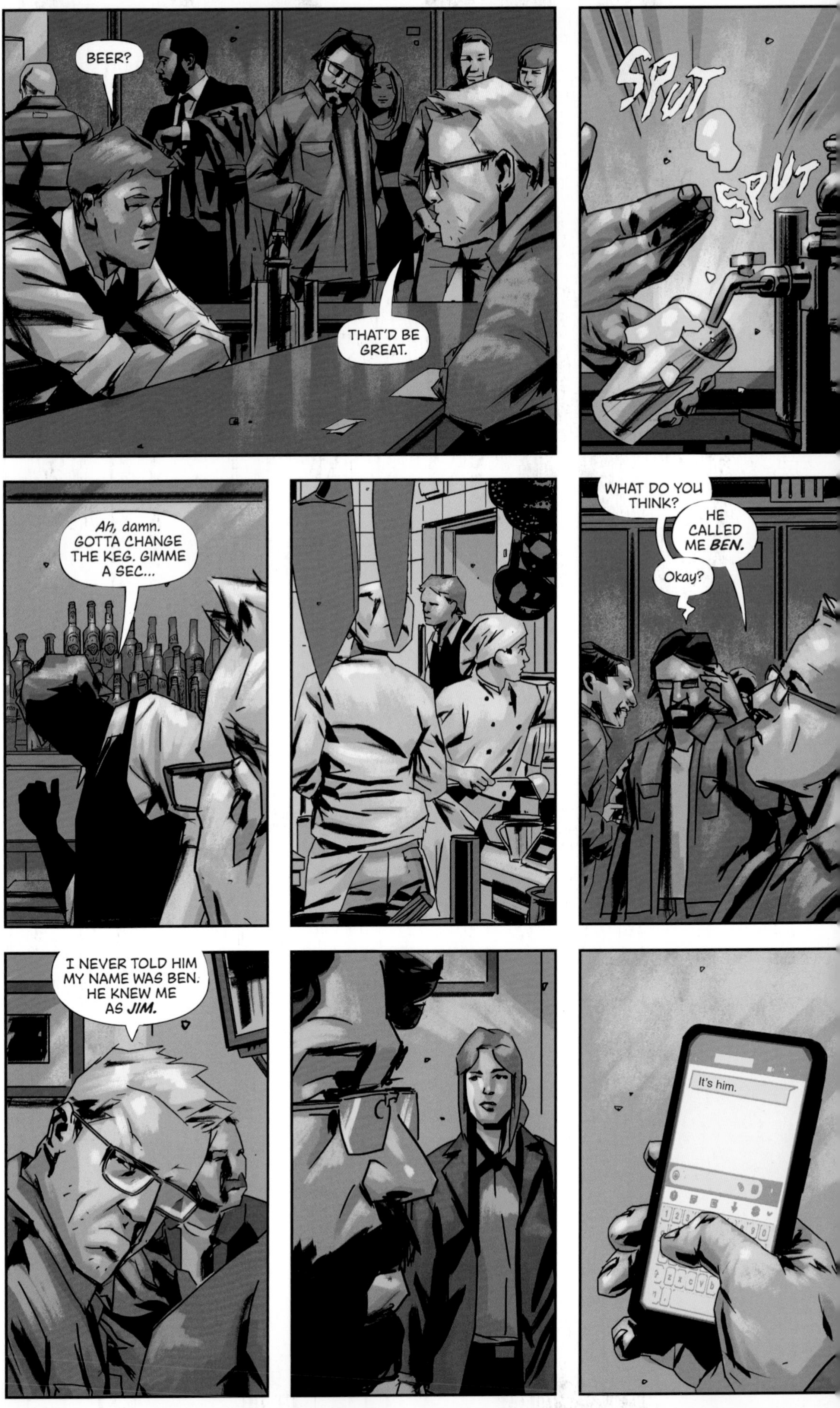
BEER?
THAT'D BE GREAT.
SPUT SPUT
Ah, damn. GOTTA CHANGE THE KEG. GIMME A SEC...
WHAT DO YOU THINK?
HE CALLED ME BEN.
Okay?
I NEVER TOLD HIM MY NAME WAS BEN. HE KNEW ME AS JIM.
It's him.

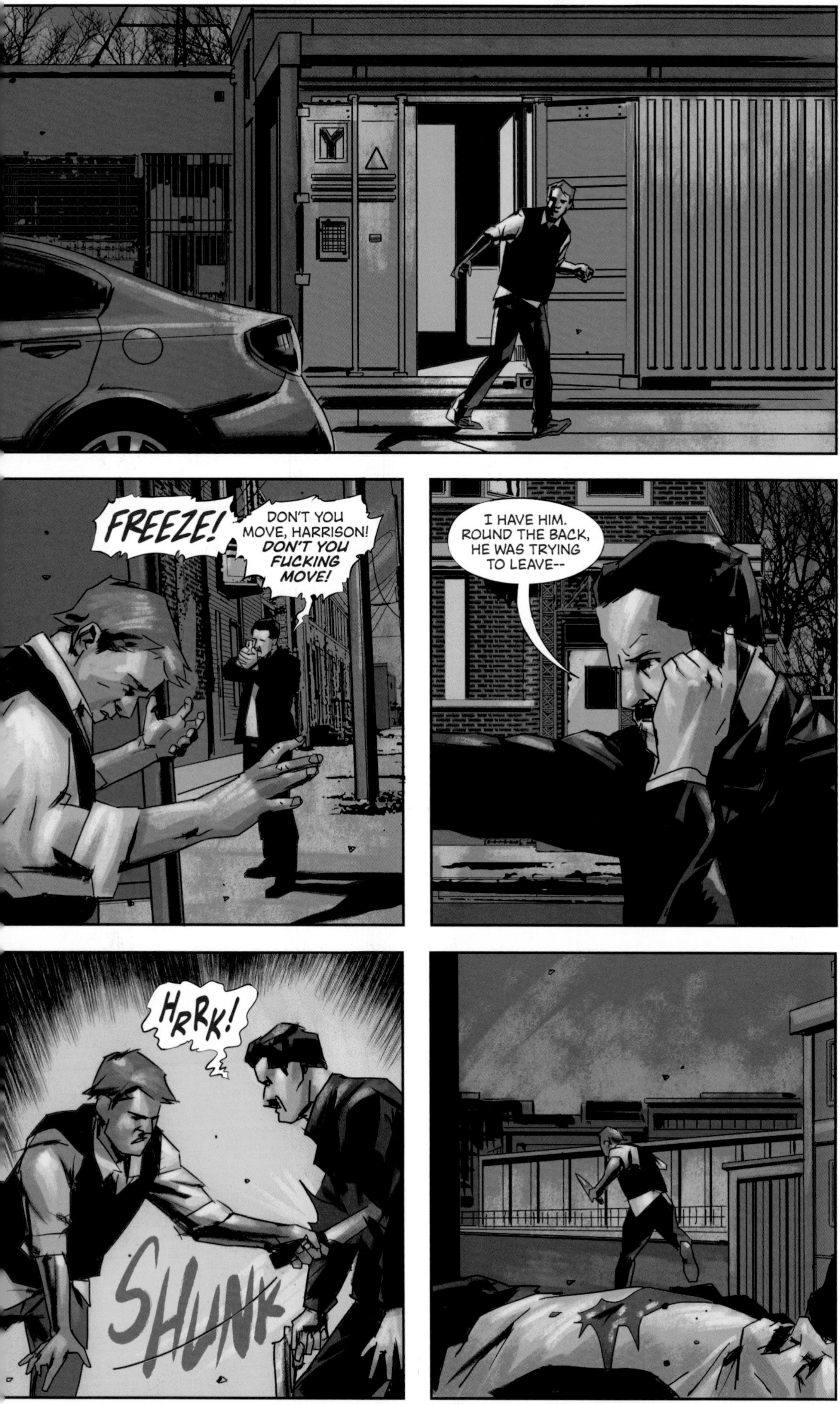
FREEZE!
DON'T YOU MOVE, HARRISON! DON'T YOU FUCKING MOVE!
I HAVE HIM. ROUND THE BACK, HE WAS TRYING TO LEAVE--
HRRK!
SHUNK

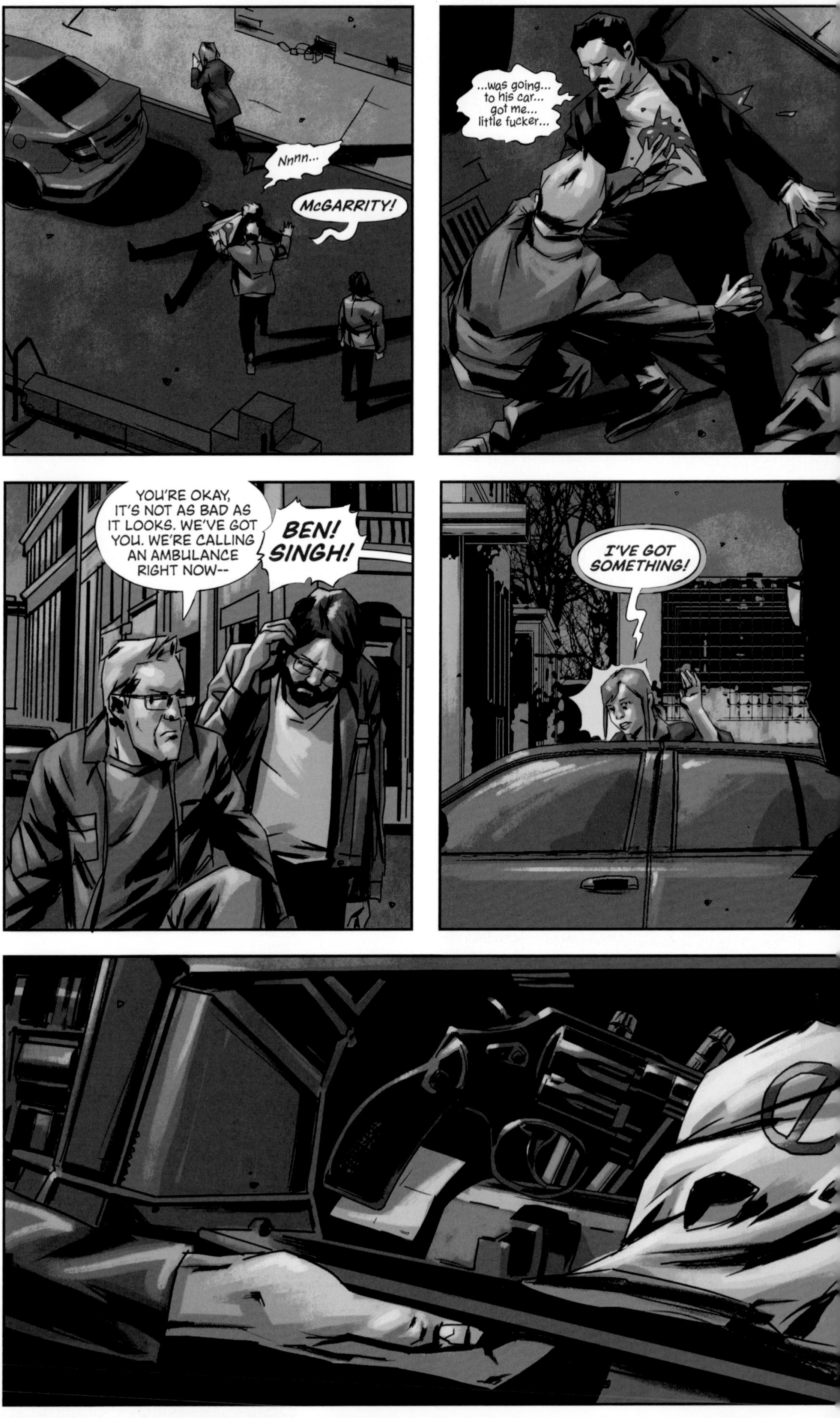
Nnnn...
McGARRITY!
...was going... to his car... got me... little fucker...
YOU'RE OKAY, IT'S NOT AS BAD AS IT LOOKS. WE'VE GOT YOU. WE'RE CALLING AN AMBULANCE RIGHT NOW--
BEN! SINGH!
I'VE GOT SOMETHING!

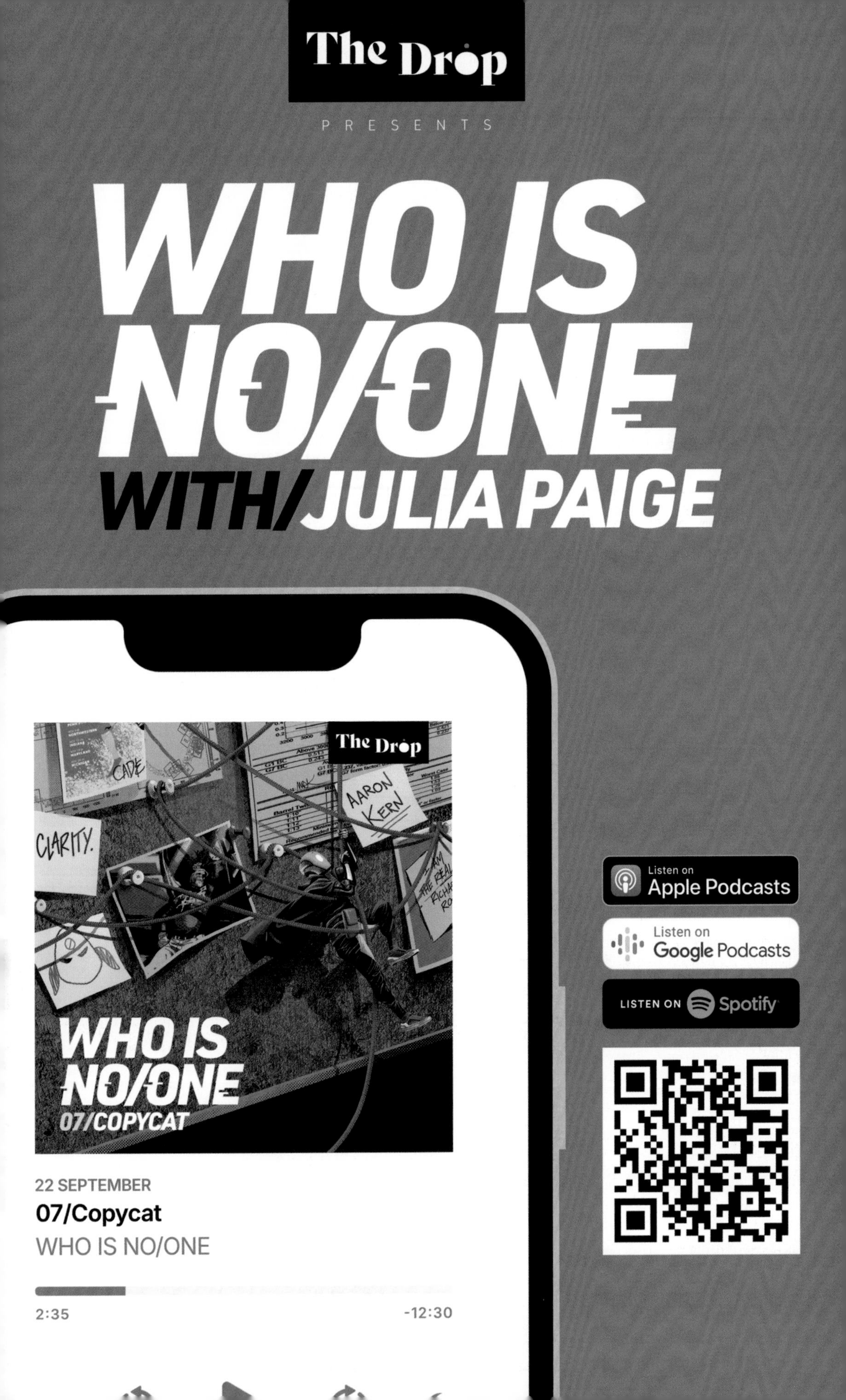

The Drop
PRESENTS
WHO IS NO/ONE
WITH/JULIA PAIGE
The Drop
CADE
AARON KERN
CLARITY.
WHO IS NO/ONE
07/COPYCAT
22 SEPTEMBER
07/Copycat
WHO IS NO/ONE
2:35
-12:30
Listen on Apple Podcasts
Listen on Google Podcasts
LISTEN ON Spotify

Manhunt for Accountability Murder suspect

Julia Paige
Pittsburgh Ledger

Pittsburgh, PA— A manhunt is currently underway for Harrison Gill, a former employee of Pittsburgh Paints and Protectives (P3), following an altercation with law enforcement outside Fitzgerald's bar, where Gill was last seen. Authorities have linked Gill to a series of chilling murders associated with the so-called "Accountability Killer," dating back to at least March of this year.

Earlier this week, investigators attempted to bring Gill in for questioning regarding his potential connection to the ongoing series of killings. However, during the operation, Gill managed to evade capture, prompting an immediate manhunt. Authorities discovered Gill's vehicle near Fitzgerald's, which contained a .38 special revolver confirmed to be the weapon used in the Richard Roe murders. In addition to real estate developer Louis Capel, Three Rivers University coach Nathan Cade, P3 executive Tobias North and Michael Kern, son of former Pittsburgh Police Assistant Chief of Operations Ben Kern, Gill is now believed to also be responsible for the killing of activist Donovan Kemp and the shooting of Officer Vince Harmon, as well as the attempted murder of journalist Alejandro Rios.

Also found in Gill's possession was a mask consistent with descriptions of the one worn by the original Richard Roe. Ben Kern, a key figure in the investigation, stated on a recent appearance on this paper's WHO IS NO/ONE podcast that "[he] saw it up close when the copycat tried to kill me. It's the same mask."

Authorities are urging the public to assist in the search for Gill, who they believe poses a significant threat. "We need your help to find this man. To stop him before he can hurt anyone else," Kern implored during his podcast appearance.

As the investigation unfolds, questions remain regarding any potential connection between Gill and Aaron Kern, the initially accused Accountability Killer, who recently recanted his confession. Aaron, who has maintained his innocence, is still regarded by many, including his father, as the original Richard Roe. Gill's use of the Richard Roe moniker raises questions about whether he was inspired by Kern or if a more direct connection exists.

"It's tough to speculate on motive at this stage," the elder Kern remarked, acknowledging the challenges in piecing together the evidence. As authorities continue their search for Gill, they emphasize the importance of public safety, advising anyone who may encounter him to refrain from engagement and instead contact law enforcement immediately.

SEPTEMBER 23 2023
PITTSBURGH LEDGER

>_ CHAPTER EIGHT
OCTOBER 2023

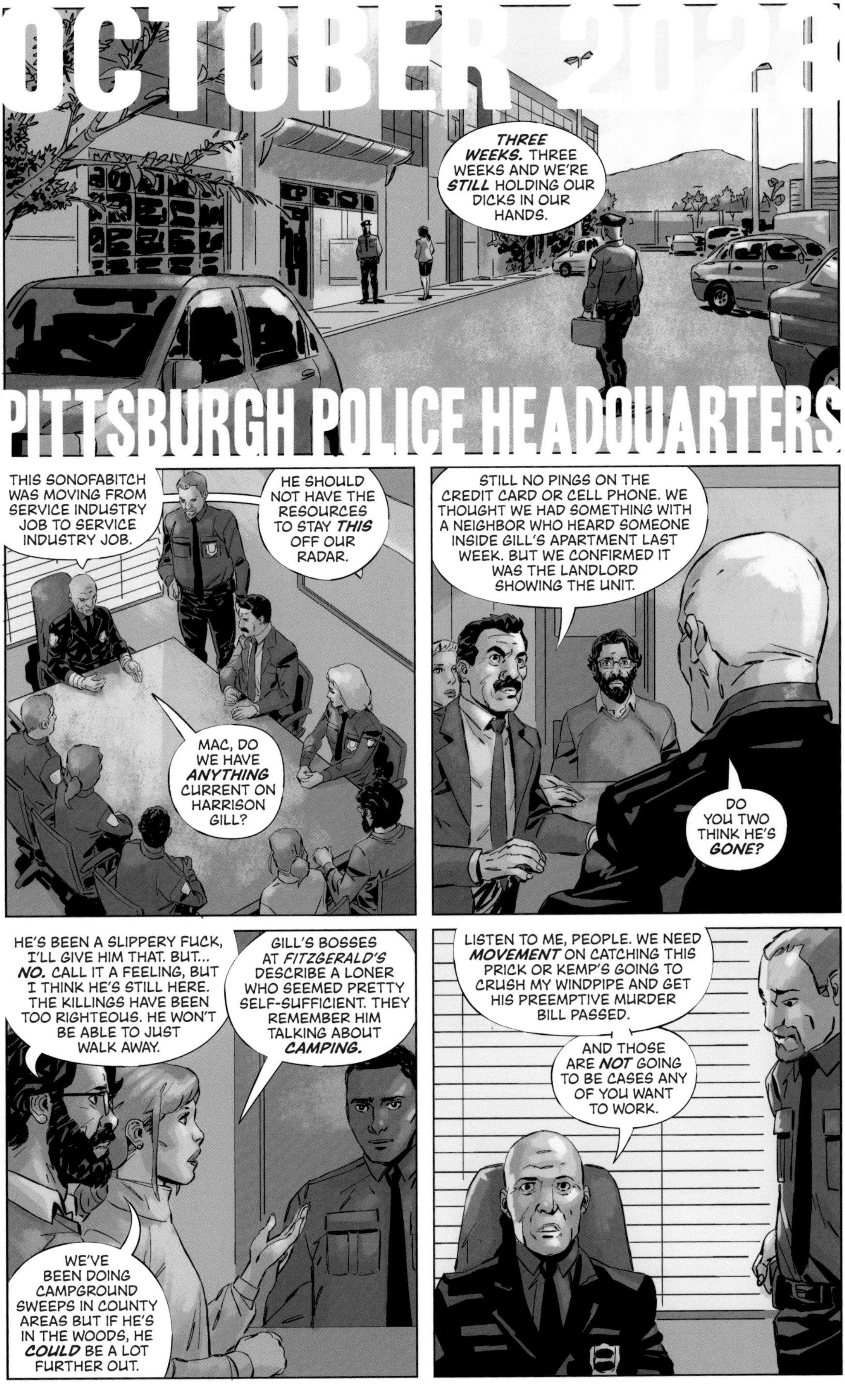
OCTOBER 2023
THREE WEEKS. THREE WEEKS AND WE'RE STILL HOLDING OUR DICKS IN OUR HANDS.
PITTSBURGH POLICE HEADQUARTERS
THIS SONOFABITCH WAS MOVING FROM SERVICE INDUSTRY JOB TO SERVICE INDUSTRY JOB.
HE SHOULD NOT HAVE THE RESOURCES TO STAY THIS OFF OUR RADAR.
MAC, DO WE HAVE ANYTHING CURRENT ON HARRISON GILL?
STILL NO PINGS ON THE CREDIT CARD OR CELL PHONE. WE THOUGHT WE HAD SOMETHING WITH A NEIGHBOR WHO HEARD SOMEONE INSIDE GILL'S APARTMENT LAST WEEK. BUT WE CONFIRMED IT WAS THE LANDLORD SHOWING THE UNIT.
DO YOU TWO THINK HE'S GONE?
HE'S BEEN A SLIPPERY FUCK, I'LL GIVE HIM THAT. BUT... NO. CALL IT A FEELING, BUT I THINK HE'S STILL HERE. THE KILLINGS HAVE BEEN TOO RIGHTEOUS. HE WON'T BE ABLE TO JUST WALK AWAY.
GILL'S BOSSES AT FITZGERALD'S DESCRIBE A LONER WHO SEEMED PRETTY SELF-SUFFICIENT. THEY REMEMBER HIM TALKING ABOUT CAMPING.
WE'VE BEEN DOING CAMPGROUND SWEEPS IN COUNTY AREAS BUT IF HE'S IN THE WOODS, HE COULD BE A LOT FURTHER OUT.
LISTEN TO ME, PEOPLE. WE NEED MOVEMENT ON CATCHING THIS PRICK OR KEMP'S GOING TO CRUSH MY WINDPIPE AND GET HIS PREEMPTIVE MURDER BILL PASSED.
AND THOSE ARE NOT GOING TO BE CASES ANY OF YOU WANT TO WORK.

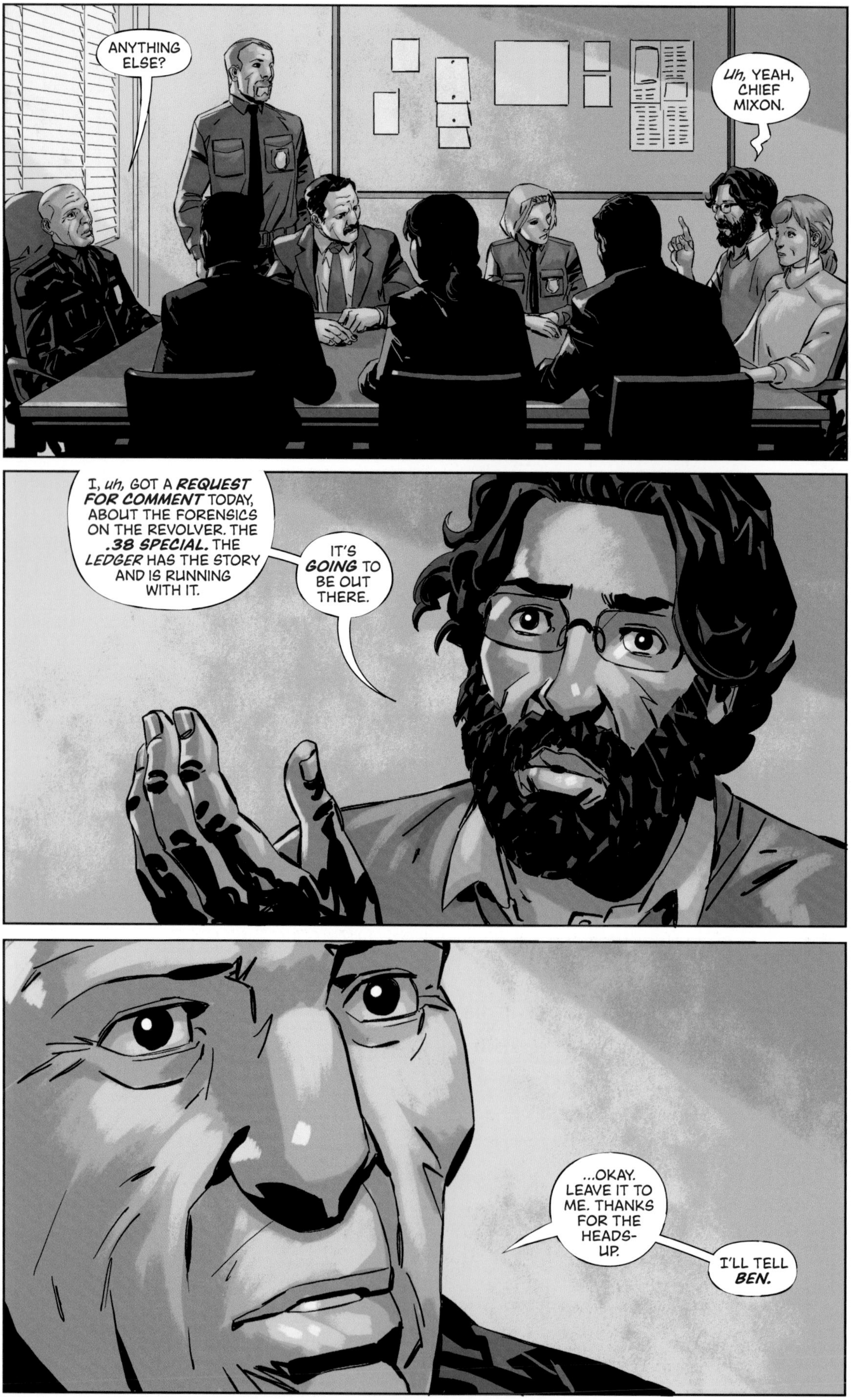
ANYTHING ELSE?
Uh, YEAH, CHIEF MIXON.
I, *uh,* GOT A ***REQUEST FOR COMMENT*** TODAY, ABOUT THE FORENSICS ON THE REVOLVER. THE ***.38 SPECIAL.*** THE *LEDGER* HAS THE STORY AND IS RUNNING WITH IT.
IT'S ***GOING*** TO BE OUT THERE.
...OKAY. LEAVE IT TO ME. THANKS FOR THE HEADS-UP.
I'LL TELL ***BEN.***

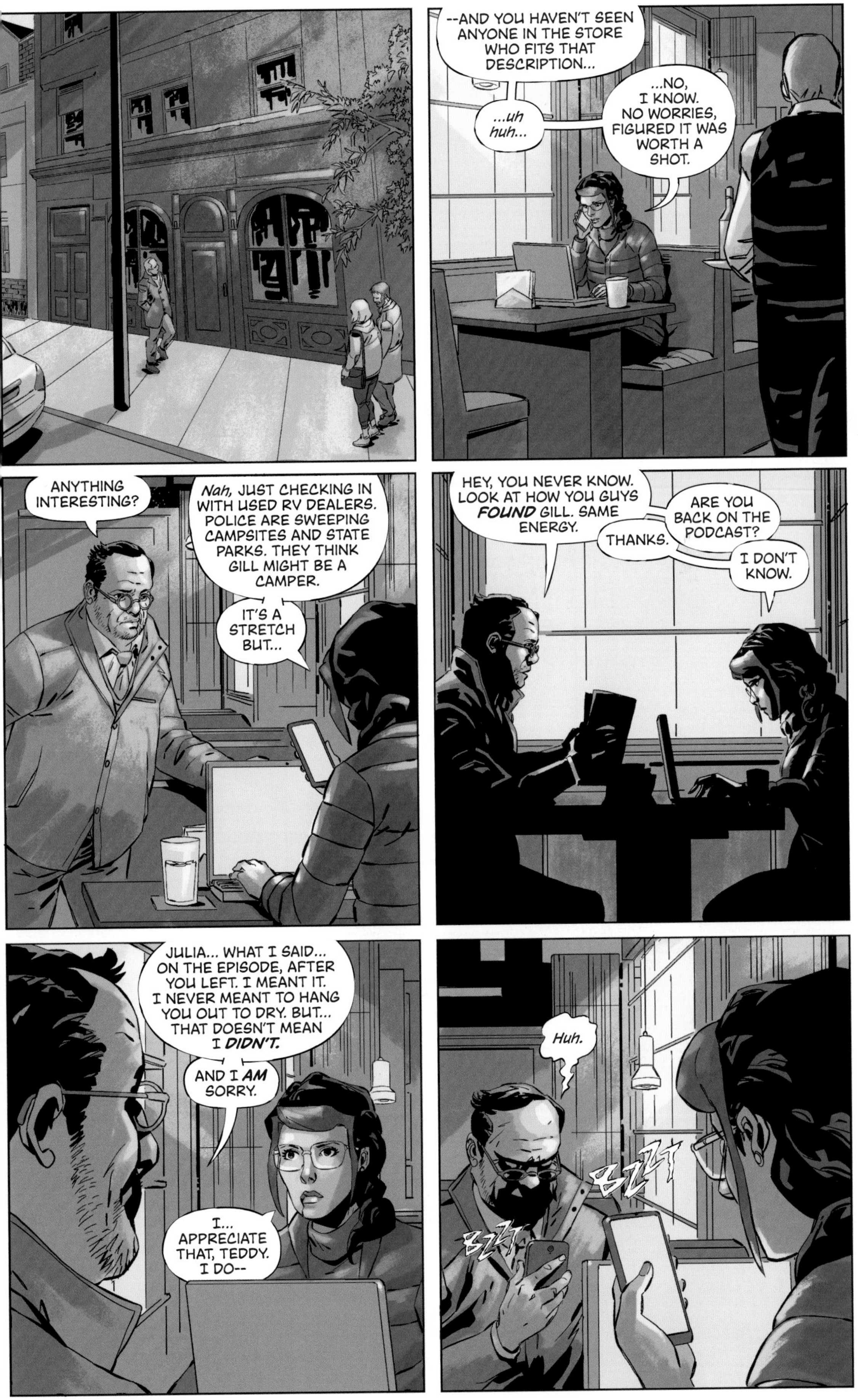
--AND YOU HAVEN'T SEEN ANYONE IN THE STORE WHO FITS THAT DESCRIPTION...
...uh huh...
...NO, I KNOW. NO WORRIES, FIGURED IT WAS WORTH A SHOT.
ANYTHING INTERESTING?
Nah, JUST CHECKING IN WITH USED RV DEALERS. POLICE ARE SWEEPING CAMPSITES AND STATE PARKS. THEY THINK GILL MIGHT BE A CAMPER.
IT'S A STRETCH BUT...
HEY, YOU NEVER KNOW. LOOK AT HOW YOU GUYS FOUND GILL. SAME ENERGY.
THANKS.
ARE YOU BACK ON THE PODCAST?
I DON'T KNOW.
JULIA... WHAT I SAID... ON THE EPISODE, AFTER YOU LEFT. I MEANT IT. I NEVER MEANT TO HANG YOU OUT TO DRY. BUT... THAT DOESN'T MEAN I DIDN'T.
AND I AM SORRY.
I... APPRECIATE THAT, TEDDY. I DO--
Huh.
BZZT
BZZT

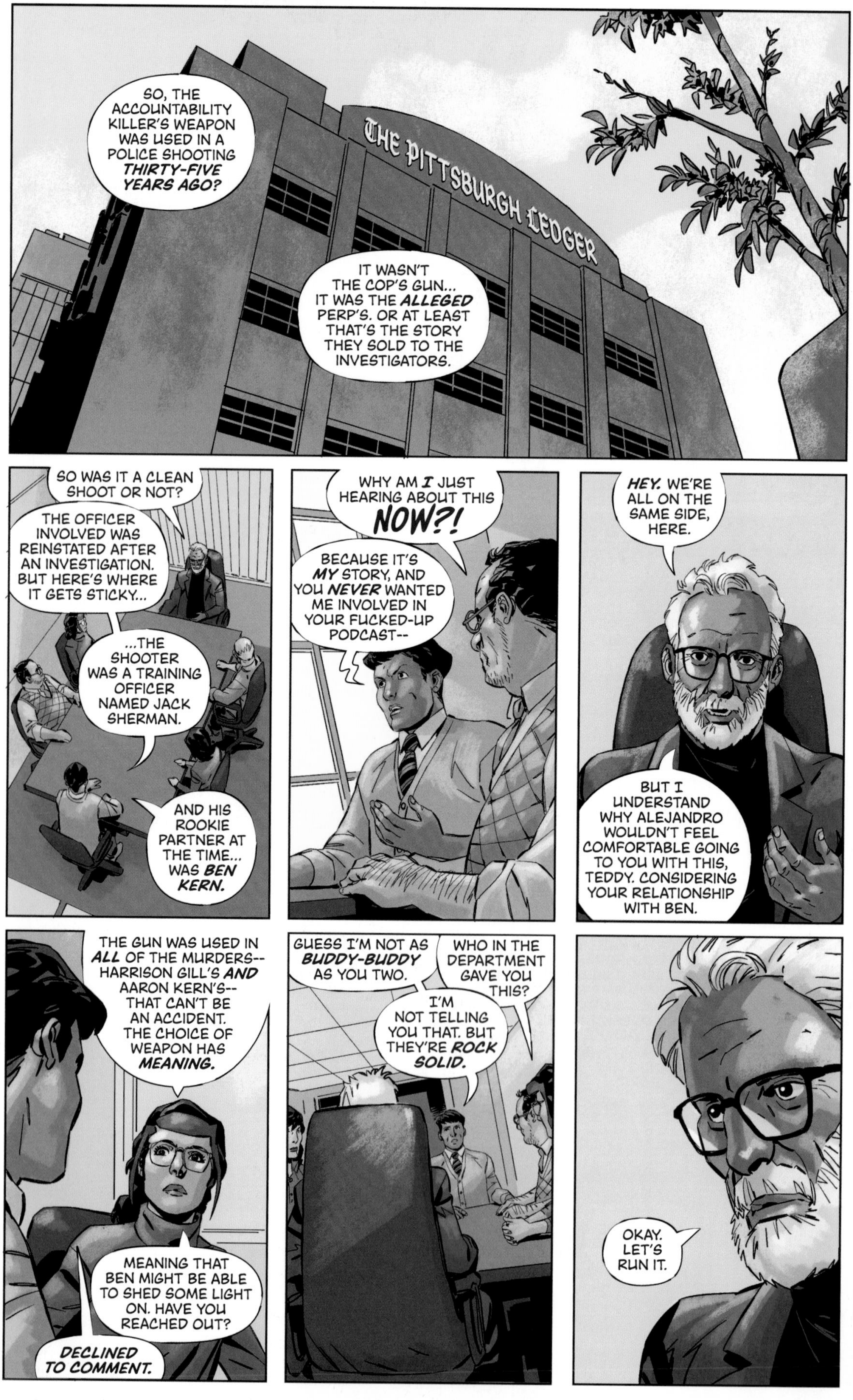

THE PITTSBURGH LEDGER
SO, THE ACCOUNTABILITY KILLER'S WEAPON WAS USED IN A POLICE SHOOTING THIRTY-FIVE YEARS AGO?
IT WASN'T THE COP'S GUN... IT WAS THE ALLEGED PERP'S. OR AT LEAST THAT'S THE STORY THEY SOLD TO THE INVESTIGATORS.
SO WAS IT A CLEAN SHOOT OR NOT?
THE OFFICER INVOLVED WAS REINSTATED AFTER AN INVESTIGATION. BUT HERE'S WHERE IT GETS STICKY...
...THE SHOOTER WAS A TRAINING OFFICER NAMED JACK SHERMAN.
AND HIS ROOKIE PARTNER AT THE TIME... WAS BEN KERN.
WHY AM I JUST HEARING ABOUT THIS NOW?!
BECAUSE IT'S MY STORY, AND YOU NEVER WANTED ME INVOLVED IN YOUR FUCKED-UP PODCAST--
HEY. WE'RE ALL ON THE SAME SIDE, HERE.
BUT I UNDERSTAND WHY ALEJANDRO WOULDN'T FEEL COMFORTABLE GOING TO YOU WITH THIS, TEDDY. CONSIDERING YOUR RELATIONSHIP WITH BEN.
THE GUN WAS USED IN ALL OF THE MURDERS-- HARRISON GILL'S AND AARON KERN'S-- THAT CAN'T BE AN ACCIDENT. THE CHOICE OF WEAPON HAS MEANING.
MEANING THAT BEN MIGHT BE ABLE TO SHED SOME LIGHT ON. HAVE YOU REACHED OUT?
DECLINED TO COMMENT.
GUESS I'M NOT AS BUDDY-BUDDY AS YOU TWO.
WHO IN THE DEPARTMENT GAVE YOU THIS?
I'M NOT TELLING YOU THAT. BUT THEY'RE ROCK SOLID.
OKAY. LET'S RUN IT.

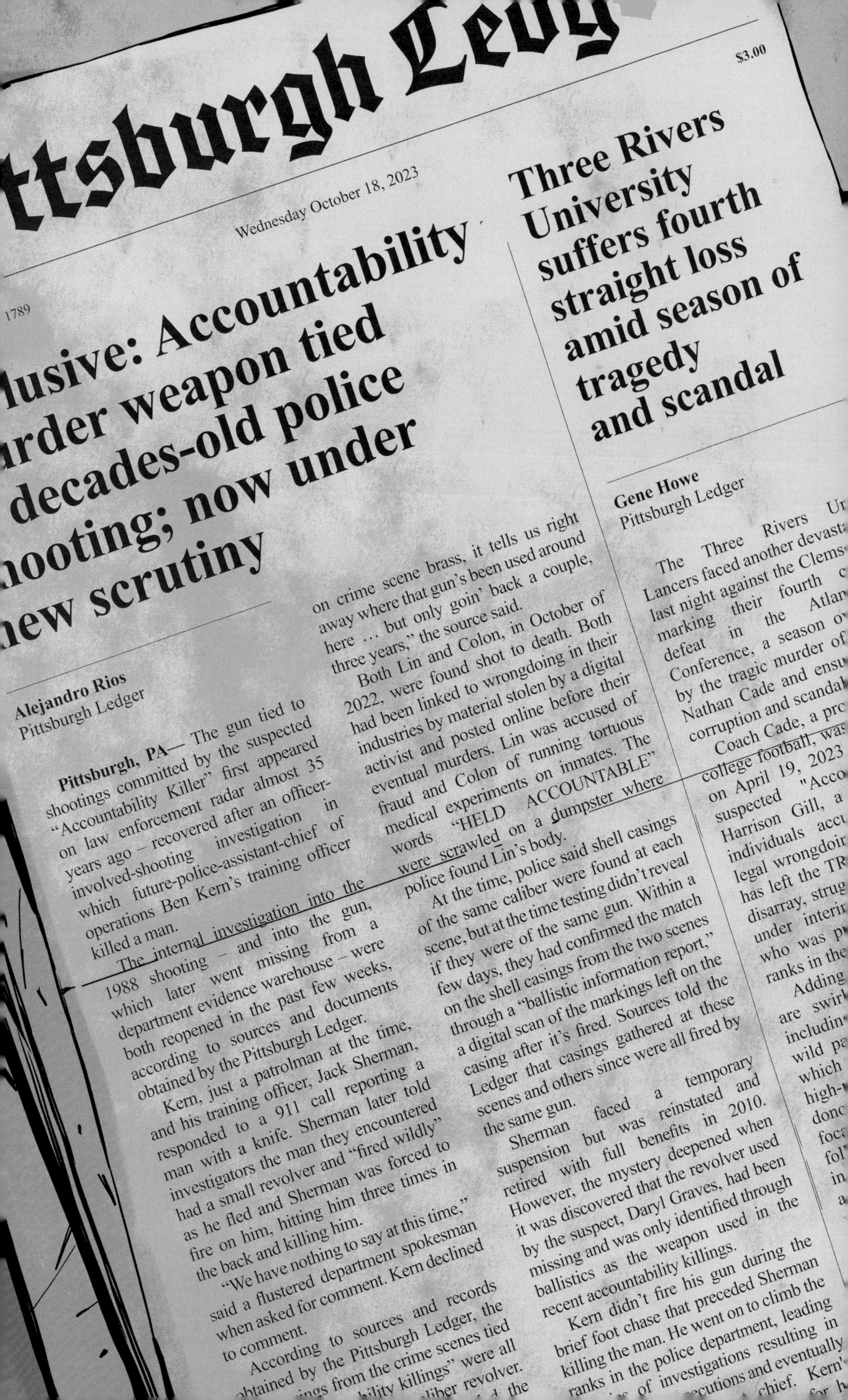

ttsburgh Ledg

$3.00

Wednesday October 18, 2023

1789

lusive: Accountability rder weapon tied decades-old police hooting; now under new scrutiny

Alejandro Rios
Pittsburgh Ledger

Pittsburgh, PA— The gun tied to shootings committed by the suspected "Accountability Killer" first appeared on law enforcement radar almost 35 years ago – recovered after an officer-involved-shooting investigation in which future-police-assistant-chief of operations Ben Kern's training officer killed a man.

The internal investigation into the 1988 shooting – and into the gun, which later went missing from a department evidence warehouse – were both reopened in the past few weeks, according to sources and documents obtained by the Pittsburgh Ledger.

Kern, just a patrolman at the time, and his training officer, Jack Sherman, responded to a 911 call reporting a man with a knife. Sherman later told investigators the man they encountered had a small revolver and "fired wildly" as he fled and Sherman was forced to fire on him, hitting him three times in the back and killing him.

"We have nothing to say at this time," said a flustered department spokesman when asked for comment. Kern declined to comment.

According to sources and records obtained by the Pittsburgh Ledger, the ...ings from the crime scenes tied ...bility killings" were all ...liber revolver. ... the

on crime scene brass, it tells us right away where that gun's been used around here … but only goin' back a couple, three years," the source said.

Both Lin and Colon, in October of 2022, were found shot to death. Both had been linked to wrongdoing in their industries by material stolen by a digital activist and posted online before their eventual murders. Lin was accused of fraud and Colon of running tortuous medical experiments on inmates. The words "HELD ACCOUNTABLE" were scrawled on a dumpster where police found Lin's body.

At the time, police said shell casings of the same caliber were found at each scene, but at the time testing didn't reveal if they were of the same gun. Within a few days, they had confirmed the match on the shell casings from the two scenes through a "ballistic information report," a digital scan of the markings left on the casing after it's fired. Sources told the Ledger that casings gathered at these scenes and others since were all fired by the same gun.

Sherman faced a temporary suspension but was reinstated and retired with full benefits in 2010. However, the mystery deepened when it was discovered that the revolver used by the suspect, Daryl Graves, had been missing and was only identified through ballistics as the weapon used in the recent accountability killings.

Kern didn't fire his gun during the brief foot chase that preceded Sherman killing the man. He went on to climb the ranks in the police department, leading ... of investigations resulting in ...ecutions and eventually ... chief. Kern'...

Three Rivers University suffers fourth straight loss amid season of tragedy and scandal

Gene Howe
Pittsburgh Ledger

The Three Rivers Ur...
Lancers faced another devast...
last night against the Clems...
marking their fourth c...
defeat in the Atlan...
Conference, a season o...
by the tragic murder of...
Nathan Cade and ensu...
corruption and scandal...
Coach Cade, a pro...
college football, was...
on April 19, 2023...
suspected "Acco...
Harrison Gill, a...
individuals accu...
legal wrongdoi...
has left the TR...
disarray, strug...
under interi...
who was p...
ranks in the...
Adding...
are swirl...
includin...
wild pa...
which...
high-...
donc...
foca...
fol...
in...
a...

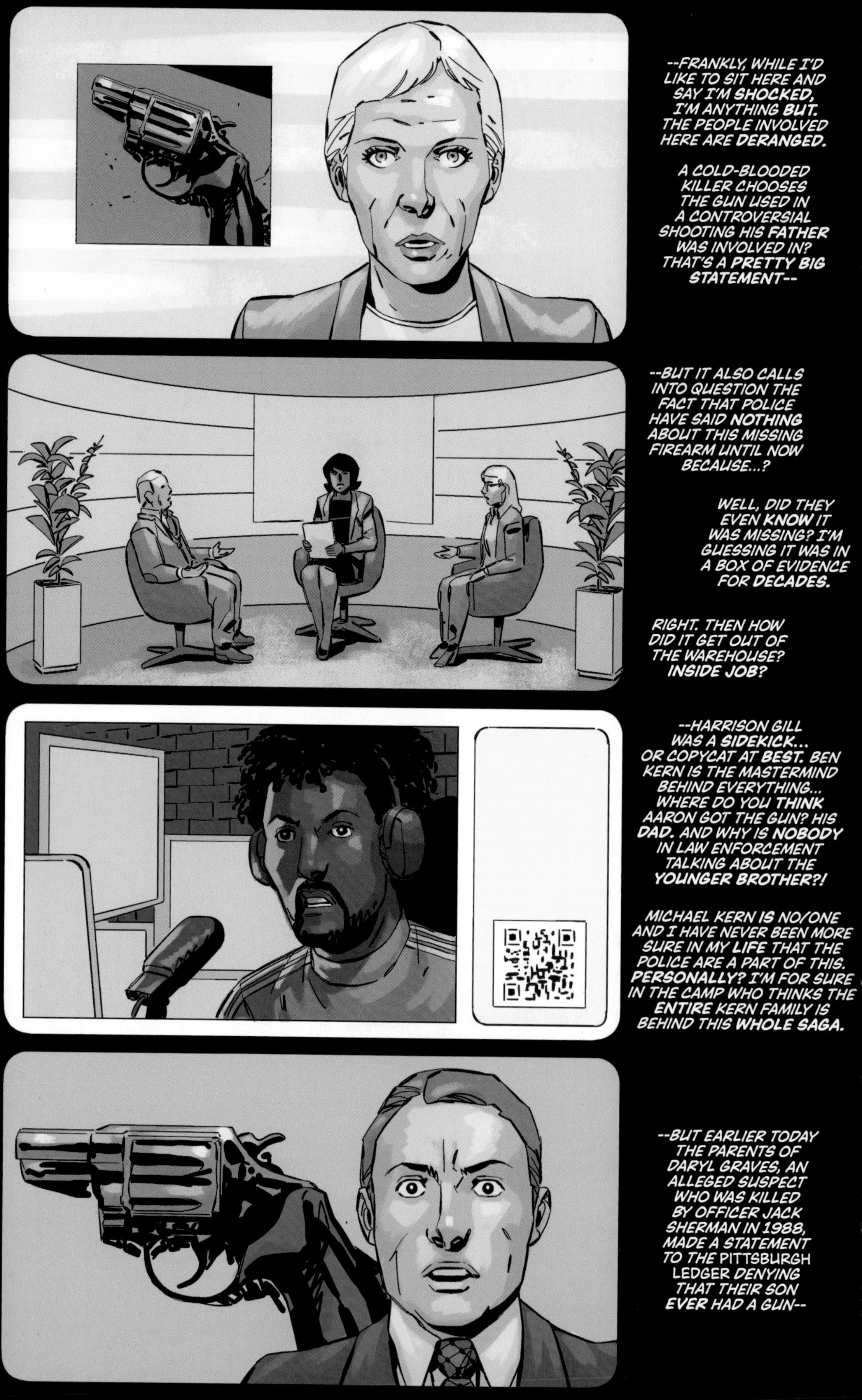
--FRANKLY, WHILE I'D LIKE TO SIT HERE AND SAY I'M **SHOCKED,** I'M ANYTHING **BUT.** THE PEOPLE INVOLVED HERE ARE **DERANGED.**
A COLD-BLOODED KILLER CHOOSES THE GUN USED IN A CONTROVERSIAL SHOOTING HIS **FATHER** WAS INVOLVED IN? THAT'S A **PRETTY BIG STATEMENT**--
--BUT IT ALSO CALLS INTO QUESTION THE FACT THAT POLICE HAVE SAID **NOTHING** ABOUT THIS MISSING FIREARM UNTIL NOW BECAUSE...?
WELL, DID THEY EVEN **KNOW** IT WAS MISSING? I'M GUESSING IT WAS IN A BOX OF EVIDENCE FOR **DECADES.**
RIGHT. THEN HOW DID IT GET OUT OF THE WAREHOUSE? **INSIDE JOB?**
--HARRISON GILL WAS A **SIDEKICK...** OR COPYCAT AT **BEST.** BEN KERN IS THE MASTERMIND BEHIND EVERYTHING... WHERE DO YOU **THINK** AARON GOT THE GUN? HIS **DAD.** AND WHY IS **NOBODY** IN LAW ENFORCEMENT TALKING ABOUT THE **YOUNGER BROTHER?!**
MICHAEL KERN **IS** NO/ONE AND I HAVE NEVER BEEN MORE SURE IN MY **LIFE** THAT THE POLICE ARE A PART OF THIS. **PERSONALLY?** I'M FOR SURE IN THE CAMP WHO THINKS THE **ENTIRE** KERN FAMILY IS BEHIND THIS **WHOLE SAGA.**
--BUT EARLIER TODAY THE PARENTS OF DARYL GRAVES, AN ALLEGED SUSPECT WHO WAS KILLED BY OFFICER JACK SHERMAN IN 1988, MADE A STATEMENT TO THE PITTSBURGH LEDGER DENYING THAT THEIR SON **EVER** HAD A GUN--

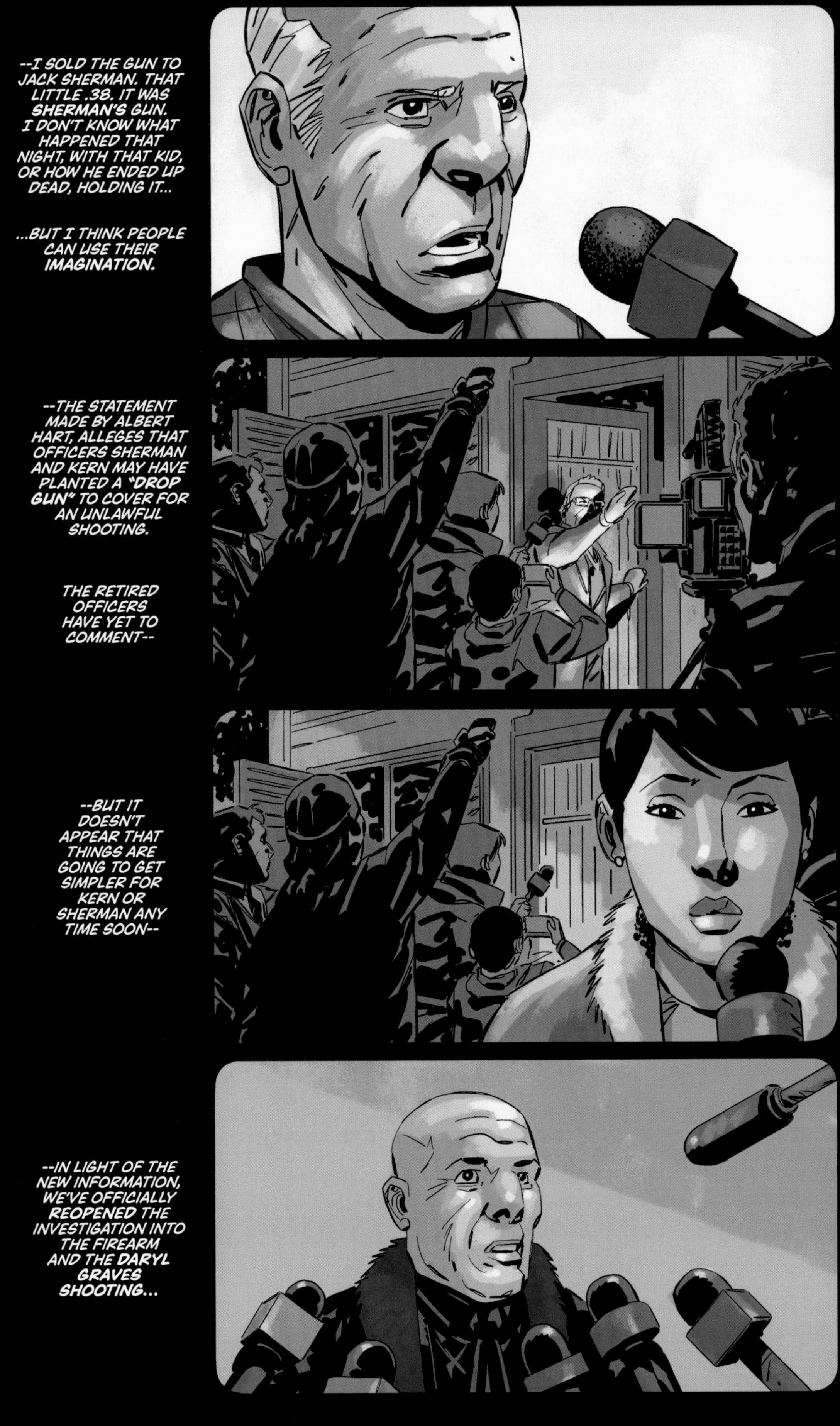
--I SOLD THE GUN TO JACK SHERMAN. THAT LITTLE .38. IT WAS SHERMAN'S GUN. I DON'T KNOW WHAT HAPPENED THAT NIGHT, WITH THAT KID, OR HOW HE ENDED UP DEAD, HOLDING IT...
...BUT I THINK PEOPLE CAN USE THEIR IMAGINATION.
--THE STATEMENT MADE BY ALBERT HART, ALLEGES THAT OFFICERS SHERMAN AND KERN MAY HAVE PLANTED A "DROP GUN" TO COVER FOR AN UNLAWFUL SHOOTING.
THE RETIRED OFFICERS HAVE YET TO COMMENT--
--BUT IT DOESN'T APPEAR THAT THINGS ARE GOING TO GET SIMPLER FOR KERN OR SHERMAN ANY TIME SOON--
--IN LIGHT OF THE NEW INFORMATION, WE'VE OFFICIALLY REOPENED THE INVESTIGATION INTO THE FIREARM AND THE DARYL GRAVES SHOOTING...

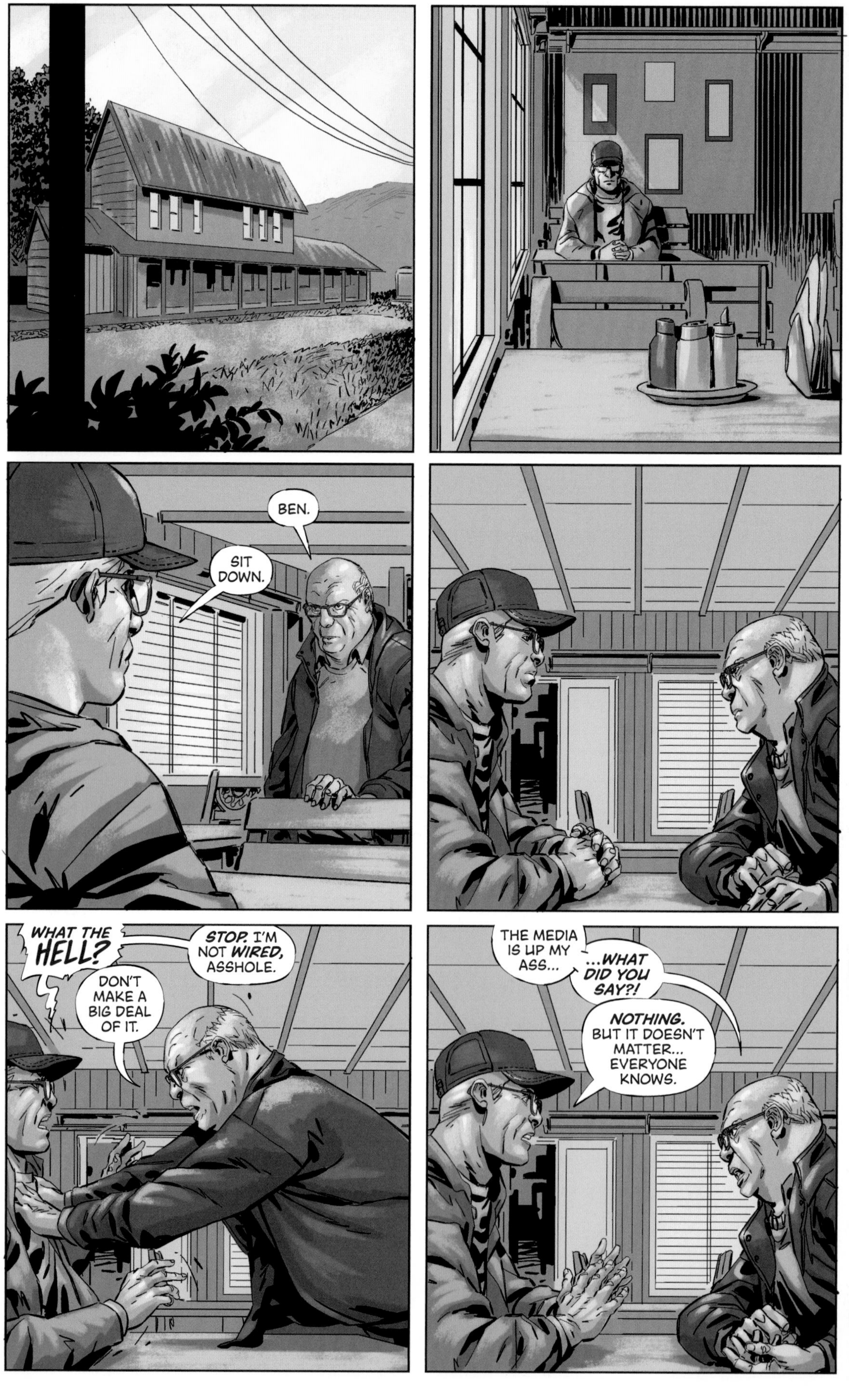
BEN.
SIT DOWN.
WHAT THE HELL?
STOP. I'M NOT WIRED, ASSHOLE.
DON'T MAKE A BIG DEAL OF IT.
THE MEDIA IS UP MY ASS...
...WHAT DID YOU SAY?!
NOTHING. BUT IT DOESN'T MATTER... EVERYONE KNOWS.

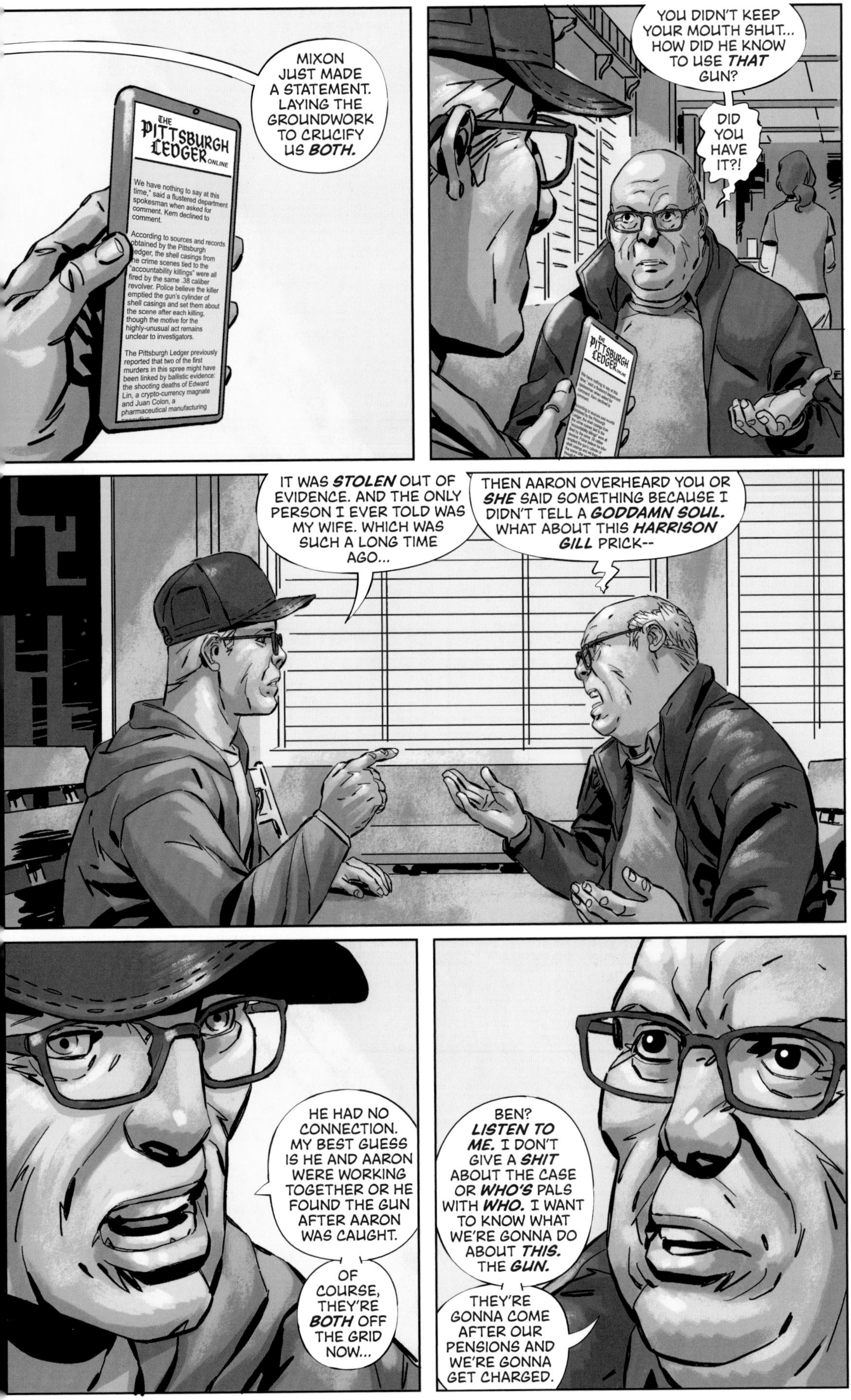
THE PITTSBURGH LEDGER ONLINE
"We have nothing to say at this time," said a flustered department spokesman when asked for comment. Kern declined to comment.
According to sources and records obtained by the Pittsburgh Ledger, the shell casings from the crime scenes tied to the "accountability killings" were all fired by the same .38 caliber revolver. Police believe the killer emptied the gun's cylinder of shell casings and set them about the scene after each killing, though the motive for the highly-unusual act remains unclear to investigators.
The Pittsburgh Ledger previously reported that two of the first murders in this spree might have been linked by ballistic evidence: the shooting deaths of Edward Lin, a crypto-currency magnate and Juan Colon, a pharmaceutical manufacturing
MIXON JUST MADE A STATEMENT. LAYING THE GROUNDWORK TO CRUCIFY US BOTH.
YOU DIDN'T KEEP YOUR MOUTH SHUT... HOW DID HE KNOW TO USE THAT GUN?
DID YOU HAVE IT?!
IT WAS STOLEN OUT OF EVIDENCE. AND THE ONLY PERSON I EVER TOLD WAS MY WIFE. WHICH WAS SUCH A LONG TIME AGO...
THEN AARON OVERHEARD YOU OR SHE SAID SOMETHING BECAUSE I DIDN'T TELL A GODDAMN SOUL. WHAT ABOUT THIS HARRISON GILL PRICK--
HE HAD NO CONNECTION. MY BEST GUESS IS HE AND AARON WERE WORKING TOGETHER OR HE FOUND THE GUN AFTER AARON WAS CAUGHT.
OF COURSE, THEY'RE BOTH OFF THE GRID NOW...
BEN? LISTEN TO ME. I DON'T GIVE A SHIT ABOUT THE CASE OR WHO'S PALS WITH WHO. I WANT TO KNOW WHAT WE'RE GONNA DO ABOUT THIS. THE GUN.
THEY'RE GONNA COME AFTER OUR PENSIONS AND WE'RE GONNA GET CHARGED.

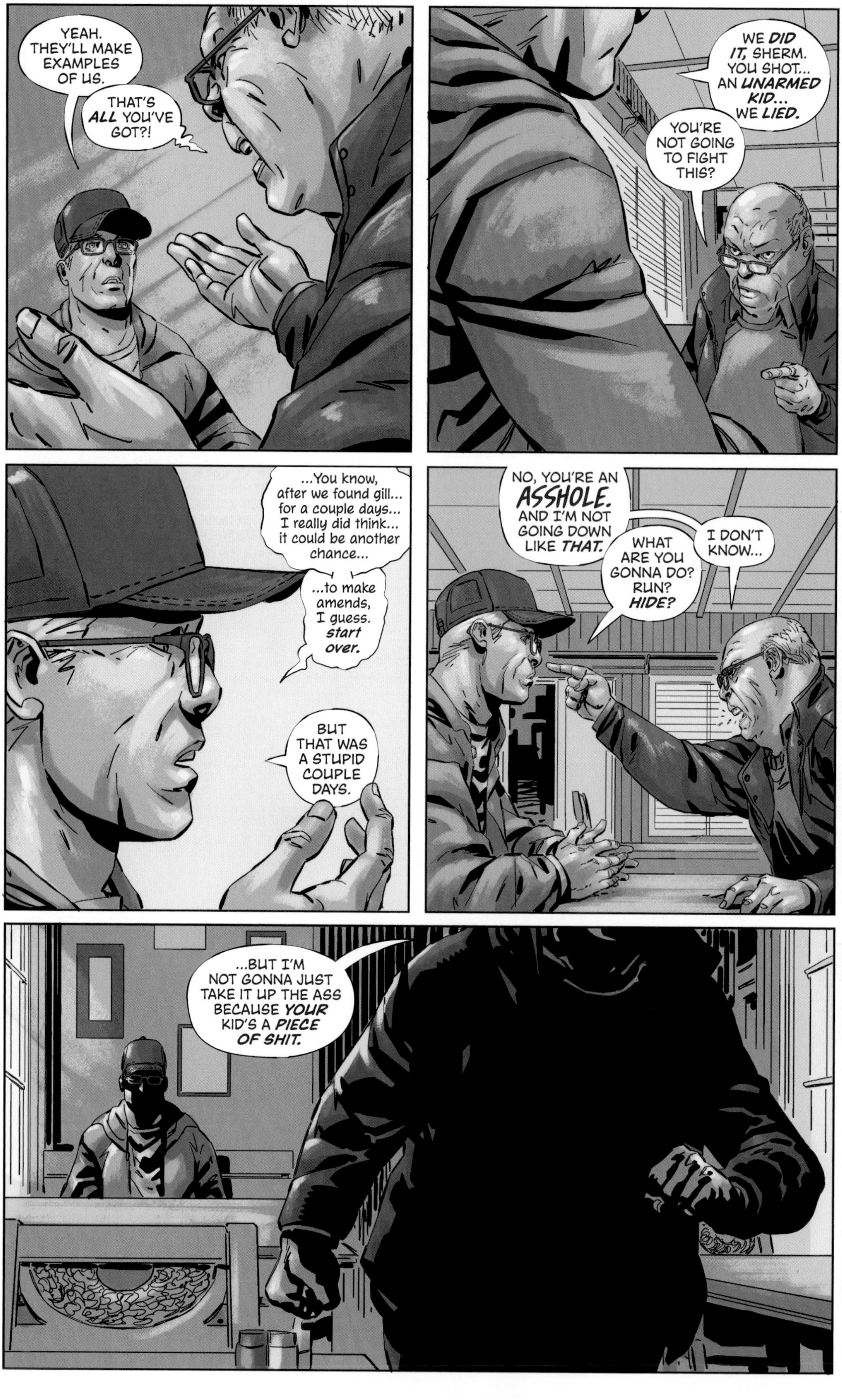
YEAH. THEY'LL MAKE EXAMPLES OF US.
THAT'S ALL YOU'VE GOT?!
WE DID IT, SHERM. YOU SHOT... AN UNARMED KID... WE LIED.
YOU'RE NOT GOING TO FIGHT THIS?
...You know, after we found gill... for a couple days... I really did think... it could be another chance...
...to make amends, I guess. start over.
BUT THAT WAS A STUPID COUPLE DAYS.
NO, YOU'RE AN ASSHOLE. AND I'M NOT GOING DOWN LIKE THAT.
WHAT ARE YOU GONNA DO? RUN? HIDE?
I DON'T KNOW...
...BUT I'M NOT GONNA JUST TAKE IT UP THE ASS BECAUSE YOUR KID'S A PIECE OF SHIT.

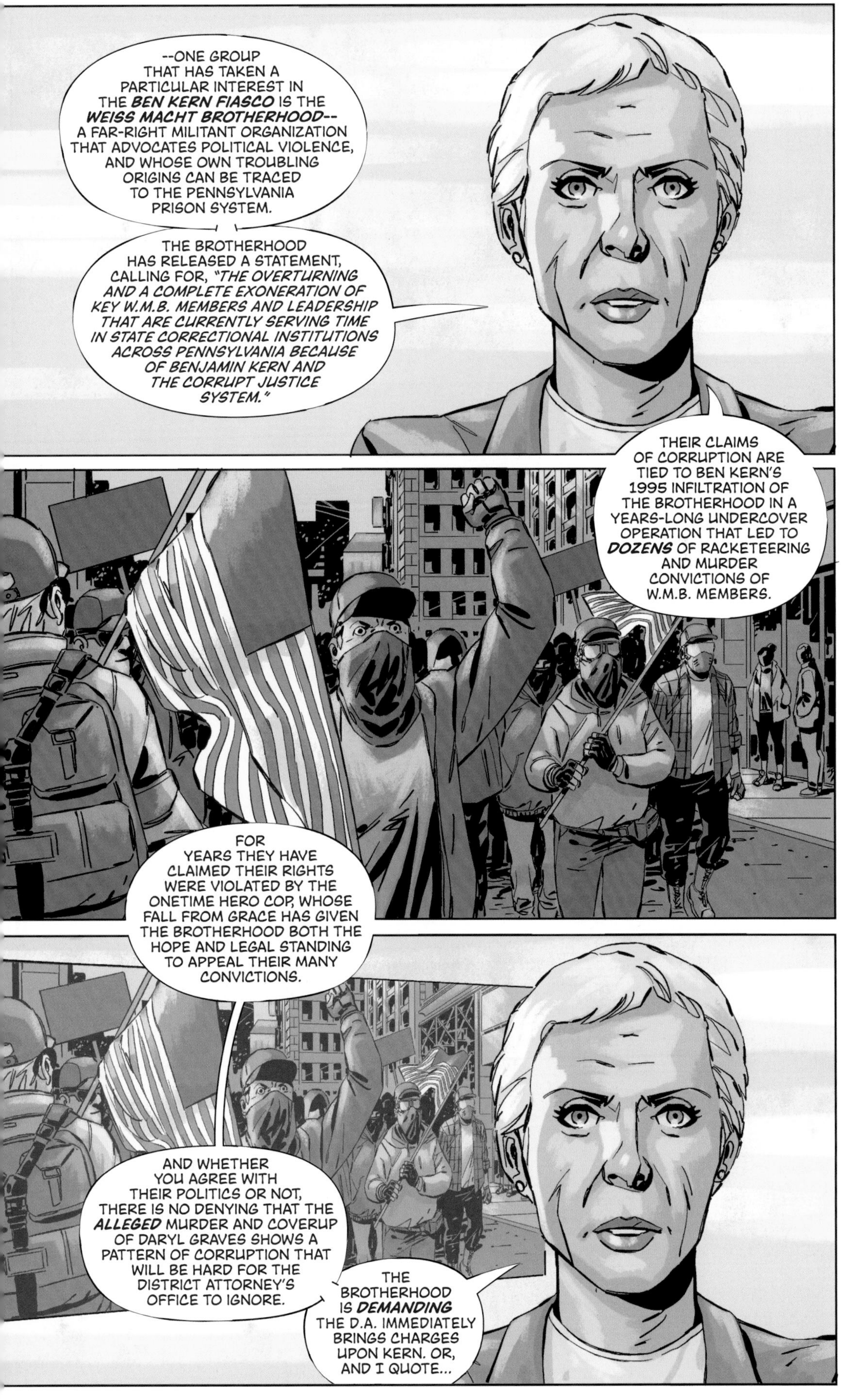
--ONE GROUP THAT HAS TAKEN A PARTICULAR INTEREST IN THE *BEN KERN FIASCO* IS THE *WEISS MACHT BROTHERHOOD*-- A FAR-RIGHT MILITANT ORGANIZATION THAT ADVOCATES POLITICAL VIOLENCE, AND WHOSE OWN TROUBLING ORIGINS CAN BE TRACED TO THE PENNSYLVANIA PRISON SYSTEM.
THE BROTHERHOOD HAS RELEASED A STATEMENT, CALLING FOR, *"THE OVERTURNING AND A COMPLETE EXONERATION OF KEY W.M.B. MEMBERS AND LEADERSHIP THAT ARE CURRENTLY SERVING TIME IN STATE CORRECTIONAL INSTITUTIONS ACROSS PENNSYLVANIA BECAUSE OF BENJAMIN KERN AND THE CORRUPT JUSTICE SYSTEM."*
THEIR CLAIMS OF CORRUPTION ARE TIED TO BEN KERN'S 1995 INFILTRATION OF THE BROTHERHOOD IN A YEARS-LONG UNDERCOVER OPERATION THAT LED TO ***DOZENS*** OF RACKETEERING AND MURDER CONVICTIONS OF W.M.B. MEMBERS.
FOR YEARS THEY HAVE CLAIMED THEIR RIGHTS WERE VIOLATED BY THE ONETIME HERO COP, WHOSE FALL FROM GRACE HAS GIVEN THE BROTHERHOOD BOTH THE HOPE AND LEGAL STANDING TO APPEAL THEIR MANY CONVICTIONS.
AND WHETHER YOU AGREE WITH THEIR POLITICS OR NOT, THERE IS NO DENYING THAT THE ***ALLEGED*** MURDER AND COVERUP OF DARYL GRAVES SHOWS A PATTERN OF CORRUPTION THAT WILL BE HARD FOR THE DISTRICT ATTORNEY'S OFFICE TO IGNORE.
THE BROTHERHOOD IS ***DEMANDING*** THE D.A. IMMEDIATELY BRINGS CHARGES UPON KERN. OR, AND I QUOTE...

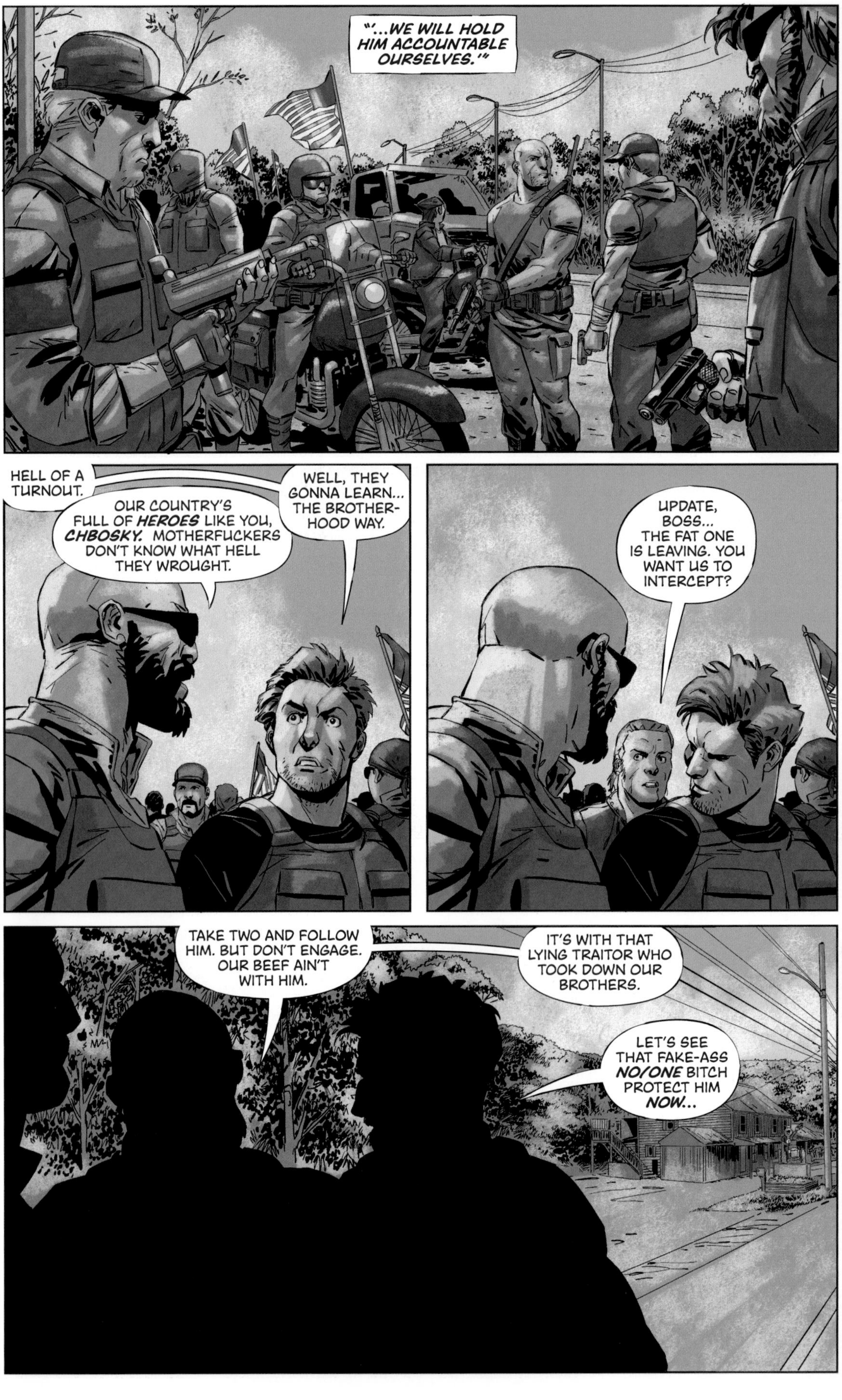
"'...WE WILL HOLD HIM ACCOUNTABLE OURSELVES.'"
HELL OF A TURNOUT.
OUR COUNTRY'S FULL OF HEROES LIKE YOU, CHBOSKY. MOTHERFUCKERS DON'T KNOW WHAT HELL THEY WROUGHT.
WELL, THEY GONNA LEARN... THE BROTHERHOOD WAY.
UPDATE, BOSS... THE FAT ONE IS LEAVING. YOU WANT US TO INTERCEPT?
TAKE TWO AND FOLLOW HIM. BUT DON'T ENGAGE. OUR BEEF AIN'T WITH HIM.
IT'S WITH THAT LYING TRAITOR WHO TOOK DOWN OUR BROTHERS.
LET'S SEE THAT FAKE-ASS NO/ONE BITCH PROTECT HIM NOW...

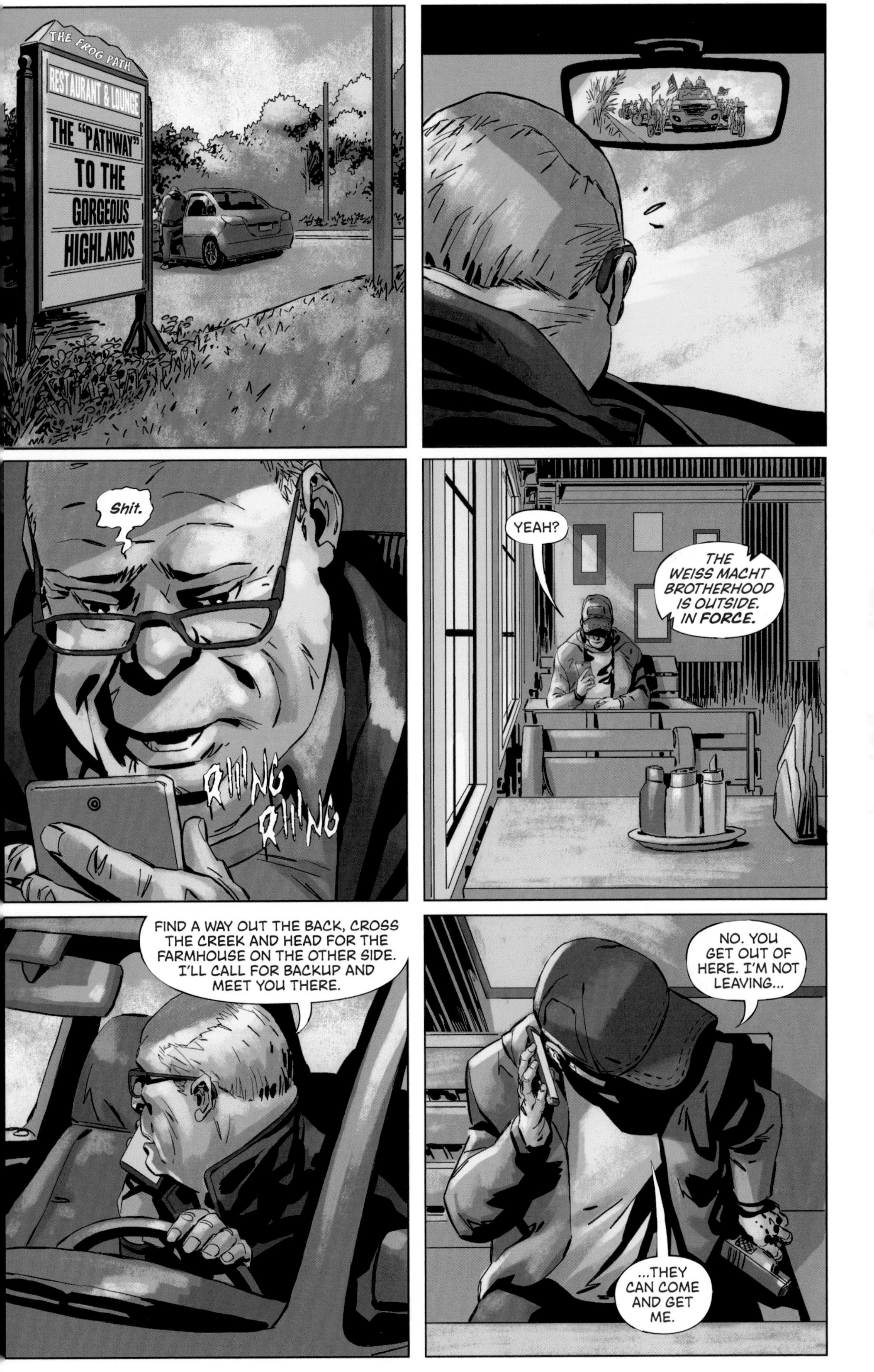
THE FROG PATH
RESTAURANT & LOUNGE
THE "PATHWAY" TO THE GORGEOUS HIGHLANDS
Shit.
RIIING RIIING
YEAH?
THE WEISS MACHT BROTHERHOOD IS OUTSIDE. IN FORCE.
FIND A WAY OUT THE BACK, CROSS THE CREEK AND HEAD FOR THE FARMHOUSE ON THE OTHER SIDE. I'LL CALL FOR BACKUP AND MEET YOU THERE.
NO. YOU GET OUT OF HERE. I'M NOT LEAVING...
...THEY CAN COME AND GET ME.

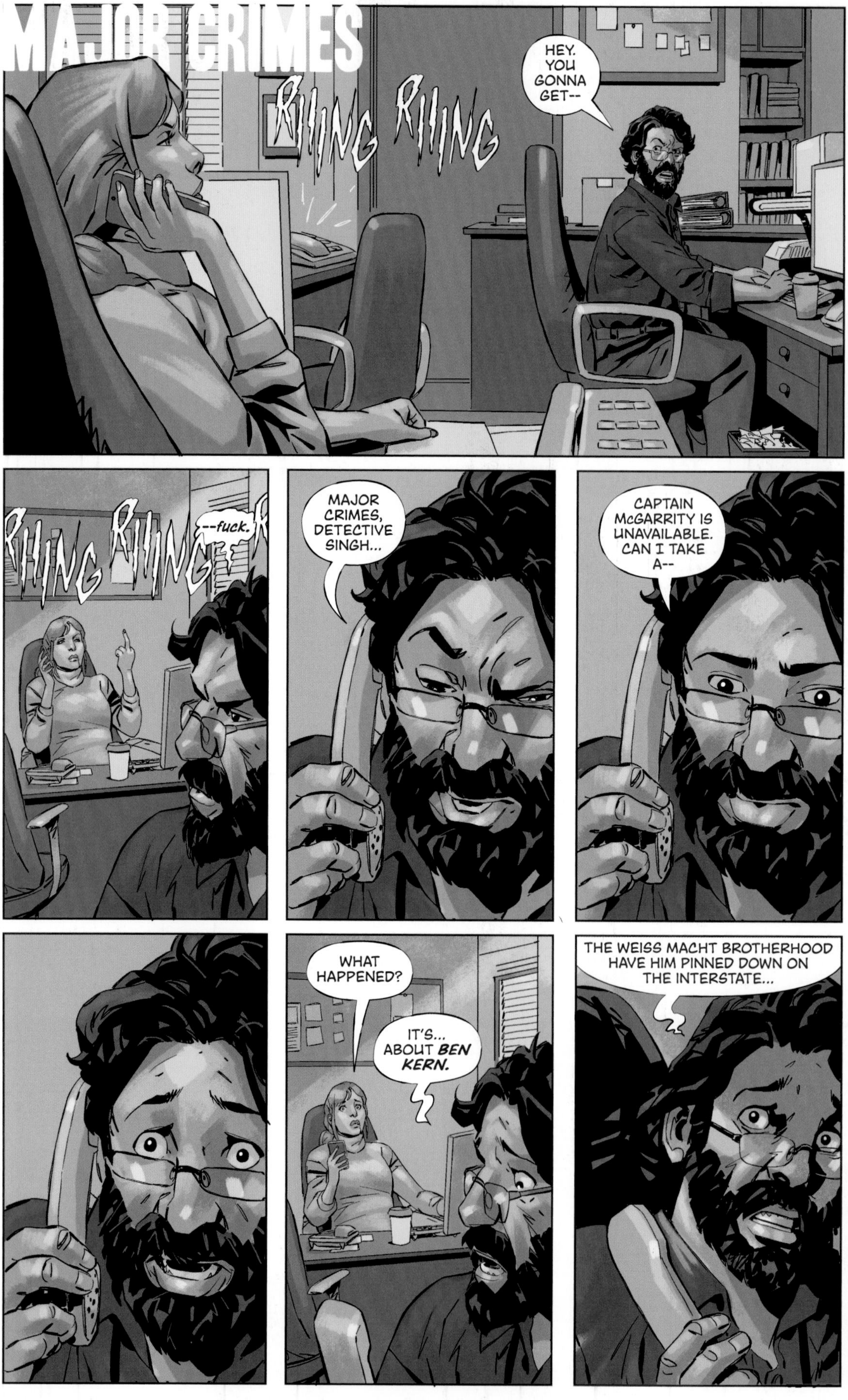

MAJOR CRIMES
RIIING RIIING
HEY. YOU GONNA GET--
RIIING RIIING
--fuck.
MAJOR CRIMES, DETECTIVE SINGH...
CAPTAIN McGARRITY IS UNAVAILABLE. CAN I TAKE A--
WHAT HAPPENED?
IT'S... ABOUT *BEN KERN.*
THE WEISS MACHT BROTHERHOOD HAVE HIM PINNED DOWN ON THE INTERSTATE...

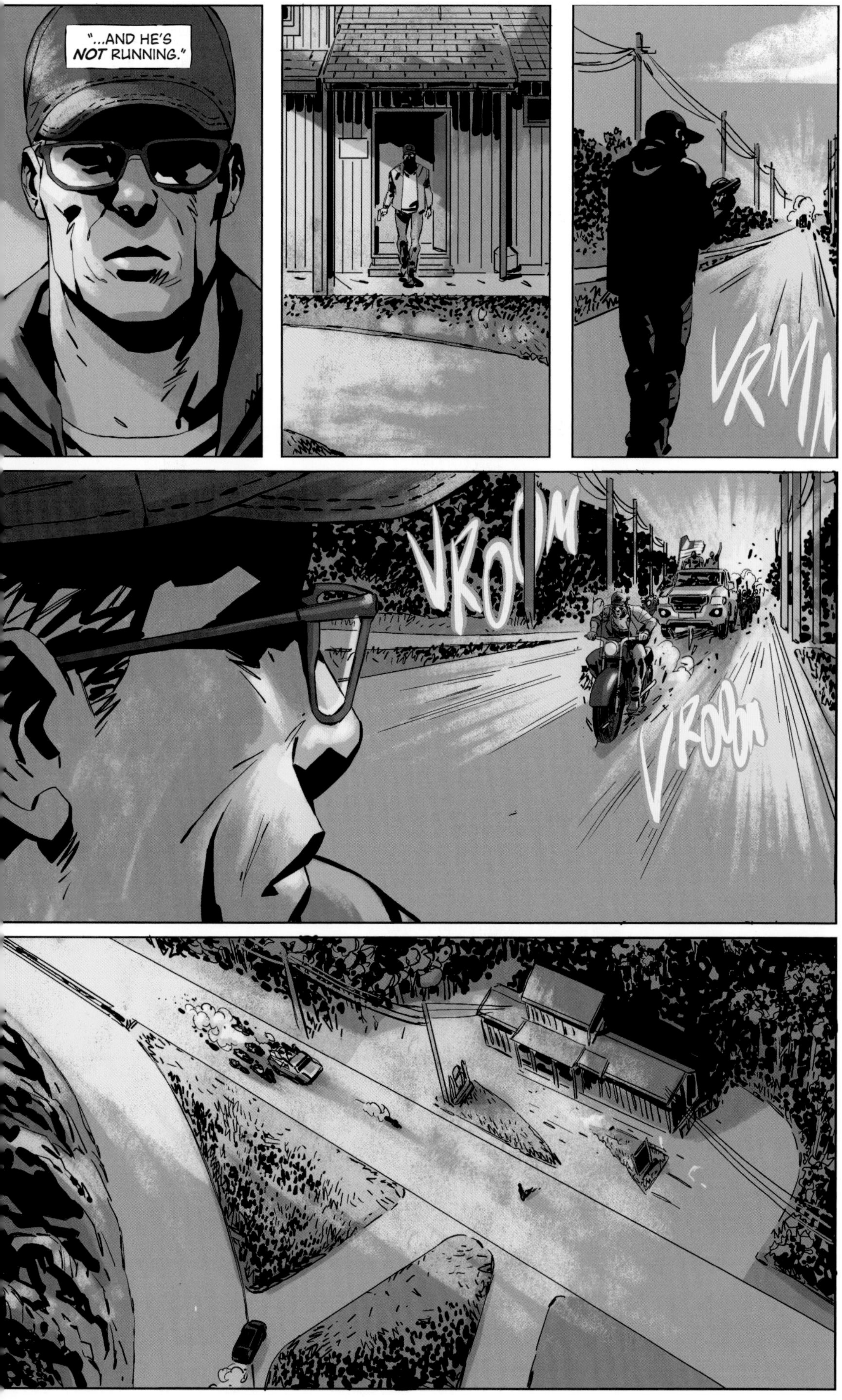
"...AND HE'S *NOT* RUNNING."
VRMM
VROOM
VROOM

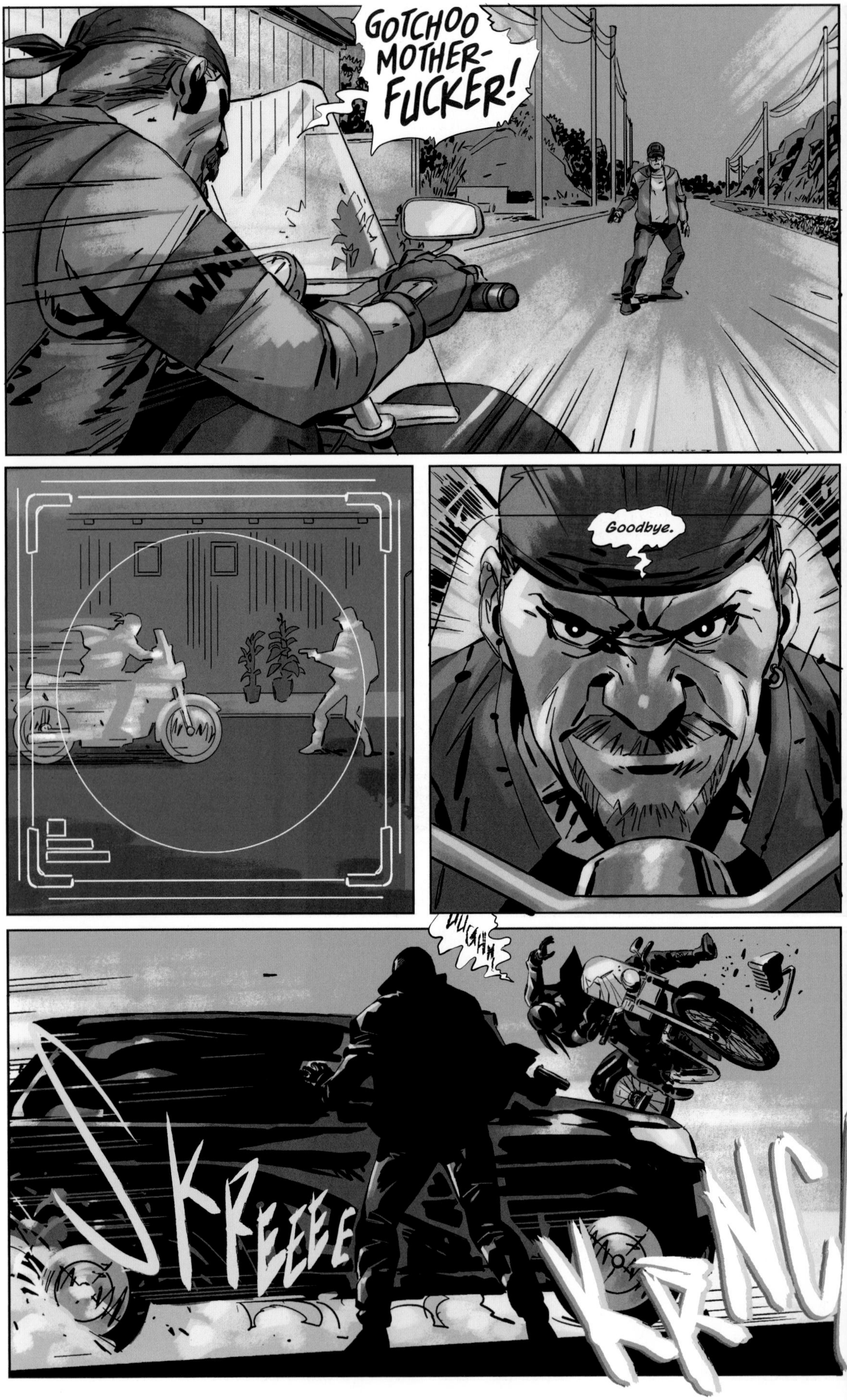
GOTCHOO MOTHER-FUCKER!
Goodbye.
UUGHH!
SKREEEE
KRNC

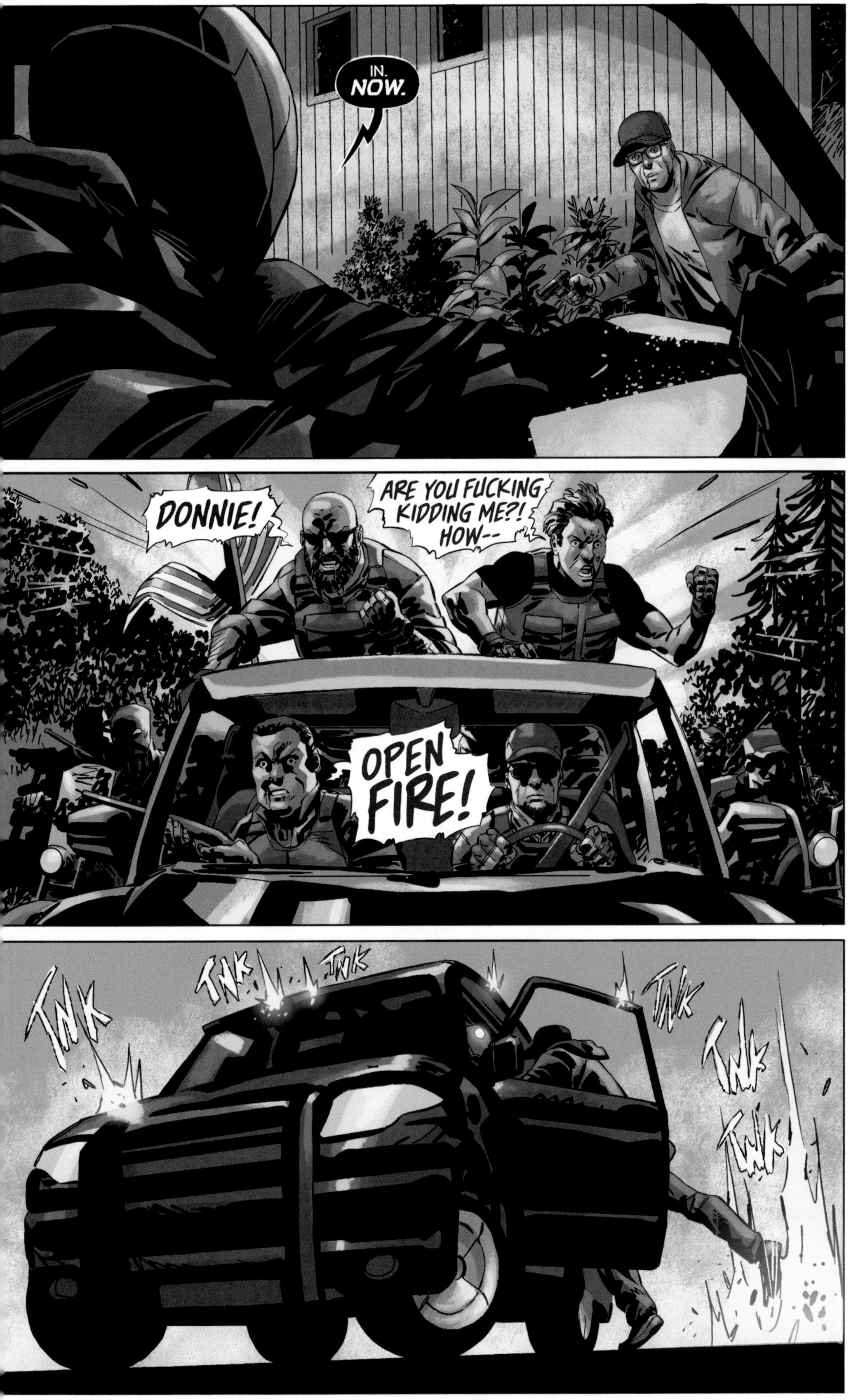
IN. NOW.
DONNIE!
ARE YOU FUCKING KIDDING ME?! HOW--
OPEN FIRE!
TNK
TNK
TNK
TNK
TNK
TWIK

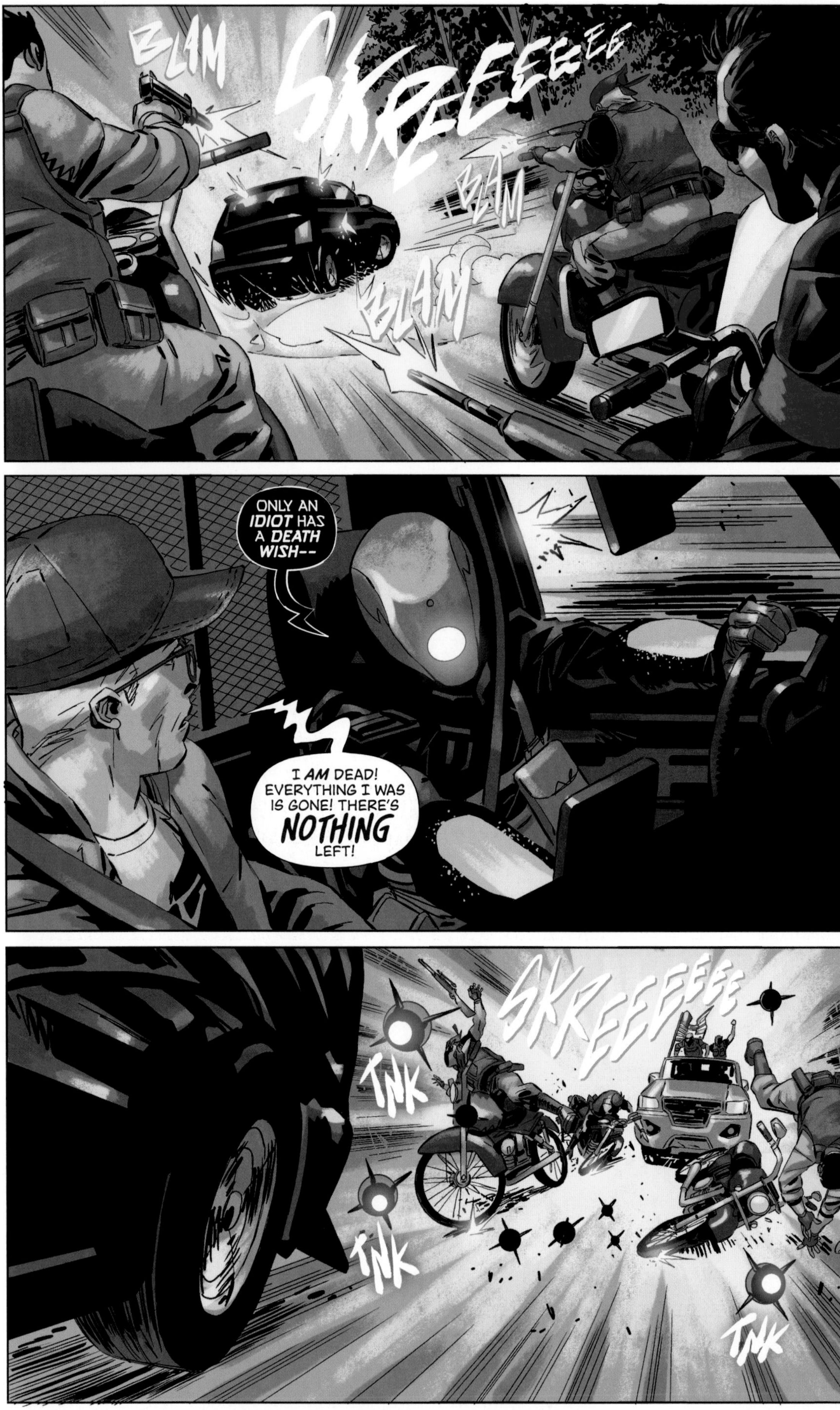
BLAM
SKREEEEEEE
BLAM
BLAM
ONLY AN IDIOT HAS A DEATH WISH--
I AM DEAD! EVERYTHING I WAS IS GONE! THERE'S NOTHING LEFT!
SKREEEEEEE
TNK
TNK
TNK

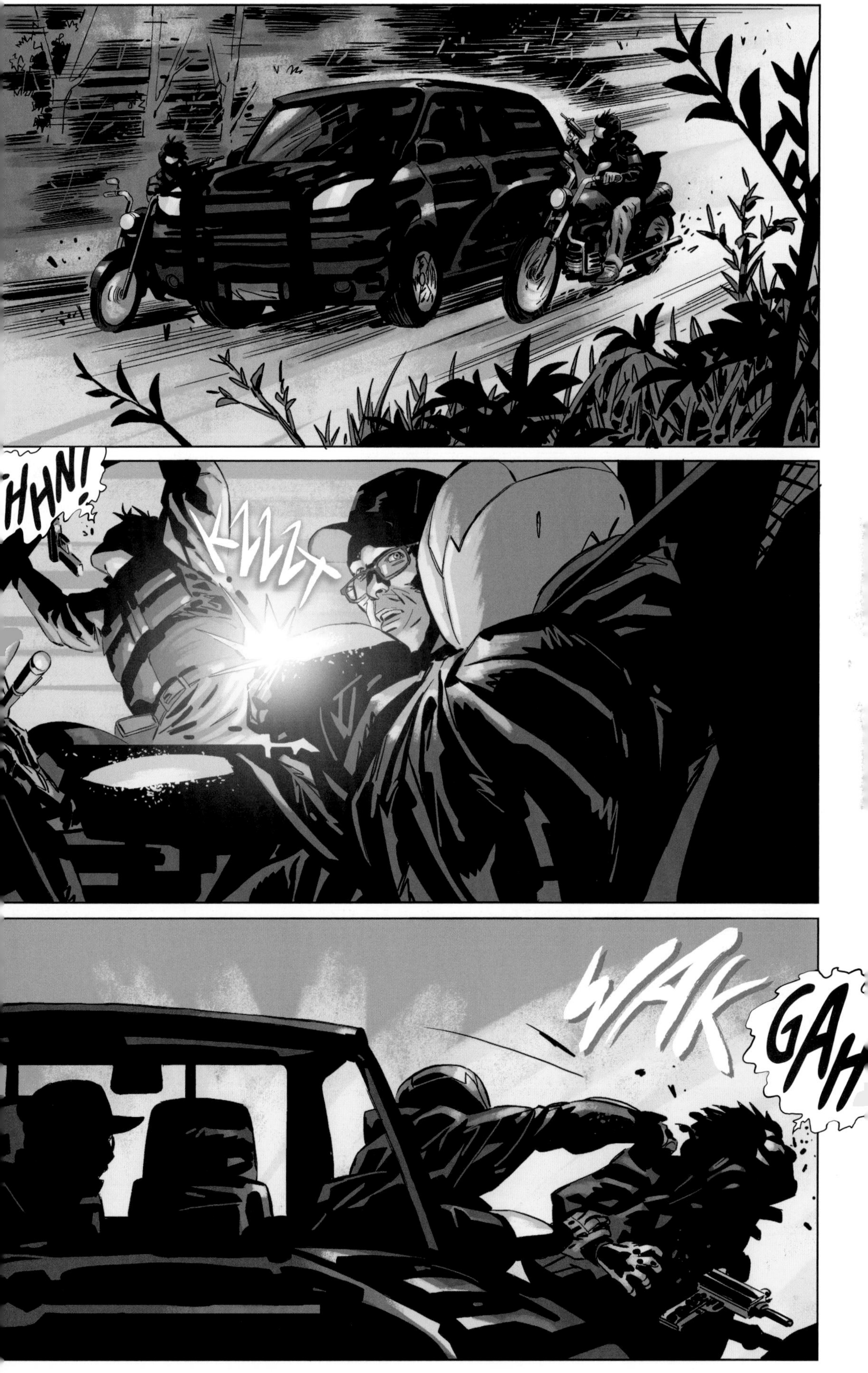
HHN!
KZZZT
WAK
GAH

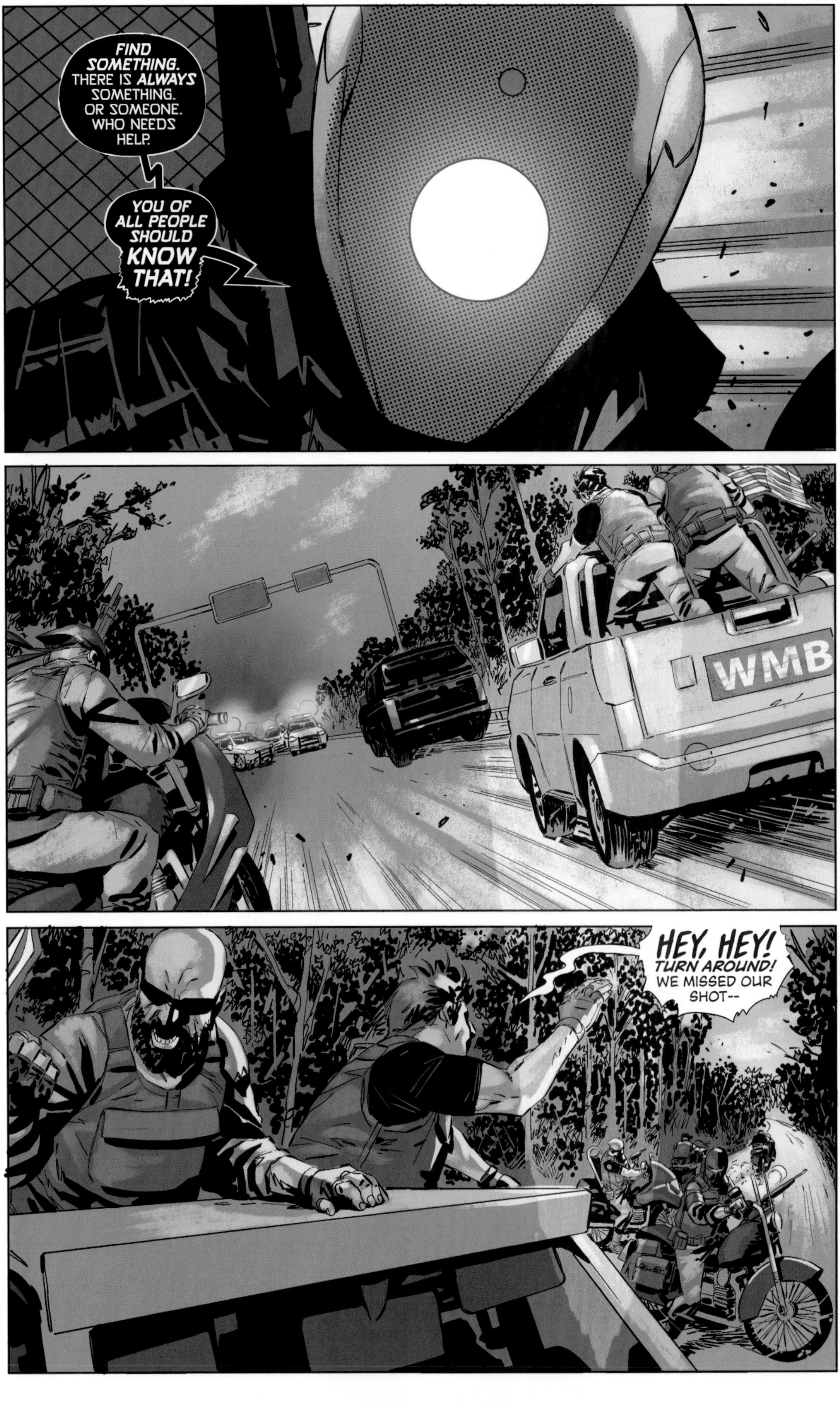
FIND SOMETHING. THERE IS ALWAYS SOMETHING. OR SOMEONE. WHO NEEDS HELP.
YOU OF ALL PEOPLE SHOULD KNOW THAT!
WMB
HEY, HEY! TURN AROUND! WE MISSED OUR SHOT--

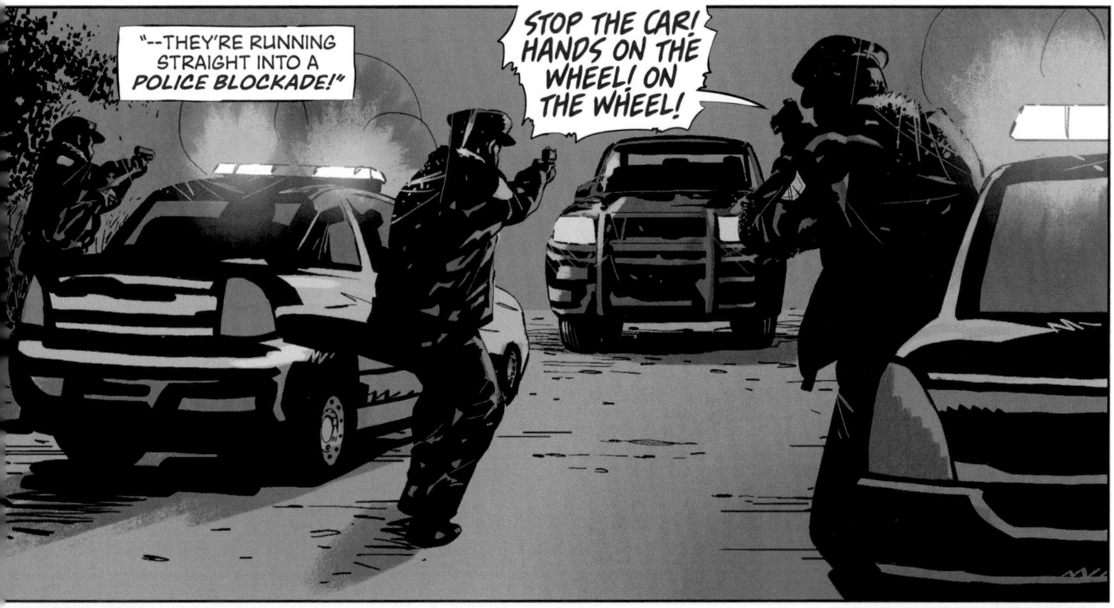
"--THEY'RE RUNNING STRAIGHT INTO A POLICE BLOCKADE!"
STOP THE CAR! HANDS ON THE WHEEL! ON THE WHEEL!

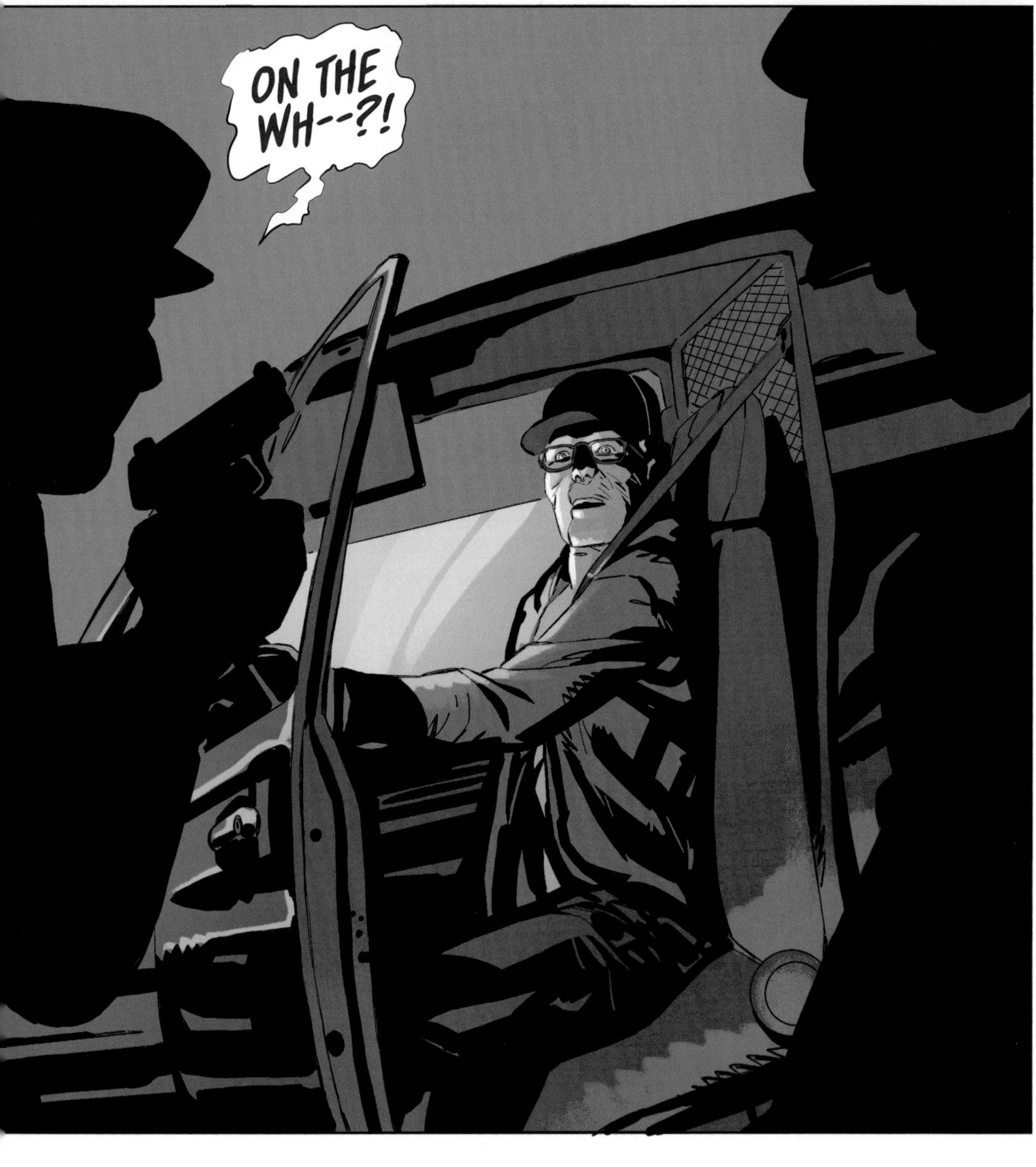
ON THE WH--?!

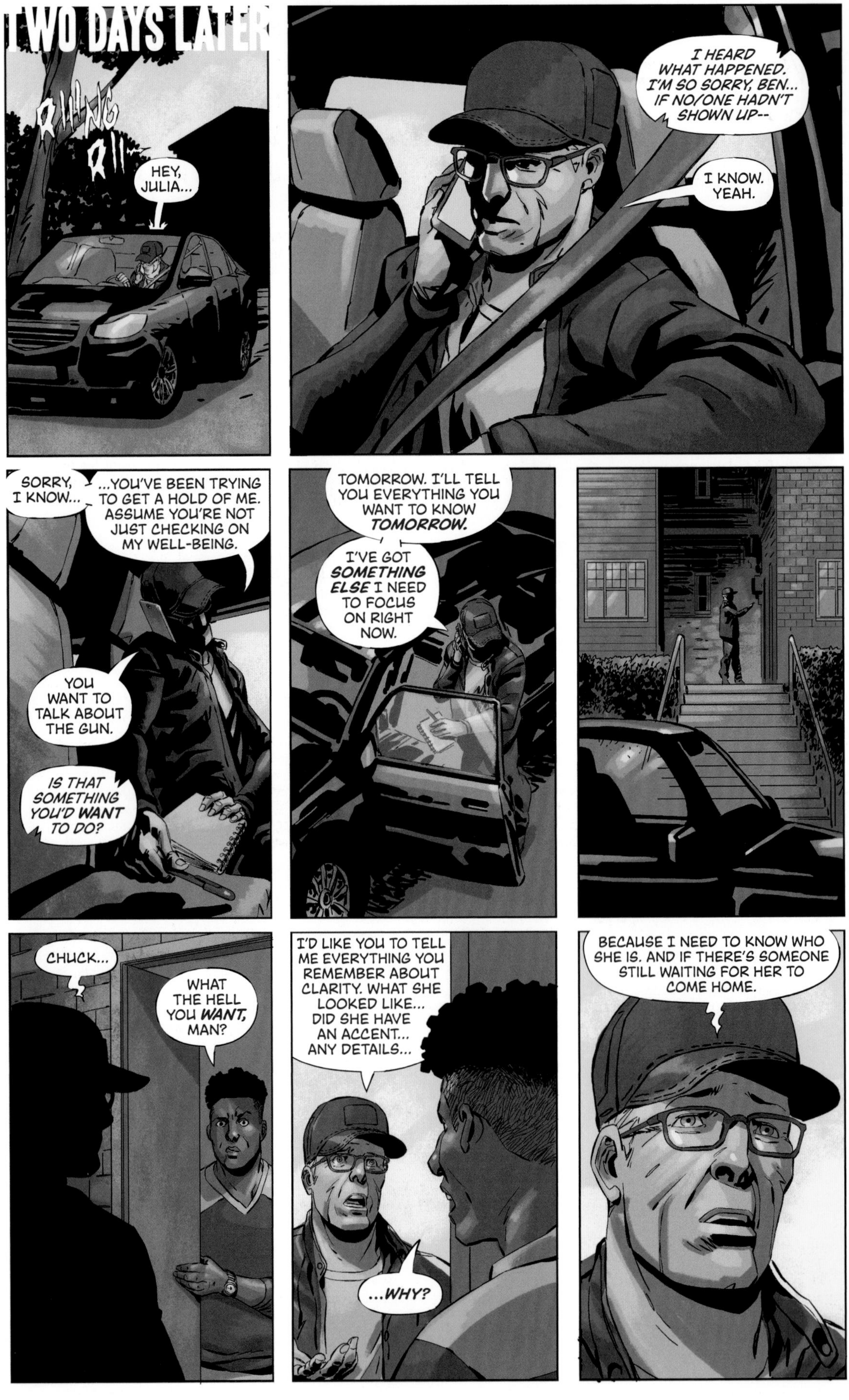
TWO DAYS LATER
RIIING
RII
HEY, JULIA...
I HEARD WHAT HAPPENED. I'M SO SORRY, BEN... IF NO/ONE HADN'T SHOWN UP--
I KNOW. YEAH.
SORRY, I KNOW...
...YOU'VE BEEN TRYING TO GET A HOLD OF ME. ASSUME YOU'RE NOT JUST CHECKING ON MY WELL-BEING.
YOU WANT TO TALK ABOUT THE GUN.
IS THAT SOMETHING YOU'D WANT TO DO?
TOMORROW. I'LL TELL YOU EVERYTHING YOU WANT TO KNOW TOMORROW.
I'VE GOT SOMETHING ELSE I NEED TO FOCUS ON RIGHT NOW.
CHUCK...
WHAT THE HELL YOU WANT, MAN?
I'D LIKE YOU TO TELL ME EVERYTHING YOU REMEMBER ABOUT CLARITY. WHAT SHE LOOKED LIKE... DID SHE HAVE AN ACCENT... ANY DETAILS...
...WHY?
BECAUSE I NEED TO KNOW WHO SHE IS. AND IF THERE'S SOMEONE STILL WAITING FOR HER TO COME HOME.

Exclusive: Accountability Murder weapon tied to decades-old police shooting; now under new scrutiny

Alejandro Rios
Pittsburgh Ledger

Pittsburgh, PA— The gun tied to shootings committed by the suspected "Accountability Killer" first appeared on law enforcement radar almost 35 years ago – recovered after an officer-involved-shooting investigation in which future-police-assistant-chief of operations Ben Kern's training officer killed a man.

The internal investigation into the 1988 shooting – and into the gun, which later went missing from a department evidence warehouse – were both reopened in the past few weeks, according to sources and documents obtained by the Pittsburgh Ledger.

Kern, just a patrolman at the time, and his training officer, Jack Sherman, responded to a 911 call reporting a man with a knife. Sherman later told investigators the man they encountered had a small revolver and "fired wildly" as he fled and Sherman was forced to fire on him, hitting him three times in the back and killing him.

"We have nothing to say at this time," said a flustered department spokesman when asked for comment. Kern declined to comment.

According to sources and records obtained by the Pittsburgh Ledger, the shell casings from the crime scenes tied to the "accountability killings" were all fired by the same .38 caliber revolver. Police believe the killer emptied the gun's cylinder of shell casings and set them about the scene after each killing, though the motive for the highly-unusual act remains unclear to investigators.

The Pittsburgh Ledger previously reported that two of the first murders in this spree might have been linked by ballistic evidence: the shooting deaths of Edward Lin, a crypto-currency magnate and Juan Colon, a pharmaceutical manufacturing executive.

That gun recovered after Sherman killed the man was test-fired after it was recovered by investigators. It's not clear what led homicide detectives to compare the casings from the murders of Lin and Colon to the 35-year-old recovered gun; sources say the department kept paper records during that time and the match wouldn't be clear unless someone went looking for it.

"Everything's digital now so when we get ballistic information alerts back on crime scene brass, it tells us right away where that gun's been used around here … but only goin' back a couple, three years," the source said.

Both Lin and Colon, in October of 2022, were found shot to death. Both had been linked to wrongdoing in their industries by material stolen by a digital activist and posted online before their eventual murders. Lin was accused of fraud and Colon of running tortuous medical experiments on inmates. The words "HELD ACCOUNTABLE" were scrawled on a dumpster where police found Lin's body.

At the time, police said shell casings of the same caliber were found at each scene, but at the time testing didn't reveal if they were of the same gun. Within a few days, they had confirmed the match on the shell casings from the two scenes through a "ballistic information report," a digital scan of the markings left on the casing after it's fired. Sources told the Ledger that casings gathered at these scenes and others since were all fired by the same gun.

Sherman faced a temporary suspension but was reinstated and retired with full benefits in 2010. However, the mystery deepened when it was discovered that the revolver used by the suspect, Daryl Graves, had been missing and was only identified through ballistics as the weapon used in the recent accountability killings.

Kern didn't fire his gun during the brief foot chase that preceded Sherman killing the man. He went on to climb the ranks in the police department, leading a series of investigations resulting in high-profile prosecutions and eventually being named assistant chief. Kern's career trajectory, once lauded for his undercover operations that led to the dismantling of the Weiss Macht Brotherhood, now faces a reputational crisis as his son, Aaron Kern, has been implicated in the killings.

The department has re-opened its internal investigation into the shooting by Sherman, though it's unclear to what end – with Sherman dead and Kern retired. A department spokesperson also said the department asked the Pennsylvania State Police to reinvestigate the missing gun, and turned over its case file from the original 1988 investigation.

The Pittsburgh Bureau of Police declined to comment. The US Attorney's office also declined to comment.

University suffers fourth straight loss amid season of tragedy and scandal

Gene Howe
Pittsburgh Ledger

The Three Rivers University Lancers faced another devastating loss last night against the Clemson Tigers, marking their fourth consecutive defeat in the Atlantic Coast Conference, a season overshadowed by the tragic murder of Head Coach Nathan Cade and ensuing rumors of corruption and scandalous conduct.

Coach Cade, a prominent figure in college football, was found murdered on April 19, 2023, at the hands of suspected "Accountability Killer" Harrison Gill, a vigilante targeting individuals accused of moral and legal wrongdoings. The loss of Cade has left the TRU football program in disarray, struggling to find its footing under interim coach Glen Dwight, who was promoted from within the ranks in the wake of the tragedy.

Adding to the team's challenges are swirling rumors of corruption, including allegations of inappropriate wild parties hosted by Coach Cade, which some claim were attended by high-profile recruits and university donors. These parties have become a focal point of the scandal, especially following allegations that Cade was involved in covering up the death of a Jane Doe known only as "Clarity", whose demise has become entangled in the lore of the team's troubled season.

The Lancers' latest loss, a 38-17 defeat to Clemson, has not only dampened the spirits of the team but also of the entire TRU community, which had hoped for a triumphant season to honor Cade's memory and bring the university together. Instead, the season has been mired in controversy, with many fans and alumni calling for a thorough investigation into the allegations and a fresh start from the program.

Interim Coach Dwight addressed the media after the game, stating "Our focus remains on football and on supporting our players through these difficult times. We are working to build a program that honors the best values of TRU, on and off the field." Yet, questions about the future of TRU football and its leadership remain, as the university grapples with the fallout from Cade's murder and the accusations that have surfaced since.

Sport Continues Page 32

Violent confrontation between ex-Police Chief and white supremacist group raises new concerns

Julia Paige
Pittsburgh Ledger

Pittsburgh, PA— Ben Kern, former Pittsburgh Police Assistant Chief of Operations, found himself embroiled in another controversy this week after a violent confrontation with the Weiss Macht Brotherhood, a white supremacist group. The altercation is the latest chapter in Kern's complex and troubled history, which includes allegations of corruption linked to a decades-old police shooting and the recent release of his son, Aaron Kern, who is still accused of being the original Richard Roe Accountability Killer. The Weiss Macht Brotherhood, long antagonistic toward Kern due to his undercover work that led to the conviction of several members, is suspected of seeking revenge as details of Kern's alleged involvement in the controversial 1988 shooting continue to surface.

During the clash, Kenneth Chbosky, a controversial figure within the Proposition 87 movement, was identified among the Weiss Macht Brotherhood members. Chbosky gained notoriety as the first person to invoke the preemptive self-defense concept in Proposition 87 to justify the shooting of Chris O'Neil, who had threatened to SWAT him during an online video game session. Chbosky's involvement has further heightened concerns, given his high-profile case and his deep connections within extremist circles. Several eye witnesses also reported a sighting of NO/ONE at the scene.

The Weiss Macht Brotherhood has been a notorious presence in Pittsburgh, known for its involvement in organized crime and extremist activities. The group's potential connection to the Accountability Killings only surfaced after the murder of defense attorney Roger Dennehy, who had represented Aaron Kern. The revelation of Kern's association with a controversial 1988 police shooting involving a .38 caliber revolver, which was allegedly used in recent Accountability Killings, has further complicated the investigation.

The revolver in question was linked to a police shooting by Officer Jack Sherman, with Kern present as a rookie under Sherman's supervision. The incident, long considered a clean shoot, is now under scrutiny, raising questions about potential corruption and cover-ups within the Pittsburgh Police Department. Kern's personal investigation and the altercation with the Weiss Macht Brotherhood have raised concerns about his impartiality and the integrity of the broader investigation into the Accountability Killings.

Sources within the police department suggest that the Brotherhood saw an opportunity to settle old scores with Kern, given his fall from grace and the ongoing legal scrutiny. "It's no secret that the Weiss Macht Brotherhood has had it out for Kern ever since his undercover work took down key members of their organization," said an anonymous source within the department. "Given the circumstances, they likely saw this as a chance to exact revenge."

As the investigation into the Accountability Killings continues, many within the department question whether Kern's involvement is helping or hindering the search for the truth. With public confidence in law enforcement already waning, the latest developments surrounding Ben Kern are likely to add to the growing sense of unease in Pittsburgh.

OCTOBER 19 2023
PITTSBURGH LEDGER

The Drop

PRESENTS

WHO IS NO/ONE
WITH/JULIA PAIGE

WHO IS NO/ONE
08/TRUST

23 OCTOBER

08/Trust

WHO IS NO/ONE

16:48   -00:41

>_ CHAPTER NINE
NOVEMBER 2023

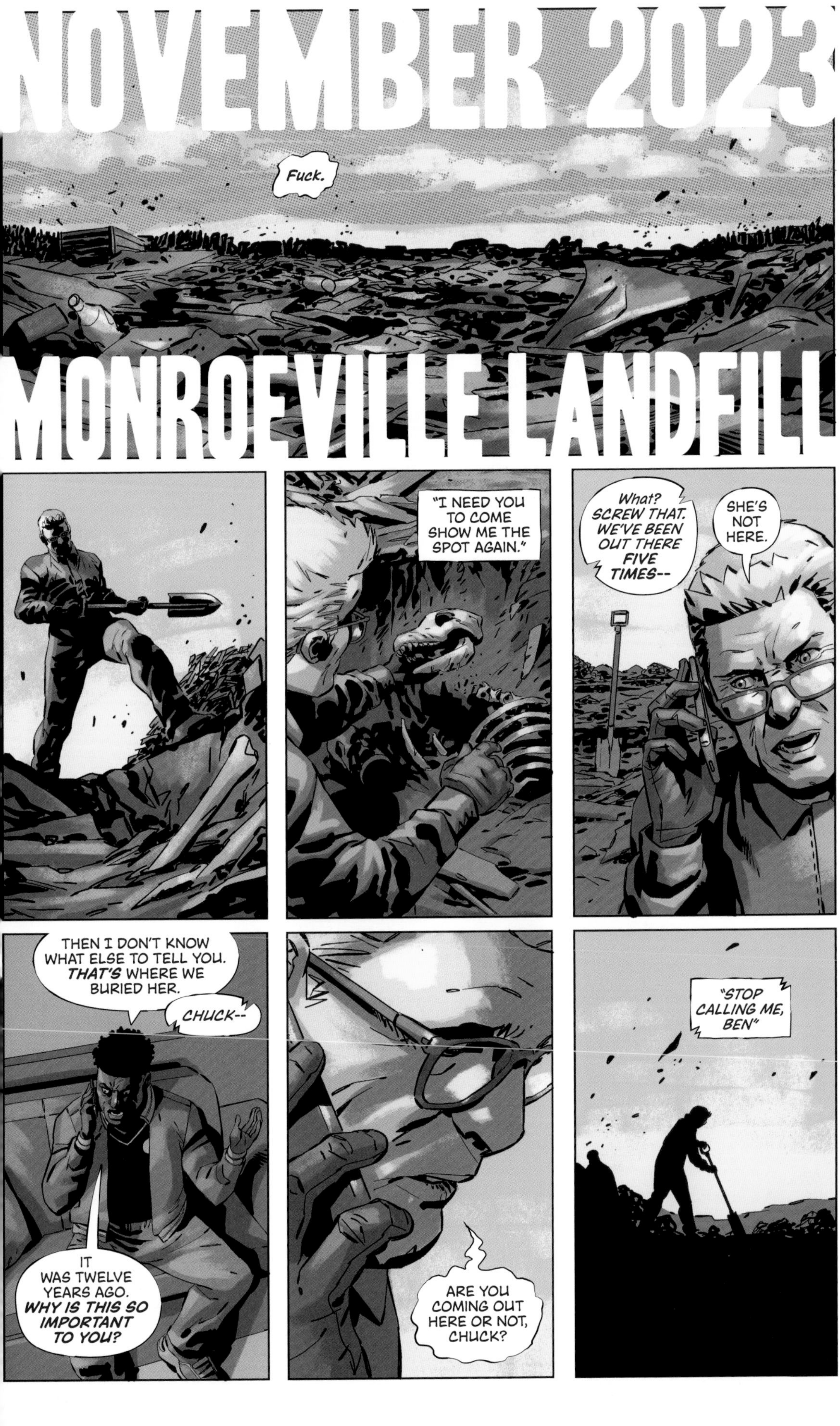
NOVEMBER 2023
Fuck.
MONROEVILLE LANDFILL
"I NEED YOU TO COME SHOW ME THE SPOT AGAIN."
What? SCREW THAT. WE'VE BEEN OUT THERE FIVE TIMES--
SHE'S NOT HERE.
THEN I DON'T KNOW WHAT ELSE TO TELL YOU. THAT'S WHERE WE BURIED HER.
CHUCK--
IT WAS TWELVE YEARS AGO. WHY IS THIS SO IMPORTANT TO YOU?
ARE YOU COMING OUT HERE OR NOT, CHUCK?
"STOP CALLING ME, BEN"

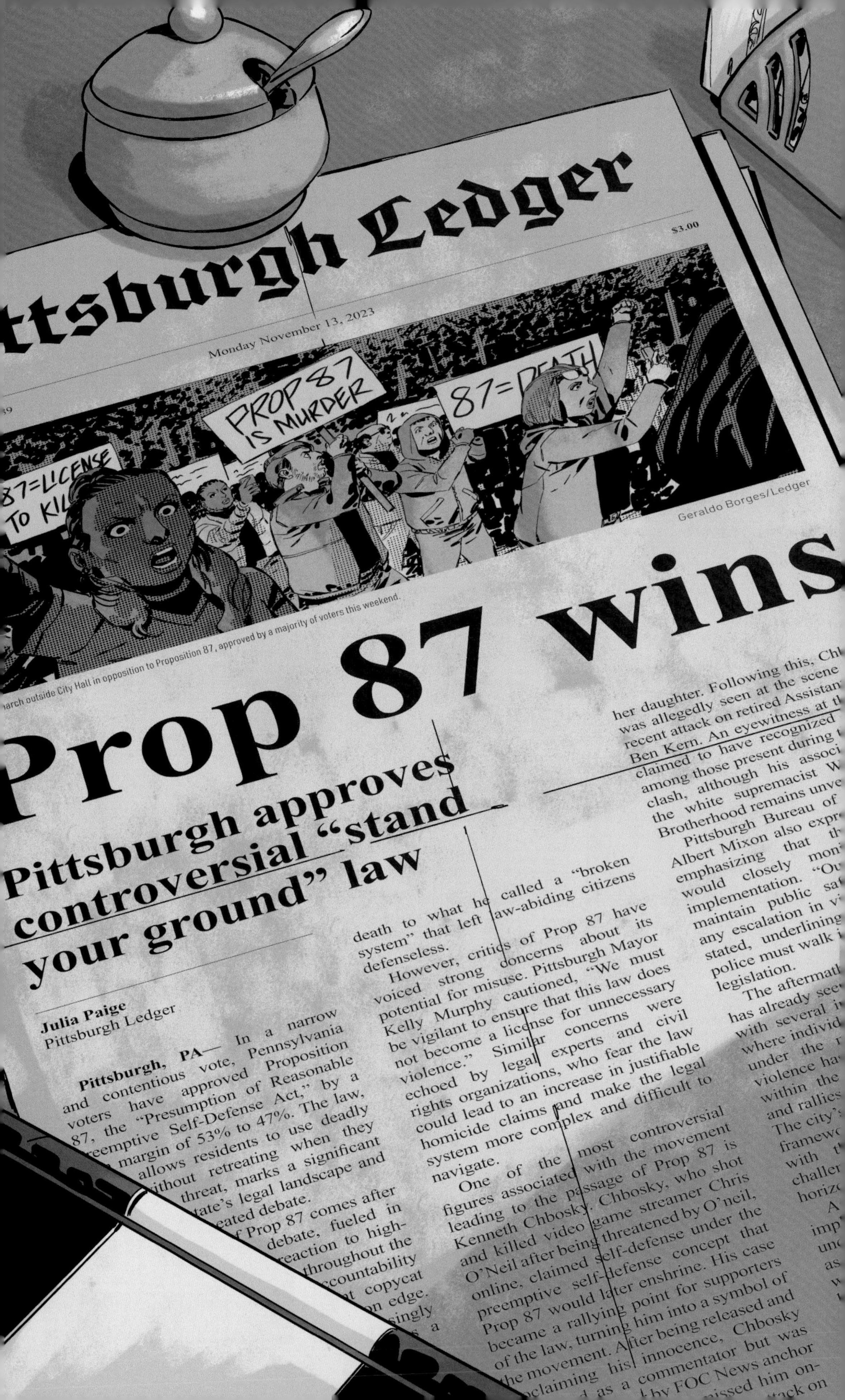
ttsburgh Ledger
$3.00
Monday November 13, 2023
PROP 87 IS MURDER
87=DEATH
87=LICENSE TO KIL
Geraldo Borges/Ledger
arch outside City Hall in opposition to Proposition 87, approved by a majority of voters this weekend.
Prop 87 wins
Pittsburgh approves controversial "stand your ground" law
Julia Paige
Pittsburgh Ledger
Pittsburgh, PA— In a narrow and contentious vote, Pennsylvania voters have approved Proposition 87, the "Presumption of Reasonable Preemptive Self-Defense Act," by a margin of 53% to 47%. The law, allows residents to use deadly ithout retreating when they threat, marks a significant tate's legal landscape and eated debate.
f Prop 87 comes after debate, fueled in reaction to high- throughout the ccountability t copycat n edge.
death to what he called a "broken system" that left law-abiding citizens defenseless.
However, critics of Prop 87 have voiced strong concerns about its potential for misuse. Pittsburgh Mayor Kelly Murphy cautioned, "We must be vigilant to ensure that this law does not become a license for unnecessary violence." Similar concerns were echoed by legal experts and civil rights organizations, who fear the law could lead to an increase in justifiable homicide claims and make the legal system more complex and difficult to navigate.
One of the most controversial figures associated with the movement leading to the passage of Prop 87 is Kenneth Chbosky. Chbosky, who shot and killed video game streamer Chris O'Neil after being threatened by O'neil, online, claimed self-defense under the preemptive self-defense concept that Prop 87 would later enshrine. His case became a rallying point for supporters of the law, turning him into a symbol of the movement. After being released and claiming his innocence, Chbosky as a commentator but was by FOC News anchor issed him on-
her daughter. Following this, Ch was allegedly seen at the scene recent attack on retired Assistan Ben Kern. An eyewitness at th claimed to have recognized among those present during clash, although his associ the white supremacist W Brotherhood remains unve Pittsburgh Bureau of Albert Mixon also expr emphasizing that th would closely mon implementation. "Ou maintain public sa any escalation in v stated, underlining police must walk legislation.
The aftermat has already see with several i where individ under the violence ha within the and rallies The city's framew with challer horiz

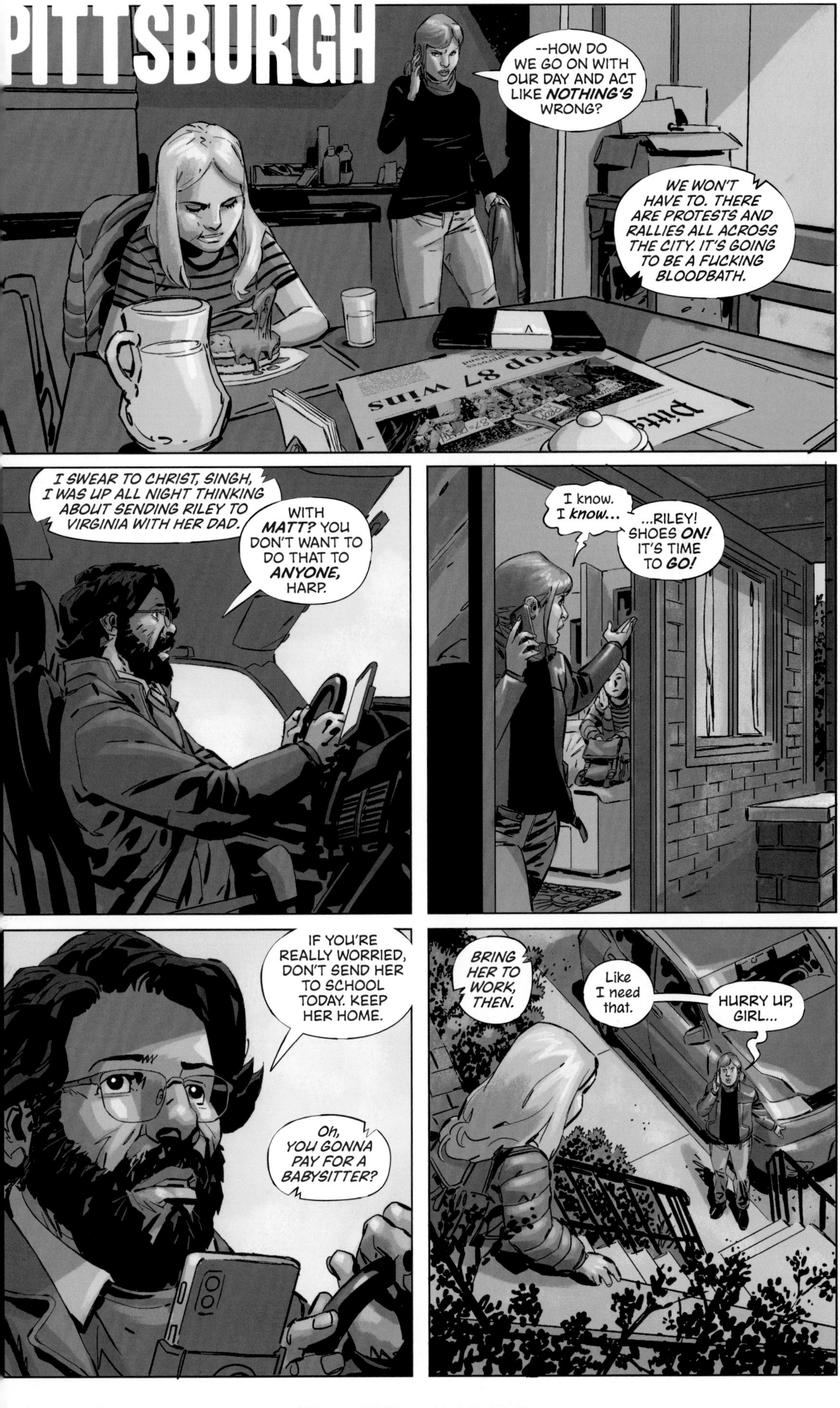
PITTSBURGH
--HOW DO WE GO ON WITH OUR DAY AND ACT LIKE NOTHING'S WRONG?
WE WON'T HAVE TO. THERE ARE PROTESTS AND RALLIES ALL ACROSS THE CITY. IT'S GOING TO BE A FUCKING BLOODBATH.
Prop 87 wins
I SWEAR TO CHRIST, SINGH, I WAS UP ALL NIGHT THINKING ABOUT SENDING RILEY TO VIRGINIA WITH HER DAD.
WITH MATT? YOU DON'T WANT TO DO THAT TO ANYONE, HARP.
I know. I know...
...RILEY! SHOES ON! IT'S TIME TO GO!
IF YOU'RE REALLY WORRIED, DON'T SEND HER TO SCHOOL TODAY. KEEP HER HOME.
Oh, YOU GONNA PAY FOR A BABYSITTER?
BRING HER TO WORK, THEN.
Like I need that.
HURRY UP, GIRL...

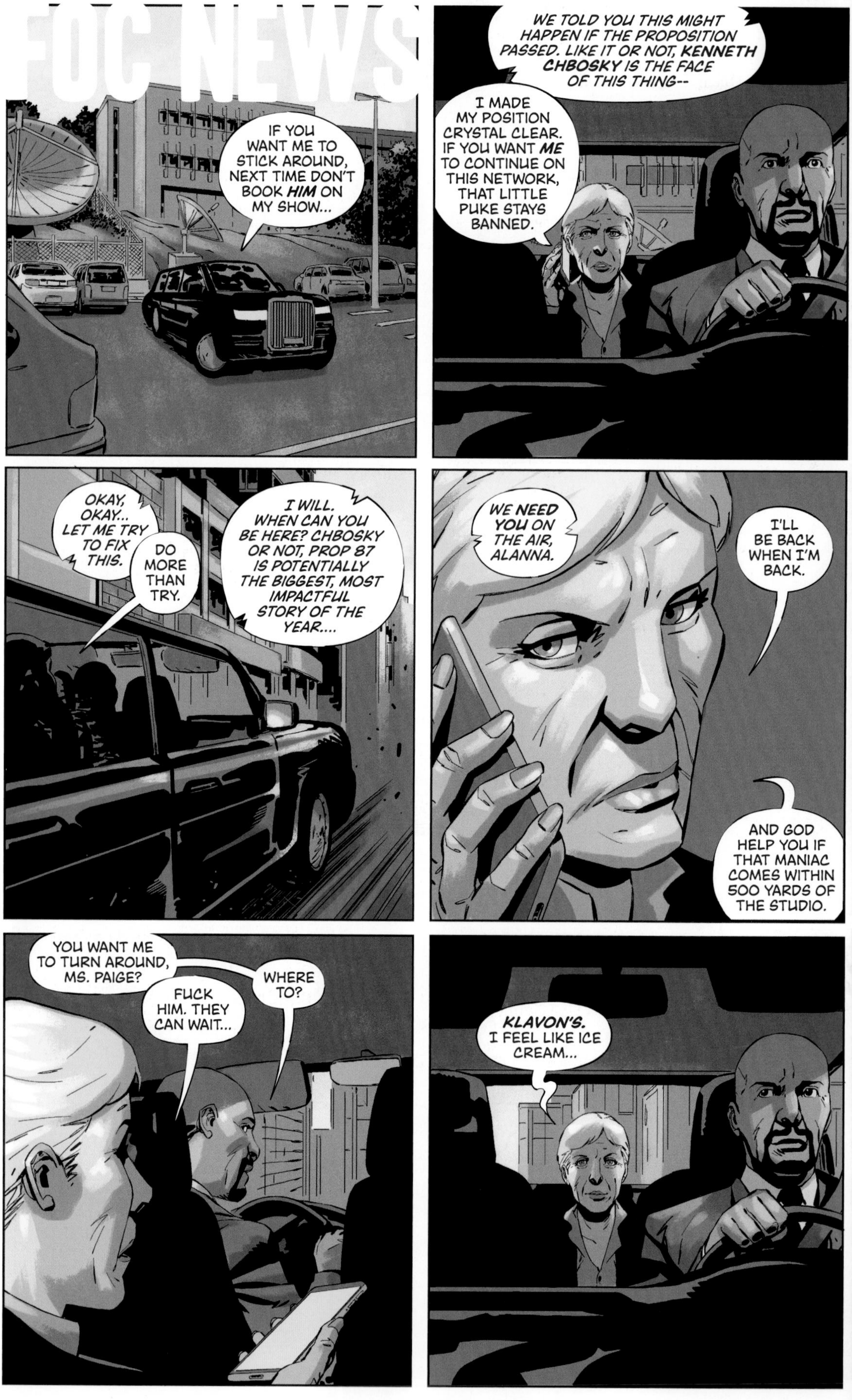
FOC NEWS
IF YOU WANT ME TO STICK AROUND, NEXT TIME DON'T BOOK *HIM* ON MY SHOW...
WE TOLD YOU THIS MIGHT HAPPEN IF THE PROPOSITION PASSED. LIKE IT OR NOT, **KENNETH CHBOSKY** IS THE FACE OF THIS THING--
I MADE MY POSITION CRYSTAL CLEAR. IF YOU WANT *ME* TO CONTINUE ON THIS NETWORK, THAT LITTLE PUKE STAYS BANNED.
OKAY, OKAY... LET ME TRY TO FIX THIS.
DO MORE THAN TRY.
I WILL. WHEN CAN YOU BE HERE? CHBOSKY OR NOT, PROP 87 IS POTENTIALLY THE BIGGEST, MOST IMPACTFUL STORY OF THE YEAR....
WE **NEED YOU** ON THE AIR, ALANNA.
I'LL BE BACK WHEN I'M BACK.
AND GOD HELP YOU IF THAT MANIAC COMES WITHIN 500 YARDS OF THE STUDIO.
YOU WANT ME TO TURN AROUND, MS. PAIGE?
FUCK HIM. THEY CAN WAIT...
WHERE TO?
KLAVON'S. I FEEL LIKE ICE CREAM...

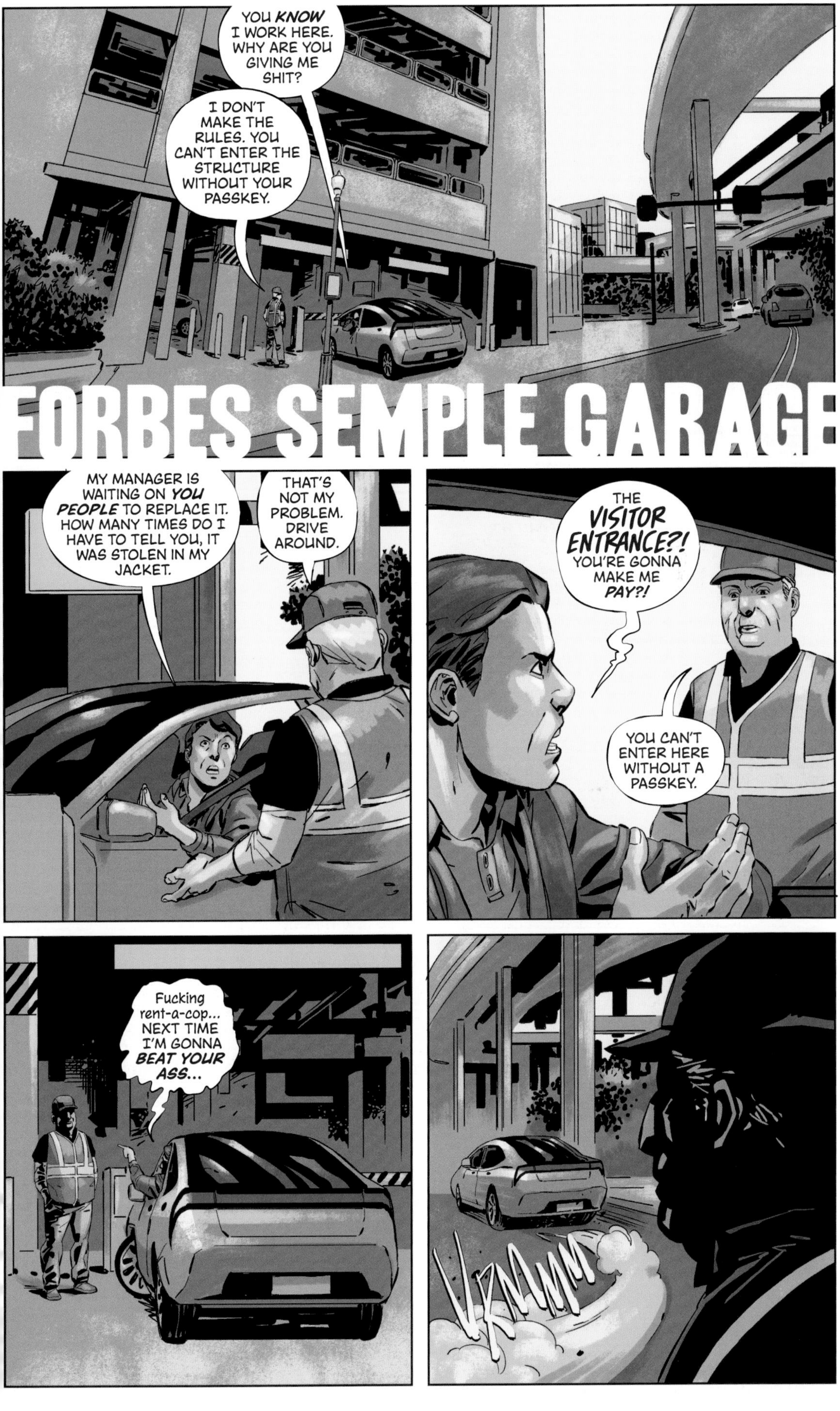
YOU KNOW I WORK HERE. WHY ARE YOU GIVING ME SHIT?
I DON'T MAKE THE RULES. YOU CAN'T ENTER THE STRUCTURE WITHOUT YOUR PASSKEY.
FORBES SEMPLE GARAGE
MY MANAGER IS WAITING ON YOU PEOPLE TO REPLACE IT. HOW MANY TIMES DO I HAVE TO TELL YOU, IT WAS STOLEN IN MY JACKET.
THAT'S NOT MY PROBLEM. DRIVE AROUND.
THE VISITOR ENTRANCE?! YOU'RE GONNA MAKE ME PAY?!
YOU CAN'T ENTER HERE WITHOUT A PASSKEY.
Fucking rent-a-cop... NEXT TIME I'M GONNA BEAT YOUR ASS...
VRMMM

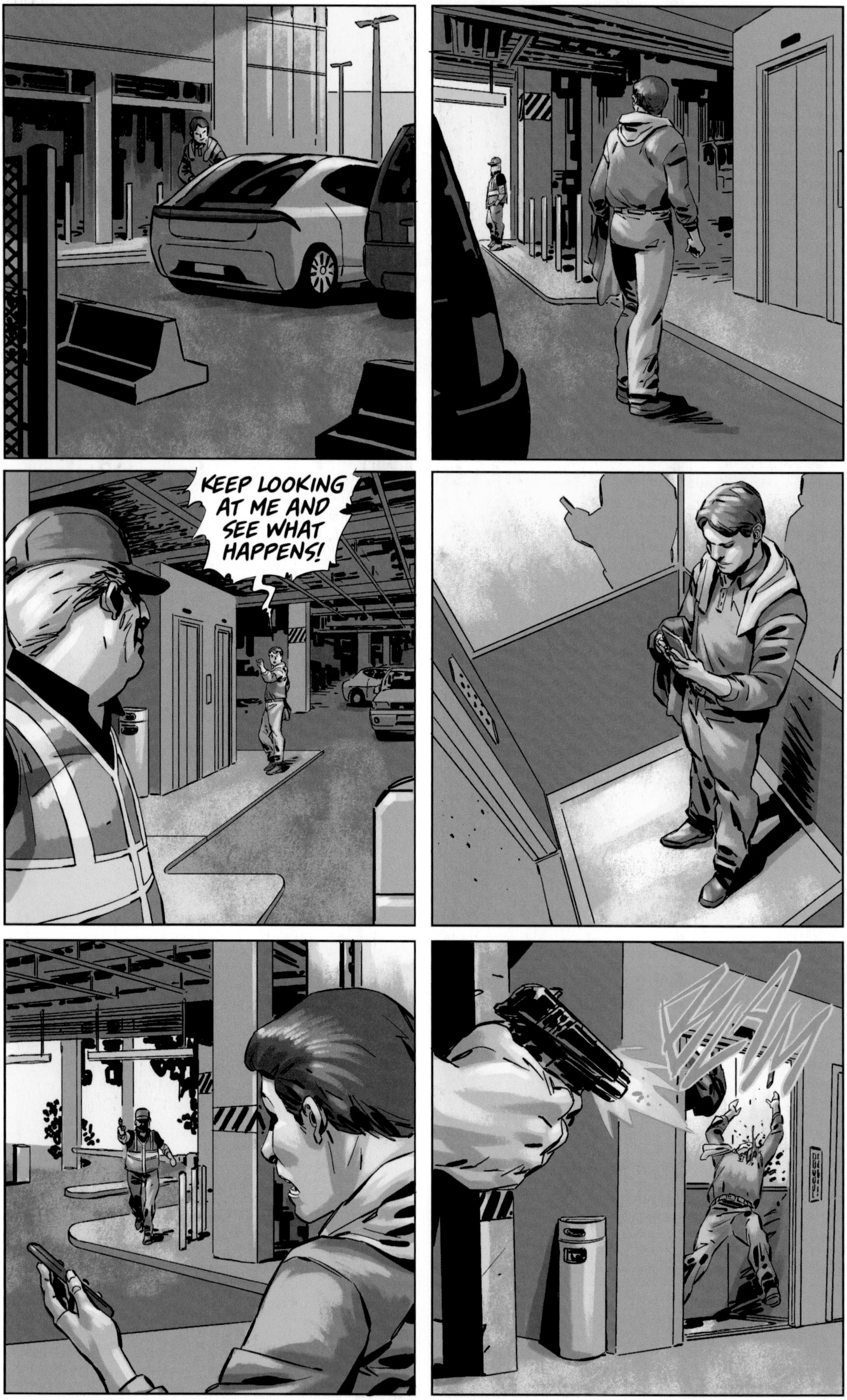
KEEP LOOKING AT ME AND SEE WHAT HAPPENS!

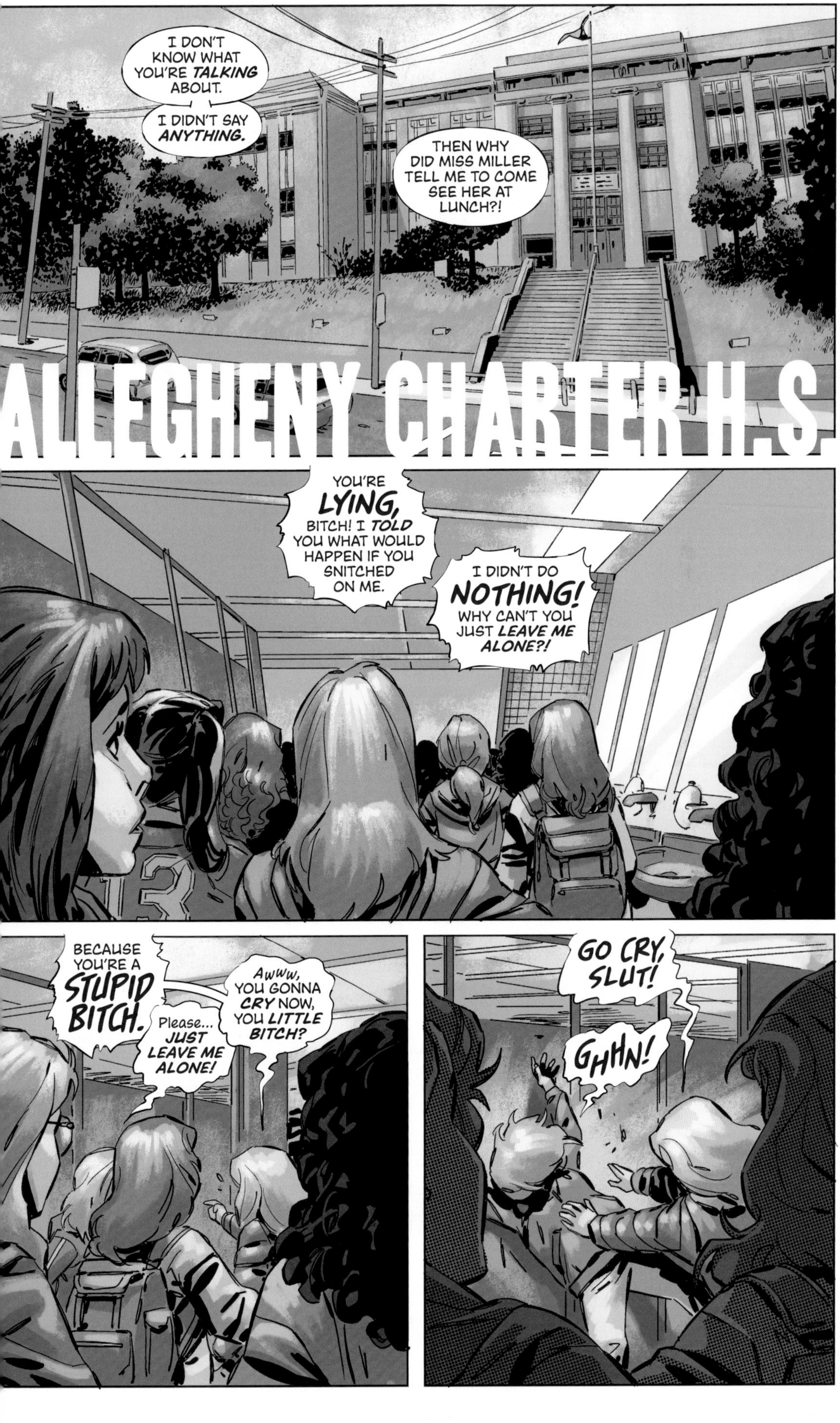
I DON'T KNOW WHAT YOU'RE TALKING ABOUT.
I DIDN'T SAY ANYTHING.
THEN WHY DID MISS MILLER TELL ME TO COME SEE HER AT LUNCH?!
ALLEGHENY CHARTER H.S.
YOU'RE LYING, BITCH! I TOLD YOU WHAT WOULD HAPPEN IF YOU SNITCHED ON ME.
I DIDN'T DO NOTHING! WHY CAN'T YOU JUST LEAVE ME ALONE?!
BECAUSE YOU'RE A STUPID BITCH.
Please... JUST LEAVE ME ALONE!
AWWW, YOU GONNA CRY NOW, YOU LITTLE BITCH?
GO CRY, SLUT!
GHHN!

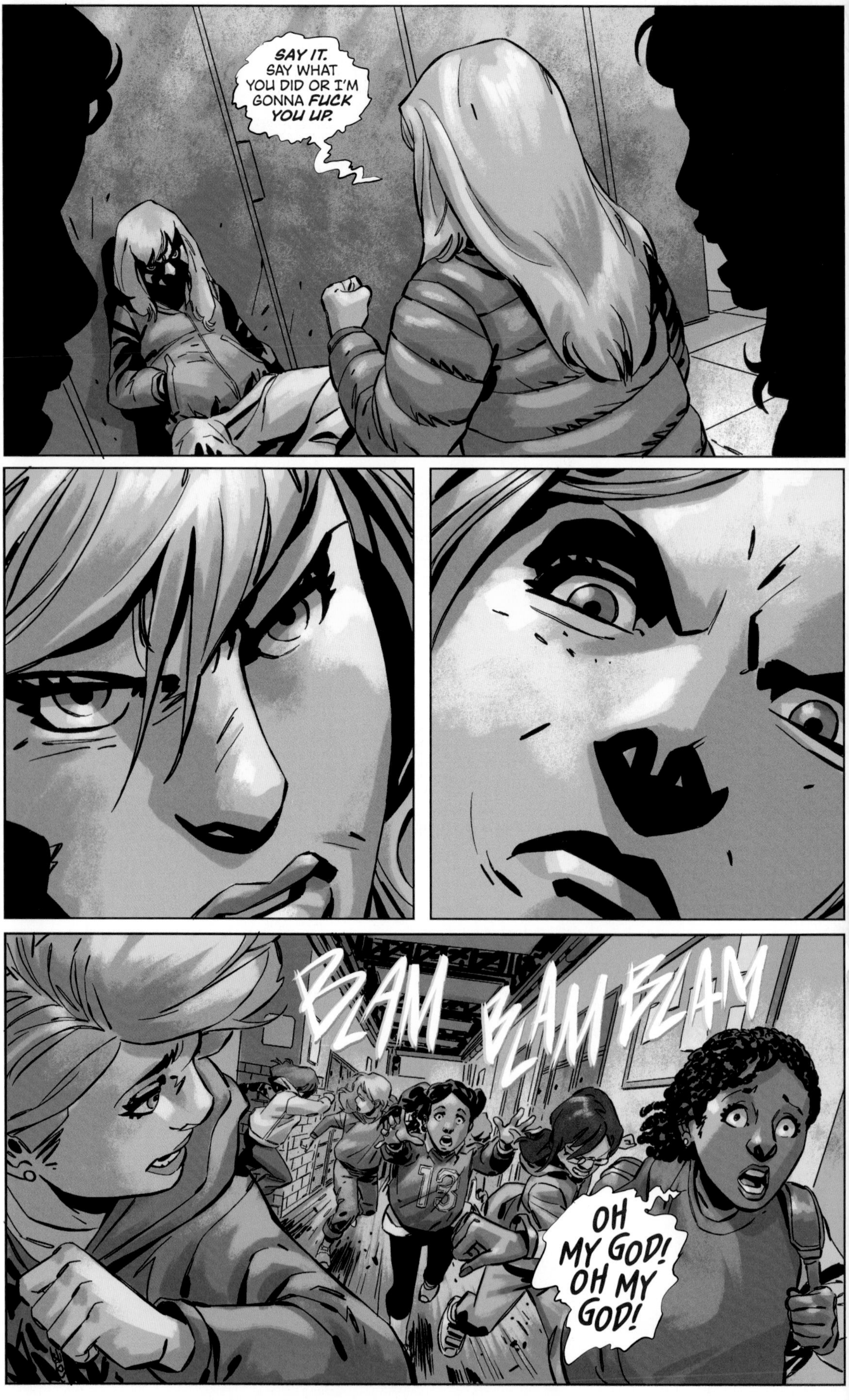
SAY IT. SAY WHAT YOU DID OR I'M GONNA FUCK YOU UP.
BLAM BLAM BLAM
OH MY GOD! OH MY GOD!

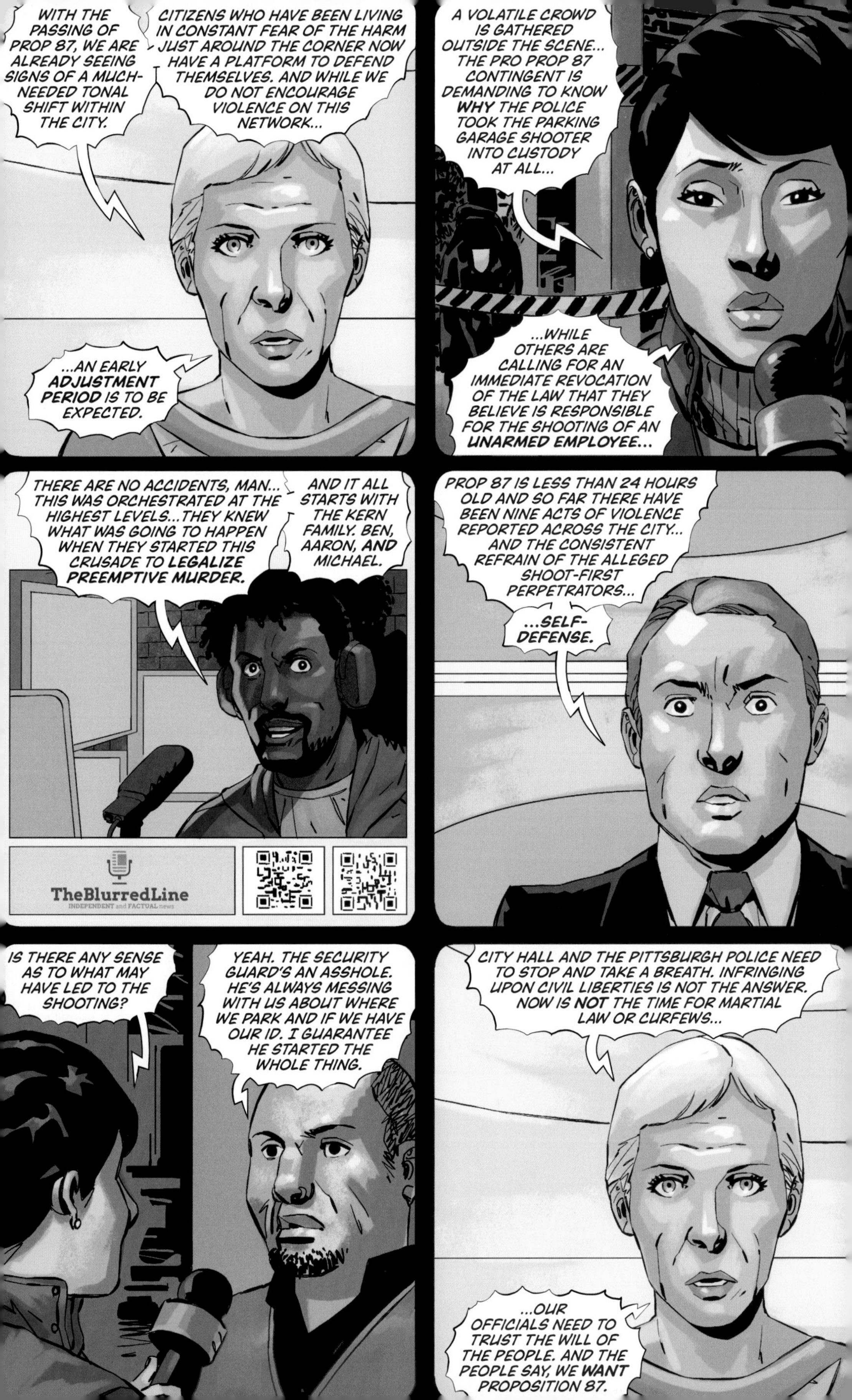

WITH THE PASSING OF PROP 87, WE ARE ALREADY SEEING SIGNS OF A MUCH-NEEDED TONAL SHIFT WITHIN THE CITY.
CITIZENS WHO HAVE BEEN LIVING IN CONSTANT FEAR OF THE HARM JUST AROUND THE CORNER NOW HAVE A PLATFORM TO DEFEND THEMSELVES. AND WHILE WE DO NOT ENCOURAGE VIOLENCE ON THIS NETWORK...
...AN EARLY **ADJUSTMENT PERIOD** IS TO BE EXPECTED.
A VOLATILE CROWD IS GATHERED OUTSIDE THE SCENE... THE PRO PROP 87 CONTINGENT IS DEMANDING TO KNOW **WHY** THE POLICE TOOK THE PARKING GARAGE SHOOTER INTO CUSTODY AT ALL...
...WHILE OTHERS ARE CALLING FOR AN IMMEDIATE REVOCATION OF THE LAW THAT THEY BELIEVE IS RESPONSIBLE FOR THE SHOOTING OF AN **UNARMED EMPLOYEE...**
THERE ARE NO ACCIDENTS, MAN... THIS WAS ORCHESTRATED AT THE HIGHEST LEVELS...THEY KNEW WHAT WAS GOING TO HAPPEN WHEN THEY STARTED THIS CRUSADE TO **LEGALIZE PREEMPTIVE MURDER.**
AND IT ALL STARTS WITH THE KERN FAMILY. BEN, AARON, **AND** MICHAEL.
TheBlurredLine
INDEPENDENT and FACTUAL news
PROP 87 IS LESS THAN 24 HOURS OLD AND SO FAR THERE HAVE BEEN NINE ACTS OF VIOLENCE REPORTED ACROSS THE CITY... AND THE CONSISTENT REFRAIN OF THE ALLEGED SHOOT-FIRST PERPETRATORS...
...SELF-DEFENSE.
IS THERE ANY SENSE AS TO WHAT MAY HAVE LED TO THE SHOOTING?
YEAH. THE SECURITY GUARD'S AN ASSHOLE. HE'S ALWAYS MESSING WITH US ABOUT WHERE WE PARK AND IF WE HAVE OUR ID. I GUARANTEE HE STARTED THE WHOLE THING.
CITY HALL AND THE PITTSBURGH POLICE NEED TO STOP AND TAKE A BREATH. INFRINGING UPON CIVIL LIBERTIES IS NOT THE ANSWER. NOW IS **NOT** THE TIME FOR MARTIAL LAW OR CURFEWS...
...OUR OFFICIALS NEED TO TRUST THE WILL OF THE PEOPLE. AND THE PEOPLE SAY, WE **WANT** PROPOSITION 87.

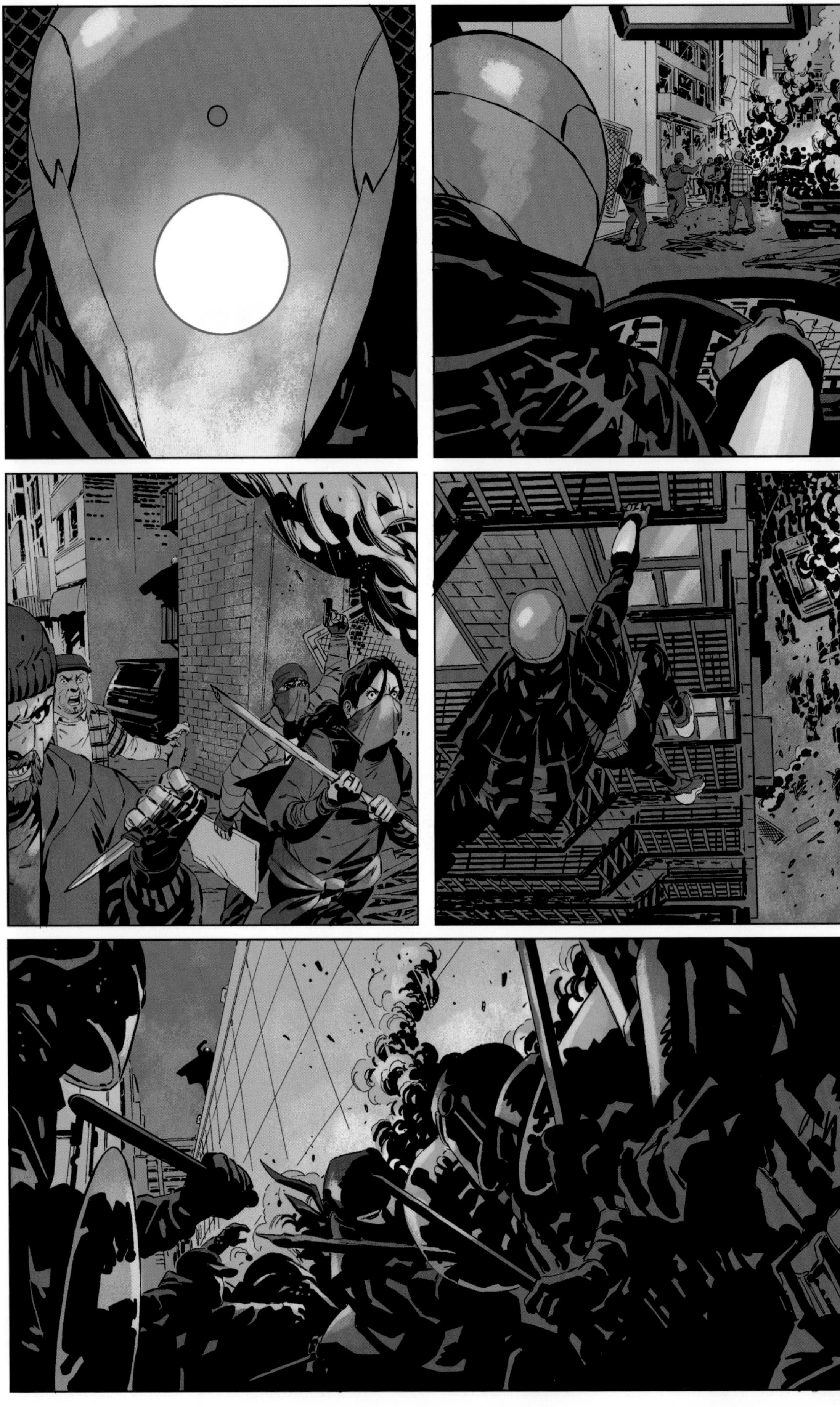

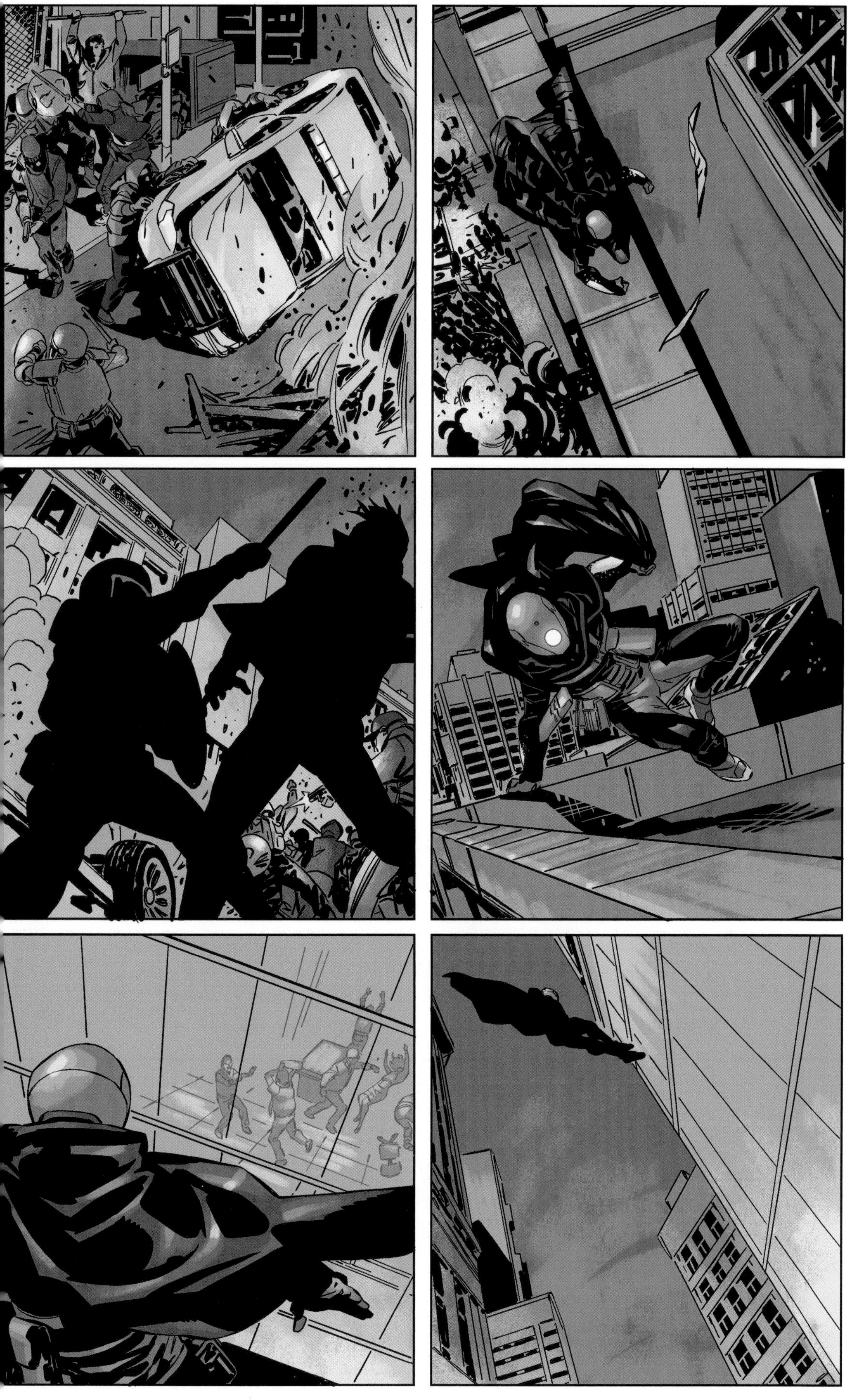

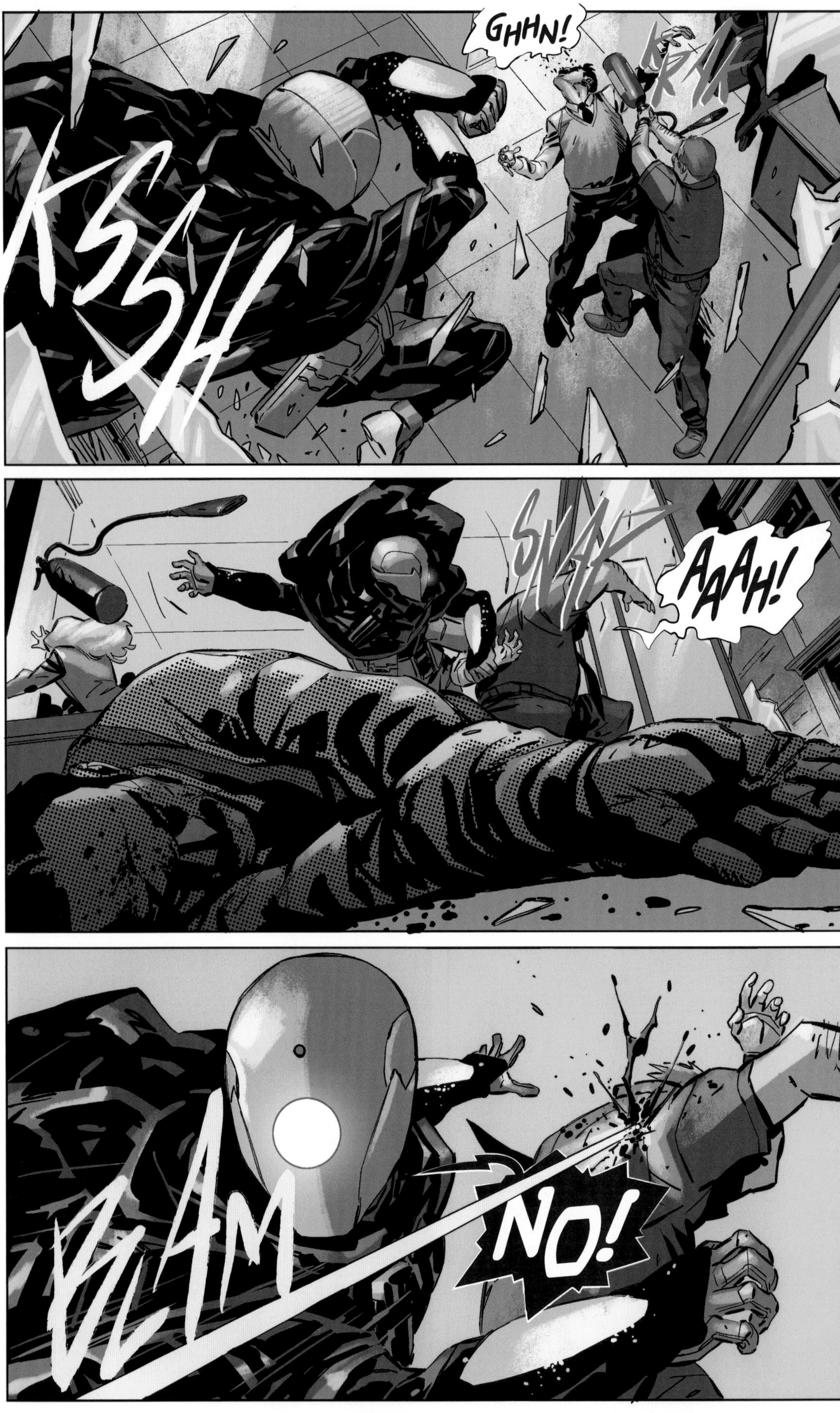
KSSH
GHHN!
KRAK
SNAK
AAAH!
BLAM
NO!

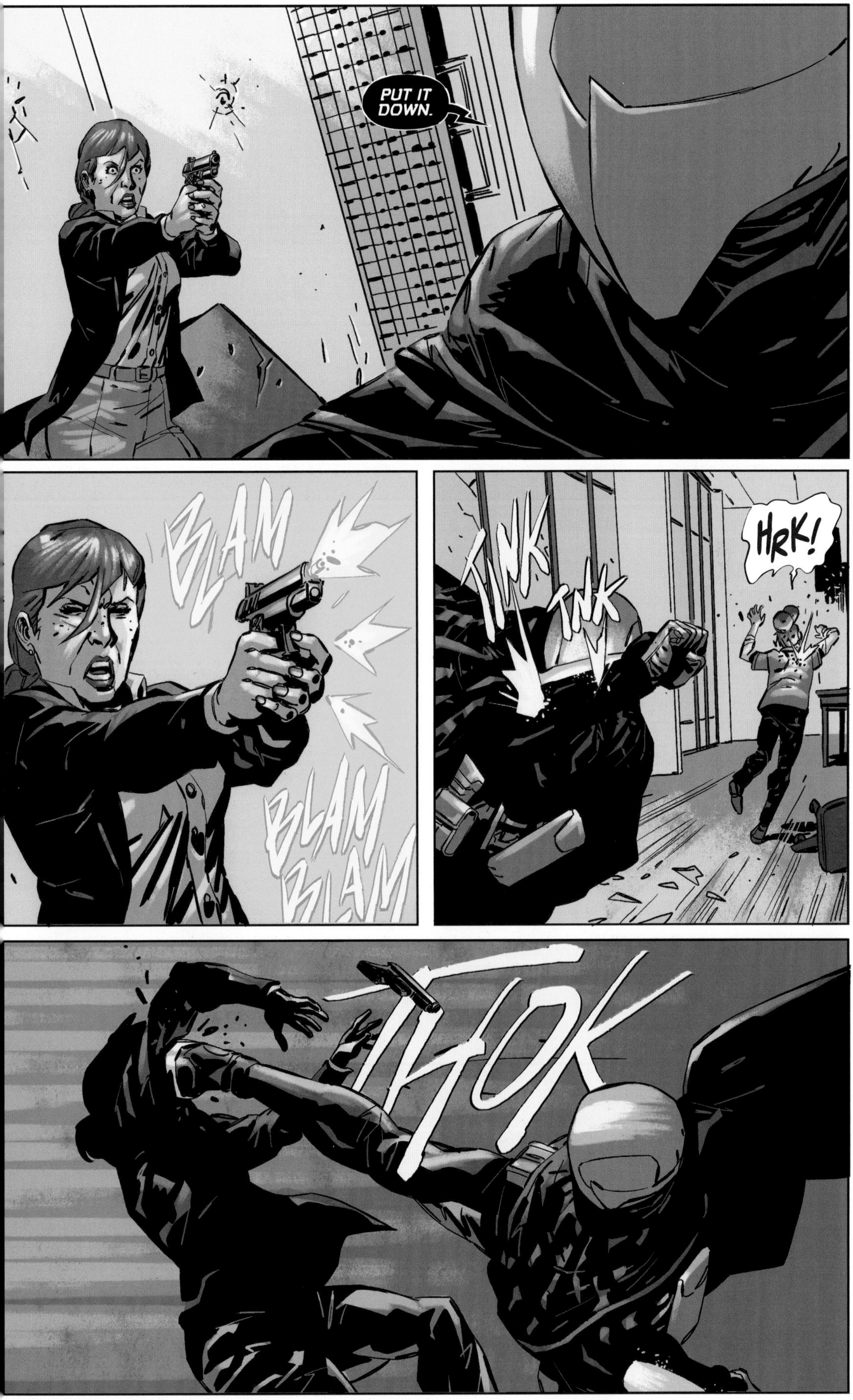

PUT IT DOWN.
BLAM
BLAM
BLAM
TINK
TNK
HRK!
THOK

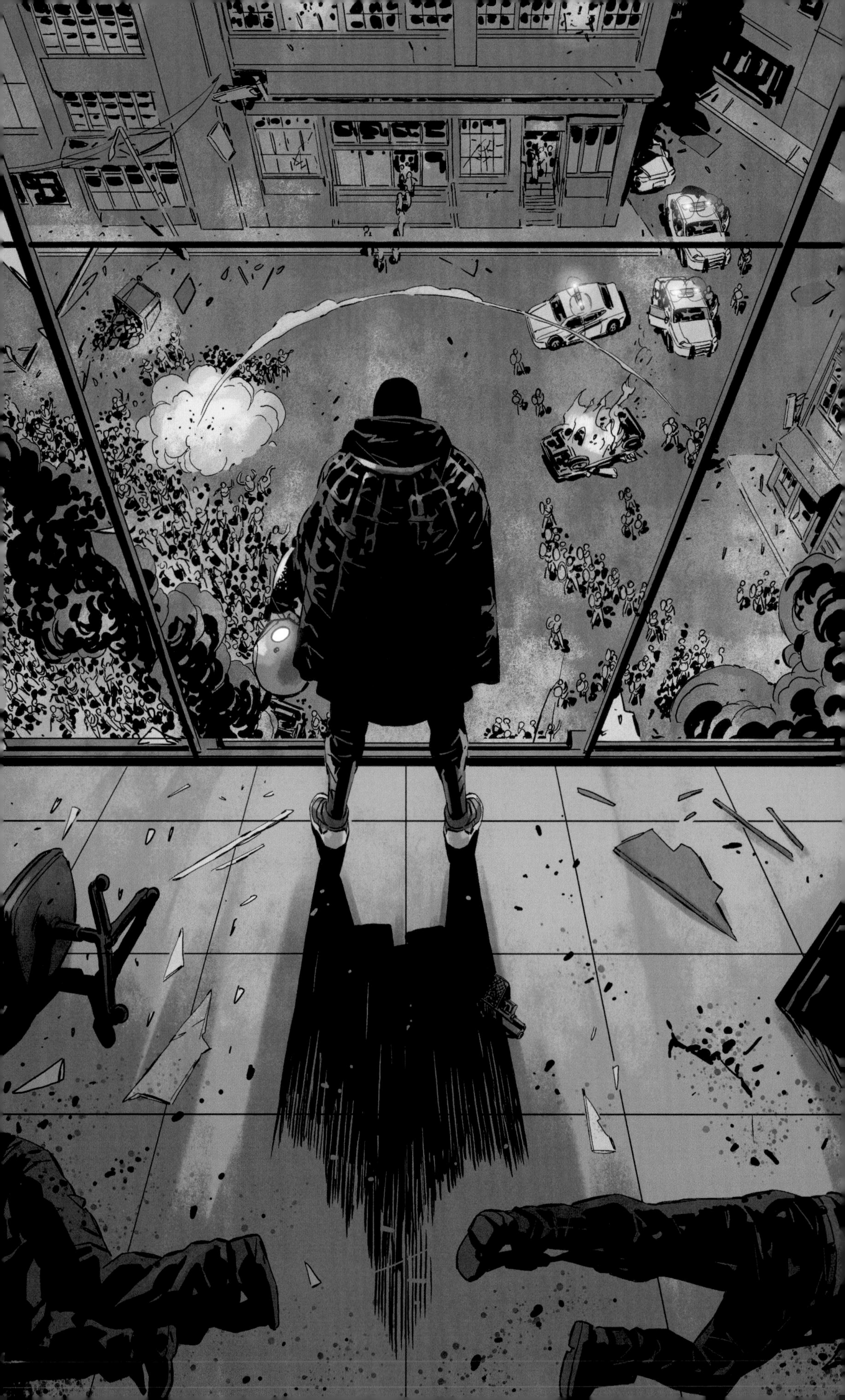

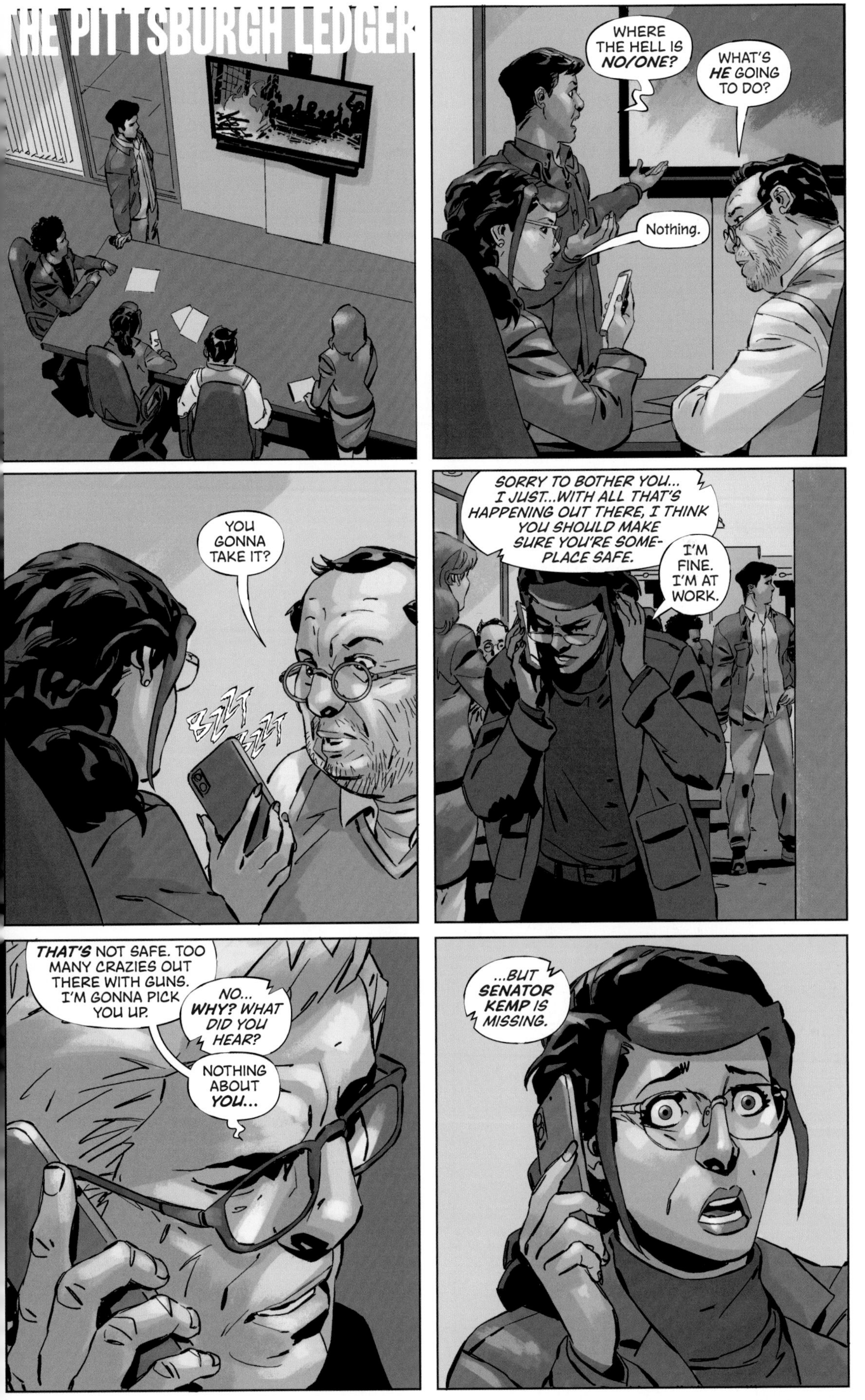
THE PITTSBURGH LEDGER
WHERE THE HELL IS NO/ONE?
WHAT'S HE GOING TO DO?
Nothing.
YOU GONNA TAKE IT?
BZZT BZZT
SORRY TO BOTHER YOU... I JUST...WITH ALL THAT'S HAPPENING OUT THERE, I THINK YOU SHOULD MAKE SURE YOU'RE SOME-PLACE SAFE.
I'M FINE. I'M AT WORK.
THAT'S NOT SAFE. TOO MANY CRAZIES OUT THERE WITH GUNS. I'M GONNA PICK YOU UP.
NO... WHY? WHAT DID YOU HEAR?
NOTHING ABOUT YOU...
...BUT SENATOR KEMP IS MISSING.

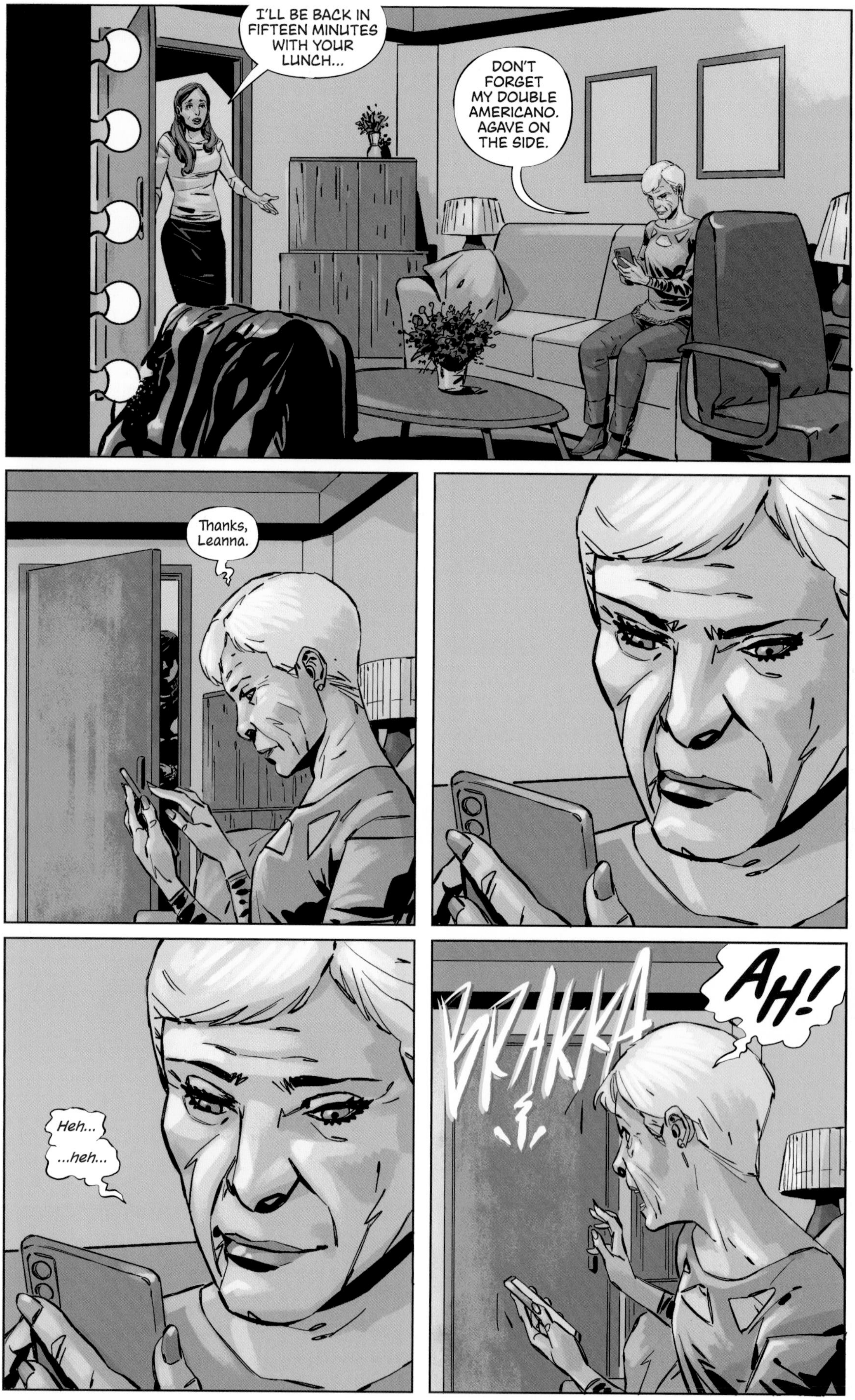
I'LL BE BACK IN FIFTEEN MINUTES WITH YOUR LUNCH...
DON'T FORGET MY DOUBLE AMERICANO. AGAVE ON THE SIDE.
Thanks, Leanna.
Heh...
...heh...
BRAKKA
AH!

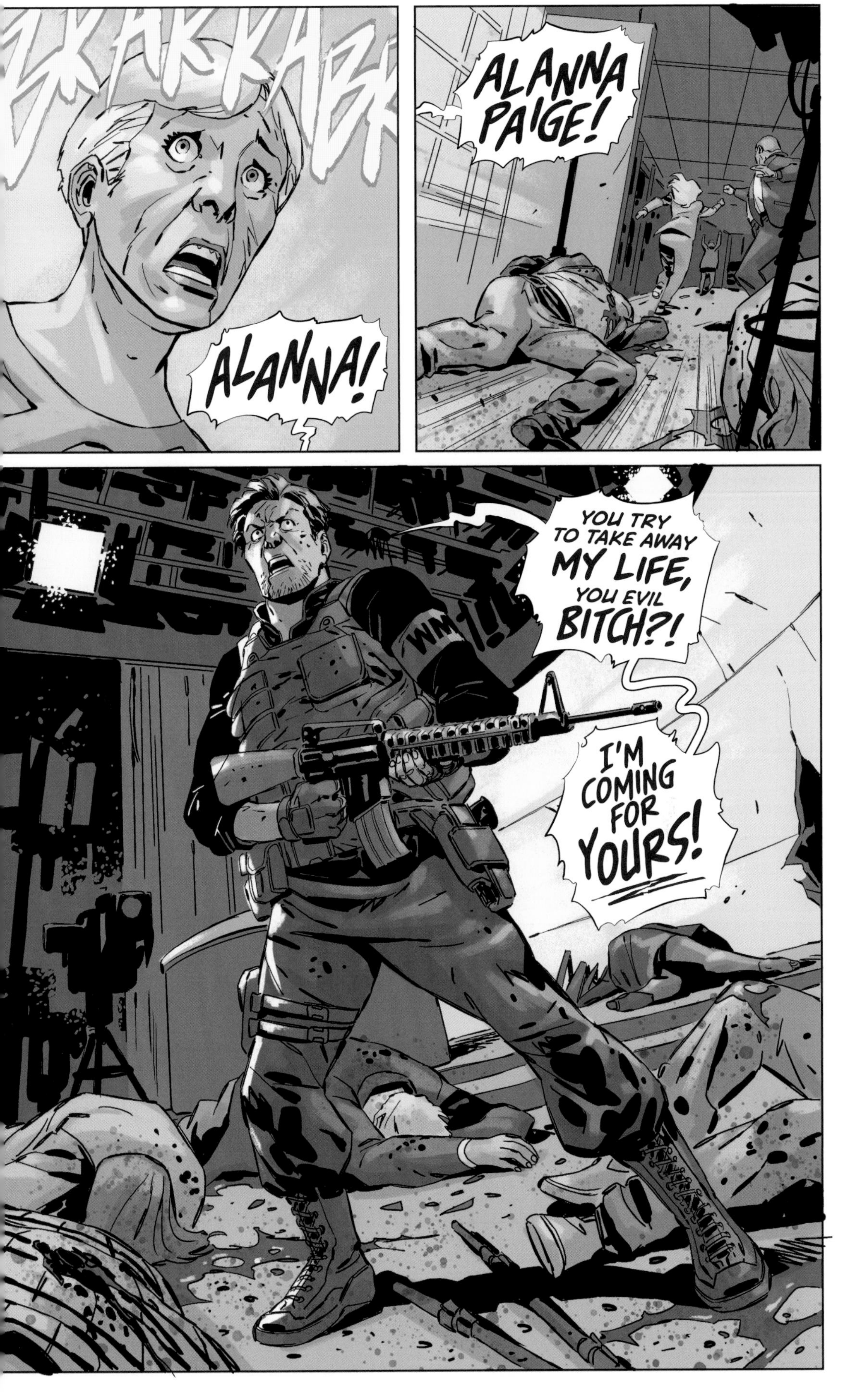

BRAKKABR
ALANNA!
ALANNA PAIGE!
YOU TRY TO TAKE AWAY MY LIFE, YOU EVIL BITCH?!
I'M COMING FOR YOURS!

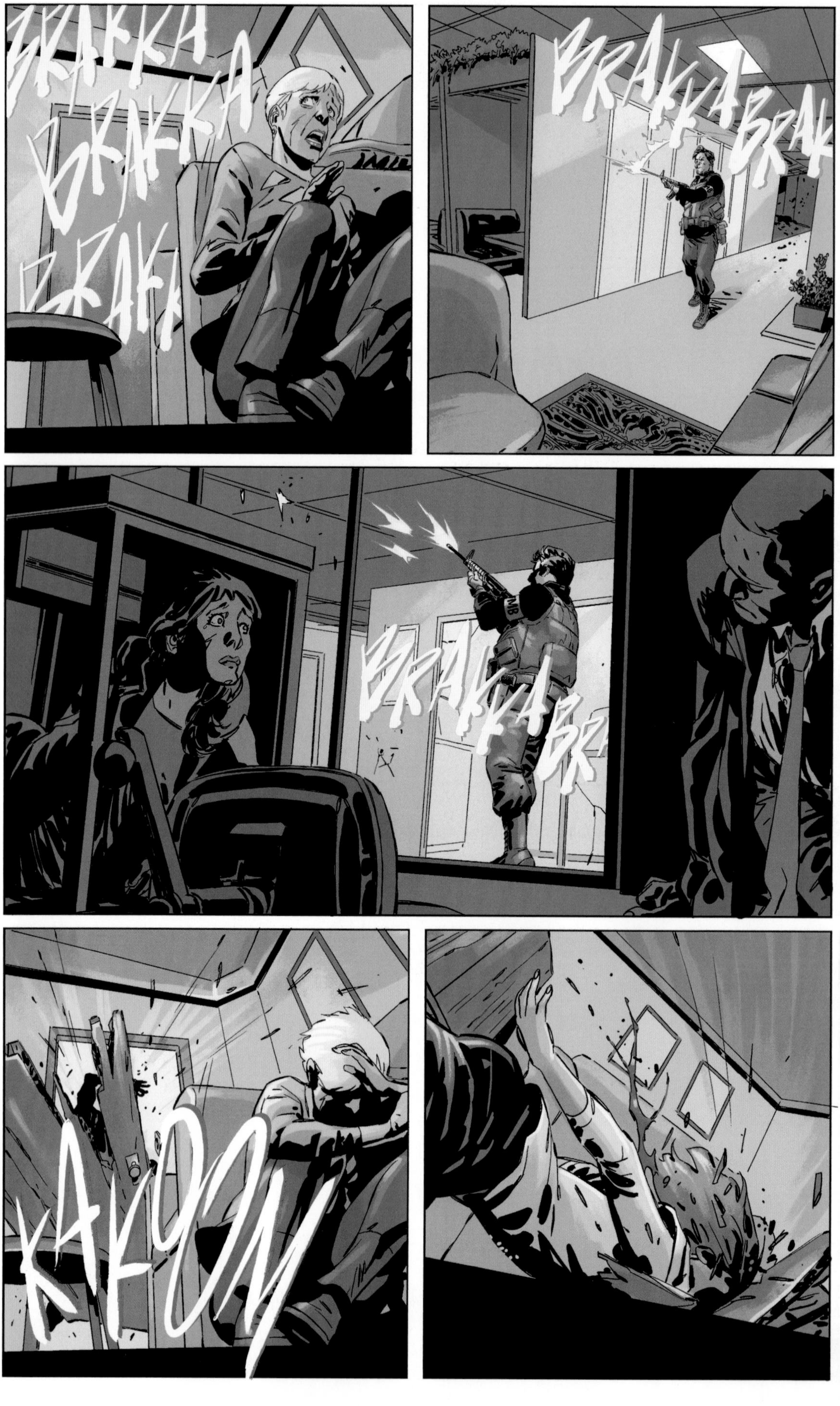
BRAKKA
BRAKKA
BRAKA
BRAKKA
BRAK
BRAKKA
BRA
KAKOOM

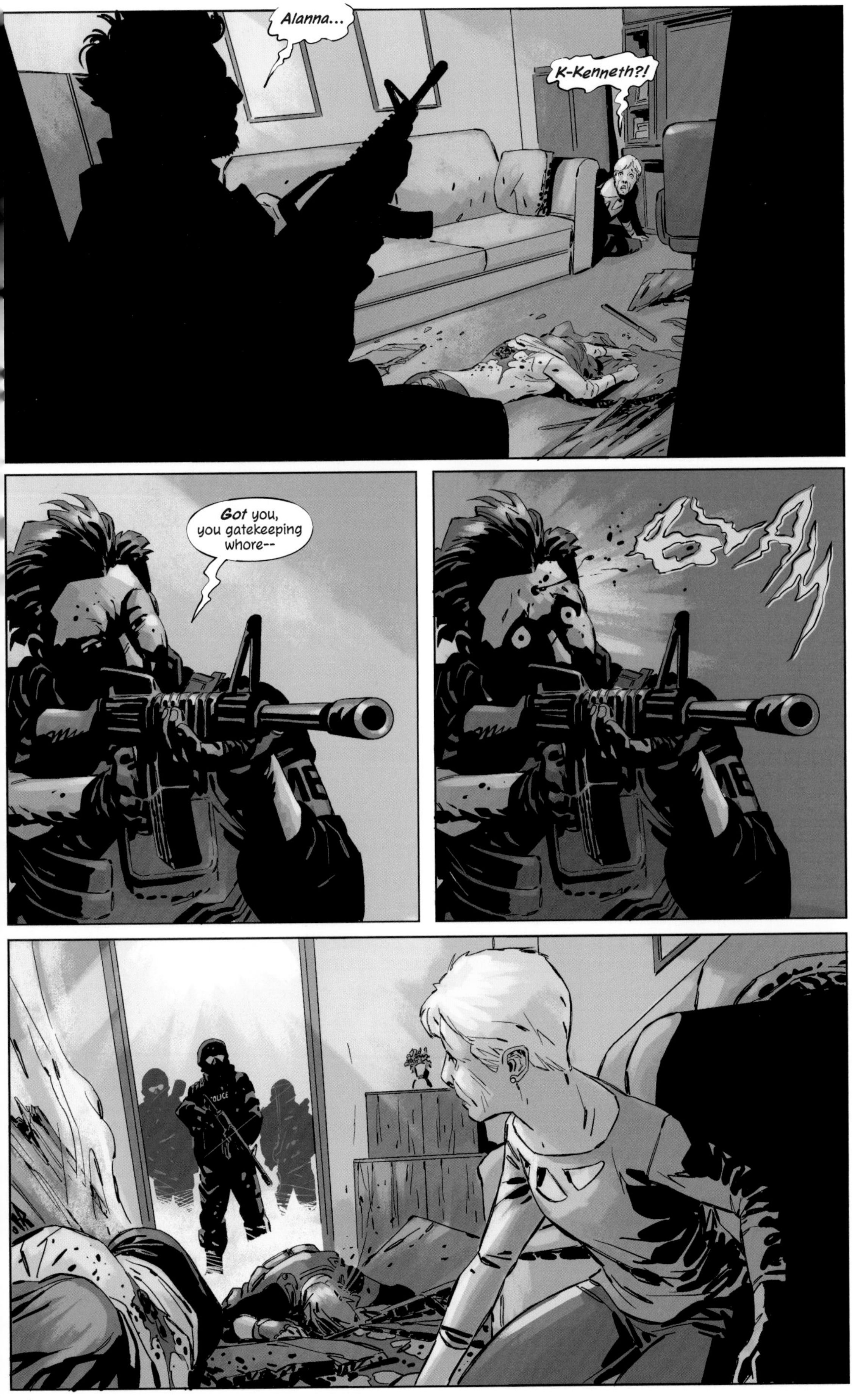
Alanna...
K-Kenneth?!
Got you, you gatekeeping whore--
BLAM

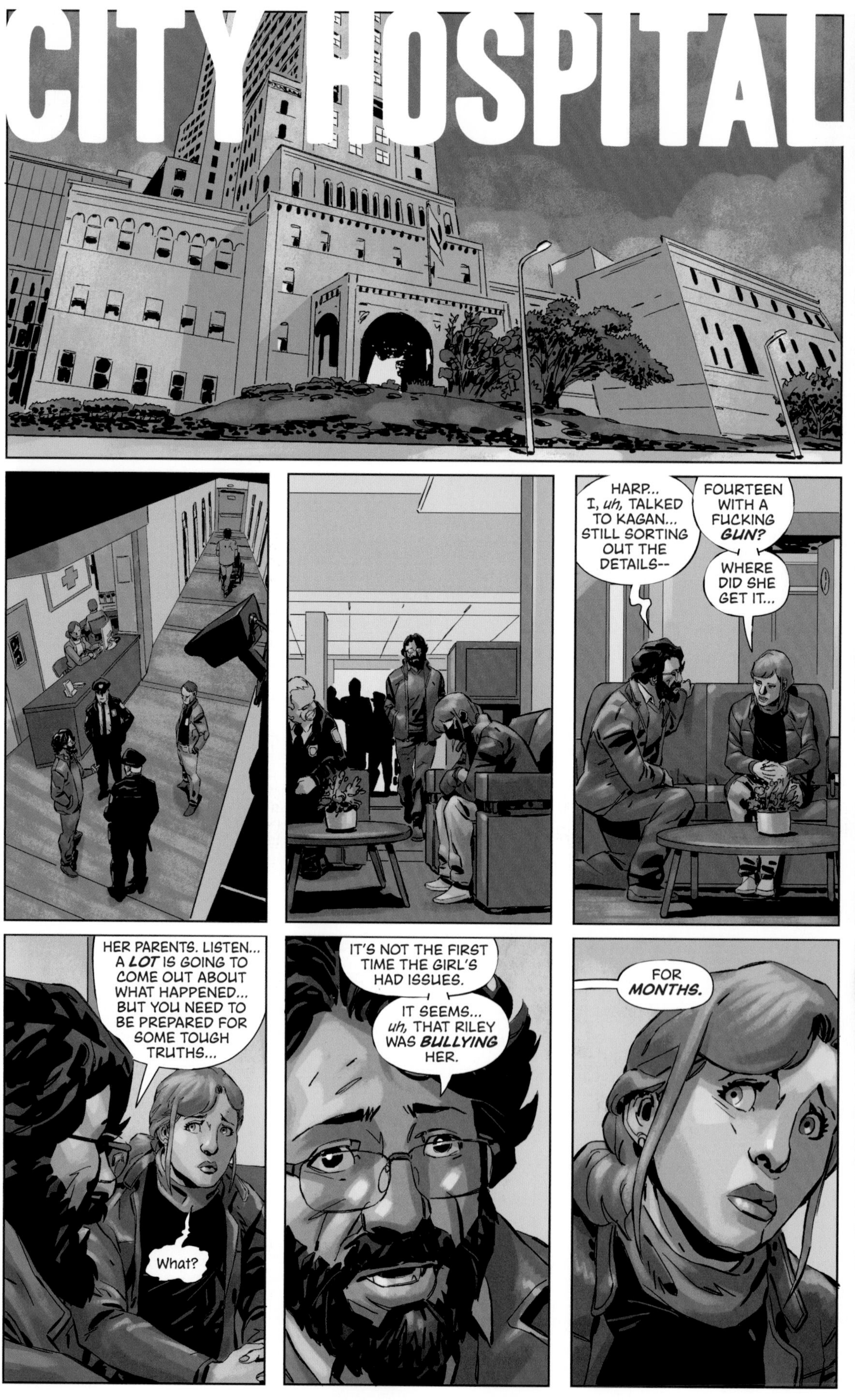
CITY HOSPITAL
HARP... I, uh, TALKED TO KAGAN... STILL SORTING OUT THE DETAILS--
FOURTEEN WITH A FUCKING GUN?
WHERE DID SHE GET IT...
HER PARENTS. LISTEN... A LOT IS GOING TO COME OUT ABOUT WHAT HAPPENED... BUT YOU NEED TO BE PREPARED FOR SOME TOUGH TRUTHS...
What?
IT'S NOT THE FIRST TIME THE GIRL'S HAD ISSUES.
IT SEEMS... uh, THAT RILEY WAS BULLYING HER.
FOR MONTHS.

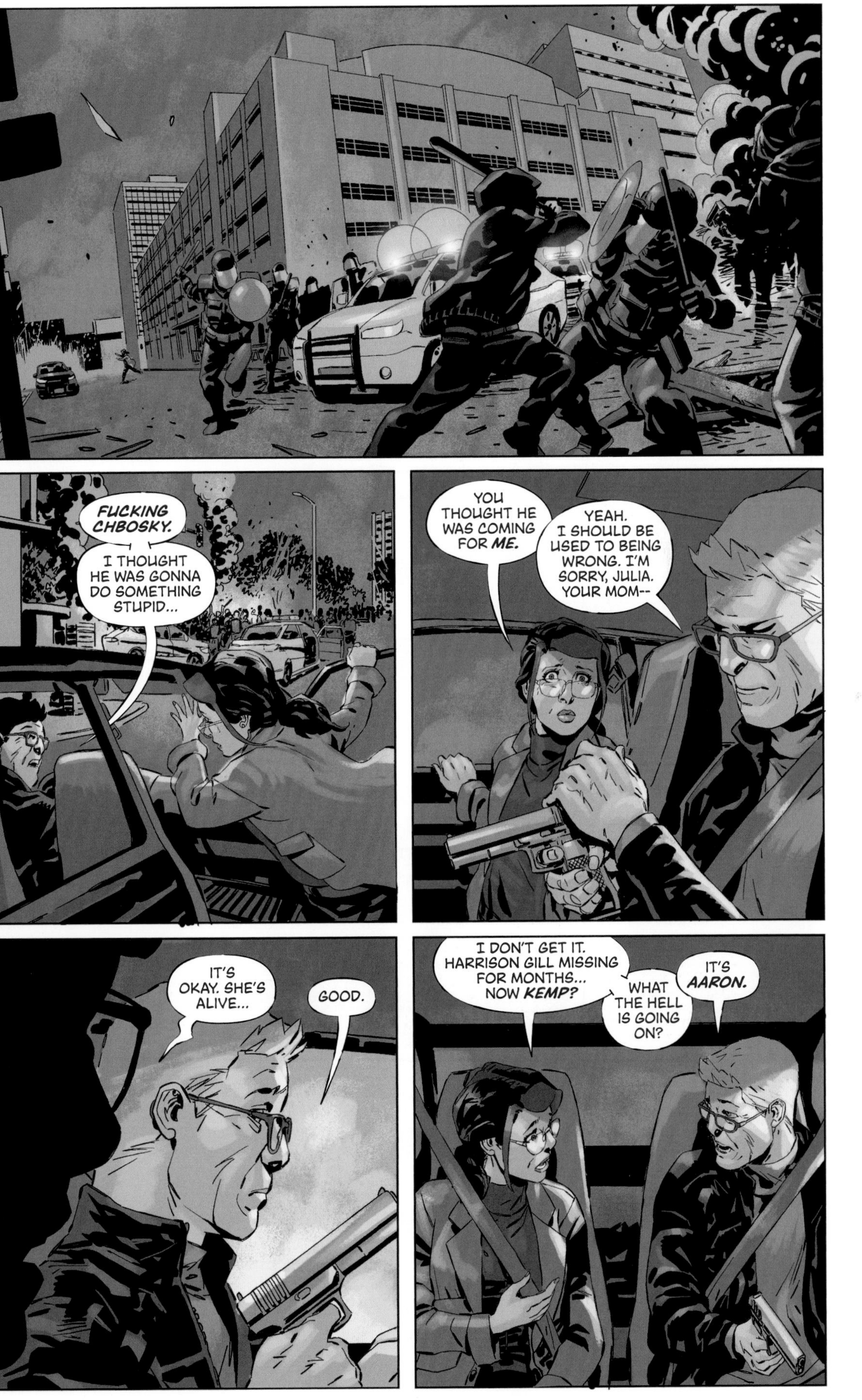

FUCKING CHBOSKY.
I THOUGHT HE WAS GONNA DO SOMETHING STUPID...
YOU THOUGHT HE WAS COMING FOR ME.
YEAH. I SHOULD BE USED TO BEING WRONG. I'M SORRY, JULIA. YOUR MOM--
IT'S OKAY. SHE'S ALIVE...
GOOD.
I DON'T GET IT. HARRISON GILL MISSING FOR MONTHS... NOW KEMP?
WHAT THE HELL IS GOING ON?
IT'S AARON.

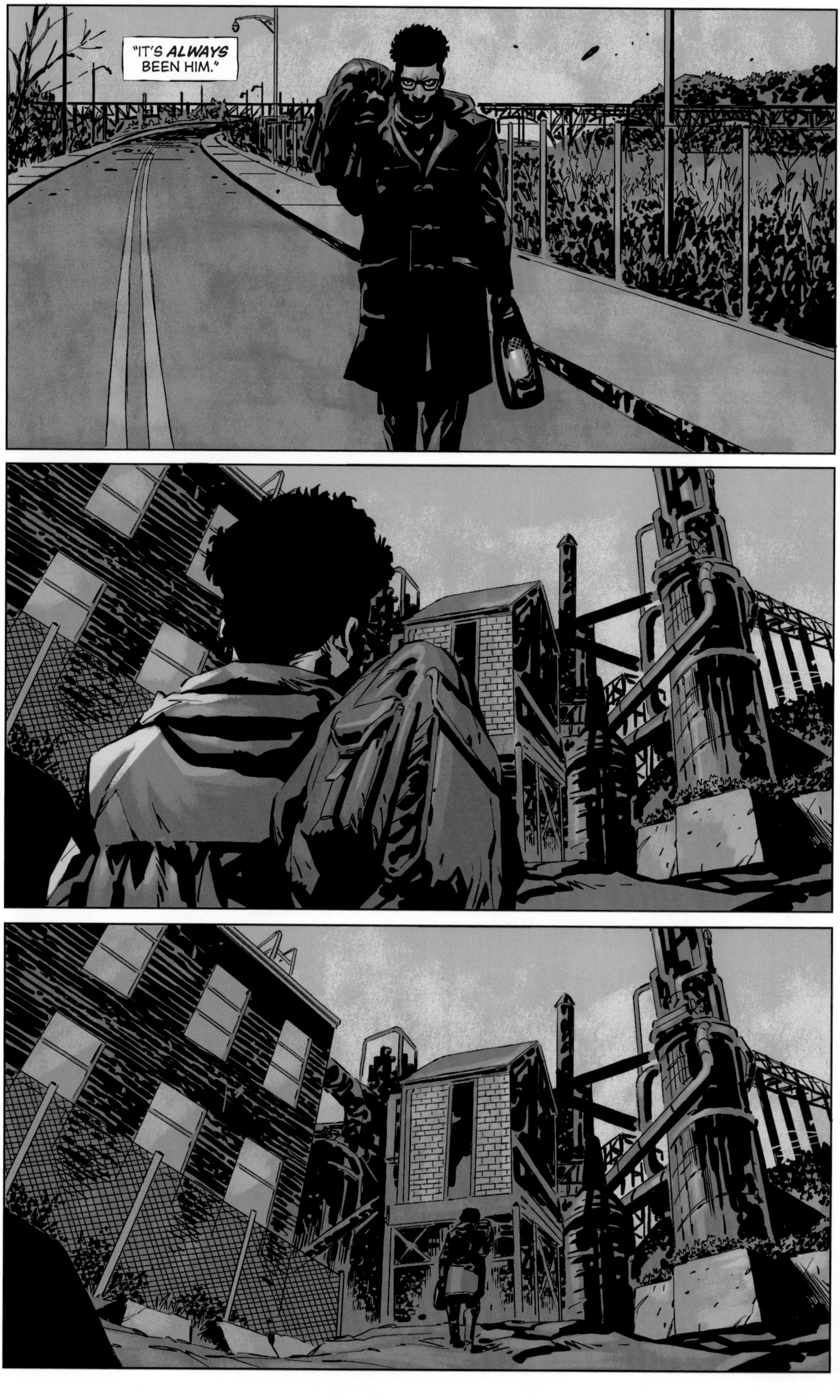
"IT'S ALWAYS BEEN HIM."

Pittsburgh Ledger

FIRST PUBLISHED 1789 Monday November 13, 2023 $3.00

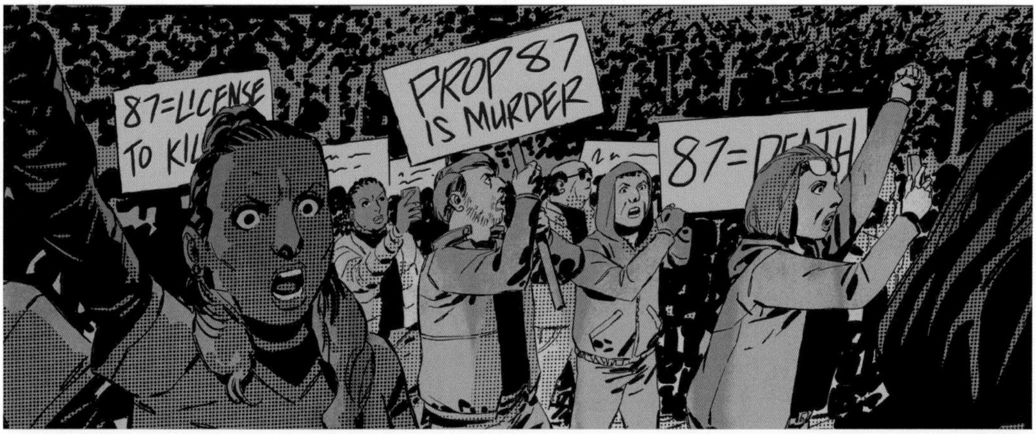
87=LICENSE
TO KIL
PROP 87
IS MURDER
87=DEATH

Protestors march outside City Hall in opposition to Proposition 87, approved by a majority of voters this weekend. Geraldo Borges/Ledger

Prop 87 wins

Pittsburgh approves controversial "stand your ground" law

Julia Paige
Pittsburgh Ledger

Pittsburgh, PA— In a narrow and contentious vote, Pennsylvania voters have approved Proposition 87, the "Presumption of Reasonable Preemptive Self-Defense Act," by a slim margin of 53% to 47%. The law, which allows residents to use deadly force without retreating when they perceive a threat, marks a significant shift in the state's legal landscape and has sparked a heated debate.

The passage of Prop 87 comes after months of intense debate, fueled in part by the public's reaction to high-profile violent incidents throughout the year, most notably the Accountability Killings and the subsequent copycat crimes that have left the city on edge. Many residents, feeling increasingly vulnerable, saw the new law as a necessary step to protect themselves.

State Senator Noah Kemp, who championed the proposition following the murder of his brother Donovan, expressed satisfaction with the outcome. "This law is a victory for all those who believe in the right to defend themselves in dangerous times," Kemp said. He linked his brother's tragic death to what he called a "broken system" that left law-abiding citizens defenseless.

However, critics of Prop 87 have voiced strong concerns about its potential for misuse. Pittsburgh Mayor Kelly Murphy cautioned, "We must be vigilant to ensure that this law does not become a license for unnecessary violence." Similar concerns were echoed by legal experts and civil rights organizations, who fear the law could lead to an increase in justifiable homicide claims and make the legal system more complex and difficult to navigate.

One of the most controversial figures associated with the movement leading to the passage of Prop 87 is Kenneth Chbosky. Chbosky, who shot and killed video game streamer Chris O'Neil after being threatened by O'neil, online, claimed self-defense under the preemptive self-defense concept that Prop 87 would later enshrine. His case became a rallying point for supporters of the law, turning him into a symbol of the movement. After being released and proclaiming his innocence, Chbosky was hired as a commentator but was fired shortly after by FOC News anchor Alanna Paige, who dismissed him on-air for his extremist views and attack on her daughter. Following this, Chbosky was allegedly seen at the scene of the recent attack on retired Assistant Chief, Ben Kern. An eyewitness at the scene claimed to have recognized Chbosky among those present during the violent clash, although his association with the white supremacist Weiss Macht Brotherhood remains unverified.

Pittsburgh Bureau of Police Chief Albert Mixon also expressed concern, emphasizing that the department would closely monitor the law's implementation. "Our priority is to maintain public safety and prevent any escalation in vigilantism," Mixon stated, underlining the fine line the police must walk in enforcing this new legislation.

The aftermath of Prop 87's passage has already seen an uptick in violence, with several incidents across the city where individuals claimed self-defense under the new law. This surge in violence has only deepened the divide within the community, with protests and rallies occurring across Pittsburgh. The city's journey under this new legal framework will be closely watched, with the potential for both legal challenges and further unrest on the horizon.

As Pittsburgh moves forward, the implications of Proposition 87 will undoubtedly shape the city's future, as both supporters and critics grapple with the law's impact on their daily lives. The Pittsburgh Ledger will continue to cover this developing story, providing updates and analysis on the consequences of this contentious new chapter in the city's history.

Pittsburgh Ledger

FIRST PUBLISHED 1789   Tuesday November 14, 2023   **$3.00**

Rioters clash with police in downtown Pittsburgh Monday night.   Geraldo Borges/Ledger

Night of chaos

FOC News shooting, citywide violence, and Riley Harper attack leave city reeling

Alejandro Rios
Pittsburgh Ledger

Pittsburgh, PA— In the wake of the controversial passage of Proposition 87, which effectively legalized preemptive self-defense, Pittsburgh descended into an unprecedented day and night of violence, culminating in what is now being described as the city's most chaotic day in recent history.

The catalyst for the violence was an incident at a downtown parking garage on the morning of November 13. A dispute between an employee and a security guard turned deadly when the guard, citing fear for his life under Prop 87, shot the unarmed employee attempting to enter the garage. The shooting sparked immediate protests at the scene, which quickly escalated into a riot. Demonstrators clashed with police, leading to widespread violence throughout the city.

As riots erupted across Pittsburgh, so did a string of unrelated self-defense killings. In one neighborhood, a long-standing dispute over loud music between two neighbors ended in tragedy when one shot the other dead, claiming self-defense. Elsewhere, a road rage incident turned fatal when a driver opened fire on another vehicle, killing the driver and seriously injuring a passenger.

One of the final, heartbreaking incidents of the afternoon involved 11-year-old Riley Harper, who was shot and killed in the girls' bathroom at Allegheny Charter Middle School. The shooting reportedly stemmed from a bullying incident. Riley Harper is the daughter of Detective Kate Harper, one of the lead investigators in the Richard Roe case, adding a deeply personal layer to the tragedy.

The violence continued to rage across the city well into the night, prompting the police to enforce a citywide curfew in a desperate attempt to restore order. Despite their efforts, sporadic clashes and instances of self-defense violence persisted, leaving the city in a state of shock and mourning.

The violence reached its tragic peak at FOC News studios when Kenneth Chbosky, the controversial figurehead who had become a symbol of the preemptive self-defense law, stormed the building in a vengeful rage. Witnesses reported that Chbosky was heard shouting for host Alanna Paige as he went on a rampage, killing three employees and injuring twelve others before Pittsburgh S.W.A.T. intervened. The S.W.A.T. team shot Chbosky before he could reach Paige, bringing an end to his violent spree but leaving a trail of devastation in its wake.

Amidst the turmoil, the vigilante NO/ONE was conspicuously absent, leading to speculation about his whereabouts and role in the night's events.

As Pittsburgh awakes to the aftermath of this devastating day and night, the city grapples with the implications of Prop 87 and the violence it has unleashed. Mayor Kelly Murphy urged calm and vowed that she would make certain, "law enforcement will do everything possible to restore peace and hold those responsible accountable for the darkness that they have swept over the city." But despite promises to stem the tide of violence, the question remains: How did Pittsburgh reach this point, and can it ever truly heal the wounds that got it here?

The Pittsburgh Ledger will continue to provide updates as the city navigates this dark chapter, striving for answers and a return to some semblance of safety and order.

The Drop

PRESENTS

WHO IS NO/ONE
WITH/JULIA PAIGE

17 NOVEMBER

09/Regrets

WHO IS NO/ONE

3:38   -10:39

>_ **WHO IS NO/ONE Episode 9 React**
NOVEMBER 18 2023

written by Danielle Gaines
published on Edge News

"So, what now, Pittsburgh? It's hard to say.
The body count keeps rising."

>_ CHAPTER TEN
DECEMBER 2023

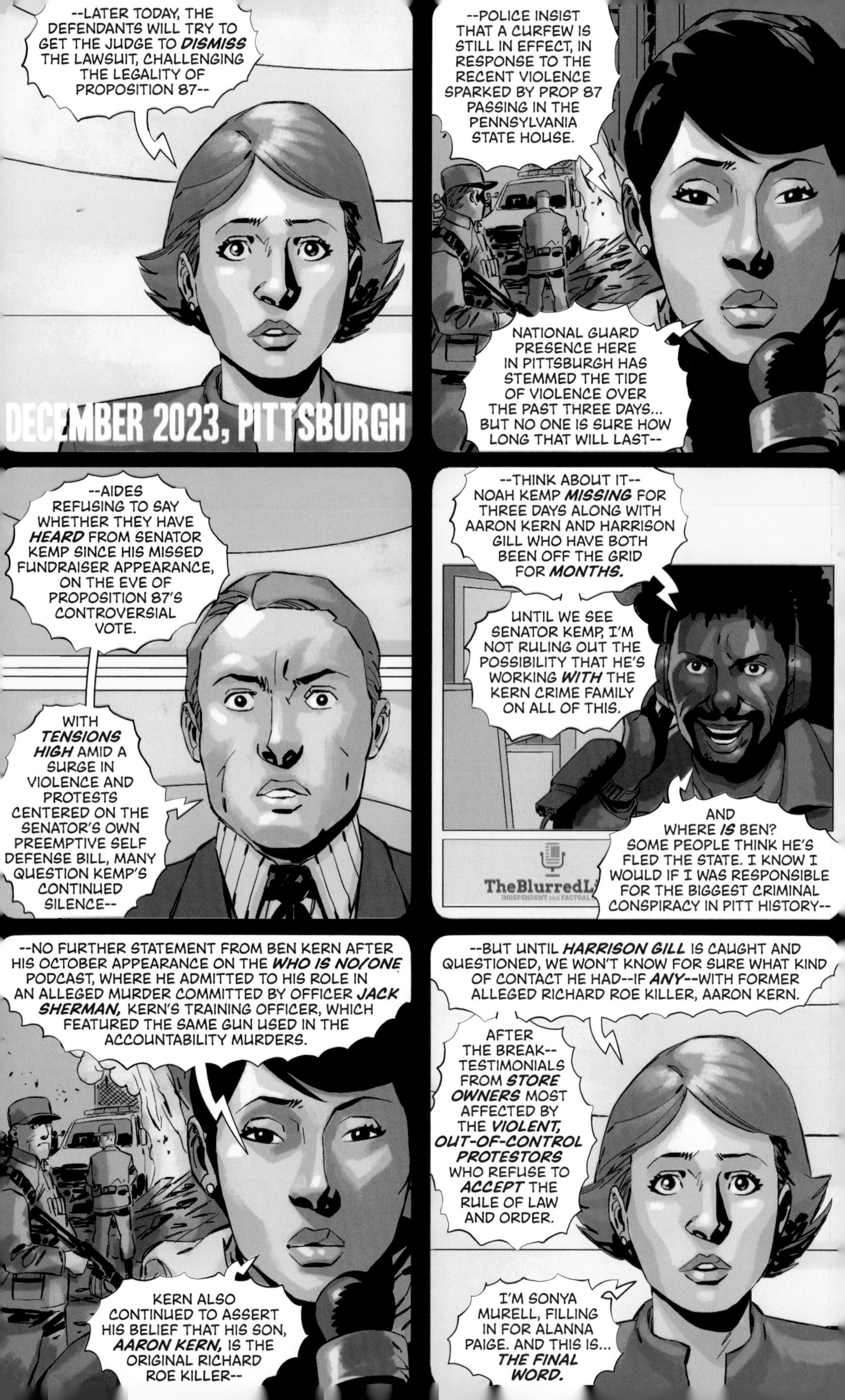
--LATER TODAY, THE DEFENDANTS WILL TRY TO GET THE JUDGE TO DISMISS THE LAWSUIT, CHALLENGING THE LEGALITY OF PROPOSITION 87--
DECEMBER 2023, PITTSBURGH
--POLICE INSIST THAT A CURFEW IS STILL IN EFFECT, IN RESPONSE TO THE RECENT VIOLENCE SPARKED BY PROP 87 PASSING IN THE PENNSYLVANIA STATE HOUSE.
NATIONAL GUARD PRESENCE HERE IN PITTSBURGH HAS STEMMED THE TIDE OF VIOLENCE OVER THE PAST THREE DAYS... BUT NO ONE IS SURE HOW LONG THAT WILL LAST--
--AIDES REFUSING TO SAY WHETHER THEY HAVE HEARD FROM SENATOR KEMP SINCE HIS MISSED FUNDRAISER APPEARANCE, ON THE EVE OF PROPOSITION 87'S CONTROVERSIAL VOTE.
WITH TENSIONS HIGH AMID A SURGE IN VIOLENCE AND PROTESTS CENTERED ON THE SENATOR'S OWN PREEMPTIVE SELF DEFENSE BILL, MANY QUESTION KEMP'S CONTINUED SILENCE--
--THINK ABOUT IT-- NOAH KEMP MISSING FOR THREE DAYS ALONG WITH AARON KERN AND HARRISON GILL WHO HAVE BOTH BEEN OFF THE GRID FOR MONTHS.
UNTIL WE SEE SENATOR KEMP, I'M NOT RULING OUT THE POSSIBILITY THAT HE'S WORKING WITH THE KERN CRIME FAMILY ON ALL OF THIS.
TheBlurredLi
INDEPENDENT and FACTUAL
AND WHERE IS BEN? SOME PEOPLE THINK HE'S FLED THE STATE. I KNOW I WOULD IF I WAS RESPONSIBLE FOR THE BIGGEST CRIMINAL CONSPIRACY IN PITT HISTORY--
--NO FURTHER STATEMENT FROM BEN KERN AFTER HIS OCTOBER APPEARANCE ON THE WHO IS NO/ONE PODCAST, WHERE HE ADMITTED TO HIS ROLE IN AN ALLEGED MURDER COMMITTED BY OFFICER JACK SHERMAN, KERN'S TRAINING OFFICER, WHICH FEATURED THE SAME GUN USED IN THE ACCOUNTABILITY MURDERS.
KERN ALSO CONTINUED TO ASSERT HIS BELIEF THAT HIS SON, AARON KERN, IS THE ORIGINAL RICHARD ROE KILLER--
--BUT UNTIL HARRISON GILL IS CAUGHT AND QUESTIONED, WE WON'T KNOW FOR SURE WHAT KIND OF CONTACT HE HAD--IF ANY--WITH FORMER ALLEGED RICHARD ROE KILLER, AARON KERN.
AFTER THE BREAK-- TESTIMONIALS FROM STORE OWNERS MOST AFFECTED BY THE VIOLENT, OUT-OF-CONTROL PROTESTORS WHO REFUSE TO ACCEPT THE RULE OF LAW AND ORDER.
I'M SONYA MURELL, FILLING IN FOR ALANNA PAIGE. AND THIS IS... THE FINAL WORD.

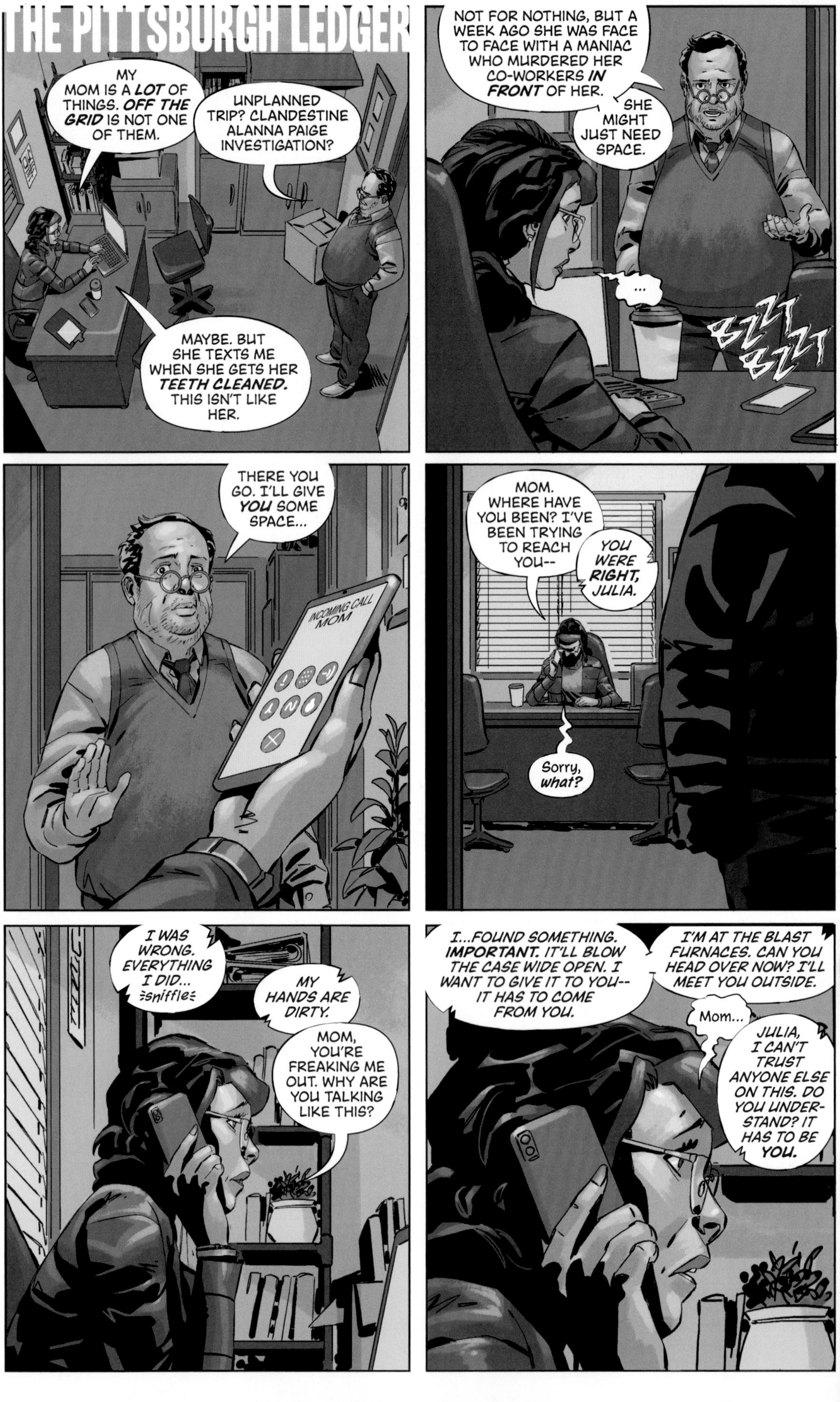
THE PITTSBURGH LEDGER
MY MOM IS A *LOT* OF THINGS. *OFF THE GRID* IS NOT ONE OF THEM.
UNPLANNED TRIP? CLANDESTINE ALANNA PAIGE INVESTIGATION?
MAYBE. BUT SHE TEXTS ME WHEN SHE GETS HER *TEETH CLEANED.* THIS ISN'T LIKE HER.
NOT FOR NOTHING, BUT A WEEK AGO SHE WAS FACE TO FACE WITH A MANIAC WHO MURDERED HER CO-WORKERS *IN FRONT* OF HER.
SHE MIGHT JUST NEED SPACE.
...
BZZZT BZZZT
THERE YOU GO. I'LL GIVE *YOU* SOME SPACE...
INCOMING CALL
MOM
MOM. WHERE HAVE YOU BEEN? I'VE BEEN TRYING TO REACH YOU--
YOU WERE RIGHT, JULIA.
Sorry, *what?*
I WAS WRONG. EVERYTHING I DID...
sniffle
MY HANDS ARE DIRTY.
MOM, YOU'RE FREAKING ME OUT. WHY ARE YOU TALKING LIKE THIS?
I...FOUND SOMETHING. IMPORTANT. IT'LL BLOW THE CASE WIDE OPEN. I WANT TO GIVE IT TO YOU-- IT HAS TO COME FROM YOU.
I'M AT THE BLAST FURNACES. CAN YOU HEAD OVER NOW? I'LL MEET YOU OUTSIDE.
Mom...
JULIA, I CAN'T TRUST ANYONE ELSE ON THIS. DO YOU UNDER-STAND? IT HAS TO BE YOU.

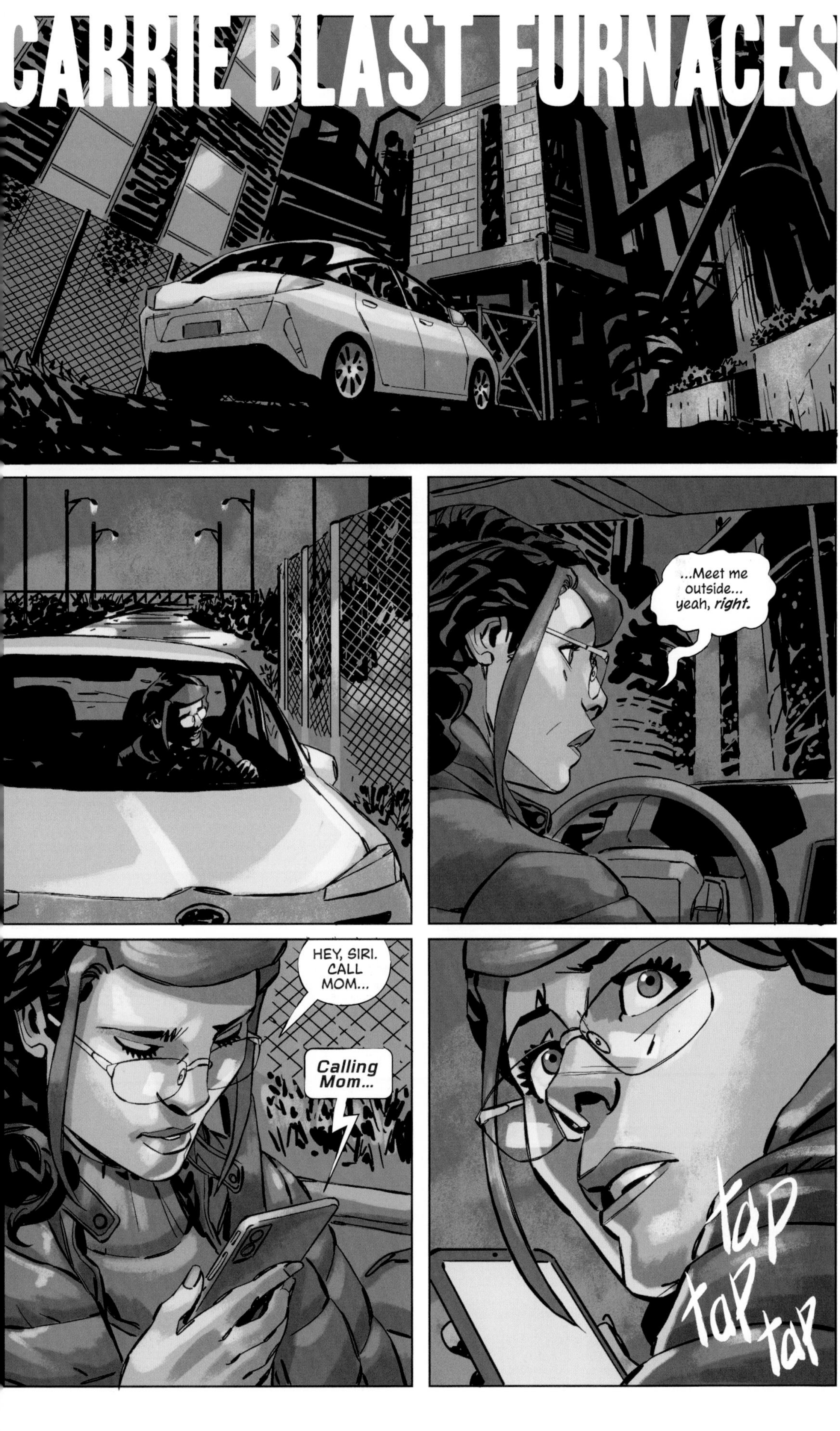
CARRIE BLAST FURNACES
...Meet me outside... yeah, *right.*
HEY, SIRI. CALL MOM...
Calling Mom...
tap tap tap

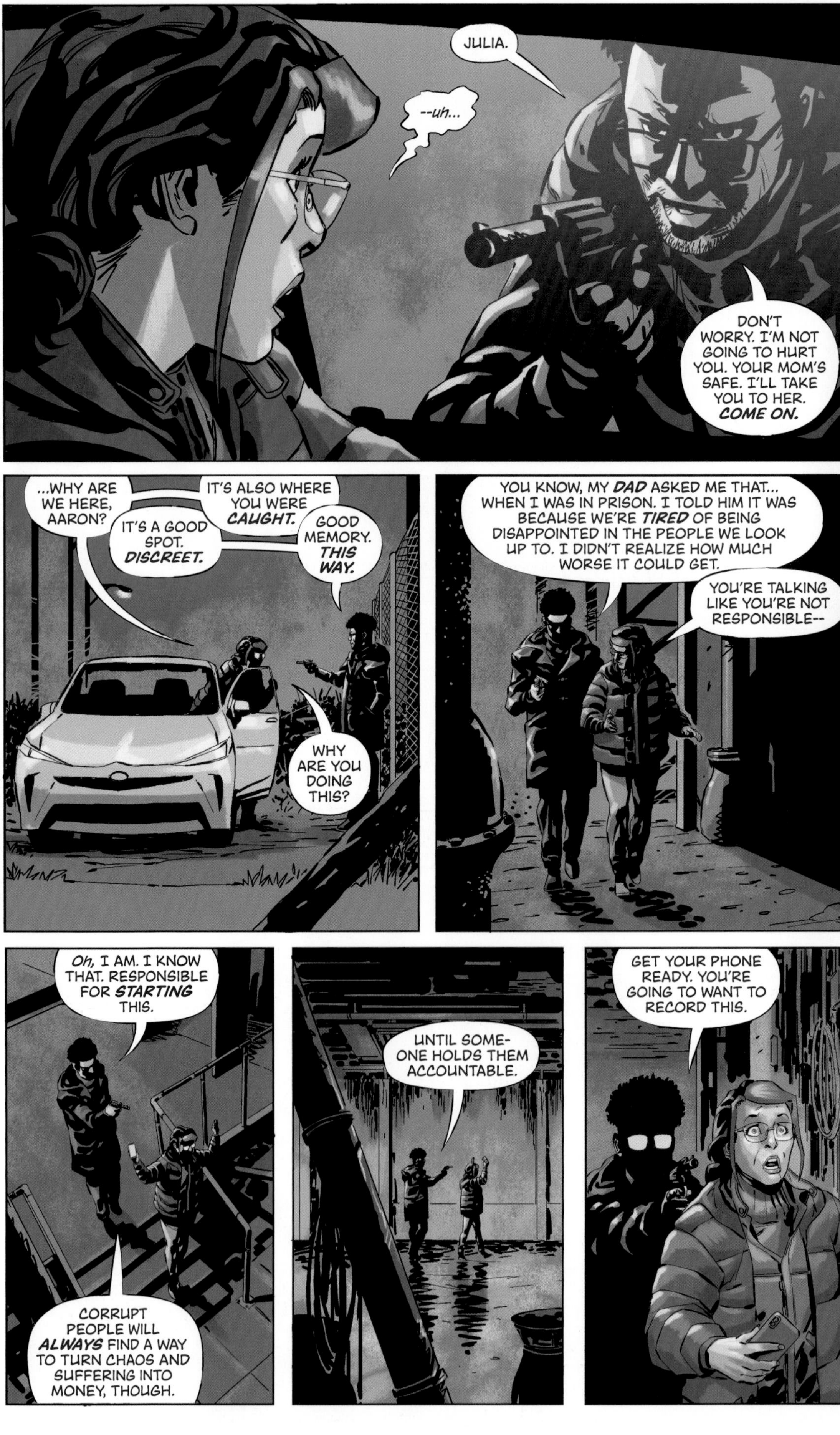
JULIA.
--uh...
DON'T WORRY. I'M NOT GOING TO HURT YOU. YOUR MOM'S SAFE. I'LL TAKE YOU TO HER. COME ON.
...WHY ARE WE HERE, AARON?
IT'S A GOOD SPOT. DISCREET.
IT'S ALSO WHERE YOU WERE CAUGHT.
GOOD MEMORY. THIS WAY.
WHY ARE YOU DOING THIS?
YOU KNOW, MY DAD ASKED ME THAT... WHEN I WAS IN PRISON. I TOLD HIM IT WAS BECAUSE WE'RE TIRED OF BEING DISAPPOINTED IN THE PEOPLE WE LOOK UP TO. I DIDN'T REALIZE HOW MUCH WORSE IT COULD GET.
YOU'RE TALKING LIKE YOU'RE NOT RESPONSIBLE--
Oh, I AM. I KNOW THAT. RESPONSIBLE FOR STARTING THIS.
CORRUPT PEOPLE WILL ALWAYS FIND A WAY TO TURN CHAOS AND SUFFERING INTO MONEY, THOUGH.
UNTIL SOME-ONE HOLDS THEM ACCOUNTABLE.
GET YOUR PHONE READY. YOU'RE GOING TO WANT TO RECORD THIS.

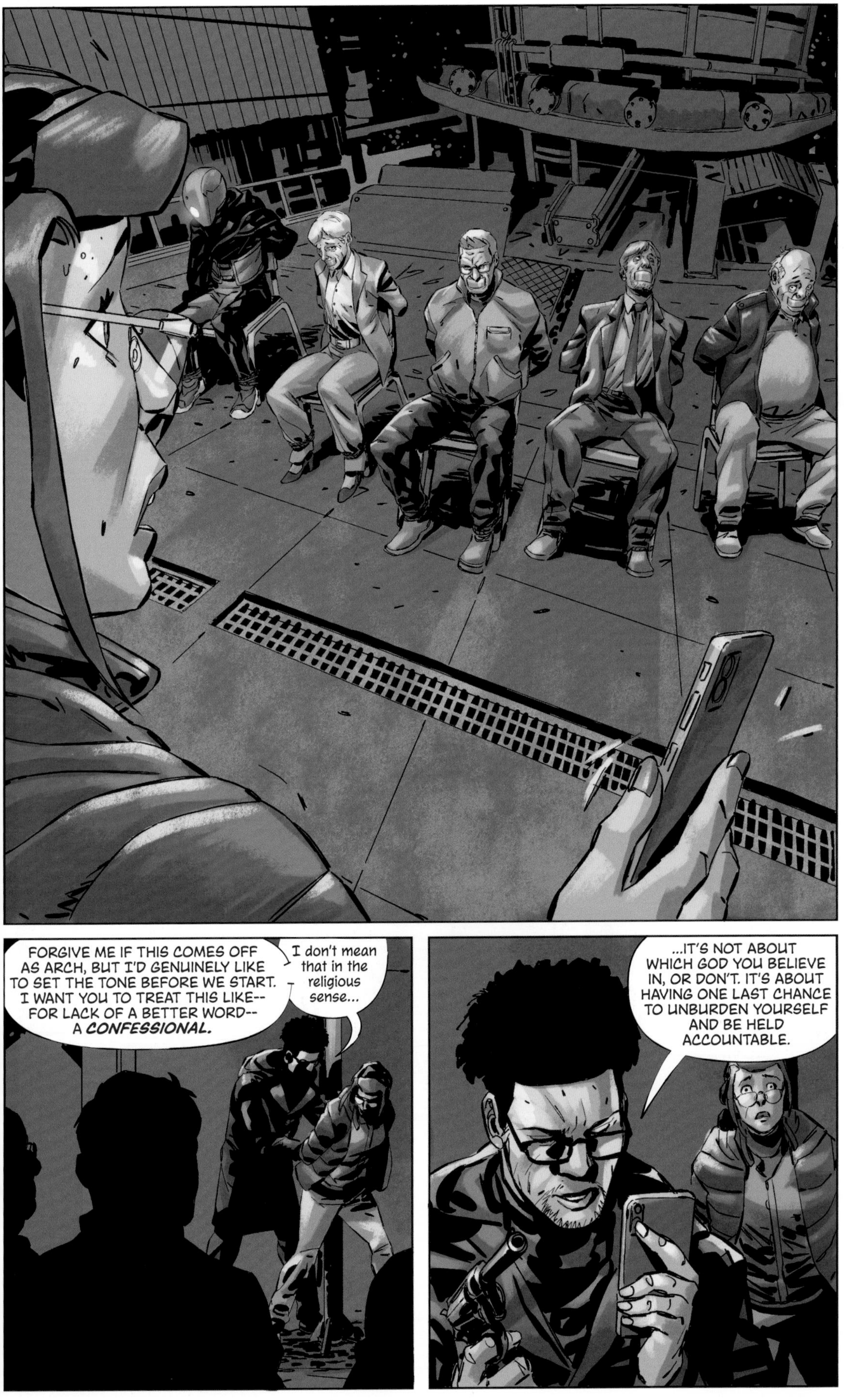
FORGIVE ME IF THIS COMES OFF AS ARCH, BUT I'D GENUINELY LIKE TO SET THE TONE BEFORE WE START. I WANT YOU TO TREAT THIS LIKE-- FOR LACK OF A BETTER WORD-- A *CONFESSIONAL.*
I don't mean that in the religious sense...
...IT'S NOT ABOUT WHICH GOD YOU BELIEVE IN, OR DON'T. IT'S ABOUT HAVING ONE LAST CHANCE TO UNBURDEN YOURSELF AND BE HELD ACCOUNTABLE.

SO, I NEED TOTAL HONESTY HERE... YOU CAN THINK OF IT AS A SAFE SPACE, EXCEPT THAT'S ONLY TRUE UP TO A POINT.

BECAUSE-- FULL DISCLOSURE-- YOU'RE *ALL* DYING HERE, TONIGHT.

ALL EXCEPT *YOU*, JULIA.

AARON... YOU CANNOT DO THIS...

LOOK, I'M SORRY YOUR MOTHER IS ONE OF THEM. BUT, MY DAD'S HERE, TOO.

THIS IS **INSANE**--

IF YOU CAN'T BE QUIET, I CAN EASILY DUCT-TAPE YOUR MOUTH...

...IS THAT WHAT YOU *WANT*?

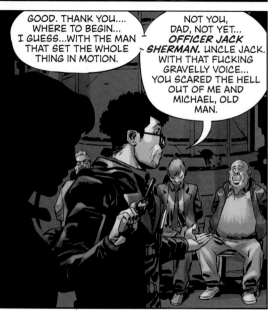

GOOD. THANK YOU.... WHERE TO BEGIN... I GUESS...WITH THE MAN THAT SET THE WHOLE THING IN MOTION.

NOT YOU, DAD, NOT YET... *OFFICER JACK SHERMAN.* UNCLE JACK. WITH THAT FUCKING GRAVELLY VOICE... YOU SCARED THE HELL OUT OF ME AND MICHAEL, OLD MAN.

UNCLE JACK. I DON'T WANT TO DRAW THIS OUT OR TURN IT INTO A DEBATE, OKAY? WHEN I TAKE OFF THE TAPE, I NEED YOU TO BE HONEST AND ANSWER MY QUESTIONS.

≈MMPPH!≈

THAT'S ALL. IF YOU DO IT MY WAY... I *PROMISE* IT WILL BE *PAINLESS.*

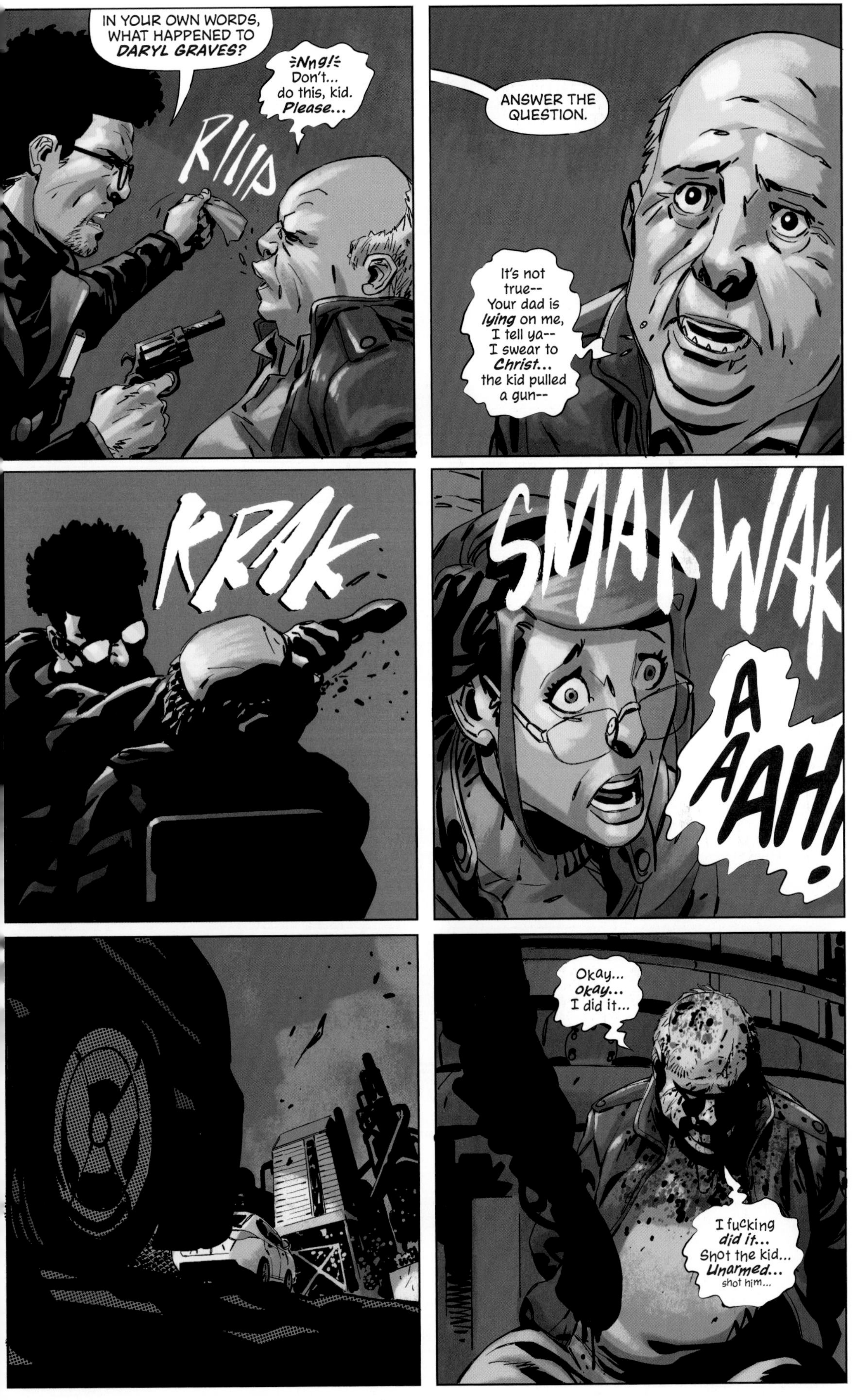
IN YOUR OWN WORDS, WHAT HAPPENED TO DARYL GRAVES?
Nng! Don't... do this, kid. Please...
RIIIP
ANSWER THE QUESTION.
It's not true-- Your dad is lying on me, I tell ya-- I swear to Christ... the kid pulled a gun--
KRAK
SMAK WAK
AAAH!
Okay... okay... I did it...
I fucking did it... Shot the kid... Unarmed... shot him...

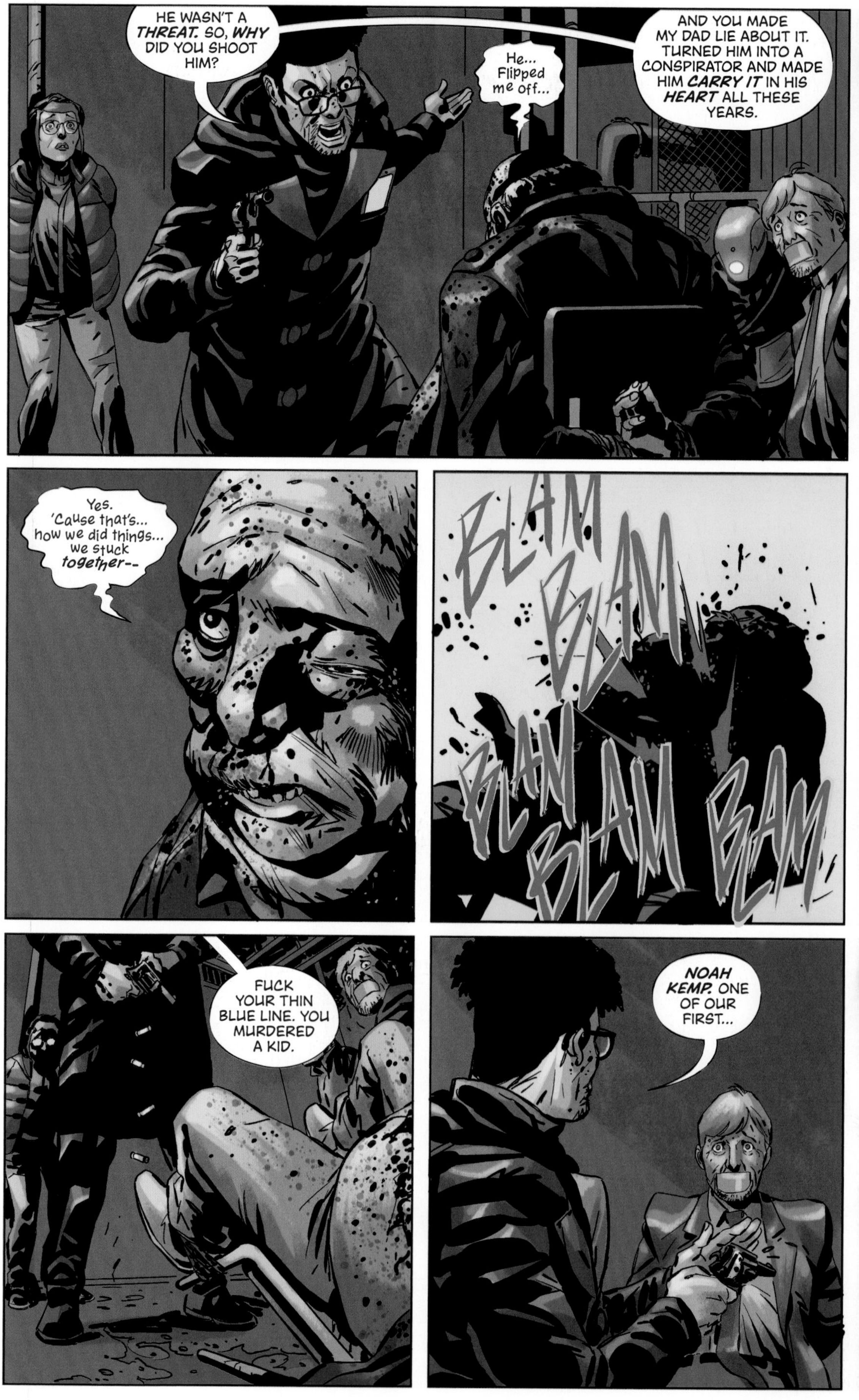
HE WASN'T A THREAT. SO, WHY DID YOU SHOOT HIM?
AND YOU MADE MY DAD LIE ABOUT IT. TURNED HIM INTO A CONSPIRATOR AND MADE HIM CARRY IT IN HIS HEART ALL THESE YEARS.
He... Flipped me off...
Yes. 'Cause that's... how we did things... we stuck together--
BLAM BLAM BLAM BLAM BLAM BLAM BAM BLAM
FUCK YOUR THIN BLUE LINE. YOU MURDERED A KID.
NOAH KEMP. ONE OF OUR FIRST...

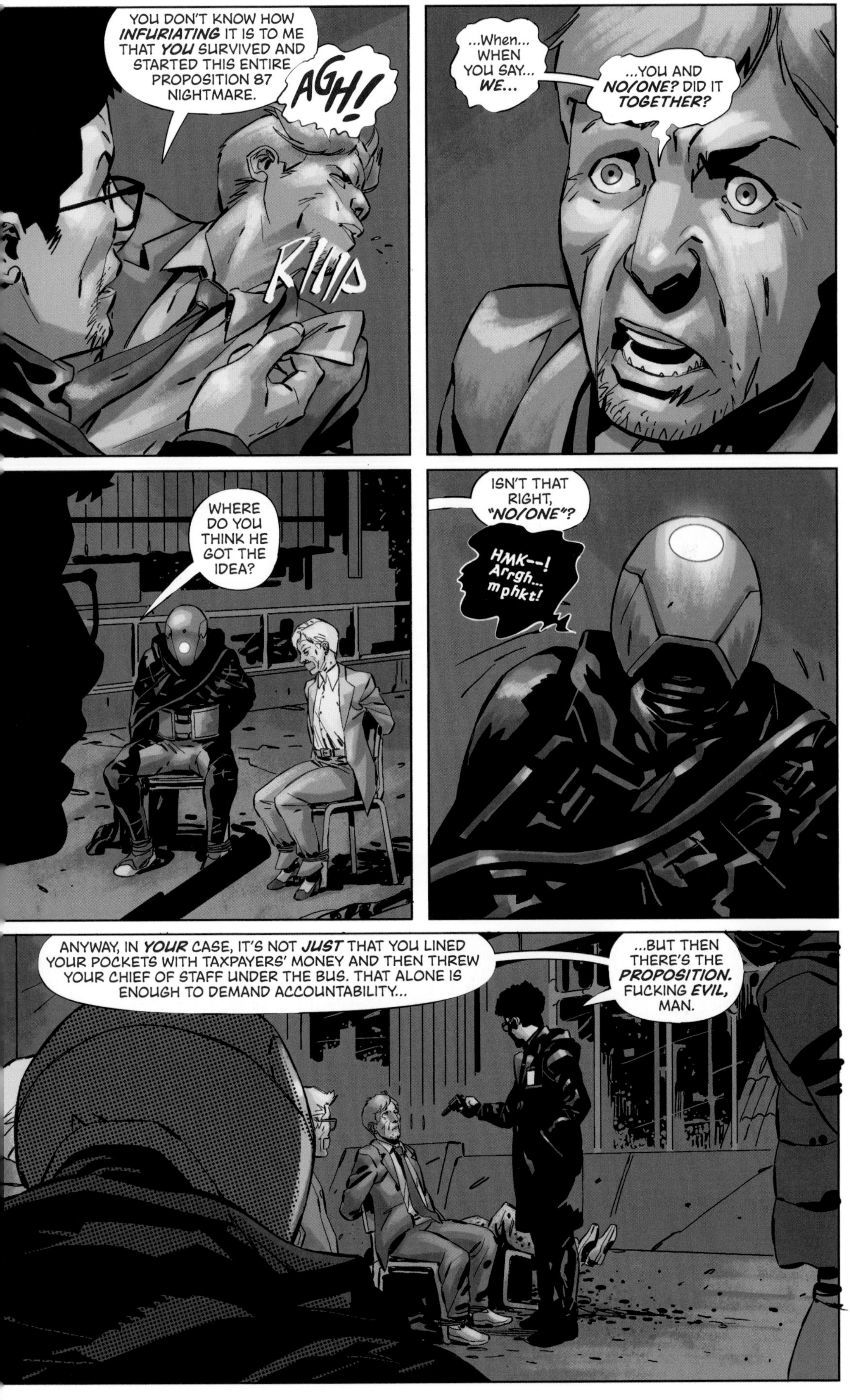
YOU DON'T KNOW HOW INFURIATING IT IS TO ME THAT YOU SURVIVED AND STARTED THIS ENTIRE PROPOSITION 87 NIGHTMARE.
AGH!
RIIIP
...When... WHEN YOU SAY... WE...
...YOU AND NO/ONE? DID IT TOGETHER?
WHERE DO YOU THINK HE GOT THE IDEA?
ISN'T THAT RIGHT, "NO/ONE"?
HMK--! Arrgh... mphkt!
ANYWAY, IN YOUR CASE, IT'S NOT JUST THAT YOU LINED YOUR POCKETS WITH TAXPAYERS' MONEY AND THEN THREW YOUR CHIEF OF STAFF UNDER THE BUS. THAT ALONE IS ENOUGH TO DEMAND ACCOUNTABILITY...
...BUT THEN THERE'S THE PROPOSITION. FUCKING EVIL, MAN.

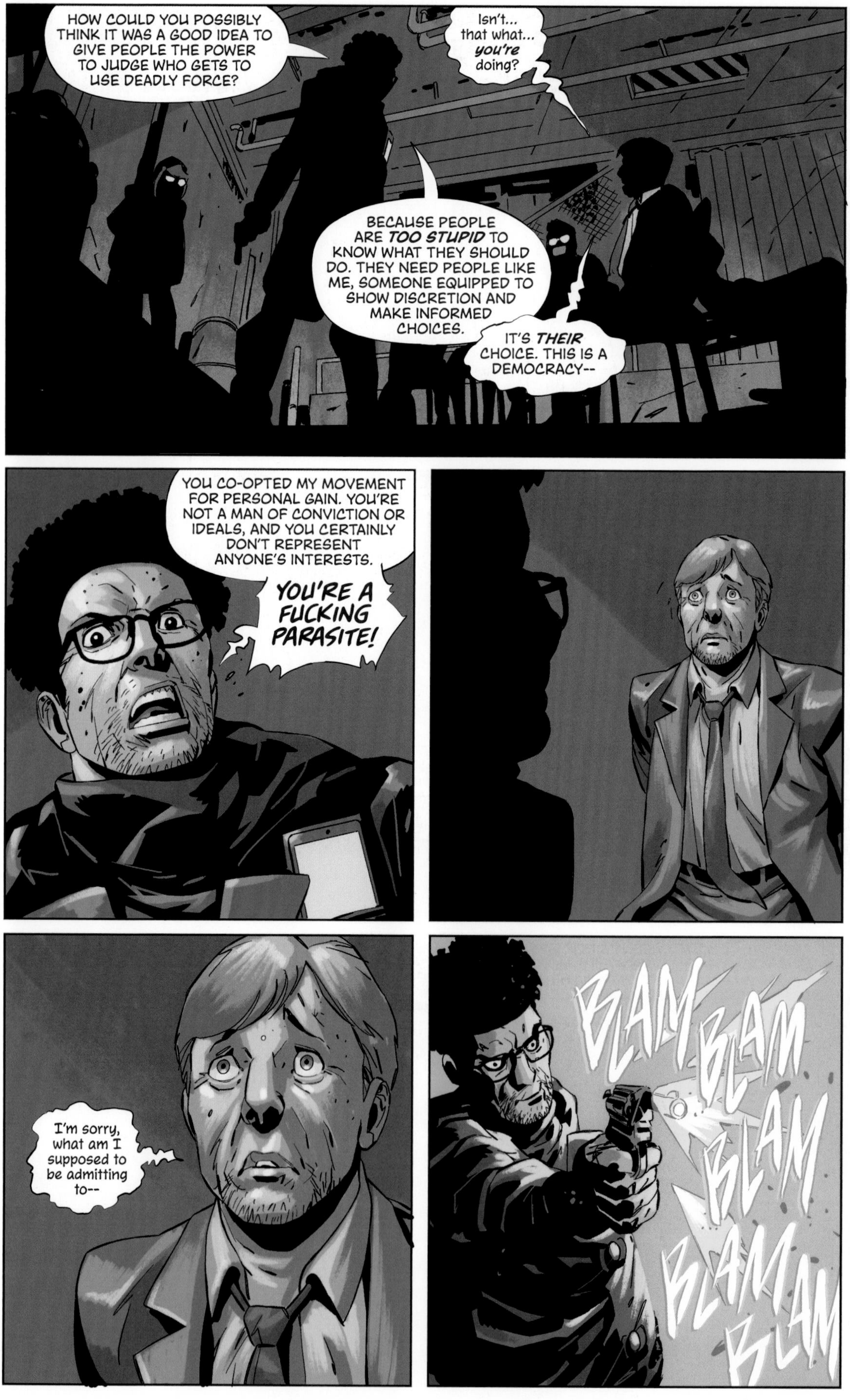
HOW COULD YOU POSSIBLY THINK IT WAS A GOOD IDEA TO GIVE PEOPLE THE POWER TO JUDGE WHO GETS TO USE DEADLY FORCE?
Isn't... that what... *you're* doing?
BECAUSE PEOPLE ARE ***TOO STUPID*** TO KNOW WHAT THEY SHOULD DO. THEY NEED PEOPLE LIKE ME, SOMEONE EQUIPPED TO SHOW DISCRETION AND MAKE INFORMED CHOICES.
IT'S ***THEIR*** CHOICE. THIS IS A DEMOCRACY--
YOU CO-OPTED MY MOVEMENT FOR PERSONAL GAIN. YOU'RE NOT A MAN OF CONVICTION OR IDEALS, AND YOU CERTAINLY DON'T REPRESENT ANYONE'S INTERESTS.
YOU'RE A FUCKING PARASITE!
I'm sorry, what am I supposed to be admitting to--
BLAM BLAM BLAM BLAM BLAM BLAM

--AGHK! GODDAMMIT... AARON!

COME ON, DON'T ACT LIKE YOU WEREN'T CHEERING JUST A TINY BIT FOR ME TO GET RID OF NOAH. THE MAN WAS A *DISGRACE.*

RIIP

THE ONLY DISGRACEFUL THING HERE IS *YOU.* THE GIANT... *BALLS* IT TAKES TO THINK YOU KNOW BETTER THAN EVERYONE ELSE WHO SHOULD BE DEALT WITH AND HOW.

What a crock of *shit...*

YOU'RE NOT *SPECIAL,* AARON. YOU'RE NOT A *GENIUS.* YOU'RE STILL THAT *TEARY-EYED LITTLE BOY* WHO COULDN'T HANDLE HIS LITTLE BROTHER CHEATING AT A BOARD GAME.

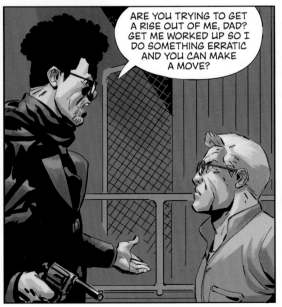

ARE YOU TRYING TO GET A RISE OUT OF ME, DAD? GET ME WORKED UP SO I DO SOMETHING ERRATIC AND YOU CAN MAKE A MOVE?

WHAT *MOVE?* YOU WANTED HONESTY, THERE'S YOUR FUCKING *HONESTY.* ALL YOU HAVE DONE IS HURT A LOT OF PEOPLE WITH THIS NONSENSE.

YOUR MOVEMENT FAILED. YOU *FAILED.*

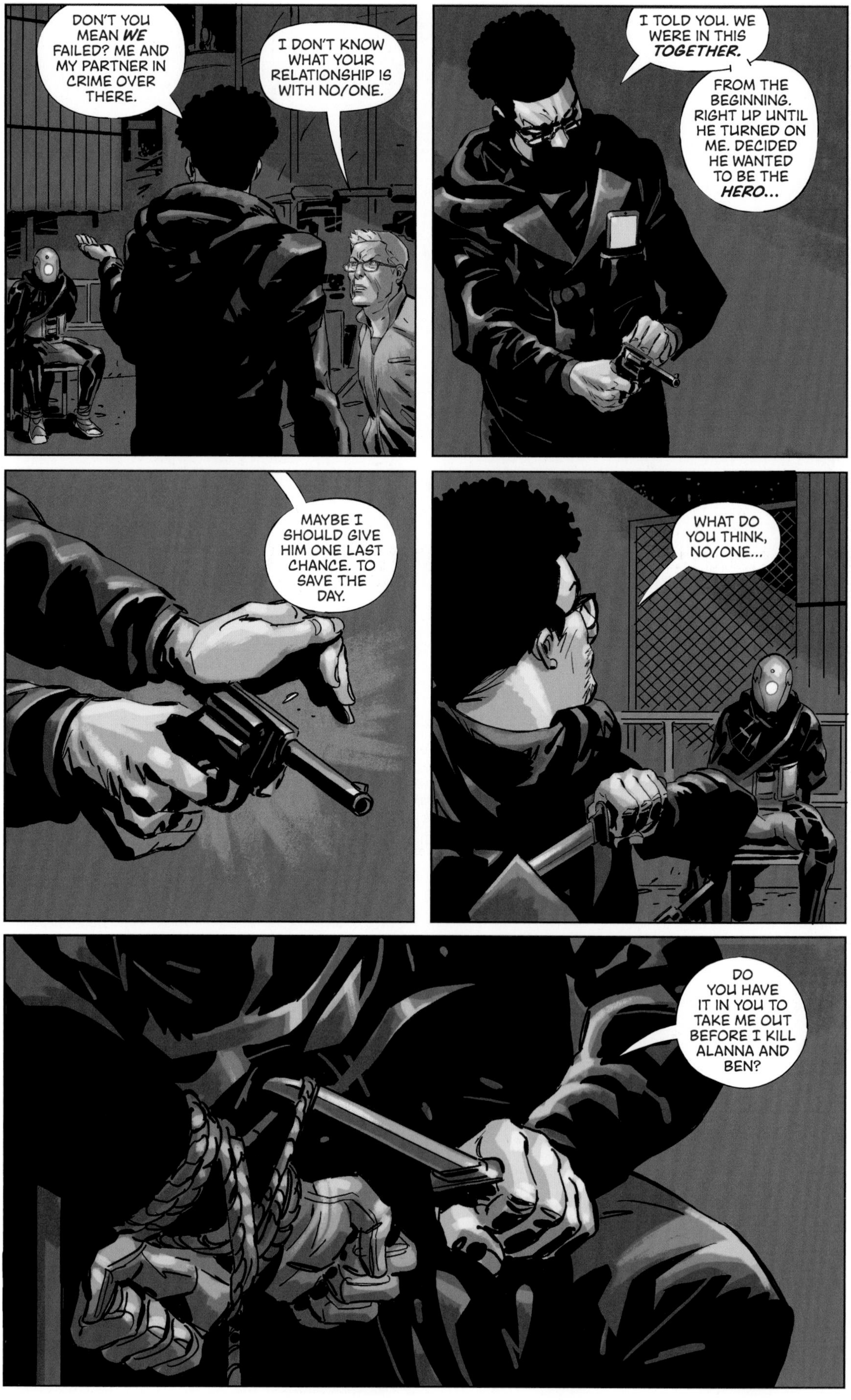
DON'T YOU MEAN ***WE*** FAILED? ME AND MY PARTNER IN CRIME OVER THERE.
I DON'T KNOW WHAT YOUR RELATIONSHIP IS WITH NO/ONE.
I TOLD YOU. WE WERE IN THIS ***TOGETHER.***
FROM THE BEGINNING. RIGHT UP UNTIL HE TURNED ON ME. DECIDED HE WANTED TO BE THE ***HERO...***
MAYBE I SHOULD GIVE HIM ONE LAST CHANCE. TO SAVE THE DAY.
WHAT DO YOU THINK, NO/ONE...
DO YOU HAVE IT IN YOU TO TAKE ME OUT BEFORE I KILL ALANNA AND BEN?

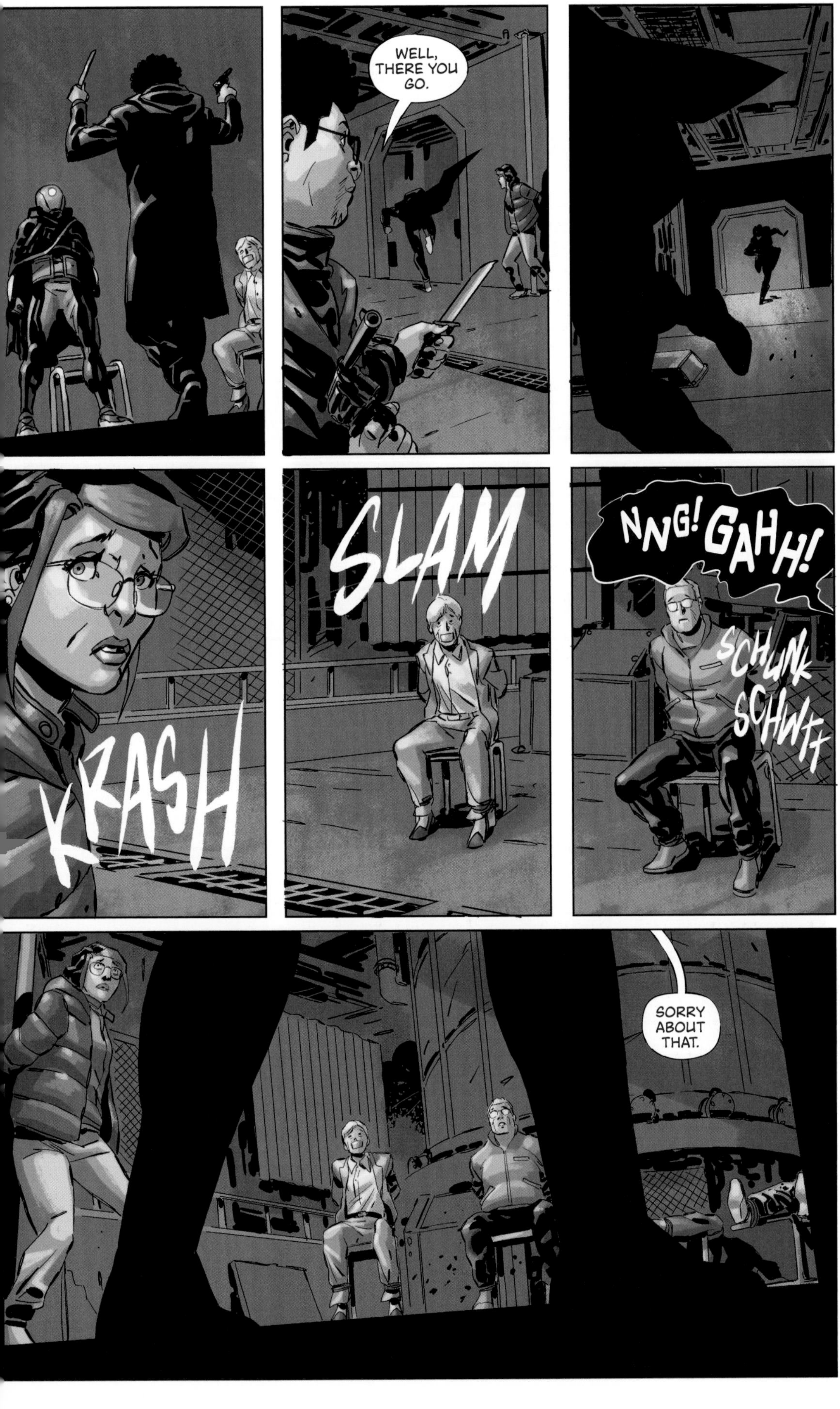
WELL, THERE YOU GO.
KRASH
SLAM
NNG! GAHH!
SCHUNK
SCHWTT
SORRY ABOUT THAT.

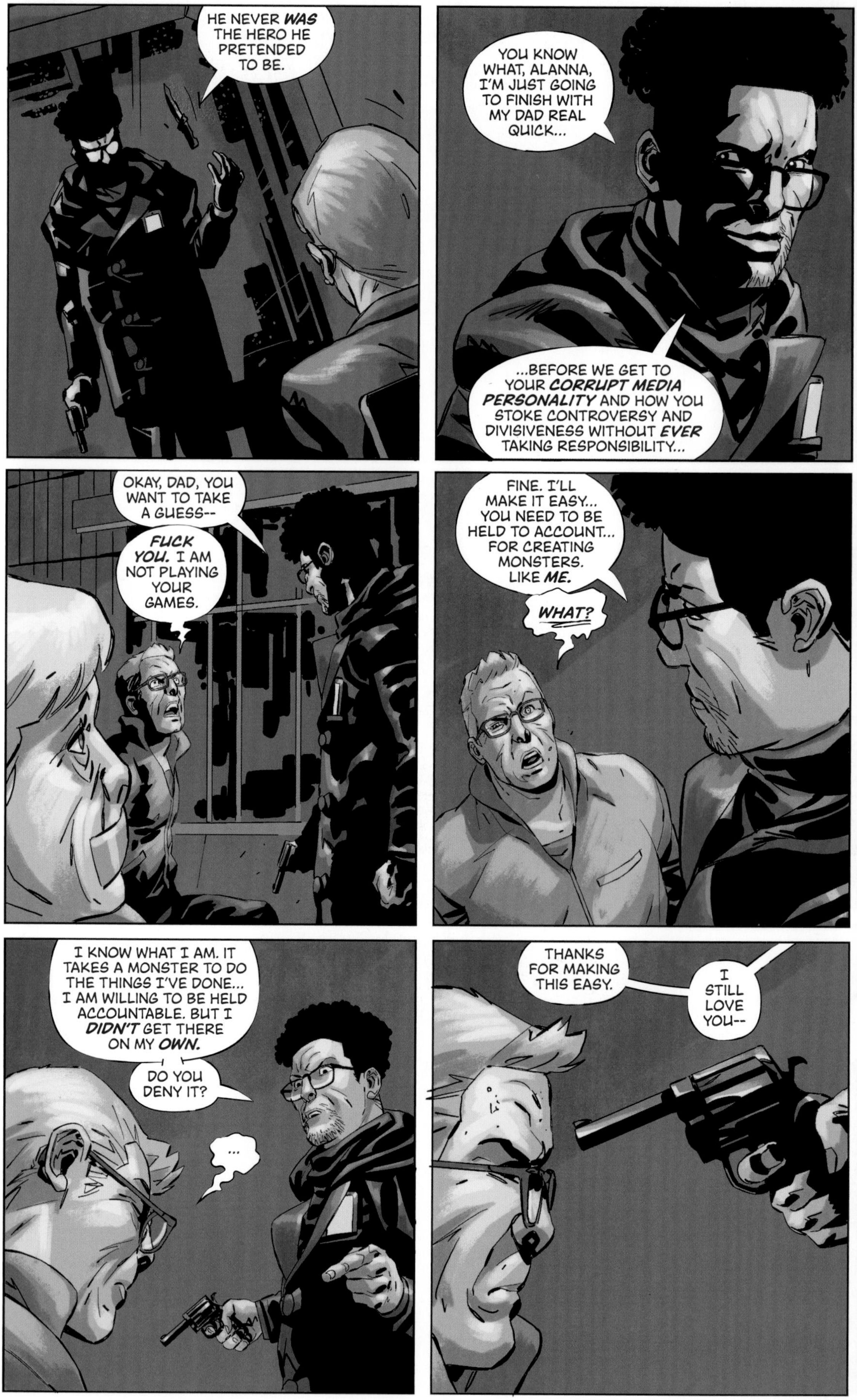
HE NEVER WAS THE HERO HE PRETENDED TO BE.
YOU KNOW WHAT, ALANNA, I'M JUST GOING TO FINISH WITH MY DAD REAL QUICK...
...BEFORE WE GET TO YOUR CORRUPT MEDIA PERSONALITY AND HOW YOU STOKE CONTROVERSY AND DIVISIVENESS WITHOUT EVER TAKING RESPONSIBILITY...
OKAY, DAD, YOU WANT TO TAKE A GUESS--
FUCK YOU. I AM NOT PLAYING YOUR GAMES.
FINE. I'LL MAKE IT EASY... YOU NEED TO BE HELD TO ACCOUNT... FOR CREATING MONSTERS. LIKE ME.
WHAT?
I KNOW WHAT I AM. IT TAKES A MONSTER TO DO THE THINGS I'VE DONE... I AM WILLING TO BE HELD ACCOUNTABLE. BUT I DIDN'T GET THERE ON MY OWN.
DO YOU DENY IT?
...
THANKS FOR MAKING THIS EASY.
I STILL LOVE YOU--

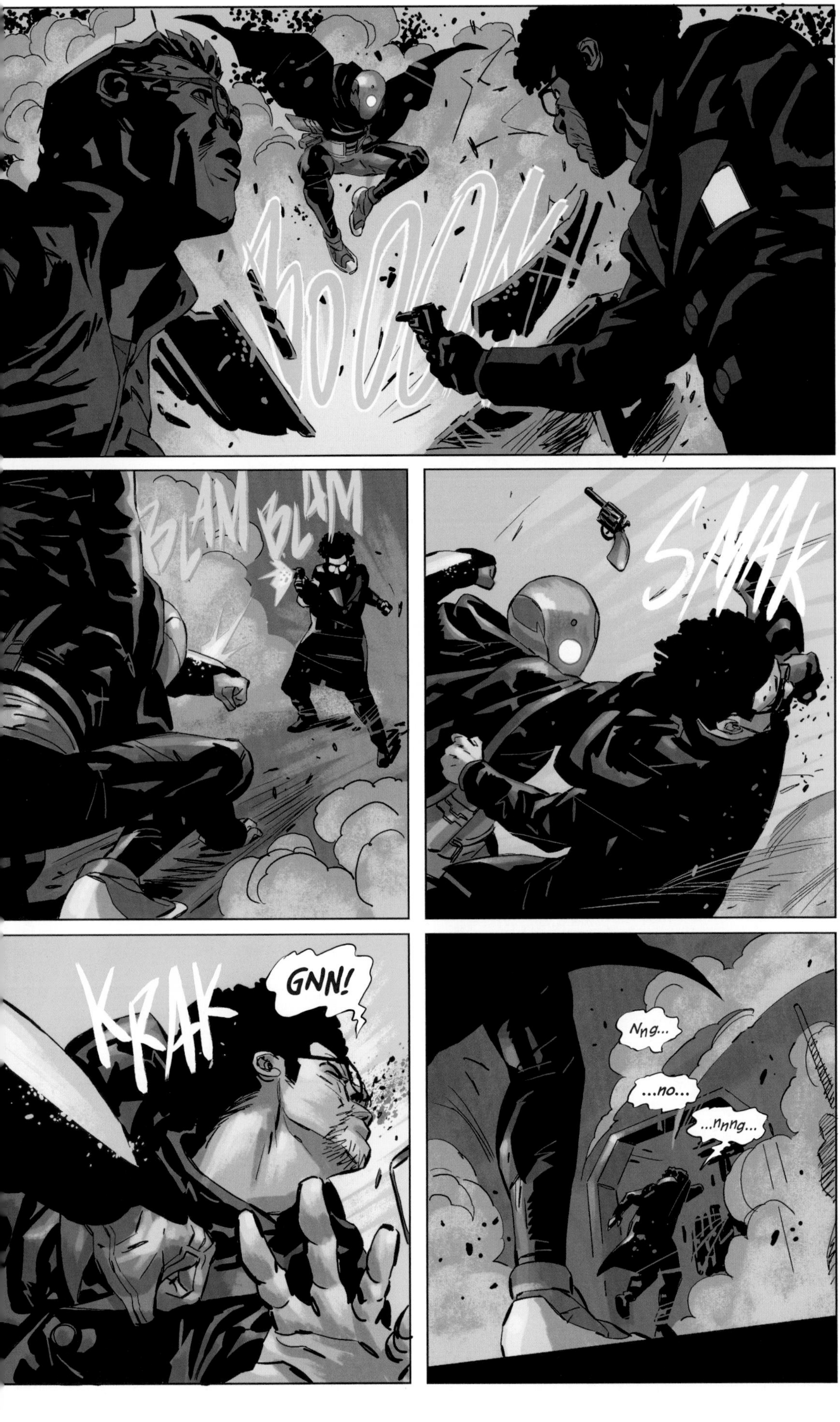
BOOOOM
BLAM BLAM
SMAK
KRAK
GNN!
Nng...
...no...
...nnng...

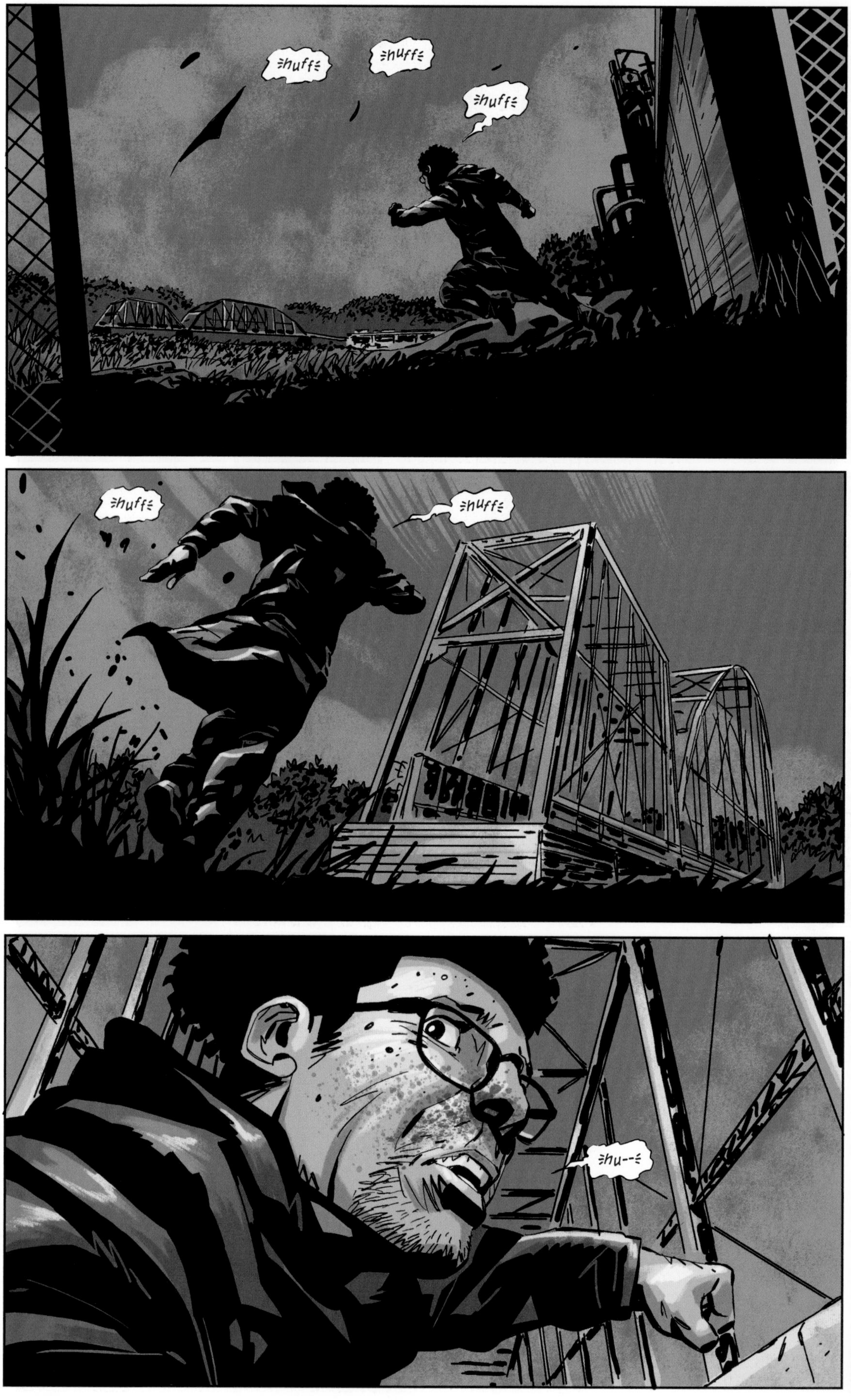
huff
huff
huff
huff
huff
hu--

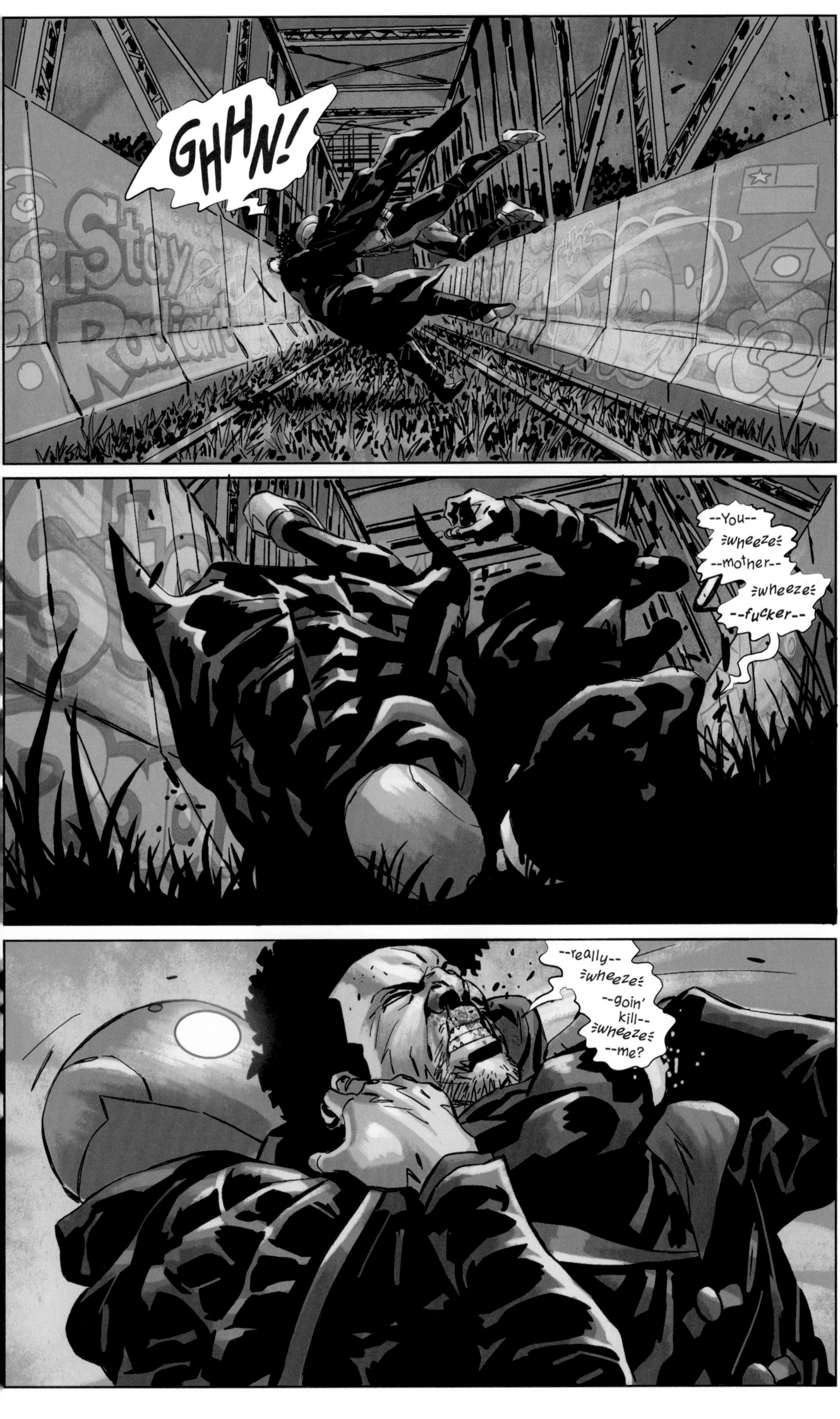
GHHN!
Stay
--You--
≡wheeze≡
--mother--
≡wheeze≡
--fucker--
--really--
≡wheeze≡
--goin' kill--
≡wheeze≡
--me?

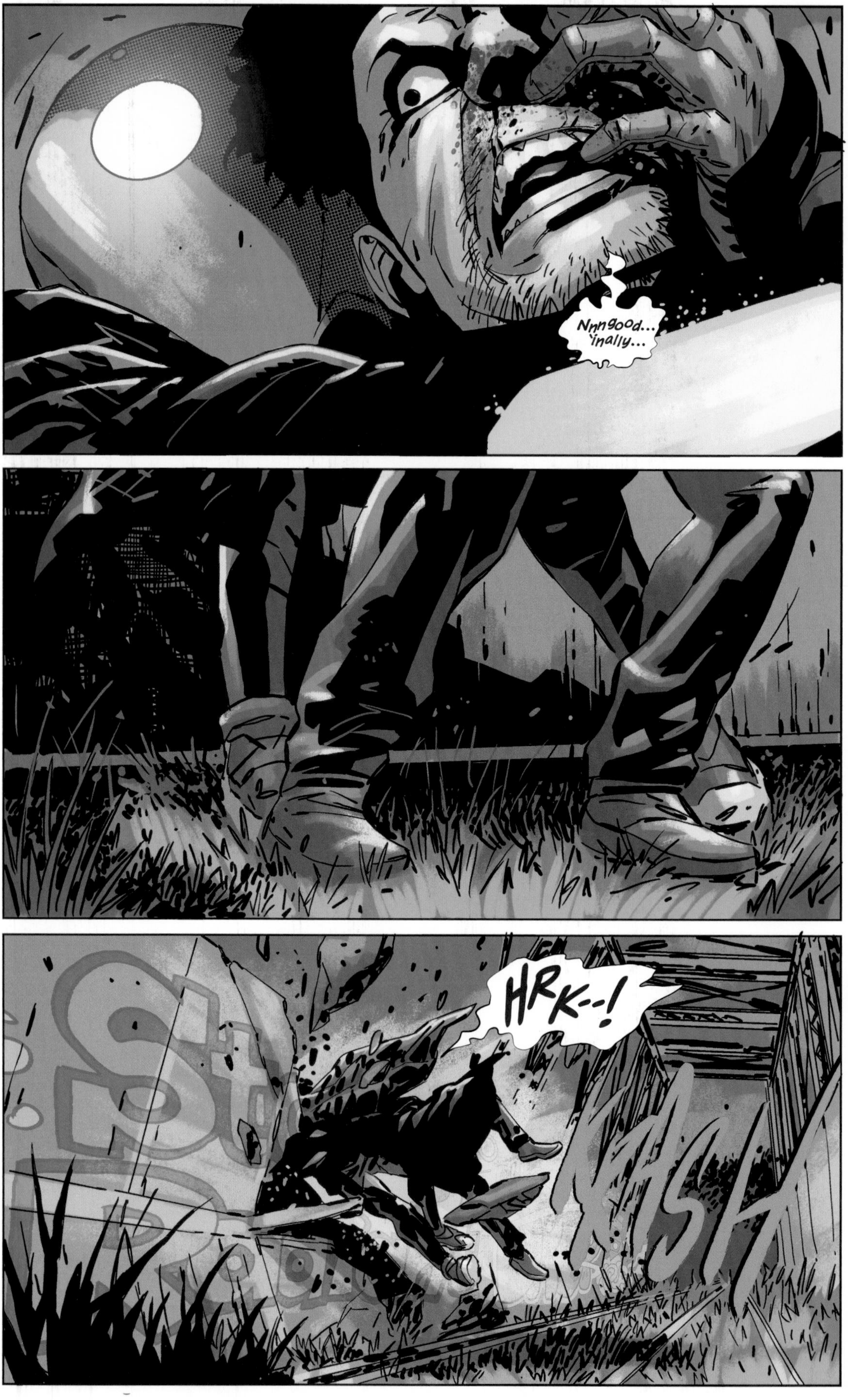
Nnngood...
'inally...
HRK--!

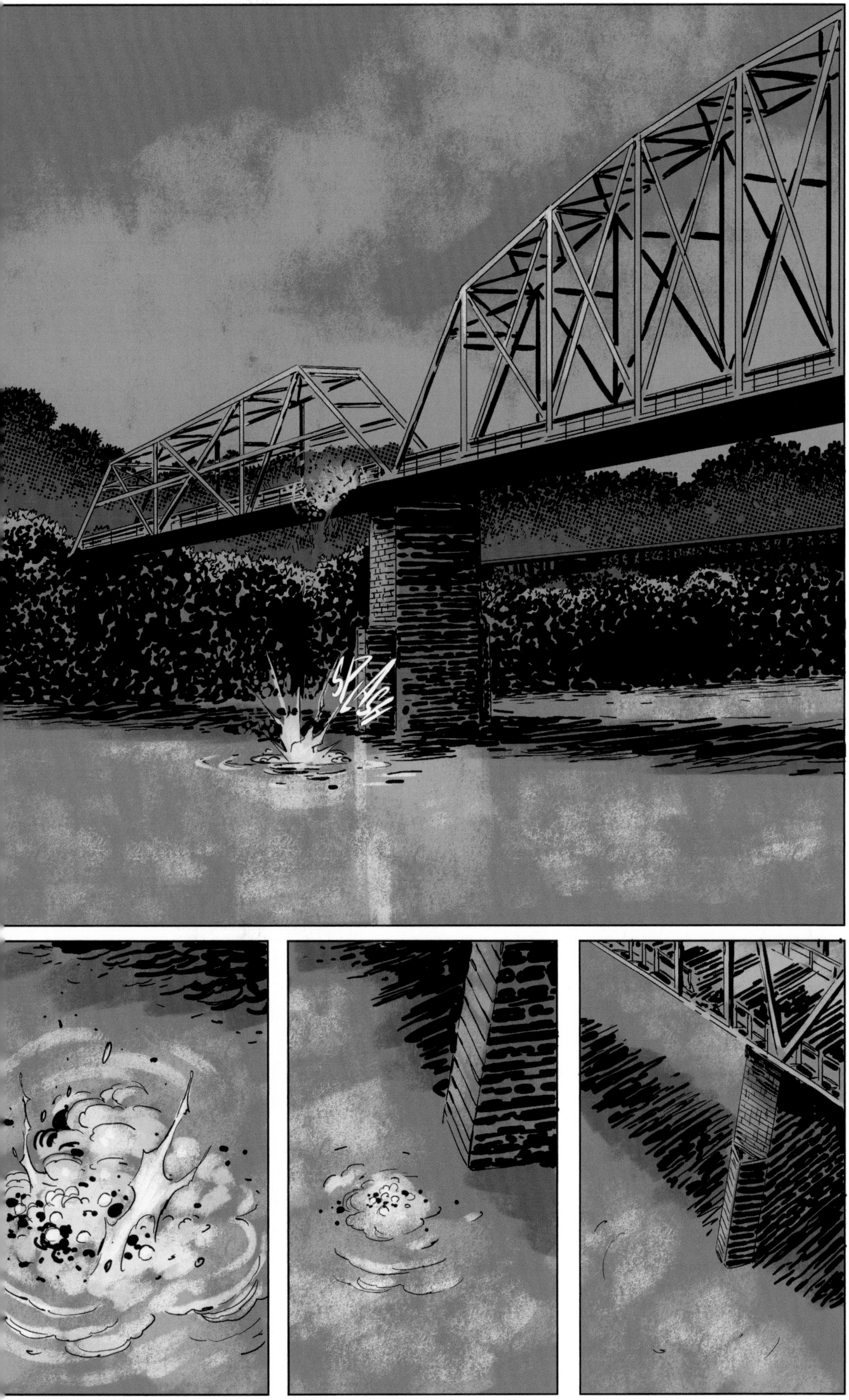
SPLASH

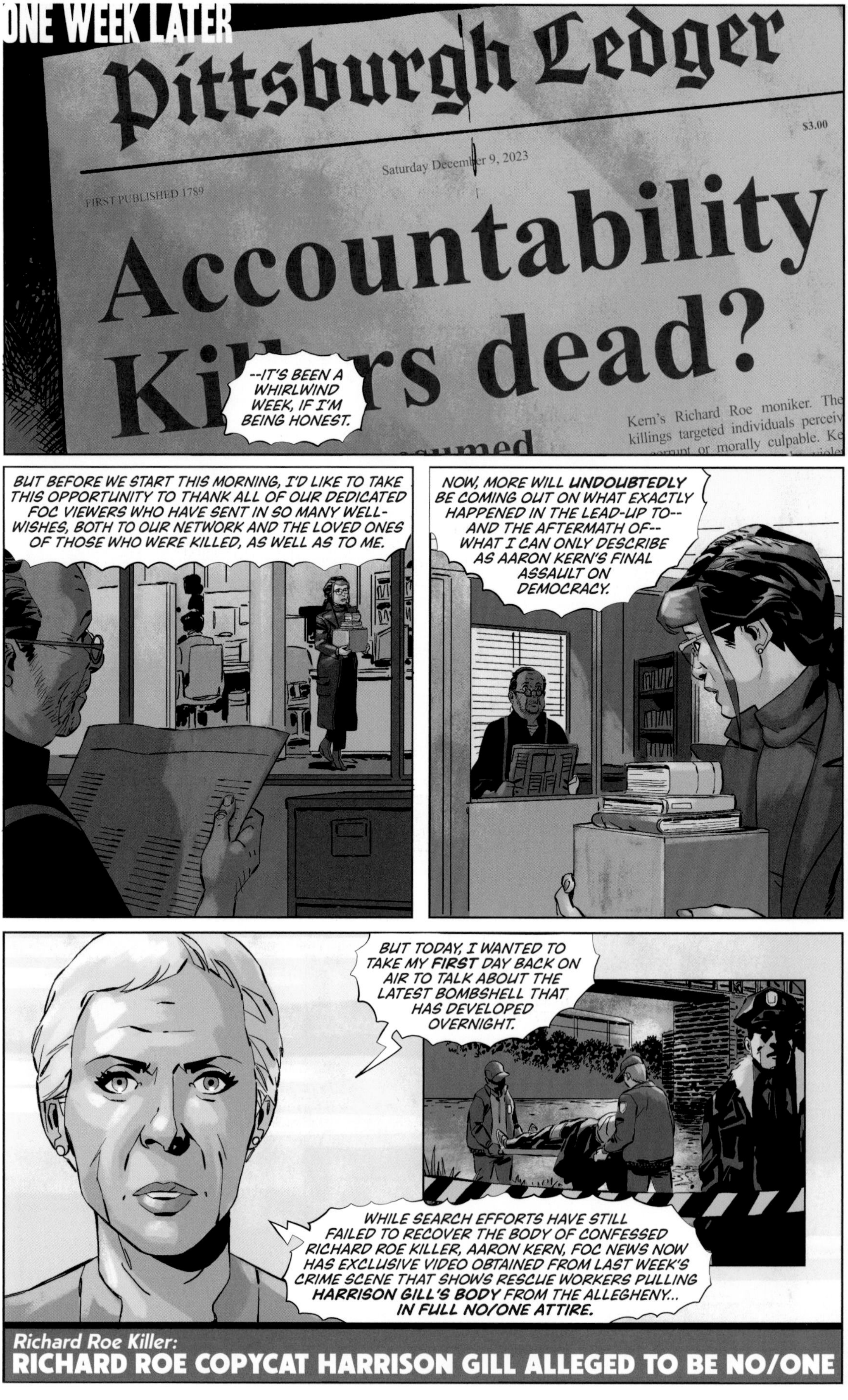

ONE WEEK LATER
Pittsburgh Ledger
$3.00
Saturday December 9, 2023
FIRST PUBLISHED 1789
Accountability
Ki rs dead?
--IT'S BEEN A WHIRLWIND WEEK, IF I'M BEING HONEST.
Kern's Richard Roe moniker. The killings targeted individuals perceiv corrupt or morally culpable. Ke
BUT BEFORE WE START THIS MORNING, I'D LIKE TO TAKE THIS OPPORTUNITY TO THANK ALL OF OUR DEDICATED FOC VIEWERS WHO HAVE SENT IN SO MANY WELL-WISHES, BOTH TO OUR NETWORK AND THE LOVED ONES OF THOSE WHO WERE KILLED, AS WELL AS TO ME.
NOW, MORE WILL **UNDOUBTEDLY** BE COMING OUT ON WHAT EXACTLY HAPPENED IN THE LEAD-UP TO-- AND THE AFTERMATH OF-- WHAT I CAN ONLY DESCRIBE AS AARON KERN'S FINAL ASSAULT ON DEMOCRACY.
BUT TODAY, I WANTED TO TAKE MY **FIRST** DAY BACK ON AIR TO TALK ABOUT THE LATEST BOMBSHELL THAT HAS DEVELOPED OVERNIGHT.
WHILE SEARCH EFFORTS HAVE STILL FAILED TO RECOVER THE BODY OF CONFESSED RICHARD ROE KILLER, AARON KERN, FOC NEWS NOW HAS EXCLUSIVE VIDEO OBTAINED FROM LAST WEEK'S CRIME SCENE THAT SHOWS RESCUE WORKERS PULLING **HARRISON GILL'S BODY** FROM THE ALLEGHENY... **IN FULL NO/ONE ATTIRE.**
Richard Roe Killer:
RICHARD ROE COPYCAT HARRISON GILL ALLEGED TO BE NO/ONE

YOU BUY *ANY* OF THIS SHIT?

NO/ONE LITERALLY USED ME AS *BAIT* TO CATCH *HARRISON GILL.*

I'M SORRY, THERE'S *NO WAY* IT'S THE SAME GUY. I DON'T CARE *WHAT* THEY'RE SAYING.

Mm. *GOOD.* YOU'RE GOING TO FIT IN AT *EDGE,* ALEJANDRO. AND DON'T WORRY-- YOU'RE *RIGHT...*

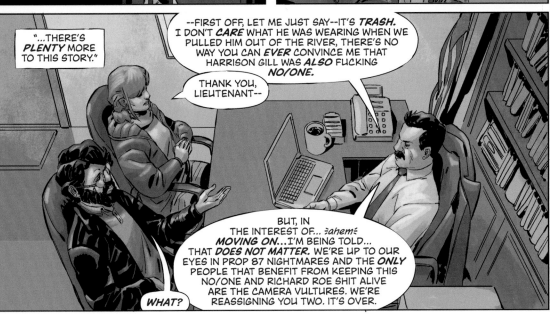

"...THERE'S *PLENTY* MORE TO THIS STORY."

--FIRST OFF, LET ME JUST SAY--IT'S *TRASH.* I DON'T *CARE* WHAT HE WAS WEARING WHEN WE PULLED HIM OUT OF THE RIVER, THERE'S NO WAY YOU CAN *EVER* CONVINCE ME THAT HARRISON GILL WAS *ALSO* FUCKING *NO/ONE.*

THANK YOU, LIEUTENANT--

BUT, IN THE INTEREST OF... ≋ahem≋ *MOVING ON...* I'M BEING TOLD... THAT *DOES NOT MATTER.* WE'RE UP TO OUR EYES IN PROP 87 NIGHTMARES AND THE *ONLY* PEOPLE THAT BENEFIT FROM KEEPING THIS NO/ONE AND RICHARD ROE SHIT ALIVE ARE THE CAMERA VULTURES. WE'RE REASSIGNING YOU TWO. IT'S OVER.

WHAT?

MAC, THIS FUCKER *STABBED YOU.* WE *KNOW* HE WAS THE COPYCAT. IT'S *IMPOSSIBLE* FOR HIM TO BE NO/ONE--

ALL DUE RESPECT, LIEUTENANT...

HOW ARE *ANY* OF US SUPPOSED TO MOVE ON?

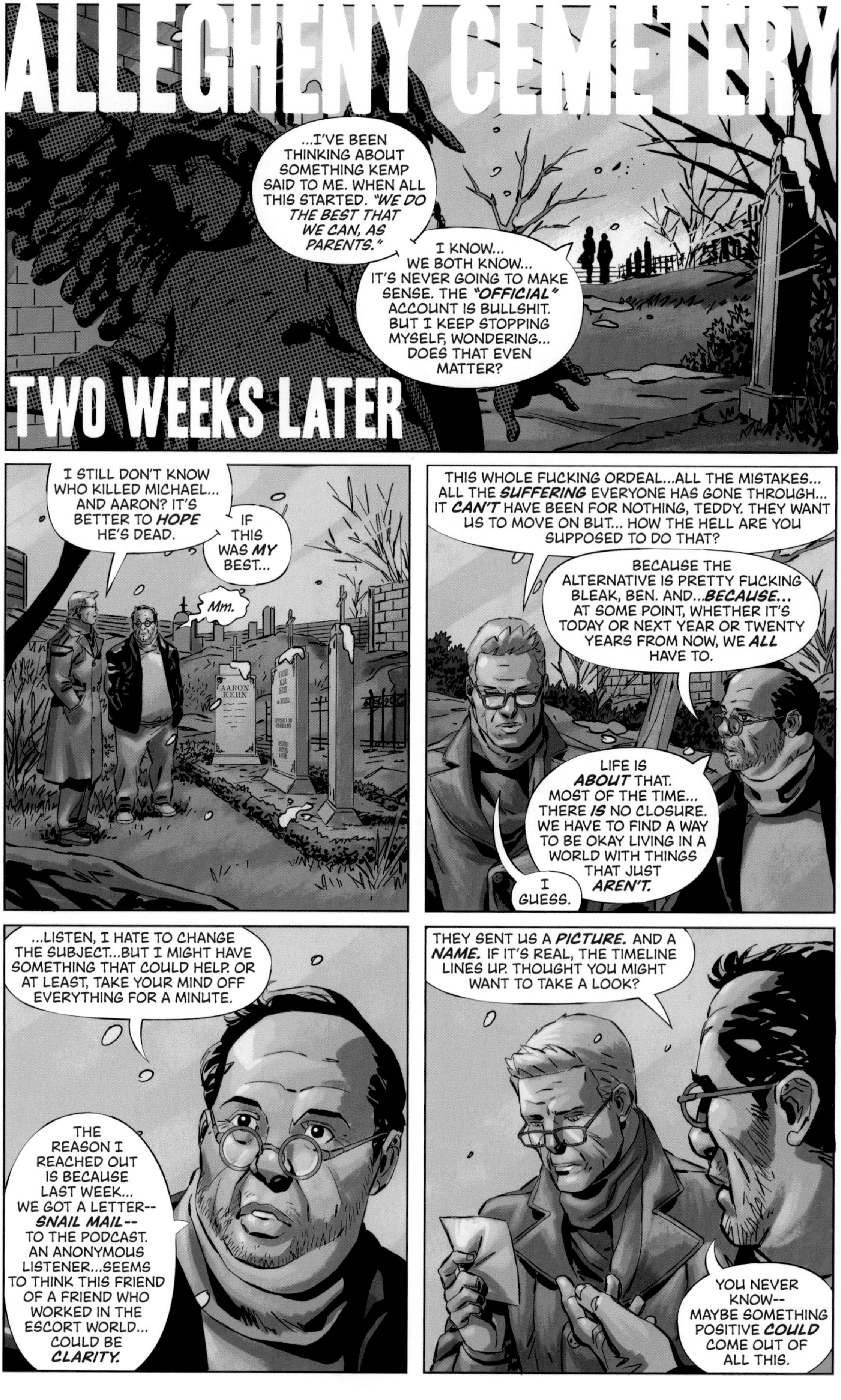
ALLEGHENY CEMETERY
...I'VE BEEN THINKING ABOUT SOMETHING KEMP SAID TO ME. WHEN ALL THIS STARTED. "WE DO THE BEST THAT WE CAN, AS PARENTS."
I KNOW... WE BOTH KNOW... IT'S NEVER GOING TO MAKE SENSE. THE "OFFICIAL" ACCOUNT IS BULLSHIT. BUT I KEEP STOPPING MYSELF, WONDERING... DOES THAT EVEN MATTER?
TWO WEEKS LATER
I STILL DON'T KNOW WHO KILLED MICHAEL... AND AARON? IT'S BETTER TO HOPE HE'S DEAD.
IF THIS WAS MY BEST...
Mm.
AARON KERN
THIS WHOLE FUCKING ORDEAL...ALL THE MISTAKES... ALL THE SUFFERING EVERYONE HAS GONE THROUGH... IT CAN'T HAVE BEEN FOR NOTHING, TEDDY. THEY WANT US TO MOVE ON BUT... HOW THE HELL ARE YOU SUPPOSED TO DO THAT?
BECAUSE THE ALTERNATIVE IS PRETTY FUCKING BLEAK, BEN. AND...BECAUSE... AT SOME POINT, WHETHER IT'S TODAY OR NEXT YEAR OR TWENTY YEARS FROM NOW, WE ALL HAVE TO.
LIFE IS ABOUT THAT. MOST OF THE TIME... THERE IS NO CLOSURE. WE HAVE TO FIND A WAY TO BE OKAY LIVING IN A WORLD WITH THINGS THAT JUST AREN'T.
I GUESS.
...LISTEN, I HATE TO CHANGE THE SUBJECT...BUT I MIGHT HAVE SOMETHING THAT COULD HELP. OR AT LEAST, TAKE YOUR MIND OFF EVERYTHING FOR A MINUTE.
THE REASON I REACHED OUT IS BECAUSE LAST WEEK... WE GOT A LETTER-- SNAIL MAIL-- TO THE PODCAST. AN ANONYMOUS LISTENER...SEEMS TO THINK THIS FRIEND OF A FRIEND WHO WORKED IN THE ESCORT WORLD... COULD BE CLARITY.
THEY SENT US A PICTURE. AND A NAME. IF IT'S REAL, THE TIMELINE LINES UP. THOUGHT YOU MIGHT WANT TO TAKE A LOOK?
YOU NEVER KNOW-- MAYBE SOMETHING POSITIVE COULD COME OUT OF ALL THIS.

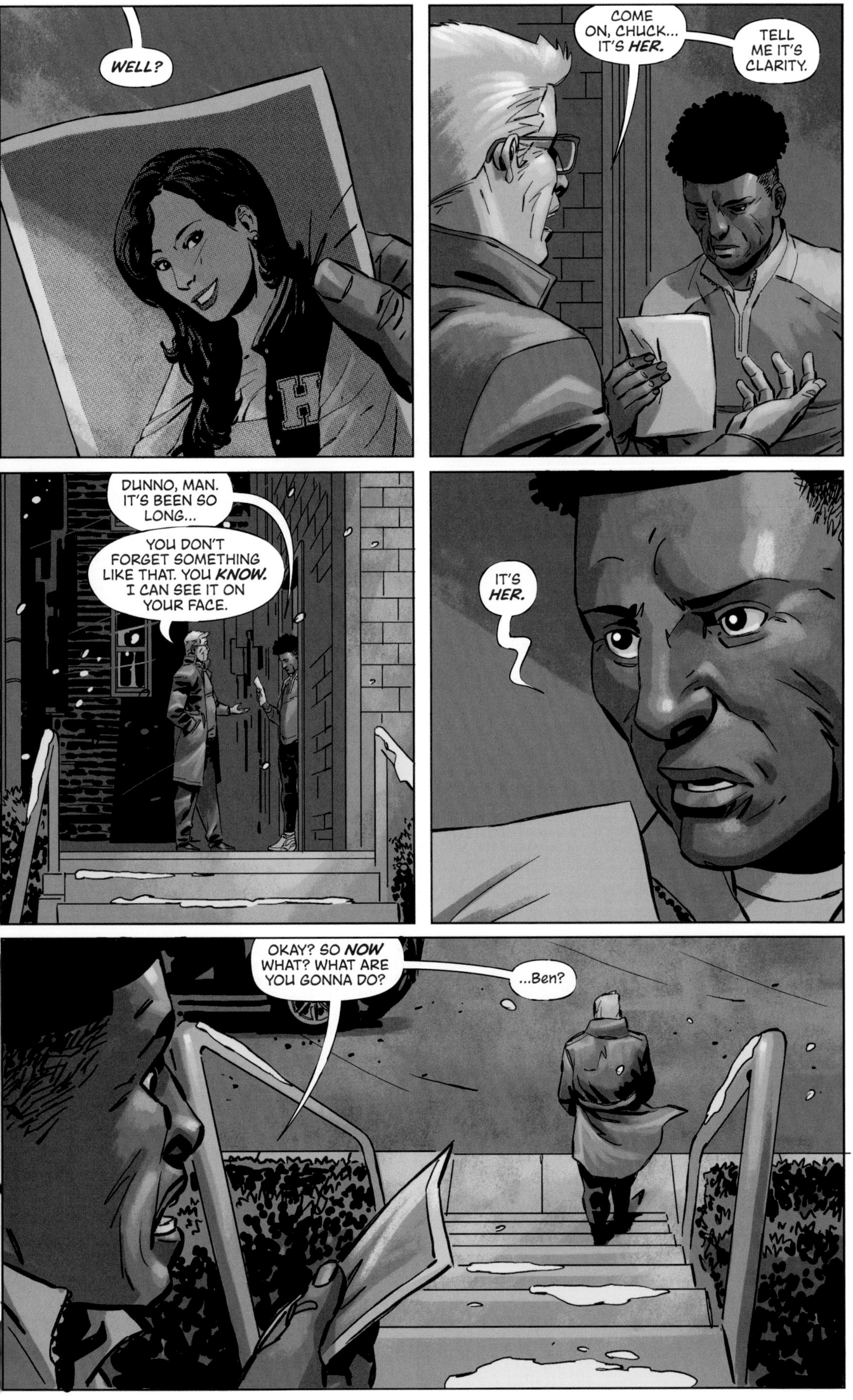
WELL?
COME ON, CHUCK... IT'S HER.
TELL ME IT'S CLARITY.
DUNNO, MAN. IT'S BEEN SO LONG...
YOU DON'T FORGET SOMETHING LIKE THAT. YOU KNOW. I CAN SEE IT ON YOUR FACE.
IT'S HER.
OKAY? SO NOW WHAT? WHAT ARE YOU GONNA DO?
...Ben?

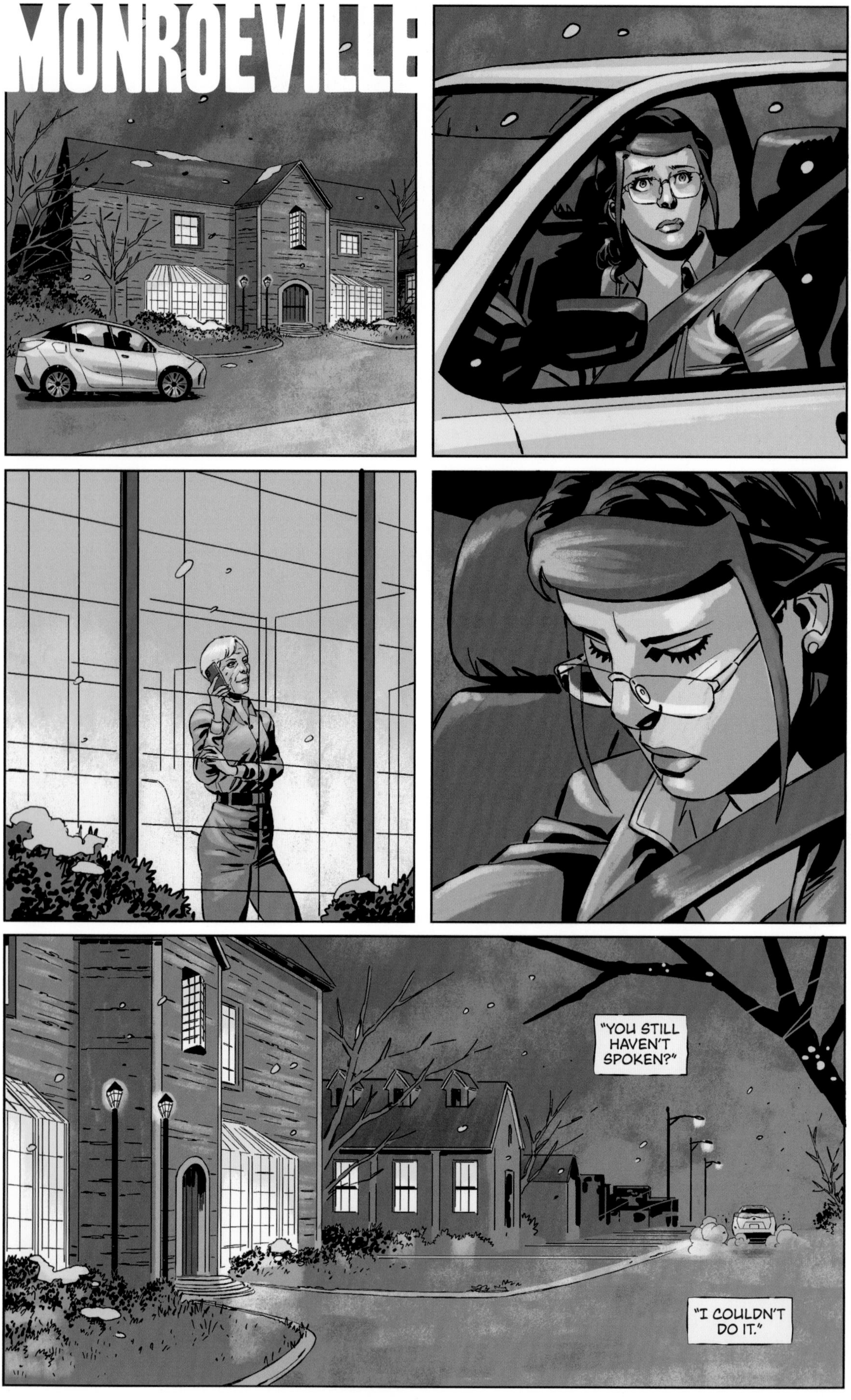
MONROEVILLE
"YOU STILL HAVEN'T SPOKEN?"
"I COULDN'T DO IT."

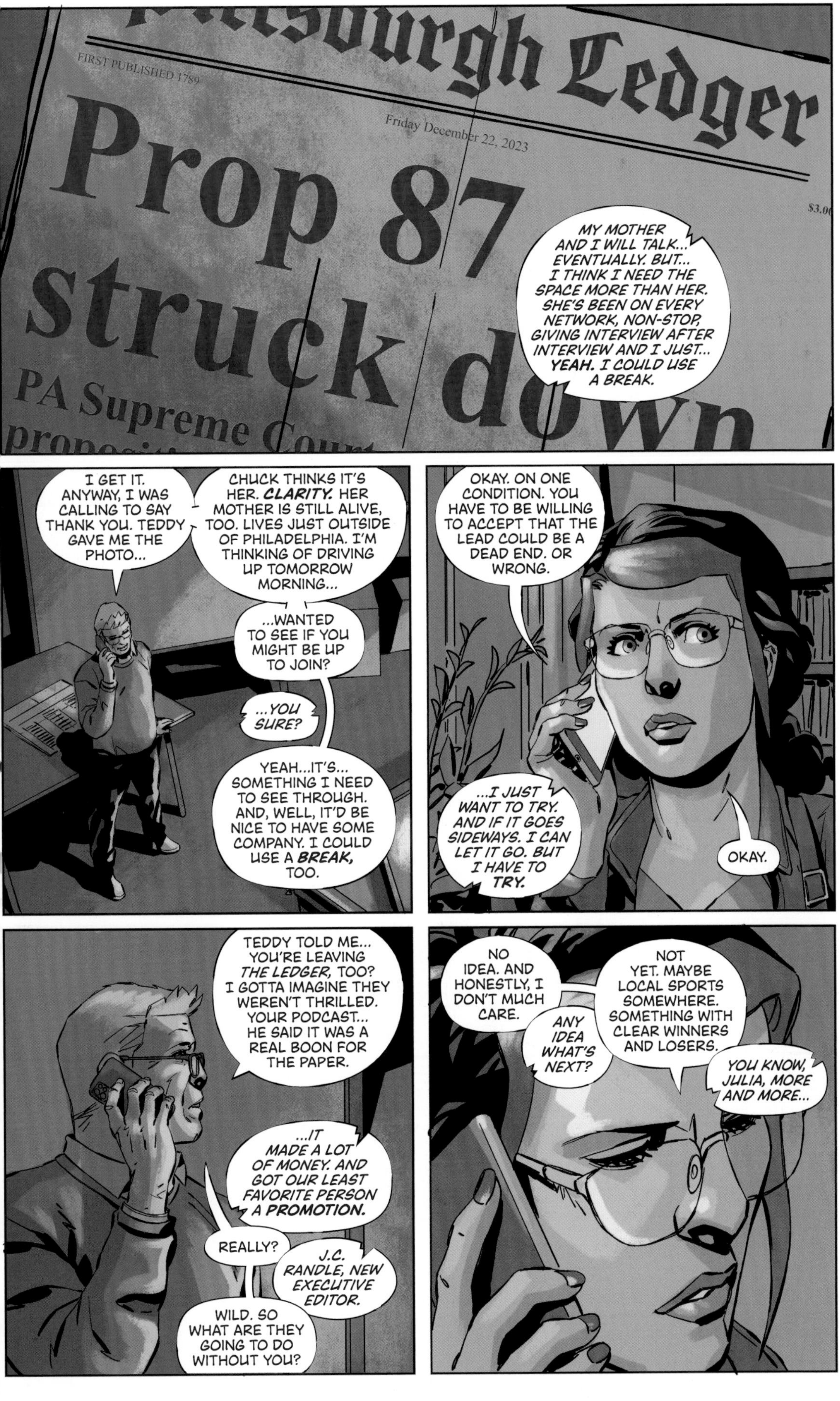
Ledger
FIRST PUBLISHED 1789
Friday December 22, 2023
Prop 87
struck down
PA Supreme
MY MOTHER AND I WILL TALK... EVENTUALLY. BUT... I THINK I NEED THE SPACE MORE THAN HER. SHE'S BEEN ON EVERY NETWORK, NON-STOP, GIVING INTERVIEW AFTER INTERVIEW AND I JUST... **YEAH.** I COULD USE A BREAK.
I GET IT. ANYWAY, I WAS CALLING TO SAY THANK YOU. TEDDY GAVE ME THE PHOTO...
CHUCK THINKS IT'S HER. ***CLARITY.*** HER MOTHER IS STILL ALIVE, TOO. LIVES JUST OUTSIDE OF PHILADELPHIA. I'M THINKING OF DRIVING UP TOMORROW MORNING...
...WANTED TO SEE IF YOU MIGHT BE UP TO JOIN?
...YOU SURE?
YEAH...IT'S... SOMETHING I NEED TO SEE THROUGH. AND, WELL, IT'D BE NICE TO HAVE SOME COMPANY. I COULD USE A ***BREAK,*** TOO.
OKAY. ON ONE CONDITION. YOU HAVE TO BE WILLING TO ACCEPT THAT THE LEAD COULD BE A DEAD END. OR WRONG.
...I JUST WANT TO TRY. AND IF IT GOES SIDEWAYS. I CAN LET IT GO. BUT I HAVE TO ***TRY.***
OKAY.
TEDDY TOLD ME... YOU'RE LEAVING *THE LEDGER,* TOO? I GOTTA IMAGINE THEY WEREN'T THRILLED. YOUR PODCAST... HE SAID IT WAS A REAL BOON FOR THE PAPER.
...IT MADE A LOT OF MONEY. AND GOT OUR LEAST FAVORITE PERSON A ***PROMOTION.***
REALLY?
J.C. RANDLE, NEW EXECUTIVE EDITOR.
WILD. SO WHAT ARE THEY GOING TO DO WITHOUT YOU?
NO IDEA. AND HONESTLY, I DON'T MUCH CARE.
ANY IDEA WHAT'S NEXT?
NOT YET. MAYBE LOCAL SPORTS SOMEWHERE. SOMETHING WITH CLEAR WINNERS AND LOSERS.
YOU KNOW, JULIA, MORE AND MORE...

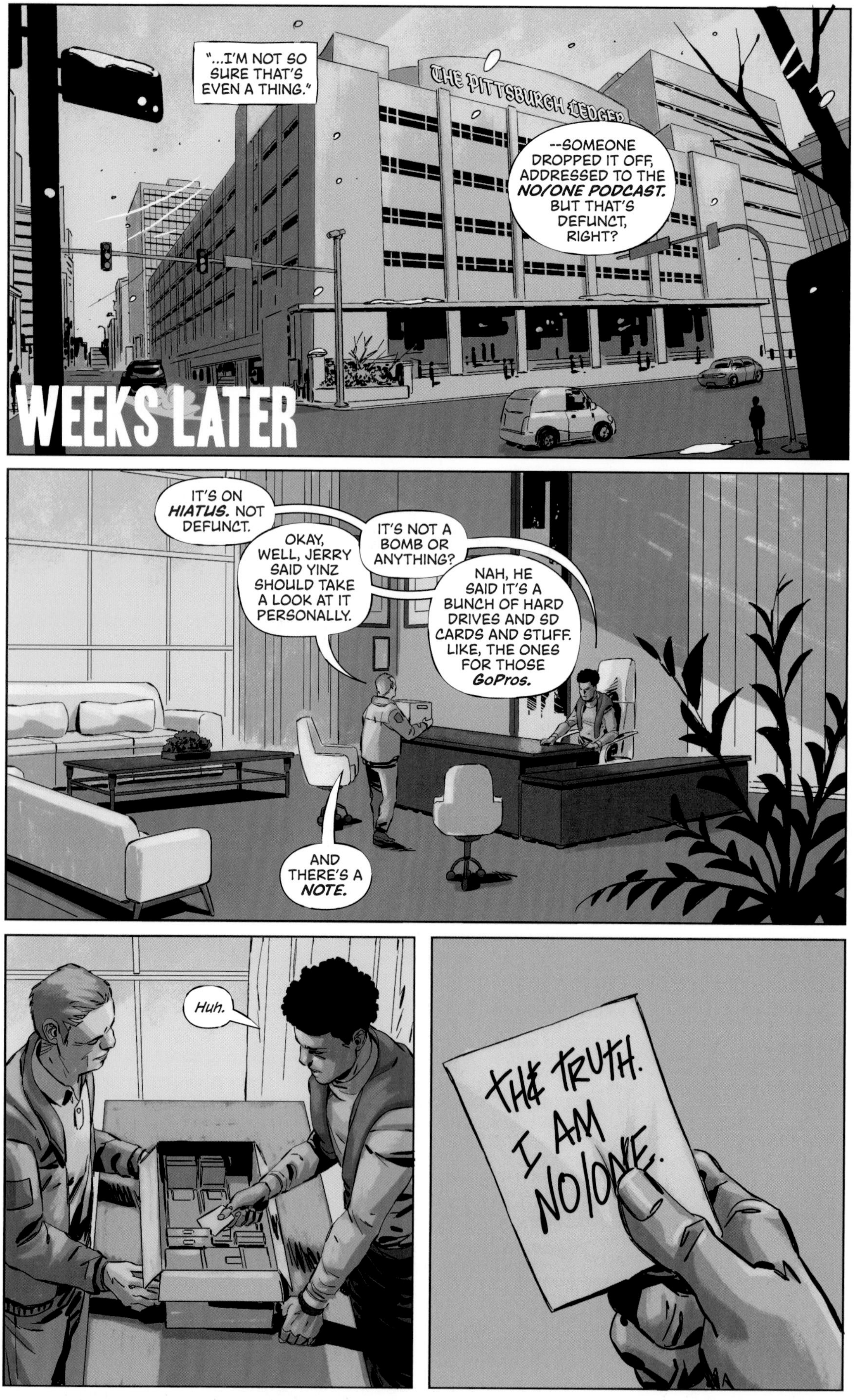
"...I'M NOT SO SURE THAT'S EVEN A THING."
THE PITTSBURGH LEDGER
--SOMEONE DROPPED IT OFF, ADDRESSED TO THE ***NO/ONE PODCAST.*** BUT THAT'S DEFUNCT, RIGHT?
WEEKS LATER
IT'S ON ***HIATUS.*** NOT DEFUNCT.
OKAY, WELL, JERRY SAID YINZ SHOULD TAKE A LOOK AT IT PERSONALLY.
IT'S NOT A BOMB OR ANYTHING?
NAH, HE SAID IT'S A BUNCH OF HARD DRIVES AND SD CARDS AND STUFF. LIKE, THE ONES FOR THOSE ***GoPros.***
AND THERE'S A ***NOTE.***
Huh.
THE TRUTH.
I AM NO/ONE.

Pittsburgh Ledger

FIRST PUBLISHED 1789 | Sunday December 3, 2023 | $3.00

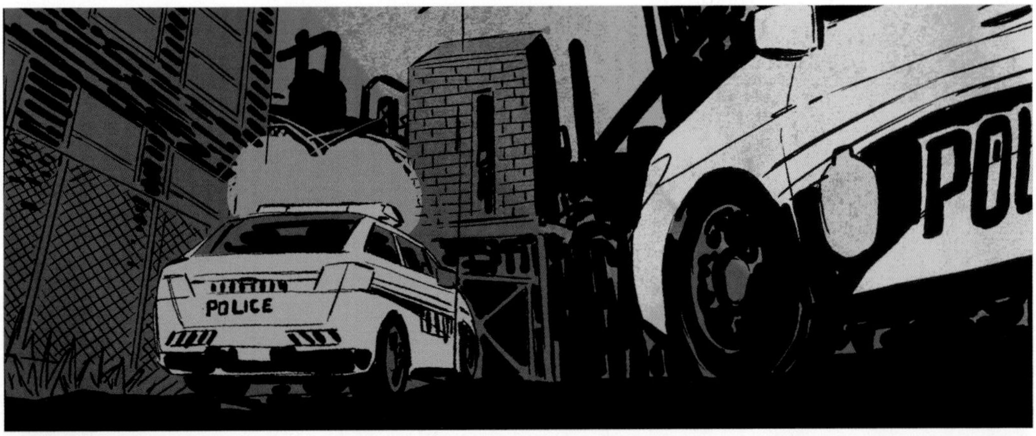
POLICE
POL

Police arrive at the Carrie Blast Furnaces yesterday. Geraldo Borges/Ledger

Accountability Killers dead?

Aaron Kern presumed dead; NO/ONE revealed as Harrison Gill in deadly confrontation

Chris Tolin
Pittsburgh Ledger

Pittsburgh, PA— In a dramatic and violent climax to a fifteen-month saga of terror, Aaron Kern, the alleged original Accountability Killer, is presumed dead following a deadly confrontation with the masked vigilante NO/ONE at the Carrie Blast Furnaces. The body of Harrison Gill, identified as both NO/ONE and a copycat killer, was recovered from the Allegheny River while Kern's remains have yet to be found; he is believed to have perished in the struggle.

The harrowing events unfolded yesterday, capping off a series of abductions and executions orchestrated by Kern over the past two weeks, and marking a grim capstone to his nearly year and a half long assault on Pittsburgh. Kern kidnapped several prominent figures, including his father, Ben Kern, State Senator Noah Kemp, media personality Alanna Paige, retired police officer Oscar Sherman, and Pittsburgh Ledger reporter, Julia Paige, holding them captive in a secret underground bunker.

In a chilling sequence, which Julia Paige was forced to record and document, Kern forced confessions from his captives before executing Kemp and Sherman. His reign of terror was abruptly interrupted by the intervention of Gill, leading to a brutal struggle that ended with both Kern and Gill plunging into the river.

This bloody conclusion follows a year of escalating violence and fear in Pittsburgh, beginning with the accountability killings attributed to Kern's Richard Roe moniker. These killings targeted individuals perceived as corrupt or morally culpable. Kern, unmasked as Roe, saw the violence continue under Gill, who allegedly operated under the guise of both NO/ONE and a copycat killer.

Tensions peaked following the controversial passage of Proposition 87, which permitted preemptive self-defense. The law's broad language incited a surge in violent confrontations, pushing the city to the brink.

In the aftermath, Mayor Kelly Murphy addressed the city, emphasizing the need for healing. "This chapter of our city's history has been dark and painful. We must now focus on rebuilding trust and ensuring justice for the victims of this senseless violence," she stated.

Police Chief Albert Mixon, whose department has been at the forefront of the investigation, vowed a thorough review of the events and renewed efforts to restore order. "Our officers are committed to bringing those responsible to justice and preventing further violence," Mixon affirmed.

As Pittsburgh grapples with the fallout of these harrowing events, the Ledger will continue to provide in-depth coverage, striving for justice and restoration in a time of profound uncertainty.

Who is Harrison Gill? Inside the secret

The Drop

PRESENTS

WHO IS NO/ONE
WITH/JULIA PAIGE

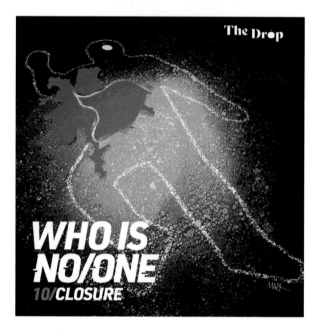

The Drop

WHO IS
NO/ONE
10/CLOSURE

15 DECEMBER
10/Closure
WHO IS NO/ONE

18:23   -2:51

Pittsburgh Ledger

FIRST PUBLISHED 1789 Friday December 22, 2023 $3.00

Prop 87 struck down

PA Supreme Court rules proposition unlawful

Chris Tolin
Pittsburgh Ledger

Pittsburgh, PA— In a decisive ruling, the Pennsylvania Supreme Court has struck down Proposition 87, known as the "Presumption of Reasonable Preemptive Self-Defense Act," following six weeks of escalating violence and chaos in Pittsburgh. This period of unrest was exacerbated by the high-profile kidnapping and murder spree perpetrated by Aaron Kern, which left several prominent individuals dead and Pittsburgh in turmoil.

The controversial legislation, which allowed individuals to use preemptive self-defense without the burden of proof, had sparked widespread unrest and numerous violent incidents across the city. The court's decision comes in response to a series of legal challenges and mounting public outcry over the law's implications.

Chief Justice Robert Walters emphasized the court's concerns about the constitutionality of Proposition 87. "The law's broad language and lack of clear limitations posed a significant threat to public safety and the rule of law," Walters stated.

Mayor Kelly Murphy, who had been a vocal critic of the proposition, welcomed the ruling. "This decision is a crucial step towards restoring order and protecting our citizens," she said. "We have seen firsthand the devastating impact of this law, and I am relieved that the court has recognized the need to uphold our legal standards."

Since the passage of Proposition 87, Pittsburgh has experienced a surge in violent confrontations, with individuals citing the law as justification for preemptive actions. The recent violence reached a peak with Aaron Kern's string of kidnappings and murders, which targeted key figures including State Senator Noah Kemp, media personality Alanna Paige, and retired officer Oscar Sherman.

Police Chief Albert Mixon reported a marked increase in shootings and altercations, leading to widespread fear and instability. "Our officers have been stretched to their limits trying to manage the fallout from this legislation," Mixon remarked. "The court's decision will allow us to refocus on maintaining public safety and order."

State Senator Gail Delmont, who had championed the proposition alongside Kemp, expressed her disappointment but called for calm and unity. "While I am disappointed by the court's ruling, I urge all citizens to respect the decision and work together to find common ground," Demont said. "Our goal has always been to protect our communities, and, in the wake of my colleague and friend's heartbreaking murder, we must now explore alternative solutions."

The court's ruling has been met with mixed reactions from the public. Some residents, like local attorney Mark Richards, view it as a necessary correction. "This law was a recipe for disaster, and the court's decision is a welcome relief," Richards commented. Others, however, fear that the ruling will leave them vulnerable. "I supported Proposition 87 because I wanted to feel safe," said Lisa Thompson, a local business owner. "Now I'm not sure what will happen."

As Pittsburgh grapples with the aftermath of Proposition 87 and the recent court decision, city leaders are calling for unity and cooperation to address the underlying issues of safety and trust. The Pittsburgh Ledger will continue to provide comprehensive coverage of the situation, keeping readers informed of further developments and the city's efforts to restore stability and security.

Prop 87 repealed: what's next?

Special Report Page 8

Veteran reporter Julia Paige bids farewell to Pittsburgh Ledger after years of covering city's darkest days

Teddy Barstow
Pittsburgh Ledger

Pittsburgh, PA— After more than a decade of fearless journalism, Julia Paige, one of Pittsburgh's most dedicated reporters– and, full disclosure, one of my favorites I've had the privilege of editing– has announced her departure from the Pittsburgh Ledger. Paige's name has become synonymous with hard-hitting investigative reporting, especially in the last year as she played a central role in unraveling the twisted web of murders and conspiracies surrounding the Richard Roe Accountability Killings. Her final column, a heartfelt farewell to the city she both loved and endured, marks the end of an era for the Ledger and for Pittsburgh's journalistic community.

"This city has been my home, my passion, and my source of inspiration," Paige wrote in her final piece. "But after everything we've been through— the murders, the violence, the fear—I find myself needing to step away, to find peace in a world that so often seems devoid of it."

Paige's decision comes after an exhausting twelve months of reporting on a story that has gripped the city and the nation. The Accountability Murders, which began with the vigilante actions of Richard Roe (later revealed to be Aaron Kern), plunged Pittsburgh into chaos. As the violence escalated, Paige became one of the city's leading voices, chronicling each grim development with determination and resolve. From the first murders that shocked the city to the eventual capture of Kern, Paige was there, covering every angle and digging into the dark truths behind the headlines.

In her farewell column, Paige reflected on the personal toll that this relentless pursuit of justice had taken on her. "It hasn't been easy," she admitted. "I've seen the best and the worst of this city, and it's left me changed in ways I never could have anticipated. It all adds up."

Paige's coverage of the Richard Roe case brought her both praise and danger. Despite the risks, Paige remained undeterred, continuing to investigate the murders and even launching a podcast that explored the deeper mysteries surrounding the Accountability Movement and the enigmatic vigilante known as NO/ONE.

But it wasn't just the external threats that weighed on Paige.

"I've always believed in the power of the press to make a difference, but there are days when I can't help but feel like we're just amplifying the horror," she confessed. "And I'm not sure I can keep doing that."

Paige's departure from the Pittsburgh Ledger leaves a significant void in the city's journalistic landscape. Over the years, Paige earned a reputation as a tenacious reporter who wasn't afraid to ask tough questions or confront uncomfortable truths. Her reporting on corruption, crime, and the underbelly of Pittsburgh's political machine has earned her numerous accolades, including multiple awards for her investigative work. And that's to say nothing of her sports coverage.

However, the pressure mounted in recent months after a disturbing incident involving her own family. Julia's mother, Alanna Paige, a controversial conservative news personality, was the target of spree shooter Kenneth Chbosky. Chbosky, emboldened by Alanna's outspoken support of Proposition 87—a preemptive "stand your ground" law—attacked her news show, killing several of her coworkers. Despite the trauma, Alanna continued to push the narrative in favor of Prop 87, further polarizing her public image and placing a greater strain on her relationship with Julia.

The incident served as a painful reminder of how deeply intertwined Julia's professional life had become with her personal struggles. It also cemented her belief that stepping away from the press was necessary for her own well-being.

"Pittsburgh will always be a part of me," she wrote. "But I need to find a way to live outside of the shadows. It's time for someone else to pick up the pen and continue the fight."

Paige's departure comes at a critical time for Pittsburgh. The Accountability Murders may have come to an end, with the presumed death of NO/ONE and the discovery of Aaron Kern's body, but the city remains deeply scarred by the violence and fear that have dominated the past year. With Paige stepping away from the newsroom, the Pittsburgh Ledger loses one of its most respected voices just when strong journalism is needed more than ever.

As she embarks on this new chapter in her life, Julia Paige leaves behind a legacy of courage, integrity, and an unwavering commitment to the truth. Her final words in the Pittsburgh Ledger reflect the complex emotions of a journalist who has given everything to her city but now seeks peace in a world that rarely offers it.

"Pittsburgh, I will always be grateful for what you've given me," she wrote. "But now, I need to find something more—a life beyond the violence, beyond the fear. Thank you for letting me tell your stories. It's time for me to write my own."

The Best of Julia Paige
Page 14

>_ **Post-Mortem: The Year That Rocked Pittsburgh**
JANUARY 29 2024

written by Danielle Gaines
published on Edge News

*"Instead of justice, we got bloodshed. And
now, there are no answers, only cover-ups."*

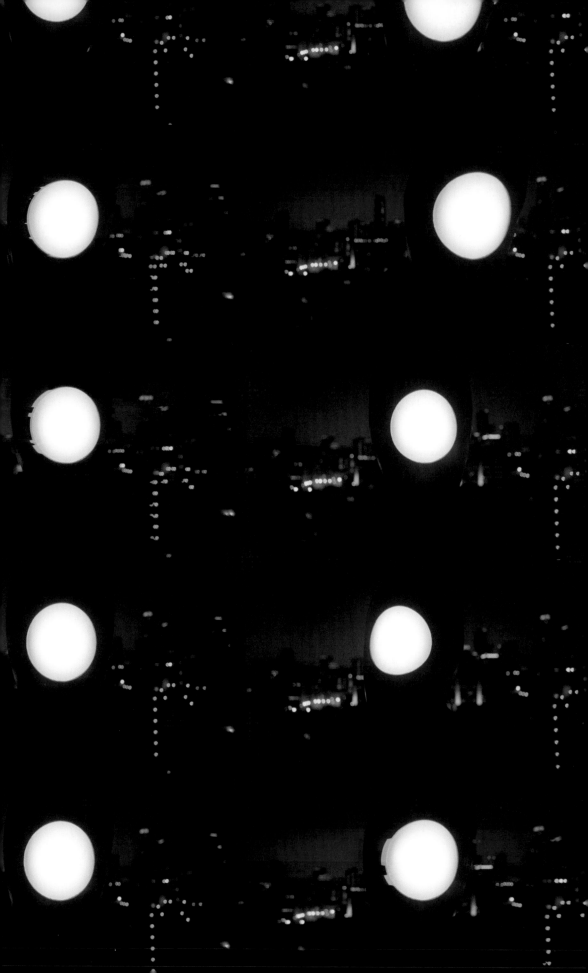

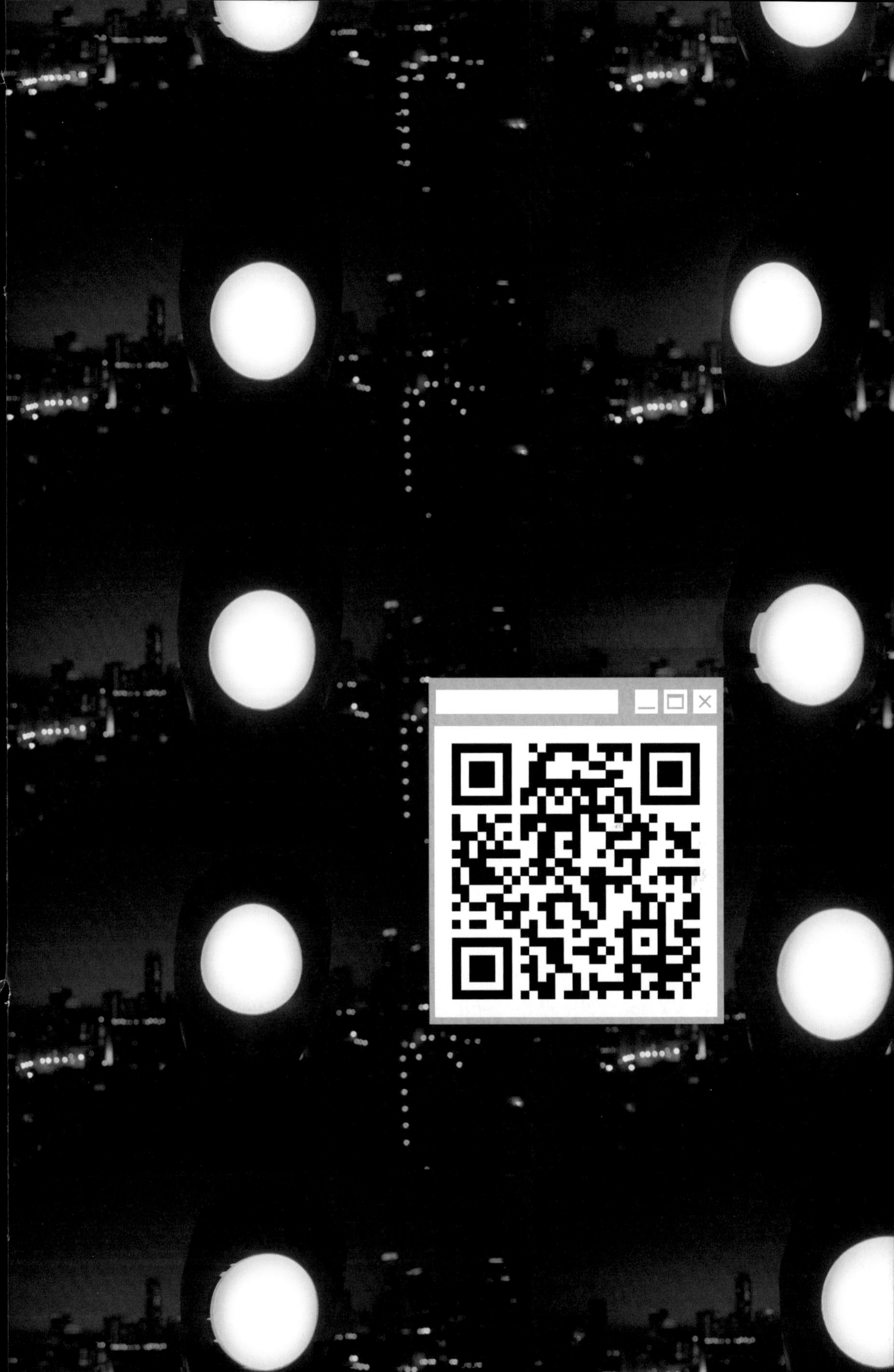

IMAGE COMICS, INC. • Robert Kirkman: Chief Operating Officer • Erik Larsen: Chief Financial Officer • Todd McFarlane: President • Marc Silvestri: Chief Executive Officer • Jim Valentino: Executive Vice President • Eric Stephenson: Publisher / Chief Creative Officer • Nicole Lapalme: Vice President of Finance • Leanna Caunter: Accounting Analyst • Sue Korpela: Accounting & HR Manager • Alex Cox: Director of Direct Market Sales • Margot Wood: Vice President of Book Market Sales • Chloe Ramos: Book Market & Library Sales Manager • Kat Salazar: Vice President of PR & Marketing • Deanna Phelps: Marketing Design Manager • Jim Viscardi: Vice President of Business Development • Lorelei Bunjes: Vice President of Digital Strategy • Emilio Bautista: Digital Sales Coordinator • Dirk Wood: Vice President of International Sales & Licensing • Ryan Brewer: International Sales & Licensing Manager • Drew Gill: Art Director • Heather Doornink: Vice President of Production • Ian Baldessari: Print Manager • Melissa Gifford: Content Manager • Drew Fitzgerald: Content Manager • Erika Schnatz: Senior Production Artist • Wesley Griffith: Production Artist • Rich Fowlks: Production Artist • Jon Schlaffman: Production Artist • IMAGECOMICS.COM

NO/ ONE

>_ WRITERS   KYLE HIGGINS
                   BRIAN BUCCELLATO
>_ ARTIST   GERALDO BORGES
                   ANTONIO FUSO [CHAPTER SEVEN]
>_ COLORIST   MARK ENGLERT
>_ LETTERER   HASSAN OTSMANE-ELHAOU
>_ PRODUCTION ARTIST   WESLEY GRIFFITH
>_ CREATIVE CONSULTANT PETER NICKEAS
>_ EDITOR & DESIGNER   MICHAEL BUSUTTIL

>_ SPECIAL THANKS   MAT GROOM   RYAN SIDOTI
                    KELLY MCMAHON   ALEC SIEGEL
                    RAMON PALERMO   JON-STEPHEN STANSEL
                    CHRIS PREKSTA   MATT TAYLOR
                    VICTOR SANTIAGO   TRACY WHITAKER

A Black Market Narrative
and ZQ Entertainment Production

Rachael Leigh Cook
Patton Oswalt

>_ WHO IS NO/ONE

>_ EXECUTIVE PRODUCERS	RACHAEL LEIGH COOK
	PATTON OSWALT
	GERALDO BORGES
	MARTIN BARAB
>_ SOUND SUPERVISOR	MATTHEW E. TAYLOR
>_ POST PRODUCER	JACOB MULLEN
>_ MUSIC BY	KRISTOPHER CARTER
>_ EDITED BY	ALEC SIEGEL
>_ CREATIVE CONSULTANT	PETER NICKEAS
>_ PRODUCED BY	KYLE HIGGINS
	BRIAN BUCCELLATO
	PETR JÁKL
	ARA KESHISHIAN
	MATTHEW E TAYLOR
>_ WRITTEN BY	KYLE HIGGINS & BRIAN BUCCELLATO
>_ WITH	JOE CLARK
	MAT GROOM
	JUSTIN PIASECKI
>_ DIRECTED BY	KYLE HIGGINS

>_CAST

Julia Paige	RACHAEL LEIGH COOK
Teddy Barstow	PATTON OSWALT
Ben Kern	TODD STASHWICK
Aaron Kern	ADAM MCARTHUR
Reporter	ALEC SIEGEL
Kenneth Chbosky	ALEX CASSIDY
Chris O'Neil	AZIM RIZK
Detective August Singh	AZIM RIZK
Police Dispatcher	CAITLIN MCKENNA
Police Dispatcher	CRISTINA VEE
Reporter	CRISTINA VEE
D.A. Foster	DAVID BLUE
Donovan Kemp	DAVID BLUE
Jack Sherman	DAVID BLUE
Julian Colon's Lawyer	DAVID BLUE
Chief Mixon	DAVID SOBOLOV
Reporter	JANE HORNER
Alejandro Rios	JONNY CRUZ
Local Resident	KARL HERLINGER
Alanna Paige	KELLY LESTER
NO/ONE	LOREN LESTER
Reporter	MICHAEL NIE
Bartender / Patrolman	RICK CRAMER
Detective Kate Harper	TARA PLATT
Chuck Tate	WALTER JONES
Senator Noah Kemp	YURI LOWENTHAL

[+]

EXPLORE THE

MASSIVE-VERSE

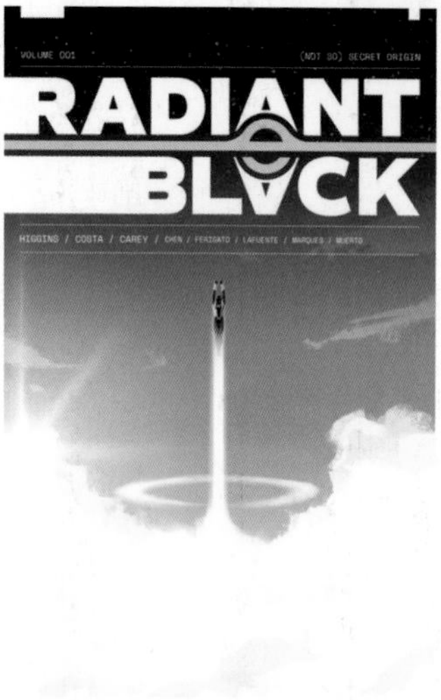

VOLUME 001
[NO7 30] SECRET ORIGIN
RADIANT BLACK
HIGGINS / COSTA / CAREY

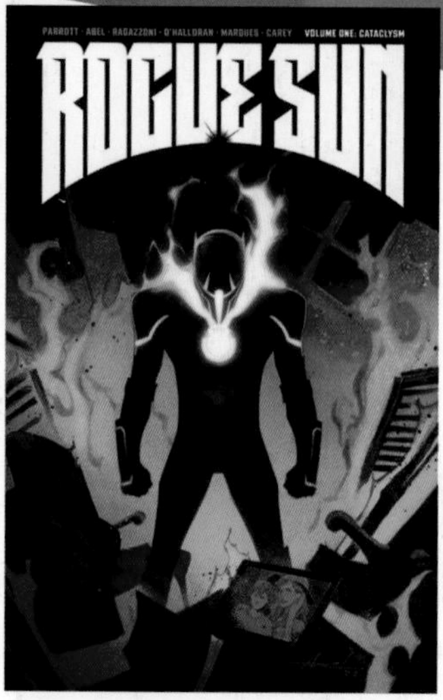

VOLUME ONE: CATACLYSM
ROGUE SUN

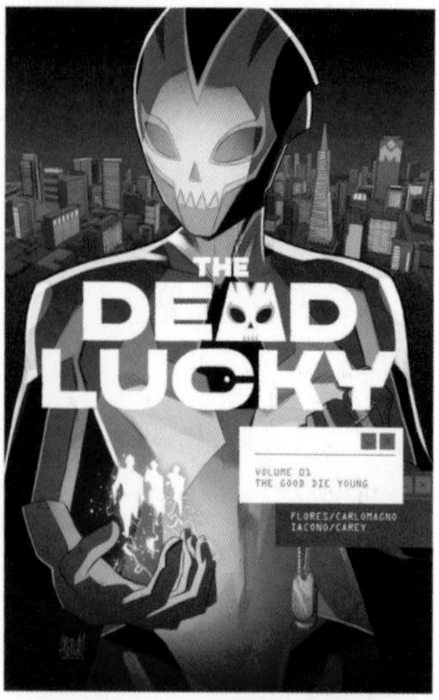

THE DEAD LUCKY
VOLUME 01
THE GOOD DIE YOUNG
FLORES/CARLOMAGNO
IACONO/CAREY

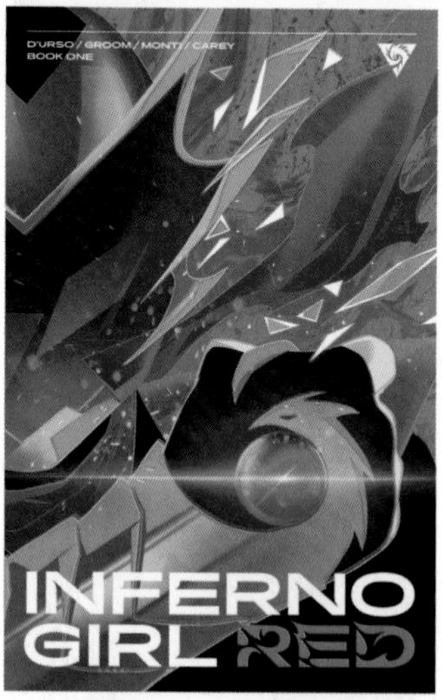

BOOK ONE
INFERNO GIRL RED

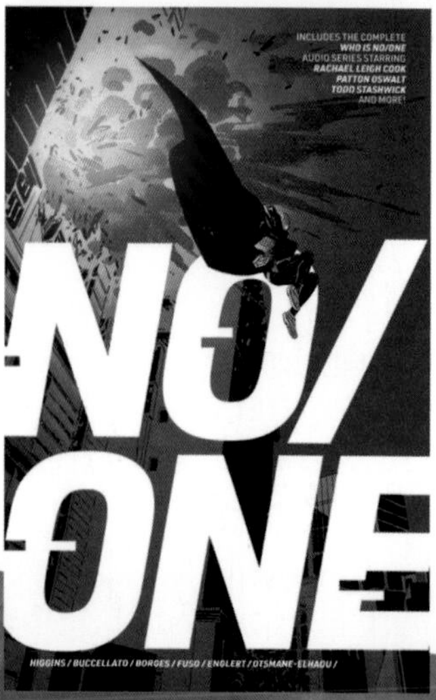

NO/ ONE

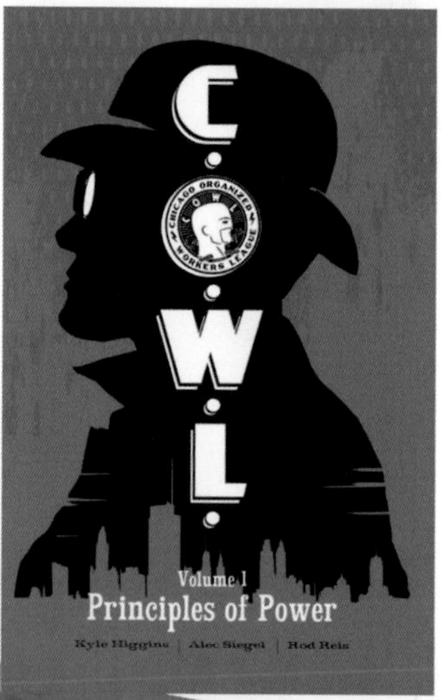

C.O.W.L.
Volume 1
Principles of Power
Kyle Higgins | Alec Siegel | Rod Reis

RADIANT BLACK

VOLUME 1	978-1-53431-916-5
VOLUME 2	978-1-53432-109-0
VOLUME 3	978-1-53432-328-5
VOLUME 4	978-1-53432-477-0
VOLUME 5	978-1-53439-725-5
VOLUME 6	978-1-53439-724-8

ROGUE SUN

VOLUME 1	978-1-53432-237-0
VOLUME 2	978-1-53432-470-1
VOLUME 3	978-1-53439-723-1

THE DEAD LUCKY

VOLUME 1	978-1-53432-466-4
VOLUME 2	978-1-53439-722-4

INFERNO GIRL RED

BOOK ONE	978-1-53432-481-7

RADIANT RED

VOLUME 1	978-1-53432-320-9

RADIANT PINK

VOLUME 1	978-1-53432-486-2

C.O.W.L.

VOLUME 1	978-1-63215-111-7
VOLUME 2	978-1-63215-326-5

NO/ONE

VOLUME 1	978-1-53439-721-7

VISIT
MASSIVE-VERSE.COM